A CROWN for COLD SILVER

A CROWN

for

COLD
SILVER

ALEX MARSHALL

www.orbitbooks.net

Orbit
Hachette Book Group
1290 Avenue of the Americas, New York, NY 10104
www.OrbitBooks.net

First Edition: April 2015

Orbit is an imprint of Hachette Book Group, Inc. The Orbit name and logo are trademarks of Little, Brown Book Group Limited.

The Hachette Speakers Bureau provides a wide range of authors for speaking events. To find out more, go to www.hachettespeakersbureau.com or call (866) 376-6591.

The publisher is not responsible for websites (or their content) that are not owned by the publisher.

Library of Congress Cataloging-in-Publication Data

Marshall, Alex (Novelist)
  A crown for cold silver / Alex Marshall.
      pages cm
  Summary: "Twenty years ago, feared general Cobalt Zosia led her five villainous captains and mercenary army into battle, wrestling monsters and toppling an empire. When there were no more titles to win and no more worlds to conquer, she retired and gave up her legend to history. Now the peace she carved for herself has been shattered by the unprovoked slaughter of her village. Seeking bloody vengeance, Zosia heads for battle once more, but to find justice she must confront grudge-bearing enemies, once-loyal allies, and an unknown army that marches under a familiar banner"—Provided by publisher.
    ISBN 978-0-316-27798-3 (hardback)—ISBN 978-0-316-27799-0 (ebook)—ISBN 978-1-4789-0345-1 (audio download) 1. Warriors—Fiction. 2. War stories—Fiction. I. Title.
    PS3613.A76993C76 2015
    813'.6—dc23
                                    2014037807

10 9 8 7 6 5 4 3 2 1

RRD-C

Printed in the United States of America

For All My Fellow Barbarians

PART I

OF MORTAL
WISHES

Friendship is the daughter of virtue. Villains may be
accomplices but not friends.

—Francisco Goya,
subtitle to ¡*Quién lo creyera!*,
in *Los Caprichos* (1799)

CHAPTER

1

It was all going so nicely, right up until the massacre.

Sir Hjortt's cavalry of two hundred spears fanned out through the small village, taking up positions between half-timbered houses in the uneven lanes that only the most charitable of surveyors would refer to as "roads." The warhorses slowed and then stopped in a decent approximation of unison, their riders sitting as stiff and straight in their saddles as the lances they braced against their stirrups. It was an unseasonably warm afternoon in the autumn, and after their long approach up the steep valley, soldier and steed alike dripped sweat, yet not a one of them removed their brass skullcap. Weapons, armor, and tack glowing in the fierce alpine sunlight, the faded crimson of their cloaks covering up the inevitable stains, the cavalry appeared to have ridden straight out of a tale, or galloped down off one of the tapestries in the mayor's house.

So they must have seemed to the villagers who peeked through their shutters, anyway. To their colonel, Sir Hjortt, they looked like hired killers on horseback barely possessed of sense to do as they were told most of the time. Had the knight been able to train wardogs to ride he should have preferred them to the Fifteenth Cavalry, given the amount of faith he placed in this lot. Not much, in other words, not very much at all.

He didn't care for dogs, either, but a dog you could trust, even if it was only to lick his balls.

The hamlet sprawled across the last stretch of grassy meadow before the collision of two steep, bald-peaked mountains. Murky forest edged in on all sides, like a snare the wilderness had set for the unwary traveler. A typical mountain town here in the Kutumban range, then, with only a low reinforced stone wall to keep out the wolves and what piddling avalanches the encircling slopes must bowl down at the settlement when the snows melted.

Sir Hjortt had led his troops straight through the open gate in the wall and up the main track to the largest house in the village… which wasn't saying a whole lot for the building. Fenced in by shedding rosebushes and standing a scant two and a half stories tall, its windowless redbrick face was broken into a grid by the black timbers that supported it. The mossy thatched roof rose up into a witch's hat, and set squarely in the center like a mouth were a great pair of doors tall and wide enough for two riders to pass through abreast without removing their helmets. As he reached the break in the hedge at the front of the house, Sir Hjortt saw that one of these oaken doors was ajar, but just as he noticed this detail the door eased shut.

Sir Hjortt smiled to himself, and, reining his horse in front of the rosebushes, called out in his deepest baritone, "I am Sir Efrain Hjortt of Azgaroth, Fifteenth Colonel of the Crimson Empire, come to counsel with the mayor's wife. I have met your lord mayor upon the road, and while he reposes at my camp—"

Someone behind him snickered at that, but when Sir Hjortt turned in his saddle he could not locate which of his troops was the culprit. It might have even come from one of his two personal Chainite guards, who had stopped their horses at the border of the thorny hedge. He gave both his guards and the riders nearest them the sort of withering scowl his father was overly fond of doling out. This was no laughing matter, as should have been perfectly obvious from the way Sir Hjortt had dealt with the hillbilly mayor of this shitburg.

"Ahem." Sir Hjortt turned back to the building and tried again. "Whilst your lord mayor reposes at my camp, I bring tidings of great import. I must speak with the mayor's wife at once."

Anything? Nothing. The whole town was silently, fearfully watching him from hiding, he could feel it in his aching thighs, but not a one braved the daylight either to confront or assist him. Peasants— what a sorry lot they were.

"I say again!" Sir Hjortt called, goading his stallion into the mayor's yard and advancing on the double doors. "As a colonel of the Crimson Empire and a knight of Azgaroth, I shall be welcomed by the family of your mayor, or—"

Both sets of doors burst open, and a wave of hulking, shaggy beasts flooded out into the sunlight—they were on top of the Azgarothian before he could wheel away or draw his sword. He heard muted bells, obviously to signal that the ambush was under way, and the hungry grunting of the pack, and—

The cattle milled about him, snuffling his horse with their broad, slimy noses, but now that they had escaped the confines of the building they betrayed no intention toward further excitement.

"Very sorry, sir," came a hillfolk-accented voice from somewhere nearby, and then a small, pale hand appeared amid the cattle, rising from between the bovine waves like the last, desperate attempt of a drowning man to catch a piece of driftwood. Then the hand seized a black coat and a blond boy of perhaps ten or twelve vaulted himself nimbly into sight, landing on the wide back of a mountain cow and twisting the creature around to face Sir Hjortt as effortlessly as the Azgarothian controlled his warhorse. Despite this manifest skill and agility at play before him, the knight remained unimpressed.

"The mayor's wife," said Sir Hjortt. "I am to meet with her. Now. Is she in?"

"I expect so," said the boy, glancing over his shoulder—checking the position of the sun against the lee of the mountains towering over the village, no doubt. "Sorry again 'bout my cows. They're feisty, sir; had to bring 'em down early on account of a horned wolf being seen a few vales over. And I, uh, didn't have the barn door locked as I should have."

"Spying on us, eh?" said Sir Hjortt. The boy grinned. "Perhaps I'll let it slide this once, if you go and fetch your mistress from inside."

"Mayoress is probably up in her house, sir, but I'm not allowed 'round there anymore, on account of my wretched behavior," said the boy with obvious pride.

"This isn't her home?" Hjortt eyed the building warily.

"No, sir. This is the barn."

Another chuckle from one of his faithless troops, but Sir Hjortt didn't give whoever it was the satisfaction of turning in his saddle a second time. He'd find the culprit after the day's business was done, and then they'd see what came of having a laugh at their commander's expense. Like the rest of the Fifteenth Regiment, the cavalry apparently thought their new colonel was green because he wasn't yet twenty, but he would soon show them that being young and being green weren't the same thing at all.

Now that their cowherd champion had engaged the invaders, gaily painted doors began to open and the braver citizenry slunk out onto their stoops, clearly awestruck at the Imperial soldiers in their midst. Sir Hjortt grunted in satisfaction—it had been so quiet in the hamlet that he had begun to wonder if the villagers had somehow been tipped off to his approach and scampered away into the mountains.

"Where's the mayor's house, then?" he said, reins squeaking in his gauntlets as he glared at the boy.

"See the trail there?" said the boy, pointing to the east. Following the lad's finger down a lane beside a longhouse, Sir Hjortt saw a small gate set in the village wall, and beyond that a faint trail leading up the grassy foot of the steepest peak in the valley.

"My glass, Portolés," said Sir Hjortt, and his bodyguard walked her horse over beside his. Sir Hjortt knew that if he carried the priceless item in his own saddlebag one of his thuggish soldiers would likely find a way of stealing it, but not a one of them would dare try that shit with the burly war nun. She handed it over and Sir Hjortt withdrew the heavy brass hawkglass from its sheath; it was the only gift his father had ever given him that wasn't a weapon of some sort, and he relished any excuse to use it. Finding the magnified trail through the instrument, he tracked it up the meadow to where the path entered the surrounding forest. A copse of yellowing aspen interrupted the pines and fir, and, scanning the hawkglass upward, he saw that this vein of gold continued up the otherwise evergreen-covered mountain.

"See it?" the cowherd said. "They live back up in there. Not far."

<hr>

Sir Hjortt gained a false summit and leaned against one of the trees. The thin trunk bowed under his weight, its copper leaves hissing at his touch, its white bark leaving dust on his cape. The series of switchbacks carved into the increasingly sheer mountainside had become too treacherous for the horses, and so Sir Hjortt and his two guards, Brother Iqbal and Sister Portolés, had proceeded up the scarps of exposed granite on foot. The possibility of a trap had not left the knight, but nothing more hostile than a hummingbird had showed itself on the hike, and now that his eyes had adjusted to the strangely diffuse light of this latest grove, he saw a modest, freshly whitewashed house perched on the lip of the next rock shelf.

Several hundred feet above them. Brother Iqbal laughed and Sister Portolés cursed, yet her outburst carried more humor in it than his. Through the trees they went, and then made the final ascent.

"Why..." puffed Iqbal, the repurposed grain satchel slung over one meaty shoulder retarding his already sluggish pace, "in all the...devils of Emeritus...would a mayor...live...so far...from his town?"

"I can think of a reason or three," said Portolés, setting the head of her weighty maul in the path and resting against its long shaft. "Take a look behind us."

Sir Hjortt paused, amenable to a break himself—even with only his comparatively light riding armor on, it was a real asshole of a hike. Turning, he let out an appreciative whistle. They had climbed quickly, and spread out below them was the painting-perfect hamlet nestled at the base of the mountains. Beyond the thin line of its walls, the lush valley fell away into the distance, a meandering brook dividing east ridge from west. Sir Hjortt was hardly a single-minded, bloodthirsty brute, and he could certainly appreciate the allure of living high above one's vassals, surrounded by the breathtaking beauty of creation. Perhaps when this unfortunate errand was over he would convert the mayor's house into a hunting lodge, wiling away his summers with sport and relaxation in the clean highland air.

"Best vantage in the valley," said Portolés. "Gives the headperson plenty of time to decide how to greet any guests."

"Do you think she's put on a kettle for us?" said Iqbal hopefully. "I could do with a spot of hunter's tea."

"About this mission, Colonel..." Portolés was looking at Sir Hjortt but not meeting his eyes. She'd been poorly covering up her discomfort with phony bravado ever since he'd informed her what needed to be done here, and the knight could well imagine what would come next. "I wonder if the order—"

"And I wonder if your church superiors gave me the use of you two anathemas so that you might hem and haw and question me at every pass, instead of respecting my command as an Imperial colonel," said Sir Hjortt, which brought bruise-hued blushes to the big woman's cheeks. "Azgaroth has been a proud and faithful servant of the Kings and Queens of Samoth for near on a century, whereas your popes seem to revolt every other feast day, so remind me again, what use have I for your counsel?"

Portolés muttered an apology, and Iqbal fidgeted with the damp sack he carried.

"Do you think I relish what we have to do? Do you think I would put my soldiers through it, if I had a choice? Why would I give such a command, if it was at all avoidable? Why—" Sir Hjortt was just warming to his lecture when a fissure of pain opened up his skull. Intense and unpleasant as the sensation was, it fled in moments, leaving him to nervously consider the witchborn pair. Had one of them somehow brought on the headache with their devilish ways? Probably not; he'd had a touch of a headache for much of the ride up, come to think of it, and he hadn't even mentioned the plan to them then.

"Come on," he said, deciding it would be best to drop the matter without further pontification. Even if his bodyguards did have reservations, this mission would prove an object lesson that it is always better to rush through any necessary unpleasantness, rather than drag your feet and overanalyze every ugly detail. "Let's be done with this. I want to be down the valley by dark, bad as that road is."

They edged around a hairpin bend in the steep trail, and then the track's crudely hewn stair delivered them to another plateau, and the mayor's house. It was similar in design to those in the hamlet, but with a porch overhanging the edge of the mild cliff and a low white fence. Pleasant enough, thought Sir Hjortt, except that the fence was made of bone, with each outwardly bowed moose-rib picket topped with the skull of a different animal. Owlbat skulls sat between those of marmot and hill fox, and above the door of the cabin rested an enormous one that had to be a horned wolf; when the cowherd had mentioned such a beast being spied in the area, Sir Hjortt had assumed the boy full of what his cows deposited, but maybe a few still prowled these lonely mountains. What a thrill it would be, to mount a hunting party for such rare game! Then the door beneath the skull creaked, and a figure stood framed in the doorway.

"Well met, friends, you've come a long way," the woman greeted them. She was brawny, though not so big as Portolés, with features as hard as the trek up to her house. She might have been fit enough once, in a country sort of way, when her long, silvery hair was blond or black or red and tied back in pigtails the way Hjortt liked . . . but now she was just an old woman, same as any other, fifty winters young at a minimum. Judging from the tangled bone fetishes hanging from the limbs of the sole tree that grew inside the fence's perimeter—a tall, black-barked aspen with leaves as hoary as her locks—she might be a sorceress, to boot.

Iqbal returned her welcome, calling, "Well met, Mum, well met indeed. I present to you Sir Hjortt of Azgaroth, Fifteenth Colonel of the Crimson Empire." The anathema glanced to his superior, but when Sir Hjortt didn't fall all over himself to charge ahead and meet a potential witch, Iqbal murmured, "She's just an old bird, sir, nothing to fret about."

"Old bird or fledgling, I wouldn't blindly stick my hand in an owlbat's nest," Portolés said, stepping past Sir Hjortt and Iqbal to address the old woman in the Crimson tongue. "In the names of the Pontiff of the West and the Queen of the Rest, I order you out here into the light, woman."

"Queen of the Rest?" The woman obliged Portolés, stepping down the creaking steps of her porch and approaching the fence. For a mayor's wife, her checked dirndl was as plain as any village girl's. "And Pontiff of the West, is it? Last peddler we had through here brought tidings that Pope Shanatu's war wasn't going so well, but I gather much has changed. Is this sovereign of the Rest, blessed whoever she be, still Queen Indsorith? And does this mean peace has once again been brokered?"

"This bird hears a lot from her tree," muttered Sir Hjortt, then asked the woman, "Are you indeed the mayor's wife?"

"I am Mayoress Vivi, wife of Leib," said she. "And I ask again, respectfully, to whom shall I direct my prayers when next I—"

"The righteous reign of Queen Indsorith continues, blessed be her name," said Sir Hjortt. "Pope Shanatu, blessed be *his* name, received word from on high that his time as Shepherd of Samoth has come to an end, and so the war is over. His niece Jirella, blessed be *her* name, has ascended to her rightful place behind the Onyx Pulpit, and taken on the title of Pope Y'Homa III, Mother of Midnight, Shepherdess of the Lost."

"I see," said the mayoress. "And in addition to accepting a rebel pope's resignation and the promotion of his kin to the same lofty post, our beloved Indsorith, long may her glory persist, has also swapped out her noble title? 'Queen of Samoth, Heart of the Star, Jewel of Diadem, Keeper of the Crimson Empire' for, ah, 'Queen of the Rest'?" The woman's faintly lined face wrinkled further as she smiled, and Portolés slyly returned it.

"Do not mistake my subordinate's peculiar sense of humor for a shift in policy—the queen's honorifics remain unchanged," said Sir Hjortt, thinking of how best to discipline Portolés. If she thought that sort of thing flew with her commanding colonel just because there were no higher-ranked clerical witnesses to her dishonorable talk, the witchborn freak had another thing coming. He almost wished she would refuse to carry out his command, so he'd have an excuse to get rid of her altogether. In High Azgarothian, he said, "Portolés, return to the village and give the order. In the time it will take you to make it down I'll have made myself clear enough."

Portolés stiffened and gave Sir Hjortt a pathetic frown that told him she'd been holding out hope that he would change his mind. Not bloody likely. Also in Azgarothian, the war nun said, "I'm… I'm just going to have a look inside before I do. Make sure it's safe, Colonel Hjortt."

"By all means, Sister Portolés, welcome, welcome," said the older woman, also in that ancient and honorable tongue of Sir Hjortt's ancestors. Unexpected, that, but then the Star had been a different place when this biddy was in her prime, and perhaps she had seen more of it than just her remote mountain. Now that she was closer he saw that her cheeks were more scarred than wrinkled, a rather gnarly one on her chin, and for the first time since their arrival, a shadow of worry played across the weathered landscape of her face. Good. "I have an old hound sleeping in the kitchen whom I should prefer you left to his dreams, but am otherwise alone. But, good Colonel, Leib was to have been at the crossroads this morning…"

Sir Hjortt ignored the mayor's wife, following Portolés through the gate onto the walkway of flat, colorful stones that crossed the yard. They were artlessly arranged; the first order of business would be to hire the mason who had done the bathrooms at his family estate in Cockspar, or maybe the woman's apprentice, if the hoity-toity artisan wasn't willing to journey a hundred leagues into the wilds to retile a walk. A mosaic of miniature animals would be nice, or maybe indigo shingles could be used to make it resemble a creek. But then they had forded a rill on their way up from the village, so why not have some-body trace it to its source and divert it this way, have an actual stream flow through the yard? It couldn't be that hard to have it come down through the trees there and then run over the cliff beside the deck, creating a miniature waterfall that—

"Empty," said Portolés, coming back outside. Sir Hjortt had lost track of himself—it had been a steep march up, and a long ride before that. Portolés silently moved behind the older woman, who stood on the walk between Sir Hjortt and her house. The matron looked nervous now, all right.

"My husband Leib, Colonel Hjortt. Did you meet him at the crossroads?" Her voice was weaker now, barely louder than the quaking aspens. That must be something to hear as one lay in bed after a hard day's hunt, the rustling of those golden leaves just outside your window.

"New plan," said Sir Hjortt, not bothering with the more formal Azgarothian, since she spoke it anyway. "Well, it's the same as the original, mostly, but instead of riding down before dark we'll bivouac here for the night." Smiling at the old woman, he said, "Do not fret, Missus Mayor, do not fret, I won't be garrisoning my soldiers in your town, I assure you. Camp them outside the wall, when they're done. We'll ride out at first"—the thought of sleeping in on a proper bed occurred to him—"noon. We ride at noon tomorrow. Report back to me when it's done."

"Whatever you're planning, sir, let us parley before you commit yourself," said the old woman, seeming to awaken from the anxious spell their presence had cast upon her. She had a stern bearing he wasn't at all sure he liked. "Your officer can surely tarry a few minutes before delivering your orders, especially if we are to have you as our guests for the night. Let us speak, you and I, and no matter what orders you may have, no matter how pressing your need, I shall make it worth your while to have listened."

Portolés's puppy-dog eyes from over the woman's shoulder turned Sir Hjortt's stomach. At least Iqbal had the decency to keep his smug gaze on the old woman.

"Whether or not she is capable of doing so, Sister Portolés will *not* wait," said Sir Hjortt shortly. "You and I are talking, and directly, make no mistake, but I see no reason to delay my subordinate."

The old woman looked back past Portolés, frowning at the open door of her cabin, and then shrugged. As if she had any say at all in how this would transpire. Flashing a patently false smile at Sir Hjortt, she said, "As you will, fine sir. I merely thought you might have use for the sister as we spoke, for we may be talking for some time."

Fallen Mother have mercy, did every single person have a better idea of how Sir Hjortt should conduct himself than he did? This would not stand.

"My good woman," he said, "it seems that we have even more to parley than I previously suspected. Sister Portolés's business is pressing, however, and so she must away before we embark on this long conversation you so desire. Fear not, however, for the terms of supplication your husband laid out to us at the crossroads shall be honored, reasonable as they undeniably are. Off with you, Portolés."

Portolés offered him one of her sardonic salutes from over the older woman's shoulder, and then stalked out of the yard, looking as petulant as he'd ever seen her. Iqbal whispered something to her as he moved out of her way by the gate, and wasn't fast enough in his retreat when she lashed out at him. The war nun flicked the malformed ear that emerged from Iqbal's pale tonsure like the outermost leaf of an overripe cabbage, rage rendering her face even less appealing, if such a thing was possible. Iqbal swung his heavy satchel at her in response, and although Portolés dodged the blow, the dark bottom of the sackcloth misted her with red droplets as it whizzed past her face. If the sister noticed the blood on her face, she didn't seem to care, dragging her feet down the precarious trail, her maul slung over one hunched shoulder.

"My husband," the matron whispered, and, turning back to her, Sir Hjortt saw that her wide eyes were fixed on Iqbal's dripping sack.

"Best if we talk inside," said Sir Hjortt, winking at Iqbal and ushering the woman toward her door. "Come, come, I have an absolutely brilliant idea about how you and your people might help with the war effort, and I'd rather discuss it over tea."

"You said the war was over," the woman said numbly, still staring at the satchel.

"So it is, so it is," said Sir Hjortt. "But the *effort* needs to be made to ensure it doesn't start up again, what? Now, what do you have to slake the thirst of servants of the Empire, home from the front?"

She balked, but there was nowhere to go, and so she led Sir Hjortt and Brother Iqbal inside. It was quiet in the yard, save for the trees and the clacking of the bone fetishes when the wind ran its palm down the mountain's stubbly cheek. The screaming didn't start until after Sister Portolés had returned to the village, and down there they were doing enough of their own to miss the echoes resonating from the mayor's house.

CHAPTER
2

Everything was dull dull *dull*, until the princess snuck away from the interminable Equinox Ceremony taking place in the Autumn Palace and went in search of spirits in the pumpkin fields surrounding the Temple of Pentacles.

Ji-hyeon Bong wasn't really *the* princess, only *a* princess. At home in her familial castle at Hwabun she was one of three, and the middle one at that. And here, in the capital, with all the court gathered, there must be more princesses than there were stars in the sky, all crammed into a multiplicity of ballrooms. Even without being the sole princess in the palace, however, getting away had proven difficult, since Princess Ji-hyeon was here in part to formally meet her fiancé for the very first time. Prince Byeong-gu of Othean, fourth son of Empress Ryuki, Keeper of the Immaculate Isles, seemed every bit as stuck-up as his title had implied, and so Ji-hyeon set herself to escape at all costs, but she never would have managed it without the help of her three guards (especially her Spirit Guard, Brother Mikal, much as he had protested the plan initially). Now the fifteen-year-old woman traipsed through tangled vines under a moon as fat as the gourds at her feet, the hubbub inside the palace walls reduced to a drone much softer than the rasping of fuzzy leaves against silk skirts.

"Your Highness," Brother Mikal called from where he and Keun-ju, the princess's Virtue Guard, strolled along one of the straight paths that cut through the field. "I wonder if you might favor to walk with us here, between the rows rather than across them? Keun-ju is concerned for your gown."

"If Keun-ju would prefer to carry my dress for safeguarding, I have no objections to walking naked on such a pleasant eve," said Ji-hyeon, happy to hear the reserved boy splutter by way of response. He hardly minded such joking when they were alone in her chambers, but in front of Brother Mikal and Choi was another matter.

"In all seriousness, Princess, I wonder if he might have a point—" Mikal began, but Ji-hyeon cut him off.

"Wonder no longer, then, for I favor my own approach," she said, but the wit of her riposte was spoiled as she tripped over a pumpkin. She would have gone down if Choi hadn't been there to catch her arm; Ji-hyeon grinned at her Martial Guard, and Choi warmly flashed her shark teeth in response. Stitched up in her own slick black gown at the ceremony, Choi could have passed for human, a princess even, if not for her petite horns. She had also looked about as comfortable as a lobster sitting on the edge of a pot, and no more talkative. Ji-hyeon preferred her wildborn guard when the woman was relaxed enough to open her deceptively small, fang-filled mouth; apparently guests to her home at Hwabun sometimes assumed the woman was mute, so rarely was she at her ease.

"Do you think we'll find one?" Ji-hyeon asked eagerly.

"The moon's full and the equinox is near," said Choi in her gruff, quiet voice. "I'll be surprised if you don't, this near to a hungry mouth."

Ji-hyeon liked Choi's sharp teeth, and her ebony horns, and her sometimes frightening speed, and even her sword lessons, exhausting though they were, but most of all the princess liked the way Choi would use the wrong words for things. It was never an error in vocabulary, Ji-hyeon knew, but rather that the wildborn thought the Immaculate tongue was often misused even by native speakers— every cat was actually a trouble, every sword a tusk, every arrow a disgrace…and every Gate a hungry mouth. Looking at the tall pearl walls of the Temple of Pentacles shining ahead of them like a lighthouse across a vegetal sea, Ji-hyeon shivered with delight. She liked being scared, a little, which was part of why she loved Choi so much.

She loved *all* of them so much, the three complementing one another every bit as much as they complemented their ward: Choi was serious, but Mikal was very funny and charming and handsome for an older foreign man, and Keun-ju, well, Keun-ju was Keun-ju, her best friend since forever, pretty much. Her Virtue Guard was almost as comely as Mikal and almost as good at swordplay as Choi, plus Keun-ju was better at dressmaking than either, which Ji-hyeon enjoyed just as much as fencing.

And once she was married to Prince Boring, she would have to leave them all behind and accept whatever new guards her husband provided for her. It made her heartsick, and she turned her mind from it, hard though it was to do when she had just met the man who would take her closest friends away from her. None of the others mentioned it, either, their numbered days the proverbial whale in the carp pond.

"Is there anything else we can do?" she asked. "Other than walk around, hoping we get lucky?"

"Luck is an excuse," said Choi. "If you kept a better vigil you would have already succeeded. I've seen three so far."

"Nuh-uh!" cried Ji-hyeon, imitating her younger sister's imitation of some yet younger cousin. "Choi! Why didn't you show me?"

Choi's eyes flashed like rubies even in the colorless pall of the moon, and she gestured to the plants at their feet. "Keep a better vigil."

"Mikal!" Ji-hyeon called a good deal louder than was necessary, knowing how much Choi despised an excess of volume... or an excess of anything, really. Other than vigilance. "Mikal, can you do something to make them appear?"

"Ji-hyeon, the brother's function is the very opposite of *that*, as you well know," said Keun-ju huffily. "Stop trying to get him in trouble."

"If my parents find out he bribed the palace guards to spirit me away from the festival, I think that will cause a lot more embarrassment than if he fulfills the dearest wish of a darling daughter," said Ji-hyeon. "Don't you think?"

"Princess, do you believe I am making sport with you when I profess my ignorance of the spirits of your land?" The path Mikal and Keun-ju followed was taking them away from Ji-hyeon and Choi, and so the pair began tramping over to their noble ward. "I would be reluctant to make any assumptions as to their character or, for that matter, their humor at being addressed by a foreigner. Why not return to the palace and ask one of your priestesses if—"

"If I wanted to talk to the nuns I would have stayed at the party," said Ji-hyeon, wishing every night could be this perfect, just she and her guards questing beneath a full moon. "I want to see a harvest devil."

"Then hush your mouth and be vigilant," said Choi.

"I am being vigilant, I just—oh!" Ji-hyeon froze, her heart plunging into ice water as if she had noticed a snake underfoot, her muddy silk shoe suspended in the air above a twisting coil of black vines. The round pumpkin at its center rolled backward in its nest, revealing the triangular eyes and jagged mouth of its face—a faint yellow glow emanated from within the gourd, pouring from maw and eyes to illuminate the gilt hem of Ji-hyeon's jet gown, shining off the silver buckle of her shoe and the abalone inlay of her dress sword's scabbard. Then, fast as she'd seen it, the saffron light faded, the eyes and mouth closed over, and it was just a pumpkin again.

Ji-hyeon squealed in delight, looked up to see if the others had seen . . . and then gasped, stumbled back, dumbstruck by what reared up in front of her, twenty feet tall, rasping, churning, spiraling. Maddening.

"Back to the palace, Princess," Choi hissed as she put herself between Ji-hyeon and the cobra-swaying monolith of vines and leering jack-o'-lanterns that had erupted from the fertile soil of the temple fields. "Now!"

CHAPTER
3

While the copper kettle came to a boil, Sir Hjortt insisted on a tour of the house. Not bad. The interior wouldn't need too much work beyond redecorating (the tacky old tapestries had to go, and fast). The wall between the kitchen and the living room ought to be punched out, though, to make the ground floor more of a hall. The mayor and mayoress had a surprisingly impressive library, no fewer than fifty tomes crammed onto a beautifully turned fir shelf, so it wasn't all doilies and bric-a-brac, although there was certainly a bit of that, too. The mantel was cluttered with wooden tubāq pipes and horsehair pottery. He would have to pick out a nice pipe for Aunt Lupitera and a vase for his father. The rest could be trashed.

Once the herbs or roots or whatever had steeped and been deemed safe for consumption by Brother Iqbal, the witchborn fatass took his tea on the deck overlooking the valley while Sir Hjortt and the mayoress convened at her kitchen table. Under the heavy walnut board dozed a lean mutt that looked as old as the woman and bore more resemblance to a coyote or bearded jackal than it did to a hound. Through the open shutters the aspens gossiped away, their inscrutable whispers as relaxing as strong fingers kneading the knots out of Sir Hjortt's saddle-cursed buttocks.

"I wish that you would speak plainly with me, sir," said the matron, all business now that the tea was poured and she was back in her domestic element. Not even the bloody satchel sitting next to the plate of scones she had put out could shake her up, the hard old cow. "All this stalling is beginning to grate."

"Is it?" said Sir Hjortt, frowning into his tea and returning the terra-cotta cup to its saucer. It smelled bitter, whatever she'd put in the pot disagreeing with his nostrils. No tea, then. Bother.

"Is that...is my husband in that bag?"

"No, not your husband," said Sir Hjortt, annoyed that she was leaping to such conclusions, stealing his show. The best he could come up with to reassert his dominance of the situation was to abruptly stand, grab the satchel, and upend its contents onto the table in front of her. It dropped out and, even better than he'd expected, bounced off the table into her lap. "Just his head."

Rather than screaming as the knight had hoped, or at least pitching it away in understandable disgust, the woman shrunk her broad shoulders inward as her callused fingers went to the severed head, turning it over to look at her husband's face. That was a cold draught, it was, seeing this grey hen gently stroke the disgusting, matted hair and gaze lovingly into the wide, horror-frozen eyes of a dead man. The smell was strong from the warm ride, and it turned Sir Hjortt's stomach.

"Go ahead and cry if you need to," said the knight, hoping to prod a more appropriate reaction from the biddy. "Perfectly understandable, given...well, obviously."

She looked up at him, and he was satisfied to see her pallid blue eyes shine with emotion. Hatred, maybe, but it was better than nothing. So quietly he barely heard her, she said, "Tears enough in time, Colonel."

The woman set the head back on the table, nesting it in the discarded satchel to keep it from rolling off again, and slowly stood. She was half a foot shorter than the knight, and more than twice his age at a minimum, but Sir Hjortt nevertheless shivered to see the wrath on her face.

A loud bark at groin level made Sir Hjortt start, but rather than attacking his codpiece the mutt shoved its muzzle out from under the table and nosed it against the knight's bare palm—he had taken off his gauntlet for tea, naturally. He was far more of a cat person, but there's only so much one can do when confronted with the pleading, rheumy eyes of an ancient dog in desperate need of a petting. He dug his fingers in behind a floppy ear, drawing forth a contented whine, but as he did he kept an eye on the mayor's widow lest she try something stupid with teapot or butter knife.

It seemed the enormity of the situation had finally sunk in, for her face fell as she watched him scratch the dog, all her rage replaced with bald terror. Sir Hjortt made no attempt to hide his smirk, and only ceased giving the beast his attention when it licked his fingers and happily tottered away of its own accord. He watched it go to the old woman, but she made no move to pet it, looking back and forth between the animal and the knight with features so wracked that Sir Hjortt wondered if she was having a heart attack right there in front of him.

Then the dog looked back over its shoulder and *smiled* at him, its chops curling back to reveal black, rotting teeth and a grub-white tongue. The ugly expression on the mutt's snout gave Sir Hjortt the chills, and then the dog circled behind the trembling woman and hobbled through the kitchen doorway, wagging its tail as it went. Wiping its now-cold slobber off his hand as he heard it nose the front door open, the knight silently repledged his allegiance to the far less disquieting feline race and decided that prolonging this affair wasn't so enjoyable after all.

"As we told your husband," he began, gesturing to the mayor's head, "the terms of—"

"What have you done?" the old woman whispered, her eyes fixed on the open kitchen door with such intensity that Sir Hjortt glanced over to make sure there wasn't someone creeping up on him. "You stupid, wretched, idiot boy, what have you done?"

"I'm not a boy," said Sir Hjortt, hating her for forcing the sulky words to leave his mouth. "I am a knight of the realm, and I—"

"To the village," she said, the fear scoured off her face by something much, much worse as she directed a ferocious stare at her guest. "By the six devils I bound, what order did you give your Chainwitch, boy? What did you tell her to do to my people?"

"Sisters of the Burnished Chain are *not* witches," Sir Hjortt huffed, all this *boy* talk putting him in a ratty mood. This old bird was about to learn a very hard lesson about respecting one's betters. "As for my orders, they involve the two hundred lances I positioned in your town before climbing up to this dump."

A distant scream rode in on the breeze just then, so perfectly timed that Sir Hjortt wondered if Brother Iqbal was eavesdropping on their conversation and had somehow given Sister Portolés a signal. Commendations all around, if so!

Sir Hjortt realized with disappointment that he had forgotten to get his hawkglass back from Portolés before sending her down to the village; how was he supposed to see anything from up here without it? She should have known he'd want it and reminded him to hold on to it. It wouldn't surprise him if she had taken it with her just to spite him. Well, even if he couldn't see the action down in the town, he could still have some fun with this old coot.

Rather than upsetting the matron, the distant scream had brought an evil grin to her chapped lips, twisting her already woodsy features into the grimace of an especially gnarled knothole. She turned to the open door leading onto the deck, where Sir Hjortt could see the chain-encircled-crown crest of the newly reunited Crimson Empire emblazoned on the back of Brother Iqbal's cloak. The witchborn was looking down over the rail at the hamlet far below, and the mayor's widow stepped out onto the deck to join him, her legs the only part of her not shivering like a plucked fiddle string.

"As I told your husband before I had him executed…" began Sir Hjortt, thinking for sure this would regain her attention. It didn't, but he went on anyway, following her to the door as she walked slowly to the railing. "I believe the terms your husband so *generously* offered our army are identical to those he brokered with Pope Shanatu's troops when this territory fell under his dominion during the civil war. On an appointed day your mayor shall deliver to the crossroads below your valley approximately one-fifth of your yearly root wines, cheeses, and marmot oil in peacetime, and one-half in times of war. In exchange your citizens shall not be pressed into service, your children shall not be enslaved, and your borders shall be defended. Did I miss anything?"

"No." Her voice was no louder than the zephyr passing through the trees as she set her hands on the thin wooden balustrade and gazed down. Brother Iqbal glanced over at the woman beside him, offering her a sympathetic grimace.

"Fair terms, Mum," said Iqbal. "Most fair."

"Why?" she asked, still not looking away, although from up here she couldn't possibly see much of the action. The distant screams and clangor had grown louder, though. "In the name of the six devils I bound, *why*?"

That weird oath of hers seemed to befuddle Iqbal, the man's perpetually snowmead-whitened lips silently repeating it as he stared at the woman. Sir Hjortt had heard stranger curses on a slow day at court. Following her as far as the doorway, he called after her, "I don't owe you any answers, woman. Besides, I'm sure that smart mouth of yours can supply one of its own."

"Maybe so," she said quietly, hands gripping the railing.

"Really, though, we're spoiled for choice, aren't we?" said Sir Hjortt. "Maybe it's because the fealty due the pontiff and queen shall *not* be decided by the hill-creatures who pay it. Maybe it's because by your husband's own admission, the citizenry of this village traded supplies to Pope Shanatu's rebel army, which makes your people traitors to the Crown. And maybe an example has to be made, for all the other backwater towns who took up arms against the rightful ruler of the Crimson Empire—bad luck on your husband's part, to be waiting at the crossroads with tribute for the losing team when our scouts spotted him."

"Before this last war we always delivered our annual tithe to agents of the queen. We trade food to those who demand it, regardless of what banners they fly—to do otherwise would provoke an assault we could never withstand. And so you're sacking a village guilty of no greater crime than common sense, and…and…*bad luck*?" She looked back at Sir Hjortt, her cobalt eyes wild as the Bitter Sea. "You're destroying everything these innocents have as *an example*?"

"That's about the shape of it," said Sir Hjortt, leaning against the doorframe. Another headache had been fomenting behind his temples ever since this nanny goat had started bleating *why-why-why* at him, and it was only growing worse. "But fret not, woman, fret not, the letter of the terms is being honored—your borders are quite secure, and my soldiers have it on my strictest orders not to flirt with a single villager, no matter how tempting, nor shackle even one of your plump little moppets, rich a price as they might fetch in Her Grace's markets."

"No?" There was the most delicious tinge of hope in her voice.

"No," said Sir Hjortt, pleased that she had given him the setup he so dearly desired. Now for the punch line. "Every single one of your townies is being put to the steel. No exceptions. Other than you, of course. You we let live."

"Is that so?" She didn't flinch—cold as the Queen of Samoth, this one.

"You are charged with a task of the utmost importance to Crown and Chain," said Sir Hjortt, a rumble in his belly turning up to keep his headache company. One of those scones might settle his stomach. "Fill her in, Iqbal."

"Good Colonel Hjortt and I discussed your future on our promenade up to your lovely home," Iqbal said genially as Sir Hjortt returned to the kitchen table. "And we came to terms that I think will be most agreeable to Chain, Crown, and, of course, yourself."

The woman muttered something Sir Hjortt couldn't quite make out, but it must have been fresh, for Brother Iqbal faked a laugh before continuing.

"Our pontiff loves you, Mum, just as she loves all those worthy martyrs below. As her sole representative on this charming veranda, I offer you, nay, *honor* you with the charge of becoming one of her apostles. You shall be a mendicant witness, traveling from burg to burg to testify of your experience here today, and—"

Sir Hjortt bit into a fluffy apple scone just as Iqbal let out a squeal, and the knight looked up from his snack in time to see the witchborn go toppling over the railing. Iqbal plummeted out of sight, and then his high-pitched wail abruptly cut off. The old woman straightened up from the half-crouch she had dropped into in order to launch the brother. Sir Hjortt laughed in surprise, crumbs flying—had that fat fool actually been murdered by a widow old enough to be his mother? This would make quite the story back in Cockspar!

What a day, Sir Hjortt thought as he drew his sword and strode back onto the deck with more enthusiasm than he had felt all campaign, scone still trapped in his teeth; what an absurd, marvelous day!

CHAPTER
4

The elders of Sullen's clan blew a lot of smoke about how you never forgot your first devil. They claimed a Horned Wolf's life was split between the nameless pup that sat at a storyteller's knee, enraptured by tales, and the adult who lived legends instead of dreaming them. The turning point from whelp to worthy member of the clan was not your first battle, your first kill, or even your naming, but the first devil you saw watching you from the darkness, the first time you looked at a beast and *knew* it was something more than mundane. Until you had squared off against a devil and stared it down, you had no right to call yourself a member of the Horned Wolf Clan.

That rite of passage had been a lot easier back when the Star teemed with devils, of course, but nowadays they were almost as rare as the clan's totem animal. Used to be folk could earn their place at the fire either way, by finding a devil or fighting a horned wolf, but such great deeds seemed near impossible in the modern age. Being as there were hardly any of the monsters left in the world—all praise the true goddess—proving your teeth to your people involved a whole lot of dicking around in the misty tundra outside of the village. Invariably the young ones went loopy from exposure or starvation, and stumbled back into town claiming to have seen all manner of bat-winged fiends perching in the boughs of what few bur oaks remained on the Frozen Savannahs. They were flogged by their parents for telling tales, and that was about it—most everyone under the age of fifty grumbled that the elders put a primacy of honor on devil sightings as a means of preventing younger members of the tribe from joining the ruling council.

Sullen couldn't recall his first devil, because for as long as he could remember they had been there, watching him. Not the corporeal ones—*the ones that counted*, according to the elders—but vague, phantasmal creatures that sometimes flitted around the edge of his vision, brightening into focus only as he was drifting off to sleep. In the Immaculate tongue his mother insisted he learn to deal with the foreign traders, these immaterial monsters were called *spirits*, but Sullen knew they were the same devils from all the songs, only ones that hadn't yet claimed a living body. Grandfather said Sullen could see the devils that nobody else could because he'd been born with the eyes of a snow lion, and the one time Sullen had broken the clan's laws about not looking at your own reflection lest one of your evil ancestors possess you, he had seen that the old man was right. Unlike the rest of his clan, whose uniformly human peepers came in various shades of brown and green, Sullen's pupils were slits in eyes the rich blue of the glaciers bordering the nearby coast where the Immaculates landed their ships. It had scared him, seeing a monster looking back at him from the still pool where he had stolen a peek at himself, and from that day on he better understood why his clan viewed him the way they did.

He actively tried to avoid thinking about his affliction, as his mother called it, for the devils never bothered him... but his grandfather, who'd been kicked off the council ages ago after getting into a row with the poison oracle, insisted that in his day Sullen would have been a great shaman, to be so marked by the gods.

"Marked by devils, you mean." Sullen's mother shuddered, making the sign of the Chain as they finished their bowls of rice and cassava porridge. "My poor boy. I don't blame you, Sullen, you know I don't."

At ten, Sullen was bigger than any other pup in the village, and by sixteen he was the tallest, broadest Horned Wolf in the clan. He could do the work of five (and frequently did), and when Old Salt's donkey pitched over dead halfway through the planting, Sullen hitched himself up and finished the field. He tried never to let his strength go to his head, and went out of his way to help those less physically blessed than himself. For all his might, he was a gentle, caring boy.

And with the exception of his mother and grandfather, every single person in his entire clan hated him and wished he would die. He was marked by the devils.

"I *mean* marked by the gods!" Sullen's grandfather crowed at his daughter, tossing his empty bowl onto the dirt floor of the hut. Sullen retrieved it so his mom wouldn't have to. "We call ourselves Horned Wolves, but here's a real beast, one of the chosen of old, and they all despise him! A boy with the blood of shamans treated like an oath-breaker, it's enough to—"

"I told you the last time, we will not speak of this again," said Sullen's mom, in her most dangerously even tone. "Our ways are the only ways, and the council has been merciful with him. With both of you."

"*Our* ways?" said Grandfather with a sneer. "Our ways are *dead*, child, ever since those toothless greypelts decided we should forsake our ancestors and start bowing before a Samothan devil. I don't even know these people anymore. Where do a pack of limp-horned Chainites get off—"

"Old man, I won't warn you again to pay me more respect," said Sullen's mother, rising from the floor with all the foreboding solemnity of a gathering storm. "Had I not shamed myself by letting you back into my hut, I would have taken another husband by now. And if I were to cast you out, who else in the clan would take you? Either of you?"

"It's all right, Fa," said Sullen, coming between the two to clear the rest of the dinner mat. "It's all just a test, is all. The Fallen Mother tests us all."

"The Fallen Mother is a lie," Grandfather hissed much later that night, when even the coals in the hearth were trying to get a little shut-eye. "A *liiiiiie*, cooked up by Imperials to take our teeth. What kind of goddess doesn't show herself to her people, eh? When the Old Watchers wanted to test us, they put a damn monster in our path to see how well we fought! None of this walking 'round with your hands at your sides, playing the anvil to those backbiting little hyenas!"

"I ain't been hit in ages," Sullen said, forgetting that his mother wanted him to pretend to be asleep when her dad went on his heretical rants. "Not since I lost my temper with Yaw Thrim all them summers back."

Yaw Thrim was now known as One-arm Yaw, on account of Sullen's slippery temper. Sullen had been fourteen at the time, Yaw twenty-three. Sullen didn't even remember what had happened after Yaw pinned him down in the permafrost and started pummeling his face; everything after that was as hazy as the devils that danced just beyond his vision. Yaw remembered, though, and his family said he still woke up screaming some nights, clutching at the twisted burl of scar tissue with his only remaining hand.

"They almost done you for that," said Grandfather. "Even with you just defending yourself, they would've done you for sure if you'd had one more hair on your balls, or that bullyboy had one less hair in his beard. Next time you stick up for yourself they'll kill you, boy, they'll kill you twice to make sure it takes."

"It'll be all right, Fa," said Sullen, rolling over to face the dark wall.

"It won't be all right until you act like a ruddy Horned Wolf and leave these pagans in your dust," said Grandfather. "When I was your age we didn't trade with no Immaculates, we raided 'em! Now we don't even build boats no more, and moved too far from the sea to hear the songs of the Deep Folk. Horned Wolves, digging fields and building churches like Red Imperials. I wish they'd had the decency to burn me alive so I didn't have to see such things come to pass. Craven knew what was coming. I've cursed him every dawn and dusk for leaving us the way he did, but now I wish he'd come back and taken me with him. He could've lashed me to his back and carried me out of here—Horned Wolves my arse, we're just plain old sheep these days."

"Do you think Uncle's still alive?" asked Sullen, forgetting he was trying to sleep and rolling back over to face his crotchety grandfather on the prickly cot they all shared.

"Might could be, might could be," said Grandfather, as though considering the possibility for the first time. Sullen's mother snorted in her sleep, and even lower than before, Grandfather said, "I don't see a man die I don't assume he's dead. The last time we seen him he was alive enough, I expect you remember that."

Sullen definitely remembered more than he cared to from the day Uncle Craven had forsaken them ... the day Sullen's father had died, the day Sullen fought his first battle against a rival clan. The day he took his first kill. He remembered how rich the air tasted before the fighting started; it was the first time he had come close enough to the Bitter Sea to smell salt and sand mingling with the scent of fresh snow. He remembered how he had pretended he was fighting alongside his ancestors in one of the old songs, how he had believed Old Black would shield them from their enemies. He remembered the glint of sunlight on the blade that ran through his father's heart, and the way the blood seemed to turn the sword to black ice when it was pulled free of his breast. He remembered how weightless his arm had felt when he threw his sun-knife, and how heavy it became when he saw his weapon enter a man's hip and bring him crashing to the ground, to be stomped and stabbed in the chaos. He remembered how the Jackal People had laughed as they fought, laughing harder as they lost, laughing until the last of them was brought low on the blood-thawed battlefield. He remembered how sad and scared he had been, remembered it like it was yesterday.

He also remembered what had come after, would remember it until his dying day. The dead eyes of his father, staring past his sobbing son and into the whiteness beyond. The gleaming eyes of the snow lions creeping in to eat the dead before the victorious Horned Wolves had even quit the scene, eyes that were the same as Sullen's. Grandfather lying howling in the gore-spattered tundra, hacked through the tail-bone by a pepper-smeared sword. And the backs of their people as the Horned Wolves headed home, his mother, Uncle Craven, and the

rest of the clan following custom by leaving his wounded grandfather
to the scavengers, and Sullen, too, when he wouldn't leave the old
man's side.

Sullen had been eight thaws old. He killed his first snow lion that
night, and started dragging his grandfather back to the village. It
had taken six days, Sullen collecting snow in the mornings for their
waterskins and frost-termites for their breakfast. By the time they'd
made it back to the disbelieving scowls of their clan, Uncle Craven
was long gone. Again.

"But you said—" Sullen paused as his mother rolled over beside
him, so excited he could barely keep his voice to a whisper. "You
said they'd ambush Uncle before he got a week out, kill him good to
make sure he couldn't shame our people ever again."

"Wishful thinking of an angry father. If those runts the council
sent after him had actually caught the boy they'd have come home
singing about it, instead of playing it too fierce to talk about. No,
my boy can't be any deader than the cold cod we got around here,"
said Grandfather longingly. "I got half a mind to see if I can't track
'im down before I find my doom, or it finds me. Fess to him he was
wise to leave, a fool to ever come back, and wiser still the second time
he lit out. Tell him . . . tell him his dad don't understand why he did
what he done, but he's finally ready to listen."

The wind whistled through the thatch of their hut, and in the
darkness Sullen squinted to see the wraithlike devils capering over
his bed. No wolf worthy of his horns would leave his pack, no matter how worthless a gang they were . . . a real horned wolf would whip
them into shape or die trying rather than turning tail. How many
times had Grandfather said that?

So this must not be the same as turning tail. Grandfather just
wanted to find Uncle Craven, and then they would come back. The
same as Uncle Craven, really, who'd gone missing as an unnamed
boy, only to return a thaw or three before Sullen was born and live
as a proper Horned Wolf up until that dark day of the battle. Even
after Uncle Craven broke their laws by leaving the first time, when
he'd come back the clan had welcomed him. That Uncle Craven had

just run away again a few years later and the clan now cursed his name more than any devil didn't matter so much, because once Sullen and Grandfather returned they'd never leave again. This would be a quest for Sullen to earn his honor, not too different from the Songs of Rakehell or the Saga of Old Black. He knew their tales by heart, kenned the heroes of old in a way he had never understood the Horned Wolves he had come of age alongside. He had always longed to have an adventure of his own, and they were thin on the ground here in the Frozen Savannahs.

The thought of meeting his uncle—of demanding to know why he'd abandoned him and Grandfather on the battlefield just to abandon the clan altogether—filled Sullen with a strange and powerful hunger. Not a small hunger, neither; no, this felt like he'd just smelled a thick slice of barley bread topped with a scoop of lye cod after the midwinter fast. He could let Grandfather talk to Uncle Craven, and then he could talk to him, and then all three of them could come home together, and Sullen would bring along such treasures as he'd found along the way as to make all the clan love him . . . or maybe just respect him a little. It wasn't as though he and Grandfather would be terribly missed—they would probably be home again before anyone noticed they were gone. Theirs would be a song worth singing, even if he only ever sang it to himself when he was sure he was alone.

Looking back and forth between his snoring mother and his eager grandfather, Sullen made up his mind. Would his mother be heartbroken when she awoke and found both her father and son gone, or would she secretly be relieved? Sullen didn't know, and as always, the not knowing made everything so much worse.

CHAPTER
5

What an absurd, appalling day.

Take some initiative, his father was always saying, like the chorus in the tragedy that was Sir Hjortt's life, *for the love of your ancestors, get off your doughy ass and take some initiative.* And the one time he took that advice, the one fucking time, where did it get him? Right fucking here, apparently. Thanks, Dad.

Sir Hjortt straddled a painful fence, split between hatred at the probably deceased Brother Iqbal for neglecting to detect the old woman's witchcraft and good old-fashioned self-pity. The mayoress clearly had the aid of devils, for she'd dodged the knight's sword with the speed of a water weasel and then broken his arm with the strength of an ox. An angry one. The steel cop covering his elbow had actually popped loose from her barehanded assault, dangling as worthlessly as the arm it had failed to protect.

The knight had been in his fair share of scrapes—well, one or two, anyway—but the agony of his arm being snapped backward had beggared belief. By the time his mind had recovered from its shock the old witch had dragged him back inside her kitchen. His sole attempt at further resistance had resulted in her frogging him in the eye with a curled finger and then twisting his broken arm until he retched from the pain of it all. After that, he did as he was told and let her tie him to a chair with the coil of thick cord she had scared up. The most that could be said for his situation was that he barely registered his headache anymore.

Now she was stomping around upstairs and Sir Hjortt's thoughts were beginning to crawl back toward rationality—she had undone both Iqbal and himself, doubtless with some fell sorcery, and now he was her prisoner. Even if Sister Portolés came straight back after giving the order to purge the town, it was a long walk up the hill. He might be alone with the old woman for a while, and had best ensure she knew what a healthy ransom he would command before she did anything regrettable. Well, anything *more* regrettable.

Footfalls on the stairs in the other room, and then she bustled back into the kitchen and deposited a pile of clothing onto the table. She paused, then picked up a linen shirt and draped it over her husband's head, covering it and the scones. Next she pulled her dirndl over her head, and then her blouse. Although she didn't seem to possess an extra breast on which her familiars might suckle or any other witchly deformities, her inexplicable stripping sat poorly with her captive.

Her head snapped in his direction, and Sir Hjortt realized with horror that he must have inadvertently made his displeasure known with a groan or something. He tried to play it off, lolling his head and staring down at his broken arm as he moaned. She walked over and backhanded him across the cheek, which was entirely uncalled for and flew in the face of all acceptable conduct regarding noble prisoners of war. He knew because he'd memorized those passages of the Crimson Codices, lest he ever find it necessary to surrender rather than die an easily avoided death on some random battlefield.

"You should have let me speak," she said, putting her face right in his, her breath stinking like that awful tea. "Instead of sending your Chainwitch down to murder my people, you should have let me have my say. You'd be counting coins right now. A lot of them. I'd follow you and kill you, of course, for what you did to Leib, but I'd have given you a few weeks to put this place behind you, lest anyone suspect the motive and return to Kypck. You might have enjoyed those extra days of easy living."

"This 'Leib' is your husband." Sir Hjortt frowned, his face stinging from her blow. "Kypck's your town."

"Leib was my husband, before you killed him. Kypck was my town, before you killed it, too. If you're not on a battlefield, you should learn the names of those you slaughter, if only to taunt any vengeful pursuers."

"From his first breath to his last, the wise general never leaves the battlefield," said Sir Hjortt sagely. "Only thus is peace won."

"Ugh," said the witch, wrinkling her nose. "They're still hammering Lord Bleak's *Ironfist* into the Crimson command? No wonder you're such a shameless bastard, swallowing that fascist dog shit."

"You've read it?" said Sir Hjortt, surprised.

"'Poor strategies should be studied as well as wise ones, for generals shall adopt the former more oft than the latter.' You know who said that?" The naked old sorceress was still leaning over him, and as one of the waves of pain rolled back out to sea he realized she was actually waiting for a response. He shook his head. "Ji-un Park," she said.

"They no more taught us the tactics of Immaculates than they did the stratagems of squirrels," said Sir Hjortt. "But I think it's high time we talked ransom, my lady, as—"

"My lady, is it?" She snorted. "You'd have been better off studying the squirrels than Lord Bleak—they have the sense to stay away from beehives, even if they are full of honey."

"I...uh." Sir Hjortt felt the heat spread from his broken arm up to his cheeks at the lewd way the matron breathed the words in his face, and he looked away from her nakedness. By all the devils and deacons of the Burnished Chain, what was she going to do, cast a spell?

Instead of ensorcelling him, the woman turned away and went back to the clothes piled on the table. After fishing out a tan pair of trousers, she squeezed into them with a grunt and then fixed a leather...thing across her bosom. Over that went a shirt or tunic or something—the knight had stopped paying attention in order to try and wriggle his ankles free, get some options going...but when she'd tied his legs to the chair she'd been thorough, and he couldn't do more than impotently squirm in his seat.

She left the room, banged around the rest of the house, and then came back into the kitchen with a stout, one-handed war hammer and an unstrung bow. Setting these on the clothes pile, she disappeared again. Sir Hjortt stared at the hammer nervously. She returned with an already bulging backpack and set to wrestling the remaining clothes into it, save for the shirt covering her husband's head.

"My lady," he said, but she ignored him, and so he tried again. It was like reasoning with his father, only worse. He hadn't thought such a thing was possible, prior to this moment. "Madame Mayoress, if I might—"

"You might shut your mouth before I decide to cut out your tongue—you could choke to death on your own blood. For all I know your Sister Portolés is halfway up the hill, and I don't intend to be here when she finds the remains of your other pet witch."

"You're the only witch here," said Sir Hjortt, although now that she mentioned it he wondered if Portolés had somehow sensed it when Iqbal died, if she was even now racing up the trail to—shit on fire, the hag was messing with his broken arm again!

"You can't know how much I hate being called that," she said, running her hand down his agonized arm, then holding up a sinew bowstring for his inspection. "But you'll find out soon enough how it feels for fools to think you're something other than what you are, for them to attribute your accomplishments to witchcraft. They'll call you a sorcerer, do you know that?"

"What are you...don't!" Sir Hjortt felt his numb thumb in her bony fingers, then the bowstring dug sharply into the base of the digit. A tear formed in the eye that wasn't swollen shut as his thumb immediately began to sing louder than its broken arm.

"They'll be wrong, of course, but it won't change things—Colonel Hjortt of Azgaroth: demonologist. Or maybe diabolist, it amounts to the same thing. Colonel Hjortt, summoner of devils best left in hell. Not bad for a young prat of a noble, eh?"

"This isn't my fault," Sir Hjortt blathered over his shoulder. "I'm a decent man, I didn't want to go into the army, I wouldn't, I'm not a bad sort, I just . . . just . . ."

"Did as you were told?" She paused in her work, her voice low. "Carried out the orders you were given?"

"Yes, exactly!" said Sir Hjortt, eager to tell her whatever she wanted to hear, anything to make her stop. "Orders! Not my idea! Never!"

"You certainly seemed reluctant to carry them out," she said, her voice hardening as she looped the bowstring around the base of his other thumb, the one on his good arm, and pulled it tight. As she deftly tied it off in a knot, an immediate, awful throbbing filled both thumbs, as though they had been stung by something highly poisonous. She stood, went to the cooling kettle, and picked up a kitchen knife she had been warming beside it on the woodstove.

"Please," Sir Hjortt gasped, his skull pounding in tandem with his arm and, worst of all, his thumbs. He tried to stay calm, but she'd tied them so tight the sensation would have been unbearable even if he hadn't guessed what she intended. "Please, there's no cause for—"

"No cause?" said the witch, coming back to him. Fallen Mother save him, the black blade of the knife in her hand was actually *smoking*. "We both know the punishment for theft in your homeland, don't we, Colonel? You've stolen my husband from me, you've stolen my friends, my *family*, so this should hardly come as a surprise. The tourniquets will keep you from bleeding too much."

"Please, I didn't have a choice, I—" But then the witch crouched behind his chair, and though he thrashed in his seat, she made short work of it. The pressure in the thumb of his broken arm was released first, and then, more palpably, he felt his other thumb sawed through in several brisk strokes. The bone gave her trouble, though, and he shrieked as she snapped it off. When he was again sensible of his surroundings, his tormentor was back in front of him, wiping the bloody knife clean on the vair collar of his cloak.

"You said you didn't have a choice," said the witch, sliding her unstrung bow into a scabbard on the side of her backpack and then shouldering it. "I believe you, boy—you're just a good little doggie doing what he's told, aren't you? An innocent lad, cursed with bad luck?"

"You evil, evil woman," Sir Hjortt whined, the fire where his thumbs had been now spreading through his hands. "I'm a colonel of the fucking Queen of Samoth! They'll find you, my father, Sister Portolés, the queen, the pope, they'll find you and—"

"And *what*, boy? And what?" She took the hammer off the table and advanced on him. "You don't know a devildamned thing about *anything*, do you? What could they do to me, eh? What could they take that you haven't already stolen?"

"You're dead!" Sir Hjortt knew he was being pathetic, that he was courting further punishment, but he couldn't stop himself. "You've fucking crippled me! How am I supposed to get on without my *hands*, you monster! It would be a mercy if you'd kill me instead!"

"Mercy. Now there's a devil I won't have any truck with, not from here until my dying day," she said, but she reached around and slipped the handle of her war hammer through a loop on the side of her backpack instead of using the weapon on Sir Hjortt. Then she went to the table, flipping the shirt off her husband's head. After a moment's pause, she picked the skull up by the hair and returned it to its satchel, which then went over a shoulder. It hung awkwardly against the backpack, and as she looked back at Sir Hjortt with those flashing blue eyes he knew what he should have from the very first— he was totally, utterly fucked.

"What can you do?" he said, his voice cracking. "What can you possibly do? Where can you go? They'll find you, they will, to make an example—"

"An example," said the witch, nodding. "That's what I'll do, make some examples. Now, let's take a look and see how the example you set for me is going."

She walked behind him, grabbing the back of his seat in both hands and dragging him out onto the deck. The legs of the chair screeched as he went. How could Iqbal have missed such obvious deviltry, a grey-haired gran capable of hauling around a fully

armored knight? What was the point of keeping witchborn bodyguards if they couldn't even recognize their own wicked kind? It was
hard to think anything so coherent, though, the pounding grief in
his hands consuming everything, all the blood that should be flowing through them instead backing up into his brain, drowning his
mind in a deluge of pain. It took some grunting and cursing, but she
finally maneuvered the chair so that he could look out over the valley.
There was a lot of smoke coming up, but he couldn't make out much
else. The mocking aspens made him reel, and if he hadn't been tied
in place he would have collapsed. Damn the Fallen Mother for her
deafness.

"Don't worry, Colonel Hjortt," she said, still standing beside him.
"If your weirdborn nun is half as clever as I expect, you'll be saved
long before the fire spreads out here. And if not, well, hopefully the
ropes will burn away first and you'll get off with a light charring. I
know masks are quite fashionable in Azgaroth, especially Cockspar.
They used to be, anyway."

He tried to speak, to beg, maybe, or threaten, but his tongue felt as
heavy as brass.

"Before, you generously offered me the freedom to weep, should
I need to," the madwoman breathed in Sir Hjortt's ear. "I think I'll
wait, though. I'm not going to cry for all those honest, blameless
people down there, much as I love some of them, much as I like most
of the rest. I'm not even going to cry for my husband."

She tousled his hair, her lips now brushing his earlobe. "The only
one I'm going to weep for, good knight, is you, and my tears will only
fall after we've been reunited. That's right, boy, once every other individual responsible for this travesty has been dealt with, after every
single one of them has been paid a visit, *then* I'll find you, wherever
you go, wherever you hide, and I will deal with you at my leisure.
Then, oh brave Hjortt of Azgaroth, Fifteenth Colonel of the Crimson Empire, *then*, when you've finally escaped my vengeance, either
through madness or death, *then* I will weep, but only because I can
no longer torment you."

"Holy shit," Sir Hjortt managed before the first sob wracked his gallant chest. From the pain, yes. And the shock of being made a cripple, certainly. Yet the true source of his misery, the thing that made him half hope that the fire she set in the house just before fleeing into the mountains would consume the deck he sat upon before Sister Portolés could rescue him, was one simple fact: he believed every word she said.

CHAPTER

6

Maroto sat atop the rim of the canyon, leaned his mace against a rock, and strapped his sandals back on. The sandstone felt warm against his bare legs with the bloody sun just peeking over the cracked plateau; in a few hours the rock he leaned against would be scalding to the touch. Even complemented by daybreak's bouquet of rose, hyacinth, and lilac, the Panteran Wastes looked even worse up here than they did in the labyrinth of ravines and gullies that cut through the desert. Down in the shadow roads there were cacti and twisted cedar, the infrequent spring surrounded by cattails and stunted willow, but nothing grew on these exposed plains and ridges save umber tufts of grass, ivory lichens, and blasted black rock formations. Maroto knew he could have found a worse place to lead his party, but doing so would have taken more work than he was willing to put in without extra pay.

Beneath him it was still too dark to see much. They had a cooking fire going, so he supposed the caravan had finished circling the wagons as best they could in the tight canyon—the gaudy convoy reminded him of an emperor centipede winding across the smoldering desert by night and then coiling up in some hole when dawn threatened. A cooking fire, in the Wastes! Maroto couldn't decide which was a greater marker of his party's absurd affluence: that they insisted on eating half a dozen hot meals a night, or that in between they snacked on sorbets and other frozen treats. Witch-powered or not, keeping the ice-wagon cool must cost a pretty princedom. Almost as much as the aquaricart, probably.

The money was good, though, so here he was. No, the money was great, princely, or else he never would have taken the gig. Repeat the mantra. As if money could ever be anything but devilish...

He really ought to start climbing back down before it got too hot, now that he had confirmed that the horizon was free of encroaching swarmclouds and the sky was clear of thunderheads, but he couldn't bear to return right away. He could (and indeed, had) slept through battles and coronations, orgies and sieges, but something about the shrill tittering of his charges kept him up long into the morning, every morning. Besides, scrambling out of the gorge as every other hold crumbled beneath his weight had given him a parched throat to go along with his raw fingers and toes, and climbing down was always far worse than coming up.

Most folk, his party included, watered down their cougar milk, but then most people, his party especially, were utterly, irredeemably weak. Knocking back his boozeskin, the draught burned like it ought to, few things restoring a man's perspective better than a pull on the licorice-sweet lava those Pertnessian alchemists cooked up. He fondly recalled a bar fight in Old Slair when a goon had swung on him with a lit torch and he'd used his flagon to breathe fire in the man's face. That he'd set his own dreadlocks alight in the process only lent the tale flavor—by all the forgotten gods of his heathen ancestors, what had he been thinking, twisting his hair into those ropes? Why not just fix a handle on your helm for people to grab hold of and sling you about...

The clattering of rocks bouncing down the ravine, and a grunt just beneath his heels. Somebody was coming up the cliff after him, and they were almost to the top. Of all the empty-skulled plays these lordlings had made, this had to be one of the worst. He'd allowed Sir Kuksi to accompany him up on their first morning out, and the ponce had slipped a mere twenty feet up the sandy slope, skinning his palms and twisting an ankle before landing in a heap of torn satin and silk at the bottom, to the jeers of his comrades. After that

Maroto had made it abundantly clear: leave the scouting to the scout. Up until this juncture they had listened, but the brats were getting surlier by the night as crossing the Wastes revealed itself to be every bit as awful an ordeal as one ought to expect, given the name of the place. They claimed to want adventure, Lady Opeth going so far as to demand a giant scorpion to battle, yet they squealed like children when they found examples of the regular variety in their shoes after a hard night's day of drinking, drugging, and gambling 'round the campfire. It took all of his willpower not to grab one of those boot scorpions in his bare hand and let it sting him into blessed oblivion.

A soft and bloody palm slapped up, manicured fingers digging into the sandstone edge of the cliff, and Maroto darted forward. He grabbed the idiot's wrist before any further weight could be put onto the dangerous handhold, before he could put any thought into whether or not it might be better just to let this moron fall to their death and serve as an example to the rest. The noble cried out as Maroto hurled them up and over the lip of the cliff, the petite lordling dangling from one of his thick hands. It was Tapai Purna, because of course it was Purna.

Even after a week in the Wastes, Maroto had no idea if this particular fop identified as man, woman, or neither. The majority of the party came from the Serpent's Circle, and there in the old-and-then-new-and-then-old-again capital of the Crimson Empire they still used the obvious titles like *Duke* and *Duchess*, *Zir* and *Sir*, so getting a rough idea of how to address someone wasn't too hard. The Ugra-kari honorific *Tapai*, on the other hand, could apply to anyone, and Maroto couldn't remember enough of his campaigns on that side of the Star to recall if the name *Purna* skewed in any particular direction. Among most of the coxcombs certain unavoidable physiological differences helped make things easy, but Purna Antimgran, Thirty-ninth Tapai of Ugrakar, was one of the exceptions. Despite looking about thirty years old, the noble didn't reveal enough in the chest or shoulders, arse or hips to give Maroto a solid clue. Tapai Purna may have hailed from a different homeland, but had adopted the Serpentine style of the rest of the nobles with gusto: an already androgynous, if handsome face was buried under lead foundation and cerulean lipstick, and the powdered wig only further befuddled matters. Purna's choice of fashion was as confounding as that of the others: the most popular attire, despite the climate, consisted of puffy lace collars, enormous ribbon bows, and layers and layers of embroidered shirts and vests tucked into frilly cream bloomers. These bloomers would have looked bad enough beneath one's clothes, but they were even worse when worn as an outer layer, Purna's admittedly shapely legs swathed in parti-colored hose and tipped with delicate, black-buckled shoes.

All of which were now scuffed or torn, stained and dripping, as Maroto set Purna down on the jagged ridgeline. Harlequin tears spattered the stone as sweat excavated gullies in the fop's makeup. Purna's garish facepaint reminded Maroto of a diva he'd performed with a time or two, way back in the bad old days, except Carla Rossi's foulmouthed drag routine was a good deal more entertaining than anything he'd yet seen out of the nobles.

"Made good time," Maroto thought out loud, almost impressed by the lordling. Almost. "You in some kind of hurry?"

"I—" Purna gasped, head shaking, and readjusted the damp wig that had migrated to the side. "Damn."

"Yeah," said Maroto, then left the panting noble to peer back down the cliff. "Any more of you coming up?"

"No," said Purna. "Water."

"That how you ask for something?" said Maroto, passing Purna his cougar milk. He grinned when the fop coughed on the liquor, then chided himself as Purna spit out a mouthful—he shouldn't waste a drop of good drink on his charges. "Ah, gave you the wrong skin—here you are, Tapai, my mistake."

"Thank you, barbarian," Purna said, after recovering enough to properly speak. "I should have brought my own. Your first rule."

"How's that?"

"You told us the first rule of the Wastes was never to leave the camp without water."

"Half right," said Maroto, remembering now. "I said the first rule was to never leave the camp, period, but if you did, never to go with-out water. Sound advice. I know what I'm talking about."

"Of course you do," said Purna. The noble unbuttoned a remov-able velvet panel and used it to mop away grime and mascara sludge from around eyes as amber as a comb of dreamhoney. These popin-jays always had something up their sleeves, if only another handker-chief. "You're even better than we were expecting."

Maroto sighed. Here it came, then. From their first night out the dirty lordlings had been trying to seduce him, which had initially flattered him. That was, until Maroto politely declined an invita-tion to share Duke Rackcleff's pleasure wagon, whereupon the jilted ninny had huffily informed him the proposition was solely due to a high-stakes wager the party had decided upon: who would be the first to bag the barbarian? Of all Maroto's wards, Purna was far from the worst on the eyes, but even if there hadn't been the pride angle, he still would have thought twice about rolling in the sand with the fop; in his experience, the upper crust were twice as likely to give you a pox as a prostitute, and half as inclined to finish you off if they came first.

"So I'm impressive, am I?" he said, eyeing the raggedy Ugrakari. "You're so impressed you came up here to what, rub my shoulders, maybe give me a token of your affection?"

"I beg your pardon?" This noble was a cool liar, no doubt—Purna almost seemed genuinely confused.

"I know about the bet, and I fear none of you stands to profit from my prick. Maroto is no whore, nor a rich lord's plaything," he said, studiously keeping his mind from the dark old nights when he had been so far down the hive that he couldn't even remember what he'd done to get his next sting.

"Oh, *gross*!" cried Purna. "I am *not* involved in that, I don't care how much lucre they put in the kitty. So disgusting!"

"Yes, well . . ." said Maroto, thinking that maybe Purna wasn't just referring to the ethics of such a wager, and flinching a little inside. "Then why follow me here? Such a climb is no place for a young, uh, person. Of distinction."

"Oh!" said Purna, eagerness replacing revulsion. "Diggelby let me use his hawkglass, and way over, ah, south of us, on this ridge, there was this great big lizard mooning itself on a rock. I thought we could hunt it!"

"Big lizard?" Maroto's sweaty skin went cold. "This ridge?"

"From where you were climbing up it looked to be just over that, what do you call it...*escarpment*? Those rocks there, I mean, over those a little bit—ah!" Purna shrieked upon noticing that he or she had pointed directly at a godguana, the horse-sized lizard watching them from atop a rock shelf some twenty yards away. It could be on top of them in three bounds of its enormous, banded legs. "There he is!"

"I see her," whispered Maroto, meeting the black gaze of the carnivorous calamity rather than glancing to where his mace rested against the stone. He knew where the weapon was, could snatch it without looking, but would give his two pinky fingers if he could avoid having to use it. Female godguanas grew bigger, could disembowel you with their hooked claws, poison you with their noxious bite, but were less territorial than the males, so maybe she was just investigating them, and when she saw that they were no—

"Get it!" howled Purna, charging past him at the godguana. Maroto didn't waste his breath on a curse as he sidestepped toward his mace. Even as his hand found it missing his eyes located it. Purna. The noble held it high, bum-rushing a creature that half a dozen experienced hunters would have balked at taking on, and ululating all the way. "Wooooo!"

It would have been better to flee down the cliff, trusting the creature to gorge herself on Purna while he made good his getaway, but that mace meant a lot to Maroto. Purna closed the distance over the rough ground, dainty shoes gliding over the rocks with admirable alacrity. The godguana hissed and rose up on her hind legs, and even at this distance the stench of her maw made Maroto's eyes water as he seized up a melon-sized chunk of sandstone.

The monster dropped down from the rock shelf, directly on top of the charging fop. Maroto hurled his rock. Purna was crushed to the ground by one of the godguana's claws, and then Maroto's missile nailed the creature's left eye with such force that the sandstone exploded in a cloud of orange dust. The godguana's head listed sharply from the blow, but only for a moment, her long, black-scaled snout straightening back out as she surveyed Maroto, one eye beady as ever, the other a raw, bleeding wound. She tensed her claws, Purna moaning as the lizard's foot ground through cloth and skin alike. Maroto hoped the idiot noble lived long enough for him to kill this monster so that he could then have the satisfaction of hurling Purna off of the cliff.

The rock had certainly gotten the creature's attention; she launched herself straight at him. Smaller godguanas had an almost silly gait, their wide-armed dash anything but graceful. There was nothing silly about a full-grown female charging him, each stride covering half a dozen feet. Maroto whipped the dagger out of his belt as the godguana bore down on him. He braced himself, and when she lunged forward he ducked to the side of her mouth and went for her spiny neck. Grabbing her in an awkward headlock with his off hand, he was carried off the ground as she jerked away.

He clung on as she attempted to buck him loose, claws narrowly missing his tucked-up legs, his head pressed against that of the direlizard. As she thrashed, the edge of his flattop caught in her gnashing jaws, and he felt the tug on his scalp as she chewed his hair, the stink of the rotten mouth bordering on the sublime. All the while Maroto plunged his dagger through the tough scales between her shoulders, over and over, nicking himself on her ridge of spines in the process, blood flowing freely down the arm he held the creature with as it ground against her sharp hide.

It was a tried-and-true approach, and would have worked, too, if the luck gods hadn't taken a shit on him in the form of a boulder onto which the godguana slammed him. He lost his strength for but a moment, and then he was off the lizard, laid out atop the rock like a human sacrifice as the bloodied, raging monster reared back up... and here she came again, crashing down like a hammer on an obstinate walnut. He tried to roll away, knowing even as he did that he was too slow, that it had taken him too long to get his wind back, and now, yes, ugh, the full weight of the lizard crashed upon him, pinning him halfway off the boulder with her chest. Woof. So much for Maroto, his guts were about to be squeezed out either end, and—

Then she was off of him, hissing louder than ever, her tail whipping the boulder a hairbreadth from his chin. The edge of the sandstone splintered off from the impact and he fell off the rock after it, landing in a crouch and bracing for the claws or bite that were surely coming. He had dropped the dagger at some point and was seeing double for the first time in years—this was it. He was irredeemably screwed.

Yet the twinned lizards shimmering in the dawn had turned their backs on him, and as his vision came back into focus he saw that one of her hind legs had been busted wide open at the haunch, the useless appendage oozing red through a mess of knotted muscle and torn scales. Purna limped just out of reach of the wounded godguana, warding off her snapping mouth with Maroto's mace rather than chancing another solid swing at it. Purna looked about as rough as the lizard, the noble's left side stained red from missing wig to torn bloomers, the priceless attire shredded to the skin and deeper still by the lizard's claws, and hold on, yes, there was a petite but decidedly feminine breast under the blood and tatters.

Even as Maroto registered this he stooped to get another missile, which stunned the godguana when it exploded against the crest on the back of her head. Purna didn't close the deal like she should have, instead using the opportunity to put more distance between herself and the lizard, so Maroto went for another rock. As he grabbed a good one the godguana gave up the fight, skittering away over the narrow ridge, trailing gore, but before she gained the shelter of a high rock formation his third stone popped her in the back, just above the tail, and, tripped up, the monster slid over the far edge of the cliff.

"Woof," said Maroto, slouching back to lean against the boulder that had almost been his gravestone. What a disaster. "You okay, Tapai?"

Purna waved the mace, then slumped her shoulders and dragged her feet over to him. She was missing a shoe, her stockings sullied and full of runs. Maroto still wanted to toss her down the ravine, but it would have been bad form, given how she'd just saved his life, so he settled for laying some hard truths on her.

"That was the dumbest damn thing one of you golden goblets has pulled yet," he growled. "And that includes bringing a fucking fish tank to the desert."

Maroto had, in fact, been rather impressed when he first saw Princess Von Yung's aquaricart, but after he learned that none of the vibrantly colored marine life was actually edible, his opinion on the matter had soured considerably.

"That was..." Purna shook her head, clearly on the edge of tears. Seeing how deep the gouges in her chest went, and the bruise rising on her scraped cheek, Maroto began to soften. Until she said, "That was the best. So fucking awesome. I saved *your ass*, barbarian! Woo!"

"You saved *my* arse?" Maroto could not believe his fucking ears. "Girl, the next time you put your head in a kiln to watch the devils dance, I'll let you look as long as you want instead of pulling you out. You nearly got us both dead!"

"Were you scared?" asked Purna. "It's okay if you were. I was scared, too. A little."

"Scared?" Maroto felt his cheeks flush, and then a fury that only escaped its bonds in his blood on the rarest occasions. But before the lordling could push him over the edge, Purna sat down on a rock, dropped the mace, and buried her head in her hands. Maroto watched her shudder with emotion for long enough to confirm that she wasn't laughing at him, and after having a gander over the far cliffside to make sure the beast was truly dead, he fetched the cougar milk to pour on their wounds. Neither had suffered a bite, but even so, godguana claws were nasty enough to carry nine kinds of plague.

When he came back Purna was sitting up straight, the mace propped against her knee, and Maroto did his best not to be too obvious in his ogling as he washed her wounds in booze. With her makeup sloughed off by the righteous trinity of blood, sweat, and tears, her stupid wig gone, and her cropped black hair spiky with lizard ichors, she looked a sight better. Not that he felt anything but scorn for the puffed-up little dandy, but few folk didn't look good with blood on their tits and a weapon at the ready.

There was a thought to please the devils. Maroto amended his musings: it wasn't that he liked the idea of an injured woman, gods no, just that warriors always looked better bloody than clean, and warriors always looked better than anyone else. Nothing wrong with thinking the truth.

"I think you've got it pretty well sorted," said Purna, standing up, and Maroto realized he'd perhaps been overly diligent in his application of the absinthe-soaked rag. "Come on, let's get you washed and then we can go after it."

"After it?" He winced as he applied the cloth to his wrist. He'd almost scraped it to the veins, riding that lizard's rough neck. "I checked; thing's busted open on a ledge fifty feet down. Even if she wasn't, though, you don't follow a wounded animal unless you have to. You think that monster put up a fight, see what one would do if you cornered her."

"Sure, sure," said Purna, fiddling with her shredded vest until she could tie a strip of it into her collar, giving her a beggar's modesty. "I just want its head. To, you know, mount? That's the whole reason we're out here, isn't it, for this sort of thing? What's the point in battling monsters if you don't get a trophy?"

"Come on," said Maroto, getting up. "We're going back before another one shows up."

"I'm not leaving without my trophy," said Purna. "If you don't climb down and get it, I will."

"Fine," said Maroto. "Good luck. I'd say I'll meet you back at camp later, except I probably won't because you'll slip and break an ankle and lie on some spit of rock crying until something comes along to eat you."

"What's your price, barbarian?" said Purna, sounding as simultaneously bored and annoyed as a noble buying their bratty kid out of trouble. "To get me the head, how much would it cost me?"

"More than you're worth," said Maroto, but he couldn't help but

feel the itch in his least honorable organ: his purse. It hadn't looked to
be too hard a climb down to the direlizard... "Ten thousand rupees."

"Let's make it twelve," said Purna with a smile, which was how
Maroto found himself cleaning off the mace he had almost lost, along
with his life, and descending to where the godguana had fallen. She
had begun to cook in the morning heat, and the stench made him
gag as he broke through her ridge of spines and the bones beneath,
mashing her shoulders into reptilian paste. Would've been a sight
easier with an ax instead of the dubious duo of mace and dagger, but
then it would've been a damn sight easier to just tell Purna where to
stick her twelve thousand rupees. He was half-baked himself by the
time he rejoined Purna on the summit, whereupon he discovered she
had drunk all his water while he was doing her dirty work. Yet not
even the realization that to get them both down safely he'd have to
carry her on his back compared to the frustration he felt when they
were at long last back on the under-roads, returning to the caravan,
and she said, "So twelve thousand rupees will take some doing, but
while we were climbing I hit on the perfect solution."

"While *we* were climbing?" Maroto tried to keep a level tone; until
he had the money in hand it wouldn't do to spook her. "You promised me something you couldn't pay, Tapai Purna? I thought you
nobles were reliable about paying your debts."

"If we were there would be far fewer of us," said Purna. "My shoulder really hurts, are you sure it's all right?"

"I'll stitch you up at the camp. But only after I've been paid."

"Ah, yes. But see, I don't have the money yet."

"When will you? I'd be quick about it, personally. You want those
sewn up right away."

"That depends on you," said Purna. "We could have it as soon as
tomorrow."

"Depends on me," said Maroto, a cannonball sort of weight settling in his guts.

"As I said, I wanted no part in their vile little wager. No part.
Bleh." Purna stuck out her tongue. "But I can go back to my chums

and enter a share, saying that after our adventure today I've warmed
to the beast, and decided to take a chance on seducing it myself."

"Seducing *it*? The *beast*?"

"Yes, that's what they call you. Not me, though. I always just call
you the barbarian."

Some improvement. "So you lay a wager, then later today or tomorrow we go off and have a screw and—"

"No, no, no!" said Purna. "What sort of a person do you take me
for? I lay the wager, then we sneak off and *pretend* to fuck, preferably
tucked away in one of these canyons where the echoes can reach the
rest, just so there's no room for doubt. Then I get paid, and in turn
you get paid."

"Absolutely not," said Maroto. "Under no circumstances. I have
pride, girl, a word unfamiliar to you so-called civilized folk, but one
dear to me as the true name of any devil."

"Have it your way," said Purna. "I think the pot's closer to twenty
thousand, so I'd go so far as to give you fifteen and keep a modest five
for the injury to my reputation, but if you'd rather be silverless and
proud, then—"

"All twenty," said Maroto, dropping Purna's reptilian trophy in the
sand. The wagons were just ahead. "All twenty, and you have to tell
them that you convinced me you weren't actually part of the wager
before I agreed to fuck you. I won't have it said I'm a whore or a rich
lord's plaything."

"Seventeen, and agreed on your condition," said Purna, squatting
down and hoisting the lizard head herself. Her arms were shaking
but she managed it. "Final offer."

"Eighteen."

"Seventeen-five, and you're no whore nor rich girl's plaything."

"Agreed," said Maroto, though he was no longer so sure about
that last bit. They returned to the campfire, the coterie of coxcombs
squawking and hooting at their bedraggled appearance and Purna's
prize. Revolting a scene as it surely was, Kōshaku Köz's valet revealed
herself to have both a barber's bag and the skill to use it. Purna was
treated first, naturally, while Maroto fended off the demands of the

rest to be taken on a dragon hunt at dusk. Later, he overheard Purna's version of events over brandy and cigars while his significantly worse injuries were tended to. He told himself that declining the valet's offer of a centipede prior to setting in was a victory, albeit a small one, but every stab of the needle and tug of the thread reminded him of his weakness, his failings; here was a man who couldn't even trust himself to take a painkiller before undergoing surgery, lest he back-slide into his old ways. And after the day he'd had, all he had to look forward to was a make-believe tryst on the morrow.

There was a time when Maroto wouldn't have entered the Panteran Wastes for the far more lucrative and enjoyable proposition of raid-ing just such a party of wealthy fools, a time when he would have laughed in the face of anyone who suggested he might end up play-ing Great Barbarian Hunter for a bunch of second-rate fops. There was a time when Maroto would have gestured at his priceless armor, his witch-touched weapons, his lands and titles and holdings, to say naught of the bloody devil that served his will—here was a man with everything silver could buy, and many things it could not.

When he squinted into the past, he could almost make out that man through the mists of bug- and drink-filtered memories and increasingly poor decisions. The simpering choir of the nobles car-ried on into the early hours of the night, and sleep was as elusive as dignity as he lay on his too-soft cot in his too-nice covered wagon, dreading the future every bit as much as he loathed the past. He told himself that once they were out of the Wastes he would never again debase himself so . . . but he'd broken that promise many, many times before and he would, sad to say, break it again.

CHAPTER
7

It was long after midnight when Choplicker caught up to Zosia in the high country. Hearing him crash through the low ring of deadfall she had piled around her camp, she drew away into the junipers, into the darkness, into the focused wrath that was the only thing that let her rioting mind relax into silence...and when the miserable scavenger appeared across the fire, she pulled her bowstring back even farther, and loosed her arrow straight at his muzzle. The missile veered off course and disappeared into the night, just like she knew it would, but she nocked another anyway, storming out of the shadows at him.

"Why?" Zosia's voice broke as she drew her bow again, just across the small fire from the beast now. "Why the fuck didn't you take it? I know you could've, I know it would've been child's play for you to honor the terms I offered, so *why*?"

Choplicker whined at her, keeping his wagging tail low to the ground the way he always did when he knew he was in trouble. This, this right here was how he'd lulled her into thinking they were all right with one another, this grotesque charade was how he'd convinced her that she had nothing to fear from him. That they were friends. And then he'd as good as murdered Leib.

Zosia almost fired her second arrow but then she noticed that Choplicker had not returned alone. The arms of a child were wrapped around his furry neck, its bloody back limp atop his own. Even freshly fed, it must have taken some effort for the old beggar to drag a corpse all the way up the mountain—and just to rub her nose in it.

Zosia relaxed her bow and tossed it onto her bedroll. Then she stalked around the fire, meaning to take Choplicker apart with her bare hands, when the child slid down his haunches, letting out a moan as he collapsed onto the cold, moss-cushioned earth. Cursing, she hurried to the boy and rolled him onto his side, the firelight turning his bloody tunic to molten gold. He moaned again as she tore the cloth and prodded the wound, a rude, deep puncture that had narrowly missed the base of his spine.

"Mayoress." The boy's voice was raspier than the junipers in the wind that stalked these heights. "It hurts."

Zosia sighed, letting out as much of her pain and rage as she could. It would only distract her now, and after the events of the day it wasn't as if she was in danger of exhausting her stores in this lifetime. She bit the inside of her cheek, focusing herself as best she could. The wound was deep, no doubt from a spear, and his long, jostling ride up the mountains couldn't have done him any boon. It would have been better if the boy had never woken up, if Choplicker had just dragged him into the underbrush and torn out his throat rather than delivering him to her. Which was the point, she supposed, and, hearing his slobbering, she scowled at the scavenger. He was licking the boy's face, plastering the lad's hair up, and if the wounded child hadn't obviously welcomed the diversion from his pain she would have murdered the beast then and there. Or tried to, anyway.

"You'll be all right," she said, straightening up. She had recognized the boy, for all the good it would do her to know his name. "I've got something in my bag to heal you, Pao Cowherd, just don't go making any trouble while I get it. Lie very still."

"Yes, ma'am," Pao whispered, trying to pet Choplicker. "Sorry, ma'am."

"Should be," said Zosia, her voice almost catching. She'd grown soft, all right—the stone was still in her somewhere, but she'd buried it so deep under years of easy happiness that she couldn't seem to find it. Tending a badly wounded child was not the time for grief or doubt, and once she would have been able to smother these things, if she felt them at all... once, but ages past. Now the deep coldness inside her teemed with a hundred different splashing, thrashing thoughts and memories and emotions, and try as she might she couldn't find the placidity that once came as natural as breathing.

Fishing in her pack, she took out a wool shirt and brought it back to the boy, cutting into it with her deer knife as she hunkered back down. He was pallid as a corpse already, and trying not to cry. "Tying off a nanny goat's tail is a dark deed, boy—you recall what I said I'd do if I caught you up by my place again?"

"Said you'd... beat the devils out of me." Even half dead, the boy grinned at her. There was blood shining between his teeth in the firelight. "Ain't my fault, ma'am. Your dog... he brung me up here."

"Well, I suppose it's all right then," said Zosia, rolling the boy farther over to examine the wound before plugging it. There hardly seemed a point at all, but he was still talking, so who knew, maybe there was some hope... "This will hurt, but it's got to be done. Then I'll stop the wound and you'll be right as rain before you know it."

"I feel sick, I—" But whatever the boy might have said next was lost as his voice turned into a gasping, gulping sob. Zosia had peeled back the soft crust that had formed over the wound and slid her index finger in, making sure there wasn't a broken arrow or spear point lodged inside. Something hard and sharp met her fingertip, but she couldn't tell if it was a piece of weapon or bone—too long since she'd rooted around in a body. Nothing she could do about it, anyway, wedged that firmly in there, alone on a dark mountainside. The boy was sucking the cold air in catfish gulps, his body basted with sweat, and she slipped her finger out.

If he lived through the night, come morning she'd clean and cauterize the wound, but for now she would spare him that ordeal. Rolling a scrap of shirt into a plug, she quickly packed it in the wound. He found enough air to let out a wail at that, then fell totally silent. She tied the remaining woolen strips tight, the boy shivering as she hoisted his hip to get the bandage all the way around his waist.

Cinching it, she watched his wracked face, wondering if this was it, if she had gone and killed the boy.

No. His face was still locked in a rictus, but his shallow breathing was evening out, his almost imperceptible whines growing in strength even as the rest of him weakened. She stood back up, the speed with which she had gained the high country after dealing with Hjortt and setting the house aflame catching up with her in a series of twinges and aches. Devils below and devils above, but her left knee was angry with her. She wanted to rinse the tacky blood off her hands, but, knowing they'd like as not be bloodied again before the night was over, decided not to waste the water just yet. She held her hands over the diminished fire, the drying blood dark on her fingers. They were still shaking. They would be shaking a lot in the nights to come, with winter on the wind that gutted her blaze.

"I'm thirsty," Pao called with more strength than she would have expected. He had curled into a ball despite the pain it must have caused to bring his knees to his chest, and she brought him both a waterskin and her flask of enzian. He coughed more on the sip of water than he did on the slug of bitter booze. "Those soldiers...they killed everyone."

"That's what I figured," said Zosia, taking a pull on the enzian herself. She gave up on trying to keep the inevitable at bay and let herself remember harvesting the plants with Leib. While she excavated the roots from the flinty alpine soil, her shirking husband strung her small, pungent crowns from the yellow flowers, setting them with the rare purple bloom. A jewel for her diadem. The smell of earth and root, the feel of cold hands slipped under the back of her blouse to provoke a squeal. She took another aromatic dram, thought of the pot-still bubbling away in its hut behind the village's communal longhouse, and wondered if the murderous Imperial soldiers were even now toasting with pillaged bottles of the same spirit. If she started back down now she could be there just before dawn, when even the sentries were caught in limbo between being drunk and being hungover...

The boy—Pao, she told herself, his name is Pao Cowherd, though she'd called the rascal other things in the past—started to cry again. She forced another drink down his throat, then sealed flask and waterskin and went back for her war hammer. Twirling in her hand, the fist-sized face and icicle-shaped pick became a steel cyclone that caught the boy's attention, and Choplicker's, too.

"Will I...am I dying?" the boy asked.

Yes.

"No." Zosia released the spinning hammer and caught it in her other hand, the familiar sting of the handle against her palm making her grimace. "I'm a witch—many times as you've called me that, I'd think you'd believe it! And enzian's a medicine, isn't it, so even if I weren't possessed of dark powers you'd be on the mend already. You'll live, boy, you'll live, and then you'll go after those soldiers who did this to you."

"I'm scared," said Pao, shuddering.

"Only because you're green," said Zosia, reckoning she'd been even younger than he was when she'd first taken up arms. "I was green once, too, but you'll firm up. Don't think we'll go after them tomorrow! Need to train you in the sword, the hammer, the bow, everything you ever pestered me and my Leib about teaching you. Need to turn you into a warrior!"

She was sure this would have cheered him, but he just stared off into the blackness between the junipers, his back to the fire. The bandage had already soaked through. Glancing at Choplicker, she could tell it was taking every drop of what little self-control the beast possessed not to lap at the sodden wool.

"You're special, Pao Cowherd," Zosia told him. "You're not like anyone else out there in the whole world. You're destined for this, boy, destined to be the one to change things, to make the Star a better place. And you do that with a sword. A magic one. That's your destiny."

That got his attention. The boy turned his head toward her, winced, the desperate hope on his shadow-cluttered face sickening. "A magic sword? My destiny?"

"That's right," said Zosia, feeling Choplicker's eager eyes boring into her but refusing to look at the beast. "Why do you think you survived, eh? Why do you think Chop brought you to me? You're a very special child, Pao, and your father trusted me to look after you, to wait until you were old enough and then teach you sword craft. To help train you up so you can rid the world of devils, restore peace, that kind of shit."

"My dad," whispered Pao. "But you always said he was a drunk asshole and that's why Mama ran him out of town."

"Of course I said that," said Zosia, seeing the resemblance to his good-for-nothing father writ in the boy's thick brows and broad nose. He would've grown up to look just like the man. Still might, she thought, but scarcely believed it. "I was trying to teach you some humility with that yarn, wasn't I? For all the good it did. Couldn't well tell you he was really a great knight and that someday I'd take you on a quest to retrieve his special sword, could I? You gave me little enough peace as it was, can't imagine how awful you'd have been if we'd told you the truth."

"I couldn't..." Pao's eyes were half-lidded, the boy drifting into some dark depth that only time would reveal to be slumber or death. "Mama..."

The wind stirred up a plume of embers, the coals pulsing, and she tucked the hammer in its loop on her backpack, put more wood on. Pao shivered on the bare, rocky ground, eyes clenched as tight as his jaw. She only had the one bedroll, and if she gave it to him it would likely be soaked in blood by morning. Choplicker rose from where he'd lain beside the fire and went to her side, his ever-thirsty tongue going to the hand that hung limp at her side. She numbly let him clean the blood off her, staring at the boy, and when he was done she offered him her other hand.

"And here I thought you hung around because you liked me," she said sadly, meeting his canine eyes and trying to convince herself this was all his fault, instead of hers. "No fool like an old fool, I suppose. Lie beside him, unless you're itching to see just how much of your wickedness I'll abide in one day. Not much more, devil, not much at all, I promise you that."

The thing that pretended to be a dog went to Pao. Even in the flickering light of the campfire she could see that all the white had left his coat, the black had left his teeth, that he was as young as when she'd first laid eyes on the fiend. Didn't take much to keep him going, didn't take much at all, but he would never be sated, not as long as the sun and the moon danced their way around the world. Maybe not even after they stopped.

Zosia left the camp, left the junipers, stumbled up the night scape of shrubs and stones above the tree line, until her fire was a distant devil's eye beneath her, and above her burned a thousand more, silver instead of gold but just as remote, just as cold. She rubbed her hands, turned, and looked down the ridge, down the mountain, down the starlit valley, out toward the highway, out toward the world she had left behind...the world that had followed her trail even to this distant hiding place.

So Choplicker hadn't taken her offer after all. In all her years, she had never heard of a bound devil turning down its freedom, but seeing was believing. She didn't claim to be the expert on the monsters that some of her old confederates were, but still, it didn't get more basic than that: you bind a devil, it has to protect you, and if you offer to set it loose, it will grant any wish. Any fucking wish. The songs were full of cunning mortals who received whole empires in exchange for setting a devil loose, and all she had wanted was to leave an empire behind.

"Just keep us safe." She repeated her wish to the darkness, the words echoing out from her broken heart twenty years after she had given them voice. "I just want to grow old with Leib, for both of us to live safe, boring lives until age claims us. Your freedom for our safety."

It was all Choplicker's fault.

As if wanting a thing was enough to make it real—didn't this whole fucking tragedy prove that wishing for something wasn't enough? No, the truth of it was that this wasn't Choplicker's fault. It was hers. After all she had seen and done when she'd led the Cobalt Company, she'd still gone and trusted her future to a devil? Trusted

her husband's life to a monster the likes of which not even the crazi-
est sorcerer on the Star wanted to treat with? Zosia had captured the
Carnelian Crown of Samoth, controlled the whole Crimson fucking
Empire, schemed and plotted against the most devious minds on the
Star to achieve her ends, and yet she'd made the most amateurish
mistake imaginable—she'd stopped watching her back.

Even when those Imperials had shown up at her door that very
morning, she hadn't believed it, had held out hope that Choplicker
would magically solve her problems. If she had attacked Hjortt and
his two weirdborn guards before the order was given to kill everyone
in Kypck, maybe the whole village would still be alive. Instead, she
was so convinced that a devil had granted her wish that she'd just sat
on her fat old ass and let the worst thing imaginable transpire under
her nose. Choplicker deserved some blame, oh yes, he fucking did...
but she deserved even more.

Except—and it was an elephantine exception—neither she nor her
devil had beheaded Leib. In twenty years of living here, neither of
them had harmed a single citizen of Kypck. Both Zosia and Choplicker would pay for their crimes eventually, but there were others to
share the blame, and until then guilt would only distract her from
some very important business. Devildamn every one of those responsible for this... but of course the devils never minded, so it was dependent on her to do the damning.

She should have killed Colonel Hjortt instead of leaving him for
later, she knew this, and she should have lain in wait at the house
until that Sister Portolés had returned and then killed the weirdborn,
too... It was sloppy, very sloppy, leaving things like this. They hadn't
seemed to know her real name, though, and she had burned the
house with all its evidence, so if she bided her time before going after
the soldiers who had massacred the villagers there was reason enough
to hope that this incident might not draw the full scrutiny of those
who might identify her.

They would know her name before it was over, that they certainly
would, but the longer it took them to put the pieces together, the less
prepared they would be to meet her retaliation...

Except this couldn't just be an unhappy accident, could it? Every hamlet on the Star did the same as Kypck had done, trading supplies to whomever came knocking. Yet of all the remote towns in the Empire, hers was the one they selected to make an example of? They hadn't even sent her a worthy enemy, just some half-grown nobody of a noble, an errand boy charged with delivering her an unmistakable message... and Zosia had a fairly keen notion of who had sent it.

She hated that it almost felt good, to realize Queen Indsorith must be behind this. Choplicker wasn't the only monster Zosia had made a deal with, and the more she thought about it, the more obvious it was that the Crimson Queen had orchestrated this entire attack. Now that it had transpired, Zosia saw how inevitable it all was—she'd been an even bigger fool to trust her successor to the Crimson Throne than she had been to trust her devil.

Quick as the flash of illumination and flush of excitement came, it was gone again, leaving Zosia cold and melancholic. Going after the sovereign of the Crimson Empire had been hard work when she was a whole lot younger, when she had her Five Villians and the rest of the Cobalt Company behind her, but now? Now she had nothing. Less than.

It should have been the boy. How many had she met who claimed to share his lot, how many songs had she heard that began this way? The sole survivor of a tribe, driven by a need for revenge, all their strength ahead of them, young enough to learn, to prepare, to adapt. Young enough to succeed. It should be this boy, who didn't deserve anything worse than a mild ass-beating for his frequent trespasses.

It should be the boy. If she had been a witch, like that idiot Colonel Hjortt had thought, if she could have given her life for his...

And predictable as a water clock, there was Choplicker, padding between the small bushy willows that sprouted here, when all other trees fell back. A smile tilted at her mouth. All she had to do was say it, *My life for his*, and then it would be done, wouldn't it? An innocent child in exchange for her black heart would entice a deal out of any devil within hearing range, especially one who despised her as much as Choplicker must, to have refused her before. The jackal-dog's eyes glittered like the stars as he approached. *My life for his.*

Maybe such an oath would work this time around, and maybe it would be but more noise on a wind-lashed mountainside, but Zosia wasn't taking any chances. She couldn't afford to, not until she had her revenge. She swallowed the sentimentalizing and cuffed Choplicker on the back of the head as she returned to camp. He snapped at her but knew better than to land a bite, just as she'd known better than to strike him as hard as she'd wanted to. They would be working together for a little while longer yet.

Sleep never arrived as she lay on the rough ground, letting her body rest even if her mind declined the offer.

In the morning the boy was dead, her only bedroll frosted with his frozen sweat and blood. She carried him to the top of the ridge and laid him out for the animals. After erecting small cairns at his head and feet, she removed the severed head of her husband from its satchel and set it next to Pao Cowherd, so that their cold brows touched. Zosia offered no prayers, only curses, and then she turned away, into the clouds that enveloped the upper reaches of the Kutumbans.

It was time to begin her last, bloody work. The thing she hated most about herself was how warm the prospect made her. Choplicker would feed well before it was over. All the devils would.

CHAPTER

8

Two days after he left home with little more than his weapons, his clothes, and his grandfather on his back, Sullen was attacked. It would have been one thing if those doing the attacking had been from a rival tribe, maybe those deranged, pink-skinned Troll Lions from the Grey Savannah, or their old enemies the Jackal People, but the sad truth was that Sullen was ambushed by members of his own clan. Shameful.

The attack came at Flywalk, the rope bridge that spanned the Agharthan Gorge. His people had hidden on the far side of the jagged trench that separated the Horned Wolf Clan's territory from that of the Falcon People, and as soon as Sullen stepped off the bridge they came at him. Due to the time-honored popularity of ambushes at this spot, the thick, mossy pines had been cleared for a good hundred yards on both sides of the crossing, and so Sullen had just enough time to process what was happening as five named Wolves and two pups rushed across the stumpfield at him.

"It's me!" Sullen announced, holding up his spear and sun-knife in a friendly gesture, hoping against hope that this was a misunderstanding. It wasn't, as evidenced by the sun-knife Oryxdoom hurled at him as the lead hunter closed the last dozen yards. Sullen sidestepped the multiflanged missile, and without putting any thought into it, really, whipped his spear around to meet Oryxdoom's charge. It sounded rather a lot like spitting a practice gourd when the weapon connected with Oryxdoom's armpit, the man's ax flying from his upraised arm as he was skewered. The other six Horned Wolves drew up short, forming a half-ring around Sullen and the ravine behind him, the hunting party in low stances, spears, axes, and throwing knives ready.

From his sling on Sullen's back, Grandfather shouted, "You've wanted the boy gone all these years, now you put up a fight when he tries to leave?"

Sullen knew Grandfather was only tying to help but blushed nevertheless. He could fight his own battles.

"I'm sorry," he said, well practiced in offering undeserved apologies to keep the peace. "I'm not leaving the clan. I just have to take Grandfather on a quest, then I'll be back. And I didn't want to hurt him. I didn't want to hurt you, Oryxdoom."

From where he lay on the black earth at Sullen's feet, Oryxdoom did not say whether or not he accepted the apology. This was probably because Oryxdoom was deader than donkey shit, the brother of One-arm Yaw sprawled on his side in the loam, blood pooling toward Sullen's flaking leather boots. Sullen tugged his spear free and took a slight step back from the mess he'd made, and would have taken another if he hadn't remembered the dropoff behind him. The bridge was just there to his left, if he broke past Swiftspear, but the two pups had taken up positions behind their older sister, and Sullen really, really didn't want to chop down the unnamed kids. And even if he somehow made it back across, what then? He'd be right back in the one place he knew his uncle wasn't—his homeland, where nobody wanted him. When none of his clanfolk broke the silence nor rushed him, he tried again to explain:

"I'm not turning tail like Uncle Craven did. I'll come back," he said, but now that he thought about it, that was exactly what his uncle had done the first time around that made the council so mad: left the clan without permission, and then came back without invitation. Looking at the mean faces of his people, he supposed they'd be fine with his following Uncle Craven's footsteps as far as leaving the Noreast Arm went; they just wanted to make sure he didn't return.

What were they waiting for, then? Wise-eye would be the alpha, with Oryxdoom dead, but she just shifted her weight from boot to boot, her spear from hand to hand. Sullen told himself they hesitated because they didn't really want to fight him. That Oryxdoom had put them up to this. That each wasn't simply reluctant to be the first one to charge, or to lose their sun-knife by throwing it at him while he stood on the edge of the gorge. He could still talk them out of this, give a speech like the one from the ballads that Old Black had given the night-rovers, when she'd convinced those monsters not to eat her during the Worst Winter...

He could do this. Clearing his throat, Sullen said, "You thought I was just running away, shaming the clan, but it's not like that! I swear on my name it's not! I'm going to find out why Uncle Craven disgraced us the way he did! I'll get a worthy answer from his lips, or bring him back to face the judgment of the council! I vow it on the names of all my ancestors!"

Wise-eye relaxed her shoulders a bit, and from the corner of his eye he saw Swiftspear look to her for guidance. Witmouth was nodding thoughtfully, no doubt recognizing the cadence of Sullen's oath from the tales he himself had sung to the boy, back before Sullen had alienated himself from his people. They were hearing him out!

"I swear on my parents I never meant to break the codes the way I did," he went on, "and I don't want to hurt nobody else. So why don't we just—"

"Kill them all!" Grandfather yowled, and Sullen stumbled to the side as the old man strapped to his back hurled one of his sun-knives at Wise-eye. She tried to dodge it, but Grandfather knew a thing or two about his business and two of the weapon's curved points caught her square in the gut. She collapsed to the ground, the other woman and two men charged, the pups hurled knives in his direction, and Sullen obeyed the wordless impulse in his panicked skull— he charged straight ahead, slashing Witmouth out of the way with his spear and fleeing toward the tree line.

Someone cut his side with something.

Grandfather was boxing his ears, commanding him to turn and fight.

A sun-knife skimmed the side of his scalp, ripping through his hair and stinging like an icebee.

Sullen ignored everything but the rough, root-slippery ground beneath his feet as he crossed the stumpfield and gained the cover of the forest, sun-knives shying off the trees around him, another thunking into the earth just between his pumping legs. Whipping through the pine boughs, he immediately crossed the trail through the Raptor Wood, ignored it, plunged back into thick timber, under-brush clawing his calves and thighs, branches scratching his face.

His clanfolk howled behind him, close, and then the downward slant of the ground sharpened considerably. Sullen cut sideways along the incline to keep his balance, but even still he began to slide down the hill, only keeping himself upright by grabbing at branches with his free hand. The descent steepened, and he half fell down the wooded mountainside, his stride lengthening with each breath as though he wore the enchanted snowshoes from the Ballad of Clev-erhands. A fallen tree reared out of the blurry forest, but he bounded over it, landing thirty feet down the slope with such force he felt it rattle his bones all the way to the marrow. He kept going until he hit a hollow in the hills and cut to his right, running up the narrow val-ley for all he was worth.

More howling came from back the way he'd come, farther off now, but he knew that only the ones in the rear would be announc-ing themselves until the lead Wolves caught him. This was not at all how he had pictured his morning. Grandfather hissed at him as a tree limb snapped at his neck, and the lad grunted an apology, barely able to hear himself over the sound of his own panting. He almost stepped on a startled armadillo, tore through sticky spiderwebs, abruptly changed direction, and plowed up the far hillside. The Rap-tor Wood was new terrain to Sullen, denser of tree than the lightly wooded steppes on the other side of the Agharthan Gorge, and beset with toe-breaking stones far fiercer than those of the Savannahs where his village lay. But then the song-singers said that all woods are home to a Horned Wolf.

"Enough," Grandfather said after they had scaled and descended half a dozen more hillocks with no sign of immediate pursuit. "Rest a moment, damn your face, rest and let me think."

"All right," said Sullen, promptly dropping into a crouch just over the crown of the newest rise and gulping the air. With a surge of nausea he realized the cramp in his side that he had been ignoring was actually a gouge that went clean through his hempen shirt and into the meat of his ribs. Half of the garment was dripping red. Prodding the wound, he wondered how he came by it. Swiftspear proving her name, probably, back when he first fled.

"You'll need to bind it before we go on," said Grandfather, leaning over Sullen's shoulder for a look at the mess. "Quick as you can, boy, they'll be on you like termites on a juicy log, and this is no place for a showdown. Never would have happened if you'd just stood your ground."

"Why would they..." Sullen tried to get his thoughts in order as Grandfather dug through the pack that strapped him to his grandson. "Why wouldn't they...Why did you...Why?"

"*Why?*" Grandfather whined, his imitation of Sullen cutting deeper than the wound in his side. "*Whhhhhhy?* Because they're not Wolves, they're dogs, that's why, dogs of their foreign masters."

That hardly seemed to explain anything. "Oryxdoom always had it in for me, but Wise-eye seemed kind enough, and Witmouth taught me every song I know. Why'd they all come so fast after us? Do they think we're cowards? Disgracing the clan?"

"Thank your uncle for that when we find him. When he came back they invented some special excuses for him, on account of all the treasure he gave the elders, but that only brought more embarrassment on the council when he quit the second time. You don't let a rabid dog flee, not when you have a chance to put it down, and since we all share the same blood, well, they assumed the worst. Fool a wolf once and all that shit." Grandfather unspooled a blanket from the pack, bit into the cloth, and tore. Passing the sizable strip to Sullen, he stowed the rest. "Oh, quit your pouting, I never said you were mad—they're the crazy ones, not us. They've suckled at the Crimson teat all right, and liked the milk. A pup like you *should* be appalled at the depths of depravity a soul will sink to, once it's been exposed to paganism, but I'm sorry to say it don't surprise me none. The only thing that caught me off guard was their waiting until we were across the bridge before springing the trap."

"I'm ready," said Sullen, tightening the bandage and tucking it in on itself. He'd packed some moss into it but already the blanket was darkening over the wound. "Hold on, I'm going to pick up the pace."

"Oh no you're not," said Grandfather, tugging on Sullen's puffy saddlehorn of hair. "Enough of this acting the oryx, laddie, it's time to be the Horned Wolf I know you are. They'll follow your trail easy, fast as you've been moving, so slow it down till we find a prime place to pounce."

"Pounce?" Sullen looked around nervously, but nothing moved on the hillside. Grandfather was making him twitchy with this talk. "Nah, Fa, I can outrun them, and they'll have to turn around at some—"

Grandfather flicked Sullen's ear, his old-man breath overpowering the smell of blood and sap and torn moss. "I told you, boy, it's not right to let a mad dog loose, not when you have the means to stop it, keep it from spreading its poison."

"Mad dog," repeated Sullen. How many times had they called him that? Still, the prospect of killing his clanfolk filled him with gloom. In all the songs he'd heard and hummed, not one had a hero doing for his own people like this. Maybe so long as he hated that he had to he could still be a decent Horned Wolf...

"You'll find me a good roost to wait in, then we'll set a trap of our own. You think a king wolf like you can handle a few rabid jackals, laddie?"

Sullen thought about all the times he had barely held in his tears when his people tormented him. Thought about all the songs he'd made up for himself, ballads where he taught them a bloody lesson. Thought about what it would mean, to lay a trap for the Horned Wolf hunting party instead of only fighting back when they cornered him. He set his jaw, and braced himself for the hardest act he had ever contemplated, something he never thought he would actually do. It would hurt, but he didn't see any alternative.

"I...I'm sorry, Fa, but there's no way I can take 'em. I want to, right, but a branch hit my head back there a-ways, and I'm having a real hard time even running straight. Forget about fighting; if I tried to I'd just fall over and get us both killed." Sullen couldn't believe he had actually lied to his grandfather, couldn't believe he was actually swaying in place a little to sell the song, acting all woozy. Couldn't believe he actually thought Grandfather would believe his stupid ruse, that he actually thought he had a choice in the matter. Grandfather was being dead silent, the way he got when he was real, real angry, but then the old man's hand gave Sullen's bushy dome of hair a gentle rap.

"All right, Sullen," said the old man softly. "If you say you can't, I believe you."

That hurt the worst, so bad Sullen almost fessed to the fib then and there, but then he remembered how scared those pups had looked after he killed Oryxdoom. He didn't want to ambush those kids. He'd always had a soft spot for the unnamed pups of the clan, maybe because while the adults had hated him as long as he could remember, he had actually had a few friends when they were all younger, before they'd come of age. He'd even been naïve enough to think Stoutest might be his wife one day, good as they got along as teenagers, but after she earned her name she stopped spending time with him, same as the rest. Small wonder that when he thought about hurting kids, about them even seeing the kind of hurt he had endured, his hands got clammy and shaky.

"Better get moving if we're really just going to run out of here instead of doing the right thing," said Grandfather. "They catch us they'll kill us, and then I'll be able to tell you I told you so."

"They won't catch us," said Sullen, and smiled, because he had half a mind that Grandfather had known he was lying and still let him get away with it. The old man loved him that much, and next time Sullen had the chance to impress Grandfather, he'd do better.

But for now he'd run like Count Raven when he was being chased out of the Seventh Void, back before the Frozen Savannahs got iced over and Sullen's ancestors had to run fast as leopards to keep their feet from being scorched on the blazing earth. A plain old Horned Wolf could never catch Sullen, if he ran that fast.

None even came close.

The next day was considerably quieter, and a week later they emerged from the Raptor Wood and stood on a hillside overlooking the withered plains that marked the border of the Crimson Empire, where Sullen's uncle had disappeared twice over. He hummed a verse of Rakehell to himself, swearing he would follow Uncle Craven's tracks only so far as they led him out into the Star and then back home, and once he returned he would never go away again. If Uncle Craven hadn't run off the second time, Sullen never would've had to leave the once.

CHAPTER
9

Winter in the north is liable to make a grumpy panther of anyone, even those fortunate enough to have a roof and a hearth to stave off the snow and wind. For those seeking shelter in the lees of rocks and the boles of ancient pines as the sleet blew straight across into their face, spoiling any hope of a campfire, it was a fair bit worse. A cave Zosia had provisioned two decades prior for just such an unhappy need had evidently been discovered and cleaned out by some lucky traveler through that desolate high country in the interim, and so while she passed the worst of the season sheltered from the constant gale, it was a lean and icy refuge. She wiled away the snowed-in weeks mourning her husband and village, plotting her vengeance, talking to herself and Choplicker, and sharpening a body gone dull with age and comfort. When the worst of winter passed, allowing her to resume her trek, her muscles popped beneath her taut skin from more than the mild starvation she'd endured.

In light of all this, Zosia's foul mood was well earned when she at last reached the border of the Immaculate Isles.

The sea was still miles away, but the persistence of the Immaculates had won them a rather tidy amount of coastline in ages past. As the recent years of internal Imperial squabbling had drawn the most able forces to the heart of the Crimson Empire, the holdings of the Immaculates had casually expanded inland. It was easy to see how far they had gotten; halfway down the foothills Zosia spied a giant fucking wall. The dark serpent of stone snaked across the whole of her vision, and it didn't take a tactician or scholar to hazard that it stretched from one end of the Norwest peninsula to the other. Nicely done.

Zosia's assumption that the wall came just short of Linkensterne proved to be off by less than a mile, as the (presumably former) Imperial city turned out to be on the far side of the fortification. *Very nicely done.* This part of the wall must have been built first, as there was none of the construction she had glimpsed farther to the east. A series of thick iron portcullises barred the tunnel through the wall, the gate absurdly narrow in contrast to the wide, ancient road. A solid defense, sure, but also a nice bite of the thumb to the Imperial traders who had once given the Immaculates such a hard time of it. As Zosia left the gorse and put her boots on the first real road she would stick to since leaving Kypck, she surmised that the encampment of caravans on this side of the gate must be a fixture of modern Imperial trade with the Immaculate.

"Mind your manners, or I'll sell your ass to the first merchant to make me an offer," Zosia told Choplicker. "Imperials have a taste for dog meat, and I doubt the Immaculate gourmands would turn their noses up at trying a new delicacy, either."

Reasoning she would have time aplenty to explore the caravan camp if they didn't let her through the gate on her first try, she made straight for the guardhouse. There wasn't one, she found, but the rampart dipped low over the gate, and as soon as she passed the last scowling merchant ensconced on his riding board at the side of the road, a guard poked her head over the edge. She couldn't have been twenty-five years old but had the simultaneously weary and haughty expression of a put-upon empress.

"Interviews are at dawn," the guard called down in Crimson. "Come back then."

"*Hello, honored friend,*" said Zosia in the Norwest vernacular. She'd been brushing up on her Immaculate over the long months in the mountains. Since she hadn't had anyone to practice with, only

Choplicker knew how much she'd actually retained, and he wasn't saying. A pleasant greeting was easy enough to remember, though, and it might be all she needed to get her toe in the gate.

"*Hello, honored friend,*" the guard replied reflexively, then scowled and reverted to Crimson. "There's the queue behind you, and some of these rats have been waiting for weeks. You'll have to bribe one of them, and heavily, if you even expect an audience tomorrow."

"What if I just bribe you now?" Zosia smiled up at the gatekeeper. "And heavily."

"Would that it were that easy," said the guard ruefully. "We'd both be happier, eh? Take your bribes to your own people."

"These cheats and scoundrels aren't my people," said Zosia, well aware that in order to be easily heard on the wall she had to shout loudly enough for the merchants at the front of the line to hear her as well. "I come on the personal request of one of your court, and he will be displeased if I am late."

"Ooooh, a noble? Well, that changes everything!" The guard leaned farther over the wall, her scale-armored forearms crossed on the rampart before her. "Sister, I'm a noble, and so's my captain, and so's his commander, and so's a thousand handmaids and houseboys on a hundred different isles. I don't suppose this noble of yours was important enough to give you a stamped invitation we could see?"

"Alas, he placed his order with me before this wall of yours went up," said Zosia. "I'm an artisan who has spent two decades aging her briar for Lord Kang-ho of Hwabun, not some button-seller seeking entry to Linkensterne."

"Kang-ho, the *Lord* of Hwabun?" said the guard, but her tone seemed to have shifted from sassy to mildly interested. "Briar, eh? His husband gives him enough allowance for that sort of luxury?"

"Lord Kang-ho paid in advance," said Zosia, pleased for a change by the gossipmongering that was endemic to the Immaculate Isles. Get two royals together and the rumor mill will turn for hours; fill a nation with nobles and it'll run till the Sunken Isle rises from the deep. "So you understand why he will be eager to see me admitted at once."

"I suppose I might," said the guard, nodding thoughtfully. "The Flower Pot's in need of some pleasant news. Tell you what, toss up that ten-mun piece I dropped and I'll run it past my captain."

Zosia rooted through her purse and fished out the smallest coin she had. "Your eyes aren't great for a wall-minder—it's a Crimson krone."

"So it is," said the guard, catching it in a gloved hand. "My captain will want to have the name of a carver so illustrious as to wait on the King of Hwabun's husband."

"Moor Clell," said Zosia, an alias she hadn't used since the Brackett entanglement some thirty years past. What a fucking fiasco that had been. There had been many times she had missed her shock of blue hair, but now that she had cause to travel incognito she gave thanks that the alchemy of age had turned what was once as cobalt as her eyes to an innocuous silver.

"Get comfortable, Mistress Clell," said the guard, disappearing from sight.

So Kang-ho was alive. He'd always been the lucky one, and she'd hoped that of all the Five Villains he, at least, was still around and kicking, which was why she'd come to the Immaculate Isles first. Nice to know it wasn't going to be a totally wasted visit, though as the sun inched low over the wall she supposed the journey wasn't over yet. Bureaucracy, be it Imperial or Raniputri, Usban or Immaculate, put her in a foul mood. This was why she had left in the first place. Even the tribes of Flintland were supposedly succumbing to the allure of pomp and pretense, though they had the decency to spice up their hoop-jumping with the odd dash of ultraviolent ritual combat. She imagined Leib sitting beside her, wearing away at her ill temper with his effortless wit, but the ghost of his memory only darkened her mood.

"She's not coming back." The merchant at the front of the encampment had descended from his gaudily painted covered wagon and approached Zosia, who sat in the wiregrass on the side of the road with Choplicker curled at her side. The trader's embroidered sarong marked him as Usban, or a dark-skinned convert to the Ten True

Gods of Trve. He had none of the paunch that merchants were notorious for, and his middle-aged face would almost have been good-looking, if not for the perpetual sneer. "I tossed that rogue, or one of them anyway, a copper dinar, and she said the same thing: wait here. It has been a week, and I am still waiting, having reached the front of the line a coin shorter and wiser, but, I fear, no quicker."

"What a song." Zosia yawned. "You have a gift for storytelling, friend."

"And yet you seem to have missed the moral," said the merchant. "While you have been lolling in the dust, waiting for the crow you fed to return with a jade ring, another train has arrived at the rear of the queue. By trying to hasten your entry, you have only delayed it further."

"The ballads just keep on coming," said Zosia. "I thank you for your concern, but if it's all the same to you I'll wait a little longer."

"In point of fact, it is not the same to me," said the merchant, crossing his beefy arms. "Nor will it be all the same to the dozen travelers behind, none of whom will be amused if you are still sitting here, at the front of the queue, come dawn. I have five stout swords in my company who will be more than happy to assist you to the rear, should you persist in this flagrant disregard for good manners."

"Or?" asked Zosia, unimpressed. "You would have brought your muscle if that was your first option, so what's the pitch?"

"My first option, as always, is those same good manners I mentioned, which seem so alien to your ear. But my second is a simple proposition, for you see, when I arrived here I had but three swords in my company. The other two I discovered some wheels behind me in the queue."

"Uh-huh," said Zosia, glancing at the dark wall. The sun had slipped behind it, but no torches were lit on the rampart. "How much does a sellsword make on your wagon, and what's to stop me from cutting loose as soon as we get through the gate?"

"Why, nothing is to stop you from going your own way once we enter the Immaculate Isles," said the merchant, his sneer teetering on the pleasant now that they were opening up negotiations. "Though I hear it is difficult to get far without an escort these days. As for payment, I regret that I will have to ask slightly more than the two men I already hired, seeing as your period of service will be so much shorter than theirs."

"Uh-huh," said Zosia, getting to her feet. Try as she had to get herself back into shape during her trek through the mountains, she still felt as haggard and run-down as a fat monk's pony after pilgrimaging to the Secret City of the Snow Leopard. "How much?"

"Hey-o!" The guard's voice came down through the gloaming. "Looks like you're coming in, Moor Clell. Step up to the front so the guards can get a good look at you."

"What's this!" cried the merchant as two guards with red paper lanterns began making their way through the small barred doors built into each portcullis. "I paid you a week ago!"

"Oh, it's you," said the guard. "Don't worry, it took some time but I've got it all worked out so you can come through first thing in the morning."

"May your kindness be rewarded in the next life, and hopefully this one as well," called up the merchant, then turned his forced smile on Zosia as the last door was opened before them. "I don't suppose you and your hound require a sword for your perilous journey through Immaculate customs? I could offer you a very competitive rate."

Once, Zosia would have laughed in his face, maybe even given him a light slap on the cheek. Once, she had been a really unpleasant, self-important kid. Now, heeding her beloved Leib's wisdom that it was much better to run into a friendly face in an unexpected location than it was to find yourself with enemies you didn't remember making, she extended her hand.

"I would if I could, friend, but we both know that won't work this time around." She nodded at the entryway cut out of the last portcullis, which wasn't wide enough for both guards to pass through abreast. "Unless you can fit your wagon through that door? I'm Moor Clell, by the by, pipemaker."

"My carriage has many marvelous properties, but that is not one of them," said the merchant as he took her by the forearm and shook. "Ardeth Karnov thanks you for the sentiment, though. Perhaps we shall meet again, Moor Clell, pipemaker, in Linkensterne, Little Heaven, or stranger markets still. I have amongst my treasures the finest latakisses, so perhaps we could sample one another's wares."

"I should like that," said Zosia, her mouth watering at the thought of the rich, smoky tubāq of the Usba. She had burned through the last of her latakiss blend on the trail and was down to flue-cured vergins and dusty deertongue; she would have lingered to discuss a purchase on the spot had the guards not barked at her to get a move on. "Safe travels, Ardeth Karnov."

"And you as well," said the merchant, turning back to his wagon.

Not much hope of that, thought Zosia as she allowed the guards to escort her into the Immaculate Isles, Choplicker wagging his tail as they went.

CHAPTER
10

Maroto went along with Purna's scheme, because of course he did.

They opted to wait a few days before enacting the plot, so as not to make it obvious. During those long nights of caravanning through the Wastes, vainly trying to scare up some sort of game for the nobles to hunt that wouldn't actually kill them, Maroto let his imagination drift through scenarios in which Purna actually wanted to screw him. Which would, as a matter of principle, actually make him a whore, but he had known many, many whores over the years, and found them to be a generally good sort. Better to be a whore than a rich girl's plaything, anyway, and she'd hardly have been the first or the worst trick he'd turned in his time.

The long nights and sleeplessly hot days seemed longer with only these thoughts buzzing around in his head like trapped icebees, especially during the desert's twilight hours when the fops were hooting and giggling under their pavilions in the shale dust. Maroto did his best to ignore the glassgazers, taking every opportunity to partake of their food and drink without actually engaging them in conversation. Setting himself up as the stoic, quiet type had been something of a coup, but as the nights had turned into weeks their patience with his taciturnity had grown thin. If he couldn't provide them with adventure, he had damn well better feed them stories of it, but he wasn't big on that, either. Such songs as he'd lived through weren't for the likes of them.

One such evening he was standing in the shade of a collapsible gazebo, picking at a freshly set table of gleaming lamprey caviar and deviled moa eggs, sipping a bloody marīam out of a gilt teacup, when Pasha Diggelby and Count Hassan sidled up on either side of him.

"What ho, Hassan, it seems our fearless leader has discovered quite the monstrous nest," Diggelby smirked, his curled goatee drooping in the heat, the bow-bedecked, alabaster-coated lapdog he held in his arm even more ridiculous looking than its master. "Pray, what sort of fell beast deposited these eggs, hmmm? And by stealing its brood, do you mean to entice the creature down upon us, so that we might at last have some of this sport you've been promising?"

"Mrumph," said Maroto. He wasn't actually saying anything, just making noise and letting half-chewed caviar run from his mouth as he spoke in the hope of repulsing these clowns into leaving him alone. "Mra mruphh mra."

It didn't work. Bracing himself on his camel-pizzle swagger stick, Hassan reached up on the tips of his suede boots and dabbed Maroto's chin with a monogrammed napkin. "It would seem our expert hunter has left his manners back on the canyon-top where he treated Purna to a private hunt. Tell us truthfully, oh veteran of a hundred wars, did she sing true when she told of your falling beneath the dragon's claws, of how she saved you from its clutches?"

"Wasn't a dragon," said Maroto, remembering too late that he didn't intend to actually talk to them. "Godguana, is all."

"A *godguana*!" said Diggelby. "Oh, that sounds even better. So when do *we* get to bring one down?"

The thought of putting these two in front of a territorial dire-lizard, with Hassan in his toga and gilded laurel wreath and Diggelby in his baggy pantaloons and carrying a bite-sized dog, brought a long-absent smile to Maroto's lips. Fuck these fucking nobles—if they wanted it so badly, he was only too happy to oblige. "Right now, lads. As soon as you retrieve your weapons and waterskins, we'll scale the far cliff there—the ripper vines will make it easy climbing, so long as you've got good gloves. Don't tell the others, though; we'll spook our quarry if there's more than a few of us along."

Hassan and Diggelby both looked skeptically at the side of the ravine in question. It was two hundred feet of vertical rock to what Maroto suspected to be a false summit. For all their talk, these two idiots didn't have much to say now, did they?

"What's all this about a climb?" said Tapai Purna, rounding the corner of the pavilion and allowing Hassan's stiff-backed Raniputri butler to pour her a frothy flute of bloody marīam. Draining his teacup, Maroto wondered where in the First Dark she had found a proper receptacle for her drink—every time he asked for glassware, be it a coupe or a flute, snifter or stein, the hovering servants brought him a teacup. Probably another of the fops' stupid pranks at his expense. "Certainly you two gibs don't mean to go off for a hunt before our guide has espied the horizon? What a fine mess that would be, if you got all the way up to the top, only to be caught by a glass storm, or even better, a swarm!"

"Yes, naturally, we had no plans for an immediate departure," said Hassan, hastily backing away from the table, Diggelby at his side. "We haven't even had breakfast yet."

"You scout the firmament, barbarian, and when you're back down, we can go up," said Diggelby. "Ta."

"Thanks for that," said Maroto. "Now I get to climb twice, assuming they don't weak out."

"You're very welcome," said Purna, sliding the empty teacup off his thick pinky with her slim, kid-gloved fingers. "Don't worry, we'll give them plenty of time to soak up some courage. First, though, let's see about getting you paid, shall we?"

Scrambling up a narrow defile with the mischievous lordling and then leaving her to make a faux lovenest while he summited the increasingly sheer slope was no fun at all. Clear skies improved his mood mildly, and coming back down to find she had packed several bottles of sparkling Eyvindian wine, a partially smushed wedge of pungent, green-veined cheese, and a crock of olives perked it up even more. "Precocious" was certainly not a word Maroto ever would have used to describe himself, but there was something undeniably amusing about sitting on the shelf of sandstone overlooking the camp and punctuating his snacking with lusty roars. Purna's moans and wails would have made a greener fellow blush, but Maroto had long since outgrown such things as being discomfited by a fake orgasm. Between mouthfuls, he gave her pointers—like most youngsters, she was overselling it.

A decent way to kill a morning, then. It brought back happy memories of his too-brief acting career, where he'd first learned how Imperials thought barbarians were supposed to behave. Those had been the days, traveling from one Arm of the Star to the next with Kiki and Carla and Two-eyed Jacques and all the rest, back before he'd ever heard of the Cobalt Company, let alone got mixed up with them . . . Back before he'd been fool enough to think he could better the world. Before he'd been fool enough to fall in love.

As was always the case, warm memories cooled quickly in Maroto's breast, and he gave a climactic bellow to refocus himself on his current endeavor, which was a lot more enjoyable than stewing in his usual barrel's worth of regrets. Not as enjoyable as actually screwing, mind, but that went without saying. Then again, Purna was slathered in her fashionable corpsepaint, midnight blue designs orbiting out around eyes and mouth, and between that and the imponderable puzzle of her stiff-ribbed petticoats he doubted he would have been able to do the deed, even if she'd been of a mood. It would be like trying to fuck an amorous ghoul after you'd rolled it up in a rug.

Guzzling the dregs from the last bottle, Maroto stood, woozier from the heat than the booze, and extended his hand to Purna. "That ought to be more than sufficient, I'd say. Let's get down before the rocks are too hot to climb."

"One last detail," said Purna, taking his hand and pulling herself to her feet. She sprang upon him with the speed of a devil, wrapping her legs around his waist and her arms around his neck, furiously kissing his throat. He nearly struck her off him in surprise, but then warmed to the ardent attack. He gingerly lowered them both back down to the steep, sandy ground—who knew if a randy ghoul in a rug might be better than your hand, until you try? On his hands and knees over the girl, her lips moved from his neck to his mouth, and Maroto gave a genuine groan at the taste of this pretty wee drag-faced noble.

Then she was away, nibbling his ear, and his fingers clumsily kneaded the layers of whalebone girding her chest, running his hand from her inaccessible bosom to her insulated groin and back up again.

"Rip it," she breathed, the salty musk of wine and olives not exactly sultry, but close enough. Yet as soon as he dug his fingers into the fabric and came away with a handful of lace, ribbons, and drawstrings, she gave a little squeal and dropped her legs and arms from around his body. He almost apologized, but then she wriggled down beneath him, hands and then head pressing up against the thickening throb in his short breeches...

And then she scooted the rest of the way out from under his legs, leaving him straddling a girl-shaped dust angel. Her voice, breathy but not heavy, put the shrivel on him like he'd been touched by a lich. "Perfect! Nobody will doubt our story now."

Clambering up, he had to fess that they both looked...tousled. He peevishly tried to wipe her makeup tracks off his crotch, but only succeeded in rubbing them in. Great. Purna beamed at him as she put her gloves back on. Maroto scowled, knowing exactly what this little tease needed, and being of half a mind to give it to her, here and now, and damn the consequences.

And why shouldn't he? She had it coming, that was beyond question, and better he just take care of the business now, while they were safely away from the rest. A strong talking-to would do her a world of good, yes it fucking would.

Of course, Maroto knew that lecturing the brat was the last way he'd ever get into her bloomers, but the old devil of his pride forced his mouth.

"Being a flirt is one thing, Tapai Purna," he said, wagging his finger at her, "but nobody likes being made the fool. It's an ugly business, leading somebody on. If you don't fancy a fellow or lady or whatever, that's fine as good wine, but making play like you do only to have a laugh at their expense is about the lowest prize you can claim. And if you truly take comfort in such sport, *well*. I'd expect such behavior from your friends, but thought better of you."

"Oh, tosh. You never would have, if I'd asked, but it was necessary," said Purna, shifting her wig so that it sat off kilter before picking up her wide-brimmed sunhat. "We'll be lucky if Duchess Din doesn't demand to inspect me for your spendings before paying out."

"Buh!" said Maroto, these nobles even loonier than he'd reckoned. Then again, they'd come too far to risk the bet now..."I mean, if you think she might..."

"If she does I'll just say you shot off in my mouth," said Purna, turning her corseted back on him and eyeing the descent. "After giving me lots and lots of scrumptious orgasms, of course. I know you've got your reputation to think of."

Maroto tried to cheer himself up by imagining what might make an orgasm scrumptious, but soon gave up. Too bloody hot for such thoughts, let alone such deeds. So he told himself, anyway. Shaking his bubbly-tickled head, he clambered back down to camp.

The plan worked. They bought the deception. What a fool Maroto was.

Before, he'd been loaded in the one currency these miserable parasites lacked: honor. And now he'd traded it all away for what amounted to a pittance of their collective material fortunes. Well, maybe he hadn't actually been that respectable to start with, but they'd certainly thought highly of him, and in any case he'd been worthier than they, refusing to play their little games.

Well, except for the little game of leading them on a dangerous adventure from which some of them might never return. *That* little game he'd signed on for without hesitation, and for not a great deal more than he'd just earned from Purna.

Be that as it may, things felt different now, and not for the better. Before, he'd pretended not to give a devil's damn that the coxcombs all whispered and pointed and giggled whenever he was around, but now the jeering note in their attention cut into his ear far more keenly. He wasn't only a rich girl's plaything, he was a lordling's object of ridicule, a second son's punch line, a zir's zinger. He wasn't just a beast, but a trained one, same as any circus bear taught to beg for his breakfast. When the crowds taunted those miserable creatures, did they dream of escaping to some deep, dark den in the Black Cascades, away from the bright lights and cruel attentions, or did they dream of having their claws back, their filed-down teeth sharp again, the chain 'round their necks broken? Did a beast fantasize of revenge on its captors, the same as a barbarian might, or a weirdborn certainly would? Those last were quick enough to turn on their tormentors, Maroto knew.

"Ho, the fancy stallion approacheth!"

It was past midnight several days after the event Maroto had come to think of as the Shaming, and he'd ridden his dromedary to the front of the caravan in hope that Captain Gilleland and his men would prove better company than the arsehole richies. Apparently not. The barb had come from the captain himself, and the dozen other chevaleresses, sellswords, and bodyguards laughed at their ringleader's jest. Unlike the anonymous lesser nobles who had jogged zero memories in Maroto, he had recognized some of their hired muscle, by reputation if nothing else, and from the grudging respect they'd given him he knew that his own ballad-worthy history was known to them as well.

Now they laughed at him, too.

"Find any wondrous caves we could plunder, stallion?"

With the nobles, it was unlikely he would ever climb back into their good graces. They had paid him for adventure, whatever the fuck *that* meant, and he had failed to deliver any of the expected fortune, glory, or excitement—only lethal heat and ugly terrain. Bad enough, but by throwing his lot in with Tapai Purna, first in a private godguana hunt and then a sexual conspiracy, he'd alienated himself further from the bulk of them by playing favorites, and with an Ugrakari to boot.

"Silent as any stud, eh?"

There was still time to patch things up with these roughnecks, though—take their burns on the chin, make a joke at his own expense. Play it off. No shame in fucking a fair young noble, unless the world had changed beyond recognition. If anything, it would humanize him to these toughs, bring the legend down to their level, make him one of them. How long had it been since he'd ridden with hard folk who thought him equal, rather than better than they, or, sure, as was more often the case of late, their lesser? Maroto sat straighter on his dromedary, giving the heavily armed outriders his stoniest stare.

"Now I know why they hired him—after the way he fucked the Crimson Empire, they figured him to be the best lay on the Star!"

But, and it was a pretty important but, *fuck these fucking fucks right in their fucking faces.* He had stared down devils, laid low mighty kingdoms, and they dared speak to him thus? He wheeled his camel away from them, knowing if he opened his mouth he would say something that would result in them stopping their steeds and demanding he fight them then and there, for honor's sake. A younger Maroto would have fallen right into the trap, but he wasn't some hornless pup anymore—he would wait until they were safely bedded down for the day, murder the lookouts, and then slit their throats, one by one, starting with the guards and working his way down through the nobles, until he was alone in the Wastes.

Except of course he wouldn't. The thought gave him enough succor to tactically retreat from the hostile situation without his mouth landing him in an unmarked grave, but once he was safely in the shadows between pleasure wagons he let the cowardly notion float up into the broiling night air. What he would actually do was wait until they arrived in Niles, take fops and fop guards alike to an inn, and then promptly instigate an epic bar fight. This would provide him with the opportunity to smash in Captain Gilleland's teeth, and the gold-flecked grills of a few nobles while he was at it, but the city militia wouldn't let it actually progress to a dozen bodyguards chopping him down in cold blood. Probably. In any event, Niles was only a few nights' ride away, and once there he would beat some manners into the lot of these highborns and their dogs.

Except of course he didn't. Before they had even unhitched the wagons and unbuttoned their ruffs at the caravansary in Niles,

Maroto strode away into the City on the Edge of Hell, shoving Purna aside when she ran after and tried to talk him into returning to the party.

"You were contracted to take us here *and back*," said Purna, shrugging off the blow far easier than Maroto expected. "You won't receive any wages for taking us across the Wastes but not providing passage home. They'll make you pay them, in all likelihood, for breaking your contract, and for the food and drink you consumed, to say naught of the inconvenience of—"

"Here." Maroto yanked the purse she had given him and threw it at her feet. He regretted it before it even hit the packed black sand of the street. "I'd rather be a poor man than a rich dog."

"You really shouldn't take everything so seriously," said Purna, making no move to retrieve the purse. More than one veiled passerby was slowing to watch the altercation. "If you like I'll see if I can discourage them from riding you so hard. It would certainly help matters if you could find someone or something for them to fight; I know I've felt worlds better about the whole affair since you and I took down that drag—"

"Lizard!" barked Maroto. "It was just a big fucking lizard, nothing more, and if I had my way I'd feed the lot of you to the godguanas!"

"So there's nothing I can do to convince you to come back?" Her glittery lips pouted. The lecture he'd given her had clearly been a waste of breath. "Tell me your price, and I'll see what I can't muster. I...I really respect you, Maroto. A lot."

"You talk about *respect* in the same breath you ask what my *price* is? There is no damn price! I'm *done* with the Wastes—I'll never set foot there again, *ever*. And as for *you*, I'd sooner float through the Sea of Devils on a raft made of meat than sail a pleasure pontoon across Lake Jucifuge with you dandies and your hired goons. You're all alike, and I'm done with you. Forever."

"I thought you were a lot smarter than this," said Purna sadly, plucking up the purse. "And what's in here won't even begin to cover what the lawyers will demand for this gross breach of bond. They'll come for their silver."

"Yes, well, first they'll have to find me," said Maroto, wishing he'd come up with something smarter even as she turned her back on him. Which was rudeness on top of rudeness, since he'd been the one storming off, yet there she went, depriving him of even a proper exit. The small crowd of Usban travelers who had gathered now wandered off, too, leaving Maroto to stand in the middle of the busy street, wishing he hadn't just given up the bulk of his money in an unappreciated gesture.

What meager funds he had left he promptly set to drinking away in the first dive he came to, a wide adobe complex a few blocks from the caravansary. Before long he'd consumed enough to convince himself that this, as with everything else that had led to this moment in his life, wasn't such a bad turnout. He could head farther down into Usba proper, hit the Honeyed Coast at Trve, and pick up work on a ship heading... well, anywhere but here. The Southern Arm was too devil-loved hot for a Flintlander out of the Frozen Savannahs.

The barkeep was evidently Geminidean, and as he served a pair of chain-draped pilgrims recently arrived from the Crimson Empire they filled him in on sundry rumors of import from back home. Maroto initially paid the tonsured women no mind, but then one of their voices sliced through his sun-stewed skull:

"...more than a few rebels, though—they're professionals, is the thought, given how effective they are, maybe a mercenary band hired by the Raniputri or Immaculates to stir up trouble."

Nothing exciting, that, but then the other pilgrim interjected:

"Hear this, though—they're led by a blue-haired general with the faceplate of a devil dog, and at least one of her captains wore the helm of a Villain, if not more. Need I tell you what color banner they flew?"

For the first time in a very long time, Maroto felt dizzy from more than the drink, and he clung to the basalt bartop.

"That story's older than my firstborn," said the barkeep, nodding at the wench serving mugs of kumis at the other end of the tavern. "I haven't heard it in ages, though; glad to hear it's making a comeback. It'd be a shame if people stopped telling it."

"That's what I told her," said the first pilgrim.

"I heard it from my sister, who heard it from her superior," argued the second. "These are holy women, not song-singers looking to attract a crowd. The company ambushed a garrison outside Agalloch not a month past."

"If not a tall tale, then clever impostors seeking to hijack a legend rather than build a reputation," said the barkeep. "Unless you believe in ghosts, sister?"

"No one knows for sure what became of the Villains after their queen was executed," said the first pilgrim. "So perhaps the captain is genuine, and their leader a fake. That way you're both right."

"I never said I believed it was really her," said the second pilgrim defensively. "Simply that mercenaries waving the Cobalt flag were seen outside Agalloch. Unlike others I could name, I prefer to repeat facts, not speculate on rumors, even when the details of such facts are admittedly scant."

There may have been more to the conversation, but Maroto did not know, for he staggered out of the tavern. From the caravansary, he quickly picked up the trail of the fops. Following their tinny cries through the baking streets, and occasionally stumbling into the walls of the tight-packed houses that scalded like the sides of a tandoor, he eventually caught up to them at an establishment of decidedly grander stature than the one at which he had drunk.

Purna had not gotten around to informing the others of Maroto's desertion, and so all seemed as he had left it. Within an hour he was contentedly asleep on the cool tile floor beneath one of the inn's plush benches, and two dusks later they were rolling back out into the desert, Maroto having successfully convinced the testy nobles that he had a hot tip on some "real adventure" to be found on the Desperate Road: the most direct, and therefore most dangerous, route back across the Panteran Wastes.

CHAPTER

11

As Zosia repacked her gear in the customs house on the far side of the wall, the guard who had brokered her admittance sauntered into the brightly lit chamber. Compared to the polished, spotlessly maintained armor of the Immaculates, Zosia's old adventuring kit looked downright shoddy. Choplicker did his tottering, just-an-old-dog-shaking-his-butt approach to the young soldier, who scratched him behind the ears and cooed to the foul monster.

"Thanks again," said Zosia as she pulled the drawstring tight and turned around to maneuver the massive pack from the table onto her aching shoulders. It was full dark now that customs had finally gotten done with her, and she still had to find an inn or flophouse in Linkensterne. "Anywhere cheap and clean you'd recommend in the city?"

"Sure," said the guard, patting Choplicker and straightening up. The fiend whined as she took her hand away. "Let's get moving. You can tell me if you're talking food and drink, men or women or what-have-you, or just a bunk."

"You're my minder?" In the old days many of the isles required an escort for visitors, but on the coast foreigners had been free to come and go as they pleased.

"Bang Lin," said the guard with the faintest suggestion of a bow, her back barely curving. "It's my neck if you're a spy or assassin. Told the captain you seemed friendly, so I get to play chaperone until you prove me right. Or wrong."

"That's one I owe you, then." Depending on how things shook out with Kang-ho it could go either way, but for all their sakes Zosia hoped she proved Bang Lin correct. Anyway, there were worse traveling companions than handsome youths . . . but as soon as her thoughts started down the path to private chambers instead of a common room, she remembered the weight of her husband's severed head in her hand, the butcher's-stall smell of his hair. The mountain crossing had been cold and lonely enough that she had actually considered letting Choplicker curl up against her when she slept, but it was still too fresh to entertain thoughts of companionship. She'd lost lovers before, plenty of them, but this was something else entirely—the ache had only grown worse with time, and though the thought that she was further fattening up Choplicker turned her stomach, there was nothing she could do to soften the hurt. Not until she had the means to go after the ones responsible for what had happened.

"So long as you don't cause any trouble, we can call it even," said Bang. "What's your dog's name? He's cute."

Choplicker barked his assent at this, nuzzling his head back under Bang's dangling palm. The soldier was delighted. Zosia grimaced.

"I call him a lot of things, but cute ain't one of them. Dumb mutt comes no matter what you say."

"So long as you don't call him late for supper, right?"

"Right," said Zosia, remembering Choplicker as he had been on campaign twenty-odd years before, feasting on the suffering of the dead and dying until his gut dragged on the ground. It might have been comical, like something you'd see on a Samothan woodcut of a half-forgotten fable, but to witness such wanton gluttony, to watch the creature's flesh warp to accommodate its appetite . . . there was nothing funny about it. "A bath, food, drink, smoke, and a bed. That order."

"We can do that," said Bang, ushering Zosia out the door. "But Linkensterne's liable to be different than you remembered, and not for the better."

"I remember it being a real shithole," said Zosia as she stepped out into the chill night.

"Then maybe it hasn't changed much," said Bang, saluting the customs officer lounging on a bench by the door as they headed up the road.

This had been farm country, but all of the old outlying ranches had been demolished, the buildings scrapped to construct barracks. A string of pink paper lanterns hung from poles leading back to the gate, and ahead of them the lights were strung from the dwarf pines and plum trees that bordered the road cutting through the overgrown fields. The city glowed at the end of the lantern string, the biggest beacon of them all.

The Immaculate influence on Linkensterne had always been stronger than just a few bun-carts and noodlehouses to offset the typical sausage-and-beerhall eateries of the Crimson Empire, and a higher proportion of Immaculate whores than you'd find in the nonspecialty brothels of Nottap or Eyvind. The city proudly displayed its bordertown lineage on its skyline, with half-timbered pagodas and stupa-based, steeple-crowned churches towering above the narrow streets, the sharply angled roofs of Imperial-styled rowhouses bumping end-tiles with the swooping curves of Immaculate construction. Far from feeling as though two cultures had been awkwardly pressed together as you saw in some cities on the Star—places in which the people and the architecture stuck to their own quarters—in Linkensterne it felt as though the city had been jointly raised in harmonious collaboration. The reason for this was simple: it had. A fire had leveled the spot some hundred years before, and a broad mix of Imperial and Immaculate interests had rebuilt it. The city stood as a testament to the potential for two peoples to come together and erect a shared future.

The city was also a total dump, with the exception of the Merchant's Quarter, which was judiciously walled off from the rest of Linkensterne and could only be entered by appointment. The rest of town was run-down and rampant with crime both petty and violent, in contrast to the more sophisticated corruption that took place among the governing merchants. The only thing worse than a royal city was a free one, where the ruling elite rarely forked over the funds for sanitation or a decent municipal militia.

When they tromped into town Zosia could see at a glance how much things had changed. They were entering the Black Earth district, which was on the opposite end of Linkensterne from the Merchant's Quarter, yet the streets were fairly clear of shit and refuse, and a pair of uniformed militia thugs stood on the corner of most intersections. Lit lanterns on lampposts were the rule instead of the exception, and four blocks in Zosia had yet to see anyone lying dead drunk—or just plain dead—on the too-clean street.

"You were right," she said, "things *have* changed."

"I heard it was a lot of fun before we incorporated it," said Bang wistfully. "Now it's just a broke-down version of an Immaculate city."

"Did a lot of merchants pull up stakes? They can't have been happy about being conquered."

"Oh, they hate the handover like you wouldn't believe, but it's not like they've got a lot of options—you know any other free cities on the Norwest Arm? Me, neither. So most of those crooks stayed put and have tried to make the best of it. Hard as a barnacle's breast, doing shady trades with Immaculate oversight, but a tough tit is better than none at all, eh?"

"That's why the caravans are lined up for days outside the wall." Zosia hadn't been back a day and was already soured on Star politics.

"Days or weeks, depends on who they're here to trade with," said Bang. "Those merchants who were more...receptive to the handover, they get invitations so their guests breeze through customs with a municipal pass instead of waiting in the queue. The merchants who aren't so amenable about Immaculate overseers, well, their goods take a little longer to clear the wall."

"And bad luck for any poor saps waiting on the merchants to provide medicine or supplies, right?" It filled Zosia's mouth with vinegar, all this familiar squabbling, with the commoners caught in the middle.

"Bad luck for some, but good luck for others," said Bang. "Merchants who were on the outs with the old Linkensterne elite have found their prospects much improved by finding new slippers to kiss."

"Bully for them. Now, a bath, food, drink, smoke, bed," said Zosia, yawning at a militiaperson who was sizing her up. "Let's get on with it."

Zosia had fond memories of Immaculate bathhouses in Linkensterne from long before the takeover, but she didn't remember any being as clean as the one Bang led her to. Jade tiles gleamed in the candlelight, the wide, terraced pools steaming like soup bowls. There were a dozen other bathers spread out in the tubs or lounging on the warm tiles, and as Zosia lowered herself into the hot water she felt true contentment for the first time since she had been forced upon this road she walked. Bang settled in beside her, and, seeing her out of her uniform, Zosia's interest in the girl increased substantially. She smiled to herself at the younger woman's flirtatious glances and offer to wash her back...but as soon as the smile arrived it wilted. Zosia dunked her face in the water and stayed down as long as she could, as if she could hide there forever from her past, and from her base nature. As if warm water and a rough sponge could scrub away what was wrong with her.

In a refreshingly dingy tavern off the main drag, Zosia and Bang were served up a steaming supper fragrant with long-missed spices. They ate at a yellowed floor table, filling their dishes from the large chipped bowl set between them. Mixing up the rice, fried quail eggs, peppery bean paste, and sautéed ferns and radish, Zosia passed the seared venison, curds, and sauerkraut to Bang—it had been decades since she had enjoyed real Immaculate cuisine, and didn't care to sully the experience with these concessions to Crimson tastes. Besides, she had eaten little else but deer jerky on her journey. She ate and she ate and she ate, offering no scraps to Choplicker even when he whined until the quail yolks turned red, the melting faces of people Zosia had killed leaking out into the rice. She raised bowl to lips and shoveled in the lot, imagining all the new victims Choplicker would haunt her with, once her work really got under way.

———

Zosia liked to drink and she liked to smoke, and she liked them best when she could enjoy them together. Once Bang had gotten the measure of her ward's preferences, they ambled through Linkensterne. They passed the tall, teetering kaldi houses (hash and bud of the saam only, please) and the fluttering silk panels of the sting warrens (insects, arachnids, and the odd kidnapping), arriving in their own full-bellied time at a longhouse that reeked of bitter beer, bitter sweat, and, sweetest of all to Zosia's nose, bitter tubāq. Even this early in the season the rice paper shutters were slid open, the chill outside mitigated by the large firepit in the center of the room and the dozens of smaller furnaces the patrons puffed upon. Cheap clay tavern pipes were bought for pfennigs from the proprietor, a reedy old gent from distant Vasarat whose longstanding devotion to his brown mistress was writ across callused lips, stained teeth, and the yellow finger he dug into his nostril as though it were an obstinate bowl clinging to its dottle.

Having the end but not the means, Zosia sidled up to the bar, shrugging off her pack as she bumped past a woolly-bearded barbarian nursing a porcelain-headed jaegerpfeiff. Up and down his arms and neck sinuous indigo tattoos wrestled with jagged white scars, his lionskin cloak stank of wet dirt and old blood, and his pipe gave off the cloying aroma of lavender. Once upon a time she would have challenged the giant to a duel for smoking his pungent aromatic weed within sniffing distance of her; once, but long ago. Pushing her wide-brimmed hat back onto her neck, she settled onto a stool and plunked her smallest purse on the lacquered bar.

"Hi, honor friend," said the proprietor, his Immaculate even worse than hers.

"Right back atcha," said Zosia in Crimson as she undid the flaps of her enormous backpack. Withdrawing a pouch smaller yet more precious than the coinpurse set before her, she removed a pipe carved in the cutty style, its gently bent antler stem as long as her hand and its smooth briar bowl canted slightly forward, like a tipsy sailor leaning against a mast. Two tiny spurs descended from the base of the bowl, allowing it to sit steady on the bartop. "I'll be filling this with your finest vergin flake, my horn with your darkest stout, a dwarf of your smoothest ryefire, and a private room. That order."

———

It was the dwarf glasses of ryefire that got her. Bang matched her tipple for tipple and horn for horn at first, the pretty soldier doing her regiment proud. As she eyed Zosia's pipe the conversation flowed into the safe waters of stormy seas and naval entanglements, of which Zosia had seen more than many in her youth. Bang obviously had the brine in her veins, and as night gave way to early morning Zosia found herself genuinely enjoying the eager young fool's company— the girl seemed intent on seeing herself washed into an early grave, and it seemed a pity to send her off to sea without a bit more sand under her nails.

"Should've said something sooner, would've been easy to arrange a bedmate," said Bang as she ducked away from Zosia at the older woman's door. "Still could see, send someone up?"

"Nah, haven't paid for it in so long I wouldn't know the etiquette," said Zosia, trying to mask her embarrassment with braggadocio. Just as she'd known that last dwarf of ryefire was a mistake before it even hit her belly, she realized now that she had totally misread the situation, that she had mistaken basic kindness and mild flirtation for something more. "Just being friendly, was all."

"I *am* flattered," said Bang. "Really. Good night, friend."

"Sure," said Zosia. "Night."

Closing the door, she looked to Choplicker. He had nosed the paper screen over and had his front paws up on the windowsill, looking out into the dark city. Much as she disliked sharing her room with him, the alternative was to let him loose on the streets of Linkensterne.

Or she could set him free once and for all, in exchange for vengeance upon all those responsible. That would take the burden from her aged shoulders and ensure that none escaped their due.

She wouldn't have to take another step into the Immaculate Isles, wouldn't have to bet her already slim chance of success on a hundred thousand variables—it had taken her over a season just to get this far; how long would it take her to achieve her ends? Why not just let the monster do what monsters did best?

"Not on your life," Zosia muttered, sprawling out on the mat. Hoartrap had claimed that devils could only speak to the sleeping and the dead, but Zosia knew better than to put faith in the word of a witch. She often wondered if the fiends couldn't also project a thought into your mind, the notion planted so surreptitiously as to make you think you'd conjured it up yourself. That would certainly explain how often she thought about turning Choplicker loose, even after he'd declined her previous offer for freedom.

And why she would have tried to screw the first available person she came across, with Leib not yet half a year dead. She remembered the wink and slap on the bottom he'd given her before riding out for the crossroads that last time and barely made it to the chamberpot in time. When she was sure that her guts were done, she wiped her mouth and looked to where Choplicker had curled up beneath the window, pretending to sleep.

Would that devils were responsible for our weakness, Zosia thought as she crawled back onto her mat. Would that there was somebody, anybody, *anything* else to blame for her lot. In the morning she would find many likely candidates, with Queen Indsorith of Samoth at the top of the list, but for now, squinting in the glare of sleeplessness, she could only twist deeper into herself, into her responsibility for the death of Leib and his village.

"My village," she whispered in the dark, "*my* village," but she never quite believed it.

CHAPTER
12

It was late spring when Sister Portolés's transgression at the village of Kypck truly caught up with her.

In the meantime, she had been lashed by Father Eddison as soon as she had led the cavalry back down the valley to rejoin the main force of the Fifteenth Regiment, the charred corpse of Sir Hjortt she had recovered from the ruins of the mayoress's house lashed to the back of his horse. She had fully expected this. She had been lashed again by the regiment's acting colonel once her clerical superior was done with her, which, again, she had both anticipated and welcomed. Finally, she had lashed herself in penance on every new moon since, but she had prayed to avoid any substantial probing into the particulars of that nobleman's ignoble death in a remote mountain town. Alas, it seemed a well-connected young colonel could not burn to death on a war nun's watch without a full inquiry taking place.

The summons came the week after she finally returned to her cell in the quadrant of Diadem's central Chainhouse known as the Dens. The Fallen Mother saw through the selfishness of Sister Portolés's prayers, and so the summons, and as the anathema read the letter in the dimness of her cell she nodded to herself. She deserved this, just as Sir Hjortt had deserved to die in the fire. Just as Portolés had judged him, now, too, would she be judged. Everything happened. Not for a reason, mind, for the Fallen Mother was beyond the need for justifications, but everything happened.

Sister Portolés set the summons down on her penitence bench and prepared herself to enter the Crimson Throne Room of Diadem. Her ablutions took the better part of the day, all of the hair on her body, and the odd patch of skin when her razor found resistance. Better to lose a little flesh than leave behind a trace of what she had been before this day. To be before Her Grace was to be reborn, and what babe comes to its mother already dressed in fur? A babe worthy of the pyre, not the teat.

Too late, she thought to call on Brother Wan, thinking he might be persuaded to sin with her one last time, the way they used to, but this was the thought of Portolés, anathema and sinner, and the penitent nun who crouched naked in the cell slapped herself across the face. Hard. And again. And now she wanted to see Brother Wan more than ever, so she stuck out her tongue and pinched it between her fingers, digging into the ridge of scar tissue that marked where the church had made her almost human when she was but a fledgling monster. She could no longer recall the tastes of the wind, of the night, but she could well remember the tang of blood and hemp as the papal barbers had sewn her forked tongue together.

A knock at her door. This was it, then. Rising, she dropped the black robe included with the summons over her stocky frame and went to meet her fate. Except instead of an escort to her judgment, it was a far more welcome visitor.

"Oh, Portolés." Brother Wan gazed up at her in the doorway. The pocked knot of flesh where his nose and upper lip should be, where his beak had been, trembled with emotion. "I would have come as soon as I heard about the summons, but thought...you might wish to come to me. Shall I go? I shall go."

"Temptation," growled Portolés, wondering if the Fallen Mother or the Deceiver had put this penultimate obstacle in her path. Not really caring either way. Kissing her brother-in-chains right there in the hall of the Dens, kissing him until her file-dulled teeth knocked against the wooden ones the church had given him, and then pulling him into her cell. They tripped over her penitence bench, came down with limbs tangled, and for what must be the final time rooted their hands beneath one another's vestments, groaning prayers together between kisses as they worked one another to forbidden rapture.

Employing only their hands did not betray the letter of the law, true, but as Brother Wan had always told her when they were done and he was regretting his weakness, their actions certainly ran against the spirit of it. He was correct that a lesser sin is still a sin, which only prompted Portolés to argue that that was all the more reason for them to consummate the greater evil their bodies craved. Everything happens, she would breathe in the humid darkness, but he always stopped her before she could damn them both.

When they were growing up together in the Dens, he had always set an example for Portolés to aspire to, and his ability to know her heart even better than she knew it herself had no doubt saved her from many a graver sin. Since becoming an attaché to Cardinal Diamond several years prior, he had soared to such lofty reaches in his piety that he had rebuked her every suggestion that they resume their discreet meetings. That he had come to her this last time filled Portolés with the buzzing ecstasy that she only ever seemed to attain through committing a new sin; what did it say about her that frigging Wan was so much more exciting, now that he was so much holier?

"What *happened* out there?" Wan whispered as they lay together when they were both finished, Portolés licking her fingers clean. "The clerks are saying all sorts of horrible things, and Cardinal Diamond—"

"Pray for me, brother," said Sister Portolés, kissing her fellow anathema on the cheek and smoothing her robe. She had to go, now, or she would tell him everything, and she cared about him too much to burden him with more of her sins. "That's what we always used to do, after."

Giving Brother Wan a final sad smile, she went to meet her queen and, holier still, her pontiff.

Sister Portolés had only been inside Diadem's Jewel once, when she had been called by Abbotess Cradofil for enlistment in the Imperial military, and on that occasion she had been surrounded by a thousand other novices in the parade grounds on the bottom level. Now she walked alone—as all mortals truly are in the eyes of the Almighty Matron—up winding stairs carved into the ossified corpse of the volcano that housed Diadem, moving from the city below to the castle above. Daunting a journey as it would have been were she only meeting her pontiff, the knowledge that the Crimson Queen would also be present filled Portolés with terror.

It was not the ferocious reputation of Queen Indsorith alone that terrified Portolés, but the anxiety that stemmed from not knowing exactly how solid the ground was beneath her feet, now that another political seismic shift had settled. For most of her life Portolés had been taught that Queen Indsorith was second only to Pope Shanatu in the eyes of the Fallen Mother, and after praying to the Black Pope every novice turned her prayers to the Crimson Queen and her royal castle in the old capital of the Serpent's Circle.

But then the Burnished Chain had declared Queen Indsorith a traitor to the Fallen Mother, and in the ensuing civil war Portolés had fought the forces of a woman she had once worshipped...only to have Pope Shanatu declare a truce, restore the queen to grace at the Council of Diadem, and then promptly retire from his post, with his niece succeeding him as Black Pope. As if matters weren't turbulent enough, after the reconciliation Queen Indsorith had moved her court back to Diadem, ruling from the Crimson Throne Room for the first time in nearly twenty years, the old queen and the new pope governing their respective spheres from the same chamber. In a few short months Portolés had gone from killing Imperials at the Battle of Brockie to serving as personal bodyguard to one of their colonels...a position she had proven woefully inadequate for.

No wonder a lowly anathema struggled with her faith even before what the summons had called the Encounter at Kypck—like all of her monstrous ilk, Portolés was born to sin, and only the intervention of the Burnished Chain brought goodness into her brutish heart. She couldn't understand how anyone, even the Crimson Queen, could be excommunicated from the church one year, only to be declared the spiritual equal of the Black Pope after the war went poorly for the Burnished Chain. Brother Wan sternly admonished her not to ask questions beyond her comprehension, but Sister Portolés couldn't help herself; she wanted the world to make sense again, the way it had when she was young. Sadly, she was losing the war she fought with her own devilish nature, and now that she had effectively murdered Colonel Hjortt there could be no saving her: the two holiest women in the world would see her for what she was, and as Portolés went to fulfill the summons she knew she would never return to the Dens, the only home she had ever known.

After being admitted through a dozen gates of narrowing width and increased guard, she was given a black candle as thick as her wrist, and with the aid of a blind officiant melted its base onto her shaven head until she was able to affix it in place. Only when it was firmly welded to her scalded skull was she permitted to proceed up the unlit avenues of Castle Diadem, her pace painfully slow lest the flame flicker out. Gargoyles leered at her from every arch and buttress, gobs of wax mingling with her tears to leave a trail for her to follow back out should she be permitted to leave after the audience. The way was known to her by the will of the Fallen Mother, channeled through the pure heart of the Black Pope, who waited with the Crimson Queen... or so the summons had alleged, but Portolés found herself guided solely by the smears of phosphorescent slime on the flagstones that directed her ever upward. Perhaps they knew her sin was so great she could no longer feel the touch of the divine, and had thus provided her another means of finding her way.

An hour passed, maybe two, stair after stair, ramp upon ramp.

Everything happens, but still Sister Portolés struggled. The echo of Brother Wan's fingers now seemed shrill between her legs, and she would have cursed her weakness had her breath not been required to keep her chant at a respectable volume. It was not for the unclean to judge any but themselves—how many times had Abbotess Cradofil made her repeat that? And yet Sister Portolés had judged Sir Hjortt, and now she would be judged. The Fallen Mother loved her, and a war-worn sister should walk with her head high, even an anathema, yet the wax dripping down her nose and cheeks made her shame public. Any hope she had felt in her cell was gone here in the house the Almighty Matron had fashioned for her hierophants.

Once Sister Portolés gained the throne room's antechamber, the lighting improved even if her mood remained dark. Candelabras illuminated a posh old man dressed in the chartreuse regalia of Azgaroth. He waited on a bench, Abbotess Cradofil beside him, and both stood as Sister Portolés shuffled down the last shadow-draped corridor. Neither appeared happy to see her.

"Sister Portolés," said Abbotess Cradofil, her lips as slick and bulging as a pair of tadpoles. "I present you to Baron Domingo Hjortt of Cockspar, Retired Fifteenth Colonel of the Crimson Empire."

"Sir." Sister Portolés bowed as best she could without risking her candle. A rivulet of wax arced across her eye, but she did not cry out. This old rooster looked just as puffed up as his broiled chick. "I pray for Sir Hjortt's soul, and trust the remains and effects I returned to the Fifteenth safely found their way home to Cockspar."

"Let's get on with this," Baron Hjortt addressed Abbotess Cradofil. "I have no desire to speak to this creature."

"Perhaps, but Sister Portolés has something to tell you of your son," said Abbotess Cradofil, those dead eyes of her cutting across Sister Portolés. "Don't you?"

"I lament the death of Sir Hjortt," said Sister Portolés, but before she could stop herself the words came rushing out of their own accord. "I believe you would have had him die a hero, not a coward. Allmother forgive him."

Well, it was the truth, though the nobleman's horrified expression confirmed that he had not come to the Imperial capital for such insight into Sir Efrain Hjortt's final moments. Abbotess Cradofil's slimy mouth pursed tight, and Sister Portolés silently apologized for the wildness in her bedeviled tongue. Perhaps it would have been better if they had just removed it altogether, as Abbotess Cradofil had always said.

"I'll watch you burn ere the moon next rises," Baron Hjortt snarled, and Sister Portolés supposed he was right. She remembered the look that had appeared on his son's face when she had not braved the burning terrace to save him, the hatred and fear and confusion… The familial resemblance was unmistakable. She wondered if she would die better. She couldn't possibly die worse.

"After all I've done for you, this is the tithe you offer," Abbotess Cradofil murmured as she ushered Sister Portolés to the great white oak doors. No guards stood sentry here, the queen decreeing that any assassin was entitled to the same chance at her throne that she had once enjoyed. In twenty years of her rule, forty-seven contenders had breached this final portal, and forty-six skulls lined the archway, grinning down at the nobleman, the abbotess, and the anathema. The one missing skull supposedly belonged to a man unworthy of a death by the queen's blade, a wastrel cast out to seek a more fitting tomb among the scavenging devils of the Star. "Fallen Mother heed me, Portolés, if you speak so freely before our pontiff, I will snap your neck myself."

"I praise your mercy, Superior, but I shall not accept it," Sister Portolés heard herself reply, and marveled that sinning had apparently become something she did on reflex. Had the deviltry she had fought her whole life to smother come loose once she let Sir Hjortt die? Was the wickedness of the Deceiver stirring this mutiny in her breast? As much as she wanted to believe such excuses, in her soul Portolés knew that her love for sin was nothing new, that hard as she had fought against her base nature, transgression gave her more succor than obedience ever had.

The Crimson Throne Room was built into the rim of the petrified volcano, a roofless half-moon of polished obsidian ending in a two-thousand-foot drop down to the gables and cupolas of the city beneath the castle. It was told in songs that the stars blazed hotter here than anywhere else in the world, even when the moon was full, as it was this night, and other than Sister Portolés's candle no earthly light disturbed the chamber. She suspected that even had she a pair of pure eyes the room would seem bright as the flush of dawn.

The Queen of Samoth, Keeper of the Crimson Empire, sprawled

across a huge throne of carven red fire glass that erupted from the obsidian floor, the flowing lines and steep curls of the seat making Her Majesty appear to float atop a plume of blood. The Black Pope, Shepherdess of the Lost, sat stiffly beside her queen in a shorter, plainer throne, this one crafted of onyx and inlaid with thick silver chains. Both women were opulently enrobed, but the queen was barefoot. The doors swung shut and Sister Portolés's candle guttered out. Three pairs of knees slipped to the hard floor, three heads bowed.

"Your Majesty and Your Grace," began Abbotess Cradofil, "I present unto you this worthy pilgrim, Sir Domingo Hjortt, Baron of Cockspar, Retired Fifteenth Colonel of the Crimson Empire, and the sister whom you seek, an anathema we have rehabilitated and given the name Portolés, for Saint—"

"Rehabilitated, you say?" came a surprisingly high voice, and Sister Portolés peeked up, one-eyed from the wax she dared not wipe away, to see if her queen or her pontiff spoke. It was Pope Y'Homa III, Voice of the Allmother, now sitting straight up, the tip of her conical hat nearly, but not quite, as high as the jagged carnelian crown of the seated queen. "This devil-spawned witch had but one purpose in the life we built her, and you dare allege she is reformed, after what befell her charge? Small wonder my cardinals counsel me to raze the Dens and be done with this ill-guided quest of yours."

"Your Grace, a single transgressor—"

"I did not call you here to debate theology." The Black Pope's pale sneer pushed through Sister Portolés's robes, into a secret tenderness she had never believed existed in her breast. That she was a sinner she readily admitted, and she prayed for punishment, but to hear that her actions might reflect upon all her wretched brethren was a poison to her nerves, a brand to blister her very soul. "You have claimed, to myself and my uncle before me, that an anathema may serve but a single purpose: to put itself between danger and the righteous. To serve as shield, however sullied. To protect the clean. Yet here we have a monster that dares return to its post not with the living pureborn it swore to serve, but his blackened bones! And as if such a travesty were not crime enough, it wears the robes I have given it, mocking this very office. And you would lecture me on the difference between one and legion?"

"Your Grace, I never meant to imply—" Abbotess Cradofil began.

"I know well the difference between a single devil and an army of them, Cradofil—the latter currently enjoy every comfort of Diadem while all across the Star faithful pureborn go hungry and cold, and the former has aroused such disgust in our queen that it has been brought here, to befoul the most sacrosanct space in all of the Empire as we ponder its punishment."

The words scourged Sister Portolés far deeper than the physical lashes she had brought upon herself, and she silently wept. Doubt was her devil, forever goading her, and she had fed the beast as eagerly as a disobedient child slipping scraps to a forbidden puppy. She had doubted Sir Hjortt, and that doubt had made her feel befouled when she had delivered the order to exterminate that village, and fouler still when she had personally executed the five members of the cavalry who refused the will of their colonel. And after the slaughter, it was her doubt that had kept her on the edge of the flames at the mayoress's house, it feeling just and good to watch Hjortt burning alive, after what he had ordered Portolés and the Fifteenth Cavalry to do . . .

Ever since Kypck she had been deceiving herself, pretending that killing the villagers was the true crime and Hjortt the true criminal, Portolés an avenging angel of the Fallen Mother, but now she recognized just how deluded she had been. Her innate corruption always perverted the truth, sin tasting sweetest upon her tongue and goodness smacking of ash and lye, which was why she had let him die, and why she had told no one of what really happened that day. Instead, during every confession after the event she had cast his death not as the result of her inaction but as the inscrutable will of the Fallen Mother. She had almost convinced herself that it wasn't a lie, not really, but of course it was, and of course the only sin that had been committed that day was her refusal to help the pureborn colonel who needed her aid. She remembered how he had thrashed in the chair he was bound to as the deck of the mayoress's house burned around him, hurling insults and promises and prayers at Sister Portolés while she watched him roast. From the corner of her eye she saw Baron Hjortt shake with silent laughter or barely contained emotion at the pope's condemnation of Portolés, and she would have whispered an apology to the grieving father had she not feared a cry would escape instead.

"That's all a bit much, isn't it?"

Sister Portolés's heart stopped, a half-birthed sob aborted in her throat. The queen had spoken. She sounded tired, her bare feet still dangling off the edge of the throne she lounged across.

"Sister Portolés, I wonder if we might hear from your lips what transpired in Kypck, and how Baron Hjortt's son met his doom there." Queen Indsorith shimmered, bathed in celestial radiance… or so she looked through the lens of Sister Portolés's tears. "My Askers have interviewed dozens of the deceased colonel's cavalry, so I have established a certain chain of events, but would have you enlighten us with your account. Mother Cradofil recounted the basics from your last confession for us, but I am interested in a more detailed telling."

Sister Portolés swallowed, willed her venomous tongue to work as her queen commanded. Finally, it managed, "If it pleases Your Grace?"

"Whether or not it pleases Y'Homa means less than nothing here, in my throne room, in my capital, in my province, in my empire," said Queen Indsorith, reclining farther into the ebon seawolf furs that bolstered her throne. "Whatever your station before you entered into the service of the Crimson Empire's armies, you are bound to heed my will. Unless you disagree?"

Sister Portolés was unsure if this last was directed at her or the pontiff, but when no response came from Pope Y'Homa, she steadied herself and began her confession, sparing no detail of her own failings. This time she would tell it true. And so she did, from her hubris to her disrespectful tongue, from her reluctance at carrying out her colonel's orders to her guilt and self-loathing at staving in the heads of the soldiers who wouldn't assist in the slaughter, and finally her doubts over the righteousness of killing the villagers in the first place. Yet just when she reached the climax, as she was about to confess how she had returned from the cleansed hamlet to find the mayoress's hut likewise aflame, the trapped Sir Hjortt wailing for help, and her own heart hard to his pleas, the queen cut her off.

"—And so when you returned to the mayoral house it was already on fire, and Sir Efrain Hjortt along with it. This is as I had heard from the men in Sir Hjortt's command, and those whom you previously confessed to. Please explain, Your Grace, how exactly does Sister Portolés's faithful enactment of the orders given her by Sir Hjortt qualify as sedition or"—the queen gasped dramatically—"deviltry?"

None spoke in the Crimson Throne Room, and then Baron Hjortt cleared his throat. When no response was elicited he tried again, and this time the queen snapped, "What do you have to say for your idiot son, Baron? Before I gave you permission to pass your command down to your boy, you always struck me as a worthy colonel, one well versed in the Crimson Codices. I believe you taught him to uphold my laws of war, did you not?"

Baron Hjortt was obviously at a loss for words, and the queen went on, finally leaning forward in her throne as she berated the retired colonel.

"Everyone in my armies from drudge to colonel knows better than to sack a single farm without my express orders, let alone an entire town, so what, pray tell, could inspire the dearly departed Sir Hjortt to commit such an atrocity? Did you accidentally tutor him in the ways of ancient barbarians instead of the civilized Empire? When you gave him your command, did you forget to mention the commandments of his queen, laws which were old when he was young?"

"Your Majesty!" Baron Hjortt finally spluttered, and then, clearly stalling, said it again: "Your Majesty!"

"Perhaps this creature blasted him with some geas or hex," supplied Pope Y'Homa, keeping her dark gaze on Sister Portolés. "That would certainly explain how a *crone*, as the anathema so eloquently put it, could murder both an experienced war monk and a knight of Azgaroth. It would be a pretty trick indeed to have Colonel Hjortt commit such evil and then dispose of him and her brother-in-chains when the crime was done."

"No!" cried Sister Portolés, surprising even herself with the out-burst. "Never! I . . . I am not pure, I have *never* been pure, it is true . . . But I strive to be as good as the Allmother allows me to be! I am no witch, nor a conspirator—I am nothing if not loyal to you! To both of you, my pope! My queen!"

"Loyal to both of us?" the queen asked, exchanging a queer smile with the pope, and Sister Portolés blushed at her own folly. "Tell me, Your Grace, do you think this wretch tells honest, or do you still believe that the rust of corruption has eaten so deeply into the Chain that even the holy soldiers you place in my service are compromised?"

The wind picked up, roaring over the high wall of the volcano and stirring the queen's long auburn hair around her haughty face. Again, none spoke for a heavy moment, the two women staring at each other, and then the pontiff threw up her hands. It was an oddly petulant gesture, and for the first time Sister Portolés appreciated that the Voice of the Fallen Mother was decades younger than the queen, the pontiff sixteen years old if she was a day.

"I leave her future in your most capable hands, Your Majesty," said the Black Pope as she rose from her throne. "For now I must away and counsel with the abbotess and my cardinals, but as always you and I are of one mind on the judgment."

"As always," said the queen, slumping back in her high seat. "Take the old man with you before I decide to attribute his son's exception-ally poor judgment to bad parenting. Rest assured, Baron, if Sister Portolés had returned in time to rescue your offspring I would cur-rently be flogging him in Diadem's square—already his actions have polluted our relations with a dozen outlying provinces. I will not see the Empire fall back into the savage cruelty of old. I never would have let you retire had I suspected your son would prove such a pitiful imi-tation of his father."

"Your Majesty," Baron Hjortt managed a final time, and then he quickly backed away toward the portico as the pontiff approached.

Abbotess Cradofil knelt until Pope Y'Homa III stopped before her and extended her jet-ringed hand for the superior to kiss. To Sister

Portolés's bafflement and delight, the pope then offered her hand to the kneeling anathema. Sister Portolés kissed the ring with more love and tenderness than she had ever kissed Brother Wan, and then the Black Pope strode out of the room, Baron Hjortt stumbling backward before her, Abbotess Cradofil scurrying after.

The doors creaked shut behind them, leaving Sister Portolés alone with her queen in the Crimson Throne Room, only the dim stars, the looming moon, and the chill wind party to what came next.

CHAPTER
13

From Linkensterne, it was a long and rocky coach ride to the coast. When they eventually hit the end of the Norwest peninsula there came the worst leg of the journey, Zosia, Choplicker, and Bang crushed together in the back of a rickshaw and carried along the miles and miles of nauseatingly high boardwalks that linked the closest of the Immaculate Isles to the mainland. When they ran out of wooden roads they rented a boat, and after a long voyage Bang finally delivered Zosia to Hwabun, the last isle before the Haunted Sea, and the family seat of her old crony Kang-ho.

Both smaller and taller than its neighbors, Hwabun did indeed resemble the flower pot it was named for, grey stone cliffs laced with pink mineral deposits rising hundreds of feet above the waves before leveling off into a plateau of variegated vegetation. Bang steered their small catamaran directly at the walls of the island, and only when they were rapidly closing in on the rocks did Zosia make out the sea cave that housed Hwabun's modest harbor. Their way lit by an enormous blubber chandelier that hung from the ceiling of the subterranean cove, Bang maneuvered the vessel around to the docks, where a dozen craft of various sizes and makes were already moored.

A white-gowned old woman helped them tie off, and after a quick Immaculate exchange with Bang, the harbor keeper directed them down the dock and up a wide staircase built into the wall of the cove. They passed through a carven tunnel and emerged into a gazebo, where they were greeted by another servant along with a pair of armed guards, all of the staff dressed in the same bright white livery as the harbor keeper. Zosia couldn't remember if white was the traditional Immaculate color of mourning, of death, or of public shame, but none of the options boded well. They were led out of the gazebo and onto a black gravel path that led through the gardens to the main house.

Kang-ho had done well for himself—he had told her at length of the sorry state his ancestral home had been in when he left, as well as the improvements he planned to make if he ever returned. The structure before her, like most of the newer Immaculate estates she had glimpsed on her voyage, fused traditional island architecture with foreign designs. Unlike many of those attempted, the castle before her actually worked as a conglomeration of Gothic Crimson, Classical Immaculate, and Modern Raniputri...though the Usban onion domes on the outbuildings might have been a bit much. At least the wind chimes were old-school Ugrakari, singing sweet songs of better days to come in the soft sea air.

A pair of servants slid open the massive bamboo screens of the main hall, and a heavyset man dressed in a starched white overcoat scurried down the wide walnut steps to intercept Zosia, Bang, and Choplicker. Another staccato exchange in Immaculate, during which Zosia heard Bang mention her alias of Moor Clell no fewer than three times. The man must have been Hwabun's majordomo, to take such a snotty tone with guests. The majordomo gestured emphatically at Zosia, who, glancing down at her raggedy attire, allowed that it would have been a good idea to buy some more appropriate clothes during her passage through the country rather than spending all of her leisure time reacquainting herself with peated rice liquor, rare tubāq blends, and spicy pickled cabbage. The majordomo spun away, his cape slapping Bang's chin, and hurried back inside.

"That could have gone better," said Bang. "But I think he'll take your request to King Jun-hwan's husband anyway. You're just lucky I know the family names this far out; nowadays most Immaculates seem to think the Isles end at Othean."

"He was always just Kang-ho to me," said Zosia, though to be honest she had probably known his full name, once. Was this how old age made itself known—the sudden, embarrassing realization that you have forgotten little niggling things, like the names of your closest friends?

"Let's just hope he remembers your name, then," said Bang, kicking idly at the gravel. "Here's a thought, though—if he doesn't, and they kick us out, what do you say about a little detour before I take you back to Linkensterne? It's a beautiful trip down and around to the Cuttlefish Cays where my family's from, and there's no sense in rushing back to the wall when we've got a cat just—"

"That didn't take long," said Zosia, noting the majordomo's almost genuine smile as he came back out.

"Hwabun welcomes the lady Moor Clell," said the majordomo with a bow, his Crimson better than Zosia's. "My Elegant Master King Jun-hwan Bong cordially invites you and your warden Bang Lin to take kaldi with his family upon the Mistward Balcony. I will have a servant house your hound in the kennels until your departure."

"Trust me, squire, you don't want him anywhere near your dogs *or* your servants." Zosia patted the majordomo's shoulder as she walked past him up the steps, Choplicker at her heels. "Don't worry, though, his paws are clean, and I won't let him out of my sight."

Cosmopolitan as the exterior of the castle was, the inside was strictly Immaculate, with the foyer nothing more than the intersection of three sparsely decorated hallways. Before the majordomo had even caught up with them, the sound of slippered feet swiftly gliding over polished hardwood floors came to Zosia from the central passage. She tried in vain to keep the smile from her face as Kang-ho slid to a stop in front of her, eyes bulging.

The Second Husband of Hwabun looked a sight better than she'd expected. His cheeks sagged a little and his hair might have been thinning, but otherwise it was Kang-ho as he'd been twenty years past. For all his whinging about how bad he looked in Immaculate fashions, he cut a dapper figure in his square horsehair hat and silk robe, the black roses embroidered on the garment's shoulders and the owlbat on the chest clearly copied from his tattoos. The only thing missing was Fellwing, but knowing Kang-ho, the devil was hiding under his hat.

"It's really you," Kang-ho breathed, looking from Zosia to Chop-licker and back again. "You're alive!"

His eyes filled with tears, and Zosia felt an unexpected tightness in her throat. The presence of Bang on one side of her and the major-domo on the other quickly helped her to suppress the awkward emo-tion, and she said hurriedly, "Yes, well . . . After my warehouse caught fire I knew rumors of my demise had spread, but I didn't expect they should have reached all the way here, to the home of one of my old customers. Fear not, good sir, the pipe you commissioned all those years ago is safe, as am I."

"Of course," said Kang-ho, blinking his eyes clear as his face brightened into a winning smile. "Moor Clell, as I live and breathe. Let us away to a private spot where we can discuss the matter at our leisure."

"His Elegance has extended an invitation to our guests for kaldi, and anticipates us directly," said the majordomo, in Crimson rather than Immaculate. "And as your annual allowance was exhausted shortly after the New Year, sir, I suspect he will want to be a party to any and all discussions you and this merchant have on the matter of new acquisitions."

If Kang-ho was irritated to have his servant call him out so bla-tantly in front of a guest, he didn't show it. "Ah, but this commission was paid for in advance, many years before our marriage, and so it will be of less than no interest to my husband—isn't that right, Mis-tress Clell?"

"Quite," said Zosia.

"Now, Hyori has been reading all sorts of military tales of late, so perhaps Mistress Clell's warden here can entertain the family at kaldi," said Kang-ho, bowing to Bang. "My youngest daughter would be delighted if you could occupy her, dame. I can assure you that your charge will be quite secure in my company."

"It would be my privilege," said Bang, bowing in return. "I am humbled to be a guest in your home. Word of Hwabun's beauty is just that; words, however poetically chosen, can never hope to match the glory of the thing itself."

The majordomo rolled his eyes but nevertheless escorted Bang away into the house, while Kang-ho took Zosia back outside and across the gardens to where a green hill rose up almost as high as the lower towers of the manse. At the summit a bench looked out over the island and the greener waves beyond, and not even the perpetual pillar of thunderclouds to the north that marked the grave of the Sunken Kingdom could cast a shadow on the serenity of the setting. So long as that drowned isle didn't choose today to fulfill the mad prophecies of the Burnished Chain and reemerge from the Haunted Sea, it was shaping up to be a lovely afternoon.

As they settled onto the seat a flock of servants came scurrying after, carrying trays of food and drink and a little table. As the staff erected the table and set it with an Usban sand bowl for the kaldi, Kang-ho and Zosia made small talk about her crossing from Linkensterne, each of them trying not to break out in another stupid grin. When the servants finally retreated back to the base of the hill, Kang-ho raised a mug at Zosia and said, "Wasn't Moor Clell what you used when we were in Brackett, just before everything went to the devils?"

"That's the one. You've got a better memory than me, brother; I couldn't even recall your family name. Hwabun stuck in the grey stuff since you looked so panicked the time you let it slip."

"The oversight in my name might be because I never told any of you what it was," said Kang-ho. "If I ever needed to betray the gang, I didn't want to make it too easy for you to find me."

"Oh, I would have found you," said Zosia, admiring the scenery. "You may live at the ends of the earth, but that's not far enough to hide from me."

"It's not you I was worried about! I'd double-cross the others, if I really had to, but I'd never be crazy enough to turn on you. Do I look like I want to die?"

"No more than usual," said Zosia, leaning down and rooting through the backpack she had fought the servants off of carrying for her. "You have a coalstick? Mine died in the mountains, and I don't think I'll be able to get a match going in this damnably refreshing sea breeze."

"It's all in the jade box there, along with my go-to mixture these days. I call it 'Thunder of Immaculate Hooves.'"

"That's a terrible name for anything, especially a tubāq blend," said Zosia.

"Bah, what's in a title!" said Kang-ho. "The point is it smokes well. It's an Oriorentine sort of mixture, and the leaf in it's as old as we are—Azmir leaf, orange and lemon vergins, and prerevolution Usban lat. Stuff's hard to come by, ever since Linkensterne got snatched by my beloved nanny state. While you're in there, why don't you pass me my—ah, thank you, Zosia."

It was the first time she had heard her true name spoken by anyone but her husband in twenty years, and even then Leib only whispered it in the dark of their bedroom as they made love. Well, there, and in their kitchen, and on their deck, and in that meadow of wildflowers above the house, and all the other places they had made time for one another... Zosia's hands shook as she removed from the velvet-lined case the long-stemmed pipe she had carved Kang-ho a quarter century past and handed it over. "You were always the cleverest, brother, so tell me—why do you think I'm here?"

"The smartest of the Five Villains? That's damning with faint praise, sister, and besides, Hoartrap was wiser than any of us."

"I didn't say wise, I said clever," countered Zosia. "To know that old serpent is to know the difference, too, so enough dodging—tell me your theory while I pack my briar, and then I'll tell you how close you are."

"Very well," said Kang-ho, launching straight into it as he watched her fill her pipe from the terra-cotta jar of campfire-scented tubāq. "You faked your own death because your life was in such danger that you didn't know any other way of thwarting your enemy. Telling anyone, even your closest friends, was too risky to yourself, and to us, so you fooled us all. Devil magic must have been involved, for there were a thousand witnesses who saw you fall, and I was one of them.

After twenty years in hiding, living under an assumed name, that threat to your person has passed, and so you return...Am I warm?"

"You got the obvious one," said Zosia. "Bungled the rest."

"Give me a bone, woman. I'm not some wildborn to peer into that ugly skull of yours! I didn't even think I was right about faking your death—why would you take such a path when you still have that hound of yours? Why not trade his freedom for a less drastic measure than abdicating your people, forsaking your friends?"

"He had his chance to be loosed," said Zosia, glaring at where Choplicker rolled in the grass a short distance down the hill, trying to provoke the servants into playing with him. "Now he'll never be free, no matter how great my need. I'd rather die. And they were never my people—they were glad to be rid of me."

"Wellllll..." Kang-ho scratched his head, grinning at her. "People don't always know what's best for them."

Zosia snorted. "I was a lot of things, but I wasn't what was best for anyone. But believe me, Kang-ho, I never forsook my friends—had it been safe to contact you, I would have."

"So I was warmer than you let on," he said. "Let's have the full account, then."

"I..." Zosia wanted to tell him everything: why she had abdicated the Crimson Throne, how she had orchestrated the deception that had fooled the entire Star, what had become of her afterward...But watching Kang-ho's face as he packed his smooth templewarden, she found she couldn't. Not yet, anyway. "In time you'll hear the whole of it, brother, but not yet. Knowing the details now would do you no good; if anything, it could bring you harm."

"A guarded reply to an open welcome." Kang-ho's familiar pout warmed her heart. By the six devils she'd bound, she had missed her friend. "When will I hear this story, I wonder? Will it be after I give you whatever you've asked for?"

"I haven't asked for anything," she said, and waited until he had his pipe lit before adding, "But since you mention it..."

Kang-ho passed her the small leather-wrapped rod he'd heated on a candle, and she put the glowing end of the coalstick to her bowl.

Puffing away on the pipe, tamping it down with the brass butt of the tool, and then lighting it again, she watched Kang-ho from the corner of her eye. His smile had returned.

"That's more like it," he said after they had both smoked in silence for a spell. "Rich tubāq on a warm spring day, old friends reuniting, the sea beneath and the heavens above. All is right in the world."

"No, it's not." And because there really wasn't any point in drawing it out, she said, "I need your help, brother. Will I have it?"

"Of course." Kang-ho sounded offended that she would even ask. "I swore an oath, didn't I?"

"And I released you from that oath," said Zosia.

"Doesn't mean I had to accept it," he said, his kindness picking at a wound on her heart that would never heal. She kept her eyes from flitting toward Choplicker but knew he must be watching her. "Then again, the oath I swore was to a woman called Cobalt Zosia, blue of hair, fiery of spirit, and cold as the Frozen Savannahs to her enemies. She was the greatest warrior I have ever fought beside or against, the first in a hundred years to take the Carnelian Crown of Samoth by her own hand, and the first in legend to take the rest of the Crimson Empire in the bargain. I saw that woman plummet to her death, Moor Clell, and unless I hear some explanation of why a humble pipemaker such as yourself would choose to impersonate my dead friend and captain, well…"

"Say I eloped, then," said Zosia, the pipe overheating in her hand as she puffed it far too vigorously. Eloped was close enough.

"And just who was the lucky lover?"

"Leib." Zosia whispered his name for fear that saying it any louder would crush her spirit anew. "Leib Kalmah."

"Leib," said Kang-ho, and he sipped his pipe until it came to him. "Not the blond stripling who worked that upscale brothel? The one in Rawg we'd always hit coming back west from the Forsaken Empire?"

"Yeah, that's him," said Zosia, the most exquisite smoke she'd tasted in twenty years turning acrid on her tongue. "Mountain boy who ran off to find adventure in the Empire, and found me instead.

The best lover I ever had, bought or otherwise. Best friend I ever chanced on."

"You expect me to believe you gave up everything, your own hard-won empire, for a whore you could have installed in your castle?"

"It was the only chance for peace," said Zosia, remembering how earnestly she had believed that. "I was a fool, Kang-ho, I see that now. I've made more mistakes than there are isles in the Immaculate Sea, but none worse than thinking I could just walk away, after all the things I'd done."

"All the things *we'd* done, you mean," said Kang-ho, patting her shoulder. "You're too smart for regrets, Zosia. We both know that the one truth on all the Star is that you possess only what you take and what you are given. Some are blessed enough to rely on gifts, but for the rest of us, well, that's why the devils gave us steel."

"The Ugrakari say the devils never meant for us to have it, that we robbed the secret of swordmaking from them," said Zosia. "They tell a tale of how a mortal crept down into the First Dark and stole a devil's ploughshare, and when the fiend tried to take it back she showed him another use for the tool."

"The Ugrakari eat their own dead," said Kang-ho. "How much stock do you put in the myths of cannibals? And I ask this having married one, mind you."

"About as much as I put in the justifications of a retired warlord who would have inherited this lovely island even if he hadn't turned to villainy."

"I would have inherited nothing if I hadn't married the man my parents selected," said Kang-ho. "Why do you think I left home in the first place? As far as barbaric customs go, forging my own destiny appealed to me quite a bit more than an arranged marriage."

"And yet here you are."

"Here I am."

"What happened after I left?" asked Zosia. "After everyone thought they saw me die at the hands of that girl, what happened?"

"We Five all owed you our titles, but really they were just a means of prolonging the dream, and with your death we woke up…some faster than others. For Samoth and the rest of the Empire, it was bad, bad as it ever was. Your death brought a lot of factions together at first—as you surmised, conquerors aren't usually held in high esteem. But any unification was short-lived. Despite what you announced before the duel, and despite Indsorith's popularity with the people after she cast you down, there were many in the Empire who thought they had a stronger claim to the Crown than some upstart girl they'd never heard of.

"Whether from loyalty to your wishes or their own interests, Hoartrap and Singh helped Indsorith solidify her rule, but Fennec sided with Pope Shanatu. After a few years of civil war both Fennec and Singh lost enough capital or gained enough sense to cut out for greener pastures. Hoartrap stuck around longer, but last I heard he'd quit Samoth, too, maybe the whole Empire. Maroto sought revenge but was too drunk or crazy to do it properly, and instead of leading a rebellion with the troops you gave him the lunkhead tried to single-handedly take on the Dread Guard of Diadem. Made it through 'em, too, and got all the way to the throne room, but then Indsorith showed him just how she'd wrested the Crown from you."

"Maroto's dead?" The news was hardly surprising, but what did catch her off guard was the sting in her chest.

"Maybe by now," said Kang-ho. "He survived the duel, though I'm not sure how exactly he slipped away after the new queen spanked him. Last time I saw him he was in a bad way. Strung out, gone to bugs if I had to guess the poison."

Well, that was better than dead, maybe, and just as plausible. Maroto would have been all right, if he ever could have gotten his shit together. "And you?"

"I left the day I saw your body land in the street," said Kang-ho, drawing a line across his throat with the stem of his pipe. "Kang-ho out, along with more loot than my family has ever known. I should have been smarter about it, taken the Empire for everything it was worth, but nobody knew what would happen next, so I got shy while the getting was good. Came home to find my mother dead and my father in poor health, and the next thing I knew I was seduced by the same stud my parents had betrothed me to as a child. Or maybe I seduced him, but the end result is the same—a new ruler with a new name at Hwabun, one nobody would associate with a certain legendary Villain who terrorized the Star for all those years."

"How's that work, exactly?" asked Zosia. "If your husband's Ugrakari and you came back rich before you even married him, why is he King of Hwabun? I thought this isle had been in your family for generations. I'm not judging here, but I thought I heard your steward back there refer to your *allowance*?"

"It's a long and boring story," said Kang-ho grumpily. "The short version is I came back rich, but Jun-hwan was *rich*. Rich enough to fix this place up, fix the family up, and still let me keep my Crimson nest egg for other investments...investments that have rotted on the vine thanks to my homeland's blatantly illegal conquest of Linkensterne, but that's an ulcer for another day. Anyway, I was happy to have him take over as King of Hwabun—even when the kingdom's small enough you can shoot an arrow from one end of it to the other, being regent is more trouble than it's worth."

"Tell me about it. Huh. Kang-ho, living happily ever after as a househusband." She looked down at the expansive garden and grounds, the picturesque sea to the south, dappled with high green islands that jutted up in single peaks like the jade teeth of some seabeast. Even the eternal storm that raged to the north over the Haunted Sea looked pretty from this distance. "Somehow it doesn't seem your style."

"What's the point of doing all the things we did if you don't get to sit back and enjoy yourself someday?" said Kang-ho. "Living comfortably and quietly, indulging my every whim, and raising a family's not such a bum deal. Beats the shit out of getting stabbed out in some pointless bar brawl or falling to my death scaling a tower to rip off some wizard's treasure."

"And the thrill of combat? The exhilaration of adventure?"

"Bad for the humors—I have an excess of bile as it is."

"We always had a lot in common, didn't we?" said Zosia, imagining

Leib sitting between them on the bench, picturing the reunion that never was but should have been. Safer to stay hidden, they had thought, yet here Kang-ho sat, secreted in plain sight, enjoying his retirement. Until her arrival, anyway—the longer she smoked with him, the more she attuned herself to his old ways, and it was obvious some underlying anxiety played at the edge of his mood. Well, there might be, she supposed, for what good could come of her reappearance in his life? She almost felt bad for him, but then he could always say no if he wanted to. "If helping me meant giving up this life you've won for yourself, would you?"

"Maybe," said Kang-ho. "I owe you a debt, of that there is no question. What sort of help would you have me give?"

"War with Samoth," she said. "I'll need an army and the element of surprise, and the Immaculate Isles can give me both. If anyone can give me the Isles, it's you."

"Oh, is that all?" Kang-ho canted his head to the side, running through the angles. "Why?"

"Leib is dead." Zosia wished her voice would break along with her heart as she told him everything that had happened when the Imperial soldiers came to Kypck, but all she felt was eagerness to hear his response. Far below, the waves crashed against the Flower Pot.

"I see," said Kang-ho at last. "But if you're right and this is all Queen Indsorith's doing, why wage war? Why not assassinate the queen and spare us all another dark age?"

"So the Burnished Chain can swoop in and fill the vacuum I leave? *Does* that sound like a good plan?" Zosia was pleased to see the grimace the prospect raised on her friend's face.

"Ouch. No, no, it does not. But you can't fight a faith, Zosia."

"Watch me."

"Damn, girl." Kang-ho shook his head. "So all you want is to take out the Crimson Queen *and* the Black Pope."

"Tell me they don't have it coming and maybe I'll reconsider."

"It's not a question of who is owed what. This is the first peace in memory, and if you start banging up Samoth and rattling the Chain, then the rest of the Empire is going to take an interest. And then the rest of the *Star* will take an interest. And then we're right back to where we started, before we even went to war against King Kaldruut, before we earned a single ally, before we won a single battle... Except we're all thirty years older."

"Thirty years wiser."

"Thirty years fatter and slower. You killed Kaldruut almost a *quarter century* ago, think about that! Hells, don't tell me you weren't feeling old *twenty* years ago, when you pulled your disappearing trick. I know I was, and I don't feel much younger now. We fought for peace, Zosia, and peace is finally here, so maybe—"

"You fought for silver, Kang-ho, silver and steel and glory and power, same as me," said Zosia, angrier than she should have been at his fair and reasonable points. "It was only later we brought peace and prosperity and a better tomorrow into it, when we started feeling the years and saw we might have a chance to do a little good after a lifetime of bad."

"Better late than never?"

"Devildamned right. And any peace they know is peace I gave them, and they betrayed me. Samoth calls itself the capital of the Crimson Empire, well, it's time I reminded them how the Empire came by that color. They brought this on themselves."

"*They* didn't do anything," said Kang-ho, that damnable conciliatory tone needling at her. "If the queen betrayed you and gave the orders to have your people killed, then she's to blame, obviously, and those soldiers who carried out the deed have blood on their hands, no denying that... But why plunge the whole Empire into chaos? The whole damn *Star*?"

"Because it's not enough to pay blood for blood." As Zosia spoke the smell rising from her neglected pipe carried the whiff of iron. "Because whoever comes after us must know what it means to be righteous—not just the next province who tries to control the Empire, either, but, as you say, the whole damn Star. All the world will learn what comes of a broken oath. I made a mistake all those years ago when I left the way I did, and I've returned to set things right. I've paid for my crimes, and I'll continue to pay for them—I'm ready for that. I deserve it. But I'm not going to hell alone, and I'll damn everyone I lay eyes on before I let the Star carry on with its business as though nothing happened. Peace was bought for a price, Kang-ho, and since Samoth has decided to renege, I'm afraid they'll have to find another means to that end."

"You would see every Arm of the Star burn alongside the Empire just to have your vengeance?" Kang-ho frowned into his dead pipe. "Well, you've set my mind to rest in one regard."

"What's that?"

"You're definitely the real Zosia."

That she was, much as she'd pretended she wasn't for the last twenty years. She felt those years now, that she surely did, and all that speechifying on an empty stomach and a fat bowl of tubāq was making her feel a little floaty. Fortunately there was only one question left to ask.

"So you'll help me?"

"And in exchange I get my daughter back, is that it?" Kang-ho didn't sound irate, only sad. "That's a cold play, even for you."

"Your daughter?" The words were fuzzy and thick on Zosia's tongue, in her mind, and she tried to stand. Fell to her knees, knocked the kaldi table over. A subtle poison, she hadn't felt anything but the pleasant prickle of strong tubāq, and then she was in the grass. Kang-ho's betrayal was less surprising than that of Choplicker—the devil had not only warned her of danger but actively protected her a thousand times over, yet now he let her fall without so much as a bark. The devil padded back up the hill to flash his bright white teeth in her face just as she lost her grip on the waking world and drifted into his realm.

CHAPTER
14

The Desperate Road ran far deeper and straighter through the Panteran Wastes than any other crossing, and consequently it was infested with perils. The only time bandits weren't lying in wait was when something even worse had fallen upon them, taking their place in the caves overlooking the road's entrances at the southern and northern edges of the desert. While the narrower, shadier canyons of the Desperate Road put off most godguanas, the far worse dunecrocs preferred the cooler sandslides and shale piles that routinely blocked the path, and wastewasps wove their barn-sized nests wherever the slightest rumor of a spring bubbled out of the rocks.

Even if one wasn't robbed, eaten, impregnated with larvae, or befallen by some worse fate still, it was weeks of long nights from either end of the Wastes to the road's only way station, the Shrine of the Hungry Sands. The lepers who ran it insisted that travelers perform a number of absurd, dangerous, and heretical rituals—on top of paying the stiff toll—before passing through their gate. Maroto had traveled the Desperate Road but once before, nearly thirty years prior, and clearly recalled promising himself that he would never again enter the Wastes if he could help it...and even if he could not, under no circumstances would he take this particular route.

He was fairly decent about keeping his promises to others, above average, even, so why was he so inconsistent with himself?

But hey, the nobles were happy with him again. It had been touch and go when he'd first proposed the Desperate Road at the tavern in

Niles, the fops having grown less easily wooed by their guide's counsel. But then Captain Gilleland and several other bodyguards had advised against that course in the strongest terms, insisting it was far too dangerous for their wards, and that was that. As they rolled out of the caravansary, the party had saluted itself with a twenty-one-cork salute.

Their first night they lost an entire wagon of supplies when a funnel python dragged the camel team into its conical pit, and during their first day four of the bodyguards standing watch were carried off, presumably by the cannibal cult that hunted the southern end of the Wastes. Of course, it might have been something worse that got them. It could always be something worse, out here. Yet Maroto's mood had never been better, not in the company of his fops, nor in the Wastes in general.

For one thing, if they were going to be ambushed by bandits, it probably would have happened already. No robber would be so mad as to eke out a living on the Desperate Road proper, rarely as it was taken in these enlightened days when one could sail down to Usba at a fraction of the cost and risk. No, any sane brigand would have made an arrangement with someone at the caravansary to be informed whenever a prime target departed, so they could dry-gulch their quarry before they entered the inhospitable desert. Rumors had been raised suggesting the local cannibal cult had once been a humble outlaw gang who tarried too long in the Wastes, but Maroto cared little for speculation.

In addition to enjoying the typical satisfaction one experiences at not being robbed, Maroto felt his spirits rise in equal measure to the declining humor of the fops, as though they sat across from one another on a dunking board. Well, the nobles were entitled to a decent pout—the clammy, sulfur-stinking canyon walls that hedged ever tighter around them would take the wind out of anyone's sails. That, and the company's temperament had never fully recovered from the shock of seeing Lady Opeth yanked wailing into the funnel python's pit when she had heroically sought to save the last crate of pâté from the sinking supply wagon. Based on the hollow stares the remaining nobles directed at the swirling sands where she'd vanished, Maroto supposed the sight of her wig being pulled down into the earth would haunt them for the rest of their days. He certainly hoped so.

Let's have an adventure in the Panteran Wastes!

Yes, yes, let's! Beyond the more immediate relief of having a good day's sleep, since the party seemed disinclined to roll dice and hoot and giggle in the perpetually dim, stagnant, and inexplicably swampy heat of the Desperate Road, there was also the bartalk that had drawn Maroto here. *A blue-haired captain with a devil dog helm.* Accompanied by one of the Five Villains, if not more, and flying the old flag. Each time he allowed the pilgrim's voice to repeat in his head he felt shivers from his toes to his elbows. Deep down, in spite of everything, Maroto had always dared to hope . . . and stranger still, some worrying sensation at the back of his brain, like a nearly forgotten dream—or an almost-remembered one—told him that he had always known this, that he had been waiting all along.

That she had not sought out Maroto before starting up the old business did not trouble him a great deal. It troubled him a *little*, because he was only human, for saints' sake, but not a *great* deal. She had surely tried to find him, but he could be a hard man to run down. Surely. Maybe she even thought he was dead—he had believed her to have fallen, so why not the reverse? It would be just like Kang-ho's sorry arse to talk her into thinking Maroto was dead as some sort of a sick joke. Well, they'd sort that out soon enough, when he—

"I'm talking to you, beast!" said Count Hassan, bouncing a grape off of Maroto's nose. The nobles and Maroto all sat around a merrily blazing fire while the servants brought them supper and the remaining guards took their posts on the edge of camp. Dawn lingered longer down here on the Desperate Road, and so they'd stopped for the day much later than usual that fifth night out from Niles; everyone had an excuse to feel worn out and grumpy. That said, throwing food at Maroto was a mistake no peasant nor princeling would make more than once. "I said—"

"If you ever do that again I'm going to give you the adventure of a lifetime, your lordship," said Maroto, so quietly that perhaps the junior patrician didn't hear, or perhaps Hassan had taken the threat as some sort of challenge. Whatever the reason, another grape plinked off of Maroto's cheek. A third fell from Count Hassan's fingers as Maroto lifted him out of his divan chair by his thin neck, having leaped over the fire in a blur of furious motion. It felt damn good to hoist a man by his throat again, and Maroto spoke loud enough for all assembled to hear, and hear well: "I've never met such a pack of middling, chickenshit gasbags in all my days, and I've spent a season or two at Diadem's Court. You runts can do whatever you like in your wagons, or when I'm not about—fuck each other, cheat each other, insult each other, even kill each other. But from here on out, there's a new king in camp, and the king demands respect."

Silence. Blessed, righteous silence. Well, except for Hassan's gurgling. He clung to Maroto's wrist, trying to take some of the pull off his neck, but the more he struggled, the more Maroto's fingers tightened. Old habits and all. He would let the noble go in a moment, but first he wanted to make sure his point had well and really, truly stuck. Looking around the fire, he supposed he was closing in on it.

Pasha Diggelby had not risen from his rattan throne but had dropped his wineglass in horror, paying no mind as the cerulean liquid soaked through his hose. Princess Von Yung had frozen in her seat, a fork-speared morsel of melon hovering at the bow of her lips. Kōshaku Köz had jumped to his feet but was clearly unsure what to do now that he was the only one up, frantically puffing on his cigar as though he could hide behind the wall of smoke. Duchess Din fanned her husband Denize, who seemed to have fainted. Zir Mana, who had talked endlessly about the expertise of this blade tutor or that martial trainer, held a pudding spoon in a defensive manner, spangled earrings clattering as the ninny shook in fear. Even Tapai Purna appeared humbled by Maroto's display, the girl numbly clinging to a silver plate even as she dropped to a crouch, ready to flee. Beyond the nobles, the bulk of their servants waited and watched, although Maroto was calming down enough to suppose that more than one had hurried off for the guards, and so decided that he had best wrap this up quick lest things take a turn.

"You wanted adventure, you cut-rate royals? The king shall pro-vide!" Maroto at last released Hassan, who had gone as green as the fashionable patina on his laurel crown. The second son collapsed gasping on his divan as Maroto cast a wagging finger over the party. "King Maroto will deliver all the entertainment you wish, ladies, lords, and lapdogs, all you need do is ask. And unless one of you cra-ven, conniving curs works up the moxie to usurp the king, my word is law. Let's call this adventure of yours 'A Mouthful of Thine Own Evil,' and see how you posturing, primping, posing little losers enjoy the taste."

A single beam of morning sunlight finally penetrated the narrow canyon, and while it shone directly in Maroto's eyes he stood still in the hope that it might reflect upon his sweaty brow like a crown of light. He couldn't decide which was odder, the fact that no guards had yet appeared to tackle him, or that no nobles had yet screamed. Squinting through the glare he saw that the expressions on most of their makeup-plastered faces were not quite what he had expected.

They no longer seemed afraid of him. They looked...disgusted. Or, in the case of Zir Mana and Princess Von Yung, enraged. Good. Fuck these twerps. Maroto snatched an open bottle of bubbly out of the ice bucket built into the arm of Hassan's divan and turned his back on them—if the devils saw fit to temporarily spare him a beating or worse at the hands of their guards, he was damn well going to enjoy the rush of having schooled these punks for as long as possible.

Count Hassan landed on Maroto's back with a shriek, his arms closing around the bigger man's bull neck while his legs wrapped around Maroto's ribs. It reminded Maroto of how Purna had pounced on him during their faux-affair, only even less effective— now that he was aboard his target, Hassan didn't seem to know what to do next. Maroto ignored his shrill stowaway and knocked back the bottle, guzzling the fizzy grape juice even as Hassan tried to squeeze his throat. There hadn't been as much bubbly left as he had hoped, so he stretched his arm back and casually rapped the empty bottle against Hassan's noggin. Something cracked, and as the noble fell away Maroto held up the bottle to make sure he had just broken the glass and not the boy's skull. Devils knew, Maroto hadn't meant to murder him, and truth be told he respected that the lordling—

Maroto's left knee buckled as a pointy patent leather shoe connected with the soft tissue there, but it wouldn't have been enough to bring him down had Purna not immediately followed the kick with a silver platter to the back of his other leg. He fell forward and landed on his knees in the rough sand, eyes widening at the improbable sight. Guards he'd expected, yes, even a bandit ambush would have made sense, but this?

"Get the king!"

The nobles bum-rushed him, and Maroto scrambled up just as the wave of taffeta and velvet broke over him. Kōshaku Kōz's cigar burned his cheek, and Duchess Din's platinum-veined fan snapped into his nose. He knocked them back, his open palm sending them rolling. Pasha Diggelby hurled a card table, which crashed into his shoulder. Princess Von Yung came at him with a bread knife. Zir Mana dove at one leg. He intercepted the knight with a kick and the princess with a punch to the jaw, but then Purna slammed a chair into the small of his back.

Maroto stumbled, fallen fops rising even as others tumbled back, and the cry came again:

"Get the king!"

There were a lot of them, was the problem. And all right, sure, some of them were better at this than he'd expected. Duchess Din went low and nearly headbutted him in the crotch, but he danced over her. He swung and missed Diggelby's ruffled throat by inches, and, cocking his elbow back for another go, smashed it into Kōshaku Kōz's painted mouth. Teeth loosened, blood flowed, and Maroto threw a second elbow, this one connecting with Kōz's temple and sending him tumbling into his comrades. Someone pulled a Hassan, landing on Maroto's back in a flurry of brocaded silk. He fell backward on top of his assailant, letting his rider break the fall as they crashed into a table. Tureens tipped and plates shattered, with

Princess Von Yung left moaning on the board as Maroto slipped back into the fray.

The punches Maroto took ranged from the pitiful to the unexpectedly painful, and in short order his shirt was shredded and bloody from the rings adorning the fists that pummeled him. There'd be some broken fingers, no doubt. He deflated Purna with a sucker punch, but as he pulled back Duchess Din seized his wrist, and Zir Mana caught his other arm. They held him in place just long enough for a deranged Pasha Diggelby to splash his face with liquor. It blinded him, burning his eyes, and the fops who clung to either arm were lifted into the air as he howled in indignation—these runts had just doused him in Pertnessian absinthe, and if so much as a spark landed on him he'd go up like one of their flambéed songbirds.

Before, he had been too amused to take the fight seriously. Now, as one coxcomb flew loose from his thrashing while the other held tight, shanking him with a fork, he realized that things were perhaps not as cut-and-dry as he'd expected. For weeks these bastards had insisted they wanted to hunt something, to catch it and kill it, and all along he had scoffed at their ambitions. He wasn't scoffing now, fighting blind and dirty, ripping wigs and tearing out piercings, as the fops yowled and hissed, mad as wet cats. What if one of them hit him with a lantern, or if he stumbled into the fire? A few years ago he would have laid these scoundrels out with one blow apiece, but his blows weren't falling as heavy as they should have, too much old muscle given over to fat, and despite his attacks the fops harried him as mercilessly as hounds barding a bear.

Blinking one eye clear of the stinging liquid as he beat Purna and Mana away from him, Maroto saw that Diggelby's use of the liquor had been well thought out, the dirty so-and-so returning from the firepit with a brand blazing. They meant to roast him alive! And after all he'd done for them, too.

Duchess Din crept up on him from the side, meaning to take advantage of his preoccupation with Purna, Mana, and Diggelby, but Maroto spied the sneaky lass and made his move. Before Din knew she'd been spotted, he had her by the bejeweled belt, and, hoisting her over his head, he hurled the squealing woman into Diggelby. Both nobles went down hard, and Maroto gave a triumphant whoop to see the brand go flying from Diggelby's hand...

Directly into the tent wall of the cooking pavilion, which quickly caught fire. Maroto hurried over to extinguish it, brutally slapping Purna and Mana aside when they tried to flank him, but he paused when he licked his lips and tasted licorice. Going anywhere near the growing inferno would be suicidal. He looked back to the fops, meaning to give the obvious order that they postpone their fight long enough to contain the conflagration before it spread to the wagons, and the magnitude of what he'd just done truly sank in. There was foolish, and then there was this...

The center of the camp was a ruined battlefield, broken furniture jutting out of the sand like crooked palisades, shattered glass, crockery, and spilled food ground into the earth like shrapnel. And everywhere he looked, bodies, bodies, bodies. Silky ones draped over tables. Satiny ones lying on the ground. Velvety ones staring at him from the dirt, blood oozing from their slack mouths. Oh *shit*.

He felt hands grab him, the long-delayed guards finally arriving to do unto him what he had done to their employers...but no, they were servants, forcibly moving the war-dazed Maroto out of the way so they could try to put out the burning pavilion. When he turned back to the carnage, letting the servants swat at the blazing tent as best they could, he saw that most of the nobles were stirring now. More servants were coming out from their hiding places, giving him a wide berth as they hurried to tend to their fallen masters. A limp hand rose from behind a crushed divan, and he saw Count Hassan wave a bloody handkerchief that might have been white, once, before everything got out of control.

"Villainy!" Captain Gilleland appeared from between the wagons closest to Maroto, four of his heaviest heavies and Princess Von Yung's valet in the wings. The muscle had their weapons in hand, and the valet pointed, rather unnecessarily, at Maroto. His eyes fell to where he had left his mace—beside his discarded dinner plate, on the far side of the fire. Now that the guard dogs had finally returned, the nobles set to groaning and moaning and crying, the post-battle calm gone along with the cooking pavilion. He stepped farther back from the blaze, but even this innocent movement was enough for a guard he hadn't noticed on the far side of the circled wagons to fire his crossbow. The bolt whipped beneath the hand Maroto was raising in peaceful protest of his innocence, passing so close that the fletching grazed his palm.

"Hey now!" Maroto said. "Let's not get carried away. This isn't what it looks like."

"Captain Gilleland," Hassan managed, a pair of servants lifting him enough to lean against his ruined chair. "Captain, get him…"

"They started it," said Maroto, as if the truth ever did a doomed man any good.

"I heard." Captain Gilleland waved Maroto silent with his broadsword. The blade glowed in the light of the collapsing tent. "Hardly the end you saw for yourself, eh, hero? Should have kept that pride of yours locked away, for all the good it's done you now. Do you think the singers will remember it was we who cut you down, or do you think it'll make a better song if they leave us out, let these richies here take the credit? Captain Maroto Devilskinner, Villain of the Noreast Arm, put in his grave by unarmed dandies!"

"Not in my grave yet," said Maroto quietly. A guard was creeping up behind him, and in three quick steps he could wheel around the sneak and have some human protection from the crossbows. "You want to be in a song, Gilleland, all you got to do is ask."

"Captain, get that man…" Hassan paused to spit out a tooth. "Buh!"

"Uh-huh." Captain Gilleland was not an ugly fellow, but one would never make the mistake of thinking him handsome. He usually looked like he was gloating, and at a time like this, when he actually was, the effect on his countenance was as off-putting as adding another ladle of oil to an already over-greased curry. "We'll just see what they sing about this night, you soft old fossil. I've been waiting a long time to—"

"*Captain Gilleland*." Count Hassan's voice had steadied a bit now that he'd taken a swig from the flute one servant held and a pull on the smoking bone the other lackey had raised to his lips. "Captain, get this man *a drink*!"

Maroto had set his foot to pivot backward and seize the creeper behind him, but was so flabbergasted by Hassan's hoarse cry that he nearly stumbled into Purna as he twisted around. It was she and not a guard who had snuck up on him, a long, curved dagger in one hand, a bottle in the other. Before Maroto could decide whether or not to put her in a headlock to use as a meatshield, the battered little lordling extended the bottle toward him, neck first, then sabered off the cork with her blade. Cold bubbly exploded in his face, going up his nose but also washing off the cougar milk.

"Huzzah!" cried Purna. "A drink for the king!"

It was difficult to say whether Maroto or Captain Gilleland was more dumbfounded when the rest of the haggard fops took up the cry, and as Maroto wiped sticky wine from his face he saw that everyone save for Duchess Din and Kōshaku Köz was cheering him from where they sat in the sand or stood propped up by their servants. And who knew, had Din and Köz been conscious, they might have joined in, too. Maroto grinned at Purna, then grinned even wider at Captain Gilleland.

"Long live the king, eh, Cap'n?" he said, licking the finest sparkling brut he'd ever tasted off his lips.

"Or not," said Captain Gilleland, and Maroto didn't like the man's wink as he turned away, not one bit.

CHAPTER
15

Zosia returned to pain, as she so often did these days. Not the familiar aching in her knees and joints, but a chisel in her brow, right between the eyes. As she had aged, hangovers had grown from annoyances into ordeals, but this was an entirely different sort of bullshit, one she had not experienced in many a thankful year: the comedown from a poisoning. The dim echoes of monstrous visions reverberated through her skull, but already the hallucinations or nightmares or whatever the fuck they were started fading, fading fast, and she had made no effort to hold on to them. Kicked away from them as hard as she could.

Opening her eyes, she found herself splayed out in a tastefully appointed bedroom. Choplicker lay beside her, but the beast had the sense to stay on the floor instead of sharing the sleeping mat. Candlelight silhouetted two figures who sat on cushions by the foot of her bed, their shadows looming halfway up the painted screen behind them. Kang-ho, and a handsome older man in sumptuous Ugrakari silks, his scarlet wig pinned up in half a dozen small buns.

"You're the King of Hwabun?" Zosia asked, trying very hard not to notice just how awful her mouth tasted. "Jun-hwan?"

The lord of one of the Star's tiniest sovereign states nodded. "Mistress Clell, I am pleased to make your acquaintance, and apologize for any misunderstanding that arose this afternoon. I hope you are recovered from your fainting spell?"

"Uh-huh." Zosia closed her eyes, willing the pain to recede. She'd actually been able to pull that sort of thing off, once upon a time, but now the grief in her skull just laughed at her presumption. "Thanks for your concern."

"Now, I have other guests to attend to, and so I will speak plainly with you and expect you to do the same with me. Do we have an understanding?"

"Absolutely," said Zosia, sitting up in the sheets and taking a better stock of the room. None of her possessions were present, save the devil who lounged beside her. Kang-ho looked nervous, as well he might—the cheek of the man, selling her out to his husband.

"We've already spoken very plainly, you and I, while you were under the influence of the harpy toxin. Do you remember what we spoke of?" Whatever face Zosia made must have pleased Jun-hwan, for he smiled all the wider. "Mistress Clell, I assure you that anything you divulged shall be kept strictly between us. Not even my husband was party to our discussion."

"No?" What in the devil's ken was this creep playing at?

"I was deeply saddened to hear of the death of your husband, Mistress Clell. I am sure that if anything happened to Kang-ho I would likewise seek justice, even if such a course was not strictly judicious."

Zosia sighed, lying back on the warm mat. So much for the element of surprise. Staring at the black-paneled ceiling, she said, "You claimed we'd speak plainly, so let's get on with it. What happens next?"

"That is entirely up to you," said Jun-hwan. "Again, I am not entirely unsympathetic to your plight. In fact, I empathize with you much more than you may suspect. You see, our daughter Ji-hyeon—"

Kang-ho interjected something fast and fresh in Immaculate but went silent at a glare from his husband. Kang-ho's frown deepened, but he did not interrupt again as Jun-hwan went on.

"Our daughter, Princess Ji-hyeon, has been missing for several months. We have reason to believe she was kidnapped by agents of Samoth. Given the history that you and my husband share where the Crimson Empire is concerned, it is most interesting to me that both your family and his have been so recently targeted by their interests, albeit in different fashions."

"Huh," said Zosia, almost forgetting her headache for a moment there. Almost. "Kidnapped princess, eh? That's obviously a sight worse than the murder of a few hundred peons, but I guess I can see how you'd draw a comparison. I'm flattered, really."

"I have no interest in pitting my grief against yours, madam, I simply point out the facts."

"And the fact is, we don't actually know it was Imperial agents who took her," said Kang-ho, fidgeting. "For all we know—"

"For all we know it was simply one of my dear husband's dear friends seeking to turn a dear profit from a ransom," said Jun-hwan. "The last time one of his *war buddies* came to call we wound up losing our daughter Ji-hyeon, so you can understand my interest in you when I was informed that yet another unexpected guest claimed to be an old acquaintance of Kang-ho."

"How's this, now?" said Zosia, eyeing Kang-ho just as hard as his husband was. "Who?"

"He introduced himself to us as Brother Mikal," said Jun-hwan. "Supposedly a missionary of the Burnished Chain, and for reasons quite beyond my understanding my husband insisted we take him on as a tutor for the girls. As I have entrusted their education to Kang-ho, I thought no more of the matter until it was too late. That my helpmeet failed to mention he knew this Brother Mikal from his time as one of the Five Villains, albeit by another name, was a most disappointing revelation."

"Hoartrap?" said Zosia, raising her eyes at Kang-ho. "You let him around your children?"

"No, Fennec," said Kang-ho quickly, his husband watching this exchange with obvious interest. "True devils and false gods know I would never let a sorcerer set foot on this isle, let alone in my home!"

"Fennec?" It hurt to smile but there was no helping it. "You installed *Fennec* in your house? That's even worse than Hoartrap! I hope you people don't put a high value on the virtue of your princesses."

"That is not our primary concern here," said Jun-hwan, looking none too happy with his husband. "But I have since learned all there is to hear of this rogue's character, and I can assure you I am unimpressed with my husband's judgment on the matter."

"I doubt you've heard all there is to know about him," Zosia said helpfully as Kang-ho squirmed. "Did you tell him about the time he seduced that Usban abbotess with the—"

"He blackmailed me into giving him the job," said Kang-ho. "Swore he just needed a place to lay low for a year or two until some storm he'd conjured blew over. I turned him down initially, but then it got ugly. I relented when he gave me his word that he would play the part of Spirit Guard and nothing more, and we used to be able to put stock in one another's oaths, didn't we? Besides, he left me no choice in the end—I couldn't afford to send him away."

"*That* is a matter of some conjecture," said Jun-hwan sharply. "What is not is that he disappeared a short time ago, along with Ji-hyeon and one of her other guardians."

"Who's the other missing guard?" asked Zosia.

"Choi," said Jun-hwan, "my daughter's Martial Guard. She had been with our house for many years before this Brother Mikal came along. Which would imply a longstanding conspiracy to abduct my daughter, or else Choi's body has yet to wash ashore. For her sake I hope it is the latter."

"So when I rolled up you assumed I was in cahoots? Maybe delivering a ransom letter?" The man didn't give his husband's friends much credit if he thought they'd send a collaborator to negotiate instead of brokering the terms from a safe distance. "It's bad for business to keep a family waiting this long without sending something— you sure she hasn't kidnapped herself? Princesses do that, I hear."

"There was a witness," said Kang-ho, though his husband was again watching him with unmistakable skepticism. "Her Virtue Guard, Keun-ju, saw Fennec and Choi carrying her off, and when he tried to stop them they threw him into the cove. He nearly drowned."

"Good thing he didn't, or you'd have nobody to tell you what happened," said Zosia.

"I expect he will give you the full account on your voyage," said Jun-hwan, standing. Peering down his nose at Zosia, he cut an imposing figure. "I want you to find my daughter, Mistress Clell, and bring her home. Then I will give you what assistance I may in your quest to bring justice against Samoth."

"A princess for an army?" Zosia's headache throbbed, spoiling any emotion this proposal might stir in her. All she wanted was to bury her face in a cool pillow for the next day or three. "And how do you know I'm not really in on it with Fennec, that this isn't how we're leveraging a martial ransom out of you? Maybe we've got her squirreled away in some Linkensterne stinghouse, and I'll be back in a week with the princess to get my payoff?"

"As I said, we spoke, you and I, when you were swimming with the harpies, and at those depths few can tell a convincing truth, let alone a convincing lie," said Jun-hwan. He nodded at Choplicker. "And if I had any doubts, your companion disavowed me of them. You always keep your word, apparently."

"That a fact?" Zosia tried to shrug off the ice water that ran down her back. The Immaculate were eerily comfortable with spirits, weirdborn, and all other sorts of horrors, but it was common knowledge that only practitioners of the black arts could truly speak with devils. Drugging and interrogating Zosia against her will was one thing, getting chummy with her fiend was quite another. "Choplicker put in a good word for me, did he?"

"*Choplicker?*" Jun-hwan looked aghast. "You should treat such a being with more reverence, Mistress Clell."

"Yeah, I bet he said as much," said Zosia, limply kicking the sheets in Choplicker's direction. "Fucker still knew better than to get on the bed with me, though, didn't he?"

Choplicker growled low in his throat, which finally inspired Zosia to sit up straight, but only so she could swat him on the nose. That was exactly what she needed, the old monster putting on airs just because some kooky Immaculate communed with his evil ass. Jun-hwan hissed through his teeth but did not comment on Zosia's treatment of her devil, and Choplicker whined reproachfully at her. She raised her palm but didn't pop him again. Staying upright took all the energy she had.

Jun-hwan reached down and petted Choplicker, his eyes on Zosia's. "It is said that in the Black Lands, the Great Dark King craved light for his subjects and so sent two fire dogs through the Gate of the Sunken Kingdom, into our world. One tried to bring back the sun, and the other, the moon. Yet the sun burned the first dog's tongue, and so she dropped it, and the moon froze the second dog's teeth, and so he dropped it. Yet knowing the Great Dark King's disposition toward failure, the two fire dogs try over and over to carry off our celestial lights, and they will continue to do so as long as the sun and the moon rise over the Star."

"Eclipses, right?" Zosia remembered the song Kang-ho had sung her nearly three decades previous, when they had taken advantage of the distracting religious hysteria the event brought on in Yennek to sneak in and rob Castle Illicitus blind. "You saying what, he's a moon-eating fire dog? If you saw the hassle his own hindparts give him when he's munching down back there you wouldn't give him so much credit!"

"I do not suggest the old myths be taken literally, but I do know they come from an age when mortals were not so alone upon the Star as we fancy ourselves now. All cultures have legends of black dogs, and while these songs are different, the universal truth is that such beings are due deference," said Jun-hwan, offering the beast another respectful nod.

"Mister, you need to lay off your fish oil," said Zosia, though the man's legend dredged up all kinds of weird memories of her harpy dream, memories that sank back down in oily blackness before she could focus on them: enormous, squirming monsters that were but fleas upon greater nightmares still, leviathans churning in the lightless center of all things...

"*Anyway*," said Kang-ho, "our honored guest was just leaving, weren't you?"

"Keun-ju will travel with you," said Jun-hwan, and when his husband gave him a wicked glare, the king shrugged. "He has been desperate to go after Ji-hyeon ever since the abduction, and what use have we for a third Virtue Guard when we have but two children left?"

"Zosia doesn't need one of our servants spying on her!"

"Mistress Clell," corrected Jun-hwan. "Though it is also true that Keun-ju can act as an interpreter for her, should the need arise, and confirm any and all reports sent to us."

"I've already got a translator," said Zosia. "The soldier brat, Bang, she can come with me. I don't need nor want anyone else tagging along."

"Keun-ju goes with you," said Jun-hwan. "If you also require the services of Lieutenant Bang Lin, I am happy to write to her commander at Linkensterne and explain my need to furlough her for a personal matter. Kang-ho, I trust you can see to sending a decommission fee to the mainland headquarters?"

An Immaculate spat was the same as any other kind—tedious—and Zosia awkwardly got to her feet in a bid to distract herself from their exchange. As she wobbled, Choplicker rose beside her, looking up at her with his hungry black eyes. She put a hand on his furry head, but only to steady herself. Princess hunting. Ugh. Nobody said bankrolling a private war would be easy, though.

———

Zosia felt marginally better that evening, but as soon as she returned to her mat she sank through it, splashing futilely in her bedding before going under. All through the night she floated higher and higher in moon-greased clouds, drifting up the haunch of a monstrosity bigger than any city, any mountain, any idea or ideal, the moon behind its many heads glowing like a silver crown... But other than the lucid dreams, it seemed a milder detox than most of her previous poisonings. It was mad to think she and Kang-ho had once smoked harpyfish oil on purpose, one wild night in Thao.

They set out the next morning, by which time Zosia was feeling invigorated, if only to get shy of the island. His Elegance Jun-hwan stayed behind to tend to his unseen guests, but Kang-ho accompanied them to Othean, known to foreigners as Little Heaven, the capital of the Immaculate Isles. After various wheelings and dealings they were admitted into the northern harbor of the massive island. White-uniformed soldiers watched them from the moment they left their small ship until they reached the walls of the Autumn Palace, and from the ramparts more hard eyes monitored their progress as they followed a gravel road out into the dead fields that surrounded the Temple of Pentacles. It was beginning to feel like old times, drawing this kind of hostile attention from the locals just by taking in a little sightseeing.

"We were here when the spirit attacked us," said Keun-ju, the missing girl's Virtue Guard. Young, veiled, and bright, the lad presumably hailed from a lower-class isle, or maybe even the mainland.

"And here I'd always thought you Immaculate were cozy with devils," said Zosia. "Who'd have thought one of them would try to gobble up a princess?"

"Respecting something is not the same as assuming it is safe," said Kang-ho. "Quite the contrary. You don't live on the sea without learning that lesson."

"If a houseboy, a couple more servants, and a teenage princess put it down, it can't have been too dread a beasty, eh?" said Bang from where she brought up the rear, Choplicker at her flank.

Neither Keun-ju nor Kang-ho seemed willing to respond to the soldier, but Zosia smiled. "So that was the first time she snuck off, was it? To go devil-hunting near a Gate, of all places—I wonder who put that idea into her head."

"Keun-ju?" asked Kang-ho, and when the Virtue Guard cast his eyes into the barren field, Kang-ho puffed out his cheeks in exasperation. "I'm hardly going to have you whipped now that she's gone, so let's have it—I can think of one or two other occasions on which Ji-hyeon was not where she was expected, so what of it?"

"He was sly about it, but I always thought Brother Mikal protested Princess Ji-hyeon's fancies a little too strongly," Keun-ju said bitterly. "He counseled against certain actions, yes, but always in the most alluring fashion possible. That night was no exception, and he was instrumental in helping us surreptitiously depart the palace. Since we all seemed in peril, and especially considering we overcame that harvest devil together, I did not suspect him of treachery until after it was too late. Now I wonder if he used Chainite witchcraft to summon the monster himself, to draw the princess closer to his confidence."

"And the other one, her Martial Guard, did she ever rub you wrong?" asked Bang, expressing more of an interest in the plot than she'd previously displayed since Zosia had filled her in.

"Choi was always beyond reproach," Keun-ju sniffed. "Right up until she threw me in the sea when I tried to stop them from abducting my princess."

"We're getting ahead of ourselves," said Zosia. "Back it up to when you four came out here, during the festival—what went down *exactly*? You snuck away, ran afoul of some devil that slipped through the Gate, beat it down, and came back to the party covered in gourd guts—that's it?"

"The expression on Jun-hwan's face when Ji-hyeon burst back into the ballroom, pumpkin string in her hair…" Kang-ho smiled sadly. "It was the last festival she attended. That was last autumn, and then a few months later she disappeared, just before the Winter Moon Ball. Fennec and Choi shoved the boat back to sea after they landed here under cover of dark, but it was spotted by a guard. They found tracks leading from the shore all the way up here, to the temple. Even with the help of Ji-hyeon's betrothed we haven't been able to unearth anything more—the trail goes cold at the Gate."

"I bet it does," said Zosia, slowing her pace even more. The paths through the fields extended like spokes from the five-sided temple they were approaching, a pearlescent stone shrine that seemed to mute the air around it, to dim even the sunlight. She had gazed into the Gates on three different parts of the Star, but had never before approached the Immaculate one. As always, she began to feel the tug in her very blood, felt the hairs on her arms all stretching toward it... "Betrothed?"

"I didn't mention she is engaged to Empress Ryuki's second son?" said Kang-ho. "Keun-ju, Bang, you two wait here while Mistress Clell and I continue our discussion a bit closer to the temple."

"Whatever you say, sir," said Bang, planting her spear and leaning against it while Keun-ju wiped under his veil with a puffy sleeve.

"Prince Byeong-gu, Ji-hyeon's husband-to-be, is beside himself," said Kang-ho when they had moved off a distance. "Our house is not the only one wearing white these past few months. It's why we haven't sent anyone else to search for her; Ji-hyeon's intended has already ordered a dozen soldiers through the Gate after them, and has personally sailed south to hunt for her in the Empire."

"He sent people *through* the Gate?" Zosia shuddered. Spooky goddamn Immaculates. "Let me guess, they never came back."

"This was shortly after Fennec and Choi carried Ji-hyeon through it, so if the soldiers all emerged somewhere else on the Star it might take them this long to send word home, either by land or sea." Kang-ho was clearly trying a little too hard to sell himself on the possibility.

"Or they're all floating at the bottom of the ocean with the rest of the Sunken Kingdom," said Zosia. "Oooh, or maybe they're off with the people of Emeritus, wherever those poor fuckers ended up, or some worse hell yet. You ever hear of anyone actually using one of these things successfully?"

"I know Fennec wouldn't jump into one if he thought there was the slightest risk to his person, not when he could just make a break for it in a boat." Kang-ho almost sounded sure of it. "They came here with purpose, not as a last resort. Which means Fennec knows how to use them."

"Or thinks he does, anyway," said Zosia, eyeing the temple. Devils below, but it was a cold sight, to contemplate the darkness beyond those mighty doors. There were Royal Guards positioned at each of the structure's five corners, which Kang-ho had told her was a new addition following Ji-hyeon's abduction. Before, any dotty Immacu-

late with the fancy could stroll right up and let themselves inside...
and never be seen again on this world. But what if Fennec really had
found the method to using the Gates to travel across the Star, stepping into this one and emerging from another a thousand miles away,
just like the legends told? "I wonder if Fleshnester had something to
do with it."

"I thought about that," said Kang-ho. "In all the time Fennec was
with us I never saw his devil, so I assumed he'd let her go long before
he came to me for sanctuary. Of course, a fly can hide anywhere, so
maybe he still had her...But why waste such a precious thing as a
devil's boon on using the Gate when you could flee by boat, save your
devil for an emergency?"

"That's it," said Zosia, sure of it—not a bad play, Fennec, not bad
at all. "Why free a devil for a one-way trip across the Star when you
could make it teach you the art of doing it yourself? I'll bet he loosed
it in exchange for the secret of using the Gates."

"You think they have such power to give?" Kang-ho looked dubi-
ously at Choplicker, who had trotted ahead and taken a seat in the
dust, staring at the temple.

"Never know until you ask, eh?" A wince at that, wondering what
she'd done wrong when she'd tried to free her own devil, and for such
a smaller wish..."Couldn't help but notice Fellwing hasn't made an
appearance; don't tell me you let yours go for a never-ending pipe
bowl, or a night with some radiant beauty? I've heard they can insert
a notion so deeply into a person's skull they never suspect the idea
wasn't their own—is that how you caught such a fine husband, by
making *him* think he wanted *you*?"

"I loosed her years ago, as soon as you loosed me, and for nothing at all," said Kang-ho, but either he'd grown worse at lying over
the years or Zosia's long absence from the subtle whiff of bullshit
had better attuned her to its bouquet. "It is wrong to bind them,
and wrong to wish upon a devil's freedom. If you seek to traffic with
such powers, you should do so with mutual exchange, not torture
and bondage."

"That right?" said Zosia, wondering if Kang-ho wasn't on to

something. Maybe she had gone about it all wrong, maybe it was all her fault Choplicker hadn't accepted her offer. Maybe, but probably not—he was just a monster, same as any devil. "You always were a bit squeamish about them, even that owlbat of yours."

"She was never mine," said Kang-ho, still watching Choplicker. "We just walked the same road for a while."

"Yeah, well, poetic as that is, me and Choplicker have a slightly different arrangement. He doesn't do what I say, and I don't do what he wants," said Zosia, watching her devil carefully. He didn't turn away from the temple when she said his name, but that only made her more certain he was eavesdropping. "Say for the moment I don't assume you set this up with Fennec as some sort of scam you're running on your husband and the Immaculate royal family—"

Kang-ho seized her coat and got in her face, eyes bulging, cheeks red, arm cocked back as he hissed, "Suggest it again, Zosia, and I'll toss you through that fucking Gate! I swear on the devils we freed, I'll do it!"

"Cool it, old man," said Zosia, slapping him lightly on the forehead as she jerked her sleeve free of his fist. "I said I *wasn't* assuming, didn't I? And since I'm not, what do you think Fennec's angle is? A payout from your kid's fiancé is obvious, with her marrying into royalty. If this Prince Byeong guy—"

"Byeong-*gu*."

"Yeah, him—if he received ransom demands, you think he'd tell you? Or would he try to handle it on his own? Maybe by going after the kidnappers instead of paying them off?"

"Why would he do such a thing?" asked Kang-ho, a little calmer, but not much.

"Shit, I don't know—honor, maybe?" Zosia shrugged.

"I don't think the prince is familiar with the word," said Kang-ho. "If the royal family had received demands for Ji-hyeon's safe return, they would have contacted us at once, if only to politely suggest we pay part of the ransom."

"Well, maybe the plan was to kidnap your kid and ransom her

back, but something went wrong, so they never got in touch," said Zosia, realizing the dark implications of her words only after they'd left her mouth. Nothing new there.

"Something like they jumped into a fucking Gate and are gone forever," said Kang-ho heavily. "The possibility has not eluded anyone."

"Well, say it's not as bad as all that. Other than the obvious ransom, why would Fennec abduct your daughter?"

"I honestly don't know, Zosia, and that's what frightens me." Kang-ho shoved his hands in his sleeves and looked heavenward. If he was peeking for portents, the encroaching rainclouds couldn't have been a great omen. "Ji-hyeon is...she's a special girl. Her sisters are equally loved, truly, but for better or worse I see myself most reflected in my middle child. Perhaps Fennec is working for one of my trading rivals, an Immaculate house that would not see the Bongs connected with the royal family. Or perhaps this is long-simmering revenge from Samoth for all my old sins, same as the attack on your village. Or perhaps Fennec seeks to cause me trouble for his own end. You know him better than I; what do you think he might want from all of this?"

"I aim to find out," said Zosia, looking back to the temple doors. To be able to strut right through there, into what realm only the devils knew, and come out from any one of the other five Gates, in the Raniputri Dominions or Flintland or even in Diadem itself, a knife's throw from the castle where Zosia's revenge patiently awaited her attention...Could there be a greater gift from the devils than the use of their Gates? If Fennec's devil had unlocked the way for him to travel with several companions, then surely turning Choplicker loose would grant her the means to bring an entire war party through—what defense could be mustered if an army appeared in the heart of Samoth's capital? She wouldn't need to raise much of a force at all, if instead of campaigns and sieges she could sack the Crimson Empire with a single attack, the work of one bloody night...

Choplicker gave a happy bark and scrambled to his paws, finally turning away from the temple. He trotted back to her, wagging his tail, excitedly nuzzling at her hand with his heavy, slobbery muzzle. She snapped the drool off her digits, wiped them on her coat sleeve. "Now why would I do a thing like that, when I can just find Fennec and make him do it for me?"

"What?" asked Kang-ho, but neither Zosia nor Choplicker responded, both turning their backs on the Temple of Pentacles and returning to the harbor. Wherever she had gotten to, it was obvious this princess wasn't going to find herself.

CHAPTER
16

After the Battle of the Extended Pinky, as the fops took to calling it, Maroto unexpectedly found himself all but adopted by the noblesse. It wasn't that he had beat some much-needed sense into them, for they seemed silly as ever, if not more so. It wasn't that he had stood up to them, because *really*, who needs a presumptuous servant? It wasn't even that he had saved the day when, midway through their passage on the Desperate Road, the party had run afoul of the leper-monks who kept the Shrine of the Hungry Sands, because all Maroto had done there was holler at them to run for it, which they'd already been doing anyway. No, it seemed to be entirely the effect of his having provided them with dearly desired entertainment, and at last a story with which to impress their friends back home: they had stood against Captain Maroto, the Fifth Villain himself, fought him in brutal combat, and lived to tell the tale.

Fine and good for those who had escaped the brunt of his blows by fleeing to a wagon or faking a concussion, but Maroto had expected Count Hassan, if no one else, to hold a grudge on account of his broken nose. Then there was Duchess Din's torn earlobe, the result of Maroto ripping out the thick turquoise plug that had graced it. Yet if anything, the fops he had been the hardest on were the friendliest, something he could not for the life of him fathom until Tapai Purna clued him in while they rode together on the satin-padded bench of her pleasure wagon. Maroto drove, his massive sandals crowding the footboard beside her dainty shoes.

"Scars, barbarian, scars." She sounded jealous as she prodded her mostly faded black eye, winced. "You've given them treasures they could never purchase, not with all their wealth or station."

"See, you're wrong there," burped Maroto, passing her the fen-brandy decanter they shared, their wagon leading the caravan through what ought to be their last sweltering night on the Desperate Road. "For the right kind of dosh, I'll give you scars a lot more impressive."

"It wouldn't be the same, though," said Purna dolefully. "Anyone can pay a barbarian to rough them up, but you're not just any thug, and you weren't doing it for coin. You were really giving it everything you had, fighting us for all you were worth. That's what makes their wounds special."

Maroto nearly coughed on his bognac, but thought better of correcting her. He shuddered to think of how different the aftermath would have played out had he put just a wee bit more effort into it. He was glad he hadn't. Far as fops went, this lot weren't as bad as some, not by half. He'd actually started to feel bad about encouraging them to take this road, especially considering what had happened to Pasha Diggelby and his guards in the Shrine of the Hungry Sands. That the pasha himself had escaped that situation physically unscathed Maroto was counting as a big win, despite the fate of the lad's would-be protectors. There was no helping it, though; if the rumor was true and Zosia lived, there wasn't a day to lose by taking the long way 'round...

"You did all right," he said, feeling more charitable than he had in...years, really. "The rest never would've got a toehold, you hadn't bumped me at the get-go, opened it up for them. And with that god-guana before, too, and then again when we got into it with those lepers at the temple over the importance of novices actually wanting to convert. Didn't take any of you pansies for being worth a kitten's claw in a tiger fight, but you've proved me wrong. I'll fess to that."

Purna vibrated from more than the rough road rocking the springs under their bench. He hadn't meant to do more than pay her what she was owed, but doubted he could have puffed her up more if he'd been trying. Soon as it came, though, she played it off, setting her empty snifter into a gold wire holder built into the riding bench and taking a snort straight from the decanter the way he did. Then she started talking weak again. *Kids.*

"You're better than I expected, too. It was my idea, you know, to hire you for the expedition. Everyone else said you were washed up, even if you'd been hard way back when, long, long ago. And for the first week we were out here I started to wonder if they were right, if you were gone to seed. If you'd ever done half the things they sing about."

Ouch. Fair, but ouch.

"I was wrong, I, um, *fess* to that. I do fess it." Purna let him take the decanter back. It got quiet on the box seat, but Maroto was tipsy enough to take the silence as a challenge: he'd been dodging the truth long enough, and what was he doing now, leading these idiots back through the Wastes by the hardest road, risking the leprous shrine-keepers and worse, if not to face the past?

"Truth is, I probably haven't done a quarter of what they sing about. The things I did don't make for good songs." Now *that* was playing the viola a little hard, wasn't it, Maroto? This girl was obviously looking for a role model, and given the company she kept she could do a sight fouler than him, so why piss on her fire? "But some of it was doubtless true...But in all the tales, what'd you hear that made you think hiring me to take you on some grand adventure was a wise investment?"

"You're the Fifth Villain!" said Purna. "What tales haven't I heard? You rode with the Stricken Queen when she was but a bandit chieftain, and from the slag of cutthroats and sellswords you forged an army. You conquered mortals, you conquered monsters, you took on the whole bloody Crimson Empire and seized it for your own. You hunted down devils and bent them to your will, you shook the very pillars of heaven, and—"

"And blehhhhhhh," said Maroto, sticking out his tongue and blowing. "Just what I thought, a pack of crap. For one thing, you'll call Queen Zosia by her name or not at all. For another, she wasn't a bandit, she was always a—how'd she put it, *revolutionary*—and the Cobalt Company weren't no cutthroats. Not all of us, anyway. For a fourth—or third, rather—for a third, we never hunted down no devils. Or I didn't, anyway, though she sung songs of doing such business all by her lonesome. Fine enough tales at their root, I'll allow, but Zosia's singing always sounded like a constipated hound howling for release. Now, the devils, we bent them to our will, as you say, but we didn't go looking for them—they came to us."

It was quiet again on the riding bench, as Maroto fumbled in the breast pocket of his tunic for the pipe he had lost years ago. Old habits to make a man blush. He missed that briar more than he missed his devil. What would this kid think of him if she knew all the awful truths?

"Go on!" said Purna.

"Light me a cigar and I will."

"You're *such* a moocher. Moochroto."

"Smart girl like you could do better. But I'll split your lip if you do."

"Promise?" Purna fished out two of the black-skinned Madros monsters she always kept close at hand. As she squirmed around and unhooded the bouncing lantern that hung on a hook above them to light the cigars, she said, "Of all the details, I thought for sure the devils were embellishments."

"And why's that?" said Maroto, removing the syrupy cigar from his lips after one puff and scowling at its familiar yet unexpected sweetness. The girl's glossy lip paint, he deduced, all papaya and pineapple and other fruits that would never grow within a thousand miles of this place. Now that he knew the cause, he popped it back in his mouth at once. "Don't you believe in devils?"

"Of course I do," said Purna, trying to blow a ring like he'd taught her to, but this close to the end of the Wastes a blessed bit of breeze finally wafted through the canyons, smearing her smoky hoop as soon as it left her lips. "But they're nothing more than animals. Rare ones, sure, but just another part of the world—monsters and devils are what people call creatures they don't have another name for. Only peasants, barbarians, and religious crazies think they're something more."

"You just jammed most of the Star and all of the Empire into three little pots," said Maroto, inhaling a hit on the cigar and immediately wishing he hadn't. It burned like a toke of dried centipede, but without any of the menthol numbness as he let it out. "Myself included."

"There's this wonderful new trend going around called 'education,' Maroto, I think you might find it interesting," said Purna, and took advantage of a lull in the gentle wind to blow a grey ring up into the canopy overhanging their seat. "The rest of the Star is catching on to what the Ugrakari and Immaculate have always known— devils aren't much different from any other animal. Calling them devils and ascribing them an infernal origin is just how scared people explain the unexplainable. Same as gods."

"Opinionated *and* a heretic," said Maroto, trying and failing to blow a smoke ring of his own. "Knew there was something I liked about you. Let's get something very clear, Purna, devils are real. I know, because I've seen 'em, and they're not just another variety of critter. As for the Immaculates and how they look at devils, what you're talking about is a translation issue—they call 'em *spirits* and say they're harmless, because they're pretty much both of those things, most of the time. Immaterial, I mean, and mostly invisible."

"Uh-huh. So *how* exactly are they dangerous fiends from hell again?"

Purna's skepticism had initially annoyed Maroto, but now that he'd gotten used to the brat he kind of liked it, truth be told. It felt strangely rewarding, to be imparting wisdom to an eager youngster. An old regret welled up in his throat; how different would his life have been if he'd gone against the clan and saved his nephew? If he'd stayed with the boy on the battlefield until his dad croaked, and then slung the youngster on his back and booked it out of there? Maybe he would've gotten clean a decade and change earlier; hells, without that added guilt pushing him into the stinghouses, maybe he never would've gotten so strung out in the first place. Maybe he'd have given that unnamed kid a name, and they'd have had all kinds of times together...But dead was dead, and he ignored the familiar throbbing at the scar tissue girding his heart. He was an old hand at suppressing such things. The key was never to let yourself look back, unless something was actively chasing you. Even then it was usually better not to know how close it was on your arse.

"Yo, Maroto?" Purna waved her hand in his face. "You in the spirit world or whatever?"

"Mmmm. What was I saying?"

"You were arguing about devils and Immaculate translations, I guess, but doing a shit job of it."

"There's this wonderful thing called education, Purna, you should try it." Clearing his throat in what he presumed was an academic manner, he went on, "So yeah, the Immaculates call devils *spirits*, on account of their not being real the way you or me are, but we're all talking about the same monsters. And the thing about devils is that they *want* to get their touch on, but they can't...until they possess something real, preferably something alive. The really strong devils can do this on their own, under special circumstances. Not being a fucking diabolist I couldn't say what those circumstances are. Anyways, when they do possess something, whether it's an animal or a plant or even a pile of rocks, they can cause all kinds of trouble for us mortals...but taking possession of something can also trap them in our world, make it so they can't flee back to whichever hell they came from. That's how binding devils works—if you summon one up from the First Dark you can offer it a living animal to inhabit, and when it takes the bait the poor fucker's bound to you. It can't go home until you let it go."

Maroto had assumed this would spook her into silence, but no dice. "So you're saying devils aren't animals themselves, but are something...intangible, imperceptible, that somehow enters a normal creature, assumes control of its body, and in this body the devil's free to do as it pleases. That about it?"

"What I just said, isn't it? Halfway, anyway. The flesh they wear gives 'em freedom to move about our world, sure, but it's also their prison: they're trapped inside whatever animal was available when they were first summoned."

Purna withdrew the cigar from her pursed lips and tapped it thoughtfully. "Are you familiar with Raniputri medicine? Plague theory?"

"Yeah, sure." Over the years and entanglements, Maroto had been stitched up, smeared with fragrant creams, and even cupped with hot glass bulbs all across the Dominions, but that was beside the point. "Were you even listening?"

"Diseases can be like that, like your description of a devil. Something invisible that gets inside you, fucks you up from the inside. Affects all your organs, your brain included, but not by accident—by design. It's intriguing, thinking about pestilence as a living creature, instead of the wrath of the Fallen Mother or the Barrowkings or whatnot. It makes sense, especially if you think about how illnesses spread through communities, and travel from one region to another along trade routes."

"You're close!" said Maroto, remembering all too well Hoartrap's plague devil, Lungfiller. Not that he'd seen it, of course, except for when they'd first bound the fiends and their true shapes were hinted at, before they entered the mortal vessels the Cobalt Company had prepared for them... "A devil can wriggle its way into something smaller than a butterfly's eyelash. You know Hoartrap the Touch, the Third Villain from the songs? He had one he kept in a bottle, so small you couldn't see it, but when he let it out, it brought death, and worse, to anyone who breathed it in. Nastiest of the nasty, that one."

"See?" said Purna. "You just proved my point. Devils are just what you call some animal you don't understand, like a disease. They don't come from any hells beneath the earth, they don't have mystical powers, they can't tell the future, or grant wishes."

"You're wrong," said Maroto, the charm of illuminating the unenlightened beginning to wear off. He'd seen devils with his own eyes, kept one within reach for over two decades, and this pup thought to talk down to him? "Devils are real, and they're more powerful than a child like you could even imagine."

"And you know because you bound one, right? That's how the song goes, you hunted it down and—"

"I told you, we didn't go looking for them. I'm stupid, not crazy. They came to us. Stalked us from battlefield to battlefield. Feeding."

"Like lions following a pack of hyenas, moving in on their kill once the dogs do the work?"

"Nothing like that," said Maroto, the booze bubbling in his stomach at the memory. "It wasn't flesh they ate. It was something else. Pain, anger, sorrow... I've heard a lot of theories, but I don't like to dwell. They didn't just feed on the dead and the dying, Purna, they fed on *us*. When we'd won, and settled in to celebrate another victory, they slunk through the shadows and drank their fill from our black hearts. If our warlock hadn't suspected them, we never would have known they were there. But Hoartrap knew, hells, maybe he summoned them in the first place. But they were invisible, hidden, until we bound them."

"How?"

"Doesn't matter," said Maroto, the cigar turning tarry in his mouth. He would never, ever speak of what had happened the night of the ritual, but even down all these years, what he'd seen—what he'd done—haunted him worse than any devil. How had they ever let Hoartrap talk them into it? Or had it been Zosia who'd first proposed it, another dire gambit by the blue-haired general so ruthless that even her own troops had taken to calling her Cold Cobalt? With everything that had come after, the lead-up to the ritual had largely fallen from memory.

"So you bound the devils," said Purna. "Sure, I've read plenty about that sort of thing."

"Have you?" What if this girl was some amateur demonologist? Eyeing her hot pink collar and chartreuse vest with heart-shaped brass sequins, Maroto decided it didn't seem likely. Not impossible, but not likely.

"Yeah yeah yeah. But isn't the whole point of binding them so you can force them to do what you want? Lead you to long-forgotten buried treasure, or write down the formula for turning coal into diamonds... or grant your wishes?"

"They only grant a wish if you let them go," said Maroto quietly. "Otherwise, they tend to be pretty sore on the person who bound them. But since I guess it goes real bad for a devil whose master dies without freeing it first, they do try to keep you safe from harm however they can, even if they hate you. How they manage it, I couldn't tell you, but it definitely ain't natural—I've seen blades coming straight at my neck suddenly fly wide of the mark, and poisoned mugs of ale start to bubble over when I went to take a sip."

"And your devil, the one that you bound—what is it?" Purna sounded right respectful now. "A pox, like that Hoartrap you rode with? The songs don't match up on that count at all."

"Crumbsnatcher," said Maroto with a smile, almost able to feel his devil squirm across his shoulder and nuzzle at the overgrown hair where his fade had been, back when he'd given half a damn about maintaining a respectable haircut. The devil had loved using its paws to trace where Zosia had shaved a stylish M into the stubble on the side of Maroto's head. "A grey rat. Smaller than you'd think."

"Can I see him?"

"I let him go," said Maroto, remembering all too vividly the horror when he came back to his senses and realized he'd loosed the fiend. The creeping black cliffs of the canyon they rolled through could have been the walls of any number of stinghouses, Maroto too stoned to move from the cot even as the world slid away from him. "Ages ago."

"So you released your devil."

"What I said," said Maroto, flicking his cigar away even though there was plenty of life in it. Bad as the taste of his memories could be, it was the bitterness of all but forgotten fuckups that had seeped into the end, poisoning its flavor—instead of a girl's gloss or strong tubāq, it smacked of stale hornet toxins oozing out of his swollen lips the morning after a bender.

"Now do you see why I'm skeptical about devils having any real supernatural powers?" said Purna.

"No," said Maroto grumpily. "You didn't even ask what I wished for."

"Unless it was to end up so broke and desperate you'd take a trashy gig leading people you despise through country you hate, I can't imagine your little devil granted it. You don't seem like the sort to squander a once-in-a-lifetime wish on something like the perfect sandwich, so there's the proof—if you'd gotten your heart's desire, you wouldn't be such a sad case, would you?"

"I . . . wait." After years of uncertainty, of fearful doubt, it finally came to Maroto, what he must have wished for back in that last stinghouse where he'd almost died repeatedly, where he'd lost weeks at a time and probably shaved years off his life. When he'd finally sobered up enough to realize his devil was gone, that he had wished it away, the possibilities had seemed endless, and mostly terrible, given the propensity for wishes to somehow turn out bad for their recipients. Realizing he'd freed a devil and couldn't even remember why had been the absolute rock bottom of a middle age riddled with potholes, and had freaked him out so badly he'd never touched insects again.

Now, though, half a year off of the bugs, it occurred to him that in a drug-blind haze he must have simply requested to be free of his dependence on the stuff. Old Black knew he'd wished to be clean enough times, when he was doing some depraved act in order to score another caterpillar or coming down from an icebee bender . . . and the last time he'd wished it, Crumbsnatcher must've heard his prayer. He should've guessed it wasn't just his iron-steady willpower that had enabled him to walk out of that last stinghouse and, after a few rough weeks of withdrawals, start his life anew.

For all the good it had done him. It hadn't returned any of the wealth he'd lost or traded, it didn't bring back dead lovers or dead dignity. He'd wished himself a new life, and, surprise surprise, it was just as shitty as the last one, only now he was far more conscious for it. Better still, it was liable to stretch on for year after miserable year, instead of abruptly terminating in a painless overdose. That was a devil's wish, all right—nothing crueler than giving people what they ask for. Why not score some firewings when he got the caravan to Katheli, see if good old Crumbsnatcher had given him the ability to handle the stuff without getting hooked all over again? That was something to look forward to...

"You all right, big chief?" asked Purna, and Maroto shook his head, realizing he'd been drifting. "Didn't mean to pry," she said.

"Yes you did, but it's no matter," said Maroto. The kid was probably getting off on talking to a legend, albeit one fallen on hard times, but the truth was it felt good to have an ear to bend about it all. "Crumbsnatcher granted my wish, Purna, though it's taken me a long time to realize it. Young as you are, you shouldn't doubt something just because you can't fully wrap your brain about it. Yet. Devils are real. Everything you've heard about them is true. And then some."

And if Cobalt's really alive, if we find her and the rest, you'll see for yourself, Maroto almost said but didn't. Telling Purna about his destination, his true motive for returning to the caravan, would surely get the girl's blood up, but he balked at repeating the rumor lest he make it false by speaking it aloud. A secret of the gods, or devils, entrusted to him, and him alone. Well, him and the pilgrim he'd heard it from, and the sister or whomever *she'd* heard it from, and on down the line, but still: you don't count pelts from untrapped cats.

Purna was giving him some sass, and he was about to put the question to her of just what the merry hob she thought the Gates were if not wells dropping straight down into hell, when something caught his notice up the road. *This* was why he insisted they take the lead vehicle and wouldn't have it any other way. They were almost out of the Wastes, the gunmetal strip of predawn sky overhead widening with the canyon, and by its faint light he saw that Captain Gilleland and his two outriders had come upon a large cart or wagon parked in the center of the road. The three guards were still on their steeds, talking down to a small cluster of silhouettes. Of all the miserable dick-kicks destiny could deliver...

Grabbing the reins and stopping their camels short, Maroto winced as one of the beasts vocally expressed its displeasure. The animals pulling the vehicles behind theirs gave similar protests as they, too, stopped, the caravan bottlenecked in the canyon. "Ambush. Kill that lantern and get everybody ready to fight. Bring the rear guard in, let them know. Fast."

"What are—"

"Now, girl. Miserable guana-fucking bandits couldn't hit us when we were going into the Wastes, no, we have to run into a crew on our way out. Wake those bums up, at this point the Giggle Collation outnumbers the guards we have left. We're already in their killzone, so anyone who wants to live is going to have to fight, and dirty. These vultures are a ways worse than a lizard or some lepers."

Purna didn't second-guess him, credit where due. They slid off the riding bench in opposite directions, Maroto pausing to root his chainmail vest out from behind the seat. Not his favorite kit by any means, but he could shrug it on fairly quickly, and once he had the armor fitted he drummed his fingers on the two handles jutting up from the recess. He decided on the ax, since he was quicker with it, and no mangy desert bandit deserved the taste of his mace anyway. Would that he still had one of his sun-knives to chuck around, but ages back he'd pawned the last couple he hadn't lost. He'd have to invest in some new ones, if he came out of this, but for now, well, it was never good to put off doing a job for want of better tools. A favorite of Zosia's mantras, trotted out whenever one of her Villains was whinging about the long odds she'd set before them.

When they finally caught up to the Cobalts, what would Zosia make of Maroto's new sidekick? For that matter, what would Purna make of Zosia, after all the songs she'd heard? Zosia was bound to be less of a disappointment than Maroto had proven!

His past and his present were barreling toward a collision, and when they connected the whole Star would tremble before the second coming of the Cobalt Company. He gave silent thanks to Crumb-snatcher for freeing him of his bug habit in time to hear about Zosia's return and pick up her scent; how tragic would it have been if she'd come back but he never knew it, too busy mourning her loss in some stinghouse?

Assuming it really was Zosia leading these mercenaries, of course, that the pilgrim's rumor was something more than gossip. But no, there'd be time aplenty for doubt in the days to come, and for now he must have faith. It *had* to be her. If anyone could cheat death this bad it would be his old general; not even a devil could bring back the dead, but leave it to Zosia to find a way back from hell.

If he wanted to see her again, though, if he wanted to introduce her to his new buddy Purna and see the rest of the old gang and, later, when they'd snuck off somewhere, hold her in his arms and breathe in her bad boozy breath and know for certain it was truly her, first he had to get past whatever death-hungry fools had blocked his path.

It felt all right, walking fast up the canyon with the ax casually slung over one shoulder. Felt like old times. In the blushing dawn he saw that Captain Gilleland and his men had dismounted, the morons, and it occurred to him that for all his fantasies of reuniting with Zosia, every single person he had led into this canyon might be dead inside of five minutes. Himself included.

And then, darker still: even if they weren't butchered, even if everyone walked out of the Wastes without a scratch beyond those he'd given them, there was Tapai Purna, the second daughter of an Ugrakari noble house he'd never heard of. Even if that girl lived out the night, when she died it would be because of him—long before he'd even met her, he'd derailed her life from its easy course, filled her with ambitions of the glory you found not at a card table but on a battleground. It wasn't just that she knew his songs that told him this, it was that she'd doubted their veracity and still sought him out—she didn't want to hear stories, she wanted to live them, and find for herself where the truth lay. That girl didn't want to play a part in some drawing-room drama, either, she wanted to star in the theater of war, and whenever death came cleaving for her, it would be all Maroto's fault.

Good for her, and good for him. A barbaric thought, something to make his ancestors proud as they sat around Old Black's Meadhall. Good for her, and good for him. Besides, whenever blame needed to fall somewhere, it always seemed to end up landing square at his feet.

Maroto walked right into the bandits' ambush, a caravan of fools behind him, and somewhere far ahead, Cold Cobalt. The Stricken Queen. Zosia. Zee.

CHAPTER
17

Sullen and Grandfather were sitting around their campfire sharing a bulging beedi of crumbly old saam rolled in a dried tubāq leaf when the witch emerged from the darkness. Neither of the keen-eared Wolves detected his approach, the gargantuan geriatric materializing out of the smoke like the Deceiver in a tale of the new faith, or a prophetic ghost in a tale of the old. One of those born-again heathens Sullen had given the slip back in the Falcon People's forest would have doubtless leaped up and begun bellowing invocations to the Fallen Mother to cast out the interloper, but Sullen and Grandfather were not heathens, and so knew that nothing happened without reason. It was better to hear out a traveler, however dubious, before deciding on a course. That, and they were both blasted out of their minds, and until Grandfather spoke Sullen wasn't sure the big man was actually there.

"The night is cold, our fire is warm, and friends are made as easy as foes," said Grandfather, and, just as in a fable, their guest responded to the ancient greeting in the true tongue:

"The night is cold, your fire is warm, and I would have friends before me than foes behind." The big man was white as a bone bleached by the sun, white as moonlight on polished ivory, white as treachery, but still Sullen felt strangely undisturbed by his grinning, withered visage. He'd killed a living man he had known all his life, so what harm could a foreign corpse do him, even one that walked and spoke? That was, until the ancient guest continued, "You pups are far from your pack, and these lands are haunted by that which even the Horned Wolf might fear."

Sullen wanted to shout this stranger down, to impress his grandfather, to impress himself, and most of all to impress upon this fucker that they feared neither witch nor devil...but nothing clever came to his tongue, and his grandfather had impressed upon him that when you have nothing to say, it is best to say nothing. Grandfather, though, always kept his cleverness close to his tongue.

"All I see by the light of my fire is a weary pilgrim, one with even more harvests than I under his back. One who would do well not to raise the ire of his hosts, lest they bash in his sly mouth so that they might again enjoy the more honest crackling of the fire." Grandfather looked pretty smug about this pronouncement, as well he should. It was solid, and Sullen felt a shiver in his marrow at discovering himself in the midst of a song in the making.

"Horned wolves," said the stranger, shrugging off a wicker-framed pack of such impressive size that the rucksack reached to his chest even when he set it on the grass at his feet. Considering how tall he was, that was some pack. "Do they still stalk the Savannahs, pray tell, or have they been hunted to ruin, all so that you might have a cloak less warm than that of the same-horned ram?"

"I wear no skins save that of the sheep," said Grandfather. It was true; Sullen remembered how he had been made to watch as Grandfather burned the hides of all the horned wolves he had killed on the day the council voted to accept the Fallen Mother and reject the Old Watchers. "You can sit down and act the role of guest at a fire you took no hand in kindling, or you can keep talking that weakness and see what happens."

The beedi had burned down to Sullen's thick fingers, scalding him, and he quickly popped the end of it in his mouth, puffing it back to hotness, the skunkiness of the bud mixing with the acrid yet earthy tubāq wrapper. Passing the smoke to his grandfather, he saw that his hand was shaking. The old giant had not sat, but he wasn't talking any more shit, either, instead watching them with that unwholesome smile on his shriveled apple of a face. Grandfather still didn't seem particularly concerned, though, so Sullen tried not to be, either. If great deeds needed doing, they'd announce themselves.

"Is it both of you, or just the boy?" said the old man. "Maroto's blood?"

Sullen's head swayed from the weight of trying to hold up this nonsense for a proper inspection. What in the name of the first fires was a Maroto? He glanced to Grandfather, who reclined against a rock with his legs folded beneath him in such a way as to give the illusion that he was just sitting down, could stand on his own anytime he wanted. Grandfather coughed on the hit he'd just taken, ground out the beedi in the dirt, and sat up straighter, his eyes narrowed.

"You've got a nose on you, to smell us out," he said.

"My nose is keen, yes, but not as sharp as that boy's eyes," said the stranger. "As I approached I saw them flashing in the firelight, and they gave me quite the fright—why, I thought a snow lion had wandered all the way down to the Empire! Now that I see you both up close I know I have nothing to fear, do I?"

"Sullen, if you have to kill this creature be sure to cut off the head," Grandfather growled. "Burn the lot of it. When the snakes and spiders try to flee the blaze, push them back in."

That dumped some water on a fellow's hearth, to be sure, and as soon as the words sunk in, Sullen found his feet already planted beneath him, his body in a tight crouch, ready to leap across the campfire at the stranger. In one of the Deeds of Boldstrut, an assassin sent by the Shaman King of Hellmouth had bewitched her around just such a campfire, and Sullen had no intention of allowing such a fate to befall him and Grandfather.

"Peace, peace, oh Horned Wolves," said the colossal man, raising a tattooed palm. "Maroto and I are friends, old friends, and I do not seek to quarrel with his family. There is a mistake, nothing more—I sought my ally, but found you instead. These things are known to happen. I assure you my nose is as plain as yours, if not plainer, and while I have been called worse things than 'creature,' I am simply a man, the same as either of you."

"You a witch, then?" demanded Grandfather. "Or do you expect us to trust that out of all the fires burning across the Star this night you just happened on ours and saw the familial resemblance?"

"There was a time in my memory, and surely yours, when those who walked both worlds were not always so cursed," said the stranger, sounding a touch nostalgic. "Now the Horned Wolves lie down with the Crimson lambs, turning their backs on the world their ancestors built for one promised after death. Such have things changed that I recently heard a traveler refer to burning a wildborn as a 'barbarian exorcism.' To think I should live to see such decline...Maroto always nodded to me, and I'd hoped his blood might, too. More's the pity."

Sullen would have lunged at the man, Grandfather having already warned this witch about talking more noise, but an epiphany breezed through his skull-smog at that very moment: this "Maroto" must be what Uncle Craven took to calling himself after he left the village. Grandfather had told Sullen there were so many Cravens in the Empire that their relation might earn himself a new name to stand out from the crowd, and they would just have to ask around for a rangy, russet-skinned wanderer with the tattoo of the Horned Wolf on his biceps. There had to be fewer of those in the Empire than there were Cravens. Still, again, what in all the songs sung by bard and beast was a Maroto, and how had Uncle Craven come into such a weird name?

Grandfather spoke again, reminding Sullen that he'd meant to attack the witch before it bestowed curses upon them. From what Grandfather was saying, though, it was all right that he had lost the moment in a saam trance. "Blunt my teeth, but it's true the respect your kind ought to command is in short supply these days. Like you say, things change, but when has change ever been good? It's just another word for rot and ruin...But there was never a time when I'd welcome some pasty Outlander to my fire without having him offer a name for himself, and never a time I'd balk at burning a shaman if he sought me harm."

"Hoartrap the Touch," said the stranger, with a bow that brought his embossed leather robes closer to the firelight so that Sullen could see that they glittered with embedded jewels and charms, an alien constellation of symbols and sigils. "And whose fire do I share this night, may I ask? Kin of Maroto's, yes, but father or uncle, son or cousin? What shall I call you?"

"You can call us both 'sir,'" said Grandfather. "I look green enough to give my name to one of your kind, whether we call you shaman or witch, mudwife or warlock?"

Hoartrap's smile began to appear strained, and Sullen's neck nodded of its own accord at Grandfather's wisdom. If anything happened to the old man, Sullen didn't imagine he'd last one day in this fallen Star, where nothing was as it should be. From the first step he'd taken outside of their ancestral lands, everything had gone to chaos; clanfolk trying to kill him, and now a witch trying to undo them with words . . . if that was even what was happening. He really wasn't sure what in the hells was going on here, other than his mouth was parched and he was squatting in front of a too-hot fire, not sure if he was blundering into an epic saga or an overlong joke.

"If you're not even willing to share your names with me, however are we going to get along on the road we must share?" *That* didn't sound like it boded well. "I told you I sought Maroto, and that he was a friend, and both of these are truths. You two likewise track him, and so it would seem best that we seek him out together . . . yet now I wonder if such a course is wise."

"Well, you might," said Grandfather warily. "Don't know if the boy and I really need to be sharing a trail with any shaman what calls himself 'the Touch.' I'll tell you straight, that's far too peculiar a handle for my liking—not one for getting touched myself, as a rule."

"So you do seek him," said Hoartrap, nodding. "You must have been between myself and Maroto, and what with your blood, our shared target, and your closer proximity, it must have thought this a suitable substitute. It's young and stupid. I'll just have to ask another."

Again, Sullen wondered if he had dozed on his feet, or if the beedi had been stronger than he'd thought—the words this witch spoke made less sense than the lowing of cattle. Before he could glance at Grandfather for clarification, though, a piece of the night tore itself loose from just behind his ear, drifting past him and over the fire to land on the witch's outstretched hand.

It was a large, hook-winged owlbat, its ebon fur and dark feathers shimmering like freshly shed blood in starlight, and Sullen fell flat on his arse, rocked to his bones by wonder so pure and profound it seemed to sober him up and make him reeling drunk all at the same time. Never before had he seen a true devil, not this close anyway, and though it mostly looked like a mundane creature, Sullen knew he was right, for beside him he heard Grandfather give an oath at the sight of the being. Sullen was not the sort of boy who divided the world into poles of beauty and ugliness, ideal and flawed, but in that instant he realized he had never before encountered something so sublimely perfect.

More than that: the songs and sagas weren't just made-up stories, the way Grandfather sometimes implied. There was more to life than dirt and blood, love and grief. Devils were real, so what else might be possible? Anything and everything, was the obvious answer.

And more than that, still: if Sullen was looking at a true devil, which seemed certain, that meant he had achieved something no Horned Wolf had in a generation. Here, without even seeking it out, he had passed that final test of the council. He gazed upon a devil made flesh, saw the creature in the shadow and *knew* it was more than just an animal, and that *meant something*. Watching the devil crawl over the old witch's knuckles, Sullen felt a knot in his throat, wishing his mother could be here to see that her son was more than just a misfit, that he deserved to be a member of the clan. Sullen wasn't a kid anymore...and yet just beholding the devil filled him with childlike wonder and delight. His first devil...

Then, before he could even sort out his feelings on the matter, Hoartrap the Touch clutched the devil in a wide fist and shoved its head into his mouth, biting down with a sickening crunch. The devil convulsed in his hand, trapped wings straining against their bonds, dark blood jetting out to hiss on the fire and spit up rainbow-colored smoke, and the witch's jaw dropped wide like a pit viper's to accom-

modate the rest of its meal in one go. Even Grandfather was dumbstruck by the appalling sight, and so there was no sound in the night
save the brittle chewing of a living creature, and then a series of thick
gulps. When next Hoartrap smiled at them, his teeth were as black as
his dripping chin.

"They always have their uses, even when they don't do as you tell
them," said the witch, smacking his lips.

"The first devil I've seen in twenty thaws, and you..." Grandfather's voice had the dangerously low tone Sullen had only heard a few
times, and he worried the old man might crawl on his belly across the
coals to get at this monster.

"If you find your kinsman, you'll see plenty more," said Hoartrap
with a leer. "Do not fret, though, even if you don't live long enough
to meet the man your Maroto has become, I can still show you what
you seek. They grow dimmer to the likes of you, old wolf, but I'm
sure your cat-eyed whelp can attest they are as plentiful as ever, lurking around us, feeding off your every movement, fattening on your
faintest sensation. If all you wish is an audience, I would be happy to
light the candles for you to see beyond the shroud of—"

"Kill him!" Grandfather barked, his voice cracking, and the desperation there chilled Sullen more than anything else he had beheld
that night. "Kill him now!"

Sullen tried, but he was too slow. Perhaps it was the saam they
had chiefed, perhaps it was some inner weakness, or perhaps it was
just the will of the Old Watchers, but by the time Sullen had scrambled to his feet and gone for Hoartrap, it was too late. Like Boldstrut
before him, he had tarried too long in the company of a witch, and
his song was sung before he could contribute a verse.

The witch wiped the devil's ichors from his face and intoned an
incomprehensible, earache-inducing phrase as he snapped his bloodied fingers, and the tip of every blade of prairie grass for fifty meters
burst into flame. A wildfire would not have frozen Sullen in his tracks,
even one incited by such witchery—fires are made to be tramped out.
No, it was what the Horned Wolf saw illuminated in the sudden

brilliance that pinned him in place so suddenly he toppled over, all the strength he had drawn to propel himself at Hoartrap banished mid-lunge. There he lay for the rest of the night, only chance sparing him from landing in the fire, too scared to even close his eyes.

They wheeled above and around and even through him, some with forms close to that of animals, others strange beyond the imagination of saga singers, and in the depths of his paralyzing dread Sullen vaguely recognized that the devils that had always haunted his dreams and played at the edge of his vision were but hatchlings to the great and terrible entities that exist beyond this world, ever waiting, ever watching. Ever feeding.

Everything Grandfather had told him about such things was wrong, he saw that now, or if not wrong, then incomplete. Naïve.

Grandfather and Hoartrap were far gone, even the grassy earth pressed against his cheek faded, and the longer he watched the more he saw, the devils dipping down through the sky and up out of the ground to bury their beaks, jaws, and proboscises in his sacrificial flesh. Yet he felt nothing at all from their bites, nothing but devastating horror that this was how his song ended, the Saga of Sullen nothing more than a cautionary tale against straying from the pack lest you spend eternity gnawed by monsters...

Until the first rays of dawn snuffed out the burning tips of the grass, and then they were gone, leaving him cramped and sore and half mad. At first he didn't believe it, couldn't believe it—the devils had fled, and he was still alive. Or close enough; his ragged body dripped translucent gore from a hundred numb wounds that opened and closed as he watched, winking at him...so he stopped looking at them. They weren't real, or at least not real in a way that would slow him down.

"New plan," Grandfather croaked when they had both recovered enough to look up and blink at one another, crumbs of blood crusted in the corners of their eyes. "We'll still find your uncle, but first we hunt down that witch and give him one of them *barbarian exorcisms.*"

Yet when the late spring sun slouched high enough for them to follow the witch's barefooted tracks, the traces only went a short distance out into the singed prairie before terminating in a wide circle of stinking grey tar. The grass and earth were covered in the foul residue, and just looking at the stuff made Sullen's neck sweat and eyes pulse.

Grandfather swore to impress the ancestors, and not just the usual bunch of heroes and hunters but even the especially pernicious ones. Sullen, to his shame, was relieved that the trail could not be followed. It was hardly a valiant sentiment worthy of the songs, but he wished he were back home in the Savannahs, where he knew at a glance who meant him harm, and where the devils kept their distance.

CHAPTER
18

The ax felt lighter on Maroto's shoulder than it had in a long time as the cluster of well-armed individuals at the stopped wagon turned to face him. A pale, scrub-bearded youth led the five new arrivals, all of whom wore sand-colored cloaks on their backs and blades on their belts. From the nervous glance this scrub shot Captain Gilleland, Maroto kenned the score in nothing flat. Rather than getting nervous at the betrayal, it put him at ease—with Gilleland having set this up, they'd be cocky, maybe even cocky enough to have all their number down here where he could reach them, instead of camped in the rocks above with bows and harquebuses. At a minimum, it meant he could finally stave in Captain Gilleland's skull before these bandits sent him screaming into whatever hell the devils had reserved just for him.

"Ho, barbarian!" said Captain Gilleland. Unlike the bandits, who were green enough to think they weren't rumbled yet, the mercenary and his two toughs drew their swords. Gilleland jovially gestured with his cavalry saber. "Just the man I was hoping to see. I must say, that chain can't be comfortable in this heat!"

It wasn't, the armor a fair bit snugger than Maroto had remembered, especially in the belly, but he said, "Don't worry on my account, I won't be wearing it long. Got some sort of problem here?"

"Nothing you can't handle, I'm sure. These pilgrims think they may have broken an axle; might you be good enough to crawl under and have a look?"

"Oh, sure," said Maroto, counting the steps between him and Gilleland, minding the loose flap of the wagon's cover where an archer or three surely watched him. Every step he took reduced his chances of being shot before he could do some good. "Always happy to help a pilgrim get where he's going. Let me see if I've got the measure of this—those guards you said got carried off by cannibals the first night, you just necked 'em and rolled 'em into a ravine?"

Gilleland's smile widened, and when Beard Bandit put a hand on the hilt of his sword the other four punks did the same. That was fine. Maroto was an easy two bounds away from Gilleland, and had come in at such an angle that the captain and his two goons were now between Maroto and the wagon, spoiling the shot of anyone inside. Not the shot of anyone hiding in the cliffs around him, granted, but you can't expect everything in life to be easy.

"Tell you what, barbarian," said Gilleland. "You stop right there and we talk through this."

Maroto obliged. He was close enough. "And in the Shrine of the Hungry Sands, you maybe put the idea to those lepers that Diggelby and his knights were interested in having a religious experience?"

"Just Zir Sisoruen and Chevaleresse Halford, actually," said Gilleland. "The Diggelby boy wandered in at an inopportune time, so you can imagine my relief that he wasn't harmed. You're smarter than your reputation, Maroto. I wonder just how smart."

"Dad, what—" Beard Bandit began, but Captain Gilleland's sharp frown cut out the boy's tongue. Oh, this was getting good, all right—the lighter the sky grew, the softer these bandits were looking. They were red with sunburn, not dark with tan. Probably hadn't been in the Wastes a week. For the first time since Maroto had made his sneering acquaintance, Captain Gilleland looked a little on edge.

"Smart enough to figure we lost everyone on the road who'd be loyal to their charges instead of going along with your plan," said Maroto.

"And here you stand, neck unslit despite your mouth," said Gilleland. "Advantages to sleeping in a noble's carriage with servants all about, instead of taking your turn on watch like the disgraced scout they thought they were hiring."

"I wondered how that red recluse got into the wagon. Lucky I always check my bedroll. Creeping things never stand a chance against the Villain Maroto—no matter how much venom they carry, a sandal settles them flat." Truth be told, it had taken a bit of will-power not to see if he could get high off the spider first.

"Game doth recognize game, Maroto," said Gilleland. "That's the only reason we're talking."

Maroto snorted. It would be bad enough if Outlanders just adopted Flintland slang, but they usually mangled the meaning. On the Frozen Savannahs, hunters meant a very different kind of game when they busted out that burn on a punk—even a scared hare knew the difference between a mouse and the maned wolf that stalked them both, was the idea.

"How would you have gotten them to take this route, if I hadn't put it out there?" Maroto recalled the captain's protests when he'd found the party at their inn and proposed the Desperate Road—he was cool as snowmead fresh out the ice-wagon, no doubt about it. "Your brat might have been waiting out here for nothing."

"Getting nobles to do what you want is simply a matter of tell-ing them that they can't," said Gilleland smugly. "Now, dawn's upon us, so let's be done with this. I know you, Maroto, and to put it plainly you're not invited to this final fete. As a token of deference for your many heroic deeds during the Cobalt War, we'll give you a head start of a hundred heartbeats. In that time you can proceed through the caravan, taking what you can carry, and then travel a respectful distance back down the road. An hour after we depart, you can follow, leaving the Wastes however you like. Simple terms, yet generous."

"Simple is definitely the word," agreed Maroto. "What if I take the opportunity to rally the troops?"

"The rear guard, who are in league with us, or the fops? Either way, it doesn't end well for you."

"And how does it end for them?" Maroto's eyes kept flicking around the canyon walls as they came into clearer sight. So far, no glint of sunlight on arrowhead or gun barrel. "Ransom?"

"*Ransom?* Those chumps?" Captain Gilleland shook his head. "Sadly, much more trouble than it's worth. They have enough on their persons to make this a handsome enough windfall without our getting greedy and complicating things."

"Point," said Maroto, weighing his options. He wasn't being offered such a bum deal here, and it would pay out nicely for all parties. Well, other than the fops. Captain Gilleland wasn't so simple after all. One minute alone in the caravan and Maroto could seize enough loot to ride all the way to Agalloch in his very own pleasure wagon. He hadn't really thought much beyond traveling with the nobles back through the Wastes, anyway—what was he going to do, lead these hooting idiots all the way over the Star to Zosia and the Cobalt Company?

He only had two plays here: swing on five greenies and three hardscrabble toughs, with more sure to follow and a decided lack of dependable support from the only ones to benefit from such a suicidal move, or take Captain Gilleland's offer. He'd have a bit more blood on his hands, but what of it? They were stained enough he'd never notice another coat. Wasn't this exactly what he'd known might happen, taking the Giggle Contingent on the Desperate Road? Wasn't this what they'd expressly *asked* for, a gritty adventure in the real world?

Fight for your lives, fops, because Maroto won't!

The old Maroto would have already taken the deal, Old Black knew. He might've been the one to set up the betrayal himself. He might be stupid, but he was no fool.

"Tapai Purna comes with me," he decided.

"Not a chance," said Gilleland. "Your word means nothing, but hers might. What if she contacts the families of those unfortunate friends of hers who are about to be lost in a swarmstorm? Come on, Maroto, we both know this doesn't work if she walks."

"Yeah, I see that." There was nothing to stop him from accepting the offer, snagging Purna on his way back through the camp anyway, and then riding away with her. Tough luck for the rest of the fops, and tough luck for Gilleland if he felt like pursuing Maroto and

Purna. That was the only move, when you got down to it—anything else was madness, and where had madness ever gotten him, other than right where he stood?

"Good. Now, that minute of yours starts now. It's been a real pleasure, hope we can do this again sometime." Gilleland waved Maroto off with his swordpoint, and his son's taut knuckles relaxed on his pommel. Beard Bandit thought Dear Old Dad had sorted everything. Well, sorted it soon would be.

"New terms," said Maroto, committing to his decision. "I'm afraid I can't give you a full minute to answer, though, just about ten beats of your chicken heart. You throw down your weapons and walk away, or I'll chop you all in half with my ax—if your own skin isn't worth the saving, Gilleland, think of your son."

Beard Bandit took a step back, bumping into one of his cronies, but Captain Gilleland was unimpressed. "Even in his prime, I doubt the Mighty Maroto could kill eight steady hands before one of them—"

"*Chop in half,*" said Maroto, trying unsuccessfully to arrest the grin crawling up his face, the ax nearly floating off his shoulder. "Didn't say I'd kill you, said I'd chop you all in half. With my ax."

"Had we the time, I might *actually* like to see you try such a—" Captain Gilleland began, but the hard man never got to finish acting his part, because Maroto took him at his word.

Maroto had heard of Gilleland long before they'd met at the outset of this ill-fated job. The wiry ginger had made a name for himself at the Siege of Old Slair—if memory served, he was the one who'd taught the survivors of the first month how to trap the rats and vultures that went after the castle's dead, so the besieged would have something other than their fellows to eat. Maybe if they'd just sucked it up and eaten their fallen comrades they could've mustered the strength to carry the day when the gate finally fell, instead of getting their half-starved arses handed to them by the Usbans. Whatever the case, the treacherous veteran was about to discover that trapping a bear takes a lot more preparation than goes into catching rats.

Captain Gilleland had enough sense not to try to parry the double-headed ax. Instead, he dodged to the side, jutting his saber out to impale the charging barbarian. It might've worked, too, if his son hadn't been underfoot. Beard Bandit spoiled his father's play, leaving Captain Gilleland nowhere near so far from harm as he'd have liked as he bounced off his boy. And then Maroto proved himself an honest man.

Captain Gilleland's swordpoint missed Maroto's side by a good six inches, and Maroto's ax snapped through the smaller man's collarbone at an angle. The weapon hewed through meat and bone, grinding to a stop in Gilleland's ribs just beneath the captain's opposite armpit. To the amateur observer it might've seemed that Maroto had failed to deliver, but then he wrenched his wrists, twisting the ax's haft in his hands and leveraging Captain Gilleland's head, arm, and shoulder completely off his ruined body. Only the undamaged flank of Gilleland's leather dress uniform kept him from falling in two easy pieces, the upper half of the bisected man flopping sideways on the hinge of armor.

There was no moment of stunned wonder as everyone considered this feat, much as Maroto would have appreciated a brief reprieve to admire his handiwork. No, the fight was well and truly on, Gilleland's two goons already on top of him. The hard man and harder-looking woman had him pinned between them, and even a star of the Immaculate ballet would have been hard pressed to dance around their flashing blades.

You wouldn't guess it to look at him, but Maroto was one devil of a dancer, and as his two new partners assailed him, his hands jerked the ax free of Gilleland's teetering wreckage and his feet spun him away. Before the captain's carcass had even hit the ground, Maroto was tagged on the cheek by the man's sword and felt the whisper of the woman's blade open breeches and thigh alike. He'd also maneuvered himself directly into the pack of stumbling, fumbling wannabe bandits, and as the two heavies pressed their advantage Maroto put the greenies between himself and the real danger. He waltzed through the cluster of youths before their steel had cleared leather, the two mercenaries barking at the kids to "Get him, get him!"

Easier said than done, a single blade managing to swat his back only to bounce off the chainmail vest. Fast as he'd launched his retreat, Maroto braced himself and heaved forward again, the side-armed arc of his ax a grey blur. It nicked the side of a stubbly, sunburned bandit on its way to its true target. As the full measure of the weapon sheared into the hip of Gilleland's hard man, the first kid struck by the weapon collapsed against his fellows, guts falling out of the modest rend in his shirt. Maroto kept his ax *sharp*.

Eight against had turned to five, and Maroto was really only counting one of those. Yet he no longer had surprise on his side, and a volley of gunfire from the halted caravan implied that the four other traitorous guards were executing the fops with due haste and might ride to the front at any moment. Gilleland's sole remaining mercenary had the sense to follow Maroto's example and insulate herself behind the four upright bandits, none of whom seemed eager to be the first to charge the barbarian now that he had darted back out of striking distance. There came the breathy pause Maroto had wanted back when he'd hewed Gilleland in twain, a moment to appreciate what he'd done—lazy as he'd been these last few years, he hadn't lost his touch!

From the corner of his eye, he saw several riders break toward them from the caravan. Better sort this lot fast, before—

Thwack. He reeled to the side, wondering how in the hells one of these runts had blindsided him, the pain in the side of his head rapidly rising from bad to White-Hot-Fucking-Agony. The arrow was still vibrating from its impact with his skull, sending dizzying waves of awfulness into the numb flesh of his ringing ear. Greenies and hard woman alike rushed him then.

Beard Bandit led with a saber clearly modeled after his father's, and Maroto went to the place he always did in a tough fight, the place from which there was no coming back, not until the last foe had fallen. His vision cleared, his heart slowed, his mind focused, even the church bell clanging in his ear fading away to a distant chime. He had made a promise to these scrubs, and he might not be able to keep an oath to himself, but he always kept those he made to his enemies.

Captain Gilleland's son came apart in a cloud of blood. Maroto's ax kept going, into a greenie behind Beard Bandit, lodging in the poor wench's rib cage. The hard woman almost nailed him but he yanked the ax free of the dying bandit girl in time to parry her slash. The noise of the world fell away into silence, save the riot his partners made for him—a grunt, a gasp, a boot heel grinding in the dust. Even deaf in one ear, Maroto heard them all so clearly he could have closed his eyes and cut them down by sound alone.

Probably. He had no intention of testing that theory at present.

Maroto danced with the bandits, with his ax, with the blades darting at him from all directions.

Chop. There went a hand, split down the middle, all the way up the wrist.

Step. There went a cutlass, skidding off his mailed chest.

Chop. There went a whole arm.

Step. There went a sunburned punk, blundering between Maroto and the hard woman.

Chop. There went the top half of a head.

Step. There went a rich spume, Maroto bringing a red rain to this parched earth.

Chop. There went Maroto, spinning away on the ground before the mercenary could hit him again with her sword. The slash across his knuckles shouldn't have been enough to make him drop the ax, but there it was, lying on the ground amid the splayed legs of felled fools. He rolled farther away from it. He'd put enough space between himself and his attacker to leap back up, but as he finished the roll the arrow in his ear dragged across the rough earth. The sensation utterly poleaxed him. It felt like wizard's lightning, his body shutting down completely, his mind as rattled as his flesh. He lay shuddering in the sand just long enough for the hard woman to tower over him, a long sword diving down to spit him . . .

First lightning out of nowhere, and now a thunderclap came just before its storm cloud, the whole order of the world running backward. The hard woman collapsed atop Maroto even as the fume of peppery gunsmoke enveloped them both. They sprawled like lovers, the contents of the mercenary's fissured skull running down into Maroto's stunned face. The cloud quickly rose, but Maroto was unable to extricate himself from the dead woman's weight. Either the arrow in his head had struck deeper than he'd thought or that first cut he'd taken to the leg was bleeding him out. Either way...

"Ho, Your Majesty, should I give you and your new friend some privacy?" Purna's voice came from far, far away, but then she leaned over him, a flintlock pistol in one hand and a kakuri in the other. Smoke rose from the muzzle of the richly filigreed gun and blood ran down the bow-shaped curve of the long knife, beading off its tip. She had clearly taken the time to apply several black and orange stripes of makeup beneath her eyes before rallying the rest of the fops to the greater cause. She wiped the blood from her blade on her victim's back, then sheathed her weapons in the black leather holsters on her studded white belt. "You two make a cute couple."

"Hey," said Maroto, his own voice seeming to drift down from somewhere high above him. "Get me up."

"Sure, I—*ugh*, is that *in* you?" Purna snatched back the hand she'd proffered him and pointed to her own ear. "Are you dying? Is it in your *brain*?"

"Get me up and I'll tell you," said Maroto, his voice even farther away now. He needed to get this done quick, before he blacked out. "Slow about it, now."

Purna obliged, rolling the dead mercenary off him with her foot and helping him up. As soon as she tried he slapped her away, collapsing back into the sand and trying not to puke. Standing hadn't been such a good idea after all. Woof.

Her voice sounded even more remote as she prattled on. "The rear guard were in on it, you know? They thought they were slick, telling us to hurry out of the wagons without even dressing. A fine thing I'd already roused everyone and told them to ready their weapons before I went looking for the guards, or who knows what would have happened! They didn't like us coming out with guns primed, and said as much, which was when I took a look with Diggelby's hawkglass, just in time to see you swing on Gilleland. I gave the order, and we shot them down."

Purna took another deep breath before concluding her account. Maroto reckoned she could probably hold her breath for minutes underwater.

"So we took their camels and rode up to help you, and Diggelby, Din, and Hassan went after the two who got away—they were hiding in that decoy wagon with crossbows, but we flushed them out. Hardly any casualties . . . other than you."

"Wonderful," groaned Maroto. Even lying flat in the dirt he felt like he was balancing on the prow of a dinghy in a hurricane, relying on chance to keep him from falling overboard. "You make an all right sidekick, kid."

"Sidekick?" Purna raised her penciled-on double brows at him. "Have you ever even *listened* to a song, Maroto? I'm the brash young hero, and you're the tired old master I have to persuade to teach me."

"Sounds awful," he said, suddenly wondering if he was going to die. Looking down the length of his numb body, he saw that his entire left leg was soaked red. "That mean you'll do what I tell you?"

"Until you die, sure," said Purna, her faint voice causing the invisible sea beneath Maroto's back to roil even fiercer. "You'll probably have to sacrifice yourself to save me before the end."

"Don't count on it," he said, the hot air tasting of blood and harsher metals.

"Well, we'll see if you last the day—you may have already gotten the jump on that part of the song."

There was a devil-blessed thought. The possibility did little to improve his outlook. "You want to be my protégée?"

"More than anything." Purna clasped one of his massive hands in both of hers. "When the time comes, I swear I'll avenge you, Maroto."

"Great," he said. "In the meantime, be a good girl and help me chop up these bodies."

"Excuse me?" Purna dropped his hand. It landed on his chest with the weight of a maul.

"In half. Every one." A nap seemed like a capital idea all of a sudden. Why didn't he take more naps? Devils knew he deserved them.

"Are you sure you don't need Köz's valet to tend you?" said Purna skeptically, and before Maroto could point out that he'd never said anything about not needing a sawbones, the darkness that forever lurks behind the eyes of mortals rushed up to give him a hug. *I missed you, too*, he thought as he blacked out in the sand, an arrow in his ear and a bloody-toothed grin straining his mouth. He still had it.

CHAPTER
19

The queues to the public booths were a constant of Diadem. Hundreds upon hundreds of citizens lined up each morning, the succession of sinners stretching out the wall of doors of the Lower Chainhouse and down the wending stairs to the streets far below. After a feast or festival, the lines numbered in the tens of thousands, the citizenry waiting all day and all night to have five minutes alone in the confession box.

The members of the clergy and the noblesse had their own booths in the Middle Chainhouse, and the wait there was rarely more than an hour. When Sister Portolés reached the front of the line and a confessional opened up, she did not wait the customary cooling time before entering. The old priest leaving the box before her had barely removed his thin, guttering candle from beneath the bench when Sister Portolés inserted her wider tallow into the alcove and entered the cramped booth. Settling onto the narrow bench, she found the iron bands of the seat still warm from the previous candle.

"Mother forgive me, for I am unclean."

Portolés never enunciated so well as when she was in the confessional. In all the corners of the Star, in all the chambers of the church, there was nowhere she felt more at home...save at her penitence bench immediately after a confession. Anticipating her sentence, she had exchanged the undergarments that usually protected her from the rough wool robes for a hair shirt and collar, tightly cinched garters of jagged glass rosaries around her legs. Each of the four thousand steps from her cell to the confessional hall had been a private hell of rasping friction, the hair of her vest turning to steel wool with the first drop of sweat, and despite the armor of calluses her chafed nipples and scarred thighs were bleeding by the time she arrived at the queue.

"How long has it been since last you cleansed yourself?" The grate separating penitent from confessor bubbled out in an iron reproduction of a face. Portolés had heard the grate was designed so that the innocent should see the benevolent visage of the Fallen Mother, Savior of Humanity, but that the guilty would instead behold the inhuman face of her brother-husband, Creator of the World, Deceiver of Angels and Mortals alike. Portolés only ever saw the one, but then she had never come to the box free of sin.

"Nearly four and twenty hours," she said, marveling at just how much the world had changed in such a short span.

"How much sin could one of the Fallen Mother's chosen accumulate in so few hours?" asked the confessor, and Portolés squirmed on the rapidly heating seat. Before Kypck, this had been the pinnacle of her desire, to come here and confess her wickedness so that she might be free of her deviltry, if only in the moments when the bench singed stripes into her robes and the flesh beneath, and after, when the scourge's chains licked her back and breasts, when the crown of barbs kissed her brow. Now her eagerness for atonement warred against the orders Queen Indsorith had given her, and despite the queen's confidence in her charge, she struggled with how to proceed.

"I defiled my temple," she began, reasoning that if she started at the beginning of the previous day she might better chart a safe path to the end. "Again."

A heavy sigh from the grate, which led Portolés to believe it was Mother Kylesa on the other side. "How many times have you committed this deed, sister, and how many times have you atoned for it?"

"I . . . I am not sure. Many times, Fallen Mother forgive me."

"She forgives those who regret their actions, and who struggle to improve their behavior." Even filtered through the molded grate, the confessor's voice carried a caustic tone. "It is a grave enough business when a lowly peasant chooses to sin and sin again, thinking so long as she confesses after she can do as she wishes. For a sister to behave so repulsively is another matter entirely."

"It's true," said Portolés, shifting from side to side on the bench despite herself. The scalding lines radiating from the seat made sitting still impossible, much as she deserved the pain. "I keep sinning despite your efforts and mine. I can overcome temptation, I can, and I do, more often than not...but sometimes I am weak, and I think it is not such an evil thing I do, so long as after I come here with an honest heart."

"What you are doing is the greatest sin of all." The Deceiver's face seemed to breathe in the heat of the box, sweat stinging Portolés's eyes. The light from the candle under her seat cast writhing shadows on the walls, as if she were already engulfed in flames. "You do not sin of ignorance, or even passion. You do not fall victim to temptation. You make a choice, sister, a choice to commit foul acts abhorrent to your Savior. You do this in spite of the example you are supposed to set for your peers and the laity, in spite of our many conversations on the matter. Yes, perhaps 'spite' is indeed the only applicable term, for why else would you continue to do this to those who love you?"

"Spite?" Of her many weaknesses, Portolés had never believed that to be one of them. She knew she had rebellious impulses, but truly believed in the goodness of the Fallen Mother with all her heart. "Mother, I swear I do not commit these acts out of ill will."

"No? And whom do you hurt with your actions? It is not only yourself, is it? You seduce your fellow anathemas, and then you come here, sin after sin, forcing we sisters who are far above such wickedness to sit audience to your crimes. I wonder, is it the sin itself or the act of rubbing my nose in it after that gives you more pleasure?"

"I'm sorry," whispered Portolés, bracing her arms on the warming walls of the narrow box and pressing herself down on the bench. The much-needed pain brought clarity, as it always did. The confessor was absolutely correct, yet try as she did to feel remorse, all Portolés felt was an eagerness for further penance. "I do try, Mother, I do, but you're right. I am base, ruined, wicked. It's what I am."

"Excuses," hissed the Deceiver, his mesh face leaning inward to Portolés, as though he meant to whisper in her ear, or steal a kiss. "It's easy, isn't it, to blame your nature? To lay all the fault on whatever ancestor of yours lay with a devil? To abuse yourself and others to sate your criminal appetites, and then shrug your shoulders and say it's a defect of birth? To blame the Fallen Mother for your own weakness?"

"Yes!" whimpered Portolés, her upper half warring with her lower to keep her buttocks pressed to the bench. She could smell the steam rising from the sweaty wool of her habit, taste the curl of smoke on her scarred tongue, and pushed herself down harder, knowing none of this yet was the worst. That would come when she had to rise from the seat. "Yes, yes, yes!"

"Of course." The Deceiver's breath stank of her musky sweat when she lay beside Brother Wan, defiling herself. "You are not so different from the pureborn, Sister Portolés, much as you deny it in your heart, much as they deny it with their tongues. Everyone wants an excuse for their bad decisions, for their selfish desires. Everyone wants to pretend they can't help themselves. Everyone wants to put the blame on the Deceiver for creating them with evil already festering in their souls instead of thanking the Mother for giving them both the awareness to know their own sins and the strength to fight them."

Too ecstatic to speak, Portolés nodded and wept. It was all true. She caught her left hand reaching down to pull up her habit and shoved the fist into her mouth, biting the knuckle until she tasted her own salty blood. Still she throbbed, and clenched her thighs together to grind the rosaries in deeper, pulling the scalded flesh free of the bench as she did. This brought on a dizzying rush far more perfect than anything she could effect with her fingers—the touch of the divine upon her wretched frame.

Before, when Portolés was at her most vulnerable, her confessor had insisted the witchborn's thirst for sin came from the Deceiver. That she sinned for base pleasure, to blaspheme. Her confessor was wrong. Here, when the candle of Portolés's faith burned away all

distractions, she knew the true motive for her own compulsive sinning: she was seeking her Savior. For a good and pious anathema
like Brother Wan, faith must come effortlessly, but Portolés never felt
the presence of the Fallen Mother during prayers or mass or carrying
out her holy duties. She had to hunt for her god, and in a lifetime
of obedience to the Burnished Chain, the only times she found her
were when she dared to transgress the holy laws, when she risked her
very soul to capture the attention of its keeper. It was the touch of the
Fallen Mother that gave Portolés the courage to sin, and it was her
touch that released Portolés from the agonies of confession. If Portolés's sins were acts of rebellion, as the superiors insisted, they were
rebellions against the Chain, not its maker; for all Portolés's doubts
in herself and her monstrous ilk and even her church, with all its
contradictions and cruelties, the one thing she never doubted was her
elusive Savior.

Fast as it came upon her, Portolés slumped back on the bench,
empty again, confused and scared as she always was after surviv-
ing another confession. She shivered, and realized the seat beneath
her had cooled, and the booth had gone dim. Her candle must have
burned lower than it ever had before. Wiping sweat from her face,
she nervously met the mute gaze of the Deceiver—had she cried out?

"You shall wear the Mother's Crown, which her jealous husbrother
forced upon her brow before casting her out of heaven," the confessor recited in her clear voice, what had appeared to be the Deceiver
again but an artfully wrought grate. "And you shall lash thyself with
the Scourge of Angels, as she was lashed by those anathemas loyal to
he who made the world with his word, instead of she who questioned
it with hers. Two score and six lashes, and the Crown until you are
next called from the Dens by a superior. Perhaps you may provide an
example yet."

Forty-six lashes. Portolés could not even offer the customary
thanks, her scarred tongue glued behind her file-corrected teeth.
Forty-six. She had never heard such a sentence. The most she had ever
received at one time was a score, and that instance had nearly killed

her. Brother Wan had tended her throughout her long recuperation. No pureborn could undergo such an ordeal and live, and Portolés doubted one of her kind could, either.

"Now, before you undergo your penance, we do need to discuss another matter. Lenience may be retroactively applied to your sentence, and indeed, those given for future infractions. All you must do is offer up the truth of what transpired last night, omitting nothing of what was said or done."

What was this, now? No wonder Mother Kylesa hadn't even asked if Portolés had more to confess before handing down the sentence— it was always going to be a fatal penance. The queen had warned Portolés that her superiors would likely pump her for information following their private meeting of the night before, but Portolés had believed they would simply ask her. This sort of low trick she had never expected, and it hardened her heart. Had Mother Kylesa plainly put the question to her before, as she was undergoing her righteous agonies, she might have ignored the orders of her queen and freely told all there was to tell. She would have betrayed the first person who had ever placed absolute trust in her, even knowing as she must that if she repeated the queen's secret to a confessor the sovereign could lose her very throne.

But now, being threatened instead of asked, Portolés found herself all too eager to accept Queen Indsorith's standing offer of absolution. The Crimson Queen of Samoth had powers of spiritual dispensation equal to the Black Pope—it was one of the Chain's major concessions to the Empire during the Council of Diadem, the parley that had ended the civil war. Portolés had never before found herself in such a precarious position, forced to make a decision that would not only affect the rest of her life but doubtless the fate of her eternal soul. This was a test of the Fallen Mother, a test every bit as dire as any found in the Chain Canticles, and until this moment Portolés herself had not known which path she would take... To refuse a confessor of the Burnished Chain was so grievous a sin that Portolés had never even fantasized of it, but now she found that like all her transgressions, it came as naturally as breathing.

"Why, Mother, to what incident might you be referring?" she said. "I cannot believe you would press me to reveal anything our queen might have spoken to me in private. Surely to betray the confidence of our sovereign is tantamount to treason."

"A crime against the state, even one punishable by death, is nothing when weighed against a crime against the church. Presuming your mortal frame can bear the weight of your mandated penance, sister, I shudder on your behalf to think of what further tolls you must incur if you blatantly go against the will of your Savior."

"Of course," said Portolés. "I understand your meaning, Mother."

"It relieves me to hear this," said the confessor. "I am ready to hear you testify as to what was discussed."

"Then you'll be waiting some time," said Portolés, ashamed of the pleasure it gave her to speak the words. It almost felt better than lifting her scalded bottom off the bench as she pressed her forehead to that of the Deceiver, a little skin coming off her buttocks like damp flesh adhered to frozen metal as she hissed into the grate, "I have a decree from our sovereign absolving me of all existing sins, and any new ones I might accrue in the service of carrying out her orders. If you wish to know what the queen and I spoke of, I suggest you ask her yourself, or wait until I am finished and return here of my own volition."

The confessor was silent, but just as Portolés put her trembling hand on the handle of the booth the woman spoke. "We count pride as a virtue, for 'twas pride that gave our beloved Allmother the strength to turn from her husbrother when he cruelly forsook her. It was pride that gave her the courage to turn her prison into paradise, to take what he crafted as a hell and transform it into heaven. It was pride that gave us this world, and the promise of salvation after. Yet like all virtues, pride can be dangerous, little sister, if it is allowed to swell beyond all dignity—you did not come here to confess, you came here to gloat, and you ought to be frightened by such compulsions. What sweeter fruit for the Deceiver than one of his children laughing in the face of those who seek to save her? What greater prize than a headstrong fool whose vulnerability is the very strength granted her by the Fallen Mother?"

"I shall pray for both of us, Mother," said Portolés, turning the knob. "For now, though, I have another appointment, and after that I fear I'll be beyond Diadem's reach."

"Oh child," said the confessor, whom Portolés was no longer sure was Mother Kylesa. "No matter how far you run on hooves, paws, or feet, you shall *never* be beyond our province. Safe roads guide you to her breast."

"Safe havens keep you at your rest," said Portolés, completing the Prayer of Exodus and hurrying out of the confessional before her accursed tongue could betray her further. The queen had expressly mentioned the importance of keeping secret her imminent departure, and what had Portolés done the first chance she got? Pathetic.

The confessor's words haunted her as she returned to her cell and changed into an unburned habit, the old one going into the Dens' sackcloth collection, where it would become a patchwork robe for a novice or orphan. It had seemed laughable at first, the idea that such a wretch as she should be prideful, yet the more she meditated upon it, the more sense the accusation made. Of course in the toxic tabernacle of her malformed body a natural virtue would be corrupted, strength becoming poison. If she truly believed her queen had the power to absolve her, why go to the confessional in the first place? And if she doubted the authority of her queen, how dare she spurn the orders of her confessor? Did she really think she could get away with turning to whichever power patted her head at the moment? Did she actually believe the Allmother would forgive her for using what ought to be atonement as a source of vile pleasure? Portolés shuddered as she rubbed twice-blessed salve into her burns, kneaded the ointment in harder to remind herself of the purpose of penance. The truth was, she never felt so close to the divine as when she was forcibly reminded of her mortality. Of her own baseness.

"Knock knock," said Brother Wan, opening her lockless door to find her kneeling on the penitent bench, habit hiked up around her waist. "Can I assist you with that, sister?"

"Would that the Fallen Mother granted us the time, brother," said

Portolés, wiping the excess salve on her hip and letting the habit fall as she rose to her feet.

"How many? Five for me." Brother Wan shuddered, having a more typical view toward penance. "I thought we could supervise each other, and fetch help if one of us atoned too fervently. When I found you last time I thought you were…I thought you had been called home."

Blunted teeth dug into Portolés's lips as she imagined herself kneeling on the bench, habit unlaced and pulled down around her waist, the scourge held in both hands to keep from dropping it in fear. Brother Wan standing over her, watching. The thought made the burns on her arse throb, and other places beside. Forty-six lashes would certainly deliver her home, and spare her from navigating the impenetrable waters where she found herself floundering. She would die performing penance, and she would take the queen's secrets with her to the hereafter—neither Crown nor Chain could fault her for divided loyalties if she made such a sacrifice. Why not put an end to all this endless stalling before damnation? Or perhaps with such an offering she might find her way to salvation yet…

Verily, if the queen had not asked for Sister Portolés's help, she would have beaten herself to death right there. Yet Queen Indsorith, Heart of the Star, Jewel of Diadem, had requested that Portolés take on this mission, and carry it out by any means necessary. She had not ordered Portolés to action, not demanded her obedience—she had asked, and that made all the difference. The forty-six lashes would be waiting whenever Portolés returned. If she returned.

"It's like you're already gone," said Brother Wan, wiping his sleeve over his mouth to catch the saliva dripping from the permanent snarl of his exposed gums. Portolés's heart ached at the thought of leaving Brother Wan again, when he had only just begun visiting her again, but then it rehardened. If he really could see into her soul, with all the secrets it carried, he might put his own life in danger if he stumbled over—

"Get out," she said. She would risk herself, her salvation, but she could not risk her innocent brother, and so she pointed to the door. "Now, Wan. You won't see me again until it's done."

"I'm not spying, Portolés, I'm just worried," protested Wan, reaching one of his gaunt hands out to her. The edges of his fingers were ridged from where the webbing had been cut. "You never let anyone help. Let me try—"

Portolés seized the collar of Wan's robe and pulled him in, her devilish tongue slithering past the defenses of his wooden teeth, and she filled her thoughts with memories of their trysts. He returned the kiss, and then she broke away, gently shoved him out the door. "I've stained you enough, brother. Safe roads guide you to her breast."

"Safe havens keep you at your rest," said Brother Wan, bowing to her and then scurrying away down the hall. Portolés could still call out, tell him to come back—after all, the queen had given her writ to conscript anyone she could trust to her mission. Brother Wan had never left Diadem, and since he was apparently indispensable to the upper echelons of Chain bureaucracy, it seemed unlikely he ever would if she didn't take him with her now. *By any means necessary...*

Together on the road, away from the ever-watchful eyes of the Dens, would it not be a worthy test for the both of them? And with the queen absolving all sins they might accrue, succumbing to temptation would never be safer. To fully know his flesh after all these years of teasing, fleeting contact, and for him to know hers... Yet the queen had said only those Portolés trusted absolutely should be taken into her company, and can any truly trust a lover who looks into your mind?

In the end, Portolés told herself she left Brother Wan behind to save his soul from her malign influence. The monk looked back down the rough obsidian corridor and offered a sad wave before rounding the bend. Again, she was alone. Never had she been more so.

CHAPTER
20

In her day Zosia had sailed every sea of the Star, and had always loved the Golden Cauldron best. Departing from Hwabun aboard Kang-ho's ship the *Crane's Bill* and sailing down along the Isles was a new experience for her, though; the sloops and galleys she had crewed had always set out west of Linkensterne at Darnielle Bay and immediately headed south to the Raniputri Dominions in order to avoid the Immaculate customs ships, who were essentially state-sanctioned pirates. Well, once or twice she had worked ships that crossed over from the Bitter Gulf and snuck through the narrow expanse of open water between Hwabun and the so-called Haunted Sea, where storms forever crashed above the Sunken Kingdom, but they had always raced far to the west before veering south into the Cauldron proper. That passage was not so scenic as this one, and a devil's load more tense. Call her superstitious, but something about the wall of lightning-torn fog that marked the watery grave of an entire civilization unsettled Zosia a bit; not even the Lost Waters or the Sea of Devils gave her the same goose bumps.

As they skirted the Isles and left both Hwabun and the Haunted Sea far behind, she finally let herself relax and enjoy being back at work on a boat—it was a long voyage down to Zygnema, where she would begin her search for the missing Princess Ji-hyeon. That fabled Dominion housed the Souwest Gate, and so it seemed the most sensible starting point; the next closest Gates were the one in Diadem, which she had no intention of visiting until she had an army at her back, and the one in the Noreast Arm, which Maroto had always said was overrun by crazed cultists, so it didn't seem likely Fennec would take the girl there. If Zygnema was a dead end they had Jun-hwan and Kang-ho's permission to sail the boat across to the Southern Gate in Usba, and if they hadn't gone through there, well, that left Emeritus...but Zosia could not believe Fennec would risk using that Gate, not after what had happened the last time they had been there.

It was actually liberating to be stuck on a boat, passing her days in honest labor and feeling her strength return with each climb up the crow's nest. It might've been different if they'd been dodging the Bal Amon reefs, but not a whole lot could go wrong on the Golden Cauldron. Except a sea monster. Those could be anywhere, though they usually preferred colder waters. Or a mutiny, for that matter, but it didn't do to dwell on worst-case scenarios—there'd be plenty of time to worry if such bad luck actually came to pass.

Which it did.

The pair of beasts that menaced the *Crane's Bill* came the night of the new moon, so there was no telling what they looked like. Wide, sticky snailtrails crisscrossed the deck where the monsters had evidently boarded and prowled the ship before someone had sounded the alarm. They dropped back into the sea as Zosia and the rest burst abovedecks to repel them, their scales flashing blacker than the waves in the starlight as they glided away across the surface of the waves. Nobody cared to speculate if the wild laughter that accompanied their departure originated from the creatures or the three members of the night watch they had carried off with them.

Well, these things happened at sea, so Zosia didn't become properly annoyed until a storm blew them off course a week later, and then half the bloody crew mutinied. It happened in the dead of night, as these things usually did, while Zosia, Bang, and Keun-ju were on night watch. The chaos erupted belowdecks and boiled over in moments, interrupting Bang's caterwauled sea shanty and forcing the trio to fight for their lives by the light of a half-moon. Even if Zosia had been sober it would've been a desperate fight, but she and Bang had been sharing her last bottle of canefire when the fighting broke out, and she nearly dropped her hammer a time or two before the killing was over. Choplicker must have been dozing in her hammock throughout, for a pair of mutineers barded Zosia into the prow and came desperately close to splitting her open, before Bang speared one through the back while Zobia clobbered the other overboard. It was hard to tell who looked more surprised, the sailor Bang had ambushed or Zosia herself, as she looked down the deck and saw Keun-ju holding his own against three.

The Virtue Guard had some serious moves, and even more serious steel to complement them—what Zosia had assumed was a humble tiger sword in his unadorned sheath revealed itself to be a three-tiger instead, the complex characters embossed in its dark blade glowing in the moonlight. Exchanging an impressed glance, Zosia and Bang raced—or rather, staggered—to his aid, and together they turned the tide of the mutiny. Alas, it was too late for Captain En-rang, who had been murdered in his bed before the fighting even started, and both of his mates, who had gone overboard in the melee.

Well, these things happened at sea. Enough crew remained to still see them safely to Zygnema, and Bang was promptly elected interim captain, so she had something to grin about all the way down the Cauldron. It made Zosia feel damn good, seeing the bossy kid earn herself the regard of an experienced crew so fast—reminded Zosia a bit of herself when she'd been that age. Given all the smoke the girl had blown back in Linkensterne and the Isles, Zosia had figured she'd been overselling herself, but coin where earned, Bang knew her way around a boat. And as far as skippers went, she was certainly a lot more pleasant than the recently departed Captain En-rang, tripling the canefire rations and sometimes leading the small crew on singalongs when the day's work was done. Celebrations were had when they sighted the northern Raniputri coast, again when they successfully rounded the Horn of the Rhino, and then a final late night was enjoyed when they neared Zygnema, on the southern side of the Souwest Arm.

Having bonded through all of this, Zosia, Bang, and even Keun-ju were all a touch closer than strangers as they approached the city-state where Fennec might have escaped with Princess Ji-hyeon and her traitorous Martial Guard, Choi. Four of the stoutest sailors rowed a dinghy to the Zygnema piers, the *Crane's Bill* waiting out in the bay. Choplicker lay under a rowbench, Zosia, Bang, and Keun-ju sat piled into the prow.

Zosia felt unexpectedly glum to be leaving the ship; she'd be back aboard it soon enough, if she couldn't find any clues here, but that she half hoped the Raniputri Dominions would be a dead end so she could spend more days and nights taking the vessel over to the next Gate at Usba probably said quite a bit about her mind-set. She should be champing at the bit to get back to tracking down her old Villains and plotting her vengeance after so long at sea, but instead she was sorry that her nights of drinking and flirting with Bang might be coming to an end—times like this, she had to admit she was a pretty rotten person. That she knew Leib would have wanted her to seek such happiness and diversion only made her feel sick.

Taking a deep breath of salty harbor air, she tried to get her head right. She had to find the princess, and here in Zygnema the key might be right under her nose... She blinked as the morning light caught the pommel of Keun-ju's sword. This close up, the hiltwork looked even nicer. If Zosia remembered her Immaculate Zodiac, three-tiger swords could only be forged on three days out of every thirteen-year cycle, on the third day of the third month of Tiger, Samjok-o, and Pulgasiri years. Regardless of the finer points of Immaculate weaponsmithing, this glorified servant wore princely steel, and wielded it with far more skill than most of the idle rich who could afford such a thing. Either Kang-ho and his husband took remarkable care of their servants, or somebody else did. Interesting.

"Lookie here," said one of the rowers, nodding over the side of the boat.

"You weren't kidding," Zosia said as their shallow vessel glided over an enormously thick chain stretched just beneath the gentle waves. "That would butcher any boat much bigger than this. I thought peace reigned throughout the Star."

"Throughout the Empire, maybe," said Bang, scratching under the kerchief she wore around her head. "But definitely not throughout the Souwest Arm. Zygnema's been at open war with two of her neighboring Dominions for the last year, so if you want in to trade you have to be willing to wait."

"Took two days, last time we were down," supplied one of the tarshirts at the oars. "Customs met us at the docks, we had to bribe 'em there. Then we had to follow 'em to their office, bribe some other ones. Then we had to bribe 'em to get the dinghy out o' the harbor impound, where they'd moved it while we were in the customs house. Then we had to take the officials out to inspect the holds and all, and, you guessed it, more bribes. Then we had to take 'em back to shore, another set o' bribes, and after all that? Still got to sit a day and a half before they lowered the chain for us to come in. All to snag a few little fishies. As if we didn't have enough trouble since Linkensterne got Immaculated!"

"Fish, huh?" Zosia glanced back at the *Crane's Bill*. That name must look good in a marina manifest next to the demarcation "fishing boat," but anyone who saw her knew she was built for two things: to be fast in a fight, and to be fast in a flight, if the fight didn't go well.

"Square mackerel," said Bang, tapping the side of her nose.

"So it's a sin to eat fish in the Raniputri Dominions, but not to sell them to foreigners?" said Keun-ju with the snotty superiority of one who had never left his homeland. "Hypocrites."

The two nearest rowers chuckled, which the Virtue Guard clearly mistook for validation. Zosia decided to set him straight rather than letting him be a punch line.

"Square mackerel is a rare breed of fish, Keun-ju, the kind you only see in the water when a customs boat is gaining on a ship that doesn't wish to be caught. Must be a dangerous catch these days, with Linkensterne regulated by Immaculate oversight."

"How's that?" Keun-ju looked at Zosia like *she* was the thick one, and the rowers laughed again.

"Whatever Kang-ho's importing from here in Zygnema—and knowing him it could be anything—it's not the sort of thing he's keen to have assessed by an officer of the law, either here or at home," said Zosia, and when Keun-ju still didn't get it Bang snorted and slapped him on the back.

"Mistress Clell's being overly polite," she said. "Smuggling, man, smuggling."

"Absurd!" said Keun-ju with that unmistakable air of misplaced certainty in his world. "King Jun-hwan would never allow his husband to engage in such behavior."

"Don't be so naïve," said Bang, throwing an arm conspiratorially around his shoulders. "We're all bloody-handed buccaneers now, aren't we? I saw the way you cut down those scurvy seadogs, and a lonely raider always has need for a fit lad or three—what do you say about joining Bad Bang's crew?"

More laughter from Zosia and the rowers as Keun-ju tried to squirm away from Bang in the cramped prow. If she could con her way into being discharged from the Immaculate army, the girl could definitely be a real captain someday, and a good one at that. She was warm to most everyone, but that warmth belied a need to break the gaze of any who dared to try and stare her down . . . exactly the sort of thing that could turn a young and talented hard-ass into a young and talented corpse. Well, if Zosia had survived her turbulent twenties, maybe Bang could, too.

"Ah, here we are," said Bang as they bobbed up to the end of the mile-long dock, one of dozens reaching out into the harbor of Zygnema like the arms of a devilfish stretching for deeper water. "Quick quick quick, those are customs agents coming up the quay, and I want our friends here rowing back to the *Crane's Bill* before the longfingers arrive to shake us down. I already worked out a signal with the bosun for when we're ready to be picked up."

Zosia was up first, and tied the dinghy's rope around a bollard to keep them in place. Keun-ju nimbly followed, and Bang passed them their bags. Choplicker deigned to let one of the sailors hoist him over the side and deposit him on the deck. The monster licked the man's hand and barked good-naturedly at his new friend. Zosia wondered what atrocities this friendly sailor had committed in his past to earn the approval of Choplicker...or maybe the man had just been sneaking him scraps of saltfish. It could go either way with the devil.

The customs agents were hurrying down the dock but still had some planks to cover. As Bang passed the last pack to Keun-ju, however, the soldier's eyes widened in their direction. "Devils have a laugh, is that who I think it is?"

"Who?" Zosia cupped her hand over her eyes to block out the Raniputri sun as she squinted at the agents. From here the figures could be anyone, and Zosia didn't think their pink saris were anything other than regulation issue...Oars splashed behind her, and she dropped her hand.

What a devildamn amateur move. It took some willpower, but she kept herself from spinning around in a tizzy and making a bigger fool of herself. Keun-ju was still peering at the customs agents, but Zosia turned back to the dinghy, which was, of course, already twice as far from the dock as she could have possibly jumped, even in her prime. The end of the cut rope hung limply from the bollard where she had tied them. Bang saluted from the prow of the dinghy, and at her word the rowers locked their oars, letting the tide slowly carry them out.

"You're smarter than this, Bang," Zosia called. "Stick with me, help me find the missing brat, and you'll be rewarded with a bigger boat than that wreck, and a full crew to boot. You have my word."

"The word of a woman who won't tell me her true name isn't worth much, I'm afraid," Bang replied cheerily. "Pretty silly, considering I figured you out before we even left Linkensterne. Everyone knows about Crafty Kang-ho's exploits, and his old commander! You're nothing like I imagined, I'll confess."

"So you know I can get you anything you want," said Zosia.

"You already have," said Bang, gesturing to the *Crane's Bill*. "I'm a humble woman. Not all of us want to be queens."

"Lieutenant Bang, you swore oaths to serve—" Keun-ju began, but Bang shouted over him.

"Did I forget to tell you guys the whole reason I ended up on wall duty was I got kicked out of the Immaculate navy? They accused me of breaking oaths, sowing dissent, and some worse crimes, but couldn't prove any of it. Probably should have mentioned that before you trusted me with your boat."

"The seas aren't wide enough to hide you once word of this betrayal comes to Hwabun," Zosia called, knowing it was fruitless but needing to shake the branch anyway. "How angry do you think Jun-hwan and Kang-ho will be when they find out you stole their ship and convinced their crew to mutiny?"

"About as mad as you'll be when you find out I stole your pipe," said Bang, taking Zosia's cutty out of her pocket and popping it in the corner of her mouth.

Zosia almost dove in the water then and there, but checked herself. "You really shouldn't have done that, Bang. Stealing the boat's one thing, I can respect that. You're young and stupid, so I'll cut you some slack. But you take that briar and I'll hunt you to the ends of the Star. You know who I am, that means you know what I've done, what I can do!"

"Tell you what, Cobalt Queen," said Bang, taking the pipe out of her mouth and pointing it at Zosia. "You catch me, I'll give you a kiss wherever you want, and your pipe back besides!"

"When I catch you, Bang, I'm going to mess you all up!" Zosia shouted to be heard, the dinghy drifting farther away. "Pirates always look better with an eye patch, so I'll give you a matching set! Hooks and peglegs, too!"

"And here I thought you wanted to give me a different sort of pegging!"

"I'll be seeing you, Bang, count on that! Gonna keelhaul your ass!"

"Then till we meet again upon the waves, fair Zosia!" called Bang, doffing an imaginary hat at Zosia as the rowers unlocked their oars. The sandaled feet of the customs agents were shaking the boardwalk as they approached.

"Or beneath them," Zosia growled, turning away from the dinghy to face the authorities. First these functionaries would be dealt with, then Princess Ji-hyeon would be tracked down, then Kang-ho would help her war against the Empire... and then Zosia would get her pipe back. First things first, though.

"Zosia?" The Virtue Guard sounded startled, and then impressed. "Cold Zosia, the Stricken Queen?"

"I am Moor Clell, a pipe-carver, come to trade my wares!" Zosia loudly announced in Immaculate to the arriving customs agents. Each Dominion had a dozen different local languages, few of which were shared with their neighbors, so most Raniputri were multilingual, and Immaculate was nigh universally used along the coasts of the Star. With a warning glare at the Virtue Guard, she said, "Moor Clell is my name, and my apprentice here is Keun-ju. Right, Keun-ju?"

"Right," said Keun-ju enthusiastically. "Definitely her apprentice."

"Then you are both under arrest," said the lead officer, stepping back and drawing a gauntlet-sword in each hand. The five other pink officers followed suit, and Keun-ju's three-tiger blade cut the air beside Zosia. Things had certainly changed, that she was the only one keeping her cool in a bad situation like this. Well, her and Choplicker—he rolled over on his back to invite a belly rub from the hostile new arrivals. "Moor Clell, tell your apprentice to sheath his weapon at once. You're both in enough trouble already."

"What's the charge?" asked Zosia, knowing they could probably take these officers, but also knowing they were on the wrong end of the territory to start chopping up government agents. It was one thing to kill a customs officer when you could just run across the border, but quite another when you had open sea behind you and an entire Dominion to cross. "And yeah, put that away, Keun-ju. You're not helping."

After giving her a doubtful look, Keun-ju did as he was told, and the customs agents visibly relaxed. They didn't sheath their weapons, though, and the leader said. "You are suspected of smuggling, conspiracy, and lying with animals."

"*Lying with animals?*" said Zosia, kicking Choplicker when he gave an amused snort. "Is this a joke?"

"Do we look like jesters?" asked the jowly leader. "Abuse your dog again and we shall show you what wages a defiler of beasts is paid in Zygnema."

Choplicker barked his support of this plan as Zosia and Keun-ju allowed the customs agents to lead them down the long dock, and Zosia whispered, "Just you wait, fleabag, just you wait."

CHAPTER
21

An anonymous black-robed priest delivered Baron Domingo Hjortt to the Middle Chainhouse confessionals, and together they waited in the shadow of a gargoyle-wreathed column for the anathema who had murdered his son to leave her booth. Here he was, sixty-five years old, veteran of a half century's worth of dangerous battles and the far deadlier arena of Imperial politics, and he felt as queasy and anxious as the day his mother had delivered him to Azgaroth's military academy in Lemi. He had been a mere boy, but one on the cusp of manhood, and with an impressive military lineage to uphold. Years later, that scene had repeated itself... to a point. *He* had hidden his fears, as he knew his mother expected, but Efrain had but poorly concealed his nerves as they'd waited outside the dean's office, the stripling shifting his weight from foot to foot as though it would somehow enable him to better carry the burden of destiny that bore down upon his narrow shoulders.

At the time, he'd been annoyed with his son's weakness, but now Domingo found himself imitating that scared little boy who haunted his heart, rocking from heel to heel in hopeless reflex. Catching himself in the act, he had to wonder if he'd always had the habit, if young Efrain had mimicked his father from the very beginning, and he'd just never been able to see it before now...

Black oak creaked as the confessional's door opened, and the bulky anathema oozed out of the narrow box. She seemed weak in the knees as she donned her mask and hurried out of the cavernous chamber. Domingo pictured himself sprinting after her and hacking her right leg out from under her with his cavalry saber. He knew the exact sound it would make, when his steel cut through flesh and shankbone, and smiled as he heard it in his mind. He imagined her screams for mercy echoing through the Middle Chainhouse, imagined her confessing it all, the truth coming out of her in bright spurts to match the crimson of her executioner's dress uniform...

"Baron?" Domingo blinked at the priest beside him, then cast a final glance at the anathema as she vanished out of the hall. He wondered if she had come clean for her crime—if there would be no need for this plot to go any further. For the first time in his life, here, in her house, he almost offered a prayer to the Fallen Mother, but caught himself. Everything happens, regardless of the hopes of mortals—on this, if nothing else, the Burnished Chain and the godless baron agreed absolutely.

The hooded priest handed Domingo a skinny candle and directed him to the booth. As he opened the slot beneath the bench he saw the anathema's far thicker tallow had burned low but still illuminated the compartment. He tossed his own in beside it and, without the slightest sense of regret or worry over blasphemy, blew them both out before closing the slot. Domingo's pain was far sharper than a hot ass, and he had felt it every devil-praised minute of every day since word of his only child's death had come to Cockspar. He felt no need to add to his misery out of lip service to the figment of some mad prophet's imagination, no matter how fashionable the delusion may have grown in recent years.

Before stepping into the confessional, he unbuckled his belt and slid off his saber so that he could actually sit in some remote proximity to comfort in the narrow box. Planting the scabbard between his feet and sitting down, he found the bench still plenty warm from its previous tenant; the confessional reminded him of the saunas of Flintland, with the added flourish of gruesome bas-reliefs etched into the wooden walls. A mesh face peered out at him from the iron grate, somewhere between masculine and feminine, angel and devil, and beyond it a shadow moved. After an awkward silence, Domingo sighed loudly enough for the woman on the other side to hear, but when she still didn't speak, he begrudgingly went through the motions.

"Mother, forgive me, for I am unclean."

"How long has it been since last you cleansed yourself?" asked the confessor, her insistence that they carry on this farce a patch of sandpaper grinding over his already bruised pride.

"Never," he said brusquely, only having known the appropriate opening from the plays his sister-in-law, Lupitera, was always dragging him to at the Iglesia Mendoza, Cockspar's only decent theater. Confessional scenes were an easy way to get information to the audience, according to Lupitera. "I didn't come here to play altar boy, Your Grace, so—"

The Black Pope hissed at him through the grate, and Domingo checked himself. Whatever his feelings on her pagan customs, she was the only one who had reached out to him, the only one who had offered him something other than a red candle to burn at Efrain's tomb. What kind of a military man was he, driving his only allies away with stubbornness?

"Mother, forgive me, for I am unclean," Domingo murmured, starting fresh. "I come here a stranger to your ways, a sinner seeking succor from the balm of the Burnished Chain. Forgive a pilgrim his weakness."

"Overselling it is even more insulting, Baron," said Pope Y'Homa III, but she sounded impish rather than irate. "I sympathize with your weakness, and have from the first. That is why I reached out to you—a good man of little faith is far worthier than a woman of the cloth who betrays her vows."

"On that we are agreed," said Domingo, though not without a twinge of guilt at what he'd done in the name of goodness that very morning, what he was conspiring to do this very moment. It was not only the clergy who could play fast and loose with their vows. "It may interest you to learn that I am once more an active colonel of the Crimson Empire and agent of the queen."

"Did she make much noise about it?" Domingo didn't like how

eager for gossip about their queen the pope was, but it certainly hammered home her humanity—Y'Homa didn't speak with the confidence of a vessel of the divine; she sounded like a teenager thirsting for canard. Which was all she was, really, but try telling that to the so-called civilized world who worshipped her as a god herself.

"Questions were put to me, alternates suggested," he said. "But the wise general never leaves the battlefield, and I am a nimble fencer with tongue and saber alike. Besides, what choice did she have but to accept my pledge? The Fifteenth is worth more to the Empire than every regiment from the Serpent's Circle to Diadem, and she wants Azgaroth's soldiers active, not twiddling their thumbs while the appointment process drags out for a new colonel."

It went without saying here as it had in the throne room that Chain-worship had broken out like a bad rash in Azgaroth, and if Queen Indsorith declined Hjortt's offer she might end up with some born-again noble leading the Fifteenth instead of an open heretic. And yet here he was, conspiring with the Black Pope—it was almost funny.

"Had my uncle enticed you into breaking your oaths sooner, the civil war would have ended faster, and to far happier result."

"I've broken no oaths," said Domingo testily. "This morn I swore to protect the Crimson Empire, the same oath I swore fifty years ago, the same oath my son...the same oath my son gave when he took over command of the Fifteenth last summer. The same oath my mother swore before me. In the hundred years we've been a part of the Crimson Empire, no colonel of Azgaroth has betrayed their duty to the Crown."

"Not to the Crown, just to the fool who wears it, eh?" Y'Homa's snide timbre grated almost as much as the truth behind her insult. "As I recall, you bucked the reign of the Stricken Queen more than any pony in the Crimson stable."

"I doubt you recall any such thing, considering you but were a twinkle in some cardinal's eye when Indsorith cast the pretender down. The vows I swore were to King Kaldruut, long before that Cobalt witch ever took up arms against him. And I rebuked her rabble at every pass until she snuck into Diadem and murdered her way into the Crown. But I'm not here to discuss her history; it's her future that interests me. Did you pry anything more out of Portolés? I saw her leaving the booth."

"Not as much as I had hoped, but her silence is just as damning as an outright confession," said Y'Homa. "She is definitely a double agent of Indsorith's, I'm sure of that now. And the anathema let slip that she's being sent out of the city . . . which can only mean that the queen has ordered her to finish the assignment your son left uncompleted in the mountains—to track down and assassinate Zosia before the rest of the Star discovers that the Stricken Queen is still alive. Indsorith must want her killed quietly in her tent, rather than risk martyring Zosia a second time on some battlefield with countless witnesses."

The hated name sent unwelcome images flashing through Domingo's mind. Bloody memories of bloody times: the rout at Yennek where the Fifteenth had stampeded over a mob of peasants, hooves and spears stained red as the riders' standards; the forest outside Eyvind, where every tree was strung with hanged soldiers captured by the Cobalts; the madness at Nattop that could only be explained by deviltry; and the worse business at Windhand that he had only heard rumors of, but the rumors were bad enough. And now Cold Cobalt had risen from her grave to murder Domingo's only child . . .

Perhaps it was payback for the difficult time Domingo had given Zosia's peasant army during the Cobalt War, or perhaps it was just a coincidence that Efrain had been the one Indsorith had sent to Kypck. It scarcely mattered. What did, what mattered more than Efrain's murder or Queen Indsorith's shielding that Chainwitch Portolés from justice, what mattered even more than the games the Crimson Queen and the Black Pope were playing with one another, was the simple fact that if Zosia had truly returned, all the Crimson Empire was in danger.

"Have your spies delivered any more news?" Domingo asked.

"My *informants* tell me they are close to a breakthrough," said the

Black Pope. "Queen Indsorith is playing this hand so close to her chest she might lose a card down her cleavage, but she is running out of time. Everyone already knows this rebel army terrorizing the south calls itself the Cobalt Company, and word is spreading that Zosia herself leads them."

"I return to Azgaroth tonight," said Domingo. "I'll have the Fifteenth ready to move before the summer's out, and then we'll run the Cobalt Company to ground and execute every single one of them. The Second Cobalt War will end before it starts."

"I thought you wanted to wait for more evidence before proceeding!"

"Consider me convinced that these rebels need to be stopped," said Domingo, not pleased to have his words parroted back at him by this girl. "I had assumed the queen's reluctance to bring the full might of the Empire down on this new Cobalt Company was a calculated move, that she was conserving our strength to take Linkensterne back from those thieving Immaculates. That explanation makes less and less sense as the Cobalts grow bolder and bolder in their attacks, and still no royal order is given for the northern regiments to free Linkensterne before the Immaculates complete their wall."

"Don't even get me started on the Immaculates," said Y'Homa. "I've received intelligence that some important princess of theirs has supposedly been kidnapped by one of my missionaries. Every isle in the Norwest Arm is frothing mad about it. I have yet to work out if Zosia took the girl to leverage the Immaculates into aiding her rebellion, or if Indsorith is behind it for her own ends."

The third possibility was that Y'Homa had stolen the noble and would use her to bring the Immaculates to her cause when the Burnished Chain made another grab for the Carnelian Crown, but that went without saying. Domingo hardly expected the Black Pope to bring him in on every scheme; no, he was already far more deeply embroiled in her plots than he was comfortable with. The Fifteenth Colonel of the Crimson Empire, conspiring with the Burnished Chain—what would Domingo's mother have said about such a scandal? Nothing appropriate for church, certainly.

"Immaculates business aside, I am glad we are in agreement on your course," said Y'Homa.

"What kind of a father would I be if I didn't consider your information?" said Domingo, flinching as he relived the pain it had brought him to hear that Efrain had been killed by none other than Cobalt Zosia, and that the Crimson Queen whom both father and son had faithfully served had known it all along. That sham interrogation of Sister Portolés in the Crimson Throne Room had only confirmed the truth—nobody else knew who had given Efrain the order to attack Zosia's village, because the order must have come directly from Queen Indsorith herself, and she would risk the entire Empire to preserve the secret that Zosia had never actually died.

"What kind of a *colonel* would you be?" said Y'Homa, clearly thinking he was every bit as pliable as he pretended to be when forced to attend court. "With the aid of the weapon I offer you, the Fifteenth alone could slaughter the Cobalts before their ranks swell any further. And with the Ninth and Third Regiments already harrying the rebels, I doubt you'll have any trouble at all. What could be better for the continued peace of the Empire than an army of thugs eradicated without mercy, rather than awaiting the machinations of the queen to allow for their fall?"

Remembering all the engagements he had taken part in over the years, Domingo could think of quite a few things better than open combat against well-armed, well-trained rebels led by the cagiest opponent he had ever faced, but he kept them to himself. Whatever her motivation, the Black Pope was right that the Cobalt Company had already quaffed barrels' worth of Imperial blood, and their thirst was unlikely to slacken as they grew in ranks and reputation. Better to kill them all, as fast as possible, for the good of the Empire. For the satisfaction it would bring him, to go deaf from their screams as his Fifteenth took them apart by inches. If all was as it seemed, and the Stricken Queen truly led this new Cobalt Company, there was the chance, however slim, to meet her on the field before the battle. And if that happened, if he had the chance to avenge his son and his old king and all the dreams of the Crimson Empire that Zosia had cast down into shit twenty-odd years ago, well, then his oath never to strike an enemy before the horns of combat have sounded might just be forgotten for a moment or two.

"And what of the weapon you promised me, Your Grace?" said Domingo. "Now that I have fulfilled your terms, it is time you fulfill mine."

"With pleasure," said the Black Pope. "When you leave the confessional pay a visit to the offices of Cardinal Diamond. He is expecting you, and will deliver something more deadly than any army. Now, before you and I never had this conversation, is there anything else I can answer for you?"

How many times had he told himself that he'd been the same way at Efrain's age, a little soft and a little spoiled and more than a little reluctant to ride to war? How many nights had Domingo lain awake telling himself that his son was worthy of his title and station? That he hadn't somehow sired the sort of colonel the grunts would sing mocking songs about, a noble who bought his medals instead of earning them? How different would their lives have been if he'd given Efrain the kitten he'd wanted for his tenth birthday instead of a sword and a library of martial philosophy? But these were not the sorts of questions a deranged poppet with pretensions of divinity could answer, so he simply said, "It's hard to believe the peasants were right all this time, isn't it? They've been chanting it ever since she first fell from Diadem's throne room: *Zosia lives.*"

"Not for much longer, Colonel Hjortt," said Pope Y'Homa III, Shepherdess of the Lost. "Not for much longer at all."

CHAPTER
22

Nobody likes to have a knife held to his face, which was why Maroto did what he did to the scout he had captured. The squirrelly little man—more of a boy, really—lay on his back hyperventilating while Maroto squatted beside him in the mossy bole of a maple, his blade nicking his captive's septum and his thumb resting on the bridge of the fellow's nose. They both knew Maroto could pare off the man's twitching, running bit of cartilage as easily as taking a wedge from an oddly shaped cheese, yet still the scout refused to give up the goods. It was almost as if the blighter knew about Maroto's oath, could tell at a glance he'd sooner cut up his own face than torture a sworn servant of Samoth.

Rare was the day where Maroto didn't regret vowing to Queen Indsorith that he'd never again raise weapons against her or her people save in self-defense; he hadn't had much choice in the matter, given the circumstances, but still, it was damned inconvenient that a poor decision made twenty years ago continued to hamstring him. He still had no idea how much use he'd be to his old general once he finally caught up to her, what with that meddlesome oath, but he'd burn that bridge when he got to it—first he had to reach Zosia. Since they had followed the trail of the Cobalt Company here to Myura, it was a safe bet she was barricaded inside the nearby castle that the Imperials were laying siege to. Now if only he could get this fucking scout to open up without opening him up.

"Come on, man," he said, hoping the knife would lend weight to his bluff. "If I have to take it off you'll scream, and if you scream I'll have to cut your throat. Who wants that?"

"I dunno what you're talking 'bout, I swear!" repeated the scout, too loudly, and Maroto sighed. He hated the very idea of taking off bits of people—if you were going to cut, not cutting to the kill was a dark business. As if he knew any other kind.

"I told you I'd give you two chances. That was your first, now your second is going to be whether or not you scream. Being noseless is better than being dead, so I'd hold it in were I you."

The scout whimpered, his bulging eyes big as goose eggs, but still didn't confess. Maroto was stumped—unless he actually cut this kid they weren't getting anything out of him, but Maroto wasn't keen to find out what happened if he broke an oath he'd sworn on the name of his devil.

"Maroto, why—" Purna began from her perch in the tree above them, but he cut her off with a hiss.

"Kiss the devils on their mouths, girl, now you've done it," he said, secretly relieved she'd set him up with the opportunity for one last play. "How many times have I told you not to use my name? I could have let this runt off with a nosing, but now...sorry, lad."

"Maroto." The scout whispered his name as reverently as that of a saint. "You...you're Maroto the Conqueror?"

"Yeah yeah," allowed Maroto. "And you're Noseless the Horribly Dying Scout if you don't—"

"The Cobalt Witch," said the scout quickly. "That's who you're lookin' for, ain't it? Your old queen."

"Your old queen, too," Maroto reminded the boy, trying to rein in his excitement at the scout's use of an epithet he hadn't heard in decades. "Although maybe you weren't born when she...while she... She's not a witch, is the point you've got to come to. Cobalt Zosia is fine, or, what was it she liked..."

"Cold Cobalt," Purna called down. "Oooh, and 'the Banshee with a Blade' is the name of one of Vuntwor of Nin's better ballads about her—that's what I'd go by, I was her. Has a wicked ring to it."

"I always just liked the sound of 'Queen Zosia,'" Maroto mused.

"But really, any such title that doesn't denigrate her character will do, and help keep your nose attached for the moment."

"It's true," said the scout, wonder seeming to have chased off some of the blind terror he'd evidenced ever since Maroto had snatched him from behind the tree and pinned him down. "It's really her, isn't it?"

"Devils lick your bones, that's what I'm asking *you*," said Maroto. "The mercenary company your regiment's cornered at Myura Castle, who leads them?"

"A woman, I told you, thass all I know for sure," said the scout. "The brass must not have toll us all for fear it'd affect morale. It's *got* to be her."

"What makes you think that?" Maroto took some of the pressure off his blade.

"I ain't seen her, let 'lone close enough to tell the color of her hair, but the flag she's run up the castle poles is blue, dark blue, with a broken red crown in the center and five silver pentacles circlin' it." The scout gulped. "One for each Villain, right?"

"That's new heraldry, but sure sounds like her style," said Maroto, trying not to grin and failing spectacularly. Five pentacles on her flag! She was expecting him! "That's information to save your nose, if not your life, scout!"

"Scout?" the scout said. "I'm not a scout."

"I told you I didn't think he was," said Purna. "And the only thing I can see from up here are more trees. Can I come down?"

"No," said Maroto, and guffawed almost convincingly. "Not a scout—and just what do you think a scout would say when captured, eh? Why's else would he be skulking around this border wood when there's a siege on in the town below, and with the Crimson sigils on his armor all blacked up? Not a scout!"

"No, Captain Maroto, sir, I'm not," insisted the scout. "Thass what I was tryin' to say when you put the knife to me—I'm not now nor 'ave I ever been a scout. I tried to cover the red on me tabard to blend into the woods, it's true, but if I was a real scout I wouldn't have just walked into your ambushin' me, yeah?"

"Maybe yes and maybe no," said Maroto, considering the boy beneath him. Not a scout? "I've caught plenty of scouts in my day."

"And what would I be scoutin' out here in the forest, miles from Myura, with the sun 'bout to set?"

"Easy," said Maroto, wondering whom he was trying to convince here. "Patrolling the hinterlands to make sure reinforcements aren't sneaking up from behind to break the siege, or deliver supplies."

"Yeah, that makes sense," the scout agreed. "I didn't think 'bout that. But if I *was* a scout don't you think I'd know that an' be ready with a better excuse?"

"You're talking into my deaf ear," said Maroto—the only good to have come out of taking that damn arrow to the head was getting to use that tired expression as much as he wanted.

"What kind of scout—"

"Shhh," said Maroto, pressing the blade firmer. Even with only one good ear he thought he'd heard—

"Someone's coming up the hill behind us," Purna stage-whispered from the maple boughs. "Shall I open fire?"

Hearing the crunch of leaves under several pairs of boots, followed by a tinkling silver bell and a high-pitched giggle, Maroto seriously considered it. Half their running crew had returned to the capital if not their familial houses before Maroto's wounded ear had even stopped oozing lymph, and most of the other nobles had fallen off along the surreptitious trail from the edge of the Panteran Wastes to Agalloch, from Agalloch to Geminides, from Geminides back around to Katheli, and finally from Katheli to here outside the castle of Myura, where the elusive Cobalt Company had been cornered by the local Imperial regiment. Those few fops who remained were the most dedicated to adventure, if not to following orders, a sad point that was made for the umpteenth time as Count Hassan, Duchess Din, and Pasha Diggelby emerged from the underbrush.

Count Hassan was dressed in his dramatically sheer fencing gown and carried an ivory-handled machete in one hand and an enormous drinking horn in the other, the sloshing vessel supposedly carved

from a megapotamus tooth. Duchess Din's thigh-high magenta
boots were fashionably gartered onto her gleaming scalemail singlet,
the prow of her wig skewered with a golden quarrel that shone in
contrast to the dull oak of the one nocked in her enormous crossbow.
Pasha Diggelby wore the leather vest and skirt he had modeled after
Maroto's own garb, a crystal waterpipe in one bony hand and a leash
in the other. At the end of the leash was the fluffy white lapdog he
insisted was a devil that his father had bought him from a Kravya-
dian diabolist but that was probably just an Ugrakari spaniel. The
bell Maroto had heard announcing their arrival hung not around the
pup's ruby-studded collar, but its master's.

"What ho," cried Diggelby. "Maroto's caught us some supper."

"Looks too lean," said the duchess. "I can abide a gamey cut, but
never a stringy one."

"Oh, fellows," said Hassan. "I do not know if I can stomach the
sight of Maroto sating his appetites, tranquil sylvan backdrop or not.
It's all too beastly."

"Didn't we tell you to wait with the wagons?" said Purna, descending from her roost.

"*We?* We! Purna, love, that's absolutely adorable," said Diggelby.
"Tell us, when are the nuptials, and shall we sit with the bride's side,
or the groom's?"

"I really ought to be merciful and cut your throat now," Maroto
told the scout.

"Who's your new playmate?" Hassan asked as Purna dropped the
last few feet to the ground. "He looks about as old as your last opponent. Good thing we arrived in time to save you another hiding."

"My name's Lukash," said the scout, beginning to squirm out from
under Maroto but freezing when the barbarian's blade tapped his face.

"His name's Noseless the Horribly Dying Scout," said Maroto,
imagining the looks on these fops' faces when he made that first
awful cut. If only he could go back and undo his vows; they needed a
reminder this wasn't all some lark, this was war, or close enough, and
this poor scout could provide just the—

"I'm not a scout," said Lukash, rather peevishly. There was some cheek there you usually didn't get from desperate fuckers.

"What are you, then?" demanded Purna, squatting down beside Maroto and putting one bark-stained thumb directly against the boy's left eye before he could blink. "Tell me now or they'll call you One-eyed Lukash the Noseless Idiot from here on out."

"I'm...a deserter," said Lukash, closing his other eye in shame. "I'm Khymsari, it's against my faith to wage war. I been lookin' for the chance to sneak off ever since the Myuran regiment drafted me."

"Uh-huh," said Purna. "Sure you are. Take off his lying lips, Maroto."

"Oh, let him up already," said Diggelby, leaning over to light his waterpipe on the match Hassan had struck for him. "This is all perfectly barbaric."

"Khymsari, huh?" Maroto reached up and pulled the boy's iron skullcap off as the fop's pipe gurgled in the background. Sure enough, there was the crown of shorn squares in his otherwise thick black hair. If Maroto hadn't stuck to his sacred oath he might have disfigured a pacifist. Wouldn't have been the first time. "Devils' mercy... Let him up, kid, he's telling the truth."

"Bravo," said Duchess Din, juggling the crossbow around in her arms to accept the smoldering waterpipe from Hassan as Diggelby coughed up a lungful of skunky smoke.

"You'll let me go, then?" asked Lukash, not daring to move from his imprint in the rotting leaves.

"Once you tell us everything there is to know about your regiment, the Siege of Myura Castle, and how one might sneak past the former into the latter...well, maybe," said Maroto. "Come on, let's get back to camp. I've got a hankering for balut, and don't expect we'll find any eggs out here."

The merry posse—for they seemed always merry, these few remaining richies, even with the last of their servants having deserted a few days past—picked their way back through the autumn woods, the brilliant topaz, amethyst, and garnet leaves that remained on the maples, oaks, and wild damsons turning the whole wood into an arboreal treasure chest. The nip in the evening air felt like a belated gift from long-absent gods to his ever-sweaty brow, and Maroto hummed an old marching song to himself as they walked. Purna followed, questioning the prisoner and thus giving Maroto a respite from her yammering, and just ahead Diggelby, Din, and Hassan argued over the wording of an anthem Maroto had never heard. Nothing could dampen his mood, not now. Sure, they'd taken a tour of the whole bloody Crimson Empire after leaving the Panteran Wastes, only to end up back here, less than a hundred leagues from where they'd first quit the desert, but that was the way of the world, wasn't it, to forever be winding up just where you'd started? There was a time when Maroto would have resented his cyclical trajectory, but at present he found it hard to complain. The reason for his excellent humor was simple: over the last few months, as they'd picked up more and more scraps of rumor along the trail of the blue-haired mercenary captain, Maroto had finally let himself believe the bartalk he'd overheard that spring night in Niles. Zosia was alive, and if the last twenty years had been him wandering out in a wide circle, wide as the whole Star and then some, now he was coming right back to the beginning. Back to her.

How? Well, she must have been imprisoned instead of killed, as everyone had claimed, and now she had escaped and rallied her old army to take back her rightful due. Impossible as it seemed, his queen, his captain, his one true love yet drew breath. And she was here, just over these hills, holed up in a castle while the forces of her former captors surrounded her.

Maroto couldn't wait to break her out.

CHAPTER
23

Come clean, Keun-ju," said Zosia for the hundredth time since they had left the Immaculate Isles, and the fourth or fifth since they'd been seized at the harbor. "You can trust me."

"Nothing to tell," said Keun-ju, turning his veiled face to the whitewashed wall of the sandy cell the customs agents had locked them in. She was wearing him down, she could tell, and he would crack eventually. "Why must you badger me so?"

"Call me a romantic, but I want to know why before they kill us," said Zosia, hitting on the idea and running with it. The Virtue Guard knew less about Raniputri culture than Zosia did about guarding one's virtue. "The crime for bestiality in these parts is execution. They don't do trials here, either, so odds are when the guards come back for us it's death by elephant—they train the beasts to take their time with it, too, so we'll be in agony for a while. I'd like to go to the devils knowing why."

"They're not going to kill us, and certainly not with *elephants*," said Keun-ju, but he didn't sound convinced. "And why do they think you would...ugh."

"It's a setup, obviously," said Zosia, thinking out loud. "Bang could've sent word somehow, I guess, via homing albatross or some other means. Definitely a good way to make sure we don't come after her."

"So why not, you know...give them your real name instead of the alias?" Keun-ju whispered the last, heathen gods of his people bless and keep him. "Why tell them to look for Moor Clell instead of Cobalt Zosia?"

"That's a good point," said Zosia. "I'd hazard the guilty party thought customs wouldn't believe such a claim, considering I'm supposed to be twenty years dead."

"Or if the locals did believe it, they probably would make a big deal out of it, yes?" said Keun-ju. "A very, very big deal, if they have any wits at all. So why don't you tell them who you are? If nothing else, they might delay the execution long enough to attract some more fanfare to the occasion."

"You think they'd believe me?" Zosia shook her head. "We're doomed, kid, so you might as well spill the royal beans, die unburdened of secrets. We both know Ji-hyeon kidnapped herself; the only thing I can't figure out is why you didn't go with her, since you obviously love her."

"I do?" Keun-ju swallowed. "I don't. I mean, yes, or rather, no... She is my mistress, of course, so I do...um."

"Wow," said Zosia, recognizing that feeling all too well. "You've got it bad. She gave you the sword, right? A tri-tiger like that must have set her back a lot more than a week's allowance."

"It's not a three-tiger, it's a four," said Keun-ju, not even trying to mask his pride. "It's been in her family for three generations, and the swordmaker was an Ugrakari who could trace her lineage back to the Sunken Kingdom. She left no heirs to her art, so there's probably no sword like it left in the world. And now it's in the hands of a filthy Raniputri, thanks to you."

"The Raniputri put a higher commodity on bathing than Immaculates, so I wouldn't go down that road were I you. And the only reason you're still alive is thanks to me—if you'd killed those agents, you never would have gotten off the dock. Those lighthouses we passed coming in? The best archers in the Dominion keep watch from up there, just waiting for an excuse to shoot some foreign idiot."

"Better to have died with her sword in my hand than with it locked in some drawer," said Keun-ju.

"Well, that would make for a better ballad, I'll admit," said Zosia.

"Personally, I can't believe they took Choplicker. The insinuation is beyond disgusting."

"What makes you think Ji-hyeon ran away instead of being taken?" asked Keun-ju, and Zosia caught her smile before it gave her away. Maybe he just wanted to talk about anything other than the crime she was accused of, but from the needy tone in his voice she guessed he might've bought the story she'd spun him about an imminent pachyderm execution. Granted, maybe they *were* about to be killed, but not for the reasons he supposed, and probably not with an elephant as the murder weapon—the beasts were rare outside of a couple of Dominions way to the east.

"Princes and princesses are always kidnapping themselves," said Zosia. "She takes after her dad, it sounds like, and that would be his style for sure. Add to that the lack of ransom note, and I'm guessing Fennec sweet-talked her into making a break for it. Fennec would be Brother Mikal to you. They're probably off somewhere fucking like rabbits while we await a grisly death."

Keun-ju crossed his arms. "No."

"No? Keun-ju, my lad, believe me when I say you don't know the first thing about it. A feisty young princess, stuck in an arranged marriage, and then along comes a silver-tongued fox with promises of a bright new future far away in Usba, or the Empire, or somewhere more exotic still? At this point he's probably impregnated her and made off with whatever treasure they nicked from Hwabun. I'd bet she's too embarrassed to come home and admit she's carrying the bastard of her tutor."

"No," said Keun-ju, more forcibly. "You don't know anything."

"I know the human heart, kid, which isn't something you learn by being a horny rich girl's sewing instructor," said Zosia, which was downright nasty but she was on the cusp of provoking him into righteous honesty, she could feel it. "I'm sure you thought you were best friends, sharing all your secrets, but the truth is a noble never shares everything with a servant, *especially* a Virtue Guard. You guys are notoriously gossipy, and—"

"We love each other," said Keun-ju, tears running down from under his veil but his voice steady as good steel. "A coldhearted crone like you could never understand that, but we do."

"Ah, the love of a lordling for her slave, and the attendant for his mistress," said Zosia, despising herself a bit in the moment—that was funny, she never used to think twice about playing people, but for some reason she was profoundly unhappy with herself over this exchange. She was already committed to it, though, so dealt the killing blow. "She's probably already forgotten you, and here you are about to be executed, all for—"

"We're lovers," said Keun-ju quietly, wiping his face and looking at the ground. Fast as Zosia had teased it out, the Virtue Guard had reeled his rage back inside. "I'll die for her, whether it's today or another, but I'll never doubt her. She hasn't forgotten me. She will never forget me."

"Lovers?" *That* was unexpected. "But…that doesn't happen, does it? Don't you have to swear some serious fucking oaths to—"

"I would rather break a thousand oaths than Ji-hyeon's heart," said Keun-ju, slumping against the wall. "I've loved her for as long as I've served her, but never dared dream it would be more than…than what you said. The affection of a mistress for a slave. Then, the night of the Autumnal Equinox, after we fended off that giant spirit in the pumpkin fields, I was helping her undress for the night, and…"

"And *what*?"

"And she made her feelings for me abundantly clear," said Keun-ju primly.

"Uh-huh," said Zosia. "Talk is cheap for moneyed kids, Keun-ju. I hate to be the bearer of bad news, but if you'd actually tried going through with something she'd have dried up faster than you can say forbidden fruit looks better than it tastes."

"And if the ripe young Lieutenant Bang had weighed down her branch enough for you to reach it, I suppose you would have polished her on your sleeve, taken one bite, then cast her aside? I saw how you were savoring her with your eyes throughout the voyage."

"And we saw how well that worked out for me, didn't we?"

"Ji-hyeon loves me, Zosia, and I love her, and even if you're so base as to believe carnal consumption is required, well...rest assured my oaths have fallen like overripe pears forsaken by even—"

"I get it, I get it," said Zosia. "What gives with all the poetry, Keun-ju? You go the whole cruise without contributing so much as a song for music night, and now we get you talking about the princess and you're laying down the fruitiest verse this side of the Othean orchards."

"I would never debase her memory by taking part in a so-called *music night*," said Keun-ju bitterly. "And I will be mindful of my language in the presence of such a discerning critic as yourself. To answer your question, yes, there are sacred vows we must swear before taking on our duty, and yes, I have broken them, and no, I am not proud that I have broken them, but..."

"Yeah, I hear you," said Zosia, contemplating the many solemn oaths she'd bent, creatively interpreted, or just plain ignored over her storied career.

"It's ridiculous, you know?" Keun-ju sounded plenty pissed, which was due. "How many nights Ji-hyeon and I stayed up afterward, whispering in bed, and how often our talk turned to you—the Arch-Villain, the one woman in all the Star who refused to take what the world offered her, who lived life on her own terms, who died rather than compromise. And here I find out you're actually still alive, and come to think we're almost friends after everything we went through together on the boat...But you aren't anything like the stories. You're just a flunky of Ji-hyeon's dads, a coward who gives up rather than fights, a creep prying into the sex lives of strangers...Were you always so pathetic? Were all the tales about you false? Were you ever the woman they said you were?"

Zosia looked down at her scarred knuckles. The sea air had played hell with them on the voyage; what had been the odd ache back in her old life in Kypck now a daily nuisance of arthritic cramping. She deserved what the kid had said about her, but all the same she felt the impulse to give him a stomping. She set her teeth until it passed, then sighed and sat down beside him.

"That's fair. I was trying to rile the truth out of you, and got a sight more than I was looking for. I'm sorry, Keun-ju." Zosia felt like she meant the words as she was saying them, but had to wonder when she finished with, "And hey, since deflowering a princess is probably a worse crime than helping one run away, why not tell me the rest? I've always known you helped her, and now I know why, so let's get the full account. You tell me the truth now and I'll see that you're reunited with Ji-hyeon."

"I thought they were going to execute us any moment?" said Keun-ju, a watery smile showing at the hem of his veil. "And aren't you supposed to return Ji-hyeon to Hwabun?"

"I've been in tighter spots than this and seen my colleagues through," said Zosia, though at present she didn't have much in the way of ideas. "And as for taking her back to her parents, that depends on if she and Fennec can make me a better offer. So long as I have my army I'm not particular about who funds it, and I'll admit to having a romantic streak."

"Oh, you definitely strike me as the sentimental sort. *Fucking like rabbits.*"

"Fair again," said Zosia, and found herself being as straight with this sad boy as she'd been with any proven friend. "I hide it better than you, but we're out here for the same reason. Love's what haunts me, Keun-ju, love for a man, a man and his people. Love for those I'll never be able to hold again, or kiss, or laugh with over a jug of strong drink." From his expression she could tell he believed, and that made her feel like he owed her now, owed her more than he'd ever know. "So that's me, and I swear on my husband's cairn I'll keep your secret till the devils take me. Now out with it, let's have the rest."

Keun-ju was silent for a time, then met her eyes. Held them. "All right, I'll tell you everything. Ji-hyeon—"

A door banged open just down the hall, and both Zosia and Keun-ju scrambled to their feet. Their iron-barred cell was one of several opening onto a narrow corridor in the rear of the customs house, and four figures strode to their door and stopped. The late afternoon light coming through the skylights made the pink of the officers' saris glow like fire coral. Zosia and Keun-ju were blindfolded and then taken from the cell.

Doors opened and closed on either side of them, and then they were on the city streets, the teasing scents of urban living hardly a match for the odors of the cramped *Crane's Bill* but the riot of sounds far more jarring. Up stairs and down ramps they were blindly marched, past the smoke and din of a tavern or tubāqhouse, and then through another door. It was much quieter in here, though Zosia could still hear the ruckus through the wall, and after stumbling on the too-soft floor, she at last had the heavy cloth pulled away from her eyes.

Blinded by green-filtered light, she wiped her eyes with the back of her hand. They had not bound either her or Keun-ju, and, keeping her hand in front of her face to conceal her glances as her sight crept back, she took in the spacious room, looking for an exit. A stinghouse, pillows carpeting the floor, the wall-mounted terrariums teeming with cockroaches, centipedes, icebees, and a dozen other varieties of intoxicating insects. Between the glass cages were masked Raniputri women of decidedly shadier character than the customs agents who had delivered them and now quickly left out the back.

"I didn't believe it when I received Kang-ho's letter, but here you are," said a familiar voice, one that caused Zosia to drop her hand from in front of her face and stare at the rear of the room, where a figure reclined in a settee. Choplicker sat at the woman's feet, and she rubbed his head as she rose to her feet. "They're going to have to come up with a new handle for you, something like The Ghost Who Walks."

"Singh," said Zosia, taking in her old confederate. Keun-ju's jaw dropped as he realized they stood in the company of another legend, the Second Villain herself. "It's been a long time, Chevaleresse."

Whereas Kang-ho had gotten soft, Singh had hardened like a suit of sunbaked leather armor. Her black sari shone with golden moons and silver suns, and her nose stud and bangled wrists glittered in the terrarium light, but despite the casual attire an imperious ferocity radiated from the woman. Her hair was black as ever, though bound in two braids instead of a bun—Zosia wondered if Singh was widowed or divorced. Her once wild, waxy mustache had finally been tamed, the luxurious, upturned lip-weasel now maintaining its lilt by habit rather than force. Still handsome if haughty, with new scars glancing off her chin, cheeks, and bare feet, the knight brought a moist weight to Zosia's dusty throat. Singh looked damn good after all these years.

"I suppose I have you to thank for the more colorful charges against us?" asked Zosia, taking a step toward Singh. One of the guards melted off the wall and put herself between Zosia and her old friend.

"I thought you'd like that," said Singh, and to Zosia's chagrin she didn't call off her muscle. "I've been waiting for you all week. Kang-ho thought you'd make better time."

"Funny, Kang-ho claimed he didn't know how to find you," said Zosia.

"*That's* what he told you? Typical. You should have looked me up first, sister; things would be very different if you had." Singh put her hand on the guard's shoulder and she stepped away, leaving Zosia to look up into the taller woman's kohl-ringed eyes.

Zosia sighed. There was no sign of Anklelance, who usually coiled herself around her mistress's neck like a dull-scaled necklace. If Singh no longer had her devil, that was something in Zosia's favor, at long bloody last. Yet of all the Villains to go up against in a barehanded fight, she would have picked any combination of the others over Singh. According to the songs, the knight had been in martial training from the time she left her cradle. Given Zosia's experiences, she'd chalk that up to understatement rather than embellishment. "Let me guess. Kang-ho didn't send you to help find his daughter?"

"Oh, Zosia," said Singh sadly. "He sent me to kill you."

"Yeah, that figures," said Zosia, and talked fast, before the knight could move on her. "I challenge you to an honorable duel, Chevaleresse.

I win, you're back to taking my orders, and you'll help me track down the others, starting with Fennec. We're going to war again."

Singh cocked her head to the side, and Zosia gave silent thanks to the insane codes of Raniputri knights. "And if you lose, General, then what—"

Zosia swung on Singh. Surprise could only take her so far, but she didn't have much else to work with. It didn't take her nearly far enough.

CHAPTER
24

Sullen and Grandfather had hoped that learning the name Uncle Craven had taken among the Outlanders would give their hunt a definite scent to pursue, but that wasn't how it panned out. It didn't help that neither Sullen nor Grandfather knew more than a few curse words of Crimson, and none of the folk they met spoke the Savannah tongue, so most of the time Sullen had to ask around until he found someone who spoke Immaculate. When he could make himself known to the Imperials, most of them had indeed heard of a powerful warrior named Maroto, but each and every taleteller sent them in a different direction. Inquiries after Hoartrap the Touch were even less fruitful, and met with anxiousness if not outright hostility. One trail took them up the cyclopean spires of Meshugg that clung to the sheerest eastern peaks of the Black Cascades like barnacles on a wrecked ship. Another brought them all the way down the Heartvein, to where the river opened onto Lake Jucifuge and spun the floating city of the Serpent's Circle in a perpetual gyre. Adventures were had, and skulls were split, and powerful foes vanquished, but if Sullen had wanted that shit he would have stayed in the Frozen Savannahs. Then, as summer gave way to fall and his spirits sank as low as the ground fog in the Temple of the Black Vigil where they again sought their quarry in vain, an unexpected lead...

While Grandfather dozed on a fallen column after declaring the mission a failure, Sullen wandered the hollow avenues, pondering the weirdness of the place. Sure, people called Emeritus the Forsaken Empire for a reason, but he still couldn't quite wrap his mind around the scope of the place. Take this temple, for example: that it was devoted to something called the Faceless Mistress had a queer ring to it, certainly, but was hardly that bizarre. Nowadays the Horned Wolf Clan bowed to the Fallen Mother, after all, which sounded close enough to beg the question of whether this Faceless Mistress was the same god as they had in Samoth and the Savannahs, just named something different. That happened a lot, according to the missionaries who had lugged the Burnished Chain up the Noreast Arm—turned out the Horned Wolves had been worshipping the Fallen Mother long before they'd converted, they'd just called her Silvereye and thought she was an ancestor of note who'd gone around slaying some giants and eventually ascending into the night sky to become the moon, instead of, you know, the One True God of All Things.

Far as the new faith went, there were some good stories, but a whole lot of it just didn't make much sense to Sullen. Inconsistencies and such, the sort of simple errors that cropped up from time to time in any tale, like how nobody could agree if the Old Watchers were gods or devils. Yet when he'd pointed out the Burnished Chain's contradictions to Father Humble, the priest had made him repeat a bunch of nonsense words and whip himself with a switch until his back bled. This was a marked contrast to how Grandfather would debate him for long hours on the particulars of any given saga or song, and thereafter Sullen kept his observations away from the ears of all but his ancient relation.

Anyway, faith was a fickle thing. You could be like Sullen, who suspected Grandfather was probably right when he said all tales had equal measures of wisdom, truth, and bullshit, or you could be like the true believers and erect whole empires to honor a single legend, like they'd done down here on the Soueast Arm. At the end of your trail, though, you all ended up rotting into the earth. Small wonder Old Black built her meadhall in the Land Beneath the Star, so that all worthy heroes might one day be reunited, or the Chainites said the Fallen Mother dwelled in a wondrous cave at the center of all things, or the Jackal Tribe worshipped the Noreast Gate, which had been carved by Rakehell when he'd escaped his infernal father-in-law. Obvious stuff, and the more stories you soaked up the more evident it became.

Anyway, they'd teased a few tales out of folk on their way down to Emeritus, but few had wanted to talk much about it at all. Odd, that, as usually people wanted to tell you all kinds of nonsense about their neighbors, but nobody wanted to talk about the Forsaken Empire, or how it got forsook, or what the deal was with their god. Matters only became stranger the day before, when Sullen and Grandfather had stumbled over an enormous, shattered statue of this Faceless Mistress. The ruined monument lay dashed in boulder-sized chunks across a four-block area, appeared to be made of charcoal, and gave off a faint buzzing that Sullen could feel in his teeth. Strange, but not unheard of.

Stranger yet was how every structure and street was drained of color, even the leaves of ornamental trees as grey as an old wolf's coat; if Grandfather hadn't displayed the same range of pigments as ever, Sullen would have assumed there was something wrong with his eyes. The crowning peculiarity about this place was the expanse of it—they called it a temple, but it was larger than most of the Outlander cities Sullen and Grandfather had visited...a temple the size of a capital, and totally deserted.

There was some bad swamp to cross at the southeast border of the Empire and the Emeritus Arm, and a few bog pearl divers had waved to them from a canoe as they picked their way along the wide, petrified boardwalks leading into the Temple of the Black Vigil. Now, after a week of scouring the empty buildings and desolate streets, there was no doubting that they were definitely the only ones alive in the whole place. No citizens nor squatters peopled this metropolis, nor beasts nor birds nor bugs. It might've been spooky, except it was the first place Sullen had ever set foot where he saw no trace of the devils that dogged him. Especially after becoming better acquainted with the fiends courtesy of that awful witch Hoartrap, this was no bad thing. Besides, Emeritus reminded him a bit of home, with the perpetual chill of the dull shadowed avenues offset by brilliant pastel skies and the orange sun of high summer; there was the world he walked through, grey and hollow, but a rich, colorful realm hovering above, just out of reach. He found himself wondering if he could talk Grandfather into prolonging their search another week, to better explore the sepulchral temple city.

Sullen had been raised better than to steal from the dead, if death was what had befallen the people who'd dwelled here. Surely there was no harm in admiring their abandoned hoards, though. Everything was in its place in the deserted storehouses and dining halls, apartments and palaces, offices and altars, with freshly prepared meals set out before shrines and waiting on many a table. The smells could be maddening, especially in one humble home where a warm pot of lentils waited on a cold stovetop, the long-absent aroma of berbere and pepper sending Sullen all the way back to his mother's kitchen...but Sullen was no thief. And besides, as disparate as the accounts of the fall of Emeritus were, the one constant was that the populace had vanished some five hundred years before. Whatever purpose kept those lentils hot and appetizing after all these centuries, Sullen doubted it was out of consideration for his homesick belly. For once, Grandfather agreed with his thinking, and they subsisted on the cold tack of the Imperials, wary of even kindling a fire from what fuel they might scrounge in this place.

Even so, exploring the temple nourished Sullen in a fashion he couldn't quite articulate. The world of the people who had dwelled in this place was obscure despite their every possession being laid out for his inspection, and long after Grandfather had relieved him on watch he would lie sleepless on the dusty street, contemplating the use of some gargantuan mechanical device or the symbolism in a lifelike painting of a weeping salmon. Grandfather seemed put off by the abandoned lives, which was why Sullen so looked forward to the old man's increasingly long midafternoon naps.

Today Sullen's wanderings took him farther and farther from their campsite in an orderly park where the great grey lawns and pregnant, pale orchards appeared carefully manicured, nary a weed sprouting in a single monochromatic flowerbed. Strolling for an hour, he turned down another nondescript boulevard, one he and Grandfather had not heretofore explored. He knew they had not come this way, for the faintly phosphorescent dust that coated every inch of the Temple of the Black Vigil here lay undisturbed by footprints. Even before he gained the intersection, he was somehow aware that this new road terminated in a great wall just a block or two down the way...

Huh. Striding out into the middle of the road, he sized up the dead end. The buildings on either side were the same austerely shaped white rowhouses that lined most every road in the temple, but instead of a wall this road ran straight into a high archway, and beyond the archway lay a Gate. Or maybe instead of ending at the Gate, this was where the road began—it was all a matter of perspective.

Sullen knew the oily pool of black mud that filled the carven-walled courtyard on the far side of the arch was a Gate because he had seen its twin, once, when he was but an unnamed pup. As he had dragged Grandfather home from the battle that had claimed his legs, they had passed within a mile or two of the Flintland Gate, a deeper patch of darkness on the horizon. The war had started because the Jackal Tribe had abducted and sacrificed several Horned Wolves, feeding them to that yawning mouth in the earth that they called the Ravenous God. Six nights later, when he was safely home in his bed, the devils had waited until he made the mistake of dreaming and then hauled him back to the Gate, carrying him as far as a plinth erected near its edge before he awoke. Horned Wolves weren't crazy savages who believed that if you died in a dream you died for real, but Sullen knew from the songs that devils could hurt you in your sleep, if they found a way past the charms hanging at your door and windows. For nine subsequent nights he had dreamt of the Gate, and each night the devils carried him closer and closer to the trembling lip of the abyss.

Then, on the tenth night, just before he fell asleep, he asked the devils not to take him back there. As a token of his earnestness, he had picked open the scabs he had acquired protecting Grandfather from a snow lion their first night in the wilds, and drifted off as the devils settled in to feed on his dripping arms. That night he dreamt of flight, but not the Gate, nor did he ever dream of it again. Strange, he hadn't remebered that in years, even after what had happened with Hoartrap on the plains…

Now he stood before a second Gate, and saw that his long-buried visions had shown true, for this portal in the earth perfectly mirrored that which he had dreamt as a boy who had never left the Frozen Savannahs. And here, in the wasted land of Emeritus, where only a Horned Wolf and his grandfather had dared to venture down many a lonely century, came all the devils he had not glimpsed since entering the temple.

Wide awake and unmolested by a witch as Sullen was, the devils materialized just the same, emerging not from the Gate but the puffs of dust rising beneath his battered boots. Up they rose, spiraling around him, the whisper of scale and fur tickling his skin and the muscles and bone beneath, and then they wheeled high into the air, winged toad and finned serpent, insectoid rodent and dog-legged crustacean, and a hundred thousand other flittering, slithering horrors. The devils came together into a squirming tornado that stretched from the dusty cobblestones high into the air.

"Aw, man," he said, not really having a lot of hope for his prospects here. Grandfather was wrong about some stuff, Grandfather was wrong about *a lot* of stuff, even, but he'd been right about one thing: *Don't go wander off and get yourself killed in this dump while I take a nap*. Sorry, Fa.

The cyclone of devils contracted further, coalesced, the awfulness of their individual parts forming an even less wholesome whole: a humanoid figure twice as tall as the surrounding buildings towered above Sullen, its pendulous breasts, featureless face, and extended fingers all writhing with unending movement as it bent down for him.

"Don't do it!" he shouted, holding up his open palms to the nightmarish giant. "I don't want to hurt you!"

As soon as he said it he recognized this was a pretty silly thing to tell a titanic, devil-spawned monster, and right enough, it didn't give the entity pause. A palm half as tall as Sullen slammed into his side, fingers as wide as his legs closing around him. The ground fell away from him and the true expanse of the temple came into sight as he was lifted several stories into the air, the Gate now but a small pool beside the giant's foot...not that he was paying much attention to the cityscape laid out beneath him. No, his focus was on the enormous face the hand held him up to, a blank oval as richly dark as the Gate itself.

As he watched, queasy from the unique experience of being lifted so high so quickly, the abyssal darkness of the face spread down the wriggling, patchwork neck. It radiated down the chest and out across the shoulders, the individual devils going rigid as the blackness seeped over and through them. The devils comprising the hand that held him became agitated as the darkness began to seep down that arm, beaks and barbs desperately prodding against him. It was as though the devils were desperate to avoid the creeping darkness and sought to crawl over or through him to escape it, but were trapped, swimming in circles around the man they grasped. Were they a captive of something greater, just as he was?

"I'll...do something," he said, speaking to himself, to the devils who bound him, and to the enormous black face. The Faceless Mistress, obviously, she to whom this temple was erected, the god of the lost people of Emeritus. One of them, anyway.

"*What will you do?*" Sullen hadn't really expected an answer, but as his ears popped and he heard his own voice pose the question, a distant constellation bloomed in the greasy depths of the giant's face. Even as these lights faded back into darkness came another question, and another flare of remote stars. "*What do you offer?*"

What did he have? It already had his person, if it wanted it, and he wasn't foolish enough to think a god would desire what few possessions he owned. Grandfather? A low thought, that one, and Sullen frowned to think that moments before he went to his ancestors he had considered selling out his most beloved kin, if only for a moment. What would Old Black or Rakehell do, if they were in such a pinch?

"Don't have much," he said, not really scared so much as...awed, maybe? Awed, sure, but not so awed he couldn't think or speak. It was like dreaming, that way. "Whatever you want, I guess."

Sullen wasn't any better versed in the ways of gods than he was in the motivations of devils, but as soon as he said it he figured that was a fairly stupid offer to make. This time, though, it seemed he might've blundered into saying the right thing, because the encroaching blackness paused at the wrist of the arm that held him and the devils holding him all went still. The gargantuan head moved closer and closer to Sullen, and, eyes or no in its light-swallowing surface, he knew he was being sized up by the Faceless Mistress.

Then, a distant twinkle of light in the heart of the void. It flickered, expanded, crackled with energy. Exploded outward, to the very edge of the blackness, so close Sullen could feel the heat...and then it contracted again, sucking the warmth back in with it, so fast and so cold that beads of sweat froze half-birthed from his pores. An ebon mountain filled his vision, though like the god's voice he couldn't tell if it was really there, or appearing only in his suddenly aching skull.

The dark mountain was hollow as a drinking horn, and brimming with people. It reminded him of nothing so much as one of the dire ant mounds back home, swarming with bizarre life. And as he watched, flaming oil bubbled up from the depths, cascading through tunnels and melting the inner walls of the mountain, incinerating all of the teeming residents, and vomiting from the top in a great spume of ash and smoke. A city even greater than this temple, populated by an incalculable number of folk, obliterated absolutely.

"Nah, not doing that," said Sullen. "Can't. Won't, even if I could. I'm a Horned Wolf, not a witch nor devil."

"*No*," said the winking stars. "*Zosia will. Unless you thwart her.*"

Zosia. Though it took a moment to sink in, Sullen recognized the name. His uncle's old boss from the first time Craven had sought his fortune on the Star, according to some of the songs they'd heard along the road. His uncle's bride, according to others, who'd died before Sullen was born. An utterly ruthless, diabolically clever, and intensely dangerous woman, according to all, a Queen of Samoth whom not even death could stop from sowing madness and sorrow, a phantom returned from the bowels of the grave to savage all of the Star.

"All right," said Sullen. "Preventing that kind of thing seems best. There's kids there, and such. Where is she?"

"*You shall meet her once you have found your uncle,*" said the god. "*Under the snapping of Cobalt banners, in the Crimson Empire.*"

"Oh," said Sullen. "Thanks."

A ring of stars flickered once, like a mouth of light smiling in the depths, and the face filled his entire world as it came in to swallow him whole. He closed his eyes, but instead of oblivion received a gentle kiss. Her lips were small and warm as those of Stoutest, before the girl had earned her name and stopped having anything to do with him. Stoutest was the only woman to have ever kissed him, and so he never had cause to doubt her counsel that one should always keep their eyes locked on their partner's when receiving such affection. Opening his eyes, he stared into the vastness of the god, and kissed her back. He felt it all the way down in his treasure, like the one time Stoutest had put her hand down there and made him feel nine kinds of heavens, followed by twelve kinds of embarrassment. This was nine thousand kinds of heavens, with none of the surprise or shame after.

And then his stomach dropped along with the rest of him as the devils holding him broke away from her black wrist, fading into the air as he fell. He landed a moment later on a steeply canted rooftop, the wind knocked out of him, and above him the Faceless Mistress went rigid. He heard the cracking of ice just before a glacier crumbled free of a fjord, and then, with slowness as impossible as the rest of her, she broke apart. The arm that had held him clipped the edge of the roof as it fell, sending splintered tiles flying into the air, but the bulk of her tipped back, crushing the building on the far side of the street. An eruption of dust and debris blanketed the temple for miles, and when it lifted nothing remained of the Faceless Mistress but another decimated statue. Sullen stared down at the wreckage and wiped his mouth on the back of his hand. It left a dark smear.

"By all the ancestors and the unborn, what happened to you?" said

Grandfather when Sullen moseyed back into the park. It was the first time he could recall the old man genuinely seeming concerned for his safety, and the novelty made him feel worse rather than better. The last thing he wanted was to worry Grandfather. "Speak, boy, are you well?"

"I'm fine, Fa," he said, giving himself a once-over to make sure he hadn't hurt himself climbing down from the building. No visible damage, so how could Grandfather tell something had happened? "You heard the...ruckus?"

"The *ruckus*?" Grandfather put a hand to his mouth, kept gawping at Sullen. "What in all the...did you stir up a devil king, laddie? Find that Hoartrap again? What *happened*?"

"I found out where Uncle is," said Sullen, hoping that would distract Grandfather. It didn't. Better to get it said and over with, then. How would one of his ancestors have told the tale, once they'd had an adventure like that? With lots of sharp words and deft rhymes, probably, but Sullen's strength was in recollecting songs, not creating them. Let someone else tell it smarter, if they thought it worth a verse at all. "And, uh...I met a god. Or a goddess, I guess?"

"Oh," said Grandfather, relaxing on his pillar as though that settled the matter. A pause. "Was she nice?"

CHAPTER
25

Told you he wasn't a scout." Maroto sneered at Purna, imitating the girl's snippy tone.

"I wasn't the one who let him go," she said, booting the stained wood of their cell door. It didn't budge. *"Durrr, he's got a Khymsari haircut, so he must be Khymsari."*

"It's a pretty terrible hairdo," said Maroto. "I couldn't see anyone but a cultist doing that to themselves on purpose. Lying little shit."

"Well, now what?" Purna turned away from the front of the sparse room to face Maroto. Even in the dimness he could see that her face was at the apex of its puffiness, lips split, cheeks bruised, one eye nearly swollen shut. The Imperials had really done a number on her before she'd gone down, but then Maroto supposed he must look even worse. He certainly *felt* worse—it wasn't a competition, mind, but she clearly felt well enough to stand and pace the cramped cell and kick at things, whereas Maroto had no intention of rising from the hay-strewn floor anytime soon. "We just wait here for them to execute us?"

"Nah," said Maroto. "They'll definitely torture us first, get any information they can. Me, they'll probably try and use to get Zosia to open the castle—that'll mean more torture, public-like, where she can watch from the ramparts. *Witch, we got your Villain down here—open the gate or we'll cut him open!"*

"Then what?"

"Then they gut me, because there's no way she's stupid enough to trust 'em—she opens the castle we're all dead, instead of just me."

"No, I mean, then what do we do, you and I, if they'll just torture us anyway—move on the guards when they come for us, or try to lure them in sooner? You look rough enough I could probably call them in now, say you've croaked and are stinking up the place. Then we snap their necks, steal their uniforms, and sneak out to rescue the others."

"Great plan," Maroto said dryly. "Assuming you even broke a neck properly, which I doubt, and we got out of here, which are longer odds yet, what better plan than risk it all to bust out those worthless scumdogs who couldn't even be bothered to fight back when the Imperials ambushed us? We might've stood a chance, they hadn't just let themselves be taken."

"What do you expect, we were all asleep! Except you, Sir I'll Take First Watch." Purna punctuated this with a withering look down at her mentor. "And maybe if we hadn't swung on them we could've avoided the whole thing, lied or bribed our way out, ever think of that?"

"Been thinking of little else," said Maroto, choosing not to remind the brat that she'd been the one to throw that fatal first punch when the Imperials had roused them—he'd been glad she had at the time, because then the Crimson soldiers had started coming at *him*, and that meant he could fight back without risking his oath... for all the good it had done them.

"If we'd played it cool you and I would probably be locked up with Diggelby and the others, if nothing else. Wherever they are I imagine the accommodations are swankier than a tavern's closet."

"That where we are?" Maroto blinked into the dimness of the musty chamber. What daylight filtered its way into the cell came from above, the thatch or whatever comprised the roof in need of repair. Maybe they weren't so doomed after all...

"Yep, a real shitkicker establishment, too, judging by the stuffed fish mounted on the walls. Just how long were you out? I figured you were faking it so they wouldn't interrogate you right away."

"Yeah, they call that method acting—learned it from some rough-and-tumble Usban players I ran with for a while. A dozen of the troupe's been hanged over the years for getting too committed to their roles. They're not bandits or killers, but if they're *playing* bandits or killers, well—"

"Rambling, Maroto."

"Listen: help me up, let's see if I can boost you to the ceiling. Maybe we can go up and out. They got the command stationed in here?"

"No, it looked like the important people were working from a temple a few blocks away. The others branched off there, but you and me got dumped in here." Purna was staring at the back wall as though she could see through the timbers and clay. "The tavern's a garrison, I guess you'd call it. Soldiers everywhere."

"Huh." Maroto's good ear couldn't pick up much. "Quiet enough now."

"There was a big to-do a few minutes ago, Snoroto. Sounded like they cleared out in a hurry."

"Doesn't get better than that," said Maroto, taking her extended hand and hauling himself upright. Not to his feet, even, just enough so he was sitting leaned against the rear wall, but even that development caused supernovas to explode in his vision and a volcano to erupt up his throat. Getting coldcocked never got easier; if anything, it seemed to be getting worse the older he got. Woof. Well, if nothing else he hadn't lost his knack for puking on himself.

"Sick!" Purna dropped his hand and danced back from him as another volley of bile came up. She grabbed the room's only furnishing, a chamberpot, and thrust it into his hands. It would have been too little too late, except the ripe contents of the pot summoned forth another devil from his belly. They must have been in here a while, for it to get so full.

Eyes shuttered from the world, icy sweat soaking his clothes, the stink of piss and shit and vomit curling his nose hairs, cooped up in a dingy, dirty cell—it was just like old times, all right. He swooned in place, thought he felt Crumbsnatcher crawling down his tunic but realized it was just a dribble of sick. The sheer abjectness seemed to transport him back over the years, into the last stinghouse he'd stumbled into, and a horrible realization broke way back behind his clenched-shut eyes, in the constipated bowels of his aching skull— none of this was real, not Purna nor the other fops nor Zosia being alive again, it was all just the bitedream of an old junkie. He'd wished away Crumbsnatcher, sure enough, but not to be free of the bugs, never that, but for something even more pathetic...and he almost remembered, could feel the rat's whiskers on his cheek as it kissed him good-bye, but then Purna intruded on his misery:

"Just...ugh. What's wrong with you? Are you ill?"

Maroto wiped tears from his cheeks. He told himself they were tears of joy at coming back to sweet, sweet reality after the waking nightmare he'd just suffered, but the sorry truth was he'd been crying before he came to his senses. Purna crouched beside him, put the back of her hand against his forehead, as though that ever did anything at all.

"Better," he said, because having the shakes and a splitting headache is undeniably better than having the shakes, a splitting headache, and actively vomiting while suffering a spiderbite flashback. He tried to set the chamberpot down gently but ended up just halfheartedly tossing it aside. Stupid numb fingers. "Been better. Been worse. Just give me a second."

More like a few hundred were eventually required, but at last Maroto was on his feet again. Purna looked skeptical when he told her to scale him, but they never had a chance to see if he could have supported her climb to the ceiling, for at that moment they clearly heard an outer door bang open and voices approaching their cell. Here came the torture. Maroto glumly supposed they wouldn't be fed first.

"Get ready," Purna hissed, snatching up the chamberpot. "I get the weapon since I'm smaller."

"All yours," said Maroto, wrinkling his nose and creeping to the side of the door. What a way to go—covered in your own puke, near blind from pain, and without so much as a half-arsed plan. He gave it a quick thought, whispered, "They'll be ready for this, so toss that pot in their eyes. Try to blind 'em before rushing out, or they'll just cut us down."

There. Now they had a half-arsed plan, or at least a quarter cheek's worth. They steadied themselves as they heard a rusty bolt slide, and then the door flew open. This was it.

On the other side were Diggelby, Din, and Hassan, all three falling back in squealing horror as Purna splashed the chamberpot in their faces. Din dropped her crossbow and pawed at her eyes, the weapon going off as it hit the floor and sending a bolt whizzing between Maroto's thighs to imbed in the back wall. If he were but a little shorter he'd have been a whole lot unhappier.

"Oh balls, sorry!" said Purna, hurrying to help their gagging saviors. Maroto followed her out of the cell, trying not to be sick again himself. Each step was hard-won. Looking past their retching companions, he saw that the repurposed common room of the tavern was empty save for dozens of bedrolls and mounds of equipment, the tables stacked up against one wall. A muted metallic clamor from just outside the tavern indicated that the soldiers had vacated their quarters just in time for some sort of entanglement.

"I told you we should have left them," Hassan told the recovering pasha and duchess, ripping off his stained lace ruff and throwing it at Purna. "Between his sleeping on watch and her provoking the Imperials when we'd already lost, they're about as useless as a eunuch at an orgy."

"I wasn't asleep, I just don't hear so good anymore," said Maroto. "And if you'd ever been to an orgy, son, you'd know eunuchs have a thousand and one uses, if you ask politely. But hey, thanks for busting us loose—how'd you do it?"

"Oh, it was ghastly, ghastly," said Diggelby, and now that the filth was either wiped off or ground into his already roughed-up finery, Maroto determined the old boy was blanched and quaking from more than the affront of Purna's attack. His lapdog Prince looked just as scared, shaking in his master's arms. "I've never...And I hope I never again!"

"An old friend of yours paid us a visit," said Duchess Din as Purna helped her up. "They took us to a Chain temple, to be interviewed by the commander. She wanted to know everything about you, and we were telling her, but then...I can't say what happened, exactly. Deviltry."

At the word the entire building trembled, the packed earth floor shivering beneath their feet. Maroto could relate. Most likely a substantial chunk of masonry had been dropped from the castle walls and struck ground somewhere close by, but even as the dust settled and everyone relaxed, he continued to shudder. *An old friend.* She was here.

"What in the cursed name of the creator is going on out there?" asked Purna, and then the oddness of it struck home—they were just outside the besieged castle, in the shantytown that had grown around its walls like dairy mites crowding on a rind of sheep cheese, so why in all the songs of Samoth would there be fighting here unless...

"They've quit the castle," said Maroto. "The she-wolf's left her den, bringing the fight to the hounds who ran her to earth."

"Madness," said Purna.

"Yep," said Maroto. "That sounds like her."

"The scout said she was badly outnumbered, and seeing the camp they brought us through, I believe it," said Purna. "Why sacrifice her only advantage?"

"Hardly her only advantage," said Hassan. "That witch—"

"Call her that again and I'll teach you some manners, Hassan," said Maroto, pointing a finger at the nobleman. "You've worked hard for my respect; don't be so quick to cast it aside now that you've earned it."

"*Her?*" said Duchess Din. "The witch we're talking about is—"

"An old, old friend," said an all too familiar voice, a hulking figure emerging from a hall that led deeper into the tavern, the enormous pack on his back scraping the top of the doorframe as he entered the room. Beneath the cowl of his yellow robes lurked the withered face of a mummy, the forearms that emerged from the garment revealing impressive sinews bulging just beneath mold-white skin. One enormous hand clutched an oaken staff topped by a carven owl pointing its wing at them, and in the other he casually dangled Maroto's mace, as though the brass-and-steel killing tool weighed no more than a carpenter's hammer.

"Oh fuckity fuckers, he followed us," squeaked Diggelby, crushing his whining dog to his chest. "Look, we don't even really know the barbarian, so—"

"*Get a grip, Digs*," said Din, switching over to Falutin, the Imperial noblecant. As with most dialects of Star slang, Maroto understood them perfectly, and so did the pale monster grinning at him with black gums. "*Why would he kill all those Imperials and let us go if he meant Maroto harm?*"

"Who..." Purna licked her puffy lips, obviously intimidated despite herself. No shame there, this was one scary motherfucker. "Who is he?"

"One scary motherfucker," said Maroto, putting every crumb of concentration into keeping his stride steady as he walked across the common room toward the terrible old wizard. "Hoartrap the Touch, as I live and breathe. They said some reeking old goatfucker had busted them loose, but that description was far too charitable for me to suspect it was you."

"We never said that," said Hassan. "I swear on my pals' lives, we never said it!"

"Maroto Devilskinner, the Barbarian Without Fear," said Hoartrap, flicking his wrist and sending Maroto's mace spinning up into the air. One of its small flanges loudly lodged in a rafter, and the heavy weapon stuck fast in the ceiling. "I'd heard you turned to bugs, so I *am* relieved to see that was just a euphemism for volunteering your orifices to degenerate nobles. Added any new specimens to your menagerie of exotic genital poxes?"

"Sorry, friend—I know you like lapping up the discharge, but

I've got nothing for you," said Maroto, looking square into Hoartrap's rheumy eyes. There weren't a lot of folk tall as Hoartrap, let alone who could meet his basilisk gaze, but Maroto wasn't a lot of folk.

"You look better than I expected," said Hoartrap, pursing his lips and nodding. "Tell you what, barbarian—for old time's sake, I'll let you cradle my balls in your mouth. Something needs to sweeten that awful breath."

Maroto couldn't come up with anything dirtier on the spot—he blamed the concussion—so he grabbed the nightmarish geriatric in a bear hug. Hoartrap creeped him out, because Hoartrap creeped everyone out, even his fellow Villains, but rather than keeping him at a distance like the others did, Maroto always just shrugged and got chummy with the wizard. If Hoartrap ever turned on them it wasn't as though proximity would save anyone; on the contrary, the only hope they'd have was if someone—and *someone* always meant *Maroto*—was close enough to lay the fucker out before he could pull one of his tricks. It had never come to that, thank the gods, and then there'd been that time in Emeritus when Maroto had pulled the sorcerer's fat from the fire and Hoartrap had loudly sworn on all his devils that since he owed Maroto his life, he would never take the barbarian's. There would be some who might point out that such a promise wasn't really much recompense, but knowing Hoartrap well as he did, Maroto had been glad to accept the oath.

Now, as the fierce old man returned Maroto's embrace with equal rib-aching vigor, the barbarian found that what had once been mostly pretext was now genuine affection. Damn if it wasn't good to see a familiar face, even an ugly one.

"Hoartrap the Touch?" Purna had slunk over while they were talking, and as soon as they broke their hug the girl bowed to the wizard. "It is an honor to meet you, sir."

"An *honor*, is it?" Hoartrap raised the snowy branches of his brows. "That's not the welcome I usually receive when strangers recognize my name. Where did you pick this one up, Maroto, and what lies have you been feeding her?"

"He hasn't been feeding me anything," said Purna, but even as Maroto began to nod in approval she went on, causing him to flinch instead. "Much as he'd like to."

"Ah, I like this one," said Hoartrap. "I see she takes after you more than those other three. Yes, hallo, I see you trying to sneak away, but believe you me, that's a bad idea. The fighting's in the streets, and I'd strongly caution against wandering outside until it's over."

"We...we..." Diggelby and the others had frozen in front of the door.

"We're locking up, so no harried soldiers could flee back in here," said Din, directing a scornful frown at Diggelby. His belled collar had given them away. Hassan sighed and miserably dropped the heavy slat in place, securing them all inside the tavern.

"That's as chickenshit a scheme as I ever heard hatched by hero or hen," said Maroto. "Brace yourselves, we're going out there to help carry the day for Zosia."

"They may be chickenshit, dear Maroto, but your scheme is pure poppycock," said Hoartrap. "You and your assistant here are barely able to stand, and after my civil attempt to parley with the Imperial command went the way of the Sunken Kingdom, I, too, am in need of a bit of sit and sip, not stand and stab."

"I have to find her," said Maroto, raising up on his tiptoes to reach the haft of his mace. "I won't wait another moment."

The next thing Maroto knew, Hoartrap and Purna were helping him back up to a sitting position. Apparently he still hadn't shaken off his beating at the hands of the sneaking Imperials. From now on he was going to gag every scout he captured before they had a chance to open their mouths, then leave them tied to a tree—if he hadn't made that stupid vow he'd just as soon kick in their heads, but when you swear on your devil you have to play by the rules or risk Old Black knew what mischief. There was no lower form of martial life than a scout; professional cowards, better at spying and fleeing than fighting fair.

"Don't worry, she'll be here soon enough," said Hoartrap.

"She sent you to rescue us?" asked Purna. "Queen Zosia?"

"So she's *Queen* Zosia to you, is she, girl? Silly old goat that I am, I thought she'd been dead and gone before you were born!"

Purna gave Hoartrap one of her imperious proclamations: "Even if she wasn't still alive, a queen like Cold Cobalt would keep her crown even in the grave."

"Oooh, she certainly sounds like you, barbarian, don't tell me you've sired another heir?"

"No, definitely not," said Maroto. Then, his head clearing by degrees, "Another? Call me an idiot, sorcerer, but don't call me a father—I've been too careful for that, unless the work I paid you to put upon my loins was naught but mummery? In which case I probably have a lot of heirs by now. And you have much to answer for."

"Trouble not your pretty head," said Hoartrap. "Like all gods, my works are eternal, so long as belief is strong. And as usual, you answer my questions without my even needing to ask them."

"And as usual, you answer every question with two or three more," said Maroto. "So let's have it straight, for a change, before I lose my patience—Zosia sent you for us? It's really her?"

"You don't know?" asked Hoartrap, helping Maroto onto a bench the fops had dragged over from the wall. With a wave and a mutter Hoartrap pulled one of the tables free from the stack and brought it skidding across the floor, kicking up a wake of bedrolls. The nobles squawked and Purna gasped, but Maroto was just happy to have something to brace his arm against.

"Don't know what, witch?" said Maroto, Hoartrap's shtick already tiresome. "I warned you about answering one question with another."

"I was earnestly asking," said Hoartrap. "I've just arrived myself, hot on your trail. I'd heard rumors of the return of the Cobalt Company, of course, everyone has, but assumed you'd caught up with her and seen for yourself. Don't tell me you were captured by the Imperials before you even reached the castle!"

"We were ambushed," said Purna. "It was ten against one."

"He was supposed to be on guard," said Hassan, he and Diggelby dragging another bench over so they could sit on the far side of the table. Din already had her cards out and was shuffling at the end of the board. "Mighty Maroto let those brigands stroll right into camp and get the drop on us."

"My hearing's not what it used to be," grumbled Maroto. "Caught an arrow in the ear while protecting these ingrates a few months back. So you haven't seen her either?"

"I was looking for you, as I said, and have been for ages. I did chance upon the pleasant company of some others who were seeking you out along the road, but I gather I've made better time than they. Here, you, deal me in—I have no great talent for such games, so pray go easy on me."

"I'll sit this one out," said Purna as the others set up their game, and asked Maroto's question for him. "Who was looking for him? Friend or foe?"

"Neither? Both? Who can tell?" said Hoartrap, winking at Maroto. "I don't think I'll spoil the surprise. They seemed...committed, so I imagine they'll catch up to you, sooner or later."

"Devils kiss me for ever missing your company," said Maroto. "Why were you chasing me down, Hoartrap, what business do we have?"

"We'll see soon enough. You've already answered most of the questions I had for you, so I suggest we just wile away the hours until our Cobalt Commander arrives. Then we'll both have our minds put to rest on a number of matters."

"Arrives?" asked Purna. "Why would she come here, if she's leading the charge outside?"

"Smart, yeah, just waiting here," said Maroto. "Whenever we'd won a town, she'd take the troops from tavern to tavern, rolling out barrels and serving the soldiers herself. If it's her, she'll come."

"I'll roll us out one to start," said Hassan, moving for the inner door Hoartrap had come through.

"Better let me help," said Hoartrap, nimbly dancing after him. Maroto couldn't decide which option was more unsettling, if Hoartrap's weirdness was cultivated or genuine. "I already settled accounts with the innkeep and his family, so it may be best if I accompany you."

As soon as the two were gone, the remaining three nobles started in on Maroto.

"Let's make a run for it," said Diggelby, and Prince yapped his agreement, maybe, or maybe he just yapped because he was one yappy fucking spaniel.

"Can we trust him?" asked Din.

"Should I cut his throat if I get the chance?" When Maroto swayed backward at Purna's question, she added, "I've heard the songs. You give me the word, and—"

A shriek came from the back of the tavern, and then Hassan staggered out of the door, paler than any foundation could ever lighten a man of his complexion. No one jumped to his aid, though most didn't have Maroto's excuse of not wanting to risk any sudden moves.

"What?" said Din, but Hassan just shook his head and wobbled over to the table. Maroto may have been the only one to notice that his tassel-toed slippers left dark wet footprints on the carpet of bedrolls.

"Some help you were," said Hoartrap when he returned shortly after, a hogshead floating after him. Most wizards kept their tricks in reserve instead of always showing off, but not Hoartrap. A train of mugs bounced through the air after the barrel, and while Purna and Diggelby stared openmouthed at the sight, Din focused all her attention on shuffling the cards. "What are the stakes, then? I only play for real wagers."

Purna helped Maroto to a drink as Hoartrap blathered at the petrified ponces. The ale was sour as tart cider, but cool on his ragged throat and feverish brow. As Maroto watched the game, Hoartrap pulled out the curved black pipe Zosia had carved for the sorcerer way back when they were all on an endless campaign against King Kaldruut, before she'd stolen his crown with little more than some well-spent silver and a whole lot of angry peasants.

What would a pipe like that be worth, Maroto wondered, hand-carved by the Stricken Queen before she conquered Samoth? Probably a whole devil-load more than he had pawned his for, back when he was suckling on the honeyed stinger—like so much from those days, he couldn't remember how he'd parted with it, only the day where he'd reached for it and found it gone, so he'd reached for another graveworm or scorpion instead. After all these months on her trail, he still harbored a tenderness over not being invited back to the Company, inventing countless scenarios for why she hadn't been able to find him...but all cards being down, it might could be she just knew what an inconstant son of a centipede he was, and thought herself better served by his absence.

"Care for a dip in my pouch?" Hoartrap said, and Maroto realized he'd been staring covetously at the sorcerer's pipe.

"Nah, I'm good." The tambo-stick Hoartrap had shaved into flakes and stuffed into his bowl was putting off a column of harsh dark smoke that smelled more like poison than tubāq, and even if he'd had his old briar there was no chance Maroto would have ghosted his bowl with that nastiness. "Looks like the duchess bluffed you, old man. You ought to pay more attention."

"Rare is the game that is made more enjoyable by being played more seriously," said Hoartrap. "A philosophy I have found applicable in literally all aspects of my existence. Ah, a worthy call, Count Hassan, a worthy call!"

Many hands later, somebody tried the door. Diggelby stood, Prince growling softly from his post under the table, but Hoartrap waved him back down without even looking up from his cards. Maroto's heart felt like he'd just provoked a bite out of a thunder wasp as he stared at the door, said aloud what he knew Hoartrap was also thinking: "If it's her, she'll force it."

The door shook again. Wood groaned. Metal began biting into it. The nobles stared along with Maroto, but Hoartrap coaxed Hassan back to the table by raising the already substantial pot three dinars.

Then the door gave. It was bright inside the tavern, Hoartrap having waved the lamps alight when the sun had set beyond the oilcloth-covered windows, but outside it was dark as a stinghouse basement, and the woman who stood before a crowd of heavily armed soldiers was silhouetted in the splintered doorway.

Maroto didn't stand so much as float to his feet, the one thing that could banish the agony in his battered skull at last before him. His vision tightened, his good ear pricked, and every inch of him tingled the way it did in the heat of battle, when all distractions fell away and the fight became everything. *Zosia.*

She strode into the room, imperious as was her due, and behind her came Fennec, the old crook. His fox helm sparkled, unblemished even after all these years, even after all the action it had seen, but Maroto's eyes passed over this in a twinkling to focus on Zosia's. It stopped his heart. A devil dog, snarling, with the twisted tendrils of a silver crown rising from the steel mask. How many hours had he spent helping her bend those tines back into shape after a battle, how many spikes had he helped replace after a close encounter with sword, ax, or hammer?

Zosia came to him, and Maroto gulped her down like a reformed drunkard tasting soju after a decade of sobriety. This was not the Zosia he remembered, this was Zosia from the portraits she had begrudgingly sat for in the Crimson Throne Room...just before their world had fallen apart.

Midnight blue riding boots came up to her knees, their cuffs banded with silver. Bare, dirtied, and perfect skin followed, her thighs shining with sweat despite the coolness of the night, nothing shielding her from assault or his eyes but a sheer loincloth of polished chainmail. Then her sculpted navel, her solid flanks, and another strip of silver links, her breasts barely constrained by the small outposts of armor. Beyond her helm and this briefest of defenses, so modest as to mock the dangers of combat rather than to offer any actual protection, she wore but a deep red cloak. Onto this burgundy cape spilled cobalt blue hair, the helm designed to let it flow wild—again, the spectacle was everything, her attire a laughing defiance of the suggestion that this woman had anything to fear in all the Star.

This was Zosia as Maroto had envisioned her ten thousand times, Zosia as she lived in his dreams long after all swore she had perished at Diadem. This was Zosia as he had always wanted her, how he had begged her to be.

In other words, whoever this masked, half-naked, blue-haired woman was, she definitely wasn't Zosia. He had let himself pretend for the last blessed months that his beloved was alive, but now, truly, he knew she was dead. Like so many others, he had been fooled by an impostor, taken in by an impossible dream. Maroto let the floor take him, as he had so many times before.

CHAPTER
26

Diadem was built before the Haunted Sea swallowed the Sunken Kingdom and shadows devoured Emeritus. More than just the capital of the province of Samoth, more, even, than serving as seat of the entire Crimson Empire and anchor of the Burnished Chain, Diadem was the last stronghold built before the Age of Wonders ended, a monument to the ingenuity of mortals and the ability of the devils they bound. Even if all the world should plunge into darkness, Diadem's radiance would continue to shine from the crown of the Star, a beacon for mortals from every corner of the Empire, from every Arm and every isle, forever and ever.

So the Chain Canticles said, anyway. Sister Portolés had come to Diadem kicking and hissing, not even an anathema then, simply a young monster in desperate need of salvation. She had received it, Fallen Mother be praised, but even after they made her nearly human, even after she learned to pray for her exterminated family instead of weeping for them, she had never seen much of Diadem beyond the Dens built into the walls of the dead volcano that enveloped the city. Even when she had ridden out to war against or beside the Imperials, she had only ever passed through a tiny section of the city.

Now she had permission to go anywhere, to see everything, and before she left the capital on her mission she decided to get her feet wet closer to home. The expectation of simply wandering Diadem with impunity filled her with as much dread as it did joy, and the prospect of visiting the Office of Answers in particular made her squirm—but that was the only place the queen expressly suggested she investigate before departing.

According to the gatekeeper who gave Portolés directions, the most direct route from the warrenlike confines of the Dens to the smoother, orderly halls of the Office of Answers took one on a tour of the capital's tunnel system, traversing steeply arched bridges over ice-rimed sewer canals and causeways that dipped low through fungal gardens. Upon leaving the Upper Chainhouse, one descended five hundred and one steps, and while crossing the Forest of Eternal Sin replaced no fewer than thirteen of the candles that had invariably burned to nubs on the countless stalactites. Then a climb of precisely five hundred steps to the black rattan gate that separated the Papal territories of Castle Diadem from the Imperial.

Sister Portolés opted to deviate from this course at the first opportunity, offering the necessary salutes and signals for the wardens to let her pass out of the surrounding walls and into the city. This exchange of time-honored gestures was more or less a formality, as the wardens' purpose was to prevent citizens from getting into the citadel, rather than to forestall officers of church or state from leaving it. The outer door opened, and beyond it lay the bursting city of Diadem.

Wide as the caldera stretched, the five-hundred-year-old settlement had quickly spread from its heart to crowd the whole expanse, until there was nowhere left to build but up. Risky business, that, both practically and socially—climb too high too quickly and your better-born neighbors might sabotage your foundations in the night. No wonder even the fickle serfs here in the capital had rallied behind the Stricken Queen, after she'd opened up the dry, spacious caverns of Castle Diadem for public use. That reform had outlived the doomed despot for all of a week, before Queen Indsorith and Pope Shanatu ran them back outside into the gloomy city. According to the older anathemas in the Dens who had lived through those tumultuous times, it had taken months for the stink of false hope and abject poverty to fade from the interior.

Stepping down the black stairs into the black mud of the streets,

Portolés smiled up into the black rain that fell onto the black cloth mask her kind wore when interacting with the pureborn. In the capital, anyway; the army put a stop to that practice as soon as they were a dozen miles outside Diadem's walls—allowing masked figures free range of your camp was asking for trouble.

Even after all these hallowed centuries since the first frame was raised, the walls of every tall, teetering building bled black in the rain, the ash of this sacred ground permeating every timber, brick, and shingle. The only color to be seen in the whole place was the steel blue scraps of storm cloud Portolés made out through chinks in the tightly clustered eaves far above her. From down here it was impossible to see the gay garments the upper classes supposedly wore to spite the grey heavens as they traversed their covered catwalks, and down here the hunched citizens thronging the narrow streets she passed through were draped in dark oilcloth robes not dissimilar from her habit. None but Portolés wore the mask of the witchborn, though, and passersby gave her a wide berth in even the tightest alley between listing estates that stretched close to a hundred feet into the air, the structures rocking ever so slightly in the keening wind. It was dimmer here, now, at midday beneath the open sky, than it ever got in the candlelit grottos of the Dens.

Portolés meandered through the ghettos of Raniputri and Usban, ate a flatfish tsire handpie she purchased from a Flintlander's cart, nodded her curt approval to a gaggle of shriven and branded Immaculate converts praying in the muck beside a line of penitents waiting to be admitted to the West Cathedral. Ashy mud plastered her sandaled feet until they resembled boots. At last, stuck to an announcement board on the covered porch of a condemned tavern, she found what she had sought: a bill printed on a drab sheet of rag paper. Two words that made the sister run hot then cold, her eyes flitting all about the dreary backstreet in nervous guilt, as though she had been the one to stick up the flyer.

ZOSIA LIVES!

There were several bundled figures lying on the porch, and once she was sure they were truly asleep Portolés reached for the bill with shaking fingers, as though it might scald her. It peeled back from the soft, damp board like an almost-ripe scab coming loose under a persistent fingernail. Folding and slipping the bill down her habit so that it was lodged in the binding that held her sweaty left breast, she hurried away. This was the sort of thing the queen had suggested she retrieve from the Office of Answers, but before she braved that dread department she had wanted to see for herself if the revolutionary propaganda was as prevalent in the wild as Her Majesty had suggested...And lo, it had taken only a bit of wandering around until she'd stumbled onto the bill, the search nowhere near so arduous as she'd expected.

Not that Portolés had possessed any cause to disbelieve Queen Indsorith on this matter, or any other, but ever since Kypck the war nun had been unable to stop herself from doubting virtually everything. This pervasive uncertainty was part of why she had agreed to honor the vows she had made to her queen, instead of those she had made to her church—Queen Indsorith alone had agreed with her that it was a sin to have executed those villagers and the disobedient soldiers, no matter who gave the order. Prior to this surprisingly liberating confirmation of Portolés's culpability, every single superior she had confessed to was primarily concerned that one of the Chain's anathemas had let an Imperial colonel die under her watch. Everything was backward, the Queen of Samoth quietly reflecting on spiritual matters while the Pope of the Burnished Chain raged over military failings.

In the end it was her doubt that propelled Portolés into the decisions she had made, decisions that had seemed so easy at the time but now stunned her with their enormity. Did her loyalty to her queen make her a traitor to her church? To the Fallen Mother? It was an unnerving experience, to trust in her intuition, as the queen had urged her, when all her life she had been taught that her impulses were not her own, that they came from the Deceiver to ensnare her soul. Yet here she had taken a first faltering step down that road, beginning her search out in the muddy streets instead of where the queen had suggested, and by giving in to her instinct she now had one less doubt to tax her cluttered skull. Curiosity, it seemed, might have its uses, despite how fervently the Chain derided that sin above all others.

She realized she had become lost, the anonymous streets giving up no hint as to which direction she stomped, and she paused at a mucky intersection. As soon as the panic of not knowing tightened her chest, though, she blew it out like so much bad air—Diadem was a ring, albeit an enormous one, and so long as she plodded forward she would find her way back to the castle in time. As if that wasn't the heaviest symbol ever to be wrought in stained glass, she thought with a smile.

Far in as she'd come, it took some time for her to get back out to the edge of town and reenter the castle. Several times as she passed higher and higher into Diadem's flanks she touched the bill that rested atop her heart; when offering the queen's writ to the guards who frequently barred her way she imagined giving them the flyer instead. She couldn't decide if those two words printed upon it were simply treason, or outright heresy.

When she was at last admitted to the open floor of the Office of Answers' Truth Chamber, the dozens of people undergoing questioning caused her stair-winded breath to catch in her tight chest. Considering there were far more individuals strapped to gurneys and chairs than there were Askers to tend them, the Office must be a bit understaffed at present.

"Raided a cell in Lower Leviathania," supplied the sweaty young clerk charged with chaperoning Portolés. "Usually we don't cram them in like this, but the holding pens are overfull, so we're making do."

Like all in the Office of Answers, he went naked while in the stiflingly warm Truth Chamber. The Askers had nothing to hide from their guests. By the light of the azure-flamed braziers reflecting off the polished floor of volcanic glass, Portolés eyed him for signs of deviltry, though she knew witchborn were forbidden from serving in the Office. That was not the way the state conducted itself. Portolés, on a real roll with thoughts both heretical and treasonous, wondered briefly if the Office would feel the same if those anathemas who could supposedly peek into minds could do so with strangers instead of only those with whom they were already intimate.

Regardless, everyone seemed to be predicting Portolés's thoughts of late, and it was making her paranoid. She jumped when an old woman's scream choked off into a gurgle as her tongue was removed with burnished shears that looked much like those used by the Papal barbers to heal the witchborn. Looking around at the other instruments in use or laid out on tables, and the dark swirling pools flowing into the numerous floor grates, she found much to compare with the operating theater where she had been rendered as pure as the church could make her. Bad memories surged up in her gorge...or maybe it was just the peanuty flatfish she'd eaten.

"They were all caught in the act?" she asked.

"A few ringleaders, and a lot of folk just looking for easy work or a dry bed." The clerk sighed. "It's always like this. Don't worry, sister, most of them will be turned over to your people soon enough."

"And all this was found in their quarters?" Portolés's heart tapped at the bill resting above it as she surveyed the table piled high with identical leaflets and several aged, weatherworn folios. "Propaganda?"

"That's one word for it," said the clerk. "I'm sure you'd call it something else. Was there someone in particular we could help you find? Even if they are not here we could have them to you in hours, I assure you."

Portolés picked up one of the folios, flipped through it, tossed it down, and picked up another. Beneath the mask that limply clung to her sweaty face she could feel her cheeks burn from more than the heat. The name of the Stricken Queen, appearing over and over, on every page...Surely the authors had known their words could land them here, and yet the text spoke to their fearlessness. Fearlessness, or a need to put it down in ink, regardless of the cost. The vellum folio in her hands was only half written, waiting to be completed in the cramped yet precise script—did the author still have her fingers, or were they already in a vise?

"I'm taking this," she said, as much to herself as to the clerk. "Do you need to make note of that before I take my leave?"

"Revered Sister, you can't—" the clerk began, then amended himself when she glanced up from the book. "That is, the Office, under direct orders of the queen, has immediate need of it. I will personally copy its contents for you and—"

"Do I need to show you my writ again, boy?" said Portolés, flushing anew with the overconfident words.

"No, Revered Sister," said the clerk, looking at his bare feet.

This was the extent of the power her queen had granted Portolés. It was staggering. She might die on the morrow, but for today she, an anathema, had authority unrivaled by any save the Crimson Queen or the Black Pope. By any means necessary meant by any means she wished, and pity the pureborn who questioned her will. Out of habit she tried to choke down her smile, but then reminded herself she was entitled to grin from ear to ear.

"I also wish to speak with the author. Someone here wrote it, yes?"

"We won't know that unless we are permitted to use it in our questioning, will we?" said the clerk with a bit more attitude than Portolés expected. It was a fair point, though.

"I did," called a teenage youth strapped to a nearby gurney. He had the ferret-eyed, rawboned look of a natural born thief to him. He leered at her. "You like my tract, witch-nun? It's all the Fallen Mom's honest truth, every blessed word of it, and—"

"That's quite enough of that," said the Asker who had been quietly talking with the woman in the next chair over. He was a scrawny man whose shaven genitals were blurred by bright red tattoos of Cascadian script, and he jabbed at the gurneyed man with his dripping three-pronged prompter. "I already have quite a few queries for you; no sense in raising more questions before we've even started."

"Believe!" said the boy. "Take off those blinders they force your kind to wear, witch-nun, read the truth and decide for yourself!"

"I'm very sorry, we'll have to continue this later," the Asker quietly told the semiconscious woman he'd been interrogating. "As for you, young man—"

"What harm would it be were it false?" cried the boy, his eyes still locked on the slits in Portolés's mask. "When's a lie ever called down such consequences, answer me that!"

Portolés had no more expected profundity in the Office of Answers than she had subtlety, but she found herself deeply moved by the boy's appeal. In this roomful of tortured dissidents and Askers employed by the Crown, only she knew that what the flyer said was true: Zosia lived, and what was more, Portolés had probably met her face-to-face in Kypck. In twenty years of rule, Queen Indsorith had told no one of the deception that had fooled the world, and only confided in Portolés because she believed that doing so could prevent another war. These rebels couldn't actually believe Zosia had survived her two-thousand-foot fall from the Crimson Throne Room and was biding her time until she launched a second Cobalt War. Their slogan of *Zosia Lives!* was just that, an anthem designed to fill their fellows with hope and their enemies with hatred...But like the boy said, if the Empire knew their rabble-rousing came from baseless beliefs, why suppress it so viciously? The queen knew there was more than a kernel of truth in their message, and this was how she dealt with it—the same way the Burnished Chain dealt with anathemas. Doubt blossomed anew in Portolés's heart as she realized that her new master could be every bit as brutal as her old one, when she felt threatened. Queen Indsorith had claimed that the mission she entrusted to Portolés would save countless lives across the Star, but even if that proved true, Portolés couldn't save the poor, naïve sinners in this room.

"You seem to be confused on the etiquette of polite discourse," the Asker told the outspoken prisoner, looming over his gurney and softly applying the points of his prompter to the ball of the youth's throat. "*I* ask, *you* answer, not the other way around. But since you're so eager to converse, why don't we just dive right in?"

For all his bluster, the young man closed his eyes and let out a whimper. He would be making a lot more noise before long. Portolés had screamed and screamed when the barbers had carved the sin out of her, screamed until they had seized her forked tongue and stitched it together, blood gurgling in the back of her throat. This heretic was going to scream, too, but with no physical signs of corruption, how would the Asker know when his work was complete? As the steel prompter reflected the brazier light, Portolés felt a flashback of fear, and just as soon a pulse of relief that it was someone else who was going to be cut instead of her. Back in the Kutumban mountains, she had executed men and women who refused to massacre peasants, and then she had overseen the purge of Kypck, and then she had watched as an Imperial colonel burned alive, but she was going to turn around and walk out of here, and this boy who had only written a political treatise probably wouldn't. Perhaps the Crimson Queen's justice wasn't so different from the Black Pope's.

"Sister?" said the clerk, reaching out for Portolés's elbow but thinking better of actually touching her.

"Mmmm," said Portolés, picturing Brother Wan strapped down where the heretic was, imagining the sounds he must have made when they removed his half-formed beak. Just like that, it happened, the anticipation of a new sin warming her chest.

"It would be best if we left Asker Vexovoid to do the queen's work. I can escort you out."

"Certainly." Portolés nodded, savoring the sensation of delay until it became unbearable. "As soon as you unstrap that heretic. He's coming with me."

Of all of them, the heretic seemed the most surprised. Asker Vexovoid ground his jaw so loudly that Portolés could hear him, but sheathed his prompter and began loosening the boy. The clerk just scowled at her. As the shock wore off, the heretic giggled nervously.

"It's no laughing matter," the Asker told him. "You'll be wishing you'd kept your mouth shut before the end. Our Mother Church has a very different methodology for gathering intelligence than this office."

"I'm not going to strip before I torture you, is what he means," said Portolés, pleased to see Asker Vexovoid's sour expression now matching that of the clerk. Already she doubted her snap decision, as she always did when she had crested the trespass and was left with nothing but the promise of penance. "I'm in a hurry, so let's get a move on."

"Would you like him like this, or is there something more the Office can do for you, sister?" asked the clerk as the heretic clambered down from the gurney and Asker Vexovoid turned away without a polite farewell.

"I would like some pants, if it's not too much trouble," said the heretic, cupping his shaking hands over his groin.

"Manacles on his wrists and ankles, connected to each other, and to a collar. Three extra locks. The same key for all of them. A long chain tether fixed to his collar. A gag in his gob and a blindfold under his hood. Plain robe," said Portolés, and then decided to be charitable. They were going to be riding for some time. "Undergarments, I suppose."

The heretic might be useful. Even if he'd been lying about writing the tract and just taken the credit to get her attention, if he'd been brought to the Office of Answers he surely knew more of the cultish veneration of the Stricken Queen than Portolés did. Any knowledge he possessed might prove valuable as she embarked on her quest to track down the woman who had escaped Kypck, the woman Queen Indsorith believed to be Cobalt Zosia. Besides, Portolés could always kill the man if he turned out to be of no use to her. She could kill him for no reason at all, if she wanted—that was the power of the authority the Crimson Queen had given her.

So she told herself, but these thoughts only took form after she had saved him from the Office of Answers.

It was after sunset and still raining when Diadem's southern gate opened for them several hours later. There was something sublimely absurd in the hundred-foot-tall, ten-foot-thick iron-banded gate rolling back just for two riders and a pack mule. The thousand soldiers who worked the winches doubtless agreed—not for nothing was the southern gate normally opened but once a day, to admit travelers during the noon hour.

The heretic had to ride sidesaddle since Portolés refused to unlock his ankle chains, but any protest he might have leveled failed to clear the gag. Their way was lit by sputtering sapphire flames of burning gas that rose from the mountain via tubes of carven obsidian flanking the wide road, torches that had never gone out since first lit at the dawn of Diadem, even in blizzard or hurricane.

Midnight found them at the last torch, and Portolés hitched their animals at the way temple beside the final beacon. It was a humble yet large one-room chamber carved into the dead rock. Only the clergy were permitted to use the refuges that spotted the Imperial highways, but based on the bashed-in door and heaps of excrement on the broken penitence bench, others had sought shelter here. Tonight, however, they had the place to themselves, and intending to keep it that way, Portolés used the ruined bench to bar the door.

"I could've died!" the youth said as soon as the gag was out, shaking his manacled hands at her. "Can't breathe good through my nose normal-like, say fuck the devils with a wet hood over my face!"

"Say fuck the devils again and I'll put it back in," said Portolés, pulling her own damp mask off and tossing it carelessly on their heaped provisions. She returned to the fire she'd kindled in the potbellied stove before tending to her prisoner. The wood let off the strong odor of urine as it burned. "My name is Sister Portolés. You will address me at all times with the respect my station commands."

"Sure, sister, the respect of your station," said the heretic, scooting on his butt over toward the fire, the chains around his ankles and wrists jingling. "Not that you asked, but my name is—"

"I will call you Heretic," said Portolés, deeply unhappy with herself for the mad compulsion that had led her to take him along. "Count yourself blessed I can call you anything other than the memory of a doomed man I left behind in the Office of Answers."

"Whatever you say," said Heretic, warming his hands. "You're the boss, I'm the heretic. Got it."

Heretic had the sense to stay quiet while Portolés boiled water to soak seaweed and beancurd in, and then they ate in silence, slurping from plain wooden bowls. Camping like this reminded her of being out in the field on campaign, first against the Imperials and then alongside them. The marked difference was that it was just her and a single other soul settling in for the night, instead of a whole regiment, and she felt an unexpected tremor of lonesomeness—she was often alone in her cell, of course, but she could never remember a time when there weren't legions of other people within shouting distance, either in Diadem or on campaign. Now it was just her and a proven criminal for miles and miles.

After they'd eaten, she looped Heretic's chain leash around the base of the stove, back through his manacles, and then secured it with one of the spare locks. He wouldn't be comfortable, bent up like that, but he would be warm.

"This isn't necessary," said Heretic. "Really!"

"The sooner you stop hoping I'm a fool the sooner you will find peace in your fate," said Portolés, stretching out to her full length on the other side of the stove. Well, he might think her a fool, given her decision to take him into her custody. When Queen Indsorith had given the war nun permission to enlist anyone she felt would help her find Zosia, so long as she kept the nature of her mission a secret, Portolés rather doubted Her Majesty could have foreseen this ill-advised conscript. This was the exact sort of thing that had always landed her the worst penance, snatching at forbidden fruit just to see what it tasted like. Mother Kylesa and Abbotess Cradofil and even Brother Wan had always warned her there would come a day when she fell too far to climb up again.

She pulled out the heretic's book to distract her from the relentless guilt that constricted her throat. No matter how convinced she was at the time that her actions were correct, within in a few hours she always arrived at this place, craving confession even worse than she had craved whatever temptation she had succumbed to. Except now she no longer even had the prospect of confession to assuage her fears—Queen Indsorith had convinced her that once she left Diadem, it would be incredibly dangerous for her to meet with any other clergy, lest word of her location reach the Black Pope and arouse her suspicions.

"This isn't what I expected," said Heretic. "You hear a lot of stories, sure, but I never...I mean, where are you taking me? Can I know that? Are you gonna publicly execute me in some dismal corner of the Empire? As an example, like?"

"Hmmm," said Portolés, opting to put another log on before settling in with the folio.

"No, that don't make sense," Heretic decided. "Maybe—"

"Heretic," said Portolés, sitting back on her bedroll and glaring at the scruffy embodiment of all her questionable decisions.

"Yes, Sister Portolés?"

"If you say another word without being spoken to I'll put your gag back in, and leave it there all night."

"Mmmmmmm," said Heretic peevishly, but he spoke no more.

As she finally settled in to read, Portolés felt some of her anxiety burn off into giddiness. Reading the contents of this tract was obviously a crime against both Crown and Chain, and it was hers to savor. What an ominous pair of days she had lived through. Who knew letting that nasty Colonel Hjortt burn to death would upend her life in such a radical direction? The Fallen Mother, obviously, and the Deceiver, surely, but not Portolés. She opened the book and read the first two pages, pages that held more heresy than she had ever thought possible to contain in such a scant space.

Look! Listen! Harken! Your Very Life is at Stake!

Look here, You! Look with Your Own Eyes! And if You be Blind, put then Your Ears to the Lips of the Wise, and Listen! Listen! However you Come to this Truth, the Only Truth in Diadem, Ponder Upon It, and do so with Your Mind. The Mind that is Yours and Only Yours. Feel the Truth with Your Heart, the Heart that is Only Yours.

Decide for Yourself. You Must Decide for Yourself.

You Bow before queen and pope. You Believe Them. You Sacrifice Yourself to them, You Sacrifice Your Children to them, Your Spouses, Your Animals, All Your Worldly Possessions. They Say this is the Price. The Price for what, We ask you? Protection of Your Body, Protection of Your Soul, that is their answer. This is The Lie.

It was Not Always So. The Burnished Chain speaks of a Deceiver in Heaven. There is a Deceiver, but he is not in Heaven, but Here, on the Star, in Diadem!

The Burnished Chain speaks of a Savior in Hell. And this is the Lie, coached in The Truth: our Savior came to liberate Diadem, and it was the Burnished Chain who cast her Down.

Queen Zosia Believed in a Diadem Free of Chains. Queen Zosia fought the Devils we now Bow before. Queen Zosia fought to Free Us. If we are Worthy of Freedom, should we Accept the Yoke of Corrupt Church and Illegitimate Queen?

If You Deserve Freedom, True Freedom to Live As You Wilt, Why Do You Wear the Collar of Your Oppressors?

Fear is the Answer. Fear for Yourself. Fear for Your Family. Fear for Your Soul.

Fear is the Sword and Scepter of the Church and the Crown. Fear is the Shackles Upon Your Limbs. Fear is the Blindfold You Wear. Fear is the Poison in Your porridge, making You Sick. Making You Die. The pope Laughs as You Weep. She drinks Your Tears. The queen smacks Her lips as You Work Yourself to Death. She drinks Your Blood.

All they Bring Us is War. War Against Whom? Barbarians to the East? Immaculates to the West? Raniputri Dominions or the Free Cities of Usba? No. They Bring War Against Ourselves. They Say Peace has been Bought, At Last, but how Many lie Dead from a Childlike Squabble between queen and pope? You Know Innocents Who Died in this War, do You not?

You, reading This Truth. You, Hearing This Truth. Answer True: how many of Your Loved Ones Perished in a Senseless War? You Tithe and You Tithe and You Tithe, All to Fund a War Against Your Own Family.

This is The Lie. The Same Tongues who spread The Lie also Claim that Queen Zosia is twenty years Dead. Do You Believe? Do You Trust the liars who Grind You to Dust? Do You Believe Queen Zosia and All She stood for can Ever Die?

There are Those Who Believe. There are Those Who Do Not. The Truth is Not that One is Right and the Other Wrong. The Truth is that Queen Zosia Lives On. Her Breath Stirs the Coals of Freedom. The Fire She kindled when She took the Throne is Dying, but is not yet Extinguished.

Does Zosia Yet Live? some ask. Did She Ever? say others.

This is not The Truth. The Truth is that She is With Us, and if We are Strong, She will Aid Us. But We must be Strong before She Returns.

There is Time. To Save Our City. To Save Our Empire. To Save Our Souls.

Stand Against the Dark. Fight Against the Dark. Stand Against the Dark.

Listen! Listen, Think, and Prepare. War is Coming, and Not the War They Wanted. We Will Not Stop Until The Cause Our Parents Died For Is Saved. Zosia Exists Forever in Your Heart—Will You Set Her Free?

Portolés closed the book and reflected for a very long time on what she had read. Then she took out the bill she had removed from the tavern wall and carefully unfolded the damp paper by the low light of the dying fire. She had seen hundreds of duplicates stacked on the table in the Truth Chamber, but still the sight of the poster sent shudders coursing through her. Even after all the queen had told her, even after seeing how plainly the Deceiver's wiles were at play in the text she had just read, these two words filled Sister Portolés with a churning, burning mixture of dread and, Allmother forgive her, excitement.

Could it be true?

Could it not, given what she now knew? A week ago the Stricken Queen had meant absolutely nothing to Portolés, a blot that both Crown and Chain agreed should be scrubbed from Imperial history.

She had never suspected that peasants the Star over apparently clung to the woman's memory, praised her as a holy symbol of resistance, and were tortured for it whenever they were caught. And most incredible of all, these dissidents were right, more right than even they suspected. Even when the fire died completely the words on the flyer floated before Portolés's vision, tattooing themselves upon her eyes:

ZOSIA LIVES!

PART II

AND THE DEVILS TO GRANT THEM

I wish to leave the world
By its natural door;
In my tomb of green leaves
They are to carry me to die.
Do not put me in the dark
To die like a traitor;
I am good, and like a good thing
I will die with my face to the sun.
　　　　　　　—José Martí,
　　　"A Morir" (To Die) (1894)

CHAPTER
1

In the plush backroom of a Zygnema stinghouse, Zosia battled Chevaleresse Singh. Neither Keun-ju nor Singh's crew were foolish enough to intervene, the Virtue Guard and the masked women side-stepping when necessary to avoid the fray. Zosia wouldn't have bet on herself in a fair fight, dead gods knew, but when a combatant is a devil up on her foe, well, that changes things. Or at least it ought to. The question was whether Singh had actually set Anklelance free in the decades since they had last seen one another, as Zosia hoped, or if the woman's devil was secreted beneath the pillows strewn around the room, waiting to strike her calf. Of all the ill-starred luck, to be saddled with a dingo of a devil when your second in command lands a carrion viper...

Singh fought like a devil, but Zosia fought like a witch trying to bind one. After Zosia's sucker punch failed to drop her, Singh tried to keep her at a distance, pummeling the older woman with her longer limbs. Zosia careened through the onslaught, deflecting what she could with her ropy forearms and shrugging off what she couldn't. She got in close, firing a chain of punches right into Singh's stomach, chest, and throat. It felt like hitting a shield, only harder.

Singh popped her knee up between them, uppercutting Zosia's left breast. Then she tackled Zosia to the ground, legs and arms coiling around her like a funnel python's rubbery tentacles and locking into place. The crook of Singh's elbow choked her, and through watering eyes Zosia looked for Choplicker. This was it. Her devil was nowhere to be seen, and no matter how she contorted herself or how viciously she jabbed with her elbows, Singh only bore down harder.

Zosia panicked. This sort of end had always been a possibility, and she'd always imagined herself going with dignity, maybe a wry last word to her executioner, but now that it was really happening she couldn't help herself. The more the strength went out of her the harder she raged, choking herself even worse in the process. What a way to go—throttled by one of your best friends, universally reviled to such a degree that even the devil bound to you would rather suffer an eternity of imprisonment over your grave than intervene to save you. Perhaps Choplicker knew she would never set him free, even if he helped her now, and so sought to get it over with rather than prolonging the inevitable...

Zosia realized these were dream musings, that her throat no longer burned, that she had floated away from Singh, from the stinghouse, from the Star. Untethered, she drifted through a moonless, starless sky...or the depths of a lightless sea. As soon as it occurred to her that she was dying, or maybe even already dead, the Diadem Gate appeared before her, the alabaster rim luminous even without sun or moon to reflect upon its etched surface. Beyond that border a deeper darkness rippled, and something colder and more primal than even the fear of death filled her lungs, stopped her heart, and caused her to impotently claw and kick the void around her as she floated inexorably toward the Gate.

Singh slapped her awake, gently-like. "Ups time, Queenie. This isn't that sort of fairy tale."

"Buh!" Zosia rasped, sitting up and shivering. They were still in the bugroom, Singh's lined face highlighted by the chaotic dimming and brightening of the firewings in the terrarium above Zosia's pillowy bower. Keun-ju and Singh's guards had left, but Choplicker remained, the furry piece of shit lying on the far side of the room, watching them. She spit blood at him, and said, "Didn't think it was possible you could hate me as much as I hate you."

Singh followed her gaze. "Devils see further and farther than mortals, you of all people know this. He wouldn't have let me kill you. No devil is *that* stubborn."

"That's what you say," said Zosia, blinking the cup in Singh's hand into focus and taking it in her own shaking fingers. Honeyed water. Warmer than she liked, and it hurt to swallow, but it soothed her raw throat. "You ever heard of a devil turning down its freedom?"

"Never," said Singh. "But they are not gods, Zosia—if a devil cannot fulfill a wish, it cannot fulfill a wish. Have you thought about why it might not have been attainable?"

"If I knew why, I'd be long shy of him," Zosia said darkly, raising her voice to make sure he heard. "Whatever his reasons, I don't think my wish was asking much at all, powerful as Hoartrap said he was. I'm starting to think the fucker's got a high opinion of himself, is holding out for a request worthy of his regard. Joke's on him, because the more I think on it the more I've come to realize the thing I want most in the whole wide world is to pay him back for all the heartache he's given me. I hope he's there when I go, so I can look him in the eye before leaving his worthless hide to rot for all time in a hell of his own making."

The silence stretched on after this pronouncement, kept stretching as if it might extend forever. Singh broke it by reaching over and hugging Zosia, saying, "Oh, sister, how I've missed you. I wore white for the week after I heard about Leib and your people, and had my sons prepare them a banquet in the Kitchen of the Gods. I am overjoyed to see you alive and hale, but would have preferred to think you dead, so long as you and yours were living happy lives."

"Thanks," said Zosia, wincing as she straightened up on the pillows. Singh had really nailed her in the tit. "Good to be missed, especially if this is the welcome I get when I visit."

"You struck me, Zosia, and in front of my children—I should have taken it, thanked you, and asked to kiss your bottom?" Singh stood and went to one of the terrariums built into the walls. "I'll get you something for the pain."

"No thanks," said Zosia. "You said Kang-ho sent you to kill me,

Singh, what should *I* have done? Next time, open with 'I'm not going to do it, but here's what's up.' Save us both some bruises."

"I'm not bruised," said Singh, shuddering on a long, fine-mailed glove and sliding open a panel above the glass cage. "And I would have hoped you'd trust me, after all we've been through. I owe you my life, General, a dozen times over."

"So does Kang-ho, and he still tried to get me dead. Maybe to his thinking if you did the backstabbing for him it wouldn't count." Talk Singh into helping, track down Fennec and Princess Ji-hyeon, ransom the girl back to Hwabun, screw Kang-ho over in the process, and then hit Samoth and its evil queen with everything she had. That order. Oh, and Bang—that punkass pirate needed to get hers, too. "I told you I don't want any bugs, Singh, don't make this weird."

Singh had reached into a narrow terrarium and, tapping her mailed pinky on the leaves of a nettle, enticed a sinuous insect from its hiding place on the plant's stem. The centipede darted forward, burying its head in the mail and coiling itself around the finger. Singh cautiously raised her hand from the glass cage and held the centipede-wrapped pinky up to her pursed lips. She slowly brushed the creature's downy back against her mouth, her lips puffing out in bright magenta blooms as she returned the insect to its enclosure and gently thumbed it off its perch. "Mmmmmm. That's much better."

"And here I'd heard Maroto was the one who'd gone buggy."

"Oh gods, Maroto! That's a tragic case, all right—Kang-ho told you what happened to him, then?"

"Only that he didn't stay on with the new queen," said Zosia, still marveling that of all her Villains Maroto had been the one to ignore her will and thrown down in her memory. "Kang-ho said you and Hoartrap were the only ones who followed orders on that count."

"Don't remind me," said Singh, swaying back over to where Zosia sat and plopping down in the cushions beside her. She rooted around and retrieved a pillow that turned out to be a thickly padded pipe-purse. "You want to borrow one of mine? I sent your things off with your boy, and I'm guessing you don't want him listening in, if he's one of Kang-ho's."

"Definitely. On the pipe, I mean, not so sure about the boy working for Kang-ho," said Zosia. "Whatever you're puffing is good—too much to hope you still have that devil I whittled you?"

"Keśi rides," said Singh, passing over the pipe Zosia had carved her during the Siege of Rondio. Whereas most of the pieces Zosia crafted aspired to beauty, Singh had expressly asked her to carve an eyesore; a pretty pipe was both provocation to pride and a target for thieves, but a beater would invite no such attention. Zosia obliged the knight, first shaping the finest billiard she had ever wrestled from the briar, and then scuffing and scratching and chipping away at it until it looked like an animal had chewed it. Instead of leaving it natural or giving it a traditional stain, she colored it sickly yellow, highlighted with splotches of green and white. The finishing touch was a short, slightly crooked stem whittled from the tusk of a devil horse they had brought down together in the acid-dripping jungles of the Forsaken Empire.

"I made the walls too thin," said Zosia, inspecting the pipe. "This must smoke hotter than a devil's fart."

"Reminds me to pace myself," said Singh, retrieving a handsome meerschaum pipe from the purse for herself. The bowl was intricately carved in the shape of a woman's face. Peering closer, Zosia saw it was modeled after Singh right down to the mustache. Heavy usage had darkened the white clay, browning it like good toast and making the resemblance uncanny. So much for chivalric humility. Singh waved it at her. "Outlandish, isn't it? The kids got it for me when I turned fifty, and I'm ashamed to say I've been relying on it of late. You don't have to rest it like briar, so on days when I need a few bowls to see me through she's a welcome sister."

Singh sliced medallions off a tawny rope of palm-wine-infused tubāq and tossed two of them to Zosia, who rubbed hers out before packing Keśi. Singh simply folded hers into the meerschaum bowl. If Zosia had been smoking with any of the other Villains she would have insisted they switch pipes now, given the trick Kang-ho had pulled on her, but Singh would never stoop to such treachery. Not if she didn't have to, anyway, and if she'd wanted to drug

Zosia she could have shoved her nose full of icebees while she was choked out.

Zosia gladly accepted the glass lamp and whangee tamp Singh offered, and once they both had their pipes well lit they relaxed back in their pillow piles and smoked in contented silence. Zosia knew sooner or later they would talk, and when they did she might not like what Singh had to say, so it was better to prolong this rare happiness as long as possible. The back of her mind roiled with a dozen questions, a hundred suspicious, but she shut them out to again bask in the companionable quiet she and Singh always found together. Not even the throbbing ache in her breast could detract from the experience. When her thirst got the better of her and she sat up to ask her host to send for a draught, Singh seemed to read her thoughts and before she could speak tugged on a bell rope. They grinned at one another through the spicy fog, it becoming a competition to see who would crack first, but it wasn't until a turbaned woman brought in a low table and a bareheaded, bun-wearing man followed with a laden tea tray that Zosia broke the silence.

"Thank you both, truly." Looking to Singh, she asked, "Yours?"

"Sriram, my second son, and Udbala, my third daughter."

"You honor me, Mahārājñī Zosia," the two said in unison, each taking a knee.

"Your kids, all right," said Zosia. "Enough of that, you two, no bowing to me. Not unless your mother does first."

The son looked confused by this, the daughter looked insulted, but Singh just waved them off. "Make sure our other guest is being looked after. And if I see you chewing betel in my house again, Udbala, I'll really make that mouth red."

Zosia waited until the children had left before saying, "I thought your teeth looked pretty clean."

"Quit gnawing that trash years ago," said Singh, pouring the chai and retrieving the pipe from where she had propped it against the tray. "Even now, though, I see them spit and I get the old craving. Hard to believe I used to have more spittoons than pipes."

"Good-looking kids—there were four girls in here when Keun-ju and I arrived; they all yours?"

"Only Udbala, the other three are nieces. My twins aren't speaking to me right now—I wouldn't support a harebrained campaign they were launching against a nearby Dominion. Even though I tried to talk them out of it they blame me for their failure. It's just too stupid for words."

"Free counsel can be pretty expensive, if you don't heed it," said Zosia.

"Hmmm," said Singh, relighting her pipe while Zosia sipped the buttery tea. "That sounds like a wise saying, but I'm not sure it actually makes much sense. Anyway, the girls are good, other than being brats. I also have a pair of sons who haven't done anything too idiotic of late. My eldest, Masood, is fomenting a rebellion in Thantifax, the capital of the next Dominion over. That's another reason Umhur and Urbar are mad at me; they think I'm playing favorites by casting my lot with him but not them. Ugh. This stinghouse belongs to the other one you just met, Sriram. It's a cover to launder money for the Dull Kriss, a revolutionary faction that we're steering away from Zygnema by offering them stakes in Thantifax."

"The nut doesn't fall far from the bush, I guess," said Zosia, biting into a biscuit. "Five kids sounds like a lot. How do you find time to work?"

"The grandchildren are where things get complicated," said Singh. "When it was just my brood, it was easy—I rode an elephant into Daar with a twin on each tit, and their father looked after them when I rappelled down the side to accept a challenge from the raja we were unseating. It's a hassle to duel with a big belly and your dugs all sore and leaking, to be sure, but it's better than fighting with a broken leg or arm, and we've both done that well enough. The grandchildren, though, for some reason I get nervous around them, more nervous than I ever was with mine. They stay with a nurse rather than riding with us into battle, and the whole blessed time I'm worrying about what might go wrong back at home—what if the nanny doesn't let the milk cool, that sort of thing. Stop smiling, it's embarrassing!"

"I'm glad you've done so well for yourself," said Zosia, and though she meant it with all her heart there came hot on its heels another thought, a darker one. Why were Singh and Kang-ho allowed to start over, in plain sight and with any riches they'd plundered from the Crimson Empire, when she and Leib had forsaken everything, even her name, and were still punished absolutely?

This wasn't a rhetorical question—*woe is Zosia, where is the justice in the world*, that kind of shit. Zosia had been queen for a full year before becoming so depressed with her ineffectuality that she preferred to fake her own death rather than continue to rule, so she would never begrudge the devils for her ill fortune, or an old friend for her better luck. No, the question of why Kang-ho and Singh were doing so well, living under their own names, demanded an answer. If Zosia had been in Indsorith's position, she would have targeted each of the Five Villains first, and only when they had all been brought down would she have gone after their leader. The captains would be easier to find, for one thing, and if the assassination of their general failed, as it had, she would not have been able to fall back on her Villains for aid. It was so obvious an oversight that it gave her pause, until she remembered what Kang-ho had said about the aftermath of her abdication—Singh and Hoartrap had helped Indsorith solidify her rule. Odds were Kang-ho had been less than forthcoming about his own involvement in aiding Indsorith...

"Kang-ho wants me dead," said Zosia, grimacing at the thought. If she couldn't trust him, how could she trust any of the Villains? Other than Maroto, anyway—it sounded like he had kept the faith...but even if he hadn't fallen off the way the others claimed, she would prefer to go it alone than waste time hunting him down for dubious reward. And really, if Singh was working the same angles as Kang-ho, Zosia would already be dead. "Chevaleresse, give me your word of honor you're not working for Queen Indsorith."

"Given," said Singh. "I left her employ some fifteen years past, and only stayed on as long as I did because it was the dying wish of my fearless leader that I do so. Remember?"

"Oh, I remember, all right," said Zosia. "But Kang-ho's working for her, that seems obvious now. I wonder if he even has a daughter—maybe everyone from Hwabun has been playing me, even the Virtue Guard."

"Zosia, Zosia, Zosia," said Singh. "You sound paranoid. The daughter's real, I assure you, although I will remind you that just a few minutes ago I cautioned against trusting the Virtue Guard. As for Kang-ho, he made off with a substantial portion of Diadem's treasury shortly after your fall—the queen must hate him even more than she hates Fennec and Maroto. I cannot imagine she is terribly pleased with Hoartrap or myself, either, considering how we left things with her. So the queen found out you were alive and went after you—that's a bad break, no question, but I wouldn't make the matter worse by imagining conspiracies."

"All right then, Singh, did Brother Kang-ho give you any other motive for ordering my assassination?" Choplicker had picked himself up and padded over to beg for a biscuit. He'd be begging for a while.

"I'm sure it has something to do with this," said Singh, hopping up from the pillows with enviable ease and retrieving a large piece of parchment from a drawer in the base of a terrarium. She shot out her hand, launching the paper through the air, and Zosia snatched it as it floated down to her. The chai curdled in her mouth as she saw what it said, and she crumpled the bill in her fist.

"What the devils is this? Kang-ho sent it?"

"No, that one I found down at the customs house—there's a board out front for flyers. They're less common in the Dominions, but I hear in the Empire they're showing up on every corner."

"What's the angle?" said Zosia, unballing the poster to make sure she hadn't missed anything. She hadn't—hard to miss much in two little words. "I don't get it. The queen's the only one who knew, so why...this? She wouldn't put them up; a bounty poster, maybe. Who's announcing my return, and why?"

"Oh, those have been around for years," explained Singh, digging through the drawer for something else. "You've heard that Indsorith banished your name, likeness, and everything else, yes? The Stricken

Queen is how you're referred to, when bringing you up at all is completely unavoidable. So that was a popular slogan for your supporters when Indsorith took over, a petty defiance. Graffiti, nothing more. Over the last year, though, it's become something quite a bit different. A rallying cry."

"My supporters," said Zosia quietly. She hadn't really believed she would be missed at all. Yet over that last year before she overthrew King Kaldruut and crowned herself the Last Queen of Samoth, they must have had fifty thousand peasants behind them, people who abandoned their farms and trades to join her cause—was it so surprising that they had really believed in her? Some of them must have known her failure to institute the Empire-wide equality she had promised stemmed not from selfishness or hypocrisy but the sheer magnitude of the task, with all her efforts snagged in the razor-sharp gears of Imperial bureaucracy. Despite her promises, despite her becoming the *fucking queen*, for the love of the Deceiver, every reform she attempted backfired, her unstable rule further weakened by sabotage from every quarter save the lowest classes—nobles, merchants, and the Chain rallied against her, ancient enemies coming together against the common threat: her.

And what of the peasantry, then? All those people who had needed her to succeed, who had bet everything on her cause, those same citizens now shouted her name in defiance, even though it might cost them their lives, even though she had failed them. All those people whom she had abandoned so that she could hide out in the hills with her favorite hooker... Zosia let herself fall back on the pillows and stared at the insectoid figures carved into the lintel over the door. Just when she thought she'd run out of reasons to be disappointed in herself.

"I didn't do it to be a martyr," she said. "I did it because I was a coward."

"You're many things, sister, but you're not that," said Singh. "Here we are. Take a look at this."

"What is it?" asked Zosia, sitting up and accepting the dossier Singh handed her.

"Everything I have on the Dull Kriss," said Singh, dumping out the dottle from her meerschaum and sitting down to repack it. "All the elements are here—we have the arms, we have the hands to wield them, and we have, at the moment, the support of several powerful cults. But we'll only have one go at it, and if that one push fails, then it will be years before the revolution recovers enough to try again. Assuming we aren't all caught and hanged."

"Sounds like old times." Zosia fingered the ribbon wrapped around the dossier. "Kang-ho wants me dead for reasons you aren't willing to spill, but you want me alive to help you plot your rebellion."

"You possess the greatest mind for tactics I've ever known," said Singh. "Sharpen the Dull Kriss with your advisement, and the Dominions will be all but united. I wonder how useful you would find it to have an entire Arm of the Star in your debt before launching an attack on the Empire?"

"Pretty useful," said Zosia, looking from the dossier to the crumpled flyer on the floor. "But even the best plans go awry."

"You have my word of honor, I will assist you in every way I can, regardless of the revolution's success."

"Well, that's something," said Zosia. "But since Kang-ho's obviously told you all about my plans, you can understand why it makes me nervous that you aren't willing to tell me why he sent you after me. He had me knocked out on his island; why not whack me there and be done with it?"

"I suspect Kang-ho and his spouse are at odds," said Singh. "Who was it that sent you after Princess Ji-hyeon?"

"Huh," said Zosia. "Kang-ho doesn't want his daughter found, does he? All that talk on Hwabun was for the benefit of he who holds the purse strings—Jun-hwan doesn't know his husband helped their daughter run away, does he?"

"If he did I expect the sweetness of affluent domesticity would sour substantially for our old friend."

"So Kang-ho helped his daughter run away, but blamed it on Fennec." Choplicker had surreptitiously scooted closer to the low table with its plate of biscuits. Planting a foot on his shoulder, Zosia smoothly shoved him back to a safe distance. "Clever enough. I wonder if the old fox was even involved."

"Definitely," said Singh. "I met with them both when they arrived here."

"Fennec and Kang-ho?"

"Fennec and Princess Ji-hyeon. There was a third with them, a wildborn woman. They wanted my help, but even if the scheme had seemed tenable, I was then as I am now occupied with my own affairs."

"And what's the scheme?" asked Zosia, relighting her low-burned pipe and taking a few embers to the tongue for the effort. That's what you got for scraping the bottom of the barrel.

"Isn't it obvious?" said Singh as her former general coughed on a mouthful of hot ash. "Zosia lives."

CHAPTER
2

Everything had been progressing smoothly until the Siege of Myura, when a couple more of Ji-hyeon's second father's old friends showed up to complicate things.

Choi's strategy had worked perfectly, the Myuran regiment never expecting Ji-hyeon's troops to charge straight out of the castle and swarm the town. The Red Imperials were caught with their codpieces down, and were routed before they'd had a chance to lace them. Ji-hyeon's pride in yet another decisive victory mingled with unease at just how little fight the Myurans had mustered—she'd barely cut down a dozen enemy soldiers before the whole lot of them fled the town. This unease deepened substantially when Choi regrouped with her after the day was won and insisted Ji-hyeon accompany her through the dusty streets to an old temple where the Imperial command had been centered.

Had. Everything seemed perfectly preserved, the beech pews neatly pushed against the walls to make space in the central chamber for two long tables. The boards were stacked with papers, maps, a small diorama of Castle Myura, and several black bottles. From the look of things, they had been no more than a day or two out from sapping their way inside—the clever bastards had dropped a tunnel straight under a shallow stretch of the river that abutted the castle's northern wall.

Ji-hyeon stepped over impossibly bent and broken weapons to get a better look at the uniforms and boots scattered around the temple. The crimson cloth and light grey kidskin were shredded by wide gashes, curious burns, and tight clusters of countless tiny holes. Instead of incense, the chamber stank of dank, deep earth, freshly tilled. Despite the obvious violence, there was no scrap of the missing officers themselves, what Ji-hyeon had thought to be a lone blood splatter on the gritty tile revealing itself to her fingernail as wax.

Choi seemed as confounded as everyone else, and even without the rest of it, seeing her usually unflappable wildborn ill at ease would have been enough to make Ji-hyeon sweat. She should have known things were going too good to last.

"What a rout! Time to add another verse to the Ballad of…" But whatever song they were to expand with their deeds went untitled as Fennec came in from the street and saw the state of the enemy command. If Choi looked on edge, Fennec appeared to have fallen clear over the side, all the color draining from his tan features and both hands shaking as he reached up and slid his visor shut, as if to insulate himself from further fright. "Oh…oh dear."

"What happened here?" Ji-hyeon asked him, staring up at where an empty scabbard had caught in the exposed rafters.

"I was…That is…Um." Fennec didn't rattle easily, either, and that both he and Choi were so uneasy did not bode well. "I supervised the left flank from the rampart, as you ordered, so this is the first I've seen of…this."

"No it's not." Ji-hyeon had learned that bluntly smashing through his lies was far more effective than trying to outfence her former tutor. "You've seen this before, haven't you? If not here, when? And who?"

"Bide." Choi had a palm up, and knowing the wildborn would never spare Fennec from an unpleasant interrogation without strong cause, Ji-hyeon did as she was asked. Choi's other hand went to the hilt of her sword, and she moved quickly but carefully across the temple floor, as though stepping on the wrong tile would trigger a calamity. Tugging her ear at Fennec, Ji-hyeon followed.

On the street, Choi huffed the air with her narrow nostrils, and immediately led them several blocks to what appeared to be a tavern or inn. The door was barricaded from within, but not for long. A hundred of her best troops backing her up, Ji-hyeon borrowed an ax from an obliging soldier and hacked down the door.

On the other side were a bunch of her dad's old gang. At first, Ji-hyeon thought the old barbarian had died right in front of her, the potbellied, high-haired ruffian staggering away from the table where his fellows sat and then biting the floor right in front of her. He looked in a rough way, to be sure. As soon as he hit the ground a small yet sturdy woman hurried to his aid, her face too freshly battered to determine much about her, save that she was no dark-skinned Flint-lander like her friend.

"My my my," said another old-timer as he looked over his shoulder, unwilling to abandon his card game despite the fact that the other three players had all stood and backed away from the table. These standing players were younger, hard-looking rogues mockingly dressed in shoddy imitation of the Imperial noblesse. One even held a tiny dog to complete the charade. The seated speaker resembled an ogre crafted out of porcelain, only bigger, paler, and uglier. "Fennec, old boy, you never fail to disappoint. This is so much better than I expected!"

"*Captain* Fennec is not in charge," said Ji-hyeon, her irritation at being ignored by this ancient ox supplanting the definite apprehension he inspired. "I am."

"Cold Cobalt," breathed the beat-up woman kneeling over the fallen barbarian, her blackened eyes wide. "Blue Zosia, the Banshee with a Blade—it's really you!"

"The devils it is," said Ji-hyeon, yanking off her helm, but rather than coming off clean it caught in her blood-matted hair and she had to wrestle it free. Hardly the dignified entrance of the future ruler of the Crimson Empire. She hated this stupid helmet, and hated Fennec for insisting she wear it. Scheming Fennec and his...his...*schemes*. "I am General Ji-hyeon, Commander of the Cobalt Company, Heiress to Glory, and the next Queen of Samoth."

The geriatric giant snorted and everyone else just looked perplexed. Choi's whisper ruffled Ji-hyeon's hair as she said, "That one is a poison. Do not let him touch you."

"Good to see rumors of your demise are only slightly exaggerated, Maroto," Fennec said to the unconscious barbarian as he stepped past him and advanced on the ogre. Ji-hyeon blinked, trying to reconcile the comatose old man on the floor with the Mighty Maroto of all the songs. "Whatever hive you dug him out of, Hoartrap, I expect it will be a wasted effort. I think he's had a heart attack, but even if he lives, what good is an old stinghound?"

"He found you, Villain," snapped the woman tending Maroto. "We've been chasing you down all summer. The Touch only caught up with us today."

"Hoartrap the Touch," said Ji-hyeon, remembering her father's stories about the sorcerer. Stories he only told when his daughters were misbehaving and he sought to frighten them into obedience. So two of the original Villains had come looking for her...but why? "The command temple, that was your doing?"

"Ah, yes," said Hoartrap, as if remembering a chore he'd taken care of the previous week. "You appreciated my help, did you?"

"What did you do to them?" asked Ji-hyeon, and at the question one of the cardplayers lurking in the background doubled over and vomited on the floor.

"There, there, Diggelby, it wasn't as bad as all that," Hoartrap told the man, then finally clambered to his feet. Even with Fennec standing between them, he easily looked over the man's head and stared Ji-hyeon in the eye. His gaze made her queasy, but she held it, told herself she was doing so because she wanted to, and not because she lacked a choice in the matter. "Do you really want to know, little general? I'd be more than happy to show you..."

"She does not," said Choi, putting herself in front of Ji-hyeon and breaking the nauseating glare. Even with a dozen of her best— and best-paid—mercenaries crowded into the tavern behind them, Ji-hyeon began to feel as though she had blundered into a dire showdown. Of all the Villains to face head-on, it had to be the sorcerer...

"Greetings, oh witchborn thug," Hoartrap told Choi. "If you will excuse us, your mistress and I were having a discussion."

"No," Fennec said firmly, having rediscovered some of the mettle he had misplaced back at the command temple. "You and I talk first, Hoartrap. We are delighted at your having assisted us this afternoon, and would discuss terms about the future before—"

"Captain Fennec, I think in your excitement at seeing old friends you have forgotten yourself," said Ji-hyeon. Each day he got bossier, and if she let him determine how things went with his old chums now she might as well resign herself to always doing what he ordered. Besides, if he had set this up, this reunion on the sly, she aimed to find out about it before the Villains could get their stories straight. "I believe a better use of your time will be to convene with Sasamaso and Kimaera. Determine how light a contingent we can leave in Myura and still hold the castle for a reasonable time when Imperial reinforcements arrive. I want the bulk of our forces marching on Cockspar two days hence."

"General," Fennec began, sliding up his vulpine faceplate. The nine months of hard campaigning had planed off most of the joviality—and double chin—he had worn as Brother Mikal. "I cannot stress how important it is that at a minimum you and I first discuss certain particulars."

"Don't, then," said Ji-hyeon, and when he clearly didn't get it she sighed and spelled it out. "If you cannot stress the importance, then don't, was the meaning. Just forget it."

"Oh, don't mind me," said Hoartrap, nudging Maroto with his bare foot. "All this fretting is unbecoming of commanders, and I don't really think there's anything to talk about until this one is up and about. For my part, I'm always delighted to assist an old friend, or an old friend's family—you *are* kin of Kang-ho's, General?"

"His second daughter," said Ji-hyeon, which caused Choi to hiss in irritation, but Ji-hyeon didn't see any utility in denying what the evil wizard already knew. She added a good line she'd been waiting to use for some time. "In another life, I was Princess Ji-hyeon Bong, betrothed to Prince Byeong-gu of Othean, fourth son of Empress Ryuki, Keeper of the Immaculate Isles, but I sought my own path. Instead of giving my hand to another I shall make it a fist to crush my enemies."

"Hey, me, too!" said the woman who had gone to Maroto's aid. She was a fighter, no doubt about that, though given the state of her face maybe not a very good one. "I mean, a second daughter seeking her own way, not the rest of it, obviously. And so are Diggelby, Din, and Hassan there—get over here, you lot, the general's just like us!"

Ji-hyeon rather doubted that was the case, but had gotten used to biting her tongue for the greater good. She nodded as the three weasely rogues came around the table, the man who had thrown up when she'd asked about Hoartrap's activities at the command temple offering her a curtsy of his battle gown and the other two bowing as they introduced themselves. The beat-up woman kneeling over Maroto rose to join her compatriots, the low dip and cocked elbows of her bow identifying her as a member of the Ugrakari noble caste... which meant if you went back far enough, she and Ji-hyeon might be related, on her first father's side.

"Tapei Purna," the Ugrakari said. "And like the Touch said, the big guy here is Maroto—you know, Maroto Devilskinner from all the old songs. He brought us here because he thought you were Queen Zosia, but you're just dressed like her, huh?"

"Yes," said Ji-hyeon icily. Legions had flocked to her blue banner, just as Fennec had said they would, but more than a few had deserted as soon as they found out that the Cobalt Queen had not actually risen from the tomb to lead her old Company. That was the worst feeling, seeing so much disappointment that she wasn't someone else. "Think of me as her successor."

"So you're after the same thing as her, too? Taking back the Crimson Throne? Well, not taking *back*, in your case, just snatching it..."

"I will succeed where Zosia failed," said Ji-hyeon. It was beginning to feel like a script, the words a variation on a dozen speeches she had given during the campaign. "No more Chain, no more Empire. I will wear the Carnelian Crown only long enough to destroy it, and then all people of the Crimson Empire will be set free."

"Sounds like a plan," said Purna. "But before I vow my allegiance to your cause, I need to clear it with Maroto. I'm sure it will be fine, though."

"A*hem*," said the woman called Din, straightening her listing wig. "Overthrowing the current regime is fine and dandy, and we are all in favor of *that*. But what's this about destroying the Empire?"

"Din...that's a Cascadian name, isn't it?" said Fennec, who had not pissed off like Ji-hyeon had told him to. "Rest assured, my lady, that those who assist the general in her quest to bring justice to the Star will not be forgotten when she is queen, regardless of their lineage."

"Then there's the niggling fact that you've just overheard enough to ensure they'll never let you leave their camp," Hoartrap supplied. "We're all with them now, friends, so why don't you come back over here so we can finish our game?"

"That's not true, is it?" said Purna, squaring her shoulders as she appraised Ji-hyeon. "You wouldn't keep us prisoner if we wanted to leave? Not after we messed up a bunch of Crimsons just to get to you?"

"No, never," said Ji-hyeon, very much wanting to lie down all of a sudden. She hadn't slept for two days, and the adrenaline that had propelled her through the day's fight had slipped away, leaving her exhausted and in the most dread of circumstances—social interactions with foreign nobles. Yawning, she waved Fennec over. "We don't have the means to properly care for prisoners, so any who would stand against us or desert our cause are hanged. Fennec, escort me back to the castle so we can have a word, and Choi, see that our new recruits are well looked after. Make sure there are plenty of guards at each entrance to their bunkhouse here, so nobody can sneak in and do them a mischief. Night, all."

Most were respectfully silent, but Hoartrap laughed and laughed as Ji-hyeon wheeled away, her silent soldiers parting for her as she stepped back out into the road. Scant protection as her armor granted her in battle, it gave her even less from the night wind, and she pulled her cape tight as she stalked back to her most recent conquest. Fennec followed after, giving her measured advice for a change instead of chiding her for this, that, and the other thing. He claimed to have no idea why they had sought her out, other than the too-convenient explanation that they, along with so many others, had believed the rumors and thought their old leader returned from the grave. That might explain why Maroto had fainted at her appearance in the doorway of the tavern, given Fennec's description of the barbarian as a sensitive soul. When they arrived in her chambers, they were agreed on the most important matter, if very little else—Hoartrap the Touch could not be trusted.

Fennec left her without even making a pass, which was another welcome development, and with a happy groan Ji-hyeon unsheathed her sweaty feet from the high boots. The Duke of Myura's bedroom had a drysink as long as an inn's bartop, and with just as many bottles cluttering it, and before allowing herself to rest Ji-hyeon called in a pair of handmaids to help her bathe. If she'd been a good little princess and married Prince Byeong-gu like her first father had wanted, she would have had a dozen maids by now, and a castle far more luxurious than Myura to call home. Instead, she had a pair of wide-eyed camp followers tending to her with stained rags and a warm bucket of soapy water in a drafty stone pile on the ass end of the Crimson Empire.

Once she was as sweet as she was liable to get without a proper tub, she sent the boy and girl away and lay back on the enormous bed to take a much-needed sabbatical from the waking world. This proved harder than she'd expected. The arrival of two more of the original Villains seemed far too convenient to be chance, and so the only question was whether her father had sent them independently of Fennec, or if the old fox was lying about what he knew. Neither possibility strained credulity. Although Chevaleresse Singh had initially declined Ji-hyeon's invitation to become a Villain in the new Cobalt Company, how long would it be until the Raniputri knight arrived at an opportune moment? Pretty soon all of the Five Villains would be riding alongside her, at which point it would scarcely matter if the woman leading them had blue hair or the right helmet. They could just stick a tame raccoon dog on a horse and call it General Fatface for all the difference it would make—people would still assume it was the reincarnation of Zosia.

After tossing and turning for a while in the moonlit tower room, she forced her mind away from the imponderable worries and onto the much nicer subject of sex. Gods, spirits, and devils, how she missed Keun-ju. Not only for that, of course not, but in trying to distract herself with pleasant memories she just reminded herself of how many months it had been since she had kissed her Virtue Guard. It was not so long ago that she would have ranked Choi as her favorite guard, followed by the funny and charming Brother Mikal, with the stiffly formal Virtue Guard coming in dead last...but then she had grown up.

She couldn't really talk to Choi, not about her heart, and though she used to find Brother Mikal a wonderful listener, she had come to discover that Fennec would use any secret to his advantage. If only Keun-ju had not abandoned her she could have had someone to talk to, someone to confide in, someone to laugh with. Among other things one can do with her mouth.

It was lonely being the Arch-Villain.

CHAPTER
3

The walleyed anathema stared at Domingo from across the sumptuously laden folding table erected in his tent, the monk's exposed, pale gums and stained wooden teeth enough to put a billy goat off his breakfast. During that winter campaign, what, twenty-three years past, Cold Cobalt's peasant army had cornered the Fifteenth on a peninsula jutting out into the toxic swamps at the border of Emeritus and they'd had to dig in and wait for reinforcements to come break the siege. Domingo had been obliged to take two weeks of meals in a fetid miasma. Black flies had swarmed the whole camp and delivered an especially virulent pox that caused gangrene to spread through the regiment like crotchrot through a Geminidean brothel, and attempts at digging latrines on that miserable spit of marsh only resulted in bubbling pools of slime that reeked worse than their intended cargo. He didn't have many fond memories of that noisome ordeal, but it had toughened his stomach from such relatively minor distractions as a hideous witchborn monk, so he tucked into his venison with little more than a passing wish that the anathema would drop dead. Preferably after suffering unimaginable agonies.

"My thanks for the invitation to dine with you, Baron Hjortt," said Brother Wan, carving his tender meat into tiny mouthfuls and spearing one into his mouth with the tip of his knife. From the rapturous expression on Wan's face as he chewed, Domingo supposed even the pope's favorite monsters didn't eat this well in the Dens. Good that someone would enjoy it, then—the doe was far gamier than Domingo preferred, but they were still a long way out from Cockspar and its kitchens. He supposed he ought to reacclimatize himself to such rough cuisine, for they would only be in the capital for as long as it took to ready the regiment for departure.

"It's Colonel out here, not Baron. And it won't do for you to dine anywhere but in the command tent once we have the Fifteenth on the move." There was a pleasant thought, weeks upon weeks of staring at that rank parody of humanity while he choked down increasingly bland fare. "Might as well get used to one another. Make sure your...subordinates are mindful never to enter without permission, nor address me directly. I know the chain of regimental command is not the leash your kind are used to, but I won't be able to excuse any oversights once we're officially in motion."

"Quite so," said Brother Wan, perhaps smiling, or perhaps not—it was damnably hard to tell, with the man's lack of an upper lip. "But the war nuns and monks under my authority have far more military experience than I, so I assure you they will not cause any embarrassment."

There was a howler if Domingo had ever heard one—three dozen robe-swinging servants of the Chain joined up as a special attaché to the Fifteenth, most of them anathemas to boot, and he shouldn't be embarrassed? Why not just let this untrained, inexperienced mutant wear his helmet and give the orders? The Fifteenth would be eating crow along with their usual rations, to be saddled with the same elite unit of witchborn clerics they'd spent many a long campaign battling all across the Star, whenever old Shanatu got it in his head that this time his brilliant coup would work.

Well, he must be the only one in the regiment not accustomed to their presence—shortly after he'd proudly passed on his command to Efrain, peace had yet again been brokered, and the Fifteenth, like all Imperial regiments, had begun employing agents of the Chain. They were probably damn useful in a bind, Domingo had to admit—given the havoc they'd caused when they were the enemy, a few powerful war monks and nuns could come in handy now that they were allies...

And then there was the dread weapon Pope Y'Homa had entrusted him with, which rolled along at the back of the caravan in a long covered wagon. For all the Black Pope's talk of it being worth more than ten thousand soldiers, it looked mundane enough to Domingo, and he knew a sight more than a teenage pontiff about war. And even if it proved as devastating as promised, it sat extremely poorly with Domingo that in order to employ it he apparently had to take Brother Wan along. When he'd been told that only one of her most trusted servants could activate the weapon, he had assumed she meant a war priest, and a pureborn one at that, given Y'Homa's outspoken revulsion for the anathemas. Instead her liaison turned out to be the monstrous assistant to one of her cardinals—she would have apparently preferred to send the cardinal himself, but attaching such a high-ranking official to a military unit would risk attracting the attention of Queen Indsorith's spies. So instead of a human fanatic who had the sole key to a weapon capable of murdering the whole Cobalt Company in one swoop, Domingo received an abominable one. Well, so long as it did what it was supposed to and carried the day with a minimum of casualties for the Fifteenth, he would take all the secret weapons he could get.

Most of them, anyway; devils would be useful in a war, too, but nobody outside the old maniacs of the Cobalt Company seemed keen on using them. Yet. Who the hells knew what the Black Pope would try next, if this debacle ended in Queen Indsorith being supplanted by some papal puppet. That thought was enough to spoil his appetite, even if the ugly little monk wasn't.

"Sir!" a voice barked from beyond the tent flaps Domingo had tied shut to keep out the wind whistling down from the northwestern extremity of the Kutumbans. "Permission to enter, Colonel?"

"Granted, granted," Domingo called, pushing his plate back on the table. "Hold a tick, Brother Wan here just needs to untie the door."

Was that narrowing of the anathema's beady eyes an invitation to dance? Domingo imagined flipping the table on top of the frail wretch and then jumping up and down on it until the mutant deflated...

"Colonel Hjortt, sir." Brother Wan admitted Captain Shea, the young woman's lean features reminding Domingo of the substandard venison congealing on his plate, and her grim expression mirroring the colonel's assessment of his meal. Her salute was as sharp as her nose, but considering that Efrain had promoted her from the ranks during his short tenure as steward of the Fifteenth, Domingo wasn't inclined to optimism where her credentials were concerned. Especially with that third button of her uniform ajar, like she was some navy hump swaggering about on shore leave... "Sir?"

"Hmmm?" Both Shea and Wan were just standing there, waiting, and Domingo cleared his throat, waved her on. "Report then, out with it."

"We have..." Shea glanced at Wan, who was watching her with the interest a gecko pays an ant, and amended herself. "That is, the witchborn outriders, who continued on while we broke for camp?" Great devils of the sea, if this captain of his framed everything as a question he'd have worse irritations than his piles to worry about on this campaign. "Well, they saw a campfire in the hills, north of the road? And they..." A ruckus was coming slowly toward the tent now, raised voices and stamping feet, and Shea spilled the rest in a rush. "They've taken prisoners, sir. Immaculate scouts, dressed for war."

Well, *that* was something! Domingo felt the old shivers at the thought of enemy spies creeping across his camp, but the ripples did not betray his delight by carrying through to the puddinglike surface of his features. Mulling it over and putting his green captain on the defensive at the same time, he said, "Why the devil would there be Immaculate scouts out here, Captain?"

"We *are* reasonably close to Linkensterne and their wall," Wan said thoughtfully, as though Domingo hadn't been the one to detour them up to this blasted northern road upon hearing the pass to Lemi was avalanched under, as though the Baron of Cockspar didn't know where the nearest foreign city lay in relation to his province's borders, as though the Immaculates' theft of Linkensterne didn't weigh down his bowels nearly as much as the death of his son.

"Yes, well, thank you very much for that brilliant intelligence," said

Domingo. "But next time don't speak out of turn—I was addressing Shea. Furthermore, Brother Wan, in the future your agents will report back here to me before carrying out any military actions at all, is that clear?"

"As you say, sir," said Wan. "Only…"

"Only?"

"Only you said my troops were to report to me, and that I would then relate any pertinent information to you. Sir." There, that was definitely a faint smile on the monster's face; Domingo could tell by the way his cheeks moved. An awkward pause followed as the colonel began envisioning another violent fantasy, but he pulled himself back before it got too involved.

"I suppose I won't lecture a Chainite monk on semantics so long as he doesn't seek to advise me on swordplay. What about you, Captain, care to point out that the moon rises in the east?"

"Yes, sir?" Shea looked back at the canvas flaps that were snapping in the wind now that Wan had left them open. "I mean, no, sir. I mean, the Immaculates' wall is still under construction, so they may be doing reconnaissance to make sure we're not rallying to take their wall and reclaim the city before they can finish their fortifications."

"Not bad," Domingo nodded. "Not the best theory, but not bad."

"It's time to put our theories through the crucible," observed Wan, as the voices outside reached the tent, followed hotly after by the stomping boots that carried them. Definitely an Immaculate whining out there, and Domingo unhappily rose to his feet to meet the prisoners. That Captain Shea's company had ridden all the way up here to meet their returning colonel at the Azgarothian border only to let these puffed-up anathemas steal the show by capturing some scouts was unfortunate. What was unforgivable was that apparently not a one of his trained officers or soldiers had told those goons to detain their prisoners elsewhere instead of bringing them to the command tent. Who to horsewhip, though, that was always the question…Looking from the sheepish Captain Shea to the reptilian Brother Wan, Domingo found himself spoiled for choice.

"Baron Domingo Hjortt," the lead war nun called into the open door of the tent, her sonorous voice at odds with her slight profile. "We have taken captive three Immaculate scouts"—there came an outburst in Immaculate from the dark silhouettes bunched behind the small woman at the word *scouts*. "One claims to be a nobleman with writs of passage, and so I deemed it best to bring them before you."

Deemed it best, did she, to ignore protocol? This anathema had cut straight to the front of the horsewhip queue, but first there was the niggling problem that an armed posse under his command seemed to have abducted a foreign dignitary. "Bring them in at once."

The war nun entered, followed by two Immaculate women and a man, and then another three anathemas, just to make sure the formerly spacious command tent now felt as tight as the Chain's confessionals. Both Immaculates and witchborn were in a bad way, faces flushed, armor smeared with dirt and blood, but the anathemas still had weapons in their scabbards, while the only metal close at hand for the Immaculates were the chains around their wrists. From the way the two Immaculate women instinctively flanked the younger man, it didn't take a clairvoyant monster to guess the pretty boy was the supposed nobleman.

"Baron Domingo Hjortt, is it?" snapped the young Immaculate fellow in stiff but precise Crimson. It seemed he trembled out of rage, not fear. "How dare you, sir, how dare you!"

"I don't quite know," Domingo drawled, "but we'll find out soon enough. And Colonel Hjortt will do fine in this tent, lad."

"Lad? *Lad!*" The handsome lad had colored the shade of the seared venison on the table between them. "I am Prince Byeong-gu of Othean"—the twin winces from the boy's bodyguards implied that his accounting himself thusly was a habit they had vainly tried to curb—"fourth son of Empress Ryuki, Keeper of the Immaculate Isles, and you dare shackle me like one of your hounds! You dare, when I have writs of passage stamped by my mother! You dare, sir!"

If there was one thing worse than a twit like Captain Shea who put everything as a query, it was a blowhard who phrased questions as proclamations. This prince was like some hammy actor overselling the role of spoiled fop.

"With due respect, Your Highness, you have no notion of what I dare, so I'd take a deep breath if I were you," said Domingo. "Now, if my guests would make themselves comfortable by sitting on the floor, we can clear up what I am confident is all just one big misunderstanding."

"Sir," said one of the witchborn in the rear as the prisoners begrudgingly lowered themselves to the ground. "We found this in one of their satchels."

"Oh? Must be this writ of passage his highness spoke of." Domingo kept his eyes on the prince as the folded cloth was passed from war monk to nun, from nun to Brother Wan, and from Wan to Captain Shea. The little jackass was squirming now, and his bodyguards stiffening. The captain unfolded the pennant on the edge of the table. A blue flag—cobalt, really—with rather obvious heraldry. "Oh. I see. It appears his highness is scouting a long way north from the rest of his company."

"You dare defile the private belongings of a member of the royal family?" A lot of the bluster had left the boy now, and he looked almost as worried as his two handlers. Almost as worried as he should be. "You have the nerve to imply we—"

"Shut up!" Domingo barked, the bodyguards twitching, the boy flinching. That was good, they were all on edge...maybe so on edge they couldn't see how rattled Domingo was. If the Immaculates were supporting the Cobalt Company, then the Crimson Empire was in a great deal more trouble than Pope Y'Homa supposed. "We catch you skulking *on my lands*, with the flag of brigands who are *terrorizing* the Empire, and you *dare* talk down to *me*? I could have you all hanged as spies and your coddling mother couldn't do a damned thing about it, Headwoman of the Aloof Isles or no!"

"We are not affiliated in any way with the Cobalt Company," the prince said firmly, meeting Domingo's glare and making no move to wipe away the spittle that had landed on his bruising cheek. "We are not spies, nor are we scouts. We are returning to the Isles, after a very long and trying journey across the Star. The flag is...evidence we recovered, not a token of our sympathies."

"Evidence of what?" asked Brother Wan, and Domingo gave him a scowl to stop his deformed heart, or at least impress upon him the importance of letting his colonel do the talking here.

"Evidence of a crime. It is a private matter, of no consequence to Azgaroth, nor the greater Empire."

"I think I will make a far better judge of that than you," said Domingo, and when the prince looked down instead of elaborating, he whipped his saber from its scabbard with a steel hiss. The bodyguard on the left nimbly hopped from her knees to a squat, but before she could move farther the flat of a witchborn's spear had slapped against her throat, freezing her in place. A trickle of blood crept down the face of the blade where it had nicked her, the other bodyguard leaning close to her prince's ear and murmuring in some unintelligible noblecant. Domingo stepped around the table and approached the prisoners, leading with his steady saber until the tip of the blade hovered an inch from the prince's left eye. The whispering bodyguard went silent, easing slowly back into a stiff-backed posture, glaring at Domingo with all the hatred a vixen bears the hound who treed her. "I'm asking you as a courtesy, Your Highness—if you don't tell me of your own accord, I'll have my Chainwitch here peer into your brain and get the truth in nothing flat."

Brother Wan cleared his throat but made no further comment. Domingo didn't have the foggiest if the Black Pope had been telling the truth when she'd said the anathema could only glimpse the secrets of those with whom he was intimately familiar, but if Domingo himself was unsure about the limits of a witchborn's power, then how certain could this princeling be? The stoic little cuss scowled silently up at Domingo, and without breaking the boy's gaze, the general moved the point of his sword closer and closer...

"All right, all right!" The prince had his eyes shut tight, and Domingo realized he'd just drawn a drop of blood from the lad's lid. He flicked his saber up so that its curved back rested casually over his shoulder, his whole body humming at how close he'd come to putting out the runt's eye. "If the wildborn can read my very thoughts, he can confirm that I am telling the whole truth as the words leave my lips. And once I have told you the sum of my account, you will release us—agreed?"

"In war, there are certain codes that all true soldiers abide," said Domingo, leaning back against the table as he considered his prisoners. "The ignorant speak of war as savage, chaotic. In truth, when open war is declared between two peoples, it is a thing of meticulously obeyed law and absolute civility. The Crimson Codices are one such guide, and having read your own Ji-un Park, I know the Immaculates view war in much the same way. Without such rules of conduct, there is no war, only theft, arson, and murder on a grand scale. The Empire does not acknowledge the Cobalt Company as a legal army, and so if you are their agent I am not bound by the usual provisions in how I treat with you. Conversely, if you only represent the Immaculate Isles, Prince Byeong-gu, than I must uphold certain standards with how you are treated in my camp...and most pertinently, if you are not working for the Cobalts I will have no reason to detain you."

"Very well," said the prince, his eyes still as low as his voice. "My Martial Guards and I came to the Crimson Empire last winter, just after the New Year. We were searching for my fiancée, the Princess Ji-hyeon Bong. We believed she was kidnapped by a missionary of the Burnished Chain."

Domingo glanced at Brother Wan, but couldn't get a read on the freak. The Black Pope had mentioned this royal abduction to Domingo in the confessional, but how much had she not told him? If Wan had the trust of not only a cardinal but even the pontiff, how much did this anathema know?

"She...she was not," the prince went on, and, returning his full attention to the noble, Domingo thought the lad's voice was on the edge of cracking. "We sought her all over the Star, at first suspecting an Imperial plot, and then a Raniputri one, until the rumor we heard more and more frequently became impossible to discount. She is with the Cobalt Company now, which is why we have that flag—it was still flying over the city when we reached Katheli, even after the Company had ridden out before your armies could catch them."

"They took a princess hostage..." Domingo mulled it over—this could be a godsend, if it provoked the Immaculates into war against the Cobalt Company, or it could be a total fucking fiasco if it convinced them to sit out the war entirely, or, worse, aid the rebellion in exchange for the return of their noble...

"Not a hostage," said the prince, his voice thick with sorrow. "A general. I interviewed dozens of survivors, and many told the same story—Ji-hyeon helped lead the charge on Katheli. We'd heard such songs before, the closer we got, but after that I could deny it no longer. I took the flag as a...memento. No, that's not the word. In Crimson I should say...a reminder, a reminder to be more cautious with my heart. To not ignore the truth simply because I abhor it."

"What about Zosia?" Domingo asked, unable to help himself though the invocation of the forbidden name definitely raised the brows of every witchborn in the room. "If your princess was the general leading the Cobalts, where was Zosia?"

"Ah, the phantom of your Stricken Queen," said the prince, shaking his head. "Yes, she was there, too, if you believe the word of a few terror-stricken peasants who swore they saw her. I was more interested in finding my fiancée than listening to ghost stories."

Domingo tried to contain his excitement; further corroboration that Zosia had returned was as welcome as it was unsettling, but a wise tactician wages one battle at a time. Prince Byeong-gu's story was interesting for more than the mention of Zosia.

"And so after finally finding your intended after all that time, you expect me to believe you just turned around and ran back home?" The prince didn't bow under Domingo's gaze. "You didn't catch up with your beloved general and have a friendly chat about old times? Maybe speculate on how your people's relations with the Crimson Empire might improve once an Immaculate noblewoman helped the Cobalt Company seize the throne?"

"*No*, I did not." The prince sounded about as warm as the waters of Desolation Sound. "She could have been my first wife, but she ran away to be a petty criminal. I have nothing to say to a lying, scheming traitor like Ji-hyeon Bong. We should have listened to my uncle when he advised Mother against the engagement, but fool that I was, I convinced her to allow it. Taming the daughter of Kang-ho Bong seemed a challenge worthy of my talents, but I see now—"

"Kang-ho?" Domingo shivered, couldn't help himself, as he imagined that smarmy Immaculate scum coming apart under his bare hands. It was one thing to face an opponent on the field and then face him across a banquet table at court, that sort of thing happened all the time with members of the inconstant clergy. Kang-ho, though, Kang-ho had never, ever even attempted to be civil to his old enemy, only taking time out of laughing behind his back to laugh in Domingo's face. He always pretended to forget Domingo's name, which was not the sort of thing that becomes amusing with repetition. "The *First Villain*, Kang-ho? Everyone knew he'd fled back to the Isles, but how in all the heathen hells of your people did that crook sire a princess?"

"He is royal by birth as a child of Hwabun, and he married into the Bong family, who are beyond reproach." The prince seemed relieved, now that they had found some common ground in hating Kang-ho with the wrath of devils. "His husband is King Jun-hwan Bong, and with the aid of a wetmother they...well. Ji-hyuen calls King Jun-hwan Bong her first father, since she resembles him more, but given her deceit I am inclined to believe it is the blood of Kang-ho that—"

"I know how babies are made," said Domingo, a glorious stratagem blossoming in his brain like a crimson lotus. And here he'd been cursing this far-flung detour but an hour before. "Kang-ho's daughter is one of the Cobalt leaders, you're sure of this?"

"Sure enough to abandon all hope of saving her from herself," said the prince forlornly. "We should have been married last spring, and by now she could be fat with our—"

"But nobody on the Isles knows what became of her, that's what you're telling me?" Domingo tried to keep the excitement out of his voice. "You found out her secret, and are going home to inform everyone—yes?"

The still-seated bodyguard's eyes opened infinitesimally wider, but the prince obliviously carried on. "By now my message will have reached Mother. I requested her to remove the white from my palace before I returned, for there is no longer cause to mourn my fiancée."

"Nothing else? Before I let you go, I would have every detail—for the safety of the Crimson Empire, what else did you tell Empress Ryuki about the Cobalt Company?"

"Your Highness," the seated bodyguard hissed, but the prince waved her quiet, all confidence now that his tale was nearly told and his captors impressed with his innocence.

"I told her everything—that I had found Ji-hyeon and that she was not kidnapped, but must have run away to become a general in this Cobalt Company. Oh, I advised her that Kang-ho ought to be questioned about his involvement in her disappearance. It hardly seems a coincidence, that she would join a mercenary army with the same name as her father's old company." The prince pursed his lips, and then decided to tell all. "I also asked Mother to ask Uncle to call the matchmakers back to Othean, since I am apparently in need of a new fiancée. And that, Baron Hjortt, is everything there is to know—you cannot fit many High Immaculate characters on an owlbat scroll, and Mother insists I never write to her in the baser tongues. I hope this intelligence has been helpful?"

The prince smiled cautiously up at Domingo, and Domingo smiled back. Then he whipped his saber down into the lad's throat. The squatting bodyguard cried out, belatedly trying to lunge in front of her lord even as the witchborn who held a spear to her neck wrenched the blade with such force it nearly decapitated the woman. The seated bodyguard bellowed at Domingo as the colonel wiggled his blade free from the shocked, dying prince's collarbone, the other bodyguard falling dead at Domingo's feet. Then one of the witchborn punched in the screaming woman's skull with a pick. It went very quiet in the command tent, save for the sound of blood running off of Prince Byeong-gu's silk robe to pat-pat-pat on the face of the dead bodyguard beneath him. After a moment, the prince toppled over to sprawl with his countrywomen on the ground.

"Fallen Mother have mercy," Captain Shea finally managed, staring at the carnage. "The prince...you...?"

"I didn't do anything," said Domingo, hardly surprised to see that every witchborn in the room wore the same stoic face, save the grimacing Brother Wan. But was it a happy grimace or a sad one?

"The codes of war," Shea whispered. "You told him—"

"I told him the truth," said Domingo, taking Brother Wan's napkin from the table to wipe his saber off. "I chose to take him on his word that he was not an agent of the Cobalt Company, and therefore not an enemy combatant deserving of all those complicated bylaws cluttering up the Crimson Codices. What a happy day for all the Empire that we have not been at open war with the Immaculate Isles for many years, despite the recent Linkensterne debacle."

"Nor will we be again anytime soon," said Brother Wan, his sharp, blue-grey tongue playing over the dry pegs in his upper jaw as he fished around under his robe. He removed a long, black-pommeled dagger and offered it to Domingo. "Next time you need to execute an enemy of the Empire, Colonel, pray use this gift of the Chain."

"I told you, Brother Wan, don't lecture me on what to do with blades and I won't lecture you on how to carry out your pagan worship." Domingo sheathed his saber and waved away the offered knife, turning his full attention to the still-shaking Captain Shea. "Captain!"

"Sir!" She stood straighter at that, but her eyes were still on the corpses. "Sir?"

"Captain, it hardly needs saying, but you are to speak to no one of this...interrogation. *No. One.* Is that clear?" She nodded, but too quickly for Domingo's liking, so he added, "As this is a matter of Imperial security, these agents of the Chain will be monitoring the camp to ensure no baseless rumors start flying around. As senior officer until we reconvene with the rest of the Fifteenth, it is dependent upon you to make sure any gossip is quashed long before it reaches the keen ears of these witchborn, or less friendly company. There is to be no gossip because there was no incident—no Immaculates were ever brought into camp. Am I clear?"

"Yes, sir!" That was what Domingo needed—a statement, not a question.

"Now, leave me with Brother Wan and his subordinates so we can clean this mess up." As Captain Shea nearly tripped over the bodies in her haste to be away, Domingo looked up from the Cobalt flag strewn over the dirty table and called after her, "And send in another round of this venison. I think I've found my appetite at last."

CHAPTER
4

Goatsdamn, but Grandfather was a pain in the arse. Or rather, the small of the back. Shrunken as the greylock was, lugging him over hill and dale for days and then weeks and finally months without end had put a whiny kink in Sullen's spine, one that troubled him even after he'd shrugged off the old man and settled in atop the mountain's ridge. Family, man, what can you do?

"Leave me to die in the mud like a common animal," grunted Grandfather as Sullen lowered him down to sit on a slab of brown stone protruding from the lichen-draped mountainside. "That's what they wanted you to do. Born-agains playing at being heathens. It's enough to make a horned wolf puke."

"Yeah, Fa," said Sullen, knowing the prospect of meeting an army was stirring up memories for the old man. "You sure this is far enough off the path?"

"It'll do," said Grandfather, closing his eyes as he panted. As though he'd been the one to haul Sullen up the steep, treeless mountain. The two men looked back down the way they had come, the crust of frost on rock and moss sparkling in the dawn. Far below, a road cut through the evergreen bamboo and browning saam groves that thrived in the valleys here, a ribbon of bare earth wound through the hair of the mountains. "They'll make through yon pass and camp in that meadowland beyond. Creeks coming down to water the animal, flat enough for tents—too posh for lambs like them to pass up."

"I still think it's best if I go myself, just at first," said Sullen. Grandfather cracked one eye at his grandson, and Sullen blundered on, knowing full well that reason never carried him nearly far enough with the stubborn old wolf. "I'm faster and quieter, and—"

"And you don't know what your uncle looks like," said Grandfather. "And even if you are a little quicker without me, so what? If some half-wit sees you creeping and gets lucky with a weakbow, where does that leave me? Up a damn mountain, waiting for a vulture to peck out my liver, or whatever mercy the Old Watchers give me for sitting out a fight. We stick to the creeks it'll cover your racket, and if they catch us 'fore we find your uncle you can always toss me on the enemy to cover your escape, you're so worried about getting away."

"I wouldn't," said Sullen. Grandfather had adamantly refused to hear his account of his encounter with the Faceless Mistress after their brief initial exchange on the subject back in Emeritus, saying if the gods wanted to involve him they'd call on him themselves, instead of sending Sullen. As a result, Sullen hadn't told the old man about his need to thwart this Zosia character from murdering an entire people, a need far more pressing than reuniting Grandfather with his ne'er-do-well son. Since that Faceless Mistress implied the two of 'em ought to be in the same camp, though, maybe it did make more sense to find Uncle Craven first. "Never mind. We'll go together."

"Oh, I hope that's not true, laddie," said Grandfather. "I hope you've got more thaws than me ahead of you yet."

"No, I mean...you know what I mean."

"Oi, there we are—not a breath too soon! Ha!"

Following Grandfather's gaze, Sullen made out a distant glint that might have been morning light striking a patch of early snow in the dying saam forest. It bobbed up the road, disappearing for stretches and then reappearing, and at last it came close enough for Sullen to decide what was what. Four riders in dark blue, the occasional twinkle coming from their bridles, which seemed to be the only edge of metal not obscured to prevent just such detection. The scouts passed far beneath them, and though Sullen knew he and Grandfather must be invisible at their perch among the high rocks, he still pressed himself flat to the frozen earth.

More shimmers and sparkles came quickly after, and then, as though the first few were but the trickles heralding a flash flood, a column of reflected light poured up the wide road. On and on the caravan came, Sullen quickly losing count of individuals, and then losing count of wagons, and finally turning to Grandfather when the stream showed no sign of stopping after close to an hour.

"Didja know there'd be so *many*?"

"One good wolf is worth a thousand sheep," said Grandfather, but even he looked rattled by the sheer size of the Cobalt Company.

Grandfather had always just looked like Grandfather, but now with the chill light of dawn striking his leathery features and the few wisps of hair left on his head and chin, Sullen had to be real: Grandfather had gotten…well, *old*. Maybe it was being away from the Savannahs, chasing rumors and false leads all across the Body of the Star, dealing with crazy Outlanders and exploring desolate ruins—Sullen felt five years older, so imagine what toll the quest must have taken on Grandfather.

Then again, Grandfather hadn't been the one touched up by a god. The old man clearly slept like a babe whenever he wasn't taking watch, and probably sometimes when he was, too, whereas Sullen hadn't gotten a good night's sleep since his encounter with the Faceless Mistress. During the months since, he had yet to unearth any information at all about her worship, the faith of the Forsaken Empire as obscure as its fate, but he did learn much of the woman she had charged him with hunting down: Cobalt Zosia. They called her the Stricken Queen now, but in her day she'd brought this land to its knees, leading an uprising of peasants against the Crimson Empire and becoming queen, only to die at the hands of her successor, Indsorith. Yet now she returned from her twenty years in the earth, and brought fresh war against the rule of her assassin.

And Sullen, armed only with his mother's spear and his father's knives, was supposed to stand against a woman whom not even death could stop, on behalf of a long-forgotten god he'd never once prayed to. If he failed, more people would die than he could even count. It was enough to get anyone down.

———

Sullen and Grandfather were spotted before they'd even cleared the second perimeter of sentries. They would've made it farther had it been darker, but the Cobalt Company kept the edges of their camp brightly lit and tightly patrolled. The shadowy creek Sullen slunk through suddenly flashed with firelight, and shouts encircled them. He wheeled about, blinded by the unhooded lanterns directed at his face, and was about to make a run back up the stream when two arrows struck the shallow water on either side of him.

"*Move* something something *you be dead*, something!" came a voice from just up the slope, and Sullen gave thanks their search for Uncle Craven had taken so long—when he'd first left the Savannahs he hadn't spoken a word of Crimson, but now he was conversant enough to get the gist of the order. He planted his spear in the creek bank and raised his empty hands as the same voice called, "Something something *wrong you back*?"

"Tell them we're here for 'Maroto,'" sighed Grandfather. "Our only hope is he's got some pull with these Outlanders and isn't just taking orders."

"*Devil!*" cried another unseen sentry.

"*No!*" said Sullen in childish Crimson, pointing at Grandfather. "*Not devil! Grandfather on back! Grandfather no walk! Not devils! Horned Wolves! Here look Maroto! Maroto family!*"

"Something something *figures*," said the first sentry. "Something *Maroto* something something?"

"*I speak small Crimson*," said Sullen, wishing for the hundredth time that the Imperials did as much trade with the Immaculate ships as the Flintland clans did—he was near fluent in Immaculate, but that hadn't come in as handy in the Empire as he'd expected. "*Maroto here, we talk Maroto. Take us Maroto. Uh, please?*"

"*Wait*," said one scout, so wait Sullen did, despite the icy water running into his worn-out boots. Walking the Frozen Savannahs could make your feet cold, but hanging out in this mountain stream was something else entirely. The lantern light didn't flicker or leave his face, so he closed his eyes and ignored Grandfather's sour mutterings about how Sullen couldn't sneak up on a deaf turtle. Oh, if the Faceless Mistress could see him now...

"Told you we shoulda just grabbed that first scout and snapped her neck," Grandfather grumbled. "Could've worn her cloak and snuck right through the lines."

Sullen didn't talk back, but really, how would *that* have worked, with Grandfather jutting up over his shoulders? Maybe if they were sneaking into a camp full of hunchbacks...

"Horned Wolves?" said a new voice in the root language of Flintland that most of the clans used for local trading. "Let's see some horns, then."

It felt so good to hear the true tongue that Sullen broke into a wide grin and flashed the secret hand signals of his people. As soon as he did, Grandfather clocked him upside the head, whispering, "That's a damn Eagle accent if I ever heard one, no kin of ours."

"All barbarians are kin out here in the Empire, cousins," said the voice, and, feeling the brightness diminish, Sullen opened his eyes again. The circle of sentries had tightened up close, but the lanterns were now directed low enough on the ground that Sullen could see the woman still wore the plumed headdress of the Crowned Eagle People, as well as a cobalt cloak. "How many more of you are up in the high country?"

"It's just us," said Sullen. "Me and Grandfather are Maroto's kin."

"Maroto didn't tell us to keep an eye out for any of his people who might sneak down under cover of night," said the Crowned Eagle. "So may I ask just what in the holy fornication of the gods you two are doing out here? If you're friendly why not enter our camp by day?"

Meeting the scouts on the road that morning, openhanded and all, was just what Sullen had wanted to do, but Grandfather wouldn't hear any of it. Sullen wasn't about to say that in front of strangers, though. "My Crimson is bad and most Imperials we've met don't speak Immaculate so good. We thought this would be a surer way of finding my uncle. I swear on my knives we mean him no harm. We're his family."

"And how can we know that?" asked the Crowned Eagle.

"Our talk is with Maroto, fledgling," said Grandfather. "Don't tell me that pup sends a bird to do his business these days? Bring him out, and then we'll hear what he has to say on the matter."

"Fa..." Sullen began, but Grandfather was in a testy mood.

"If he's not wolf enough to face his kin we'll just turn around now and have no more to do with him. Would give him a second chance, but if this is the welcome he offers, well, they can keep him and we'll just head home."

"We'll see what's what when Maroto returns," said the Crowned Eagle. "But until then you two aren't going anywhere. I've got a dozen of my best checking the countryside as we speak, so if you forgot to mention any other of your kinfolk who might be hiding up there, now's the time to make it right."

"Call us liars again and I'll bend your beak all the way back to your cloaca, see if I—"

"Just us." Sullen spoke quick and loud, talking over Grandfather. "You go north up the ridge to the first saddle, our gear's stowed under the glacier lip there, behind some rocks. Be obliged if your people could fetch it for us."

"That's just great," said Grandfather, probably pissed at Sullen. Again. "Take us to whoever's in charge while Maroto's away, then."

The woman laughed. "I'll be in charge of you till he returns, and we'll leave it at that. I am Chevaleresse Sasamaso, acting captain of the general's bodyguard."

"I'm Sullen," said Sullen. "And my grandfather's Ruthless."

"There's a joke in there somewhere, I'm sure," said Chevaleresse Sasamaso. "I'm going to come take your weapons now, all right?"

Sullen worried that Grandfather was going to make a stink about it, but the old man stayed quiet as the Crowned Eagle took Sullen's spear and knife bandolier. Had the woman tried to disarm Grandfather of his toothpick there might have been trouble, but she pretended not to notice the sheath poking out of his harness. Finally, she stepped back and invited Sullen out of the creek. The night air of the mountain felt colder on his damp ankles than the water had.

"A chevaleresse's what they call a warrior out here, right?" asked Sullen as she led them into the camp proper, a few of the sentries accompanying them but most hooding their lanterns and returning to patrol. "But you're a Crowned Eagle."

"A chevaleresse is more than just a fighter," said their friendly captor. "It is a title with much honor among both the Raniputri Dominions and the Imperial provinces, one they rarely bestow on foreigners. It signifies nobility of spirit as well as martial prowess."

"Is my uncle a chevaleresse?"

"Maroto? No, he's no knight, though it's said they offered him the privilege many times over, had he wanted it. Turned it down every time."

"Why would he?" Sullen tried not to gape as they were led through the thronged camp, regal-looking folk in spotless metal armor sitting around fires with bare-chested soldiers so grubby and disheveled they looked like beggars.

"They have rules, don't you?" said Grandfather. "Calling yourself *knight* means no more fighting dirty, no lying or cheating, eh?"

"To name but a few of the codes of conduct," said Chevaleresse Sasamaso with a smirk.

"There's your answer," said Grandfather, settling back in his harness. "He'd have no part of *that*, not our Craven."

"Craven?" Chevaleresse Sasamaso looked delighted. "I knew Maroto wasn't a Horned Wolf name. *Craven.* Well!"

"These are the spies?" A new woman strode toward them through a break in the tents. She addressed them in Immaculate rather than Crimson, thank the Old Watchers. The guards flanking her were impressive enough, with their crablike plates of armor and steel helmets shaped like dog skulls, but as the prisoners stopped to meet the woman by the shifting light of a bonfire and Sullen caught better sight of her, he felt his throat close and his hands sweat.

It wasn't that he was knocked off guard by her scant attire, though her sparse patches of chainmail did catch his eye—despite enjoying warmer climes than Flintland, most Outlanders swaddled themselves in more sweltering layers than a newborn with pneumonia. It wasn't a stirring at her beauty, though she was decidedly fleet. No, it was the rich blue of the long hair framing her face, the severe slash of her bangs casting her dark eyes in shade that not even the bonfire could banish. She was exactly as the stories of Cold Zosia had described her, a ferocious swordswoman with cobalt hair who led devils as well as armies.

This was who Sullen had to stop, before she used her witchcraft to destroy an empire. Zosia. As if punctuating his realization, a small owlbat flapped overhead, its wings shining ebon in the firelight.

"We look like spies to you?" said Grandfather, conversant enough in Immaculate despite all his shit talking of their shipwrights, rice spirits, and general style. "We're here for Maroto."

"Kinfolk of his, they say," said Chevaleresse Sasamaso. "For what it's worth, I believe them." Switching over to Crimson, she added, "Something something *foolish enough* something something."

"I'll take Maroto over the rest of the old guard," said the blue-haired woman, again in Immaculate. Then, bafflingly, she bowed. "Welcome to my camp, kin of Maroto. I am General Ji-hyeon Bong, Commander of the Cobalt Company."

"I'm Sullen," said Sullen, though at present he felt anything but. No, he was happier than he'd been in a very long time that he wouldn't have to throw down on this woman. Especially since he was positive the owlbat wheeling overhead was a devil that was looking out for her. Not sure how he knew it was bound to her, but he did. "And my Grandfather's called Ruthless. We're Horned Wolves. Or we were, aren't no more. Might be again someday, I guess. Depending." Sullen was many things, but he had never before found himself a babbler, so he cleared his throat and finished with, "Anyway, we come down from the Frozen Savannahs."

"The tundra of Flintland?" asked this Ji-hyeon.

"Did he stutter?" said Grandfather. "It's called the Frozen Savannahs, girl, and you'll show it the respect it's due by calling it such."

Sullen blushed, but to his relief Ji-hyeon smiled at the admonishment.

"My apologies, Master Ruthless, I meant no disrespect. Quite the contrary, that's a long way to travel with no steed but your grandson."

Sullen's blush heated up, and he weakly explained, "Wolves don't ride."

"I would like to accept your apology," said Grandfather. "But so long as we're your prisoner I don't think I will."

"Old wolf, you ought—" began Chevaleresse Sasamaso as one of Ji-hyeon's guards took a step toward them, but Sullen got to it first. There would be hells to pay later, especially since he said it in Immaculate, but the words were out before he could stop them.

"By the heathen god and the true ancestors, Fa, just say thank you! They caught us sneaking in here like lions trying to carry off a baby, and you expect 'em not to be wary? What would you do if you nabbed a Jackal man coming through our window some night? Offer him a cup of snowmead?"

Grandfather went rigid on Sullen's back, but did not speak. Again Ji-hyeon smiled, and as the wind stirred up the fire he saw her eyes better, and found they were not so dark as he'd first thought. While those shining gems stayed on Sullen, she addressed Grandfather. "Ruthless of the Horned Wolf Tribe, if I have your word that you and your grandson will cause no evil, you are welcome to stay as guests instead of prisoners."

"Given," sniffed Grandfather, relaxing a bit in his harness. "And I warmly accept your gracious apology, General."

"Excellent," said Ji-hyeon. "Chevaleresse, see that a private tent is erected for them. When Maroto returns from his expedition I'll see that he is sent to you at once, whereupon you will have to make the decision to move on or swear allegiance to our cause. Much as I might like to provide for you indefinitely, with winter fast approaching I can only afford to supply those who are in my employ. Welcome to my camp, gentlemen."

General Ji-hyeon gave a clipped nod and walked past them; likely she had not actually been looking for them but on her way somewhere else when they had crossed her path. There was no parting smile for Sullen, not that he expected one . . . but he missed its absence enough to risk acting the fool, and pivoted around.

"Hold up now," he said, feeling pretty confident for a change. That confidence evaporated as the general turned back and he saw how annoyed she looked. "I, uh, was going to say we ought to burn one together. You and me."

Her expression didn't make it seem likely, and Grandfather snorted on Sullen's back, but he plunged ahead, trying not to sound as desperate as he felt right then. "I can tell you're a busy woman, so there's no need rushing it. In your own time, then, in your own time."

"I don't smoke tubāq," said Ji-hyeon, and Sullen could tell she'd be gone in an instant if he didn't say something witty. Wit, though, was no kin of his, so he just spoke the truth, as he always did. For all the good the truth had ever done him.

"Me, neither, nasty stuff. Fa rolls the beedies in it sometimes, but I've got no stomach for it straight. I'm not some sheep, to be living off poison weeds. I was talkin' about saam, yeah?" There it was! All cautious-like, just peeking out the corner of the general's lips like a wary fox testing the air outside her den, the faintest hint of a smile.

"You want me to smoke drugs with you, is that what you're asking me?" Fast as he'd seen it, that smile was gone. "You want me to take time out of war-waging to get high with you, barbarian?"

Chevaleresse Sasamaso covered her mouth with a mailed hand, and Grandfather rocked on Sullen's back with silent laughter. This was a disaster.

"Saam isn't a drug, it's a medicine," said Sullen lamely.

"And what malady does it treat?"

"Bad moods?" he said. He'd never really thought about the practical applications before, but knew mudworkers and poison oracles used it. Admitting that he had in fact just been asking if she wanted to get high with him seemed a bit low, though.

"Master Ruthless, I have a request to make regarding your grandson," said Ji-hyeon, and while that almost-there smile was back, she was giving Grandfather her full attention now. Sullen had really stepped in it this time.

"He's a good lad, General, just not used to conversing with warlords," said Grandfather. "So long as you don't aim to flog him for his impudence, though, I could see my way into letting him take a little discipline for his cheek."

"Good," said Ji-hyeon. "With your permission I would like to take kaldi with him sometime in the next few days. In private. I hope you understand?"

"Oh, I understand," said Grandfather, which was good, because Sullen certainly didn't. "I'll give you leave to talk to the boy, but nothing more than that. He's still a virgin, and I aim to keep him that way—big, smart lad as he is, he'll catch quite the groomprice if I can arrange a marriage somewheres along the line without him—"

"Great fucking devils, Fa, shut the fuck up!" Sullen wished the old man had straight up murdered him, instead of talking this shit. "I don't . . . She doesn't . . . devildamn it!"

"I assure you his chastity will be preserved," said Ji-hyeon, giving them a final bow. Her smile was out in force now, but Sullen was no longer so delighted to see it. Fucking Grandfather, man . . .

CHAPTER
5

T his is bullshit," panted Duchess Din, plopping her mohair-swaddled bottom down on a boulder near the one Maroto and Purna occupied. The pass they had reached was less than a dozen feet wide, the rugged peaks on either side wasting no time in jabbing straight up to poke heaven in the eyes. With the whistling wind delivering a slurry of early snow and rock dust, it was hardly an ideal picnic spot. On either side of the narrow saddle, rough talus slopes sharply dropped a thousand feet before leveling off a bit, and if anything, the side they were to descend looked even steeper than the way they'd come up.

"Testify, sister!" said Purna, raising a fist and lowering her head. "If I'd known this was the work we'd be doing I would have just had the Cobalts execute me as a traitor. If I wanted to play marmot I never would have left Ugrakar."

"Puhhhhhh," gasped Diggelby as Hassan helped him up the last jagged rise, even his mean little dog wheezing as it scrambled up the rocks ahead of them.

Yet Maroto was pleased, which he hadn't been in . . . weeks, maybe a whole month. Old Black knew, he probably hadn't cracked a smile since he'd found out the blue-haired girl everyone thought was Zosia was just Kang-ho's brat, with Fennec her faithful puppeteer. Now, though, he felt genuinely happy. The reason was propped up against another boulder, as though the three scouts were huddled into a windbreak, and not, you know, dead. Maroto wasn't such a baddie as to rejoice at seeing random corpses—hells, if he were that sort of man he'd rarely stop smiling, living the life he'd lived. No, his bliss—and bliss was really the only word for it—was that he recognized one of the scouts Choi had dispatched just before dawn, when he and the others were still way down at the misty bottom of the pass. It was Lukash the Nearly Noseless Scout, that lying fucker who had repaid Maroto's mercy by bringing a whole platoon of Imperial toughs down on them outside Myura, just before they'd finally found the Cobalt Company. Maroto only wished he had been here to watch Choi do the deed. Maybe advise her to be a bit slower about it. His oft-regretted vow prevented him from torturing agents of the Crimson Empire, sure, but that was no reason why he couldn't offer his professional oversight to such activities. Same reason he could guide a scouting party to spy on the Imperials but not lead an open charge against 'em—a man has to keep his word to his enemies, if no one else, but that's no reason not to get creative with interpretations.

"Don't get comfortable," he called to Diggelby and Hassan as they collapsed onto the harsh brown summit of the saddle. "Soon as Choi shows herself we're moving out, and fast. Too exposed up here."

"They need a rest, Maroto," said Purna, her own face ruddy and sleek with sweat. The fops had learned to leave the makeup in its case on mornings that started with a steady climb up an exposed mountainside. "Look at them. You think we're going slow now, wait until someone snaps an ankle because you're pushing them too hard."

"Take it up with Choi," said Maroto, eyeing the alpine meadows into which the slope poured its talus like a waterfall of sharp stones. Somewhere down there the weirdborn was creeping around, and as soon as they got her signal they could—

"Stay here until dark," came Choi's voice from above them. Except for her modest horns, which were mostly hidden by her mesh hat, the white-haired weirdborn looked enough like a normal woman, sitting around camp with the rest of the crew . . . but nobody watching her melt down the sheer peak beside them could mistake her for human. Too fast, too surefooted, too damn devilish. "There's a regiment nesting in the next meadow, and they will have more scouts down there watching the descent from this pass. If we come down now we will be witnessed."

Duchess Din whistled appreciatively. "So much for Maroto's assessment of the Imperial colonels being, what was it, 'too damn thick to cover their front, let alone their arse'? I've lost track of how many times you've proven him wrong, Choi."

"Things have changed," grumbled Maroto. Which was true enough, whether it referred to the Imperial brass sharpening up or Maroto growing dull from neglect. "A lot."

"Since the days when you were one of said colonels, you mean?" asked Purna, and even though Diggelby and Hassan were too far away to hear what she was saying, the contrary bastards tittered right on cue. Then again, they both had two working ears, so maybe they heard her perfectly.

"Get down from there, move around back," said Choi, walking past them and squatting down on the far end of the boulder, overlooking the way they'd come. "If a change of guard comes we do not want them to see us until they reach the top."

Maroto joined Purna and Din in groaning theatrically as they clambered down from their sunny perch and dug in against the cold backside of rock. Quick as Maroto's good humor had been restored, it was gone again. He'd felt like a dead man, wandering the Cobalt camp like an unwelcome ghost after meeting General Ji-hyeon and Fennec in Myura, unwilling to take the oaths of fealty that the rest were falling over themselves to swear. Well, not so much unwilling as unable—that was the thing about oaths, you swear one and all of a sudden it becomes a lot harder to swear any more—but in the end he'd found a sort of compromise. He hadn't relented out of any long-dormant loyalty to his old comrades and their ascendant offspring, but due solely to Purna's pestering—she wanted to offer her services to General Ji-hyeon, but wouldn't until Maroto agreed to do the same.

"Here's the rub," he'd told her. "I can't raise a sword against the Queen of Samoth."

"Whaaaaaaat?" she'd said. "Why the devils not? You hate the

Crimson Empire, you've said it a hundred times! And you dragged us all over the Star looking for this army, who are obviously *at war* with the Empire, and you can't be at war with an empire without also being at war with its capital providence, can you? 'Fighting the good fight,' you said it a *thousand* times! Now, I know the Cobalt leader isn't who you expected, but we're here, and we can help, and what else would you do—go back to hosting hunting parties in the Panteran Wastes?"

"I swore an oath," said Maroto, as unhappy about the situation as he'd ever been. More so, probably. "Long ago, to Queen Indsorith, and I won't break a vow, not even one I regret. I came here chasing a dream, Purna, and now it's time to wake up."

"So swear a new oath," Purna had said, knowing him well enough not to dig at subjects he didn't want dredged. "To help me! If you're defending me from Imperial swords, that's hardly the same as, um, raising a blade against the queen."

"Hmmm," Maroto had said, because he had no intention of going along with any more of her brilliant plans but knew *her* well enough not to say no outright.

And yet here he was, weeks into a scouting expedition ordered by General Ji-hyeon. Maroto's insider knowledge of the Imperial military made him an obvious choice, and anywhere he went there went Purna, and wherever Purna went there went Din, Hassan, and Diggelby. Choi had been assigned to the mission because General Ji-hyeon evidently had the sense not to trust any of her new recruits further than she could have them shot, and so the weirdborn was put in charge of their band. Maroto hadn't thought anything could reduce the nobles from a merry band to the regular kind, but the sharp-toothed Choi had done wonders to dampen everyone's spirits: no fires, no feasts, no fighting, if they could help it, and, cruelest of all, no singing. It had been a long, joyless slog through the mountains, and while they had gained quite a bit of information on the Imperial forces moving in to surround the Cobalt Company, Maroto hadn't been properly drunk since leaving Myura. Worse things than not drinking, though—he could barely remember the last time he'd gotten laid, to think of one. It'd been before he'd taken on the lordlings; devils' delight, what had happened to the Mighty Maroto, that he'd go the better part of a year without so much as a suck? Getting old beat getting dead, but not much else, and not by much.

And at last they were almost back to the Cobalts, but of all the idiot fates, another Imperial contingent was smack between them and a proper drink, and if Maroto was lucky, a roll with a camp-whore. Not that he was all that lucky, these days...

"Hey look, a goat!" said Purna, spoiling Maroto's nap. You'd think an Ugrakari girl would be long over the novelty of seeing the animals universally regarded as the second-biggest arseholes on the mountain, but apparently not. "What a beard! He must be older than Maroto!"

"Not as horny, though," said Hassan, leaving Diggelby and his dog to doze on the smaller, sharper stones while he climbed the last dozen yards up the slope to join Maroto, Purna, and Din in the lee of the boulder. Now that the flurry had blown over, the afternoon brightness of the mountain sun made Maroto's eyes water, and every bone in his arse ached as he sat up straighter and wiped drool from his stubbly chin.

"Choi keeping an eye on the other side of the pass?" he asked. "Or did she run off again and you clowns decided we didn't need a lookout of our own?"

"What's to watch for, at the top of a bloody mountain?" grumbled Din, whetting the ornately hooked heads of her crossbow bolts.

"That's probably what the last scouts to hold this post thought," said Maroto, jerking a thumb in the direction of Lukash the Nearly Noseless Scout and the other corpses. "Don't all volunteer at once."

"Man, that old boy is making straight for Diggelby," said Purna. "I've got five dinars that says it's on top of him before he wakes up!"

"I'll pledge six thousand rupees that Prince wakes up first," said Hassan.

"No fool's taking that bet," said Din. "The dog wakes before Diggelby, whatever else the outcome... but I see Prince waking and rousing his master before the goat is within pissing distance. So I take your wager, Purna."

"Damn," said Purna. "Hadn't thought about the dog. As far as a goat can spit, or as far as a person?"

"As we determined in the Wastes, dromedaries can spit some distance indeed," said Hassan. "But I am unversed in the range of goats."

"Where's an avalanche when you need one?" said Maroto, his joints popping as he rose to a crouch. "I'll take first watch, then, so as…"

Idly glancing down the mountainside they had earlier scaled, he saw the so-called goat in question. Maroto felt his guts turn to iron, the weight threatening to rip out through his taint. He blinked, licked his lips, willed his suddenly trembling legs to be still. They ignored him. For the first time since waking he noticed that the wind had died completely, and the sun now buried its face in a tuft of cottony cloud. In the stillness it must have picked up the scent of their trail, and in the shade the creature's eyes would be as sharp as its teeth. And it was only a hundred yards down the steep slope, clip-clopping straight toward the snoozing Diggelby.

"…five that it wakes the dog from the distance of a practiced human spitter for Hassan, then, and five for Din that it's a camel's range before—"

"Shut your fucking mouths," said Maroto, dead calm in the way he only got in the heat of a battle and other mortal-fucking-circumstances. "Crawl around the rock. Now. Purna, you open up the belly of one of those dead scouts. Then you all go down the other side, quiet as you can. Now."

"Are you serious?" asked Din. "Is he serious? What is it?"

"Fucking go," growled Maroto. "I'll crawl down and grab Diggelby. Be right behind you."

"Is it Choi?" asked Purna, looking everywhere but at the beast meandering up the mountain.

"What are we looking for?" asked Hassan. "Is it near the goat?"

"That's not a goat, damn your eyes," said Maroto, shuddering. "It's a horned wolf."

The other three went quiet, and Maroto snatched up a sizable pebble. Shying this off Diggelby would be safer than crawling out in the open, but just as he flicked the stone at his target, Din and Hassan burst out laughing. His missile went wide, clattering loudly across the stones. Their guffaws would echo, he knew, and the horned wolf went stock-still, cocking its snout in the air.

"You had me, Mar—" Din began, but Maroto lunged over and clapped a hand over her mouth.

"Maroto, have you ever actually *seen* a goat before?" whispered Purna, pointing at the creature. "Because I'm telling you, *that* is a goat."

A bark brought them up short, but then Hassan was snickering again as they all realized it was just Prince. Diggelby's dog scrambled up in a cloud of dust as though he'd been stung by a bee, yipping in earnest now. His nominal master groaned and swatted at him but didn't rise. Then Prince stopped yapping, took a big sniff in the direction of the horned wolf, and turned tail on master and monster, his leash bouncing along after him.

"Prince! Prince!" hissed Din, but the dog ignored her, shooting past their boulder and disappearing down the other side of the pass. The horned wolf had stopped moving when Din and Hassan had made their racket, and had stayed rooted to the mountain the whole time Prince yapped at it, but now it was on the move again, dropping its belly close to the ground and quickly slinking up the mountain in a decidedly uncaprine fashion, its legs now splayed out at right angles like the scuttling appendages of a spider. That must have got Din to appreciate the severity of their situation, as she carefully set down the bolt she'd been sharpening and started to string her crossbow with equally deliberate slowness.

Purna had also come around, although to predictable outcome: "Oh devils yes, let's take this beast! Should we flank it, or—"

"Shhhhh," whispered Maroto. "I told you, we run. He's too fat to be sick and too fast to be old, and that means he has a pack laid up in some cave around here. We go, now, and hope the dead scouts keep him happy."

"Diggelby," said Hassan. "We can't just leave him."

"If you'd listened to me, I would've had him over my shoulder already," said Maroto, the bottom threatening to drop out of his bowels as he watched the horned wolf slither up the steep mountainside. There was no way he could grab the dozing noble in time.

"Sacrifice," said Purna, which even Maroto thought was harsh. "No time to talk, come on. Trust me."

Purna squirmed around the edge of the boulder, Din and Hassan following tight on her heels. The horned wolf was close enough now that Maroto could see it had two pairs of horns, one going out and up and the other curving in and down. This was no mere animal, this was a monster out of legend. Sacrifice, Purna had said, but while he knew he'd saved Diggelby's hams a dozen times over since meeting the callow twerp, he couldn't shake the memory of throwing open the cell door when he and Purna were locked up in Myura and seeing that chump on the other side...

So maybe it was gratitude that took Maroto to his feet, or maybe it was a deep-seated refusal to just hand this rich kid the best death a warrior could ask for, while he snuck away to find an inferior demise. Craven, they had called him, when he'd guiltily returned to the clan after all his adventures with Zosia, and a different Maroto had deserved that name... but he was no longer the sort of Horned Wolf who turned tail rather than bearing fangs at the avatar of his people. This was it, then—it was time for him to come home. It was enough to drip glacier water down a man's crack; as far as he'd journeyed, from the Frozen Savannahs and back and then away again, to here on the southwest edge of the Crimson Empire, it still came down to a horned wolf catching his scent on a still day.

For just a moment, Maroto let himself pretend this monster was Dad, returned from the dead in the guise of the Old Watchers to retrieve the son who had abandoned him twice. The first time he'd forsaken his father Maroto had been but a boy, so desperate to hide his shame at fleeing from a horned wolf he'd seen by the fields that he'd kept running until he reached Samoth. The second time had been even worse, with his wee nephew there, watching him go...

But no, the past is a trap as sharp as a horned wolf's tooth, and Maroto shook himself free of the guilt that had stalked him for years.

Going back to the Frozen Savannahs after Zosia's death had been a mistake; he would not compound the error by revisiting it in his mind. All tolls would be paid in the end.

He stepped out of the shadows of the boulder, the great big world spread out as far as the eye could see. Mace up, head down, he made his peace, such as it was, with whatever invisible ears still cocked in his direction, be they divine or infernal, so long as they were listening. Then he pursed his lips to whistle a challenge, when clattering rocks to his side made him spin around—he'd been flanked by the monster's pack-mate!

No, it was Purna, Din, and Hassan crabwalking across the saddle, the body of Lukash the Almost Noseless Scout in their arms. Before Maroto could step forward to help, they had stumbled past him, and with a muttered "heave!" they did just that, launching the corpse over the lip of the ridgeline. He landed a short way down with a snap and a crunch, but slid to a stop on the jagged earth rather than picking up momentum and rolling on. The horned wolf stopped in its tracks, looking not at the broken body that had landed a scant dozen feet from where it crouched, but at the humans who had thrown him one of their kind.

It was so quiet on the mountain that they could hear a distant wheeze from the creature's throat, the patter of its drool landing on the rocks. This close, it was easy to see why Maroto's heathen ancestors had thought these beasts were devils, if not outright gods: there was a regal bearing in its pale woolly shoulders, something otherworldly in the twin rows of black teeth gleaming in its nightmarishly long mouth. Finally, those disturbingly bright eyes looked away from the four breathless people standing above it, passed over the sleeping shape of their comrade, and settled on the offering. It extended one sharp, splayed hoof toward the corpse . . .

"Will you shut *up*!" said Diggelby, sitting straight up from his rocky bed. "Oh, a goat!"

The horned wolf's hackles flew up and it ducked back into a crouch, growling low in its throat, eyes fixed on Diggelby. All of Maroto's relief rushed out of him in a cold sweat. The wind came back, now that it couldn't help them by smearing their scent, and Diggelby scrambled to his feet in a foolishly hasty fashion.

"What do *you* want, goat? I don't have any old cans, if—" Diggelby began, but then the horned wolf was flying up the rocks toward him, and his chiding rose to a panicked, "—Eeeeep!"

Usually time didn't seem to slow and then crystallize, like honey settling at the bottom of a jug, until Maroto was in the thick of a fight, with a few blows already traded. This time, though, everything was already in focus, the action blocked even before he swung. Purna's hands were fluttering up, pistol and kakuri a second away from being useful; Din was dropping to a knee before shooting her crossbow, but her foot was on loose rocks and it would take her a moment to stabilize before firing; Hassan's saw-toothed sword was cocked back, but in taking a wide charge to not interfere with the girls' shots he would never reach Diggelby in time. None of them would . . . but Maroto launched himself anyway, bounding over and down, his only hope that the beast would see him coming and redirect its attack toward the bigger threat . . .

It did, but not at him. Choi appeared like a devil in a summoning circle, shoving past Diggelby and down to meet the beast's charge, her limbs too quick for even Maroto's eye to track. Yet not too quick for the horned wolf, the creature dipping to the side to avoid her jabbing sword and then slamming its skull into her wheeling legs. One of its upper horns gored her thigh, upending her even as its slavering mouth closed on her ankle. It caught her out of the air and flipped her onto her back, more like a Raniputri wrestler than an animal.

Maroto smelled Purna's gunpowder, and then the report rattled the stones beneath his floating feet, and a tiny puff of white hair bloomed on the creature's arched back where the ball grazed it. Din's missile fared better, a quarrel gliding softly into the horned wolf's haunch as it furiously banged Choi against the rocks by her bloodied boot. It didn't take notice of the bolt quivering in its flesh, even when the red began to pulse out and stain its leg. Choi must be dead, she must be, but even as Maroto watched her limp body flop up off the steep ground she reared forward, as though trying to touch her toes, and stuck the creature in the muzzle with the sword she still clung to. It slammed her back down even harder, and the sword clattered away down the mountainside.

The rocks came up to meet Maroto, and he made his final bounce off a granite springboard, this last bound taking him directly on top of the horned wolf...which suddenly jerked its enormous head and released Choi, flinging the bloodied woman directly into Maroto's path. Just before they collided he saw the horned wolf tense, and then Maroto and Choi crashed into one another. Something cracked in his right elbow as he landed on the merciless slope, pain jolting him alert even as his left knee was flensed near to the bone by a sharp stone edge. They tumbled a bit, Choi tangled in his arms, the mace dropped lest he bludgeon one of them in their slide, a soft whine coming from either him or the woman, he couldn't tell which. Snarling drowned out the whine, and he slapped out the one hand that was still doing as he asked, wedging his fingers in a rocky crack to arrest their slide and loosening a few fingernails in the process.

His plan was to roll away from Choi, dividing the horned wolf's attention, but even as they jerked to a stop the woman sprang away first. Well, shit. Just lifting his surprisingly heavy head took more work than he'd expected, and when the swirling mountain slowed its orbit in front of his vision he saw that neither Choi nor himself were in immediate danger: the horned wolf had mounted the saddle after the nobles, rather than following Maroto and Choi down the mountain. From here he couldn't see anything but the lip of the ridge and hear the screams. That explained why the horned wolf hadn't charged them from the first, then; from just a short ways down the slope one couldn't see much of the summit.

"You can move," said Choi, hunched over him. It didn't sound much like a question. Looking up at the weirdborn, he saw that her whole face was bloodied and raw, and one of her horns had snapped off near the tip, marrow and blood running down its length. One arm hung limp, while the other caught his good elbow and helped him up. Putting weight on his skinned knee, he felt queasy and terrible, but he didn't fall over or pass out, so it wasn't shattered. Hopefully. "Move!"

Move they did, though not nearly as fast as either of them probably wanted. Retrieving his mace and using it as a short, clumsy cane, Maroto hobbled after the limping weirdborn. They both left bloody tracks as they scaled the saddle for the second time that day, Maroto glancing behind them every few steps and thanking the old gods and the new every time he saw nothing but a lonely mountainside at their backs. Choi strafed to the side, plucking her chipped sword out of the rocks. Then, a dozen feet beneath the summit, a tooth-rattling howl overpowered the screams and grunts of the nobles. It trailed off, and when it was gone not even the low groans of the dying lordlings could be heard. Choi and Maroto both stopped, braced themselves for the inevitable attack.

"Not a bad death," he told himself, and though he wasn't sure he'd even said it aloud, the weirdborn seemed to hear him.

"None of them are," she said, and, glancing over at the battered barbarian, grinned at him despite the oozing sockets where her sharp teeth had been knocked out. Maroto saluted her with his mace. Worse ways to go, certainly.

"That," came Diggelby's voice from the saddle above, "is *definitely* not a goat."

"Maroto! Choi!" Purna appeared like one of the Burnished Chain's angels, shining from on high. "They're alive!"

"More than can be said for me," said Hassan, stumbling into view and dropping his bloody sword with a shudder. "I think it's killed me."

"Get down there and help them," said Din, for once following her own counsel and nimbly climbing down to Choi. "They've had the worst of it."

"Where's Prince?" said Diggelby. "Prince? Priiiiiiiince!"

"Shut it," Maroto gasped. Every time he thought he was done for, too tired to move, these nobles did something so idiotic it pumped him full of nervous energy. As the fop's voice echoed out behind them, Maroto staggered on with newfound strength. "For the love of devils, shut the fuck up!"

"Don't worry, boss, it didn't get away," Purna said smugly as she helped him the rest of the way up. She was a hard one, all right: the horned wolf had taken a mouthful out of her forearm, her leather gauntlet sheared through as though it were silk and a dark bandage already leaking. "Put one in the brain, just like you always say."

"No such thing..." he panted, teetering on the edge of the saddle even with her support and then collapsing onto the summit. He stared at the limp mountain of fur and horns splayed out in the dusty pass, rivulets of blood extending in a mandala around it. "No such thing...as..."

"As a carnivorous goat?" said Hassan. "I would have agreed, if not for our little fete with this fellow. We appreciate your softening him up for us, Choi. Diggelby never could have laid him out if not for your opening salvo."

"I could, too!" said Diggelby. "But more important, where's my dog?"

"The other side," said Choi, all action even after tangling with a monster. "Go and spy. Now. The Imperials will have heard Purna's attention-getter."

"Run," said Maroto, waving them all away before it was too late. "Go. Down the other side. Hoof it, you fucking fools, hoof it!"

"But the Imperial camp—" began Hassan, when Din, having heeded Choi's order, called from the other end of the boulder:

"Are coming up, maybe a dozen of them! They're just at the meadow now, but as soon as we take a step down they'll see us."

"Retreat, or dig in?" asked Purna. "But if we stay and take these ones out, the main body will still know something's afoot, won't they?"

"Retreat," said Choi, crouching over a pack and rooting through it with her good hand. "Even wounded we'll be back down before they're up. You, help me tie a sling, and you, bandage Maroto's knee. Then we retreat."

"But Prince!" protested Diggelby.

"Fuck your stupid dog," said Hassan, retrieving his sword and wiping it off on his friend's exposed back. "Pack us up while I tend to our wounded heroes."

"No," said Maroto, shaking his head and feeling his brains slosh around, as though his skull were so swollen the grey stuff had more room to breathe. "Straight down on top of them. Two of you put on those scouts' uniforms, might buy us some time until they're close enough to see you're impostors."

"Why—" Purna started, but then a distant howl silenced her. Followed by another, and then another, and then a dozen more. From back down the way they'd come. Far off, but not nearly far enough.

"Because there's no such thing as a lone horned wolf," said Maroto, flopping back on the coarse stones and staring at the clouds. They were tinted with red now that the sun was brushing the far peaks. "A pack'll have a dozen of the monsters, maybe even two. And that one you killed? Either a pup or a runt. His parents will be bigger, faster, smarter, meaner. We're all dead."

Nobody had anything to say, which was nice—he could hear the howling of the horned wolves better this way. Then Purna crouched beside him, slapped a bandage on his seeping, grit-stubbled knee, and began wrapping it tight. Hassan came to his other side with one of Din's bolts, broke off the head, and set to strapping it against his sore, pulsing elbow.

"I'll see to myself," he heard Choi tell Din. "You and Diggelby put on those dead women's uniforms. Fast. We're going down."

"Better to make a stand here," said Maroto, sitting up as best he could. "You don't know horned wolves, weirdborn. They'll be on us—"

"Her name's Choi," said Purna, cinching the bandage painfully in place. "Don't be an asshole, Maroto, you know better than to call her anything but her name. Now, if you want to be soft as a firstborn royal and wait up here for the easiest death you can find, you're welcome to it, but the rest of us are going to bring hell down on those Imperials before we go. The least we can do is lead a pack of pissed-off goats straight to their camp."

Looking around, Maroto saw Choi nod, lick blood off her lips, smile at him in a way what got him eager to stand, if only to be the closer to a fit woman with red smears on her cheeks and a red sword in her hand. Saw the fucking ponces he'd led both ways across the worst desert of the Star watching him, crazed grins playing on faces painted with grime and blood instead of makeup. Hassan put one hand under the armpit of his jacked-up arm, and Purna took his other. Together they hoisted him up.

"So what's it going to be?" asked Purna, as if it was even a fucking question.

Maroto put his head back and howled like the horned wolf he was.

"That's more like it," sniffed Diggelby. "Now let's find Prince!"

CHAPTER
6

Zosia lived, all right, as a saddle sore on the thigh of every rider in the Imperial regiments tasked with pursuing the Cobalt Company. The timing was right for it to be the mayoress that Sister Portolés had met, the Cobalts showing up in regional complaints and then official reports just a few months after the massacre at Kypck. Depending on who you talked to, they were a band of mercenaries hired to stir up trouble, unusually effective revolutionaries, or bandits who'd gotten organized. Considering they had gone from raiding outposts and border garrisons to sacking whole castles and pillaging provinces, the threat the Cobalt Company posed to the newly won tranquility of the Crimson Empire would have been immediate and severe regardless of their leader, but if it was truly the Stricken Queen returned, well, Fallen Mother have mercy on them all.

Portolés did her best to keep her mind on these more practical, definitive problems, rather than on the slippery questions of why the story Queen Indsorith sang her in the throne room was so different from everything she had grown up believing. That she was sworn to secrecy on the truth of how Cold Cobalt lost her crown, even where her superiors in the church were concerned, did little to relax her worries. Nor, for that matter, did all the finer points in Heretic's propaganda that supported some of what Queen Indsorith had told her. Baiting her companion into sharing even more minutiae on Blue Zosia turned out to be as simple as not beating him silent whenever he opened his mouth, which was often.

"...which makes a lot of sense, when you put it all together," he said as their boat bobbed across the waves toward the gleaming cliffs of Hwabun. "You can just murder a woman, but then you make her a martyr. But by concocting a version of events where she's meeting your marionette in a fair fight, and loses, then you've stripped her of one of her key strengths: her skill in combat."

"So you don't think it was a fair fight?" asked Portolés, fanning him on. "That Indsorith, what, poisoned Zosia before the duel?"

"That the duel never even happened!" said Heretic. "Whose word do we have that it did? The letters signed by Zosia that confirm it are just that, letters, easily forged. Open your eyes, sister, you've been duped, just like the rest of the Chain, the rest of the Empire."

The Immaculate escort they had been assigned at the border didn't even try to conceal his amusement as he directed the two sailors to bring them into Hwabun's harbor. Let Heretic and this infidel have their smiles. Portolés was discovering that by checking her pride she was gaining far more insight into popular sentiments than she ever would have by checking his cheek. With any luck, she was about to discover a lot more about the Stricken Queen.

Hwabun. The Immaculate Isle where Kang-ho had fled two decades past was the sensible first stop on their search. According to Queen Insdorith, she and Zosia had agreed that the plot could only work if not a single other soul knew the truth, and so even her most trusted captains thought their Cobalt general dead. Upon coming out of hiding she would likely reveal herself to her Five Villains in hope of enlisting their aid—if nobody suspected Zosia was alive, how could she have raised an army so soon after the attack on her village without the help of some old friends? The timing was too close for Zosia to have done everything on her own.

Most of the other Villains would be hard to find, if they were even still alive; Chevaleresse Singh bounced around the Raniputri Dominions, and the rest could be anywhere. Kang-ho was the easy one, having settled down here, and if Queen Indsorith knew that, it was a safe bet that Zosia did, too. Not that Portolés expected to get the truth out of any of the Stricken Queen's cohorts, but considering the Cobalt Company would be as tough to catch up to as any of the other Villains, she might as well start close to home.

If the woman from Kypck had been Zosia, of course, and if the same woman was indeed leading the mercenary company that currently terrorized the southern end of the Empire... but Queen Indsorith had been convinced by Portolés's description of the woman and the concurrent appearance of a new Cobalt Company. Convinced enough to risk her throne by bringing Portolés into her confidence. When the queen had asked Portolés if the mayoress had a scar on her chin, the war nun had remembered that detail, vivid as she remembered the first time she had convinced Brother Wan to touch her... but now the old worm of doubt was gnawing at her, making her question if she had actually remembered the telltale scar, or if she just thought she had, prompted by Queen Indsorith's obvious need for the suspected woman to have had such a mark. *If* she had the scar, and a strange dog, and had seemed far too educated for a country mayoress in the Kutumbans, then she might be Zosia, and that possibility was too dire for Queen Indsorith to dismiss out of hand. That Portolés was the only person who would be able to recognize Kypck's mayoress at a glance made her the only candidate for hunting her down before the Crimson Empire found itself embroiled in a second Cobalt War.

Portolés would soon find out if it was truly Zosia, or at least have more to go on than the speculation of a lone woman. Even if said lone woman was the Crimson Queen, one of the most powerful individuals on the Star, a little corroborating evidence never hurt.

As Portolés, Heretic, and their Immaculate escort were led across the isle and into the manse by a coterie of servants, the first thing the war nun noticed was all the white lanterns and candles—the family was in mourning according to her guide. Her request for an audience with Kang-ho was met with less surprise and stalling from the majordomo than she might have expected a foreign cleric to garner, even with all her diplomatic writs, but the gentleman who came out to greet her was regally attired in Ugrakari fashion, not Immaculate. Kang-ho's husband, King Jun-hwan Bong.

"To what do we owe the pleasure of this visitation?" he asked straightaway, cocking his high-domed skullcap at the road-weary Imperial nun and her scuzzy assistant. The glossy bird-of-paradise feathers set in the hat were probably worth more than the heavy silver bracelets around his wrists. "Surely my husband did not anticipate your arrival, or he should have made himself available."

"My name is Sister Portolés, and I seek an audience with you, King Jun-hwan," said Portolés, and, knowing every lie goes down smoother with a dollop of truth on top, added, "Your husband is not expecting me."

"I see." This monarch's sovereign nation might be a single island that was substantially smaller than the Queen of Samoth's summer castle, but he was still a king, and if he decided to send them away there wasn't a thing Portolés could do about it... "Shall we take kaldi? I have business this evening, I am afraid, but can certainly spare an hour for a representative of our Chainite friends."

"An hour is fine," said Portolés, trying not to reveal her relief. "If your servants can entertain my escort and keep an eye on my prisoner here I would be obliged."

Eyebrows went up all around at that, and Heretic laughed, shaking his manacled wrists at them. "That's right, I'm a desperate criminal. These irons won't hold me for long, so mind a tight watch or I'll plunder your pockets to the seams."

"This way, Sister Portolés," said Jun-hwan, and she followed him through several corridors vaulted with delicately painted rafters until they emerged on a long balcony. From up here the crashing waves sounded faint as a whispered chant, and off to the north, Portolés saw the spectral fogbank that must mark the farthest extremity of the Haunted Sea. To think, during the Age of Wonders she could have looked from this very spot and gazed upon Jex Toth, before it became the Sunken Kingdom. As distant as she now felt from the church itself, its teachings would always be at the front of her mind, and she felt a joyful tremor at beholding such a hallowed place. Some said there was a maelstrom at the heart of the Haunted Sea, others spoke of a leviathan that patrolled its depths. Neither seemed beyond the realm of the possible to Portolés—you wrap your kingdom up in devil worship and black magic, and you could hardly claim surprise when the ocean swallowed you whole, belching up further darkness where your land had once been.

Yet even the foulest pit could nurture a seed of goodness, like a rosebush springing from a midden heap; who knew that better than Portolés? And just as the Fallen Mother found purchase in the corrupted flesh of an anathema, so, too, would she transform the iniquitous Sunken Kingdom into a garden of the blessed, once the Star had proven itself worthy of the honor. When that happened, the storms would cease and the fog would clear and the Haunted Sea would part, a host of angels raising the Sunken Kingdom back to the surface, the holy land scrubbed free of its ancient sins and ready to welcome those deserving of its bounty. The Chain Canticles said on that Day of Becoming, the faithful pureborn would be called home, the few deserving anathemas would be healed, and all the sinners and devils would inherit the ruined Star. On that day, even a monster might finally see the face of the Fallen Mother, but even if she was deemed unworthy, she now knew there was a place upon the Star where the damned could look out upon the habitation of the saved and reflect upon their fate…

Then again, the Chain had foretold the return of the Sunken Kingdom for over a hundred years, and here was proof with her own eyes that nothing lay out there but rough seas and bad weather.

"What does the Burnished Chain believe happened there?" King Jun-hwan asked, following Portolés's gaze. "Witchcraft? A ritual gone awry? The wrath of the gods?"

"Something like that," Portolés croaked, her momentary elation transmuted into dejection as she turned to the low lacquer table. "The Sunken Kingdom is often in our prayers. And what do the Immaculates say?"

"Witchcraft. A ritual gone awry. The wrath of the gods." Jun-hwan smiled. "Superstition is universal, sister."

Portolés hated the word "superstition," hated how snidely it dismissed the miraculous and reduced the faithful to the feebleminded.

"And what does a learned gentleman believe, living so close to where it all happened?"

"A weapon beyond our ken," King Jun-hwan said in the easy manner of one discussing the weather. "There was a war between the ancient kingdom Jex Toth and the Star. Surely I cannot conjecture on the source of the conflict, but whatever the cause, both factions lost. They sought to control the uncontrollable. Jex Toth sank into the waves, and even from this great distance they dragged the people of Emeritus down with them. An end to war, and an end to the Age of Wonders, at a cost greater than anyone living or dead could conceive. The tragedy of our ancestors."

"Don't the Immaculates say time is one big mill wheel?" asked Portolés, trying to get her mind back on track—she was here for answers about the present, not the past. "What do you think that bodes for the Empire's current trouble?"

"Another matter beyond my ken," said Jun-hwan, and Portolés realized she was expected to sit first. Very well. Pulling out a cushion, she made herself comfortable on the floor as more servants flitted out of the screened door like so many drones leaving the nest. Kaldi was, of course, forbidden, but with a writ of absolvence in her pocket, she savored the heady smell of the decoction in her porcelain bowl. Besides, it didn't do to be rude.

"Besides," Jun-hwan went on, "you have your pagan heresies mixed up. It is the Ugrakari who think of time as a mill wheel. The Immaculates envision it more as a river, rushing along, with eddies and pools and a very strong current."

"It must have been your bracelets that threw me," said Portolés. "Do you ever miss the mountains of your homeland?"

Jun-hwan smiled, touching the silver serpent that guarded one lithe wrist. "Here I have both stones and sea. Furthermore, I was born on the Isles, to an Immaculate father. My mother was Ugrakari. These belonged to her. But did you come here to discuss genealogy or theology, sister?"

"Everything is theology," said Portolés, sipping the kaldi. It was far more bitter than she'd expected from the smell. "I came here because

I'm looking to stop another war. Ugrakari, Immaculate, or Imperial, surely we can agree war does little good."

"It depends upon the war, I suppose," said Jun-hwan, stirring cream into his bowl.

"Spoken like a general," said Portolés. "Well, we need generals as much as nuns, I suppose."

"Mmmmm," said Jun-hwan, daintily sipping his kaldi.

"I will speak frankly, King Jun-hwan," said Portolés, and played her bluff. "I am here on the express orders of Queen Indsorith. She is curious to know what came of your husband's meeting with a woman claiming to be Blue Zosia, and whether Samoth ought to be concerned."

Some stiffening there, in the hand that held the king's bowl, but no other trace of acknowledgment. It was enough to convince Portolés she had struck true, she was sure of it—Brother Wan was always talking about how if you paid close enough attention, you didn't even need to have the second sight to know when people were lying. Jun-hwan tried to play dumb, but it was too late. "You speak of my husband's former commander, the woman your queen personally executed two decades ago?"

"That is she," said Portolés, and decided to add some details to her wild speculation—so long as she didn't overdo it, she had him, she could feel it. "Sharp a fellow as you are, King Jun-hwan, surely you deduced the identity of your husband's guest? Forgive any seeming impertinence, but it will help to avoid an international incident if you are forthright with me on this matter. We know ohe met with Kang-ho, what we don't know is what came of this conversation. That the man himself is absent when I call, well…surely you understand our concern. Especially considering that Hwabun sent no word to Diadem following Zosia's visit. The Crimson Empire has always counted the Immaculate Isles as dear and faithful allies, but first you exploited our recent domestic troubles to illegally seize Linkensterne, and now this matter…Suffice to say, Queen Indsorith is curious what exactly she has done to offend."

"And for such a critical diplomatic mission, the Queen of Samoth sends a lone wildborn war nun as her envoy? And this envoy is sent first to call upon my husband at Hwabun, instead of to Othean to meet with Empress Ryuki?" Jun-hwan carefully put his bowl back on the table. "You are fishing, Sister Portolés."

So much for her cunning ruse. "I am. And I shall catch something, here or elsewhere, but I have no intention of returning home hungry."

"Well, never let it be said the Immaculate waters are barren," said Jun-hwan. "Perhaps your bait is lacking, sister. What if you tried another lure?"

"Forgive me, King Jun-hwan, but I am no more a courtier than I am a fisher. Talk in riddles if you must, but don't expect a humble nun to decipher them." Portolés drained her bowl and stood, hoping she had aroused the man's curiosity enough that he'd try to talk her back down. During the card games Heretic had taught her around their campfires, he had chided her for following up one bad bluff with another, but Portolés didn't have any other strategies here. "I was sent here to ask a question. You've given me one answer, and I expect to receive a different one from the Empress of the Immaculate Isles when I meet with her two days hence. Both shall be returned to the queen, unfiltered by the simple mind of the messenger."

Jun-hwan stood as well, not nearly as ruffled as Portolés would have liked. "May you find better luck casting your line in Othean. The Autumn Palace has many pools for you to plumb."

"If you or your husband do happen to run into a dead woman who goes by the name of Zosia, let her know that I'm looking for her," said Portolés. "It's important. Tell her..."

Tell her what? That Queen Indsorith had nothing to do with the slaughter at Kypck, that this was an obvious plot to set Zosia against the Crimson Empire? That Queen Indsorith suspected the Burnished Chain had found out about Zosia and sent Colonel Hjortt to kill her people to create this very situation, where Stricken Queen sought vengeance against Crimson, and the church could rule absolutely after they had destroyed each other? That the Crimson Queen had sent Portolés to alert Zosia to all this, so that another needless war could be avoided? The only thing more insane than the truth was the notion that Portolés say anything more to Jun-hwan on the subject; already she had given too much away. "Just tell her Sister Portolés needs to parley."

"I say again, I believe you are confused, Sister Portolés—I do not know this woman you speak of."

"Thanks for the kaldi." Portolés looked back to the distant fog-bank, and Jun-hwan stepped around the table. In a low voice, so low Portolés barely heard him, King Jun-hwan said:

"There are others you could ask, sister."

"I told you, I'm no good at riddles," said Portolés, holding his gaze. Now, at last, there was something more than an impenetrable mirror meeting her eyes—eagerness.

"The schools of harpyfish swim farther and deeper than any creature in the Isles," Jun-hwan said as he leaned down, popping open a hidden recess in the center of the table and retrieving a tiny, pink-lidded cream pitcher. "As deep as the Sunken Kingdom, some say. Those who drink of their essence are granted a deep communion with friend and foe alike, and stranger folk still. There is no deception in the realm of the harpies—we could share everything with one another, and know that our exchange was equal."

Portolés took the miniature carafe and opened the hinged lid with her thumb. The oil within shimmered as black as the Gate in Diadem, into which all anathemas had to cast any devilish scraps the Papal barbers had removed from their malformed bodies before first being admitted to the Dens. It smelled of kelp turned up on desolate spits of rock, and the draught sang to Portolés's scarred tongue, setting her blunted teeth on edge...

"But would I remember a damn thing afterward?" Portolés smiled as she poured the harpy toxin over the balcony, into the sea far below. It hurt so good to refuse the temptation. "I've heard of your devil milk, King Jun-hwan, and politely decline the invitation."

Jun-hwan hissed through his teeth; even for a highborn gentleman of the Isles that stuff must be worth a fortune. "I had hoped one of your descent would have a more enlightened view."

"Hope isn't really a dependable purview," said Portolés, shaking out the last few drops before gingerly returning the ceramic vessel to the table. "Faith, well, that's something you can fall back on, when hope doesn't pan out."

"There is war coming, sister, but not the one you're expecting," said Jun-hwan, his smile just a hair too wild for Portolés's liking. "Your superiors in the Chain are busy as wastewasps with their preparations, even if they keep their plotting far from the ears of the wildborn they convert through mutilation. Or the queen, for that matter. You could have learned much, if you hadn't stopped your ears with divine mud."

"Divine mud, huh?" she said, already aching inside at her decision to dump out the drug—she always regretted the sins she had passed up more than those she had indulged. But she couldn't risk revealing the weapon Queen Indsorith had entrusted her with, even for something as tempting as a taste of the black brine that flowed through the Sunken Kingdom. "Mud's dependable, too. I put stock in the ground beneath my feet, even when it's soft, rather than jumping over yon railing and *hoping* the sea air is more to my liking."

"Good afternoon, Sister Portolés," said King Jun-hwan, and two servants sprang out of the door like wooden dolls on a Cascadian cuckoo clock. "See that our guest and her, ah, prisoner are escorted directly back to their ship. They are in a haste to be away on other business."

"Thanks again," said Portolés, following the servants.

"And do give my regards to Empress Ryuki," Jun-hwan called after her, which put Portolés in half a mind to actually sail straight to the capital—with her paperwork, she might actually be able to finagle an audience. But that wouldn't do her any good, and would show the queen's hand more than Portolés already had. Ah well, if nothing else she'd finally gotten to try kaldi, though as far as sins went that one hardly ranked.

CHAPTER
7

Plotting and executing a coup isn't the sort of thing you can rush into willy-nilly, but Zosia thought she'd done an impressive job given her tight time frame. Better still, she got to spend some time catching up with Singh and properly meeting her children. The reunion almost made her happy to ride a week in the wrong bloody direction to get the revolution started in Thantifax, the targeted Dominion even farther out on the Souwest Arm than Zygnema. Almost.

Now, though, it was time to escape the city and let the Dull Kriss revolutionaries do all the heavy lifting. Past time, if she wanted to be pedantic.

Outside, in the narrow warrens of Thantifax's streets, the fighting was well under way, the wattle walls of the temple shaking as another explosion tore through the city. Inside, Zosia took one more hard pull on the familiar pipe Singh had scared up for her, a poker-shaped briar piece she'd meticulously rusticated and stained to resemble a piece of Flintland frost coral. That had been a quarter century back, and it'd apparently been gathering dust on Singh's pipe rack for the better part of a decade.

It hurt to know Maroto had pawned the pipe she had spent so many hours carving for him, but she was relieved he'd had the decency to sell it to another Villain. Knocking the bowl out against her thigh to make sure she didn't set her purse on fire, she stowed it and shouldered her pack. Choplicker whined and scratched at the hollow altar in the back of the temple, no doubt peeved he wasn't permitted more than a taste of all the desperation wafting off of the hidden orphans Zosia and Singh had led here just before the rebellion began in earnest.

"I'm going to stay and help," said Singh, cinching her breastplate tight. "I understand if you'd prefer not to, and we can reconvene in—"

"I'm not hearing this, Chevaleresse," said Zosia, expecting this bullshit but nevertheless perturbed at the aroma. "A deal is a deal is a deal, here as anywhere on the Star, or beyond, as far as I know. Don't tell me Raniputri knights started reneging on their oaths while I was away."

The barricaded doors shuddered, and not from another bomb. Idols teetered on their shelves, and the priestesses prayed all the louder as they lifted their writhing snakes toward the graven rafters. Singh tried to stare Zosia down. As fucking if.

"My oath was to help you only after you helped me, and until we can be sure Thantifax falls you haven't fulfilled your end of the bargain." Singh tucked the ends of her mustache under the chinstrap of her spiked helm. "My children—"

"Will win this war with their own blades," said Zosia. "Or lose it, I don't really care. I spent weeks planning the attacks with Masood, and wheedling your daughters' allegiances to boot, which wasn't part of the original agreement. Nor was laying the explosives myself, nor was herding up all those brats and shepherding them to this safehouse. Don't think I'm too thick to realize we're in the worst loyalist quarter of the damn city, either. Just getting out on the road to the Empire is going to involve a whole lot of killing. I haven't bellyached once, Singh, so don't you dare try this shit on me now, just so you can gloat over the success of your brood."

"It's not gloating," said Singh sternly, then softened. "Well, maybe a little. It's just so good to see the family come together for once. Give me this boon, Zosia, and I'll see that a hundred riders accompany us to the Crimson Empire—surely that's worth dallying another day, to do what you do best?"

"If you'd asked me outright..." said Zosia, looking to Keun-ju.

The Virtue Guard shrugged, and with shaking fingers cupped one of Singh's wasps to his neck, shivering as it administered its dreamy kiss. He still looked peaked from the bloodbath of the morning. Apparently for all his fighting of cantaloupe devils or whatever back home, shedding human blood wasn't something he was used to. Give him time. "Curse me for a sentimental old fool. Two hundred Raniputri dragoons, Singh, and not a hump in the bunch—we'll need real riders where we're going, not loafers or greenies still figuring out their straw foot from their right."

"You didn't even make me say please," said Singh as the doors began to buckle. "Soft as a kitten's belly, as I've always said."

"Softer than that, but only for you, sister," said Zosia, whistling to Choplicker. The dog looked up at her but made no move to leave the shrine. "Hey there, old buddy! Hey! You ready to be a good doggie? Maybe not just sit there and watch me get knocked the fuck out for the third time in a row?"

Choplicker beat his tail on the floor in time with the wailing of the snake-handling priestesses, his thin canine lips pulled back to show his full array of slimy yellow teeth.

"Yeah yeah, what's in it for you?" Zosia brandished her war hammer and strutted to the rattling door. "Come on, then, might as well feed the dog if we're not leaving right away."

"Thank you, sister," said Singh. "We'll be on the road in two days, at the farthest."

"You hear that, Keun-ju?" said Zosia. "You want to see your Princess Pumpkin again, you'll get off your bee-stung ass and use that two-tiger of yours."

"Four-tiger," said Keun-ju, all energy now that the wasp was in him. "Let them bring their sharpest steel and their fiercest devils. Nothing, not even their pagan gods, will stop me from meeting my bride."

"Yeah, well, pagan gods have their ways of reuniting lovers that aren't reliant on all parties being alive," muttered Zosia. "First things first: we fight until the fighting's done, have a victory feast with the chevaleresse's family, ride out with our new cavalry, and deliver you to your girlie. That order."

The doors splintered wide, an arm wriggled through and shoved the bar open, and then raging loyalists poured into the temple even faster than the sunlight at their backs. Time for Zosia to do what Zosia did best.

———

If the Thantifax loyalists had been sensible and led their attack on the temple with a volley of arrows or simply rolled in a bomb, things might have turned out very differently. To be fair, they only expected to find a gaggle of priestesses and refugees, so Zosia could forgive them their rash tactics. Most of the charging loyalists wielded short katars, but a few had khandas much like the heavy serrated sword flashing in Singh's hand.

None wielded their blades as well as the chevaleresse, however, as was made intensely clear when the first man was deftly deflected by Singh, her sword bouncing off his and cleaving neatly through his finely ornamented helmet. When one of his fellows tried to seize the moment and hack into Singh's exposed armpit he discovered that Keun-ju's thin four-tiger sword might not pierce a bronze helm but could certainly glide through an eye-slit and skewer a skull. Zosia covered the chevaleresse's other flank, the insatiable pick on the back of her hammer punching through a breastplate and sending the woman who wore it tumbling back into her fellows. Despite their superior numbers, the flood of raging loyalists broke upon the three defenders and then fell back like a retreating wave rebuked by a seawall.

They were well armed and armored, these warriors, most wearing the deep purple and violent green of minor Thantifax nobility, and not as foolhardy as they'd initially seemed—with Zosia and company pressing their advantage, the bulk of the loyalists quickly pulled back to the street. Their fallen and falling comrades slowed Zosia, Keun-ju, and Singh just long enough for the loyalists to pass around a stack of chakram, and as the three rebels burst out of the temple doors they were greeted by half a dozen grinning bastards brandishing the wide, razor-edged rings. An especially cocky fucker was twirling one on her finger.

Keun-ju and Singh ducked back around the ruined doors as the loyalists launched their missiles, but with Choplicker at her side Zosia stood proud, raising her arms in a shameless display of bravado. Well, what was the point of putting up with a devil if you couldn't show off? The chakram aimed at Singh and Keun-ju embedded in the doorframe or flew into the temple, but even as Zosia heard them bouncing through the building the ones thrown at her continued to float slowly toward her, their speed undone by Choplicker. All but one abruptly dropped to the street, but the final chakram drifted into Zosia's reach. Jaws dropped, as well they fucking might. Passing her hammer to her off hand, she plucked the deadly, lazily spinning circular blade out of the air with her right...yet as she closed her hand on it, Choplicker released it from his wiles, and it sped up enough to cut her palm before she'd held it fast. Dirty fucking devil.

"That's right, children," Zosia said, hefting the familiar weight. "You've gone and fucked the pooch but good this time."

Zosia pitched it back into the crowd, and Choplicker must have put some extra spin on it, as it took off the forearm of the girl who raised a hand to shield herself and carried past her, bisecting the face of a man behind her. Then Singh and Keun-ju were following Zosia as she led the charge, a pair of sensible girls in the back turning tail before the trio even reached the front-runners. Steel met steel, and steel met flesh, and pretty soon all parties were sliding around on the bloody cobblestones. The bravest of the bunch came at Zosia with a whip-sword, and would have made short work of her light armor if Choplicker hadn't repelled the weapon back on its wielder, the three lithe blades winding around his throat and digging in. An obstinate chunk of his spine kept him from being decapitated, but just barely.

"Damn," said Zosia, as they cleaned their weapons on the corpses after. "I'd almost forgotten how much fun this could be."

"Almost?" asked Singh.

"Almost." Zosia smiled.

"Blurgh," said Keun-ju, hunching over and vomiting onto the street.

"Come on," said Zosia, patting Choplicker's head with her wounded palm. "There's plenty more where these came from."

———

They'd dragged in tables from all over the palace, setting them up in the courtyard so there'd be enough room for everyone, from Singh's family all the way down to the formerly untouchable weirdborn who had planted the bombs under the barracks and guardhouses. It was just like the long march on Diadem, royalty and ragamuffins sharing food and drink beneath the stars. Except they were eating a hell of a lot better this time around, with hundreds of piping-hot dishes set out on the scuffed boards. Apparently the revolution was popular in the royal kitchens.

"I take back everything I said about Raniputri cooking," said Keun-ju, piling his third plate of coconut rice with nothing but pickles. "Everything, except I wish there was some fish, squid, *something*."

"Yeah, well, nobody's pickier than a beggar," said Zosia, sipping on her mahua. The flower wine reminded her of the early days with Singh, nothing to their names but the swords at their sides and a small bottle to share along the dusty road. Beside her, Singh's elder son, Masood, drained a Flintlander horn of Samothan red and clapped her on the back.

"No beggars tonight, madam, only mahārājñīs and mahārājas of a new Raniputri dynasty!"

"Uh-huh," said Zosia, eyeing his mother across the table. "And what about tomorrow?"

"We're all beggars when the sun rises," said Masood, punctuating his wisdom with a burp. "It's what we are when night falls that counts."

Thank you, Singh mouthed, and, watching her old comrade mend fences with her family, Zosia was glad she'd agreed to stay and help carry the day instead of holding Singh to her word that they'd head out as soon as the fighting started. The chevaleresse threw an arm around one of her twins, Zosia had already forgotten which one. "You remind your brother of his sagacity when next his luck changes, and he goes to bed in an alley with only his fat tongue for a pillow."

"I'll remind him now that the city never would have fallen if not for my soldiers," said the girl, squirming away from her mother's embrace, but not earnestly enough to fool Zosia. "What, dear Masood, do you have to say on that matter?"

"*Dearest* Urbar," Masood said, sloshing wine onto the table and his dhoti as he gestured roughly in her direction, "I say I would rather fight a dozen Thantifax armies by myself than get on your bad side by pointing out what a peacock you are, wearing diamonds to a war!"

They bickered on, though good-naturedly, and when a warm jug of bhang replaced Zosia's liquor, she drank deeply of the draught, and soon floated above the table. The stuff used to provide escape, but now it imprisoned her in her own heart, the droning laughter of the Raniputri and Keun-ju drowned out by the chiding in her mind. Why hadn't she and Leib taken this road, hiding in the open where friends could watch their backs, instead of fleeing to the mountains and pretending they were different people?

They had come to believe the lie as much as those they told it to, a small-town boy returning to the tranquil hamlet of his birth and bringing a foreign bride with him. Working the modest fields of their neighbors, tending their animals, harvesting roots for the pot-stills. Becoming joint mayors when the old mayoress passed away and insisted they take on her duties. Passing the years with songs and mundane sorrows and the annual pilgrimage down to the jade-tinged foothills to offer alms to the Empire, instead of actually living the lives they were born to—lives tinged not green but red, blood-shed in the ruddy dawn, and dark wine spilling everywhere by the evening…

Perhaps there was a table like this in some hell or another, where she would rejoin her husband and all the others whose lives had ended violently on her behalf. Perhaps she would someday fill Leib's cup with congealed blood, and they would eat ashes among the tombs. Perhaps many things, in the grave, to go on Choplicker's knowing glance from the shadows at her ankle. He was fatter than he'd been that morning, his coat lustrous, his teeth again white as the ivory stud in Singh's nose.

The courtyard echoed with songs and boasts and jests and even a dance or three until dawn finally intruded over the palace walls, but Zosia neither sang nor bragged, nor laughed again that night, and kept counsel only with the sated devil at her feet, silently staring back into his dark eyes until her head hit the table.

They traversed twilit deserts and beside bright rivers, through cool forests and over blazing hills where the red-tipped grass waved like a sea of burning silk. Once they spied the ruins of a tower atop a spire of white rock in the midst of a black jungle; based on Choplicker's keening insistence they investigate it, Zosia presumed it was devil haunted, but wasn't about to go close enough to confirm it. They rode on, over creaking bridges built when the Empire was young and through passes in the mountains hewed by the very gods, to believe Singh . . . or strong winds, to believe her children. Her daughter Udbala and her son Sriram accompanied them, with a hundred and one riders each, and their passage from the tip of the Raniputri Dominions to the Heart of the Star was as easy a ride as Zosia could remember. Stampeding through the pickets at the understaffed garrison of the Imperial border outside Azgaroth, she dared hope it could all be as easy as this: a whoop and a cry and a pell-mell race past slack-mouthed young fools, to victory!

As if life were ever so easy. Half a day later they discovered why the border station was so lightly patrolled; an Imperial regiment, recently bulked up from the garrison, sat camped in the middle of the road. Judging by the prodigious dustcloud that chased them when they cut across the foothills to ride up and over the northern Pass of Blodtørst, the regiment had a sizable cavalry to boot. No Azgarothian stallion could match the Thantifax mares, but even without risk of immediate engagement Zosia's jaw set and her eyes narrowed: the Crimson Empire was already mustering for something, and she could imagine what. Or, rather, whom. Cobalt Company *indeed*, as if any army had a right to that name without her leadership—this Princess Ji-hyeon had some bloody nerve, if Singh's account of the girl's plan was remotely accurate.

The village of Blodtørst lay on the edges of a mirror-still pond three days' ride up the treacherous trails of the western Kutumbans. It was a pilgrimage site for both the Burnished Chain and Ugrakari worshippers, and each summer the town of several hundred swelled to the thousands. Stupas lined the western banks, inverted wooden crosses the east. The Raniputri cavalry arrived at nightfall and were given a hero's welcome, as Blodtørstians, being sensible people, welcomed all marching armies, regardless of their pennants.

"Girl, get over here," Singh said, beckoning Zosia to the shrine wall in the common room of the headwoman's hostel, once they were all settled into their shanty rooms for the night. "There's something you don't see as much down in the Dominions."

The hostel was as simple as everything else in Blodtørst, its neatly stacked stone walls unadorned by windows or even tapestries, but early winter being a full season out from any major Chainite pilgrimages, the proprietor had the curtains pulled back from her shrine. It consisted of several plain wooden shelves cluttered with idols, the Ugrakari having almost as many gods and devils as the Flintland tribes had legendary ancestors. Singh was meaningfully eyeballing one of the small statues.

The feminine figure sat on the upper shelf, beside the ferocious wargod of the Ugrakari and an ursine fellow Zosia almost remembered the name of, but not quite. Unlike her neighbors, she was decidedly human in shape, with neither extra limbs nor animal features. In fact, with that hammer and sword she looked almost like...

"No fucking way," whispered Zosia, a funny feeling spreading through her chest as she picked up the idol. It was crafted of heavy wood, briar or she was no pipe-carver, and the hair...the hair was painted robin's egg blue. "You're having me on. This is..."

"Cold Cobalt," said the headwoman, setting her tea tray down on a table and bustling over. "Please, respectfully, put her back. She is wroth to be touched."

"Oh is she ever," said Singh, putting her palms in the air and stepping back to further implicate Zosia for the crime. "Better be careful, friend, or you'll get a curse, disrespecting the Blue Queen that way."

"I don't believe it," said Zosia, looking down at the statue before remembering her manners and putting the figurine back in its place. "I mean, sorry, I meant no disrespect to your shrine."

"Doesn't bother me," said the headwoman, pushing a few errant grey hairs back under her head scarf. "The queen, though, can be testy, especially to foreigners."

"Really?" asked Zosia, relieved that Choplicker had obeyed her order to stay in their room. She never would've lived it down, if he'd been here for this. Keun-ju, too, for that matter—good that he was already sleeping off the day's ride. "You don't...I mean, you pray to her?"

"Pray?" The headwoman barked a laugh, rubbing her gnarled wrists as she stared at the statue. "She doesn't listen. But that's all the more reason to stay on her good side, eh?"

"She's..." Zosia tried not to smile. "Do you...she's not a god of your village, your people?"

"Bah," said the headwoman, probably a little freer with her tongue since they'd all drunk chaang together during the communal dinner. "Of course not! Just a woman, like all of us. Only a fool would bow to her...and only a damn fool would call her a devil, like the Imperials do. They say she's back, you know, and the Cobalt Company is big as it ever was, but I don't believe it's her. Can't be. That's the one truth of this world, the dead stay dead, praise the mercy of gods and weakness of devils."

"Well, I say she—" But whatever Singh was going to say was cut off by Zosia's glare.

"I knew her," said the old woman sadly, and Zosia felt a stab of shame at still having no bloody idea who this woman was, until she said, "Well, not to speak to, as we are. But I was with her, as a girl. The Cobalts came through, quick quick quick, but not quick enough for my mother to keep me from running away with them. Ah, what an adventure!"

As a girl? Zosia chided herself for thinking this woman old—she must be a few years her junior, so what did that make Zosia? Singh was giving her a look, prodding her with her eyes to take a bow, but fuck that. Instead, Zosia said, "How many folk died on that adventure, do you think? I've heard thousands starved or got weatherbit into the grave, not counting the actual fighting."

"Thousands?" said the headwoman, sitting down on a bench at the low table and pouring herself yak butter tea. She nudged the cast-iron pot in the direction of her still-standing guests. She wasn't smiling anymore. "More like tens of thousands. Maybe as many as half our number. I don't know. People I'd known from the cribhouse dropping all around me. I was lucky to only lose a few toes. And we who weren't stout enough for war with the Imperials were charged with foraging supplies. You know what that meant? Robbing farms that wouldn't donate everything they had. Storming towns not too different from this one, hoping the locals wouldn't join up so we could steal enough to feed ourselves. We fought as hard as any soldier, I tell you true, with rocks and sticks! Not even her Villains were fierce as us, farmgirls, village boys, and plenty of others, all drunk on a dream..."

"Some adventure," said Zosia, sitting down on the opposite bench with a groan. Her ass and thighs certainly hadn't missed the saddle, even if the rest of her had.

"Ah, but it was!" said the headwoman, blowing on her tea. "I met my wife on the Long March, made friends who still pilgrimage here from year to year. Maybe Cobalt was a devil, as the Imperials say, and it was a ruthless business, no mistake. But she fought for us. Me, you, and most of all the Imperials themselves, though many were too blind to see it. She wanted to remake the world, to liberate the poor, to—"

"Bullshit," said Zosia with more venom than she thought she had in her. "She was a killer and a coward, same as every king or queen before her, and same as every one since."

"You're wrong," said the headwoman. "She was a killer, true, but she *tried*, she did—if you'd but heard her speak to us, you would believe it was more than lust for power or wealth that spurred her. She would have brought change, too, if not for the assassins of Samoth. Things would be different."

"I noticed you didn't have a statue of Queen Indsorith on your wall." Singh smirked as she sat down beside Zosia and poured herself a cup of the rich tea.

"Do not mistake one thing for another," said the headwoman, as though they were contrary children. "I keep the Crimson Queen in my heart, and her idol above my bed. Less...*ambitious* than Queen Zosia? Yes, yes, yes. But her soldiers are well behaved when they pass through, and it was she who designated Lake Blodtørst a holy site, not those...clerics of the Burnished Chain. Things are not so good as they would be had Zosia lived, but are not as bad as they could be."

"I think I'd better lie down," said Zosia, rising from her seat. "I feel like I'm already dreaming. Thank you for your hospitality, madam, and for sharing your tales with us."

"We're riding early, of course," said Singh. "I'll give the knock when it's time."

"May your time with the devils pass swiftly," the headwoman called after her, and Zosia walked stiffly to her room. Glancing back down the dark corridor, to where only a tea candle lit the room where Singh and the headwoman still sat, she let out a long, sad sigh. They would be gone before the sun rose, but if the Imperial cavalry still pursued them they would arrive in this village ere the moon next rose. When that happened, would they be as respectful as the headwoman supposed, or would they punish the helpless populace for aiding and abetting a crew of border-jumpers? Would they all be wiped out as an example, the way Kypck had? Had she damned another village just by setting foot in it? And how many more villages would she pass through on her ride to Diadem? How many more poor fools who bought into her myth would die with idiot grins on their faces, in war or crueler deaths, believing they martyred themselves for something other than a selfish woman's ambition, her conviction that she alone knew what the world deserved?

Choplicker nosed the door open and snuffled her hand in the dark hallway. She pushed him back into the black room and shut the door behind them.

—————

They caught sight of the would-be Cobalt Company within a week of leaving Blodtørst, as they crested one of the Kutumban range's seemingly infinite passes. They were miles off, caravans crossing the Bridge of Grails, which spanned the Trench of Mordlust. From up here, they looked like an enormous mass of maggots swarming over the exposed ribs of the mountains. Yet this vantage also showed another force, albeit a smaller one: the same Imperial regiment they had eluded by the border. It looked to be just the infantry; even on foot, the Imperials had made much better time than Zosia's crew by taking the Black Tar Pass directly over the front range. The mass of soldiers marched between Zosia's Raniputri riders and the distant Cobalt Company, winding along the main road through the mountains. Even after Singh watched the dips and rises of the remote road for half an hour through her hawkglass, not a rider of the heavy Imperial cavalry appeared... which meant they were probably still in pursuit, coming up through Blodtørst Pass after them. Not only were Zosia and her warriors cut off from the Cobalt Company, they were being scissored between the Imperial riders and their main force.

"So close," said Keun-ju wistfully, staring out over the ocean of air to where his beloved led her army over the four bridges. "Why don't we... I mean, couldn't we..."

"Lead the Imperial riders all over the devil-kissed mountains until we find a way to go around their infantry?" said Singh, spitting a ruby that splattered on the rocks. Not a full season on campaign and she was already back on the betel. "Won't be the first time, what?"

"No," said Zosia, "though if we're lucky it will be the last."

When not taking the narrow highway carved through the Kutumbans, walking was hard enough, and riding was nearly impossible. Many a summit and decline was traversed with the Raniputri leading their nervous animals by the bridle, boots and hooves sliding on snow and dust-slick rocks. In the weeks that followed they never hit on a way to circumnavigate the Imperial infantry, and so it wasn't until the Cobalt Company came down in the Witchfinder Plains that the Raniputri dragoons were able to break north and come in for a parley. As they neared the end of their long hunt, Zosia wondered if she showed her nervousness as badly as Keun-ju. What did he have to sweat over? All he had to do was be reunited with the love of his life... Zosia was the one who might very well have to kick her ass.

CHAPTER

8

That Ji-hyeon girl, man. When Sullen sat down for kaldi in her tent he'd been thirteen kinds of happy, and then fourteen kinds of disappointed when the first question she'd asked him was about his hair. Not that he wasn't proud of the high ball he'd been able to tease up with his mom's old pick—if secretly horrified that of late only white hairs came loose from the comb, instead of the black strands of his youth. No, the thing was, ever since they'd left the Savannahs, Outlanders kept wanting to talk about his hair, and a few had even been so bold as to ask if they could touch it. Some didn't even ask before reaching for his head, and a bar fight had erupted in some Kvelertakan shithole when a woman at the next table had reached over and tugged on it for no reason at all. The result of all this was Sullen would've been happier than a baby-fattened lion to talk about anything at all with this lady, *except* his hair.

"Nah," he said, because technically she'd asked *if she could ask him* about it, in that roundabout Immaculate way. She was meeting his gaze with both of those blood-dark eyes, and he dropped his to the delicate kaldi bowl in his hands. "I mean...what about it?"

"Has it always been that way?" asked Ji-hyeon, but before he could roll his eyes at her she said something that stopped him short. "White, I mean?"

All that ivory in his mom's pick. Without really thinking about the company he was keeping, Sullen reached up and gave a tug. The pair of curly strands he held up were as pale as everything he'd picked out of the comb. "Um...no."

"You've passed through, too, haven't you?" asked Ji-hyeon, her eagerness not at all what he'd expected from a hardened general. With that Fennec creep and the rest all booted out of the tent, she seemed...girlish, almost. "Did you keep your eyes open? I didn't. I wish I had, now. Which one did you enter? Where did you come out?"

"Um..." What the devils was she talking about? "What?"

"That *is* what happened, isn't it? To your hair? You went through a Gate?"

"Nah!" *Through* a Gate? There was a thought to keep you up nights. But when had his hair changed, and why hadn't Grandfather said something? When...the Faceless Mistress. Sullen remembered the look on Grandfather's face when he'd come back to camp in Emeritus, how the old man had just known something weird had gone down. He patted his hair. "It...it ain't *all* white?"

"Oh yeah," said Ji-hyeon, holding up the polished silver kaldi press. "Same as mine, under all this dye."

Even in the blurred reflection he could see. His whole damn dome had gone snowy! He knew he should be freaked out, to say the least, but truth be told he thought it looked pretty swift. Glancing over the press at the general, he asked, "Dye?"

"Immaculate girls don't come with blue hair, Master Sullen," said Ji-hyeon, and he thought she sounded a mite sore about it. "When we came out of the Gate in Zygnema, every black strand of it was white as yours. Could be a lot worse, though, and it takes the blue better like this. I don't know how we would've colored it otherwise."

"So, um..." Part of Sullen didn't want to know, but another part of him had to. He felt the same giddy terror he experienced whenever he really thought about his encounter with the Faceless Mistress. "What's on the other side of a Gate? And how did you get out again, once you went in?"

"You've heard of the First Dark, haven't you?" said Ji-hyeon, leaning in close and lowering her voice like she was telling a ghost story.

"I know the Burnished Chain says it's hell, and plenty of other cults agree, but I don't think that's what it is at all. I think it's . . . I think it's like a secret ocean, kind of? A living, breathing ocean, and the Gates are the shores? So when we went into it, I just felt . . . *weird*, really, *really* weird, and smelled, like, burning oil, and felt these . . . *things*, lots of things . . ."

Sullen felt the hairs all over his body stand up watching her tell it, her eyes closed as she reached back for whatever she'd felt in that place. The Horned Wolves definitely knew all about the First Dark, but it wasn't any kind of ocean. The First Dark was what had been here before his first ancestor was born, before the Old Watchers who made her, before even the Star—it was called the First Dark because in the beginning that's all there was, blackness, and from this blackness grew all the monsters of the world . . .

"Anyway, it was over before I knew it," said Ji-hyeon, straightening up and shaking her hair out. "We went in the one in the Isles, and before I knew it we stepped out of the one on the Soueast Arm. It was . . . an experience, but not one I'll ever repeat. I don't think it's very safe, passing through them like that. Fennec said he knew how to use them, but considering what happened to *him*, well, I'm just glad my hair was the only thing that changed. It'll be easy to dye black again."

"I think the blue looks fleet, fleet as a fox," said Sullen, regretting the compliment as soon as he said it—he'd been saving it up, to use at an opportune time, but this damn sure wasn't it. He'd gotten all keyed up, imagining Ji-hyeon jumping into a Gate, and his bowl sloshed hot kaldi in his lap from his suddenly shaking hands. To change the topic, and fast, he blurted out, "Mine must've changed this one time I met a god."

Stupid, Sullen, real stupid. He wasn't trying to show off, but how else could it come across? She'd think he was either bragging or crazy, or both.

"Which god?" asked Ji-hyeon, sipping her kaldi and tactfully pretending not to notice the mess he'd made with his.

"Faceless Mistress," said Sullen, wondering if he shouldn't be spreading that around just as he said it.

"Faceless Mistress?" Ji-hyeon furrowed eyebrows that Sullen now noticed didn't match the bangs above them. "I've heard of spirits like that, ghosts from the Sunken Kingdom. How do you know she was a god? What's she the god of? Does she have other names?"

Sullen shrugged.

"Where was she? Who worships her?"

"Forsaken Empire," said Sullen.

"*The* Forsaken Empire?" Ji-hyeon's tone told him she wasn't convinced. "Nothing's there anymore. Nothing but ghosts and devils and bad luck."

"We were there," said Sullen. "Grandfather and me. Didn't see any ghosts, I don't think. And the only devils...the only devils showed up when she did. When she went, so did they."

"Sounds like you have quite the song to sing," said Ji-hyeon.

"Uh..." Sullen bit the inside of his cheek, watched the woman warm up her bowl from the press. He shouldn't trust her, not some fiery general who matched up in all but name to the descriptions of this Zosia woman he was supposed to thwart...but he wanted to trust her. Wanted to do a lot more than just trust. Who in all the Savannahs would've guessed he would end up halfway across the Star, with a beautiful foreign warlord asking him to sing her a song, because she sensed his song was worth a listen? If he had learned one thing from the sagas, though, it was you let your host take the first boast; that was just good manners. "After you, General."

"After me what?" asked Ji-hyeon, nodding the kaldi press in the direction of Sullen's bowl. Jittery as he was already from the fruity, acidic brew, he quickly held it out for her to fill. "And in private you can drop the 'general,' Sullen."

"Yeah?" Sullen's heart didn't skip a beat so much as vault over a solid dozen of them.

"Yes. 'Princess' will do just fine," said Ji-hyeon primly, and bizarre gods of exotic empires take pity on him, he couldn't tell if she was being serious or joking. "Now, what should I do first?"

"Oh. I just meant that since I'm a guest in your tent, you should tell the first story. Everyone thinks you're this Zosia," said Sullen, and *that* put the seed in her beedi, no doubt, but he went on. "Me and Grandfather trekked all over the Star, looking for my uncle, and heard a hundred songs about her. Zosia, Cold Cobalt, and other names beside. You even look like what we heard about her."

"Just like Zosia, eh?"

From the look on her face, he'd made things even worse, so he quickly added, "I'm happy you're not her. I'm...delighted."

Delighted? He could almost hear Grandfather snickering from halfway across the camp. But for once he'd said the right thing, maybe, because all the building irritation left Ji-hyeon in one obvious sigh.

"You're the only one," she said. "You can't know the toll it takes, seeing how disappointed they all are when I lift the visor and I'm not her, just some hooligan down from the Isles to stir up trouble."

"Hooligan?" asked Sullen, his Immaculate pretty good but maybe not what it could be.

"Yes, it means, like...a thug?"

"You don't look like a thug," said Sullen. "I can't figure anyone calling you a thug."

"Oh, they call me a lot worse things than thug or hooligan, but you probably don't want to hear those."

"No," agreed Sullen gravely. "I don't."

She laughed, as if he'd said something clever, so he laughed, too. Why not? Something doesn't have to be funny to laugh at it, so long as you're laughing with good company. Just when things didn't look like they could get any better, she slid open a drawer in her table and pulled out a small pipe packed full of red-haired skunk flowers, and even offered him first puff.

"Ah, come on," he said, taking the pipe, "after you gave me that look for asking you to chief with me the other night?"

"I'm sure I don't know what look you mean," said Ji-hyeon, giving him *the exact same look*, all fierce with one eyebrow up near her bangs. "Now get that going, I want it to air out in here before my next meeting. Fennec is such a whiner, says it clouds my mind—unlike all the cider he puts away."

Sullen was getting it bad for this girl; he couldn't ask for things to be better.

"Well, isn't this cozy!" came a voice from the back of the tent, and a dreadful, familiar shape stepped out of the shadows. This was a nightmare, it had to be—before accepting his seat on an embroidered cushion Sullen had surreptitiously looked all around the tent to make sure they were alone, and yet here stood that awful witch from the grasslands. Hoartrap the Touch.

"You!" Sullen dropped the pipe and nearly tipped the kaldi table as he leaped to his feet. "You!"

"The one, the only," said Hoartrap, bowing low. Devils above and gods below, but the witch was even bigger than Sullen remembered, his brow nearly brushing the blue canvas canopy. "So happy to see you again, Morose."

"His name is Sullen," said Ji-hyeon, scowling at the witch but not bothering to stand. "I've cautioned you before about your sneaking and spying, sorcerer. Do you want to die?"

"I *am* sorry," said Hoartrap, about as sincere in his contrition as a dog who's stolen dinner off its master's plate. "I assure you, my dear general, I had no intention to sneak or to spy. If I had, I would hardly announce my presence, would I? No, I have urgent business to discuss...*private* business, Sullen my boy."

"You..." Sullen looked back and forth between Hoartrap and Ji-hyeon. It broke his heart that she knew this creature, trafficked with him.

"Yes, yes, you said that already," said Hoartrap. "Now be a good pup and go back to licking your grandfather's arse. The adults need to talk."

Had anyone else taken such a tone, Sullen would have been inclined to educate them on proper comportment. With Hoartrap, though, he was simply relieved to have an excuse to leave. He'd left his weapons back at his tent, and Grandfather said nothing but cold metal could stop a witch...

"Treat him like that again, sorcerer, and I'll—"

"Cut my lungs out yourself, yes, yes, I know," said Hoartrap.

"Apologies, apologies, Master Sullen, sometimes my sense of humor doesn't translate. But we do need to talk tactics, m'dear—my little friends tell me we have a Raniputri problem to the north, on top of a possible Imperial complication, and we really should start to—"

"All right already," said Ji-hyeon, waving the hulking monster quiet and then hopping lightly to her feet. "Sullen, I am sorry to truncate our conversation. Another time, spirits willing."

"No doubt," said Sullen, trying not to color under the mirthful gaze of the witch. "Whenever. I'll be ready."

"Give my regards to your grandfather," said Hoartrap. "I'm looking forward to seeing him again, just as soon as Maroto returns to camp. That's a reunion I wouldn't miss for all the devils in hell."

The witch was trying to spook Sullen, obviously, but the memory of their last meeting kicked up something different in his mind. Glancing to the tent pole where Ji-hyeon's devil roosted among the folds of canvas, he said, "Mind your devil around him. He eats them."

Ji-hyeon froze mid–parting bow, straightening quickly. She looked . . . frightened? Good if she was, hanging around with a witch. "Who told you?"

"I saw him do it, out in the plains. An owlbat, just like Fellwing."

"No, no, how did you know she's a devil?"

"Oh, our Sullen's full of surprises, aren't you?" said Hoartrap, and for the first time there was real anger behind his casually nasty smile. "He's witchborn, General, or hadn't you noticed? And more than that; since last we met he's been peeking into dark corners best left lightless, or I'm no judge at all of deviltry. I'm also looking forward to hearing how you came by that creamy coif, pup."

Sullen felt deadly cold all of a sudden, and said, "Call my mom a witch again. Call me whatever, but Ma? Nah."

"A lovely woman, I'm sure," said Hoartrap. "There I go again, with my clumsy translations. I simply meant you've got, oh, how do you people put it . . . the blood of shamans, is that right?"

"Oh," said Sullen, too confused to stay angry. First the witch insulted his mother, now he was doling out compliments. Crazy old monster. "Yeah. Maybe. Not for me to say."

"I happen to find your eyes very handsome," Ji-hyeon told Sullen, which wasn't something he had ever expected to hear. Coming from her, it burned his cheeks right up, even with the witch looming over them. "And Choi's wildborn, too. My second. She's with your uncle, but you'll meet her as soon as she's back."

"*Uncle* Maroto, is it?" said Hoartrap. "And that makes your grand-father...well, I suspected as much, but those two were very cagey about the whole subject when last we met! Glad to finally know how the blood flows."

"We've got plenty of other wildborn in the ranks besides Choi," said Ji-hyeon, ignoring Hoartrap, though Sullen was unnerved by how much interest the sorcerer took in his family tree. "They've got more reason than many to march against the Crimson Empire. Some of the best we have. Good people, not like others in this company, who have more questionable motivations."

"Oh, how your words sting!" said Hoartrap, clutching a burly hand to his chest. "But really, now, that kaldi's not getting any hotter, and we do have the trifling matter of waging a war to consider. So might I bend your ear, General?"

Now that he'd gotten some licks in, Hoartrap wouldn't even look at Sullen, but Ji-hyeon was all classy about it, as she seemed to be about most everything. "I was enjoying myself, Sullen, before we were interrupted. Please give my regards to your grandfather, but inform him we may be moving on sooner than expected. If we leave before your uncle returns, you may carry on with the Company until he reconvenes with us."

"Thanks," said Sullen, imitating her bow. "Really. A lot. And I'd tell you again to be careful, but you're clever enough to know that without me beating the mule. Wouldn't leave my worst enemy alone with him, I could help it."

As he left, Sullen wondered if her smile was triggered by his words or Hoartrap's obvious displeasure at them. Didn't really care much either way. It was that kind of smile.

CHAPTER
9

Ask me again, Wan, and you'll have a different answer, I promise you that. Ask away. *Please.*" Domingo was in better humor than he'd been since he'd dispatched that Immaculate prince back on the Azgarothian border. After the many rump-wrecking leagues of riding over the worst country the Star had to offer, headache-inducing meetings with the Ninth Regiment's interim colonel when they joined the Myuran force, a steadily worsening diet, and now the infuriating revelation regarding the nature of the weapon the Black Pope had given him, the prospect of stomping the anathema greatly appealed to Domingo. Adamant as Brother Wan was regarding the prospect, could he resist a final prod? If he did keep harping on the subject, Domingo would give his hideous dinnermate a final prod of his own—only by setting rules for oneself could order be preserved, after all, and Domingo had set a rule that he would not murder Brother Wan unless the witchborn stepped over one of the many lines the colonel had set before him. So far Wan had always drawn up short, but here, at last, in this miserable camp in the barren heights of the eastern Kutumbans, with a full-on engagement with the Cobalt Company a foregone conclusion and the monster's toe hovering over this last border, maybe he would dare to take that final step and...

"Forgive me, Colonel, I meant no disrespect," said Brother Wan, in a tone that carried plenty of what he verbally disavowed. He swirled his grappa, flicked his lizardlike tongue into the glass. "When you accepted Pope Y'Homa III's weapon, I naïvely assumed that you intended to use it. My lack of experience with actual combat has again embarrassed me."

"I took her so-called weapon, and I took on you, Brother Wan, under false pretenses," said Domingo. "I will admit I was disappointed when I peeked in that wagon and saw that this great and terrible weapon was nothing more than crocks of oil. But no matter, I thought, oil can come in handy in a battle, and maybe we can erect a means of launching them into the Cobalts. Fine. Hardly revolutionary, but fine. Setting the enemy on fire is a time-honored tradition, but this, *this* I will not allow."

"There is something to the proposal, though, isn't there?" asked Colonel Wheatley, even more cautious than usual in his tone. Daft as the green Myuran seemed, he'd evidently come to appreciate that being co-commander of this joint operation was strictly an honorable formality, and on matters military he was not to speak out of turn. "I mean, we have the stuff, it couldn't hurt to try, could it? Might be just the thing for morale, if nothing else."

"Morale is boosted by stalwart command, not magic potions," said Domingo, drunk enough to speechify but not so far gone as to overdo it. "No Azgarothian in living memory has allowed their soldiers to poison their blades, nor slather themselves with Chain grease, and I have no intention of being the first. Long before we called ourselves the Fifteenth, we were noble enough to fight fair, even against those of less chivalrous disposition. What sort of a knight would I be, if I took to using deviltry when we already had strength of numbers and advantage of terrain? We will obliterate the Cobalt rebels absolutely, and with nothing more than cold steel and iron resolve."

"Whether or not the Fifteenth takes part, I will allow any troopers in the Ninth who desire the Chain's succor to be anointed before the battle," said Wheatley, the sudden display of backbone as surprising in this command tent as it would have been in an octopus. Apparently the bronze iron chain around the man's throat represented something more than a memento from a pious uncle or aunt. "Thank you, Brother Wan."

"Yes, yes, thank you for sowing criminal notions in the fertile soil of a greenie's empty helm," said Domingo with a sneer at both the anathema and his human sympathizer. "Since you were but recently promoted to your position, *Colonel* Wheatley, I will pretend I did not hear your suggestion that your soldiers poison their weapons before engaging with the enemy, in clear violation of no fewer than three of the internationally recognized codes governing ethical warfare."

"In open war with an honorable opponent, yes," said Wheatley, quick enough to reply that Domingo would have bet his last biscuit that Brother Wan had coached him on the topic. "The Cobalt Company is not a legal army, though, so wouldn't there be some wiggle room—"

"There's no fucking wiggle room in my tent," said Domingo curtly. "I am amazed you could locate the errata on rebel factions in the Crimson Codices, Wheatley, when you couldn't find your own fucking command at the Siege of Myura. How fortunate for us you were off digging latrines when every other ranking officer was caught by the Cobalts, otherwise we would have had to promote some grunt with actual military experience to the post!"

"I was overseeing the sapping operation," Wheatley said, having gone the color of Wan's naked gums as the anathema gnawed at a piece of sheep cheese, watching the two colonels. "Not *digging latrines*. And the colonel and lieutenants and other captains weren't captured. They say . . . they say they vanished."

"Spirited away, were they, maybe by ghosts or devils?" Wheatley was making this too easy for Domingo—it felt even better to be shaving parts of this boy off with his tongue than it would have to do so with his saber! "They were caught with their greaves unbuckled, Wheatley, not once, but twice—bad enough old lady Culpepper fell for the oldest trick in the songs, sending the whole Ninth out of Myura after an obvious decoy, but then she couldn't even take back her own fucking city. While you were down in the dirt trying to . . . trying to . . ." Domingo was trying not to laugh, ". . . trying to blow open your own colonel's castle, the Cobalts swooped in and butchered the whole command. They vanished, all right, into an unmarked grave somewhere off the road between here and Myura.

Another old Cobalt trick—if the bodies of your enemies are never found, superstitious humps will start whispering about how they weren't killed, they'll say…" Domingo lowered his voice in a passable imitation of the lad, looked back and forth between the livid Colonel Wheatley and the frowning Brother Wan. "They say…they say they *vanished.*"

To say that the silence that followed was awkward would be a bit like saying gangrene was unpleasant: accurate, but nowhere close to capturing the severity of the condition. Domingo watched the trembling, wide-eyed Wheatley very carefully, in case he pounced across the table to attack him with his fork. That's what Domingo would have done, if any of his peers had talked that way to him, even in his youth. Especially in his youth.

"As I said, I mistakenly believed you intended to use Her Grace's weapon because you brought the wagonload of oil all the way here from Diadem, and me along with it," said Brother Wan snottily. Domingo had never seen the witchborn so blatantly annoyed, which, considering the innumerable times he had baited the anathema, seemed yet another feather in Domingo's already many-plumed helm. "If you had refused her gift, I never would have raised the subject, because I never would have had the pleasure of making your acquaintance, to say nothing of riding all over the Empire with you and your army."

"Good steel has a little bend in it, and so does a good colonel," said Domingo. "You are correct that I accepted the Black Pope's weapon, but I have changed my mind. I am allowed to do that. I would rather risk the lives of every soldier in this regiment by fighting the Cobalts fairly than risk their souls by using your devilish magic."

"After all of your lectures on the matter I assumed you didn't believe in an everlasting soul, Colonel," said Wan.

"See here," said Wheatley, "the Burnished Chain does not practice black magic!"

"One fellow's faith is another's heresy," said Hjortt, which didn't sound as clever as he'd thought once he said it, but no matter. He was in charge; he didn't have to be clever.

"There is no more powerful weapon than faith, Colonel—" Wheatley began.

"Codswallop! I've been hearing that line from loonies my whole life—faith is the strongest weapon, the truth is a weapon, blah blah blah. You hit me with your faith and I'll hit you with my fist and we'll see which one's a weapon!"

"Colonel Hjortt," Wan said with poorly contained frustration, "a great many of your soldiers have already asked my brethren if they will be permitted to receive the Burnished Chain's blessing before they see combat. If we could compromise, and I could anoint only those soldiers who request—"

"I don't give a quick fuck what they asked you for, Wan. A soldier will ask for enough beer to drink herself blind and enough cheese to constipate himself for a week, but that doesn't mean they should have it," said Domingo, winking at Wheatley. "Even without the Third coming over from Thao to cut the Cobalts off, between my regiment and Wheatley's we've got more than enough stiff fingers to pluck every blue pansy in the Company. The horse I sent after those Raniputri riders should rejoin us any day, and then, well! It will be a massacre, that's the only word for it—they may have devils and witches and who knows what else, but our combined forces outnumber them two to one. That's all that matters, when the horns blow, not the Black Pope's dread weapon of holy slime and fatuous prayers."

"Thank you for dinner, Colonel," said Wheatley, stiffly rising and dropping his napkin over his barely touched beans. "I think...I think I had better see if the squad I sent to check on that odd signal from the western scouts has returned."

"See that you do," said Domingo, leaning back in his chair rather than standing. Fuck *Colonel* Wheatley. "If it turns out one of your scouts dropped his rifle and alerted the whole bloody mountain range to our presence, have the blighter hanged. That will do wonders for your *morale*, believe you me, nobody in the Ninth will discharge their weapon without—"

But Wheatley had turned without a salute and all but dashed out of the tent. "Well, Colonel..." the witchborn said, refilling Domingo's glass. "If anointing the rank and file is out, I hope it is not too much of an imposition to ask that I bless our armies when the horns sound? Just a few quick words to—"

"It *is* too much to ask, Wan, it damn well is. No Chain nonsense where the Fifteenth is concerned, nor the Ninth, nor any regiment within a hundred leagues of me, and that's final. I won't have you waving your rosaries around and then thieving all the credit when my intense planning and our hardworking troops bring us to victory. The queen's extra-special holy oil gets to ride right back to Diadem, along with news of our honest win over the Cobalts," said Domingo, knocking his glass back in one lusty swallow. Smacking his lips, he dealt the finishing blow: "If you really must have a prayer for them, Wan, I do give you leave to skulk about the latrines blessing the sounding of their farts... But ask for nothing more, or risk my discipline."

The anathema looked like he might squirt a tear, or even better, lose his temper... why, Domingo might have pushed Wan into saying something truly stupid, in which case that horsewhip might get some use after all. And even if it didn't, well, the warmth in Domingo's belly proved that a good tongue-beating could be even more rewarding than the traditional kind. But as he set down his glass a heart-stopping howl tripped his hand, causing the goblet to topple and roll off the table. It wasn't the first howl heard that evening, but it was a damn bit closer than the last few had been.

"Just a coyote, nothing to be alarmed about?" Brother Wan echoed Domingo's words from before, to his profound irritation. It was a low, common sort of thing indeed, mimicking a man.

"Coyote my eye, no mangy hilldog would come so close to a bustling camp," said Domingo, drumming his fingers on the table as he considered the possibilities. First Wheatley's scouts on the western ridge and their mysterious single gunshot, and now this... He rose to his feet. "If you'll excuse me, brother, I intend to go see just what in the merry hells is going on out there. I can't expect much of Wheatley, obviously, but Captain Shea should have something to report about all this caterwauling."

"Of course, sir," said Brother Wan, rising as well and offering a sharp salute. What had Domingo done to deserve this, where the anathemas were better disciplined than his own officers? "Shall I accompany you, or will you have one of the war nuns?"

"Think I'm safe walking around my own bloody camp," said Domingo, though another, closer howl took some of the scorn out of his step as he left the tent, a hand on the hilt of his saber. There was quite a bit of commotion now, as he stepped out into the chill, torchlit evening. Soldiers rushed between the rows of tents, but without betraying any definite purpose. Several gunshots came from the western edge of camp, and then a whole volley went off, the rising walls of the high valley flashing with muzzle blasts. Shouts. Screams. Howls. The pair of war nuns to the left of the tent's entrance were evidencing far less alarm than the pair of burly pureborn soldiers Domingo had stationed on the right, but all four guards looked to him for insight into what was happening, or failing that, an order. "You there, stop, stop at once, damn you!"

The bedraggled squad staggering past the command tent was a rum lot, no doubt about that, but they halted at his command. Wheatley's people, without a doubt—not the lowliest pike lass in the Fifteenth would go around in such a shoddy state. One man was being clumsily carried by three of his comrades, and the other two women supported each other, smeared with blood and dirt from top to bottom, but seeing a little action was no excuse to let your uniforms flap around half-buttoned. "Just what in the yellow hells is happening?"

None of the bedraggled morons spoke at first, trading guilty looks, and then they all started blathering at once:

"Wolves!"

"A whole pack!"

"Big as oxen!"

"Hot on our heels!"

"Enough!" shouted Domingo. "Who's got rank here?"

"Him," said all three of the soldiers carrying the big man with the bloodied leg, nodding at their human cargo. The man raised a drowsy head, saluted in Domingo's direction as best he could with two men holding him up by the shoulders, and slumped back into the arms of his fellows. Domingo recognized him at once, but couldn't place which squad of Wheatley's the man led... No matter, he wouldn't be standing at the front of the ranks when this mess was over, Domingo would see to that—this idiot was getting busted down to stable duty for dereliction of duty, failure to wear a uniform, and... and... something pawed at the back of Domingo's mind, something about this wounded squad leader...

"Begging your pardon, sir, but we need to get him to the sawbones—he's going to lose the leg as it is," said the younger of the two women leaning against one another. Domingo looked her full in the face now, then took a long, hard look at the other one, who was even stranger—her hood bulged out at the top, and beneath the cowl he made out white hair and a flash of red eyes. What the hell was Wheatley thinking, letting his witchborn wear normal cloaks instead of Chain robes? You needed to know at a glance whether someone was a normal soldier or an anathema, that was just common sense.

Another howl ripped at Domingo's nerves, from just the other side of the officers' tents, and he shooed the shirkers away without another thought. Between their maimed squad leader's ridiculous flattop and the white-haired anathema they'd be an easy enough bunch to locate for disciplinary action once things calmed down, but for now it sounded like the beasts had actually stormed his camp. He drew his saber and nodded at his four guards to accompany him on the hunt—he'd never heard of anything so absurd, a pack of wolves attacking—

He froze, having taken only two steps toward the howl, the wounded squad shuffling off in the opposite direction. It wasn't that their parting salutes had been sloppy—that would have been typical for the Ninth Regiment—but not even Wheatley would have soldiers so poorly disciplined that half of them used their right bloody hands. Ill-fitting or missing uniforms. Furtive glances. Heading east when the sawbones' pavilion was north. Domingo was slipping, to have let it go this far, but he made up for the sloppiness with a burst of insight so keen it rattled him to the tips of his boots. *That* was where he had seen the squad leader. Unbelievable.

Pivoting on his heel, he walked leisurely after the squad. They weren't going anywhere, not laden down with their injured leader and their anathema limping along with the help of the young Ugra-kari girl. Domingo's saber felt light as a baton as he closed the ground behind himself and the fleeing spies. "Oh, one more thing."

The squad lurched to a stop again, but not a one of them looked back to meet Domingo's eye. The Ugrakari called, "Yes, sir?"

"I wonder if you would be so good as to drop Captain Maroto on the ground for me, so I don't have to cut him out of your arms." Not bad, Domingo, though at his root he knew he could have done better, if he hadn't been caught so off guard by seeing one of his old nemeses here in his camp...Then, to his further amazement, the men and woman carrying the big man did as he ordered, dropping the so-called Devilskinner onto the trampled meadow grass of the camp.

The witchborn guards behind Domingo shouted in unison, and well they might, but Domingo had seen things that would make a dead man squirm, and he kept his cool even as the monstrous silhouette stepped around the far end of the command tent, cutting off the spies. They'd dropped Maroto because they had seen it first, and slowly drew weapons as the gargantuan horned wolf stalked toward them. This should be quite the show!

Still, he was close enough as it was, and he took a step back, bumping into one of his guards. When he glanced at the girl to tell her to buck up, he saw that she was gawping behind them. He followed her eyes just in time to catch a second horned wolf shooting out from a gap between the officers' tents, burying his bigger witchborn guard in a wave of furious white fur. The other witchborn darted in to help her friend, but even with the speed of devils she was no match for the horned wolf; it snapped its head around to meet her charge, the straightest of its three horns punching neatly through robes, the armor beneath, and into her stomach. It reared back on its hind legs, standing as tall as the tents as it pranced on the first witchborn it had tackled, kicking its front hooves at the impaled woman who hung limply from its horn. A solid shove of a splayed hoof and she slid off, falling through the roof of the command tent and bringing the canvas down around her as the creature dropped back onto all fours.

The horned wolf looked at its next victim, and Domingo looked into the face of death. Maroto's spies were wrong; it wasn't as big as an ox, it was bigger. His last two guards screamed for help as the behemoth took a wary step toward them, but their voices seemed remote to Domingo, as remote as the shouts of Brother Wan inside the collapsing tent, as distant as the clamoring behind him where the other horned wolf rendered Maroto's spies into offal. The only thing Domingo heard clearly was Efrain crying over the kitten his father had refused him, and then the monster charged.

What saved him was not the bravery of his guards, but their cowardice. The man and woman both tried to run but crashed into one another, limbs tangling, and, unable to resist the flurry of motion, the horned wolf careened into the pair. One of its horns speared through both the guards, but as the animal drew up short to dislodge the annoyance from its face, Domingo took a wide step around the side and stabbed it through the eye. It didn't matter if it was mortal, devil, or something in between; a distracted opponent was a dead opponent when Domingo had his saber in hand.

Except deep as his saber went, it didn't go far enough to kill it outright, apparently, for the monster reared away, wrenching his saber out of his hand and snapping his wrist in the process. Pulled to his knees by the momentum, he blinked in surprise, and before his eyes had reopened he felt a battering ram catch him in the left hip. He was in the air, pinwheels of torch and starlight all around him, and then he landed in a roll, extremities crunching and then going dead as he bounced along and finally slid to a stop. Only one eye would open, but as the world stopped reeling he saw the horned wolf that had headbutted him was crashing drunkenly through the tangled canvas of the collapsed command tent, Domingo's saber still jutting from its eye, both guards still caught on its horns. A faint slapping sound, and then another, and black blooms spread on either side of its blind eye. It died abruptly, and Domingo closed his eye and gave silent thanks to the Fifteenth, those brave children of Azgaroth who had saved their father, even when he had been unable to save his son.

"Oi!" A stick prodded at his aching chest, and he tried to sit up and assault his assailant, but barely managed to reopen his eye. He hadn't recognized the voice because he had only ever seen him across the battlefield and had never parleyed with the man during the long war, never spoken to him in peace. There could be no doubt, though, that he had remembered true: the man standing over him was Mighty Maroto, the Fifth Villain of the Cold Cobalt. Well, not standing so much as tottering on the walking stick he had poked Domingo with, the man's black-bandaged knee apparently not just a crafty disguise. "I know you, friend?"

"Yes...Colonel..." he managed through ribs that were surely broken, but then lost his air. He might never speak another word...

"Hmmm," said Maroto, biting his bottom lip as he stared down at Domingo. "Nope. Sorry, friend, I can't say I remember."

"Fifteenth Regiment, out of Azgaroth," said Domingo, clear as the lymph oozing out of him now that rage had overridden agony. After all the times they had matched wits during Cobalt Zosia's war on the Empire, this moron didn't even remember him?

"Ah!" Maroto brightened considerably, snapped his fingers. "At Ensiferum, right before Zosia snuck into Diadem and got Kaldruut with the old sneak-and-shank! You would have had us for sure, if Hoartrap hadn't—"

"Thirteenth," Domingo hissed through gritted teeth. "The Thirteenth met you at Ensiferum, not us. We fought at—"

"Got it loose!" The Ugrakari woman entered Domingo's narrow, black-speckled field of vision. She looked to be holding a huge, wet rug, blood dripping from it to patter against Domingo's cheek. Peering down at the name badge his sister-in-law had sewn on his breast pocket, she said, "Bad news, Colonel Hjortt—looks like the Cobalt Company just jacked your shit *all* up."

"We kind of did, I guess?" Maroto lowered his voice as he leaned closer to the prone Domingo. "Make sure the queen knows I didn't mean to, you know—"

"Time to go!" one of the other spies called.

"Past time!" said another, and, offering him a blood-handed wave, the Ugrakari trotted away.

"Sorry?" Maroto offered Domingo an apologetic smile. "Sure it'll come to me, where we met. Probably right after I leave, you know?"

"Now, Maroto!"

"Right, sure. Like I said, really sorry about this—Colonel Hjortt, was it? Won't forget again, promise."

Domingo shut his throbbing eye—he'd always thought he'd be ready to look head-on at his own demise, but ignoble as it had turned out to be, he wanted no part in it. Killed by a ravenous monster in the mountains, that he could have done…but the truth was he'd been murdered by the incompetence of his own soldiers, who had let a pack of overgrown devil dogs into his camp, and a crew of obvious spies in the bargain. And now, at the very end, he was to be executed by a man who didn't even remember him. He tried to think of his murdered son, tried to think of the wife who had left them both to become an ambassador to Usba, but all he could think about was how fucking terrible it was that he should come this far, only to…

"Colonel?" Hjortt cracked his eye, and immediately regretted it. He wouldn't live out the night, bashed-in as he felt, and now the last thing he would ever see was Brother Wan's grisly visage. The anathema swam in and out of focus. "Sir, I know it must be hard to speak, but who were those soldiers who saved you? Come what may, I know you'll want commendations for them."

"They're…dead." Domingo's tongue felt heavier than his eyelid. *Stop them. Arrest them. Spies.* But no more words would leave his mouth that night, nor for several days to come. When he finally returned to consciousness and found Brother Wan at his bedside, the long-delayed intelligence came streaming out.

"Did you stop them, Wan? Are they in chains? Maroto's spies?"

"Um…" Brother Wan didn't have to give more answer than that, and Domingo let out a protracted groan, the pain of his weakness in not clinging to consciousness a few moments longer overshadowing the throbbing aches that occupied most of his body. "Is there anything I can get you, Colonel?"

"Yes," said Domingo, trying to sit up and spasming instead. "Every drop of the Black Pope's poison. And if you've got any devils or spells, those as well. Call on your heathen god, call on the Deceiver, call on every power. We're going to use your weapon, Wan, and we're going to kill every Cobalt we can find, and we're not going to be nice about it."

CHAPTER
10

That Sullen boy. *Damn.* It wasn't just that Ji-hyeon could tell he was into her, if only a little. She wasn't as pathetic as *that.* Dozens of people had made passes at her, especially as her small band of mercenaries became a large one, and finally grew big enough to call themselves the Cobalt Company. Once there was a Cobalt Empire, she'd be beating them off with the blunt end of an ax, even her advisors. Especially her advisors.

She wasn't callow enough to think most of these advances arose from earnest interest in her mind, body, or soul, though suitors had called on every conceivable combination of the three. Any idiot could see she was no more than a year out from a decisive conquest of Samoth, and everyone knew if you took Samoth you took the Empire. What's more, she'd do it without any of that wandering-the-wilderness business of her spiritual predecessor. No, what it had taken Zosia half a decade to accomplish, Ji-hyeon would see completed in under two years, and without thousands of her followers starving in the process. Ji-hyeon's victory was inevitable, which surely had something to do with all these attempts on her love life—get in before she was queen, before she realized people were just after her for power. As if she were that stupid.

Sullen wasn't like that, but it was more than just his earnest attention that appealed. After all, some of the others had probably been genuine in their affection, too. In part it was his attitude, respectful but not overly so. Maybe it was just pig ignorance on the boy's part, as Fennec suggested every chance he could, but to Ji-hyeon it seemed...real, as though she'd actually impressed him without even trying. Well, maybe she'd been trying a little, because she was always on, it seemed, trying to astound everyone, trying to fill the greaves of a woman whose death had elevated her from leader to god. Yet those quiet afternoons when she had him alone in her tent, taking kaldi with the quiet barbarian, she actually felt like herself again— not like Zosia Returned, as Fennec and the rest wanted, and not like Princess Ji-hyeon Bong of Hwabun, Betrothed of Prince Byeong-gu of Othean, etcetera, as her first father had wanted, but just like... Ji-hyeon. She didn't like to think of it that way, but something in Sullen's sincere interest in her moods instead of her ambitions, in her past instead of her future, reminded her of how things could be...of what she'd had with Keun-ju.

Keun-ju. It almost didn't hurt to think of him now. Not that she was some moonstruck kid, hung up on the first boy to reach under her dress, but she had really loved him, and even now she caught herself daydreaming explanations for his duplicity, envisioning scenarios to explain his actions. It wasn't like Sullen had come along and all of a sudden Keun-ju was forgotten; anything but. She thought of Keun-ju more than ever now, and, strangest of all, Sullen encouraged her. When she had told him about their relationship, and how Keun-ju had betrayed Ji-hyeon to her first father, almost foiling her escape from Hwabun, he had nodded sympathetically and said:

"That's bad. I've been bit by beasts, and I've been bit by...by loved ones, and loved ones bite worst. Sorry, Ji-hyeon."

Sorry, Ji-hyeon. Simple, heartfelt, and oh so welcome. They'd been talking over kaldi, and even as the bowl went cold in her cupped hands he hadn't pressed her for more or tried to talk everything better, the way Fennec would have. She couldn't wait for him to meet Choi—when the laconic met the terse, who knew what might go unsaid?

A week later, another report came back that Keun-ju still hadn't sent word. It was the same shitty news she had received each and every month since she'd first left Hwabun with only two of her three guards. It was the not knowing where he was or what had really happened that made the pain of missing him so much worse.

"Nah," said Sullen, when she imperfectly articulated all this to him. "Pain's good. It's how you know you've been stuck, but also how you know you'll heal. Only thing that doesn't hurt is being dead."

"You sure about that?" Ji-hyeon eyed him skeptically over her ryefire.

"Devils, I hope so," said Sullen, blowing out his cheeks. "If being dead hurts, I don't want no part of it."

So he was funny, in an effortless sort of way, on top of the rest. But there was something else, too, and if it made her a shallow person, well, she had been called worse. What it was, simply, was this: Sullen was damn easy on the eyes.

Tall wasn't always her thing, and lanky but tight-muscled could go either way, but combine all that with his rich, dark skin, wide, striking features, and that halo of shocking white hair? Spirits keep her in check. Then there were those eyes... they were closer to a cat's than a man's, with inky pupils arching all the way up the cornflower blue orbs, the sparkling brightness a pleasing contrast to his perpetually serious jaw line. He had his fair share of scars, and some more besides, his nose had been broken so many times it looked off-center, and his enormous puffball of hair could do with some shaping, but still: the boy looked damn good.

She almost kissed those velvety lips, too, the night of drunken nonsense, but then Fennec had burst in with more news on the small Raniputri force that had been dogging their cat, and so she was saved the conundrum of what to do after a first kiss. For now. Gods, devils, and spirits willing, she wouldn't be spared that puzzle for too much longer. When Hoartrap informed her that the Raniputri riders would catch up to their slowly marching company within a day or two, and that his devils told him Choi, Maroto, and his noble entourage were but a few days out themselves, she decided it was time. What Sullen would do when his uncle returned had been left unsaid, as had the particulars of both her rise to power and his quest for his uncle—for all the time they'd logged since he'd crashed her camp, they had yet to revisit the aborted topic of their first conversation. It was time for that, too. Definitely.

Well, maybe.

"Did you name her?" Sullen asked, watching Fellwing squirm her way around the nearby heap of Ji-hyeon's chainmail. The owlbat loved crawling across her armor, hooking tiny talons in the links.

"My father did," said Ji-hyeon. "She was his before she was mine. They all bound their devils together, I guess—Dad, your uncle, Fennec, Hoartrap, the chevaleresse, and Zosia."

"My uncle...has *a devil*?" It took little to arouse Sullen's curiosity but quite a bit to surprise him.

"Not anymore, or else he's good enough at hiding him to fool even Hoartrap. But they all captured the creatures together, before they captured Samoth." Fellwing landed on her arm as she spoke.

"Horned Wolves don't bind devils," said Sullen glumly. "Not supposed to, anyway."

"Nor do the Immaculate, as a rule," said Ji-hyeon. "The royal family have some, but most people still think it's disrespectful."

"That's one word for it," said Sullen. "Disrespectful. The Jackal People take slaves, other clans, too, but not the Horned Wolves."

"A devil's not the same as a slave," said Ji-hyeon, stroking Fellwing and summoning a throaty croak from her beak.

"Then set her free, and see if she stays," said Sullen, which pissed Ji-hyeon right off.

"Is a horse a slave, then? What about cattle, or other livestock? I don't intend to eat Fellwing, so I'd say she's doing better than most beasts."

"Huh," said Sullen. "You're right."

"Of course I am," said Ji-hyeon, pouring them more malty liquor.

"Horned Wolves raise cattle and fowl, and trade for mules. We don't call them that, but they're slaves, just as you said. Not so different from others, much as we like to pretend. We're as bad as the rest of you."

"Well, it's nice to hear Saint Sullen admit such a mortal weakness."

"What?" Sullen blinked at her. He could be thick sometimes, the same as anyone. "Oh. Ha, no. Yes. Didn't mean to be a jerk. I'm bad, too, Ji-hyeon. Most people are, I guess. I've broken the laws of my clan. Killed one of my own people. Did everything wrong, and all because I was trying to do right. It's not easy, doing good."

It was hard to imagine the gentle, earnest man sitting across from her attacking anyone, let alone a fellow Horned Wolf. But he'd done something to come by those scars, and that white hair of his. Much as she liked him as an enigma, it was long past time she heard his tale. But that meant she had to go first.

"I've talked your ear off about Keun-ju, but you've never asked why I ran away from home, about what came before or after."

Sullen fidgeted on his cushion, knocked back his drink with a grimace. "Yeah...Sorry. I'd like to hear, I would, but didn't want to push you. I hate being pushed. Love Grandfather, but he's pushy, and much as I want to be like him some ways, that ain't one of 'em."

"Oh hells, I wasn't complaining! Quite the contrary," said Ji-hyeon, brushing Fellwing off her. The devil flitted over to Sullen, and he stuck out a finger for her to perch on. She'd never seen her owlbat land on anyone else, and like everything else in this world, that could probably be an omen. "I would call you many things, Sullen, but not pushy. You'd really like to hear?"

"Definitely," said the man, offering a sugarcube to the devil on his finger.

"So you know I'm a princess, and all that. Hwabun was a great place to grow up, though I didn't appreciate what I had until I left. Is that how the Frozen Savannahs are for you?"

"Huh. Not exactly," said Sullen, scratching his crooked nose. "See it different now that I'm gone, though. And I miss my mom. A lot."

"I miss my first father, Jun-hwan, though the last year I was there we couldn't stand each other. Yunjin, my older sister, said it was like that for them, too, when she was my age. Things get strained, especially when one of your dads is trying to marry you off. And I told you about Keun-ju, and what he meant to me. One of the conditions of the marriage my first father brokered was that Keun-ju wasn't to come with me—it would be rude, he said, for me to take my own servant into a nicer house, and my fiancé was the son of the ruler of the Immaculate Isles. Houses don't come nicer than that."

Fellwing finally got her beak around Sullen's sugarcube and carried it up to a crossbeam in the tent poles.

"So I'm supposed to leave behind my favorite guard, to marry this nebbish I've met all of zero times. The idea turned my stomach—I *loved* Keun-ju, even though I didn't know he loved me back, not then. And so the same night I finally met my fiancé for the first time, I snuck off by myself. Well, not alone, my guards were there—Fennec, but back then I thought he was just a Chainite missionary named Mikal, and Choi, who you'll meet soon, I hope, and there was Keun-ju. And we were out in some fields looking for spirits, near the Temple of Pentacles. That's where the Immaculate Gate is, the one I ended up escaping through when I ran away a few months later—I told you about going through the Gate, right?"

"Uh-huh," said Sullen, touching his hair with a wince. "I mean, a little. The first time we took kaldi you said it was kinda like going into a sea, only the sea was the First Dark."

"Ha, I said that? Well, yeah, it kind of was…Anyway, we were real close to the one on the Isles, the Temple of Pentacles, and all of a sudden this…this spirit monster attacked us! There were smaller spirits in the field, in the pumpkins, but this one…this was like a bunch of them all mashed up together to make something huge, huge and scary and dangerous."

"I can picture that," said Sullen, nervously licking his lips. Oh, he had a song to sing when it was his turn to tell how his hair turned white, she knew it!

"So we fought it, the four of us against a monster straight out of the bedtime stories my second father would tell us about his adventures with Zosia and the rest of the Villains. And we won! It was… well, you've been in fights before, so you know what it's like. First you're too scared to move, and then something takes over, all your training wakes up, and your sword's in your hand before you know it! And you're fighting, fighting for your life! And it's just…so…"

"Terrible," said Sullen, looking into his ryefire bowl.

"Yes! No! I mean, it's scary, but it's also kind of wonderful, isn't it? Dodging out of the way at the last minute, cleaving into your enemy, fighting alongside your friends and working together like you were born to do this and nothing more! Not even thinking, just...doing, and doing it so freaking good! Hack, slash, parry, dodge, hack again! Devils above, I get tingly just thinking about it."

"Have you talked to a barber about that?" asked Sullen, and given his general demeanor, it was only by his sly smile that she knew he was joking.

"I know you've felt it, Sullen, I know it."

"Well...maybe. Yeah."

"Anyway, when it was done, and the spirit king slain, we went back to the Autumn Palace, and everything after that was just so... *dull*. And not just dull like it'd been before, but poisonously so. I was depressed for weeks after, and not just from the lecture I got from my first dad on the boat ride back to Hwabun. I think he would have been happier if it'd eaten me than he was to have me come back in to the festivities the way I did. He said I was an embarrassment, and when I asked if it was embarrassing that my other dad was one of Zosia's Villains for all those years he said yes, that was embarrassing, too. What's embarrassing about buying your life back from Death herself, with your own sword?"

"Hmmmm," said Sullen, giving it his full consideration. "Nothing, to my mind."

"Nor mine! So it was inevitable, really, that I'd decide to do what I did, even without Fennec whispering in my ear. I see now he had his own motivations for counseling me on such a course, but I'm still glad he did. Choi wouldn't even talk to me about it, as in, *at all*. When I first brought it up she said, 'I swore an oath to serve your martial needs, and will do so until I die. Do not ask me to advise on other matters, but be sure you always consider all possibilities, and do not be swayed by any heart but your own.' That doesn't sound like much, but I've never heard her say so much in one go, or so clearly, either before or since. I even wrote it down right away, because I knew I'd forget it otherwise, and forced myself to memorize it, because that's some serious, sutra-level wisdom, isn't it?"

"It is," said Sullen thoughtfully, as though he were still digesting the words.

"But yeah, I never expected Choi to come along so easily. And while Keun-ju balked at first, once I persuaded him it was the only way for us to be together he came around. I *thought*. It's not too long a sail from Hwabun to the Temple of Pentacles, and from there a few seconds to any Arm of the Star, if you know how to use the Gates, so it should have been easy to leave before anyone knew we were gone."

"So how does it work?" Sullen asked. It took a lot to freak out a wildborn, but freaked out the man definitely looked. "The first time you invited me here you told me about going through, but...but I can't even *think* about that without feeling sick."

"Obviously it wouldn't have worked if I'd just tried to strut through on my own," said Ji-hyeon. "Who knows where I would've ended up, probably some obscure hell I've never even heard of. But long before he came to Hwabun, Fennec did some work for Hoar-trap in exchange for the secret of the Gates. Now he can step into any Gate, and after a few paces come out any other, and bring along anyone he wants. As for how it works, I don't have the slightest damn notion, it was all Fennec's doing...and I don't think he's quite the expert he claimed to be, either, all things considered. What's really weird, though, is nothing happened to Choi—my hair turned white, Fennec's hands changed, but Choi's still Choi. Then again, she had white hair and horns and fangs to begin with..."

"Hmmmm," said Sullen. It was less a contemplative sound and more the noise of a dog displeased at being roused from a doze.

"Anyway, the Gate was where we were headed when Keun-ju pulled that shit I told you about," said Ji-hyeon. "I've kept telling myself it was a coincidence, that he didn't deceive us...But from inception, we all agreed that if something happened and we couldn't all go together, then whoever was left behind would send a coded message to a certain Linkensterne merchant who owes my second father a great boon. We're coming up on a year since I left, and Keun-ju's sent nothing...so maybe it's about time I made myself accept the truth about him, don't you think?"

"The truth," said Sullen, pursing his lips as Ji-hyeon rose. She used the pretext of fetching a blanket to sit down beside him when she returned. She'd thought it warm across from him, but here, with their knees brushing as she settled onto a cushion and pulled the unnecessary blanket around her shoulders, it was downright smoldering. "How do you know the truth of Keun-ju?"

This hadn't been what Ji-hyeon expected him to latch onto; surely *Don't you think I should get over my ex?* was a more intriguing question for him to consider? Unless she had totally misread his surreptitious glances and shy smiles..."I told you, he was late meeting us at the boat, despite how many times we went over the plan, and then... then when he did come down to the dock, all smiles, every other guard on Hwabun was sneaking just behind him. If Choi hadn't spotted them we never would have launched in time; as it was, Keun-ju barely missed the boat when he jumped after us!"

"Yeah, but how do you know? I mean, what he was thinking? That he brought the guards on purpose?"

The memory stank, and Ji-hyeon stole Sullen's lukewarm bowl of ryefire to clear her nostrils with its hot scent. "You mean besides him shouting 'stop, stop!' just before he dove off the pier after us? Fennec saw him leaving my first father's chambers that very morning, and in all the years he was in our house he had never set foot there before. Later that day he bathed me before afternoon prayers, and didn't say a single word about what would have been quite the oddity, had it been unrelated. We shared everything, and the only reason he wouldn't mention my first father calling him in for an audience would be if he had something to hide. I didn't want to believe it, either, I still don't..."

"So don't," said Sullen, sounding like the words stung him but needing them out all the same. "I wouldn't, unless I had to. And right now you don't."

"What do you mean?" Ji-hyeon shivered, and, no doubt misreading it as arising from her being cold, Sullen slowly extended his arm over her back and gave her far shoulder an endearingly self-conscious squeeze. Oh, how she wanted him to keep his hand there, but he quickly retrieved the appendage and, obviously not quite sure what to do with it, flopped it in his lap.

"It's all Fennec's word," said Sullen. Mistaking her expression for confusion, he elaborated: "That Keun-ju was with your dad, your first dad, and that the merchant in wherever would deliver a message from Keun-ju, if he tried sending one. Last time we talked you said Keun-ju and Fennec didn't like each other much, and clever as Fennec is, maybe he figured a way to bite Keun-ju without making it obvious... I'm not saying nothing, just, you know, thinking. You don't seem like you trust Fennec as much as I'd expect you to trust someone who's got as much pull as he does with your people... So yeah, if you don't trust him altogether, I don't trust him at all. Especially seeing how tight he is with Hoartrap."

Sullen clamped his mouth shut, perhaps remembering that Ji-hyeon herself took the sorcerer's counsel. Perhaps he realized he'd just suggested the general's closest advisor might have played her for a chump. Or perhaps he was just embarrassed at having spoken as much in a minute as he usually said all night. Whatever the cause, he no longer seemed able to look at her, let alone meet the stare she turned at him. Not being an imbecile, she had lost many a night's sleep pondering that very question, but had always assumed it irrational, to put it kindly, and crazy fucking paranoid, to put it bluntly. That it was the first possibility an objective listener came to after hearing even a truncated version of events raised some sticky questions indeed.

Even studiously inspecting the tent poles where Fellwing nested, Sullen must have sensed that Ji-hyeon was trembling all over, because his hand crept back across her shoulder. Quite without her meaning to, her back rose to meet his fingers, pressing firmly into his cautious touch. This time he kept his arm around her after offering a squeeze, gently kneading her shoulder. His arm pulled her hair a little, but whatever.

"Are you a good judge of honesty?" asked Ji-hyeon, when she could bring herself to talk, her mind racing her thundering heart and coming out a nose ahead. "I'd like you to be here in any event, when I sit Fennec down for a talk. I want you to watch him, and if he doesn't come clean at once tell me right then and there if you think he's lying."

Sullen's hand stopped its slight prodding, his whole arm going rigid. He gulped, but still wouldn't look at her. Afire with movement all at once, he stood, his fingers swimming upstream through her hair in a rush and then falling lamely at his side. "Let's go find him, then. With a natural liar like him it won't be easy, but together we can crack him. I know it."

"Wait," said Ji-hyeon, grabbing his wrist and hoisting herself up, the blanket slipping off her shoulders. The blue-skirted, bell-shaped dress she wore around her tent suddenly felt constrictive despite its bagginess, and for a change she longed to be in her sexy, chafing armor instead of comfortable clothes. Even more confused about her feelings than she'd been when she mostly believed that Keun-ju had betrayed them, she did what she'd always done when at an impasse—charged straight ahead, hoping for the best. In this case, she blundered straight into a handsome Flintlander, still holding his limp wrist in one hand and sliding her other across his striped tunic, his muscles twitching under her touch and tightening up even more as she ran her hand over and down to his hip, until she could firmly turn him to face her. Ridiculously, he still wasn't looking at her, his chin cocked up in the air and his eyes fixed on her dozing devil. Ji-hyeon gulped, scared all over again that she'd sussed things totally wrong...Nothing to do but ask, then. "Are you going to make me climb you like a tree to steal a kiss?"

With wonderful, terrible slowness, he turned down to look her in the face. Devils below, he looked in fear of his life! "You...you don't have to steal it. But...well, what if I'm right?"

"Then we better be fast about this, just in case you are," said Ji-hyeon, and stood on her tiptoes even as Sullen leaned down. He tasted of ryefire and stale smoke, and was as bad a kisser as she'd been before Keun-ju had taught her. She fucking loved it, her hands eagerly exploring his chest, wondering what would happen now that they'd shared a first kiss and were already working on a second, a third, a fourth, forgotten gods of the Sunken Kingdom, did he feel good under her fingers…

And having the matter decided for her when a throat cleared at the entrance to her tent. She wheeled away from Sullen, barking a shin on the kaldi table, ready to bellow at Chevaleresse Sasamaso or one of the other guards for not announcing herself before barging in, when she saw Fennec himself standing there, holding the canvas flap open with a slightly shaky hand. He looked uncharacteristically nervous, his face flushed. "General, we need to speak, immediately, about—"

"Oh yes, yes, we all need to speak, and immediately at that," said Hoartrap, striding in past Fennec, whose eyes went wider at the old giant's appearance. Behind her, Ji-hyeon heard Sullen crack his fingers, his warming shadow crossing her as he stepped over the kaldi table to have a clear path to the sorcerer who said, "I wondered if you'd run for the general or the hills when you got a good look at her, Fennec old boy, and there's my answer."

"Riddles are never welcome in my tent, gentlemen," said Ji-hyeon, giving each of them her best worst scowl. "What unholy horror do I have to thank for not one but both of you bursting in here in such a rude fashion? Unless the matter is grave indeed—"

"Grave is certainly the word!" said Hoartrap, clearly overjoyed. "General Ji-hyeon Bong of the Cobalt Company, may I introduce you to the Raniputri emissaries who have been hot on our heels these many days."

Three hooded figures came striding into her tent like they'd been invited, and Ji-hyeon's fists balled at the insult. She hadn't even had time to pull on a vest over her simple dress, to say naught of actually changing into something more formal. Emissaries or emperors, Hoartrap and Fennec would have much to answer for once these foreigners were dealt with...but for now Ji-hyeon forced a pleased expression onto her face and, dipping low into a bow, greeted the emissaries in High Immaculate:

"Welcome to my camp, honored guests. I am General Ji-hyeon Bong of the Cobalt Company, and would have your names in turn so that we might—"

"Ji-hyeon!" The smallest of the hooded emissaries charged forward, crying her name, and Sullen darted between them, holding up a palm as if that were all it took to thwart an assassin. As it happened, the man *did* stop, throwing back his hood and veil to give Sullen a familiar glare as he said, "Ji-hyeon, it's me!"

"Keun-ju?" Keun-ju! Sullen tripped over the kaldi table in his haste to get out of the way, and as Ji-hyeon embraced her old lover she heard her new one curse under his breath as he hopped on one foot. Keun-ju pressed his lips to her cheek, hard, and then she felt a tear dribble off his lips and down her chin. It was really him...

"This is just great," said one of the other emissaries, and though it pained her, Ji-hyeon quickly stepped back from Keun-ju, looking to the two older women who had accompanied him. They both had their hoods back now, and although she couldn't tell the speaker's nationality, the other woman was obviously Raniputri. "You even went for the hair. Well, why not, if you're taking everything else. By the six devils I bound, young'un, for an impostor you look perfect as a portrait."

"I am indebted to you for returning my Virtue Guard to me," said Ji-hyeon through gritted teeth. "Impostor" was not a word that got easier on the ears. "Even if your manners leave something to be desired, Auntie. Who do I have the honor of offering my thanks?"

"Ha!" The Raniputri belatedly put a mailed hand to her mouth. "Oh hells, this is too much."

"Ji-hyeon," began Keun-ju, but the silver-haired emissary's booming voice cut him off as she took a step forward:

"Who am *I*? Girl, I'm the woman your fathers hired to take you home."

Ji-hyeon's eyes flicked to Keun-ju's sheepish expression—he had betrayed her after all! Strangely, neither Hoartrap nor Fennec made a move to stop the older woman's advance, and the futility of it all sunk in. She'd been set up, and this was how it all ended. Well, not without a fight. Before she could deliver the first punch to Keun-ju's stupid face, however, the woman said something else, something that pinned Ji-hyeon in place:

"More than that, though, I'm *you*, you devildamned brat—or don't you recognize me? I'm Cobalt Zosia, returned from the fucking grave."

From the far side of the tent where Sullen had retreated after tripping on the kaldi table, Ji-hyeon saw the man go totally still, his eyes wide as hers must be. It couldn't be her, of course it couldn't, of all the laws of mortals, gods, and even devils, there was no coming back from death...But looking into the woman's cold cobalt eyes, Ji-hyeon believed her.

CHAPTER

11

Zosia didn't much think of herself as a proud person, but devils knew it felt good to shut down Kang-ho's brat. The runaway looked the part, all right, severe bangs giving way to waterfalls of longer hair, her pretty young face framed in cobalt. Her Immaculate dress was plain, as much as those garments could be, so maybe all her success hadn't gone to her head yet. Add to that her entertaining a hunky, white-haired Flintlander alone in her tent at this hour, and you had a girl after Zosia's own heart.

"It's really her," Keun-ju told the slack-mouthed girl. "I'm sure of it. She met your fathers on Hwabun, and, well, it's a long story."

"Queen Zosia," breathed Ji-hyeon, and, dropping to one knee, lowered her head. "I am honored to bow before you."

"General," said Fennec, somewhat frantically. "There's no need for all that, I'm sure. As our guest Zosia is owed hospitality, of course, but—"

"Out, Captain," said Ji-hyeon, looking up but staying on one knee. She had the ridiculous seriousness of the young and sincere etched on her fine features. "All of you, save the queen."

"Ji-hyeon..." Keun-ju said plaintively, and even knowing this girl for all of two minutes, Zosia could tell that was the wrong tack to take with her.

"Everyone out. Now."

"General, let's take a moment before deciding anything," Fennec tried again, the old fox sly as ever. He hadn't met Zosia's eyes once since he'd seen her, Keun-ju, and Singh being led to the general's tent by a dozen guards, the rest of the Raniputri waiting a few miles outside of camp. Instead, he'd swiveled on his heel and booked it back here, no doubt trying to get in a word with Ji-hyeon before they arrived. Hoartrap's crazy ass had the decency to walk them in, making his usual absurd small talk, though she could tell even he was taken aback to see her alive and well.

"Did I give an order or ask a question, Fennec?" demanded Ji-hyeon. "I'll send word when I want you back here. For now, I wish to speak with the queen. Alone."

The sinewy Flintlander nearly tripped over his feet again in his haste to be gone; he was trying just as hard as Fennec not to look at Zosia. Weird—he was certainly too young for their paths ever to have crossed before, but then again her reputation certainly seemed to precede her everywhere she went. As he passed her, she noticed a familiar tattoo on his arm, and flashed him a smile.

"Nice meeting you, too, Horned Wolf," she said in the trading tongue of the Savannahs. "No relation of Maroto's, are you?"

"Sullen nephew," he mumbled, and then was away into the night. What the hell was a sullen nephew? Maybe just some obscure Horned Wolf Tribe greeting or apology or something, though he looked enough like Maroto to be kinfolk.

"So *good* to have you both back," purred Hoartrap, but when he moved to pet Choplicker the devil whined and avoided him, hustling to a far corner of the spacious tent with his tail tucked. There wasn't much to recommend about the crazy old wizard, but the fear he always put into Choplicker endeared Zosia to the man. Or so she tried to tell herself, anyway; if she were being real with herself, it unnerved her a bit. "We have so much to discuss, once you're all caught up with our fearless general. It's been too long, Zosia."

"Uh-huh," said Zosia, knocking fists with Hoartrap and turning to Fennec as the old behemoth left the tent, Singh accompanying him out. "Hey, Fennec! It's me! Your old friend! Happy to see you, too, fucker!"

After his initial cringing at her volume, Fennec finally faced her, smiling sheepishly. "If I'd known you were still around, Cobalt, I would have played it differently. Much differently. I'm glad you're alive."

"Hey now, don't fall apart on me," said Zosia, clapping the man in a tight hug. He'd put on some pounds, his sharply dashing features smoothed out by the years, but otherwise he'd aged a sight better than Hoartrap, Kang-ho, or even Singh. Or herself, for that matter. Slapping his back a bit harder than he probably liked, she released him. "Now beat it, me and Ji-hyeon here have lots to talk about, I don't doubt."

"Ji-hyeon, if I could stay, too, and—" Keun-ju began, but Ji-hyeon stiffly rose from her bow and laid what looked like a neck-breaking kiss on the Virtue Guard. Fennec coughed softly and, patting Zosia's shoulder, exited as well. Breaking off from her lover, Ji-hyeon pushed his chest with two fingers.

"Don't think you get to dance back in here without an explanation," she said, her voice betraying only the slightest quaver. "I'd start working on a damn good lie, if I were you. Now scat."

Keun-ju offered Zosia a weak smile as he left, the boy practically floating out of the tent. She was finally alone with the princess. Might as well start things off on the right boot.

"Looks like you've got a tidy setup here, Ji-hyeon. You can dress a pig in armor and lead him to the front, but that doesn't mean he'll be anything but bacon when the war starts."

"Auntie," said the girl, all trace of humility gone now that they were alone. "I must have misheard you. It sounded like you just called me a sow."

Zosia shrugged. "You're winning battles, it sounds like. Picking up plenty of volunteers, as well as the mercenaries you've bought from sacking all those Imperial cities. So you tell me, girl—is this, ahem, *Cobalt Company* of yours doing so well on account of its brilliant general, or are a bunch of dusty old men whispering in a piglet's floppy ear?"

"Now that's just not very friendly," sniffed the girl, turning her back on Zosia and squatting down in front of the tent's low table.

She was mucking about with a mortar and pestle, as though she were some witch preparing a philter...but then Zosia heard the kaldi beans crunch and smelled their soft bouquet, and a powerful thirst tickled her throat. It had been way too damn long since she'd had a decent cup of kaldi, the Raniputri preferring a hundred different teas. Without looking up from her preparation, Ji-hyeon said, "Grab a cushion, Auntie, I've got just the thing to sweeten that tart tongue of yours."

"Much obliged," said Zosia, but just as she was about to plant herself on the biggest, least saddlelike pillow in the tent, she saw something that stopped her short. Choplicker was sitting perfectly still on his butt, his front legs straight, his eyes fixed on the small owlbat that perched on the tip of his snout, staring back at him. "Is that...that's Fellwing, isn't it?"

"Oh yes, you know her, don't you?" said Ji-hyeon, looking up as she dumped the grounds into a silver press. There were already three dirty ones on the table. This girl put away some kaldi, to be sure. "He is...Mouthlicker?"

"Close enough," said Zosia, sitting. Watching devils commune was as creepy as camping in front of a Gate. "Your bad dad gave him to you, huh? Wasn't expecting that."

"No?" said Ji-hyeon, filling a kettle from a small cask and resting it atop the brass stove that was heating the tent. "I wonder what you were expecting, Auntie. Other than a pig in armor, of course."

"Look, let's just level here," said Zosia, all the months catching up to her now that she was sitting in a tent with Princess Ji-hyeon Bong. She'd logged over a thousand miles, and racked up quite a few more dead bodies, all to end up in a disturbingly familiar rebel camp a few hundred leagues south of Kypck. A whole year of bouncing around the Star, and she was right back where she'd started. "I don't give a shit what either of your fathers want. I don't give *half* a shit what *you* want. But I think that right here, right now, we can both help each other out. And to do that we have to be more honest than we'd ever be with Hoartrap, Fennec, or any of the others. Yeah?"

"Maybe," said Ji-hyeon, smiling for the first time as she settled in across from Zosia. "I guess that remains to be determined, doesn't it? You see, Blue Zosia, I know everything there is to know about you, but you don't know the first thing about me. So how can you so be so sure you have anything to offer me, or my army?"

"I know enough, Princess," said Zosia, and as much to wipe the simper off the brat's face as anything else she launched right into it. One advantage of months upon months of stormy seas and windy mountains was you had plenty of time to think. "Your daddy Kang-ho's been a part of this scheme since the beginning, not that the fucker told me so. He gave me the same sob story he gave your other dad, about your being carried off by big, bad Fennec. I don't think Jun-hwan buys it any more than I did, for what it's worth."

"Oh," said Ji-hyeon. Then, not surprisingly, given her age, she asked, "Is he all right? My first father? And sisters? Nobody's too upset, are they? They don't have any right to be, shabbily as they treated me... Hey, don't light that up in here. I don't want my tent stinking like tubāq."

"Eh?" Zosia glanced down at the pipe she'd pulled out without even thinking about it. "Really?"

"Really," said Ji-hyeon.

"You sure you're Kang-ho's kid?" asked Zosia, but she put the piece away. Ji-hyeon rose and picked a camel hair blanket up off the floor, wrapping it around her shoulders as the kettle began its keening. Once the kaldi was steeping, she settled back down, legs and arms crossed as she watched Zosia. Her air was of a difficult child demanding a proper bedtime story.

"You got anything to put in the kaldi?" asked Zosia.

"I can send for some ghee, or—"

"No, no, soju or potato wine or something?"

"Ah, sure," said Ji-hyeon, waving at a jug on the table. Ryefire, thank the devils who love us. It was almost empty, but better than nothing. "You were telling me about my family?"

"Oh yeah. They're full of shit, all of them, but you probably know that. Kang-ho helped you and Fennec run off, along with, um, what's her name, the weirdborn?"

"Choi prefers the term *wildborn*," said Ji-hyeon, not arguing the point about her dad.

"Right, Choi's your Martial Guard. Where is she, anyway? I heard she never left your side."

"She's with another of your Villains, Maroto. They're on a reconnaissance mission, but should be back soon. Should've been back already, in fact."

"Maroto!" Improbably, Zosia found herself delighted to hear that he was slinking around somewhere, working for Ji-hyeon. From the way Kang-ho and Singh had talked about him, she'd assumed he had stung himself to death, or was close enough to it as made no difference. Good for him, getting honest work again! "But I was saying— Keun-ju was supposed to come with you, Fennec, and Choi, all the princess's guards defecting along with their mistress. But even though Keun-ju didn't know your dad was helping facilitate the escape, your dad definitely knew you were banging the Virtue Guard."

"I say!" said Ji-hyeon, her cheeks turning as red as Samothan wine.

"Sure you do. So, Fennec helped Kang-ho pull the rug out from under Keun-ju at the last moment, stopped him from splitting with you. Then he went one further and tried to have your lover executed." Zosia watched Ji-hyeon carefully as she tried this gambit. It wouldn't hold up once Keun-ju and Ji-hyeon had a proper sit-down and he gave her his account, but right here and now Zosia needed to slide as big a wedge as possible between the princess and her second father. To cover her tail for later she shrugged, and amended herself: "Or exiled or something. The point is, your dad did him dirty—must not have approved of his little girl shacking up with a slave."

"He's not a slave," said Ji-hyeon with all the sickeningly sweet naïveté of the young and spoiled.

"Sure, sure. Anyway, your other dad must've believed that Keun-ju was innocent, or maybe just more valuable kept alive and close at hand. Since Jun-hwan obviously wears the hat on Hwabun, your boy toy stayed on in the house, twiddling his thumbs till I came along. Like I said, Kang-ho tried to play dumb with me, but Jun-hwan's more devious than his husband gives him credit. So your first father sent me off to bring you back, with Keun-ju along for the ride. Of course your second dad tried to have us bumped off along the way, but I don't bump so easy. That's me, following you, up to this magical evening."

Ji-hyeon poured the kaldi, clearly considering some new kernel of information Zosia had dropped. Good. You have to feed a chicken if you expect to take her eggs. Huffing her bowl, Zosia said, "On your word as a noble girl and a fellow warrior, there's no harpy juice in here, is there?"

"Like father like daughter? No," said Ji-hyeon, "I hate that stuff, wouldn't wish it on an enemy. My second father gave me this seaweed you can take to keep you from getting the full effect of that shit. Let's you keep your secrets, but even still it's always a rough ride."

"I've had worse," said Zosia, taking a sip of the delightful black draught. "This is nice. Earth Ripper?"

"Only the best Usban beans go into my press," Ji-hyeon said in the snobby tone you only ever hear when someone's talking about kaldi, art, or tubāq. She rolled her eyes when Zosia smirked at this, and put her bowl back on the table. "So let's see, now that you've sung your verses you'd like me to tell you my side of this, yes? Answer all your questions?"

"Oh, don't trouble yourself," said Zosia, enjoying the girl's obvious annoyance. "I put most of it together on the boat, and the rest I added up riding over here from the Dominions. You're a pretty easy case, Princess, not much to you at all."

"And this is the part in the ballad when I spill my guts, right?" asked Ji-hyeon. "You've cunningly baited me into telling you everything, Auntie Zosia, let me sing, sing, sing!"

"You think I'm bluffing?" Damn but this kaldi was good.

"Yup," said Ji-hyeon.

"Fine, Princess," said Zosia, settling in. She'd been bullshitting a little, sure, since most of the pieces hadn't actually slid into place until she'd entered this tent, but a few details notwithstanding, she had enough to impress the impostor. She hoped. "Let's start with your second dad's angle in all this. I came to Hwabun looking to get his help resolving some personal affairs of mine. Without boring you with the details, my business involves Queen Indsorith of Samoth; specifically, her ass on a platter. So when I got down to the Dominions and Singh told me good old Kang-ho wanted me dead before I could find you, it threw me. I mean, if you're trying to take on the whole Crimson Empire, and he's backing you up on that play, why not enlist me to help you out, the way he did with Fennec and the rest?"

A pleased smile from the girl told Zosia she'd fudged something here, and she thought she could imagine what.

"Or maybe Hoartrap and Maroto just showed up unannounced and have stuck around for their own reasons." From the sinking of the brat's smile, Zosia had nailed it. "Doesn't matter. Point is, your first father wants you back because he set you up with some local royalty, and your other dad helped you run away because he's got larger ambitions...but not so large as taking on the whole Crimson Empire, even if they are softened up from infighting."

There we go—General Ji-hyeon definitely pouted like a princess, but she was still trying to play it cool, sipping on her kaldi.

"Now, obviously the whole Star's abuzz about how I've returned from the dead and my Cobalt Company is bigger and badder than ever, sticking it to the Empire with both spurs. Fennec and your dad probably convinced you to go that route to lend you an instant reputation, though I appreciate you not using my name anymore—your people calling you General Ji-hyeon is more than I expected. I guess a blue-haired badass leading an army stocked up with my Villains turned out to be enough, eh?"

"If I'd known you were alive I wouldn't..." The girl seemed embarrassed. "I mean, I've always loved your songs. But I never would have done more than the hair, if not for...And I never used your name, not once, much as Fennec insisted. And the hair, helm, and armor were only because I thought it looked damn fleet, really."

"Armor?" Zosia glanced down at her dusty hauberk and kneepads. "I've worn a lot of different kits in my day, so what...Oh hells, don't tell me you wear that!"

Zosia had followed Ji-hyeon's eyes and landed on the chainmail brassiere and panties that were laid out on another table. The pieces were so small she'd overlooked them before, assuming they were scrap metal or maybe some new style of steel doilies. Looking back at the girl, she shook her head in amazement.

"I didn't think it possible, but I actually feel bad for you, half pint," she said. "Fennec talked you into *using* that? In battle?"

"Obviously it doesn't provide as much protection as some gear," Ji-hyeon said defensively, ignoring Zosia's snort. "But the mobility it allows for—"

Zosia snorted louder. "Wearing that you'd be dead in five minutes, you didn't have your daddy's devil watching out for you."

"But I do," said Ji-hyeon. "Fellwing's better than a suit of steel plate, and not being weighed down I fight faster and fiercer than any chevaleresse."

"Devils can't be everywhere at once," said Zosia. "You think me, your dad, and every other asshole with a devil got the scars we wear before binding those fiends? As soon as you go up against someone else with a devil you're naked as a babe, or maybe that owlbat just gets distracted by a tasty morsel and you catch an arrow to the gut. You don't listen to anything else I say, save that shit for your private meetings with Keun-ju or that Flintlander kid and invest in something sensible for the field."

"Why, Auntie, do I sense some jealousy that you can't pull off that ensemble anymore?" Ji-hyeon sneered.

"Oh, I bet I could, if I felt like snagging my pubes in chainmail on a regular basis," said Zosia, pouring herself some more kaldi.

"Did you have something to say on matters other than my wardrobe, or are we done here?"

"Hmph," said Zosia. "Yes, actually. Most of your army thinks you're after the Crimson Empire, and with good reason, the way you've been carrying on. But if that were true, Kang-ho would've tried to get me on board before double-crossing me—after all, I want revenge against the Empire, so why not see if I'll help his brat take the throne? That's the smart play, and the safer one, and Kang-ho likes smart and safe more than he likes Azmir tubāq in a templewarden."

Ji-hyeon was smiling again, but Zosia couldn't tell if the girl was impressed or contemptuous.

"So it's obvious you're not really doing what everyone thinks you are. What, then, are you up to?"

"You tell me."

"Sure. Linkensterne," said Zosia, savoring the girl's petulant expression even more than the kaldi. She waited, and sure enough Ji-hyeon cracked.

"Who told you? Fennec?" It was kind of cute, watching the girl try to figure it out. "No... Dad and Fennec tried to bring Singh in on it, but she decided to put her lance with you instead, yes? She told you everything?"

"Nope. A chevaleresse's honor is such she never gave me more than a few hints, even if she knew everything. Don't know, and don't care. Figured it all out myself, as I said. See, when I came up to Hwabun I passed through Linkensterne, and my escort told me how pissed off the merchants are that it's been incorporated into the Isles. Back when the Crimson Empire held it, if you could even call it that, it was a smuggler's paradise, Lawless Linkensterne. Now, not so much, not so much at all. Even if I couldn't guess Kang-ho was running all sorts of shady business through there prior to the handover, some of your family's sailors told me exactly that in plain terms. Ever since, Kang-ho's had a bad time of it—must be a shame to wake up a house-husband, when you've grown accustomed to a certain lifestyle."

"Not bad," admitted Ji-hyeon.

"Not bad!" Zosia cocked her kaldi bowl at the princess. "Brilliant is I think the term you're looking for. The only thing I can't figure out is how you used the Immaculate Gate to whisk yourselves down to the Dominions. I figured your old man set his devil free for the ability, but seeing as Fellwing's still around, that can't be it. Fennec's devil?"

"He's not had a devil as long as I've known him," said Ji-hyeon. "But you're half right. Fennec's the one who knows how to use the Gates. I couldn't do it on my own, and won't do it again at all, if I can help it."

"See, you're a smarter girl than I gave you credit for," said Zosia, the idea of walking into a Gate still giving her the shivers. "Far as your plot goes, I've got to admit: whip up the populace, put the fear into Samoth, and then offer a truce—look the other way when we take Linkensterne back from the Immaculates, and bam! A free city for the princess to rule, business is back on for your dad, and better than ever since he engineered the reclamation of Linkensterne. All his merchant buddies will be awfully indebted to the family that gave them their city back."

"Close," said Ji-hyeon. "Close enough, anyway. The plan isn't just to get the Imperials to step back, it's to enlist them. Losing Linkensterne's got to be a sore spot for the queen, and in exchange for restoring free trade to the Crimson Empire she'll be all too happy to lend us a few regiments. That wall they're building is still incomplete on the eastern coast, so we'll ride up and around and capture it from behind. Once we have the wall, we'll complete the construction ourselves, including a northern loop to shield Linkensterne from the Isles. Easy as that, we have a solid wall, and Linkensterne's insulated from both the Immaculates and the Empire."

"You call erecting leagues and leagues of substantial defenses before the full weight of the Immaculate Isles comes slamming down on your heads 'easy'? Assuming you can even take the wall, of course. Easy, she says."

"Easier than you think," said Ji-hyeon smugly. "We have people inside the Immaculate army, working the wall, and we've got way more inside Linkensterne—the merchants want this to happen even more than we do. They've been preparing all year, and when we take the wall they'll take the city. Then the citizens of Linkensterne all pitch in to help finish the wall while my coalition of Cobalts and Imperials defend the construction and hold the border from the

Immaculates—the wall will be completed by this time next year. And after that, Linkensterne is its own republic, guarded by the Cobalt Company, with freedom and fortune for all."

"That's good," said Zosia, impressed. "Really good. Your first father might not be too pleased, seeing as he's got that loyalty for his Arm as you only get from an immigrant's kid, but for a dyed-in-the-wool double-crosser like your other dad, it's a huge get. Fennec and the rest earn a healthy cut of the profits, so nobody's complaining there, since they all know by now a small victory is better than a huge almost. Looking back, maybe that was my problem—I dreamt too big. Maybe instead of going after the Crimson Empire I should have contented myself with a smaller conquest, one I could have managed better."

"Except…" said Ji-hyeon, unable to stop herself from smiling as cheekily as her father. There was the family resemblance, right enough.

Zosia thought about it, came up with nothing. "Except what?"

"Except a daughter isn't some devil you can order about."

"No," said Zosia, twirling it around some more and still not getting much. "So what's your angle, then? Squeeze your old man out, take Linkensterne for yourself?"

"Ha!" Ji-hyeon shook her head, as though she were the smartest woman in the room. "Now, just what prize do you think a powerful warlord would pursue, a woman weaned on songs of the Cobalt Queen? A general with an army willing to ride after her into a Gate, if she asked them, armed with devils and black magic, at a time when a bloated empire is weak from civil war? What would *you* do, Zosia, faced with the dilemma of familial piety or something far more glorious?"

Well, well, well. Zosia found herself grinning as wide as the girl sitting across from her. "Samoth."

"Yup," said Ji-hyeon, looking more like a general than a princess as she reached under the table and pulled out a map, followed by another jug. "And since you have your own business with the Empire, I'm more than willing to bring you on as one of my captains. You can be one of General Ji-hyeon's captains...or should I start calling you and your friends my new Villians?"

Zosia bridled at the girl's choice of words, but what came next was too tasty to spit out for the sake of pride.

"Whatever I call you, Queen Indsorith is yours, Zosia, as I imagine you have unfinished business with her from that time she executed you. Whoever else you want is yours in the bargain, so long as you come clean with me about what happened back then, and any other pertinent details you might have. Pledge yourself to my flag, Zosia, and let's remind those Crimson cowards why they fear the Cobalt twilight!"

"That's quite the offer," said Zosia, getting more excited the more she thought about it. This could work out really damn well for both of them. "Shit. So long as that chainmail lingerie of yours isn't the mandatory uniform, I'm in. Where does a long-in-the-tooth recruit sign up?"

"Pack that pipe of yours, Captain Zosia," said Ji-hyeon, clearing the table and unfurling the map. "We planned on capturing Cockspar next, but their regiment cut us off in the mountains, and so we beat a retreat down here."

"The Azgarothian regiment, you know who's leading them?" asked Zosia, her heart quickening. She couldn't believe of all the luck—

"Uh-huh, I wrote it down here," said Ji-hyeon, pointing to some chickenscratch on the corner of the map. "Heart? No, Hjortt, Colonel Hjortt—he's leading the Azgarothians, but my scouts said there were Myuran flags flying over part of the army, and I don't know who they've got in charge."

"Doesn't matter," said Zosia, licking her lips. This day just kept getting better and better—she'd be seeing her old chum the thumbless colonel a lot sooner than she'd hoped, and this time she wouldn't let her theatrical streak get in the way of what needed doing. Efrain Hjortt was a dead man. "What's your strategy?"

"Well, the Imperial regiments can't be more than a few days behind us, so Fennec wants us to pack up and get moving now, but

I think the Cobalt Company might be done running. You're the expert, though, so I'd appreciate your insight."

"I think Fennec's a coward, and you're set up nicely to meet the Imperials in open combat," said Zosia, trying not to let her eagerness show. "Better put on some more beans, then, it's going to be a long night."

Zosia hunkered over the map, relieved she'd let Hjortt off the first time, so she could have the pleasure of getting him now. The only thing that tempered her excitement was the two devils in the corner, silently staring into each other's eyes.

CHAPTER
12

War was indeed coming, and you didn't need to drink Immaculate devil milk to gain that insight. The signs became increasingly obvious as Sister Portolés and Heretic left the Isles and cut back across the Empire, making for the highway that would take them down to the southern provinces, where the Cobalt Company was causing so much trouble. Open towns that she had paraded through with her Imperial regiment but a year before had erected new walls; way stations that had once welcomed all travelers now viewed even a war nun of Diadem with suspicion. Everywhere she traveled with Heretic, motley militias performed drills in barren fields instead of harvesting ripe ones, and everywhere they were questioned as to their business, and scowled at when Portolés sternly rebuffed all queries.

That King Jun-hwan had claimed it wouldn't be the war they were expecting worried at the back of Portolés's mind, like the urge to sin. She had done a good thing, as far as that went, not taking Brother Wan with her. Yet in her soul she knew Queen Indsorith had been right to advise her to view even her brethren and superiors as potential saboteurs—if the Burnished Chain had sent Efrain Hjortt to Kypck as a means of provoking Zosia into attacking the Empire, they would have a vested interest in preventing Portolés from finding her and telling her the truth. This distressing possibility was given credence when she and Heretic crested a grassy butte overlooking the languid Heartvein and caught sight of four black-robed riders racing up the road after them. They weren't much more than a mile off.

"Hmmmm," she said, surveying their surroundings for a defensible position. Portolés had fought well for the Chain during the civil war, and after the reconciliation she had worked just as hard to earn the right to serve with the Fifteenth Regiment. Her time first warring against the Imperials and then working for them had honed her natural intelligence toward self-preservation. Alas, the butte was as gentle a hilltop as a lazy pony could hope for, with a lone stand of poplars set just off the road, and nothing on the far side of the rise but a leisurely ride down to a tranquil valley. "They've timed it right—probably waited all morning for us to clear the forest."

"How's that?" Heretic looked back, forth, up, down, everywhere the nun had tilted her head. "What is it?"

"My people," said Portolés. "Come on, let's picket the horses in those trees before they're on us."

"Was wondering when you'd stop for a pray," said Heretic. "You expecting them, or is this an impromptu service?"

"Heretic," said Portolés as she dismounted, "how would you like the opportunity to kill some clergy?"

"Um." Heretic glanced back over his shoulder. From here the inclined approach and its riders were obscured by the wide top of the butte. "Not sure how you want me to answer that, Sister Portolés. It might surprise you to know I'm not really a hardened killer so much as a, um, gentle knave?"

"I didn't ask if you had killed, I asked if you wanted to," said Portolés, tying her horse and the pack mule to the thickest tree. "Hop down so I can unlock you."

"This…" Heretic looked genuinely nervous for the first time since she had freed him from the Office of Answers. "I'll level with you, sister, if this is a test I'm bound to fail. So if you're looking for an excuse to do me after all our time together, I'd prefer you just looked me in the eye when you put that hammer to my skull."

"Heretic," said Portolés as she tied his horse, "if you aren't willing to fight next to me, I'll do just that, right now."

"No need to rush into these things," said Heretic, dismounting so quickly he almost fell. She'd taken to letting him ride with his legs unshackled, and in a moment his hands were free. "I don't suppose—"

"Take those two crossbows I bought in Linkensterne, string, nock, and load them, then set them on that wide stump back there," said Portolés. "The short sword in the bedroll looked to be about your size. Now."

"Sure, sister," said Heretic, rubbing his red wrists. "But, um, you are going to talk to them first, yes? It might not come to anything, right?"

"Doubtful. In a Chainhouse or the Dens we debate with our tongues, out here I expect the saints will do the talking." Portolés hefted her maul. "Saint Orakulum here died at the Encounter of the Condemned Earth, thirty-three years ago. His bones stoked the forge, and his spirit dwells ever more in its steel. He will provide a stirring counterpoint to any argument my fellows lodge."

"This right here," said Heretic as he quickly removed the weapons from the back of the pack mule, "*this* is why people fear the Chain. If you settle your internal differences this way, what hope is there for dissent among the common folk?"

"You're smarter than you let on," said Portolés. "I'll parley with them, but you'll see soon enough the way the wind blows. Bows on the stump, sword in the ground beside them, and then lay a saddle blanket over them so they're hidden but easy to get out. And mind the safeties are—"

The bow Heretic had loaded with shaky hands went off, an arrow launching up through the rustling poplar branches. Portolés didn't look to see where it landed.

"On second thought, forget the blanket. Stand in front of the stump to obscure them with your body, until you need to start shooting."

"I thought the Chain forbade crossbows, sister?"

"Haven't you cottoned on yet?" Portolés showed him her file-blunted teeth. "I'm a bit of a heretic myself."

"Yeah?" Heretic wiped sweat from his face, almost dropped the bow as he did. This was shaping up to be a right proper martyrdom.

"If we fight, we kill, and if we kill one, we kill them all. If any escape they'll soon be back, with a local posse or two. If that happens the writs I carry mean very little to the illiterate. Be ready to fire at the ones in the rear. Less chance of your shooting me that way."

"If I . . . how will I know when to—"

"You'll know," said Portolés, and, hefting her hammer, she stepped out into the wide dirt track. Above her, dollops of puffy cream clouds floated across the afternoon sky. Beneath her, the browning grass in the center of the road was beaten down from countless hooves and feet that had recently traveled this way. Before her, a cowled rider crested the butte and slowed, the other three quickly appearing behind the first and reining in their horses as well.

With enough time, she could have strung a rope across the road, secured it to a rock on one end, and wrapped it around a tree on the other, so Heretic could pull it tight and trip the first horse.

With enough time, she could have dug a trench to effect the same.

With enough time, all the sinners on the Star could repent, and when the Sunken Kingdom returned from the waves there'd be no more need for hell.

When you were short on time, all you had was action, and the belief your action would work. Here, on this crisp autumn day so much like the one in Kypck, Portolés believed that Heretic wouldn't shoot her in the back in hopes of endearing himself to their pursuers— faith in a man whom she wouldn't have trusted not to murder her in her sleep when they'd first set out. How had it come to this, arming a confessed heretic and traitor to help her fight against her own people? In a few short years she'd gone from fighting alongside her brethren against Imperials during the civil war to riding alongside the Crimson soldiers, and now she was preparing to battle other war clerics in the service of the Queen of Samoth.

Well, everything happens.

And verily, it did.

As Portolés expected, there was no pretense. Why should there be, among servants of the Burnished Chain? The Chain Canticles warned that any anathema might harbor the talent for looking into

the thoughts of another, and with even a sliver of a chance that Portolés could smell their deception, they wouldn't risk coming down
from their horses to talk. Instead, they made to ride her down in the
road.

The lead rider wore the mask of an anathema, as did two of the
three behind him. Over his head buzzed the wide, smoking halo of
a censer-star he swung in a deadly gyre, which explained why his
fellows gave him a healthy lead. As he bore down on Portolés, a crossbow bolt flew under his steed's thundering hooves, and then a second missed horse and rider by an even wider margin. So much for
Portolés's order that Heretic fire on the clerics in the back. The first
rider was almost on her, the chain of his weapon still whisking the air
above him.

As soon as Portolés made a step to evade in either direction he
would bank his horse to pass her on the opposite side and bring the
enormous iron censer down upon her.

So she waited in the center of the road, forcing him to make the
choice of which side to pass her on. Twenty yards out, the horse
veered into the right-hand wagon rut. At ten yards Portolés darted to
that side as well, and then passed the rut, even as the horse flew down
like an avenging devil. She pivoted, putting all of her might into the
swing, blind for a moment to everything but the wide, empty butte
before her, and then came back around with her maul. The two-
handed hammer struck the charging horse, but where, she could not
tell, for her maul was sent flying from the impact, and, refusing to
release the handle of the weapon, she flew along with it.

The first bounce on the solid turf knocked her senseless, but the
second restored her, and the third turned into a roll across the grass.
She was on her feet, then, but immediately toppled back onto her
arse, the world spinning as furiously as the first rider's censer-star,
the chain of which had wrapped tight around both horse and rider
as they fell from her hammer. She staggered upright and took in this
miracle, the monk broken and bound to his steed's mighty neck by
the long chain that had ensnared them both, the smoking head of
the censer partially embedded in his side. Then the other three riders

surrounded her, their horses stamping as they were slowed to a walk, and the time for contemplating miracles was passed.

It was as Portolés had feared—they meant to take her alive, the first rider intending to lay her out or disarm her with his long, blunt weapon rather than execute her. That hadn't worked, so now the others quickly glided off their horses. One of the anathemas broke into a sprint toward the trees where Heretic lurked, the other two clerics slowly advancing on Portolés. The masked anathema was slight but quick, his scimitar flashing in the sun, and the barefaced pureborn man had shoulders nearly as wide as Portolés's to power his mace. From the poplars, Heretic screamed. Soon two-on-one would become three against, and dizzy or not, Portolés knew her only chance was in not waiting a moment longer.

She made as though she were heaving her massive hammer at the pureborn, but as the anathema darted in to gut her with his curved blade she reversed her swing, bringing the butt of the weapon up instead of the head down. The long handle of the hammer connected with his sword, slowing it enough that when its blade slid up the shaft and into the bottom of her fist it only clipped off her pinky and ring fingers, instead of doing worse damage.

She flicked her injured hand out, and her remaining fingers hooked the anathema by his dangling rosary and jerked him into her. She brought her skull down like a comet, striking him between the eyes. The point of his scimitar jabbed into her side, rooted around as she headbutted him again. He went limp, but by then the pureborn was atop her with his mace. She had no choice but to choose between the falling anathema or her maul. With a wounded hand, the lighter weapon was preferable, so she clumsily tossed her hammer into the oncoming mace. The pureborn's weapon clattered against her maul, knocked it from the air, and concluded its trajectory, dull metal crushing the bones in the forearm she brought up to block her face.

The pain sent her reeling, despite her training, despite her intimate familiarity with the sensation of being destroyed by her church. Twisting her thumb and the two remaining fingers of her only responsive arm into the woolen cassock of the limp anathema who still dangled in her grasp, she set her heel and slung him around. The mace came down again, faster than she could track it, but this time it collided with the dazed anathema she put between herself and the pureborn. He didn't make a sound as the weapon clobbered him. Instead of falling back at this unexpected defense, the pureborn pressed his advantage, meaning to beat his colleague out of Portolés's hand.

She met his assault with one of her own, shoving the drooping body into the pureborn's path, and then following after it with the last of her wobbly momentum. Slinging her numb, broken arm out and releasing the anathema with her other, she tackled the pureborn. Big man he was, but Portolés was bigger, and with the added weight of the anathema to aid her, she took him to the ground.

Grunts, and a groan. The pureborn tried to roll free, the blood-slickened wedge of the anathema between them making him slipperier than a Tangordrim catfish... but before being taken into the church, Portolés had fed herself and her sisters on fish she pulled barehanded from under rocks in the River Tangor. The sisters the Burnished Chain had burned alive, deeming them far too corrupted for even the salvation of the ecclesiastical surgeons. Portolés could no longer recall their names.

She caught the pureborn by the belt as he squirmed free of the anathema, and, launching herself after him like one of the swifter fish pursuing a fly darting above the river's surface, she bellyflopped back down atop him. He had a dagger or something, shanked her in the chest and gut, but then she was level with his wracked face, looking at him eye to eye... and then she did for him as she'd done for the anathema.

His skull was harder than the first man's. Portolés's was harder. After the second headbutt his knife stopped poking her, and after the fourth his eyes crossed, his split nose warm against her crown as she brought it down again. And again. And again. She only stopped when a sharp boot caught her in the armpit and rolled her off him, quickly delivering a series of kicks to her stab-riddled stomach. The last anathema...

Blinking the stinging blood out of her eyes, Portolés stared up at her assassin. The anathema reached up and pulled down her mask, revealing a face scarred with pits from where they must have scoured away her fur or scales.

"Safe roads guide you to her breast," said the sister. She raised her weapon, the silver crescent winking, and Portolés tried to prepare herself for whatever awaited her on the other side of the ax. Despite everything she thought she believed, she was scared. So much for taking her alive.

The anathema yipped and stumbled back. Portolés squinted at the small arrow that had appeared in her assailant's shoulder. Fast as the anathema had faltered, she dashed forward, out of Portolés's sight— the tall, dying grass in which she lay on her back veiled everything but the reddening sky. Night was falling, and jackals would be out on the buttes soon. She thought she heard a crossbow twang, but couldn't be sure. It was quiet, save for her wheezing breaths. She willed herself to sit up, but when she tried the hot slits in her side, stomach, and chest pulsed wetly, her arm shuddered, and she collapsed back down. The battle haze was lifting, and the angels of suffering were planting their kisses all across her body. What a terrible way to die...

She felt herself drifting off, and forced herself to think of Kypck. It was how she kept herself awake when she was exhausted on watch. Guilt and shame has a way of perking one up. All those ignorant people, cut down for no reason they could ken, screaming as they were sent to their judgment. Portolés giving the order as sedately as if she were overseeing drills on a parade ground. Using her maul, a relic of the Burnished Chain and symbol of her devotion to a greater good, to bash in the skulls of the five wide-eyed, shaking Azgarothians who refused to follow her command. Not killing a single villager herself, as though that kept her clean, instead of making her just as bad as Colonel Hjortt.

Boots crunched the gritty track of the road beside her, and she focused on Hjortt, his face bubbling like the wax of a freshly lit candle in the confessionals, his ringlets flashing up like burning scrolls. She thought of Queen Indsorith, her long hair waving like a pennant in the winds that forever lash the Crown of Diadem. Maybe Portolés had done some good in the end. Maybe she'd done enough. Maybe. A living shadow fell over her, the devil of death blotting out the sky, the promise of salvation...

"Well, well, well," Heretic said, leaning over her. "You look in a bad way, sister."

"I'll bleed out if you don't tie me." Portolés found the words pouring out of her in a rush, despite how sluggish her tongue felt. "On the mule, there's a bag for this, this...a bag of bandages, a pot of ointment. Smelling salts. You've got to pack me, pack my wounds, got to..."

"I know where it is," said Heretic. He looked remarkably hale for a man who had squared off against an anathema.

"The last one, the anathema, she'll be back..."

"I see that happen and I'll convert," said Heretic, directing the crossbow in his arms down at Portolés. "Now I know why your pope outlawed these things. Gotta be evil, if it lets a common sinner like me take down the Chain's holy monsters."

"You fought...good, Heretic. Better than I believed."

"Fought? Lady, I ran for it, soon as that witchborn came after me! Led her on a hunt, and fast as I am, she soon gave up and doubled back. I figured she'd get a horse and catch me for sure, so I cut back, too, along the edge of the bluff. None too soon for your benefit, neither!"

"And now?" Portolés swallowed blood, staring up at the crossbow. "Listen to me, Heretic—I know you want to know why."

"Why?"

"Why this. Why I took you, what we've been doing, where we're going. Why this fight. Why everything."

"What makes you think I give a shit, so long as I'm free?" Heretic seemed delirious. "Free, with horses and loot and the open road in all directions! *Why*, sister, would I care about your songs?"

"Because you're a heretic," said Portolés, shivering in the cold, wet grass. "And being curious is how good folk become heretics in the first place."

"You think you know me, huh?" Heretic pulled the trigger on the crossbow, the bolt thudding into the corpse of the pureborn beside her. "You think 'cause you read my tract you've got me pegged? Tell you what, sister—say right here and now you hate the Fallen Mother, that you love the Deceiver, and I'll listen to anything you want to tell me."

"I hate the Fallen Mother," said Portolés through gritted teeth. It wasn't the voicing of heresy that disturbed her, for without belief words are nothing; it was Heretic's utter stupidity. If he actually wanted to hear anything, he'd better stop wasting time. "I love the Deceiver. Now stanch these before I bleed out."

"Sure." Heretic suddenly seemed chastened. "Of course, right. Hold on, hold on."

He returned with the chains she had bound him with instead of bandages. He kept apologizing, his hands shaking as he secured the bonds. She didn't struggle, and he didn't look her in the eye. Only when her broken wrist was manacled to her bloody one did he fetch the barber's bag. After that he followed her instructions adequately. When he was done he propped her up on the body of the pureborn monk and returned to the horses. He came back atop her bay, wearing the soiled robes of one of the anathemas.

"All right then, sister," he said, his voice quavering. He had probably never killed anyone before, to be so shaken up about it. He made the sign of the Chain, offering her a loony smile as he did. "I'd say we're even now. Don't wait up for me."

Then he was gone, leaving Portolés with a pureborn for a pillow and the bloody heavens for a blanket. She deserved this, she knew, but the Empire didn't deserve to have Zosia wage war upon it for the crimes of an overly obedient war nun and her rogue colonel. She prayed then not for herself, but for the Star, that she might recover just long enough to complete her quest. The color bled from the sky, her words slurred, and her prayers trailed off. She might have died, or maybe it was just sleep, she could hardly tell the difference as she closed her eyes and fell under, into the First Dark.

CHAPTER
13

Purna looked right smart in her horned wolf hood, Maroto had to fess. Choi had helped her rig it up proper from the smallest hide, so the four horns jutted out from the girl's head in imitation of the weirdborn, and the horned wolf's limp snout hung down between Purna's eyes. Diggelby and Hassan had split the other hides into matching mantles, and Din made a crude tiara from the teeth. Neither Maroto nor Choi had taken trophies from their encounter with the horned wolves, other than a clutch of new scars. The wounds they'd picked up from the confused Imperial recon squad on their way down from the pass were scratches in comparison, and would like as not leave little lasting reminder of their barmy dash to the enemy encampment. Thinking back on all his wild days with Zosia and her Villains, here at last was a deed to match those adventures of old, and surpass a good many of them. Whatever Imperials had made it through the night would have songs to last down through the ages, ballads to commemorate the time a gaggle of rebels led a pack of horned wolves crashing down onto their regiment...

For his part, the only ditty Maroto was singing was "Give Me a Cot, a Bottle, and Four Whores." As they ought to be given a hero's welcome back at the camp of General Ji-hyeon, it seemed one of his songs was going to come true, for a change. There was nothing like returning to camp with all of the people you left with, and good information to boot.

For as many miles of hard ground Maroto and his scouts had

covered over the preceding weeks, the Cobalt Company hadn't progressed much—after Myura they'd gone up into the Kutumban mountains to throw the Imperials off their trail and spent a few weeks resting their army in the Secret City of the Snow Leopard. When they left the kind nuns of that mountain sanctuary the Cobalts had meant to come crashing down on Azgaroth, but then the regiment from that self-important province unexpectedly appeared on the horizon to intercept them. The Cobalts had been obliged to cross the Bridge of Grails and double back east rather than risk tangling with a larger force that held the high ground. If only the general had known her valiant scouts were wrecking the shit out of that very Azgarothian regiment, she could have had the Cobalts come up from behind and hit 'em while they were still pulling wolf teeth out of their arses, but that was war for you—the best tactics oft revealed themselves in a moment of desperation, rather than coming in early enough to let you get your ducks in a row.

The Cobalts had marched down into the Witchfinder Plains, not a terribly long way north of where they'd started, and still many leagues from Diadem. Maroto was surprised to see that the Cobalt Company had made a proper camp in the high foothills a mere five leagues north of the road that had taken them down from the Kutumbans, rather than making all haste to put more distance between themselves and the Azgarothians. But then the general seemed dead set against following the example Zosia had laid down two decades prior of cutting and running from the Imperials for years on end, whittling away at the Crimson hordes and slowly swelling her rebel ranks as she led them on a wild chase from one end of the Star to the other, and back again. No, after less than a year of rabble-rousing and small victories, General Ji-hyeon was taking the fight straight to the Imperials—no other reason for digging in at this spot unless she meant to greet the pursuing regiments that had harried her through the mountains.

Couldn't rightly blame her for picking a defensible spot to make a stand, though, since Maroto had finally remembered where he knew Hjortt's face—and the Fifteenth—from; those were the mad bastards who had kept the original Cobalt Company on the run for well over a year straight, shaving pieces off their rebel army every time they stopped to catch their breath. Hjortt must push his crew like a devil pushing at a mortal's temptation, sacrificing any goodwill he might have fostered with his soldiers to get them marching early and keep them marching late when the chase was on, all day every day. You simply couldn't expect a bunch of volunteers and sellswords to put in hours like that, which made the Azgarothians the fastest regiment on the Star.

So yeah, even taking time to recover from their wolf bites, the Azgarothians could probably catch the Cobalts before they reached the Haunted Forest or any other populated region where they could replenish their supplies. That was the problem with being so successful so fast—before you knew it you had more mouths than you could feed, and no teat to stick 'em on. General Ji-hyeon probably hoped to take down a few owlbats with one bow, by leading the Azgarothians into a serious engagement—check another Imperial regiment off her list, and steal their stores when the day was won.

If the day was won. Assuming they hadn't lost or gained many heads in the Kutumbans, the Cobalt Company had eight thousand pikers, stickers, hackers, and other broke-arse, poorly armored foot; a thousand archers, crossbowers, and gunners; five hundreds chevaleresses, knights, and other folk who could ride worth a damn and had a horse to do it on; another hundred or so weirdborn of various abilities; and three out of the Five Villains. Even if you took into account that Hoartrap was as dread a fucker as he'd ever been, those weren't great numbers, especially since by all accounts the Church of the Burnished Chain had a few of their own sorcerers, though they called them cardinals instead of witches. Whether or not one of those creeps was with Colonel Hjortt's company, the two scary robed fuckers who'd gotten the worst of the horned wolf attack in the Imperial camp were definitely weirdborn, so apparently the church had reversed its decision to burn all so-called anathemas since the last time Maroto had encountered the Burnished Chain. Under King Kaldruut those arseholes had wanted to burn everyone, it seemed, the whole bloody Star, presumably as part of some hideous ritual to summon that mother of devils they worshipped or some equal insanity, but maybe they'd figured out it was better to let the Star burn itself, and weirdborn wield torches as well as anyone.

During their reconnaissance, Maroto, Choi, and the nobles—Maroto's Moochers, as Fennec had dubbed them when they'd set out, despite Maroto's insistence that they should be called the Dandy Dogs—had counted enough Imperial heads to know the odds were long indeed even without Chain-indentured weirdborn taking part. They had seen the still-sizable remnants of the regiment they had spanked at Myura taking a southern pass through the Kutumbans, and while the Cobalts rested up and planned strategy in the City of the Snow Leopard those Myurans must have looped up to merge with the marching Azgarothians. On their own a few thousand Myuran soldiers wouldn't have posed much threat, but when Maroto's Moochers had led the ornery horned wolves through the Imperial camp they'd had an unprecedented peek at the true power of the joint regiments:

Twice as many grunts as the Cobalt Company.

Twice as many gunners and bowfolk.

A cavalry to match the Cobalts, and then some.

Add to that the two cavalries of no less than two hundred riders each the scouts had glimpsed at various points on the distant slopes, no doubt coming in to beef up the Azgarothians, and it was shaping up to be a real shitshow in the plains.

Not that Maroto gave a devil's damn; he'd let Purna have her fun, putting in real time as a bought killer, and now that the stupid part of every war was fast approaching it was time to cut out. He'd been thinking, ever since their run-in with the horned wolves, that adventuring was a lot more fun than he remembered. Sure, he was nine kinds of injured—even before one had been sliced open on a rock, his knees had started complaining about all the fucking hiking—but so long as they laid up somewhere for a while before setting out in earnest he'd be off this stupid crutch. And it might have been his imagination, but he was sure his paunch had shrunk a bit since the Panteran Wastes, so that was as clear a sign as any poison oracle's prophecy that he was on the right track. Hells, he'd even put it to Choi, see if she might be willing to buy out whatever contract she had with the general—she was as eerie as waking up to seeing your devil sitting on your chest, watching you sleep, the way Crumbsnatcher used to do, but eerie could be good...eerie could be damn appealing, in fact. He'd put in his time with countless lovers of most any and every sort, but he'd never had a weirdborn so far as he'd known...

Wildborn, he reminded himself, not weirdborn. Coming up in the Isles she'd prefer that, no doubt. He wondered if she liked having her horns touched...once the left one healed up, of course. She was almost as bad off as he was, after that tumble down the mountainside, but had sprung back a sight spryer than he'd managed. Impressive as any miracle, the way she'd danced over those mountains, facing monsters without a flinch. Maroto could get behind a woman as good in a pinch as she was. So to speak.

"What are you leering about?" asked Purna as they saluted their way past the innermost ring of sentries, and Maroto checked himself. Some weird—wildborn, wildborn, some *wildborn*—could peek in a fellow's mind, they said, and so no more thoughts like that. Not as long as Choi was walking with them, anyway, instead of a mile off on point.

"Wild game," said Maroto, licking his lips as he watched Choi's heavy brigandine skirt sway back and forth across the back of her knees as she crested the foothill they climbed. Could hardly tell she had a limp from that horned wolf. "Hungry, is all."

"I know, right?" said Purna, following his gaze. "A freebooter can't live on beans alone. What I'd give to roast that rump..."

"Shut it!" hissed Maroto. "She'll hear you."

"Worse things than letting a lass know your intentions," said Purna. "If you don't make a move on that, I will."

"Careful, barbarian," said Diggelby, coming up between them, Prince cradled in his arms. He had barely put the dog down for so much as a shit ever since they caught up to the cur on the edge of the Imperial camp. "Our Purna's not the sort to share her supper, even with a starving man."

"Oh grow up, you two," said Maroto, his eyes back on *that arse...* but then Choi glanced back over her shoulder, and Maroto blushed as Purna cackled.

"I'll report to Ji-hyeon," said Choi, eyeing them with little amusement. "You can come, or not."

"Not!" said Din and Hassan in unison from where they took up the rear, and Din added, "Party tonight in our tent, Choi, come by after you're done."

"We all have some *serious* drinking and drugging to catch up on," said Hassan as they all stopped atop the last hill and could take in the tent city of the Cobalt Company spread halfway up the first serious slope of the Kutumbans, what few grasses that weren't trampled flat swaying in the balmy lowland breeze. "You most of all, oh tireless leader."

After a contemplative silence, Choi nodded once, looking almost amused for a change. "Yes. I'll come."

"Huzzah!" cried the nobles and Maroto as one, and Purna threw her arm around the broader woman's shoulders and gave her a squeeze meant to pass for comradely. Maroto knew that move well, had used it a hundred times himself, but smiled to think himself above such things now. This wildborn would surely appreciate a mature, respectful lover far more than some fumbling teenager.

"You should all see barbers first," said Choi, inelegantly withdrawing from Purna's embrace. "The white tents."

"You more than us," said Maroto, not about to be outmaneuvered by a pup like Purna. "I can give Ji-hyeon the basics while you get patched up. I'd feel better if you'd see yourself tended to before bothering with a simple report, Choi."

Purna rolled her eyes and Choi looked rightly cautious. "I am... fine. We can give the report together, if you like."

"I would like that," said Maroto, nodding seriously as Purna mugged from the other side of Choi. "We'll go together."

"Have fun!" chirped Diggelby. "I've got ten taels that says I'm through a parcel of Agonist cheroots before you're free of the command tent."

"I'll take that," said Hassan. "I can't wait to see you puke up your guts after a month off the stuff."

"Double up with me?" asked Din, and Diggelby frowned when Hassan readily accepted. "You're about to be down twenty, Count; Diggelby's been lining his panties with tubāq leaves every morning since we left."

"Spying on a gentleperson during their toilet?" said Diggelby, abashed. "You have no shame, Duchess!"

"Not really, no," said Din, spitting a brown clod onto her friend's boot. "I've just been chewing mine, since Choi said smoking was off-limits."

"It's got to itch, absorbing it through your treasure," said Hassan thoughtfully. "But I expect Diggelby's long accustomed to that sensation in his knickers."

Choi resumed walking, Purna keeping pace with her, and Maroto hobbled quickly after, saying, "Surely you don't have any interest in a stuffy tactical meeting, Tapai Purna?"

"Quite the contrary," said Purna, pulling her hood back a bit. It was still far too raw for her to be wearing it, and the stink must be singeing her nose hairs. "You've got to start somewhere, eh, Maroto? You wait and see, I'll be one of Ji-hyeon's Villains before this campaign is won!"

"Huh," said Maroto, waving at a gaggle of rough-looking camp followers who crouched around a breakfast fire at the outskirts of the tents. "I actually had some things I wanted to talk about, before any plans for the future get hammered hard. It concerns the both of you."

Choi looked as intrigued as Purna, for a welcome change. Purna asked, "And what might those *things* be? I've told you every day since we set out, Maroto, you're a fine ally, but I'll not be a rich man's plaything. And as much as you say you'd like to have Choi right there on her knees beside me, sharing the load, I doubt she—"

"Deceiver's wounds, I never said that!" cried Maroto. "I'm being serious here, Purna!"

Choi's expression was unreadable, but she was definitely giving Maroto her full attention now. Purna winked at Choi and said, "Not that I don't find you most comely, Captain Choi, because I verily do, but anything involving Maroto's womb-hammer—"

"Purna," said Maroto, closing his eyes. A brilliant if wicked play on her part. "Please."

"*Fine*," said Purna. "What's the story?"

"War's no good," said Maroto, having to wing it because his carefully prepared speech was completely forgotten, now that Purna had flustered him. "I've been in enough of them to know that, and know it well. And besides that, I took an oath to Queen Indsorith long ago that I'd not take up arms against her. I've been playing that promise way too loose until now, by pledging to defend you, Purna, but once the battles really begin I won't be able to pretend I'm not breaking my vow. Not so long as I'm with this army."

"This oath," said Choi, her expression all too readable now. "You never spoke of it to Ji-hyeon."

"No," said Maroto. "But not because I'm working for that Crimson arsehole, nor will I ever. Fuck Queen Indsorith, and double-fuck her Empire. Not the good kind of fucks, neither. But I swore an oath on my devil, and that's the end of the matter—truth be told I don't know what'll happen if I take one more step over the line, so I don't mean to find out."

"Why?" asked Choi, then seemed genuinely taken aback for the first time since he'd met her. "I apologize. It is your past."

"No, no," said Maroto, having picked up enough of Choi's odd way of speech to know *past* meant *private business* to the wildborn. "I don't owe either of you the tale, sure, but I'll freely tell it, since we're friends. And since I expect you to trust me."

"Damn," said Purna, punching Choi's arm to the woman's confusion. "I've been trying to pry this verse of the song out of him since the Panteran Wastes. He must really want to get into your—"

"Purna!"

"Sorry, sorry, go on!"

"I'll make it short, give you the full version some night around a fire," said Maroto, since they were already getting into the camp and he wanted to make his play before they reached Ji-hyeon's tent. "My...Zosia, Cobalt Zosia, you all know about her, that we were..."

"Your general, yes?" asked Choi.

"That," said Maroto, the despair of her passing hitting him all over again, in this blue-bedecked camp that should have been hers. "And...I loved her. Truly. Like no other, before or after. And she loved me, too, I know it. Old Watchers keep me, I love her still."

"From the songs, I figured..." said Purna after they walked a ways in silence, both women slowing their paces to Maroto's relief. Even with Choi's ministrations it felt like his knee was going to rip open again from all this limping about on it. "I'm so sorry, Maroto."

"Dusty as it is, the wound still feels fresh," said Maroto, and snorted. "It's the stuff of songs, all right, and that'll teach you to aspire to such glories. The good ones all end in tears for everyone but the bard. If she and I had but a wee bit more time...shit. Anyway, she died. Queen Indsorith cut her down in a duel and threw her corpse off the top of Castle Diadem, earned her crown the same way Zosia won hers. You all know that, it's ancient history."

By Old Black's teeth, this was harder than Maroto expected. He cleared his throat, cleared it again. "I was away from Diadem when it went down, but you'd best believe I returned as soon as I heard. Meant to tear down the whole fucking place, meant to make the castle itself bleed out and drown the city in blood, till it reached the very throne room...But Indsorith was ready for me. Offered me the same as Zosia had offered her. A duel to decide the matter. Fair terms. She didn't even want to toss me down onto the city after, if I couldn't lay her low, just my oath I'd be done making trouble for her...and...and I fucking *lost*."

Devils, was that his voice breaking? They stopped walking, and Purna put a hand on his shoulder. Cracking his neck, he pulled himself together. "So that's it. The short version. Why I can't in good faith keep on with General Ji-hyeon. Really, though, even if I could, I wouldn't."

"Yellow as a canary's marrow," said Purna, trying to help him wash down the lump in his throat with a swig of her sass. Daring to glance at Choi, he saw neither suspicion nor scorn in her ruby pupils, but maybe... sorrow? It cut him, that look, like strange as he'd thought her up until recently, the wildborn was no different from him, that she knew nothing could be worse than failing those you've sworn to save. Then Purna slapped him on the back again, said, "So what you're telling us is you've got an excuse, but even if you didn't, you'd still be too fear-footed to throw down."

"There's being scared, then there's being smart, and while I'll fess the two are often confederates, this ain't about being scared of a scrap." Maroto waved his hand at a crowd of youths running sword drills in one of the camp's clearings. "Once the Imperials come down on us, all of them are dead."

He pointed past the practicing soldiers to one of the kitchen tents beyond. "All them. And everyone there, and there, and there, too. To Ji-hyeon's credit, it won't be as bad as when Zosia led us. Things were real dark then, on account of the Imperials burning any village they didn't trust, and they didn't trust many by the end, so it wasn't just fighters in our camps, it was all their families, too, young and old. So it won't be that bad... but it'll be bad enough."

As they passed the drilling boys and girls, an Usban knight leading them, Purna said, "Really, it can't be as hopeless as all that! Everyone dies? I don't think so."

"Maybe not everyone," said Maroto. "But it'll be worse for the survivors, believe me. And even if we pay so high a price that Ji-hyeon wins her war, what then? You think the Imperial provinces will just hand over their titles and castles to another conquerer? You think she'll be able to rule, without killing a hundred thousand more, be they soldiers or serfs? Even after all Zosia did, or tried to do, once she had the throne it was like she wasn't even there. Orders she gave got mistranslated or mysteriously lost; her move to fix the crooked system by sending the rich folks to work the fields was a fucking disaster of epic proportions. More died in her reforms than died in the war, I reckon. Not that it was all her fault: the whole ruddy Empire worked against her. You want to bring a land together, give them a common enemy, and for the merchants, nobles, and politicians, that's exactly what she was. Why would it be any different this time around? I won't say there aren't folk who benefit from a well-fought war, but you rarely find them within a hundred leagues of the front."

Devils, but Maroto was parched after that sermon. They'd come up on the busy cooks, and he dug around in his purse for a suitable bribe. Choi and Purna waited until he'd talked a furry-faced wench into selling him a wineskin of retsina before they continued on their way, Choi surprising him again by cutting straight to his bone. So to speak.

"You would have us disgraced with you, before we even give the Imperials a chance to repay us for the wolves?" She didn't sound mean about it, so much as . . . perplexed.

"Nothing disgraceful about avoiding a pointless war," said Maroto, offering her the skin after he'd drained half of the pinewine in one tug. "Not suggesting we go off and join a Khymsari monastery, neither—there's more battles than you could ever hope to wage, just waiting out there for you. For us. We work well together, don't say we don't. The three of us, and Diggelby, Din, and Hassan, if they're game, could be the Six Chums or what the fuck ever, seeking out adventure on every arm of the Star. Monsters and maniacs, devils and darker things yet are lurking in forgotten ruins and dungeons, and we could—"

"No," said Choi, though she'd taken a slug of his wine willingly enough before passing it to Purna. Then, thoughtfully, she added, "Thank you, Maroto."

"Yeah, I dunno, either," said Purna apologetically. "This is . . . I mean, the Star will always be there, right, but a war like this doesn't come along often! It's easy for you to say they're no fun, since you've already had your sport. I'd prefer to fight one myself, a'thank you very much."

"That's not why," said Choi, though whether she was speaking for her own reasons or Maroto's he never knew, because just then Chevaleresse Sasamaso emerged from a tent, and after doing a double take, hurried over to them.

"Here's a sight to please the gods of war and wine! What news from our flanks, friends?"

"News that first goes to General Ji-hyeon," said Choi, and it was only the resurgence of her frostiness that reminded Maroto it had thawed for a few clement days. "We have only now returned."

"Really?" Chevaleresse Sasamaso gave Maroto a sly grin. Fucking Crowned Eagle People, always with that *knowing look* shit. "Well, let's not waste any time, then! I'll show you to the general's tent; since we settled in here I've been moving her nightly, as you ordered, Captain Choi."

Chevaleresse Sasamaso led them at a sweaty canter through the camp, ill-respecting the fact that Maroto and his people had just spent a month doing little but hustle around on aching legs. Neither Choi nor Purna responded to his frequent glances. Well, so much for happily ever after, anywhere but here. Making matters worse, when they got to Ji-hyeon's tent they were informed by the guards that she was still carrying on a private meeting with a Raniputri emissary who had arrived the night before, and not even Choi was permitted to enter. Awkward.

Chevaleresse Sasamaso insisted they follow her to meet some other visiting dignitaries, but Maroto was only half listening. As was always the case when a pass or a business proposal failed spectacularly, all he could think about was getting away from Choi for a while...but really, looking at the whole tapestry here, what the fuck was he supposed to do? Wander off on his own again, swinging his mace by his own bad self as though he were some punk kid waving his treasure around? That was a loser's play, right there, and Maroto was no—

"Craven!"

Maroto tripped over his walking stick at the outburst, looked frantically around at the tents hemming them in. Felt like an idiot as he did; this exact scene had played out a couple of times over the years, when he'd be drinking in some tavern or squirming in some stinghouse and a random punter from the Noreast Arm would insult one of his companions with the term, but Maroto would jump up, thinking somebody had recognized him from—

"God of devils," he whispered as his eyes landed on his father. His *dead* father, mind, his long, long-dead father. Considering the old bastard was supposed to be twenty years with his ancestors yet towered over half a dozen feet in the air, strapped to some mule-faced kid's back, Maroto figured he could be excused for not noticing him immediately.

"Oh, how you'll be wishing it was she instead of your daddy," said Da, his smile wicked as those of the horned wolves who had harried them down the mountains. The old man's mount stepped fully out of the shade of a tent now, and Maroto nodded in appreciation of the young pup's vigor. He didn't look like much, but the casual way he moved, as though he didn't have a mean old fucker tied to his shoulders, implied a certain ferocity. That, and silver where due, his big snow-white helmet of hair looked fleet as fuck. "Craven, Craven, Craven, you've let yourself go, m'boy! Look at that gut! Are you with child? Has one of those women put a baby in your belly?"

"You..." Maroto wiped his face with the back of his hand, blinked at the stony kid supporting his dad. Could it be? Could it not? Who else but... "Nephew?"

"Sullen," supplied Da, and right enough, the kid's mug tightened even more as he stared down Maroto. He'd earned that name, to be sure. Recognizing that other folk accompanied Maroto and they had stopped as well, Da switched over to Immaculate, probably trying to make his shaming all the more public. "He did what my own son was too *craven* to try. He stayed with me, saved me, carried me home, tended my back when even your sister refused to help. Took on the wrath of every Horned Wolf to see me through. He's the son I never had."

"Damn," said Maroto, not put out in the slightest by his father's vitriol; how could he be, when it was proof that this was really his old man? That both of his kin had somehow survived that terrible day, in spite of his cowardice? The three of them had songs for one another, no doubt, but for now he raised a fist to knock against his nephew's knuckles for having the strength to do what he had not. "You're either crazy or stupid, kid—both times I broke clan law I took off with the quickness, and still barely made it out alive. Can't imagine trying to live a week around those arseholes once you got on their bad side, say fuck-all of coming up in the village, staying to earn a name and a few thaws after, to look at you."

Sullen didn't say a damn word, and didn't meet Maroto's fist, either. Left him hanging like a fucking punk. That would be enough for a fight, right there, between two proper Horned Wolves, family or no...but they weren't Horned Wolves anymore, not really. Maroto dropped his fist. Give the pup a bone and all...

"It's an honor to meet you both," said Purna, stepping up next to Maroto. "I am Tapai Purna, a—"

"Ruddy heretic!" gasped Da, pointing at the telltale horns jutting from the hood Purna had pulled back on her shoulders. "We're all exiles now, Craven, but to dress your grungy lover in the hide of your people? Where is your decency, man? Where is your *shame*?"

"I'm not his lover, and if you call me *grungy* again I'll wear your skin instead," said Purna, as easy as she'd offered the introduction. Her hands rested casually on the hilt of her kakuri and the butt of her pistol. "Maybe bridle up that big boy of yours when I'm done—looks like you could talk a whole cart's worth of shit from up there, out of reach of repercussions."

Sullen's beefy fingers rolled up into fists, but Da just smirked and patted his grandson's shoulder. "Well, that's about as respectful a tone as I'd expect from one of Craven's confederates. I think I heard that a tapai is a prince of the Farthest Mountains, aye? Tell me Prince Purna, how much did your royal jester here trade you for that pelt?"

"She—" Maroto began, but Purna spoke for herself.

"Took it myself, not a week past. I'll fess your son helped, and our comrade Choi here, too, but it was me who delivered the beast back to the First Dark, so it's me who wears his crown. If you know my people, you know we don't wear what we don't kill...So are you an old fool who's forgotten what little he once knew, or are you just an asshole looking to get his face broken in?"

Da had his smile on now, the hungry one he wore just before taking a bite of you, but Sullen of all people intervened.

"Tapai Purna," he grumbled. "Grandfather's had his say, you've had yours, and all with ears ken the victor. Let it be enough."

"First my feckless son leaves me for dead, and now my grandson would light the pyre," clucked Da. "Very well, very well, peace to you, Prince Purna—after all, can't say Sullen here's had the opportunity to claim such a prize as you wear like a silk scarf wrapped 'round the fat neck of a trader's spoiled husband. Where we come from that means you deserve more respect than I showed ya. Peace to you, Tapai, from Ruthless of the Horned Wolves—we'll wrestle properly in Old Black's Meadhall someday, when I have my legs again."

Purna was clearly elated, but praise whoever listens that she held her tongue and bowed to the old windbag. It was queer as a devil's smile, seeing the kin he'd given up for dead so long ago, but queerest of all was that rather than feeling relief or joy he was just pissed off that Da was already being such a fucker, and his nephew was clearly harboring some hard thoughts toward him. All he could do was be righteous and hope for the best.

"Da, Sullen, I figure you already know the Crowned Eagle, since she led us here," he said. "And the rest of my crew's getting stitched up, but yeah, this here is Choi. She's wildborn, same as you, Sullen."

Sullen tensed up, maybe on account of his being able to pass better than the prong-horned Immaculate and riled that Maroto would out him so casually. The boy had grown into his huge, bestial eyes, so unless you were looking you might not even notice he wasn't strictly human. Choi came forward and offered a sharp, curt bow.

"Choi Bo-yung, Martial Guard to General Ji-hyeon," she said, her sharp little teeth clicking in that way Maroto was getting seriously into.

"Ain't wild," said Sullen defensively, though he had the sense to curtsy back. "No offense, yeah, but I'm shaman blood, not wild-what-have-you. Ji-hyeon, she speaks proud of you, ma'am. Honored to bow to you."

"You've spoken with the general?" said Maroto, wondering just what these two savages had told Ji-hyeon...and just what they were doing here in the first place, far as obvious questions went.

"Oh, they're right cozy," said Da. "Though the hours he's out, don't reckon there's a lot of talk involved, am I right, laddie? If that general was as serious about leading this army as she is about wooing him, then—"

And just like that, easy as skipping a stone, Choi's sword appeared in her hand. Sullen's jaw fell loose, the boy paralyzed with mortification. Chevaleresse Sasamaso stepped right up, too, the head of her glaive swishing down to point at Da's sneering face. The Crowned Eagle knight said, "I told you the last time, old wolf, what would happen if you disrespected our future queen."

"Last time?" said Choi, and that tore it, right there—you didn't say Ji-hyeon's chamberpot smelled of anything but fresh-baked cakes around Choi, not if you valued your vitals. Before Da could open his evil mouth again, though, another voice spoke, one that filled Maroto with relief. He was dreaming, was all, and since none of this was real there was nothing to be concerned with. Should've known, soon as the ghosts of his father and nephew appeared. Might as well enjoy it before he woke up, and he turned to her as she casually insulted him.

"A Maroto family reunion? I'd heard there were destinies worse than death, and now I know there's truth in the old sayings."

Usually when he dreamt Zosia, she was as he'd last seen her, young and hale, if haggard around the eyes by the long campaign to take Diadem, and then the harder campaign to rule the Empire after she'd won the Crimson Throne. In dreams her hair shone like its namesake, as dark a blue as the waters of the Bitter Sea crashing into the Noreast fjords, and she usually appeared in a similar garment to the chainmail kit her successor actually wore...if not significantly less. Choplicker rarely made an appearance in his dreams, thankfully.

Now, though, he dreamt Zosia as she'd probably be if none of the badness had ever happened—older and sharper, her hair molten silver instead of cobalt, those delicate lines around her eyes now spread down to the corners of her mouth. A simple hauberk, much like those she'd favored in the early days, hung from her broad shoulders, baggy woolen trousers in the Raniputri style bunched over her thick legs. And looking not a day older than the last time they'd met,

Choplicker stood at her knee, offering a good-natured bark and then rushing him.

"Zosia." He breathed her name as a prayer to stay asleep a little longer, and dimly realized that Purna, Choi, and Sasamaso were all taking a knee at the invocation of her name, only Sullen too stupid to bow before her. It felt so good, he said it again. "Zosia."

She shrugged, her barely contained grin now sloshing out at either side of her mouth. Reflexively, his hands went down to push the snuffling devil away from his crotch, as though Choplicker were a real dog, and that was when it sunk in—the devil's nose was cold as the grave against his palm, the slobber that greased his fingers warm as a beating heart. He felt it, he felt everything. No dream, not even one bought from a centipede dealer, could be this real.

"You going to play with that fiend all day or are you going to give me a hug?" Zosia asked, that perfect smile that had become so rare in the last few years of her life now splitting her mouth wide. She stomped over to him in her heavy boots, instead of gliding above the hard-packed earth. Not a dream. Not a ghost. *Zosia*. She raised her arms, palms up in a *What are ya gonna do?* expression, and Maroto took a breath, something he hadn't done since hearing her voice for the first time in twenty years. "You look like shit, old man, if I didn't—"

Maroto seized her in his arms, dipped her low, and kissed her full upon the mouth, the way he'd always meant to. She tasted of whatever curried lunch she'd had, of stale kaldi and stale tubāq. She tasted alive, and he kissed her harder, hands squeezing her as firmly as he dared, savoring this delicious moment of surprise before her tongue unlocked itself and kissed him back, kissed him the way she'd always wanted to...

Instead, she bit his tongue, jerked her head away, and kneed him viciously in the crotch.

CHAPTER
14

Devildamn Maroto to the worst hell, and devildamn Zosia for thinking fondly of him, even once! She laid the lecherous bastard out on the ground, returning his saliva to him in a glob that spattered into a freshly scarred ear. He stared up at her, wide-eyed and stupid as ever at her response to his most unwelcome advances. She would have kicked his teeth in if a short girl with an awfully big flintlock pistol hadn't scrambled to her feet and pointed her weapon at her.

"You ever touch me again and I'll kill you, Maroto," growled Zosia, ignoring the gun-toting tot. "By the six devils I bound, I mean it."

Was he...was he *crying*? Maroto turned his eyes to the ground before she could be sure. On closer inspection he did look in a bad way, worse by far than any of the other Villains in general, and freshly torn up around the leg, arm, and face. Maybe she'd really hurt him...

Whatever, that was a long time coming.

"You didn't need to lay him out!" said the girl with the gun. "He's just happy to see you!"

"That excuse might work for Choplicker humping your leg, but I expect a sight more from anyone who walks on two legs," said Zosia, and let out a big breath as Choplicker growled at her suggestion. She couldn't remember the last time she'd stayed up all night planning out tactics; back in the Dominions they'd done their plotting by daylight, as chevaleresses deemed it dishonorable to do so at any other time. Glaring down at her old Villain, she saw he was still inspecting the dirt at her boots instead of apologizing. "Same old fucking Maroto, eh? Devils keep us."

"Captain," said one of the guards Ji-hyeon had assigned Zosia, "if I might show you to your tent now, I believe Maroto and Captain Choi need to report in with the general."

"Sure," said Zosia, sizing up Maroto's people. That stern Noreast kid from Ji-hyeon's tent was there, wearing a mean-faced old man like a backpack. There was another Flintlander, this one a chevaleresse in banded plate, and a po-faced broad with hair paler than Zosia's, and small black horns to boot. This last was giving Zosia the devil eye, an easy enough trick when you've got red eyes by birth. None of them said shit, though. Returning the wildborn's stare, she said, "You're Choi, then? On behalf of my fellow Villains I apologize for any harassment you had to endure from this creep whilst patrolling."

"Unnecessary," the woman said, her pointed teeth looking as sharp as her tone.

Well, all you can do is try to be nice. Zosia turned her back on them, Choplicker falling in with her and the guards. A cool cot in a dark tent was sounding even nicer than it had before.

"*Captain* Zosia?" she overheard the Ugrakari girl mutter as she helped Maroto up. "Devils keep *us*."

———

Zosia knew better than to nap for more than a few hours. Between the position of the sun and the pounding in her skull when Choplicker roused her with a sticky lick to the cheek, she supposed he was actually honoring her requests for a change. Well, he might be in a good mood; the monster had eaten more over the last year than he had in the previous twenty, and with war imminent, he'd be feasting plenty more in the days to come. She'd barely finished getting up and packing a bowl before the guard outside called:

"A visitor for you, Captain."

"Care to place a bet on which one?" Zosia asked Choplicker. "You're not acting the piddly puppy, so it can't be Hoartrap. Maroto will need to have a proper drunk on before he shows his face again, so that leaves Singh looking to see why I was in the general's tent all night, or Fennec eager to learn the same. Hmmm. Coming!"

Yet, parting the flap, she saw it was none of the Villains, but that Ugrakari pal of Maroto's. The guard handled the introduction, since the fiery-eyed sprat didn't seem inclined. "Tapai Purna to see you, Captain."

"Royalty, to see a lowly captain?" Zosia winked at the girl. "Let's see a salute, Your Highness, and you can come on in."

Tapai Purna stiffly raised a fist beside her freshly washed face, and Zosia held open the tent for her. As rich kids went she looked ground pretty sharp, a poorly tanned horned wolf hide wrapped around her shoulders, the rest of her kit a motley, well-worn assortment of ring-mail and spider lace, bronze caps and leather straps that probably passed for fashionable in this brave new world. She looked less like a tapai playing soldier and more like a soldier playing tapai. Nice legs, too, emerging from the bottom of her pelt—Maroto had an eye for quality, give the old dog his due. "To what do I owe the pleasure, friend?"

"I hope it will be a pleasure," said the girl, making straight for Zosia's table and plunking down a flask she'd had up her sleeve. "I've brought Immaculate peatfire and Madros sticks, if you'd care to break cork and wrapper with me."

"Quickest way to my good graces," said Zosia. "I can guess why Maroto sent you, so—"

"Maroto doesn't know I'm here," said the tapai, offering Zosia a cigar and flicking the end off her own with the blade of an enormous kakuri. Zosia was almost impressed—this generation of adventurers seemed harder than hers had ever been. Then again, they had stellar examples to follow. "He'll be even more ashamed than he already is, if he knows I came on his behalf. So unless you're an even big-ger, sloppier asshole than everybody already thinks, you'll keep this between us."

"You're a real charmer, Tapai," said Zosia, putting her full pipe down on the table and accepting the cigar.

"Purna," said the girl. "Tapai's my mother, or my brothers. I'm just

Purna to you, Captain. I didn't buy my way into this army, I earned it. Same as you."

"Same as me?"

"Those Raniputri who just arrived are yours, right? We've been watching you off and on for weeks, coming through the mountains. Assumed you were a mercenary vanguard of the Imperials you were ahead of, but I guess they were just chasing you?"

"That's the shape of it, but I wouldn't call the Raniputri mine. If anything goes cockeyed, they'll side with Singh over me."

"I wondered if that old knight was her." Purna opened the door in the hanging lantern and lit her cigar. As Zosia followed suit, Purna said, "So that means the only missing Villain is Kang-ho. Quite the reunion."

"I'd say his daughter fills in just fine," said Zosia, doing her best to downplay how fucking rapturous it felt to have a genuine Madros cigar back between her teeth. The strong, earthy black wrapper tasted like coming home. "She makes a better general than he ever would, that's for damn sure. Don't tell me you grew up on the songs of Cold Cobalt, too."

"Can sing them in three different dialects," said Purna, and there at the perimeter of the girl's hard-ass act was a quick flash of excitement, eagerness. "It's warm in here, mind if I shed my skin?"

"Sure," said Zosia, taking the girl's hood and slinging in onto her cot. Purna was boyish enough to give Zosia a nice little tingle, but nice little tingles quickly turned into queasy guilt as she thought of Leib. Tried to remember the sensation of his hands, really *feel* them . . . and found that like so much else about him, she was losing that, too. He'd never begrudge her a fling, of course, not now that he couldn't help relieve her tension himself. He would want her to have some fun, forget her burdens for an hour or two, but knowing that only made her miss him more. Besides, the last person to give her a nice little tingle had stolen her pipe, the only thing of Leib's she'd had left, and now she was stuck with Maroto's discarded briar, and a cigar from Maroto's little friend. "What do you want, Purna? I'm a busy woman."

Purna laughed. It sounded almost real. "Anything I want, I take. You probably think I'm sniffing around for gossip. How's the Cobalt Queen still alive? Why are all the Villains back together? Are we on the cusp of another golden age?"

"And you're not a little curious?" Zosia opened the girl's flask, and when a glance at Choplicker provoked no warning bark, she took a deep swig. Like he'd told her the last time she'd been poisoned. Ah, smoky cigars and smokier peatfire for breakfast. Just like old times, right enough.

"Woman, I couldn't give a bad vindaloo shit," said Purna. "It's all *very* exciting, of course, but I didn't come here to listen to you gloat about past glories, or promise me new ones. I came here to talk about Maroto."

"Look, girl, I don't know what he's whispered in your ear—"

"He hasn't whispered anything in my ear," snapped Purna, taking a puff to calm herself and then blowing a perfect smoke ring right at Zosia. "We talk. As friends. Comrades. And I can't say why you crawled out of whatever hole you've been hiding in, and I can't guess why so many of the Villains have assembled, but I know exactly why Maroto's here: because of you."

"Is *that* what he told you?" Zosia passed the flask over and idled back over to her cot, sitting down with a grunt at the twinges in her knees and back. "It's bullshit, Purna. Nobody in this camp knew I was alive until I rode in last night."

"Exactly," said Purna, taking a pull and swishing it around her mouth before continuing. "We were way the fuck out in no-one's-land, past the Panteran Wastes, when he heard some bartalk that you were back from the dead and raising hell in the Empire. He fell for the same line most everyone has, thinking General Ji-hyeon was the dread Zosia returned. So Maroto led me and my friends on a tour of the whole fucking Star trying to find you, only to end up more miserable than ever when we finally caught up to the Cobalt Company a month or so back. Broke his heart all over again, and he only stuck around because he didn't have anywhere else to go, and I wanted to see what the mercenary life was all about."

"So?" Zosia looked up at the naïve girl. "Am I supposed to be touched?"

"So he's probably the only one in this camp who's actually happy to see you," said Purna, which put a run in Zosia's cigar, all right. "The others might be overjoyed to have a living legend roll into camp, because its good for morale and all that shit, but do you think anyone else cares about you? He's loved you since before I was out of short trousers, and when he finally sees you again he gets carried away, and you punk him in front of everyone!"

"Damn right, and I'd do it again without thinking twice," said Zosia, wondering how in all the Usban names for hell this runt had actually made her feel a stab of guilt for what was clearly a justified reaction. "Maybe he's changed in every other way a person can, but from where I sit he's an even bigger asshole than ever. I offered him a *hug*, as I'm sure you noticed."

"Hugging's nice," said Purna, coming over and sitting down beside Zosia on the cot. Close enough to make a hard-up widow wonder, then looking sidelong at Zosia in a way that took a lot of the wonder out of the equation. "You've never got carried away, wanted something so much you didn't care who might be watching?"

Zosia glanced at Choplicker, who had the courtesy to totter off to a corner and sit down facing the wall of the tent. Damn, but Purna wasn't wasting any time—that was a welcome change of pace. If they were still talking about Maroto then Zosia was a devil's auntie. And if she was reading this wrong, better to get it cleared up now, lest she be strung along the way she had with Bang. Tossing her cigar on the dirt floor of her tent, she patted the girl on a convenient break in her armor between kneepad and mail skirt. Her flesh felt warm as the peatfire.

"Zosia," Purna said, her bangs falling in front of her eyes as she slowly leaned forward, tossing her own cigar onto the floor. "I didn't come here to..."

"We can have it any way you want, Purna," said Zosia, feeling her heart start to gallop as she caught a whiff of the girl's fresh sweat mixed with the smoky fragrances of Madros and the Isles. "I can talk for hours about what a bastard Maroto was, always with a smart word about my body, constantly trying to talk me into a pity-fuck, or you and me could pass the time some other way, maybe."

"You..." Something she'd said had snagged Purna just off the edge, and the girl took a swig off the flask instead of Zosia. Wiping her mouth, she sat up a little straighter. Away from Zosia. What the devils had she said wrong? "I mean, obviously, you and Maroto...you had something, once. Right? Even if you don't want to anymore?"

"So you would rather talk about him," said Zosia, wondering, hoping, praying, and doubting that by clearing the air where that pervert was concerned they could get back to whatever had almost happened. "Sure, we had something once—we were friends. Then he decided he wanted to fuck me more than he cared about most anything else, as far as I could tell. Hells, maybe we were never even really friends."

Zoisa took the flask back and emptied it before continuing. "You know he would never spar with me? Ever. Said he was worried he'd mess up my pretty face. So then I told him I only slept with those who had bested me in combat, and the next fucking day he had the dull irons out, pushing me to duel him. After that I had to fight him not to fight him, if you follow, but he never got lucky enough to beat me, praise the gods of steel. So that's what we had—a very, very sick relationship, contrary to whatever lies he told."

"He never *said* anything happened," said Purna. She seemed as heartbroken as old Maroto, lying in the dust. Nothing less sexy than sadness. "I just thought he was being discreet. Romantic."

"Oh, girl," said Zosia ruefully. "Maroto's been called a lot of things in his day, by me and others, but I don't think he's ever been accused of either discretion or romance."

"Shit," said Purna, slumping a little. "Shit and damn. I really wanted to...Never mind."

"Really wanted to what, patch things up between us? You can't patch something that doesn't exist to be rent in the first place. And if you thought enticing me into some devil's three-way with you and him was ever going to—"

"Ew, no!" said Purna. "I do *not* want that!"

"So if we're done talking about him, then..." said Zosia, giving it one last go and sliding her hand back onto Purna's leg. Even a low fire can be banked up after all.

"Shit shit shit," said Purna, scrambling to her feet. Her cheeks were as red as Maroto's had been when she'd rebuked his kiss. "Shit! Don't get me wrong, I'd love to, you're even hotter than I imagined. But...shit!"

"Purna," said Zosia, "take a deep breath, now. This doesn't have anything to do with anything; we're just two women talking in a tent."

"If you and he had...even once, that would be one thing!" said Purna, grabbing her hood from beside Zosia. "But I can't, not now. Of course he can be a creep, and a jerk, and a hundred other things, but he's also my best friend. I can't do this, much as I'd like to. It would kill him. Shit!"

"You don't owe him anything," said Zosia, but she could tell the girl was long gone, even as she stood there kneading her cloak in her hands. "Neither of us do."

"No," said Purna, all her boldness gone. "Please don't tell him we even...Bye!"

And just like that, Zosia was alone in her tent again. This was getting really fucking old—she'd never had so much trouble getting laid in her life. It was coming up on a year...from the first time on, had she ever gone a year? A month? Not a week, if she could help it.

On the bright side, according to Ji-hyeon the Imperial regiment pursuing the Cobalt Company was none other than the Fifteenth out of Azgaroth, led by Colonel Hjortt himself, so as far as the vengeance game went, Zosia couldn't have prayed for a better hand. She was keenly looking forward to seeing the thumbless murderer again, and breaking the shit out of her oath to kill him last—him, and his entire cavalry, and his big war nun bodyguard. It was almost too perfect an offering, a regular Kypck reunion.

Had Indsorith sent her pawns here as a sacrifice to appease Zosia, as though she were some ravenous devil that could be sated? Doubtful. It was far more likely the Fifteenth Regiment was set out as bait to draw her into a trap, but that was just fine with her—the Crimson Queen of Samoth wasn't the only one who could sacrifice an army for the sake of a personal vendetta, and if the Cobalt Company had a rough time of it when the battle raged, that was a small price to pay for vengeance against those who had killed her husband, her people. Then, long after the smoke had cleared and no sign was found of Cold Cobalt, the queen might be alone one night in her throne room, when an unexpected guest joined her...

Choplicker whined, and Zosia reached for Purna's smoldering cigar butt to throw at him when she saw the real cause of his outburst: Hoartrap had appeared in the opposite corner of her tent, smiling like a freshly freed devil.

"Just when you think it can't get any worse," said Zosia. "Don't tell me you've learned how to materialize out of thin air."

"Would that it were so," said Hoartrap, wiping dust off the front of his robes. "I unpin tent posts and squirm under just like everyone else, I'm afraid. The key is doing so when the occupants are too busy to notice."

"There's mercy in hell, then," said Zosia. "I don't suppose you can conjure some booze?"

"Ah, now there is a trick within my talents," said Hoartrap, removing a small bottle from the cavernous pockets of his saffron robes. "Care for a puff as well as a tipple?"

"Since it worked out so well the last time, why not?" said Zosia. With a sigh, she looked at Choplicker. "Fine. You're off until he is, but if I catch one word that you've been into any mischief at all—"

But the devil didn't wait to hear the rest of her oath, shooting out of the tent and away from the wizard as fast as his legs could carry him.

"I don't think he missed me," said Hoartrap. "A pity, I've thought of him often since you both disappeared."

"All right, Hoartrap." Zosia hopped up from her cot in a quick, pantherlike motion that she'd be feeling in her hips for hours to come. She strutted toward him with a bravado that felt as patently false as Purna's, hoping it wouldn't come down to her and Hoartrap. Hoping for once Choplicker hadn't strayed far. "I need you to be totally straight with me for the first time in your miserable life. Did you put those Imperials onto me at Kypck, or was it the queen? Lie to me and it'll be a lot worse for you."

"I never even suspected you were alive," said Hoartrap, patting a hand to his breast. "I swear it on all the devils I've eaten. Don't think I didn't check, either! Choplicker kept you well hidden—did you manage to bind him a second time, or did he do that out of love?"

"He tricked me," said Zosia, relieved to feel all the fight slough out of her. "Kept me hidden, all right, just as long as it suited his needs. Wondered why he stuck around for nigh on twenty years after I offered him an out, and now I know—he turned it down. You ever hear of a devil saying no to an easy wish?"

"No," said Hoartrap, scratching at a boil on his bullish neck. "Which makes one wonder if the wording of your wish was such that he honored it without your notice, and is indeed a free devil. There are songs of ancients in Emeritus who befriended devils, rather than binding them."

"If that were true Choplicker could do whatever he wanted, whenever he wanted," said Zosia. "*There's* a cheery thought."

In a great swirl of robes, dust, and mighty-thewed legs, Hoartrap sat down on his ass in the middle of the tent. From an inner pocket he removed the pipe Zosia had carved him thirty years past from a black gnarl of nigh-petrified oak he had brought her, claiming to have dredged it from a swamp. It took ages for that oak to dry, and the peaty bouquet of the bog never quite left the wood, but Hoartrap seemed delighted in the result. The downward curve of its yellow horn stem was inlaid with leopard palm where it joined the black oak shank, the wood carrying downward another inch before swooping back up and out into a bowl shaped like a half-bloomed tulip. The rough stratifications of the unique wood made it look less like a pipe and more like a grotesque snail shell or ebon stinkhorn. As he packed the piece from a ratty leather purse, he said, "We have so, so much to discuss, old friend."

"Mmmm," said Zosia, retrieving from the table the bowl she'd packed earlier. She remembered how touched Maroto had been when she'd given it to him at that kaldi house back in Linkensterne, just a year or two before he helped her become Queen of Samoth, Keeper of the Crimson Empire. "Another time, old Touch, I'm about talked out at present. You amenable to a more meditative meeting?"

"Oh sure," said Hoartrap jovially. "You know I love nothing more than sitting and staring silently at you for hours, occasionally murmuring portentously."

"So long as you don't talk," said Zosia, canting her pipe to accept the floating flame Hoartrap offered her. Light. Puff. Tamp. Light. Puff.

That order.

As far as plans went, this one succeeded wildly, and Zosia settled back on her bed with a groan. What a fucking day. The best part was that even after staying up all night with Ji-hyeon planning strategy, even with the better terrain, she was still unconvinced any of their tactics could overcome a much larger force with military experience—the Imperials had the numbers, like they always did, and even with that green kid Colonel Hjortt leading them, the new Cobalts were still in for one tearjerker of a song. She had helped talk Ji-hyeon into throwing down here and now because if the Cobalts carried the day, she could have her vengeance on both the cavalry that had slaughtered Kypck and the colonel she had foolishly let slip through her fingers, but if the Cobalts couldn't pull this off, it might be one of her last days on earth.

And how was she spending it? Sexually frustrated, smoking a pipe that she had thought peerless when she'd carved it but now saw it for the crude work that it was, a pipe that was burning far too hot due to the Oriorentine blend having dried out in her purse. Her only companion was the evilest man she'd ever met, and adding insult to injury, his bottle contained crème de violette and his pipe smelled more flowery still, packed with a mixture of astringent, powerful tambo and some soapy brown flakes that made the whole tent reek like a geriatric's perfumed undergarments. Cold Zosia, former Queen of Samoth, this is what a year of hard work and heartache gets you: exactly what you deserve.

Just like old times, sure enough.

After a substantial interval of pungent contemplation, Hoartrap broke his promised silence. "Want to go to a party later?"

CHAPTER
15

There had been times when Domingo hated his son. Not the sort of thing any father cares to admit, but there it was. No matter which way you sliced it, when you got to the bone of the boy you found marrow of the purest yellow. Efrain Hjortt wasn't just a coward, either, he was also a weakling. And a sniveler. Hard as Domingo had tried to help the lad become worthy of his mother's house, firm as the Azgarothian Academy had been with the boy, nothing seemed to help—he had the spine of a jellied eel, and the vicious selfishness of a living member of that species. Away on campaign for months at a stretch, if not longer, Domingo saw the boy grow in great bounds, but never to discernible benefit. Each time he returned and saw Efrain the boy's sneering smile was broader, as was his belly, but while he eventually became somewhat adequate with a sword, there was no doubt this indolent teenager would never be fit for commanding anything more important than a dinner party. He wanted to blame his sister-in-law Lupitera for retarding Efrain's maturity, he wanted to blame Concilia for casting off her family and moving to Trve, but at his heart Domingo knew that his son's weakness stemmed from neither the influence of his aunt nor the absence of his mother.

Yet still he had told himself his son would come into his own, that all he needed was that push into the saddle. And Domingo Hjortt, decorated Colonel of the Crimson Empire, Baron of Cockspar, a shrewd ruler in peace and war alike, was totally, utterly wrong. For most of the boy's life, Domingo had vacillated between lying to himself about Efrain's quality and despising the child for possessing none. What a waste.

Now, as Domingo lay broken and battered in the back of a wagon, bouncing down a seemingly eternal mountain road, he was done with delusions about Efrain, and all that remained was hatred. Efrain was the reason he was here, and thus Efrain was the reason his left hip had shattered under a horned wolf's headbutt. Efrain was the reason he'd lost all feeling in his right arm. Efrain was the reason half his head was so swollen from slamming face-first into the ground that he still couldn't see out of one eye, a full week after the attack. Efrain was a chump who never should have been in charge of a modest kitchen, let alone a regiment, but that was no excuse for getting himself wrapped up in ridiculous plots and then murdered for his trouble.

Really, how did any ranking officer get himself killed, in this day and age? Once again Efrain had scraped new lows, bringing his aged father down with him, and the only way for Domingo to restore his honor was to avenge his son. He was as bound by familial duty to catch Efrain's killer as Efrain had been to lead the Fifteenth, come to think it, both men destroying themselves in the name of the other, and there was another nasty bump in the road to aid him in shedding a few tears over the tragedy of it all. If only Lupitera had been here to witness it all, she'd have given him a standing ovation—the shows down at the Iglesia Mendoza didn't have a red herring on the drama of the Hjortts.

Unlike most of those tragedies, this bit of overwrought theater would have a happy ending: drenched in blood, the old hero unmasks his enemies, and executes most of the cast. His maneuver with the Immaculate prince turned out to be unneeded, but then a little comedy to break things up always made the serious bits hit harder. To think he had actually been worried that the pope was wrong, that all the rumors were false and Zosia was as dead as she deserved to be. That this new Cobalt Company was just a band of phonies, led by the runaway Immaculate girl that Prince Byeong-gu had been chasing. Funnier still, even in his current condition Domingo was relieved to know that the Stricken Queen had indeed cheated death, that she was the one who had murdered his son, that she was the one who had ordered the horned wolf attack on his camp. Even without catching her old Villain Maroto sneaking past his tent, Domingo would have recognized that insane tactic as bearing the stamp of Zosia—no one else in all the songs of today, tomorrow, or yesterday would have dared such a deranged, suicidal maneuver.

Much as it hurt to admit it, he could learn a trick or two from his blue-haired archenemy—her gambit had paid off. Even if she had sacrificed a few soldiers in the course of luring the monsters down from the mountain, the Fifteenth had lost over a hundred foot soldiers, fifty-some archers and gunners, and their two best witchborn guards...and that wasn't even getting into the Ninth's losses, or the horses the retreating wolves had carried off when their blood thirst was sated, or the panic that the attack had caused. Another fifty soldiers had deserted that very night, and running them down and hanging them had wasted a full day they should have been on the march. How do you wage war against such madness? Countering with some deranged, devilish maneuvers of his own was just the thing to bring Zosia down for good, and make it take this time... Not like he had much to lose, unable to ride a horse of his own and needing an anathema to help him so much as take a piss. As the Burnished Chain became increasingly popular in the Azgarothian court as it did everywhere else, Domingo's insistent hewing to the godless ways of his ancestors was viewed as increasingly eccentric, so it would probably come as quite the relief to everyone back home when they heard he had destroyed the Cobalt Company with the help of the church.

"Sir?" Splayed in his deep nest of padding and pillow in the wagon bed and unable to move his neck without extreme distress, Domingo kept his gaze on the crimson twilight leaching into the high peak looming over them but knew who had ridden up beside him without needing to see her.

"What is it, Shea? I'm a very busy man."

"The witchborn scouts? They've returned with news."

Domingo closed his eye, speaking with more patience than he thought he possessed. "And what is the news, Shea?"

"The Cobalt Company, sir? We've found them. They appear to be fortifying a camp?"

"Where?" Domingo's heart soared into the darkening sky; he had anticipated another agonizing pursuit all over the Star, but maybe twenty-odd years on, Zosia was as tired of running as he was of chasing her.

"Where the road comes down into the plains? They cut north as soon as the ground evened out enough for their wagons. Their camp is where the foothills back into some famous mountain...It's called the Lark's Tongue?"

"I've ridden past it," said Domingo, remembering, remembering... "Good position. Not great, but good. Steep ridges come out on either side of where they'll camp at the base, so we won't be able to flank them, but that also means they'll have nowhere to run—the mountain's too sheer to safely climb away." Thinking, thinking... "Smarter than I thought. The Cobalt Company's burning their boats so the volunteers can't flee if the battle takes a turn. She's transforming her little blue mice into cornered rats. Just when I think I've got you figured out..."

"Sir?"

"Just pondering, Shea. A colonel mustn't be afraid of a good ponder from time to time." It wasn't right, her digging in for a last stand already. Zosia was changing up on him, so he would have to do the same to stay ahead. "How far are we from their camp? At earliest?"

"If we go the usual extra hour tonight? We're overlooking the plains now, so we should be down by late afternoon tomorrow, and from the foothills another solid day will take us within engaging distance. But we're still waiting on the all clear from Diadem, and the last owlbat we received from Colonel Waits said that the Third are still most of a week out from—"

"If I wanted to know where the Thaoan regiment was I'd have asked, Captain, and as far as the queen's written permission to engage the enemy goes, I daresay it's a bit late to get hung up on every formality," said Domingo, his mind swooping through the haze of time and memory and toward the silhouette of the Lark's Tongue overlooking the Witchfinder Plains. Cold Zosia wasn't the only one who could pull a trick to surprise the devils, and while he certainly hoped the Black Pope's weapon proved as devastating as advertised, a little insurance never hurt. "Inform the men we'll be stopping in half an hour for dinner."

"Very good, sir, an early night will still put us—"

"Three hours' rest, cold rations, and then we're marching through the night—just like the old days," said Domingo, wishing he could crane his neck to catch Shea's frown but wanting to save his strength for rarer game. "We won't catch the Cobalt Company with snoring troopers, Captain. Now find Colonel Wheatley and have him join me on the command wagon. There's a certain suicidally risky tactic I need to consult with him about."

"Sir?"

"Slip of the Lark's Tongue, Captain," said Domingo, groaning as the wagon bounced and his entire body warred to see which bit could cause him the most discomfort. "Be a good officer and keep it to yourself, lest I find myself in need of volunteers. By the time Waits limps in from Thao we're going to have every Cobalt head on a pike, save Zosia's—that one's going back to Azgaroth in a box. I'm going to mount it over my son's tomb."

"Zosia, sir?" Shea sounded as incredulous as she always did when he mentioned the Stricken Queen, like her old colonel was going soft in the helm. "You don't think the rumors—"

"You don't think at all, if you know what's good for you," said Domingo. "You're a soldier, damn it, not a bloody philosopher. Now fetch Wheatley, and bring along Wan, too—when you're bringing hell down on a pack of sinners, you can't have too many devils to help deliver the goods."

CHAPTER
16

The villagers Heretic impressed from the nearest hamlet brought a wagon with them. Portolés and the corpses of the other clerics all went into the bed, and then they were brought back downstream and taken over a rattley bridge. They passed through the hovels clustered on the riverside and then left the road, bouncing over a marshy field until they reached a great heap of wood the local children had gathered. The corpses went onto the pyre, and then oil went onto the corpses, and then the morning sky was obscured behind a wall of black smoke. Half-conscious in the back of the wagon, Portolés imagined she could see the Sunken Kingdom rising out of the mists of the Haunted Sea, but when a gust parted the smoke she saw it was just the thatched roof of a nearby hut on the far side of the pyre.

As her brethren burned, Heretic led the villagers in a bizarre dance around the blaze, the billowy cassock hanging off his lanky body making him resemble a living scarecrow. Portolés assumed it must be some pagan rite, but found out later that Heretic had successfully passed himself off as a brother of the Burnished Chain and told the ignorant villagers they were helping him in a funerary ritual for fallen clerics. He thought this a lot more amusing than she did. He explained all this in a hut set back on the willowed banks of the Heartvein, after the local mudhusband had tended to Portolés with a liberal mix of medicine, miracles, and mummery.

Heretic kept up his deception for the length of Portolés's recovery, and lest she give the game away, he only removed her gag at mealtimes. He told the mudhusband she was the ringleader of a renegade band of heretics, and must be healed in order to stand trial in Diadem. Portolés's former prisoner had quite the time of it, dining and gossiping with their elderly host and the man's daughter, dozing his days away by the river with a bottle of their best plum brandy, explaining that he couldn't offer any prayer services in the village as he was a war monk, better suited to acts of worship unfit for a friendly town. Portolés lay locked in the root cellar, alone with her prayers.

"Don't think they believed me, mind," said Heretic as they walked their horses around a frozen bog on the misty morning when they finally left. "Sure they saw right through me, but were happy enough to help the revolution, so long as they could honestly deny it after the fact."

Even without the gag Portolés wouldn't have spoken. Partly to deny Heretic the satisfaction, since he seemed of a mood to keep her as oblivious to his intentions as she had kept him to hers. Partly because riding a horse was agony, a perpetual stitch in her side and a tender throbbing in her guts and mangled hand. The stab wounds to her chest hurt like the worst kind of penance but had failed to puncture a lung, praise the Fallen Mother, and cinched as it was against a wooden brace, her broken arm only hurt when she moved. All told, she felt worse now than she had lying on the twilight butte, unsure if Heretic planned on returning.

"You know what he said, old Dafhaven back there? He said you were lucky he was also an animal mender, or he wouldn't have known what to do with you. Said under the skin you were more beast than woman, and that's what saved you—said a real person got worked over the way you did, their vitals would be too bad off to tend. Praise the Black Pope you were born a monster, yeah?"

The gag was so tight it hurt to smile, the straps cutting into the corners of Portolés's lips. For a time the only sound was of hooves cracking through hoarfrost and ice-capped puddles, frozen reeds snapping off against their flanks. On the far side of the fen they rejoined the road, but only long enough to cross it before plunging back into the cold, damp woodland on the far side. Heretic knew enough to keep them off the highways, after what had happened on the butte, and lest they encounter more agents of the Chain, he had them both change out of their robes and into plain linen and wool garments. Portolés had never felt so naked and vulnerable as she did in the heavy peasant's frock Heretic gave her, but it also brought the familiar tickle of the profane to her breast. She had no idea what gear remained on the pack mule, if her writs were safe, but she noticed he had salvaged her maul. A fine omen of his intent, that. Maybe.

"You know, when we first set out I wondered if you were one of us," he said when they'd made camp for the night on a soggy knoll jutting up from another expanse of miserable marshland. "There's a bigger concentration of support in the Dens than anywhere else in Diadem, you know that? Might seem odd to a pious maid like yourself, but a lot of your kind aren't happy with being called anathemas, treated worse than devils, by the same church that expects them to die in the name of the Savior. To sacrifice your whole life, serving an institution built to oppress you... Hey, are you asleep?"

Sitting with her back against the stump he'd chained her to, Portolés opened her eyes and gestured at the gag with her manacled hands. When he frowned across the small fire but did not rise to remove it she closed her eyes again. He could talk, but he couldn't make her listen—something he'd taught her, early in their acquaintance. Then she heard him squelching toward her, and held in a word of thanks as his grimy fingers pried the gag out of her mouth.

"I'm right curious, as you said back on the hill," said Heretic, holding a waterskin to her lips. She took it, and didn't spit it out when she tasted the sweet and flat barleywine of the Heartvein provinces. No sin there, so long as she didn't ask for it. "Denied it at first, so's not to give you the satisfaction. Wasn't planning on coming back for you, neither, not at first, but when I hit that river town a couple leagues out I couldn't help myself. Wasn't just that you saved me from the Office of Answers, or just that you'd fight your own kind without so much as squeezing out a fart by way of parley... But both together, well, that'd raise the interest of anyone. I can't read the hightalk on those documents you flash around whenever someone gives you lip, but I recognize the Royal Crimson Seal from the warrants they waved when they arrested me. So what is it you're after, Sister Portolés? What's your mission, up in the Isles, and now taking us all over the Empire? Why'd you bust me out, and keep me with you this whole time, instead of bringing along Imperial loyals, or Chain folk? You really one of us?"

"Cut this gag off for good and I'll tell you," said Portolés. Heretic considered this, then shrugged and sawed it off with the same knife that had punctured Portolés's bosom. He tossed the hated thing on the fire, her saliva popping and hissing as the gag twisted in the flames like a serpent. "All right, Heretic. You have many questions, but I'll do my best to answer some of them."

"My name's Boris, damn your tongue," said Heretic. "*Boris.* After all we've been through you could do me that courtesy, calling me by the name my mother gave me."

"I took you with me because the Fallen Mother put you in my path," said Portolés. "I fought my brethren alongside you because the Deceiver turned them against me. What I am after, my mission, as you say, is to do the will of the Savior, be it in the Isles, the Empire, or in hell itself. And as for whether I am, as you say, *one of you*, well, only the Fallen Mother or the Deceiver can say for sure—we are all mortal wretches born to die, *Heretic*, so in that respect, yes: I am one of you."

Heretic shook his head, frustrated as she'd yet seen him. "You... you've either got a better sense of humor than I expected, or you're even crazier than the rest of your kind."

"*My kind* meaning anathemas? I told you, Heretic, I am one of *you.*"

"Your kind meaning Chainite crazies. It'll go better for you if you're up-front with me, Portolés, here and now, before anyone else gets involved."

"That sounds awfully familiar," said Portolés, enjoying herself for the first time since the Battle of the Butte. For all his high and mighty posturing, as soon as he had the chance he'd treated her even worse than she'd treated him. "I wonder where I've heard that sort of talk before. Oh yes, it was in the Office of Answers—the Askers said something similar to your friends. How many of them confessed, I wonder. And how much of a difference do you think it made in the end?"

"Try to be nice…" Heretic shook his head. "Just to show you I'm not the same as Imperials, or war nuns, for that matter, I'll keep my word where the gag's concerned. But when I turn you over you'll wish you'd leveled with me."

"I don't doubt you, Asker Boris," said Portolés, denying him the satisfaction of her asking whom he intended to turn her over to, and in the process giving herself a faint and fleeting thrill. "And I thank you for your mercy. Now, shall I take first watch, or did you have more questions for the accused?"

Heretic didn't have much else to say, either that night or the ones that followed, and as they broke away from the river and moved west Portolés contemplated the best way to escape. Outside the city of Black Moth she almost managed it, when he left her chained around the trunk of a cypress in the surrounding woodland before riding into town. By the time he got back, laden with supplies, she had sawn partway through the tree with her chain, her wrist dripping black in the light of his lantern. He sighed theatrically and moved her to a bigger tree before settling in for the night. She'd assumed he'd be meeting with other traitors, tracking down underworld sorts who would have a standing bounty on Imperial or Chain officers, but he'd come back far too quick… meaning he'd just been restocking on food and beer, as he'd said.

"You're a naughty nun, no mistake," said Heretic. "You know they call this place the Haunted Forest? I hurried back on account I was worried for your safety, leaving you tied up in such a place."

"My savior," said Portolés.

"Only one you'll find in these woods. Here, thought you'd find this interesting." He passed over a torn flyer, and by the light of their fire she saw two familiar words blackening its surface. Even now they made her throb with something approaching awe. She looked Heretic in the eye. "You believe, do you?"

"I believe in what she stands for," said Heretic, setting their camp cauldron on its tripod. "Got you some bean mush and weeds, since I know how much you hate the saltpork we've been living off, pious girl like you."

"And what does Zosia stand for, then?" Portolés thought she had a fair understanding already, but it never hurt to ask for more details. "Freedom from the yoke of the oppressor? For your comrades, anyway?"

"Freedom for all," said Heretic. "No gods, devils, nor other scapegoats. No queens, popes, nor other vampires. Just people, helping each other."

"And if you have to kill a few hundred thousand people who disagree with you, well, that's not a bad cost, is it?" Portolés rather enjoyed playing his part, could see the sport he'd found in baiting her. "Open your eyes, Heretic; she was just another despot, peddling the same old story under a new name. Nothing more."

"Nothing less, either," said Heretic, looking up to where the paltry light of their fire faded into a darkness that was all the deeper for their having kindled a flame. As if he saw the answer there, in the night, he said, "Thing is, sister, I'm beginning to wonder if some of the crackpots in our party weren't on to something. The ones who say she's still alive. People really believe it out here in the Empire, too, you can tell they do—maybe she's rotting in some Diadem dungeon. Maybe death was too good for her, by Indsorith's thinking. When the overlords start reading your tracts instead of just burning them, you have to wonder..."

Portolés did wonder, as she had most every day since setting out, how Heretic would react if she told him the simple truth: Zosia lived. This knowledge she so easily carried within her sullied, bestial body was a weapon so powerful it might change the fate of the Empire, the fate of the Star. She had stumbled on a secret, *the* secret, and through the trust of her queen, an anonymous anathema had become transformed into a force of unspeakable influence. Like all weapons, she could be destroyed or cast aside, but if she could reach Zosia in time and convince her that the queen hadn't ordered Hjortt to attack Kypyk, she could win a war before it was even fought. Not bad for a chained-up witchborn who still had nightmares of screaming peasants dying under her orders.

"You've got that look again, Portolés," said Heretic, watching her closely. "That look like maybe you know something of what I speak? Like maybe that's why you wanted a rebel to ride with you, and not just because you could rely on me to fight any Imperials or Chainites that came after you. You wanted an expert on all things Cobalt."

"Now what would make you say such a thing, Heretic?"

"You're the worst damned bluffer I've ever seen. Here's a confession for you, sister, and it's been a long time coming..." Portolés perked up, couldn't help herself. "That book you've been reading down to the fibers, the one you took from the Office..."

"The one you wrote, Heretic?" Portolés hungered for his revelation the way she still hungered for Brother Wan. "That book?"

"That's the one," said Heretic, and like many who offer a confession, he looked half gleeful, half disgusted. "I didn't write it. Haven't even read it. Was an old bird in our party, Eluveitie, was working on it. She was in the Asking Chamber, too, though I didn't see where."

"Confession sets us free to see the Fallen Mother," said Portolés soberly, liking Heretic more than ever. "Did you take the credit to spare her especial attention from the Askers, or to gamble on finding yourself a way out?"

"I..." Heretic spit, which gave her answer enough. He didn't know himself. "Doesn't matter. We'll both hear some answers right quick, sister. Some lasses I met in town said they'd been hunting along the front of the Kutumbans, but beat it across the plains because the Cobalt Company's pitched a camp right in front of some mountain they call Bird Tongue."

Portolés felt the darkness at the edge of their firelight contract, as though the night itself had held its breath. She'd prayed, of course, prayed hard and long that Heretic would take this road. He was curious enough that it seemed possible, but she hadn't let herself believe, not until she heard the words from his own lips, but now that he'd said it she knew there had never been a question. What Queen Indsorith had planted inside Portolés could only be released when she met Zosia, and recognized her for the old mayoress. Then and only then would Portolés ascend from too-faithful servant and admittedly lousy messenger to savior of incalculable lives. Or destroyer, it was all a matter of perspective—once Zosia heard that the Black Pope had probably sent Hjortt to murder her husband and raze her town, would she seek an alliance with Queen Indsorith to go after the true perpetrator? Would the information Portolés delivered prevent the coming war between the Cobalt Company and the Crimson Empire but bring about a final, fatal civil war between the Empire and the Burnished Chain, with Zosia's army marching alongside Imperial regiments? Would she prevent an imminent massacre, only to cause a greater one? The seed cannot predict if it will become wheat or snakeroot, or what use its crop will be put to...

"You all right, sister?" Heretic looked concerned, but not concerned enough to leave his steaming stew pot.

"Never better," said Portolés, wiping tears from her cheeks. "You mentioned... the Cobalt Company?"

"Aye, I'm sure you've heard enough to know the stories behind them. A flesh-and-blood army led by a blue-haired ghost. If you believe the legends, which I'm not so sure I do. Whoever truly leads them, though, they'll be happy to have a war nun delivered to their door, especially one on a secret mission for Diadem. Seems like my people back in the capital have the same enemy and the same strategy, so why not throw in with these Cobalts?" Heretic watched her intently. "Nothing to say to that?"

Portolés fought to keep the relief off her face. She should have just freed Heretic from the onset and followed him after her quarry, trusting that higher powers had set him in her path as a human bloodhound. The uncertainty of what would happen when she finally caught Zosia filled her with unspeakable raptures, uncertainty about whether she brought miraculous peace or delivered infernal war, and she shuddered against her bonds. "I say you were dead right from the first, Asker Boris: we'll both have some answers before much longer. Now what do you say you loosen these chains enough so we can play some cards?"

CHAPTER
17

Maroto's wounds hadn't festered and none of his bones were broken, but other than the barber's welcome report he didn't have much to feel good about. Of all the hells he'd waded through, of all the nightmares he'd lived, he'd never imagined one as dread as this. Zosia, beautiful, brilliant Zosia, alive... and she hated him.

Well, to get real about it, that wasn't quite right. But bloody well close enough. If she'd hated him she would have thought of him from time to time. This was so much worse—she'd been off somewhere for twenty years, doing devils knew what, with devils knew whom, and she'd never once dropped him a clue that she was still alive, because he didn't even warrant her notice. If he'd died back when she was Cobalt Queen—or if he'd seemed to, anyway—she wouldn't have carried a candle for him, wouldn't have missed him every day, the way he had for her. She didn't give an easy shit about him. Never had, like as not.

"Come on, old man, I thought it was your kin over there they called Sullen, not you!" Diggelby swayed in front of the bonfire, dancing shapes limned against the night behind him. He held out a bottle, and Maroto took it, though he'd already drained enough to fell a dozen lesser drunks. Scowling across the fire at him was Sullen, though the pup hadn't brought Da to the party. Maroto waggled the bottle at his kin, who spit into the fire and looked away. Right, it was time to get something more than a shit-eyed stare out of that punk, find out what his beef was, and how bloody a cut it was...

"Whoa, steady on, man!" said Diggelby, catching Maroto as he took a wobbly step and nearly pitched into the fire. "Here, you lazy lumps, clear a seat! Dance for your captain's pleasure, or pay the price!"

Din and Hassan dutifully rose from a nearby divan, clapping Maroto on the back and saying the sort of overly cheerful crap you always fed to people you felt sorry for. Maroto wondered if there was a single cart horse or guard dog that hadn't heard about his encounter with Zosia that morning. Collapsing onto the couch, Diggelby pressed something into his hand. Something wriggling.

"A graveworm. Magica, the best!" whispered Diggelby. "It's good for what ails you, Captain. Just make sure not to chew it!"

"Know what to do with it," grumbled Maroto, the old hunger upon him as soon as he felt its carapace in his palm. It'd been right around a year since he'd been stung, so a graveworm would be just the creepy-crawly to ease him back into the habit...Though at his prime he'd gulped a dozen at a time, when he couldn't find bees or centipedes, and barely felt a thing.

"Good chap," said Diggelby, doing a clumsy Mustakrakish two-step away from the recumbent Maroto. "Don't forget who gave him to you, once the cryptcrawler's in your legs and you're ready for a first dance!"

"Uh-huh," said Maroto, opening his hand and watching the graveworm squirm in his fist. Purna bumped into Diggelby, danced off him with far better moves, and after a few twists and turns, she practically fell on top of Maroto.

"What've you got there, Moochroto?" she asked, sitting on the arm of the seat and rubbing his shoulder. "Whoa, hey, Diggelby give you that? No call for that shit, man, you told me you were off the bugs for good."

"Told you lots of stuff," said Maroto, admiring the way its papery shell shimmered in the firelight.

"Yeah, you did," said Purna. "Look, I know...I know it sucks, right, but banging bugs over a girl? That's not your style, Maroto. You're better than that."

"Better than what?" sneered Maroto, and popped the grave-worm into his mouth. It tickled his tongue, and he dry-swallowed it, savoring the way it fought against the inevitable even as it went down. Just like people, bugs were, once you got acquainted with them. He regretted it even before Purna bolted up, slapped the back of his head.

"I love you, man, but you need to grow the fuck up already," she snapped.

"That's rich, coming from a brat who wants to play war because she thinks murdering people's a laugh." He regretted that, too, but she didn't hit him again. If anything, she softened a little.

"Look. You decide to stop feeling sorry for yourself tomorrow, let me know and we'll split this waste before lunch. Go to any Arm you want. But I won't ride out with a stinghound. Think about it, Maroto—adventure with me and the gang, or kill yourself with bugs because you can't let go of a dream. It's up to you, buddy."

"Yeah?" Getting the fuck away from here definitely sounded like a plan.

"Yeah. You take tonight to throw yourself the biggest pity-party you ever had, and in the morning we go. Promise." She looked like he must, heartbroken for no good reason, and, giving his hand a squeeze, she set her shoulders and got down to some serious dancing.

Maroto felt better already, the graveworm hitting him harder, faster, meaner than he expected. Good old Diggelby probably had a crate of cemetery dirt loaded with the things, and once they were free and clear of the Cobalt Company, who knew what sort of sport they could find? Ride over the mountains and knock off some Dominion stinghouses, set up a mobile operation...invest in a rolling aquarium like they'd had in the Wastes, but stocked with centipede warrens. Ooh, or maybe combine the design with an ice cart to keep the icebees cool, have a whole bloody apiary on wheels. Nice.

And there she fucking was again, appearing by the fire with Hoar-trap. Girl knew how to suck the air from a party, bringing that monster. She caught sight of him, and he bobbed his bottle at her, fully expecting her to turn away, give him the low visor all night. That was how she'd always played it in the old days, after a kind word or gesture on his part got taken the wrong way. Instead, she made a bee-line for him, and he hauled himself upright to meet her charge. Get ready, you fuckers, the night's entertainment has arrived, another stupid fight for no reason at all…

"Hey," said Zosia, standing in front of the divan. "Got enough room for a big-boned broad on that couch?"

"Sure," he said, wondering if the graveworm was giving him the walking dreams. Eat enough of those things and you'll see all kinds of shit. "Yeah, definitely."

She sat down next to him, stiff as a lance. She was stiff, like, not him…Devils, but this worm had turned since last he'd gulped one; he could barely keep his thoughts out of his mouth, or his mouth out of…Devils. He took a pull from the bottle to sober himself up, tasted every grain and hop that had gone into the pale Raniputri ale, handed it to her. She took a swig, then another. Smiled at him.

"Sorry about earlier," she said. "I'm…shit, man."

"Yeah, definitely," said Maroto again, nodding. "I mean, me, too. I was…I was excited to see you, was all. Didn't mean anything by it."

Her look told him this wasn't quite doing it, so he dug deeper, tried harder, hooked some of the stuff Purna had laid on him earlier that afternoon in his tent.

"Nobody likes getting grabbed like that. I wouldn't, Diggelby kissed me like that. Me being happy to see you's no excuse."

There was the smile again, and she huffed in that cute way that let him know they were in the mend-things-up stage, and in record time. Maybe she *had* missed him! "Which one's Diggelby?"

"That crustfop, dancing with Purna."

"Wow. Yeah, he looks terrible."

"Diggelby's all right. They all are. Solid."

"So it's true, then?" Zosia took out a pipe and pouch from her hip-bag, blind-packed it while overlooking the crowd of revelers. "Mighty Maroto took a pack of princelings under his wing?"

"Kids saved my life, no joke," he said, nervous she would ask him what had happened to the briar she'd carved him.

"I heard you lot saddled up a pack of horned wolves and rode them into an Imperial camp last week. Any truth in that?"

Maroto laughed, almost couldn't stop, then calmed his happy arse down. "Not much. A good song, though."

"Definitely," said Zosia. "Be right back, I'm going to get this going. You have one you want me to light?"

Shit shit shit. Anxiously scratching the side of his flattop, he inadvertently dislodged a cigarillo he'd bummed off Din earlier in the evening and tucked behind his ear. Salvation! "Sure, fire this dog for me."

"And I thought you only sucked sticks for coin," said Zosia with a wink, and headed over to the fire. She still had those legs, and her arse had filled out nicely, still tight with muscle but widened with age. Dark thoughts, Maroto, dark indeed—she looked a sight better than he did these days. When she returned, he took the cigarillo and puffed contentedly on it.

"What's with your kid? He got it in for me to make a name for himself, or what?"

"Kid?" Maroto followed her gaze and saw that Sullen was still glaring at them. Hard to believe it possible, but the kid looked even meaner, now that Maroto had some company. "Nephew. And I'm the one he's coming hard at."

"Yeah? The way Choplicker's been nodding at him, I thought for sure it was me he was sore on, for some reason I've long forgot or never knew. That ball-licking devil's always liked you, though, so maybe that's all it is, Choplicker looking out for his old litter mate." Zosia waved at Sullen, beckoned him over, but he pretended not to see her. "Aw, he's playing hard to get. Think you're going to live another night, Maroto."

"Scary fucking savage is giving me the death eyes and she says it's nothing to worry about." Maroto shook his head happily. He had half a mind to go give Sullen a hug. "Where is Slopchops, anyway? Didn't used to let him out of your sight."

"You know how they get when Hoartrap comes around, decided to go easy on him," she said, the unasked question of Crumbsnatcher dangling between them. Let it fucking dangle all the way down to the lowest hell. "Anyway, what's the nephew's story? That your dad I saw riding him before?"

"Yeah, that's Da," said Maroto, trying to blow a smoke ring and fucking it all up. "Still haven't figured out what their song is. That was the first I knew they were alive, when you decided to haunt my arse. Hadn't said ten words to 'em, and haven't said one since."

"No shit?"

"Not even a toot," said Maroto, delighted to see her shake her head and grin at his wit. "They were the whole reason I cut out on my clan the second time 'round, you know? Thought about it lots, sure, but never would have left if..."

"Second time 'round? You went back?" She poked him in the ribs. "Come on, dish."

"Shit, where to start?" Where to start indeed—maybe with Zosia playing him so hard he'd wrecked his life trying to avenge her, when she hadn't even had the decency to really die? He had half a mind to make her sing first, but this was his couch, sort of, and that made him host, and hosts take the first round. Some rules can't be bent. "Um...okay, yeah, so a ways back, I...I got burned out on, well, everything, so I decided to head back to the Savannahs. Go home, you know? Start over."

"You always said they'd kill you if they ever saw that ugly mug again." Zosia blew a perfect smoke ring with those perfect lips.

"Oh, they wanted to, and they would have, definitely," said Maroto, feeling the glares of the Horned Wolf council burning at him from across time and space. "But I figured the one thing that would settle me with the old bastards who run the clan was a big show of contrition. Of the physical sort, yeah? So I brought along what was left of my nest egg and laid it at their feet, told 'em that ever since I ran away as a pup I'd been working up enough dosh to come back and atone. Wonder of wonders, they let me back in."

"Some things are the same the Star over."

"True. I had to duel the meanest Wolf in the clan, too, but I think Da went easy on me, so it weren't no thing." Weren't no thing but a mark on his belly where his father had nearly gutted him in the honor pit, but what family didn't leave its scars? "Um, and since I'd left before I'd earned my name, I had to take the one they decided on for me."

"Which was..." From the gleam in Zosia's eye he wondered if she already knew.

"Not important. Anyway, after all that, I was a Horned Wolf again. Was *weird*, you know? Going from who I was when I rode with you, sleeping in palaces, to sharing the old floor cot with Da and my sister and her babe...That'd be Sullen, there, when he was but an ankle-biter. Sweetest kid I ever saw, too, wonder what soured him so."

Except Maroto knew, of course, knew without a doubt: it was him. Who else? The closer he got to folk the deeper their frowns, and you don't get closer than blood.

"I gather your retirement didn't go much better than mine," said Zosia, teasing him like she always did with the promise of a good song.

"Definitely not. At first things were better than I expected—I wasn't just trying to fit in, I was trying to be the best Horned Wolf in the clan. Followed every little rule." Which was true to the letter; the clan never imagined a Horned Wolf would intentionally stick his arm in the hives on a daily basis, and so there was no law forbidding it—why get yourself stung when the snowmead they produced was a far milder and nicer buzz? Da had told Maroto only the shamans of old ever let the icebees kiss their flesh, bringing them portents in peace or vigor in war, so the first time had just been an experiment, see if the bugs of his people were anything like the stinging insects he'd used a time or two during the Cobalt War, when one of the Villains needed field surgery but didn't need to feel it...Turned out icebees agreed with Maroto like few things ever had, rendering the sharp memories of his murdered beloved and his failure to avenge her into a dull dream, transforming a washed-up loser who did nothing but ponder the mistakes of the past into a proper Horned Wolf who pondered nothing at all, doing only what was expected of him—he'd floated through his days and nights in the Savannahs like a man resigned to drowning, drifting through the numbing depths of the freezing sea...

"You still with me, Maroto?" said Zosia, nudging him with the bottle.

"Sure, sure," said Maroto, accepting the warm beer and draining the witchpiss in the bottom. Damn graveworm hadn't ridden him this hard since he didn't know when—the kids must get better bugs in the old capital than he'd ever been able to afford. "Just getting my thoughts sorted. See, I did some dumb stuff after you...after I thought you died. Felt pretty low, and wanted to prove to myself I could still be of worth, somewhere, to someone, even if it was just the craziest fucking clan on the Noreast Arm. And I fell right back into it, which was even stranger because some of my people had converted since the time I'd left."

"Converted to what?"

"The Chain, man, the Burnished Chain—you believe that shit? While I ran off to raise devils in every other Arm but home, some missionaries had worn down the council, struck some deals to get a church built right back behind the meadhall. Craziness."

"Something tells me the Noreast denomination is a little different from what they practice in Diadem," said Zosia.

"Not as much as you'd think! But yeah, they hadn't gone all the way over, still kept a lot of the old ways...which was just confusing 'cause Da *hated* all that shit, so he'd be lecturing me on how I was a disgrace to the clan at the same time he'd be running the clan down for allowing the conversions. And I..." Was high as balls constantly. "...wasn't quite myself, 'cause I was trying to play it straight as a Horned Wolf when there was some debate over what that even meant anymore, so when shit went down and I had to make a choice, I fucked it all up. Bad. Like, the worst."

"The Mighty Maroto made a mistake?" Zosia dug around under the divan and retrieved another of Diggelby's bottles. "I don't believe it."

"This was epic even as far as my fuckups go. We were warring with another clan, some devil-worshipping nutters called the Jackal People who guard the Noreast Gate. Scary bastards, pale as snow and twice as cold. They'd been stealing some of our people, throwing them through."

"Damn! They tried that shit on the Horned Wolves?"

"Not more than the once." Maroto grinned. "We brought it down on them, hard. Sullen there was his dad's knife-bearer. Couldn't have been more than six or seven. It got bloody, as war does, and we won, as we usually did. But Sullen's dad got killed, and Da took one square across the back, the kind that kills slow—the Jackal People grease their swords with this pepper oil, so it's even worse than it sounds. Just wrecked his arse."

"Damn. Takes a special kind of asshole to poison up before a battle."

"Yeah. I wanted to carry Da back, see if we could mend him, but Horned Wolves...It ain't done. So we left him, and when my nephew wouldn't leave his granddad's side, we left him, too. Left them to the ghost bears and snow lions and any of the Jackals who fled that might come back and find them."

"Cold. That doesn't sound like your people," said Zosia. "Doesn't sound like you, anyway."

"Horned Wolves are fucking savages," said Maroto bitterly. "Crowned Eagle People, Walrus Folk, Snow Lion Tribe, Orcas, and a hundred other clans are all decent, and I don't have to tell you that the free cities of the Noreast Arm are the most civilized on the Star. I mean, West Mastodon's as stunning a metropolis as any in the Isles, and the poet-philosophers of Reh give the Raniputri a run for their hemlock...But the Horned Wolves are just as barbaric as the Troll Lions or Jackal People, only difference is they gave up on human sacrifice. Last week, sure, but they did away with it."

"Wait, your old man and the kid were *sacrifices*?"

"They wouldn't call it that, but yeah, that's about the shape of it. No such thing as a crippled Horned Wolf, or an old one—you can't run with the pack, you get left behind it. It's fucking stupid. And I was wigging out, big-time, Da screaming his jaw off from the pepper in his spine, Sullen just staring up at me with his witchy cat eyes, and I didn't know what to do. I didn't have any fucking idea. But then my sister said good-bye to her son and our father, going back with the rest of our people, and I told myself if she could walk away from her own child and the dad who praised her every day of her life, I ought to do the same to a nephew I barely knew and the old man who'd never wasted a breath whistling he could use on running me down. I left them, Zosia, left them to die."

Even without the graveworm making him all emotional he would've needed a minute then, watching Sullen watch him from across the party with murder in his leonine eyes. Zosia puffed her pipe, let him come to it in his own time, instead of pushing him like the other Villains would have. Devils, how he'd missed her.

"I went back for them, Zosia, I did." Maroto closed his eyes, gritted his teeth. "Three days later. Took me that many nights of lying awake all night, hearing Da screaming in my ears while my sister slept like a babe, that many days of folk finally treating me with respect around the village, to figure out what you've known since I first started talking, what I'd known when I'd quit them the first time—the Horned Wolves are fucking crazy. And crazy as I was right then, I wasn't crazy enough to ever be right with that kind of bullshit. So I left. Again. For good. But I ran all the way back to the Jackal People's lands before I did."

The cigarillo had gone out in his fingers and Maroto flicked it away.

"I figured I'd give them…an apology, if they were dead, or take them with me, if they'd managed to live. I prayed, Zosia, for the only time in my whole fucking life, I actually prayed they'd lived out those nights, prayed to my ancestor Old Black, prayed to the Fallen Mother, prayed to darker things best left unnamed—anyone who would listen. Even told Crumbsnatcher I'd let him go if I got back and they were waiting for me, offered him his freedom if I trotted onto the battlefield and even just my nephew was sitting there, alive and hale and able to come with me. Should've known when the rat didn't take the cheese that it was hopeless, but I prayed on…

"The lions and vultures had been all over that field. Da and Sullen weren't the only ones whose bodies were gone. And I knew if I'd worked up the courage to do what I knew was right a few days earlier, they'd be alive. I could have kept them safe. So I said a few empty words, shed a few guilty tears, and said good-bye to the Savannahs. Some Horned Wolves came after me near the border, trying to cut me down so I couldn't shame them twice by leaving again, but they couldn't catch me. I hit the Body of the Star and never looked back."

Maroto took the bottle Zosia offered him and drained the whole thing, not noticing it was one of Hassan's nasty sour ales until the contents were in his belly.

"Who saved them, then?" Zosia asked. "You know that much?"

"They saved themselves, I guess." Maroto smiled across at Sullen, a real warm smile, but the kid just stood and walked off into the night. "Sounds like Sullen dragged Da all the way back to the village as I was getting up the moxie to leave, and then they got back right after I left to look for them. Wide as the Savannahs are, we missed each other, two riders in a fog going different ways. When they returned, the clan couldn't very well deny them their place at the fires, seeing as they'd pulled themselves back on their own, but I imagine it wasn't the welcomest way for Sullen to come up. Horned Wolves don't appreciate being proven wrong. And now they're here. That's all I've got."

"That's enough," she said, and when he felt behind his ear for the cigarillo he'd already smoked she passed him her briar. Zosia was always good that way, too good to an arsehole like Maroto. Another storm of wizard fire exploded in his chest as he realized her pipe was the same tankard shape as the one she'd made him, the one he'd lost or sold or broken while he'd been so strung out he hadn't known his arse from a hole in his heart—Zosia had carved two identical pipes, then, one for herself and one for him, something she'd never done for any of the other Villains, something he had never even noticed, too busy eyeing her haunches or tips to look at her personal briar. She had cared about him, even if it wasn't in the way he'd hoped. Still did, to see the emotion on her face as he put his lips to the black stem, shivered to taste her saliva and the tang of tar on the end of the pipe. The graveworm did its dance in his belly, from one pole to the other, happy then sad then happy again.

"You need to talk to them, Maroto. You tell it to them like you did to me, not a word out of place, and you'll need to come up with another name for that kid, because Sullen won't suit him anymore."

"Yeah, I will. Tomorrow, when I'm clearheaded." Of course, being off the bugs so long he'd be all kinds of hungover, but another worm from Diggelby would help get him up and able—only cure for a graveworm before bed was another one for breakfast. After that, though, he'd be done with 'em for good. He'd promised Purna, and a man has to keep his promises. "What about you, Zee? Never heard how you came up."

"Hmmmm," she said, not looking any more amenable to the topic now than she had the dozen times he'd tried to pry it out of her over the years.

"Hey, no need for that face." The last thing he wanted was to spoil things, now that they were looking up. He gave her back her pipe with a final twinge. He'd smoked plenty of tubāq since losing her gift, but never from a pipe—penance for his folly, and smoking a pipe was a lot easier to give up than the bugs that had caused him to lose the dearly loved briar in the first place. "How 'bout the song of your resurrection, then? What the devils happened, Zosia? Did they lock you up in Diadem instead of icing you? Or have you been in on this new Cobalt Company scheme from the get-go, biding your time, waiting to spring from the shadows like the Allmother returned? Both?"

Shit, that hadn't been a wise move at all—she looked even unhappier now, but with a big sigh, laid it on him: "I chickened out, Maroto, after that first year on the throne. I *fled*. Made it look like I died so no one could come after me. Set myself up with a new life. Our victories and our failures, *my* failures, I tried to put it all behind me. Should've known it wouldn't work."

She was quiet, and as much as Maroto knew she'd prefer to come to it in her own time, his mouth did its thing, as it always did, when he had the worm in him. It was the graveworm's fault, not his. "So what, you caught wind of Fennec's play and couldn't resist coming out of retirement? Setting the record straight? Having one more adventure? Trust me, I can relate, even after I found out it wasn't you leading the new army, I stuck around for my buddy Purna's sake, and now that we've been up to our old exploits my taste for the stuff is coming back in a big—"

"They killed my husband, Maroto. Our whole village. Children. Animals. Everyone."

Shit. Shit shit shit. No damned wonder she didn't welcome his kiss, she was in mourning, she—

"I thought it might have been one of you," she said quietly. "Not you, obviously—you were the only Villain I was sure about, Maroto. And now I'm sure it wasn't any of the others, either. I was right from the start: Queen Indsorith went back on her word. Gave me enough time to hope it had worked, gave me enough time to relax, really invest myself in a place, in people, let me believe I had won...and then she did me just like I did her. She must have led a happy life before I became queen, before my efforts to fix the system wiped out her family, and nearly killed her, too. So when it was her turn to be queen she gave me a happy life, and a family, and...and then gave me exactly what I deserved. Just over a year ago, now."

"Wait, what—the queen? She did that? I don't get it..." Maroto struggled for something, anything to say. "...but I don't need to. I know you didn't deserve that, though, nobody deserves that."

"No, they don't," said Zosia softly, looking a lot older right then. "A lesson I learned too late."

"She double-crossed you," said Maroto, the graveworm making him smarter, sharper. "You gave her the Crown to leave you alone, and she double-crossed you. That's what happened."

"Yeah," said Zosia. "That's it. Pretty damned simple."

"And now you're going to get her, right? Now you're going to teach her what fucking wages Cold Cobalt pays a double-crosser, yeah?"

"That's the idea," said Zosia, scratching her silver hair. "Cold Cobalt returns, and all of Samoth trembles."

"All of the fucking Star!" said Maroto, standing up. "We'll make the world remember us! Make the devils shrink back into their holes! Kick the Crimson Empire's teeth in! Yeah?"

"Yeah," said Zosia, getting up, too, and handing him her pipe. "But in the morning. I'm dead on my feet. You want to finish this?"

"Sure, yeah," said Maroto, taking it greedily, when a dire thought reasserted itself. "Except...shit."

"Shit?"

"Shit shit shit!" Maroto wheeled around and stomped the divan, meaning to splinter it in his rage. His heel bounced off the springy seat and he fell flat on his back, his busted knee throbbing. Brays of laughter from a dozen arseholes looking to get their heads split, but score one for Maroto: he'd made Zosia smile again as she helped him up.

"You doing okay, oh conqueror of ales?"

"Yeah. No. Look, Zosia, after I heard you died, I did something stupid. Really stupid."

"I heard you fought the queen," said Zosia, not even trying to hide her smile. "Despite the express orders I left that my Villains were to serve her in my stead."

"Orders don't mean shit," said Maroto. "I mean coming from you, of course they do, but how'd I know they weren't fakes? Anyway, I played it all wrong—left Crumbsnatcher out of it, got her to take me on in a square duel. I won, I won. And she won, I'd pledge not to hassle her ever again. And...and..."

"And the girl can fight, can't she?" Zosia stood on her tiptoes and kissed Maroto on the cheek. It was the first time her lips had ever voluntarily touched him, and it felt better than anything he'd ever won or stolen. "We'll figure something out, Maroto, we always do."

"Yeah," he said, relieved he hadn't wrecked the divan as he collapsed back onto it. "We always do."

"Oh, and try not to lose that again," Zosia said, winking at him, and it took Maroto a moment to realize she was talking about the pipe in his hand. What? No, it couldn't be... But turning the pipe over for the first time since she'd let him hit it, he saw that the bottom of the bowl still bore the two marks she had carefully etched into the wood all those years ago: a Z, for the carver, and an M, for the intended owner. His hands started shaking so badly he nearly dropped it, and he looked up at his old friend with tear-filled eyes, wondering how in all the devils she'd found it, but not wanting to risk breaking the spell by asking.

"I've been a fool," was all he could manage, but it seemed to be enough.

"Every day since I've known you, but then you've had ample company."

"Maybe…" Maroto rocked his head back and forth, but nothing shook loose. "Maybe I'll have a better comeback in the morning."

"It's really, really good to see you, Maroto," said Zosia, turning away, but at her words the graveworm turned to ice in his belly, spreading its chill to every part of his body. He felt sick. "Sleep well, brother."

He couldn't respond, couldn't do anything but cling to the pipe he didn't deserve and sink into the divan, shaking all over. He watched her go, watched Cobalt Zosia, the woman he loved, sway over to the fire and exchange a few words with Singh and Fennec, and then disappear back into the camp. But she had been here, beside him, no vision nor ghost, but Zosia. And maybe it was the graveworm and maybe it was some sick game of the devils, now that the bargain was fulfilled, but he knew beyond any doubt at all that this was what Crumbsnatcher had given him in exchange for his freedom. Maroto was on the divan in the center of the Cobalt Company and he was simultaneously in a Pendleton stinghouse, strung out on bad bugs, pressing his lips to his devil's velvety ear, whispering the words that had doomed them all:

"Bring her back to me. Just let me see her again and I'll let you go. Please, please, just bring her back to me."

And Crumbsnatcher had granted his wish, just like devils were supposed to. The rat couldn't resurrect someone who had died—that was the one wish not even a devil could grant—but reuniting two old friends would be short work for a creature that could see into the future the way mortals look into the past. Zosia thought

Queen Indsorith had ordered her soldiers to go after her as part of a long-simmering revenge plot, but Maroto was sure Indsorith had only sent her assassins because Crumbsnatcher had made the queen think it was a brilliant idea. The queen, or someone else, it scarcely mattered—whoever had decided to target Zosia and her people, they had only done so because Maroto's devil had made them. Everybody had heard songs about devils planting evil thoughts in the minds of mortals, and even if a devil couldn't make you do something that wasn't in your nature, the Star was brimming with bloody-handed reavers who wouldn't take much more than a nudge to go after a vulnerable village, the Queen of Samoth included.

Maroto was coming up on a year clean of the bugs—well, he would be, if not for tonight's one-off—but point being, it was last autumn that he had sobered up one morning and discovered Crumbsnatcher missing. Zosia had said her husband and all their people were murdered around that time. It was the only explanation; Crumbsnatcher had burrowed into someone's brain and made them decide to kill Zosia's people... Hells, the executioners might not have even known it was Cobalt Zosia they were targeting.

Zosia was ready to tear the Empire apart for vengeance against Queen Indsorith, and she had just kissed Maroto on the cheek. Maroto had as good as slit the throat of Zosia's husband when he'd loosed his devil, as good as chopped down anyone else who had died along the way. He had destroyed the world of the woman he loved more than his own life, and all because he was so fucked up on bugs he'd made a wish that no sane mortal would ask of a devil: to bring back the dead.

"Bring her back to me. Just let me see her again and I'll let you go. Please, please, just bring her back to me."

CHAPTER

18

Grandfather said the Old Watchers only took notice of humans when they were bored and in need of sport, and this was the same reason mortals first turned to the devils. Grandfather said it was up to shamans to interpret the words of the divine as they came down through the rustling of leadwood leaves in autumn and new grasses in spring, to unravel the whispers of the infernal from the crackling of a wildfire some hot summer's night, or read the lacing of ice on a chamberpot some cold winter's morn. Grandfather said when a devil spoke a mortal listened, but only a shaman could reply. Grandfather said when a god spoke only a shaman could hear, and a wise one wouldn't talk back.

But Grandfather also said the tastiest treat under heaven was creamed honey badger, and Sullen knew for a fact that shit was *nasty*. And Grandfather also said the Horned Wolf way was best, that all other peoples of all other lands were wicked or corrupted or dastardly or just plain arseholes . . . But if that was true, and the Horned Wolves were the chosen people, why had they been so down on Sullen and Grandfather? What did it say about *them*, that the Horned Wolves had hated them so much they'd tried to kill them rather than just letting them go?

And sure, getting really real here, but what did it say about Sullen, that he kept deferring to Grandfather even though the old man seemed increasingly full of shit? When they'd finally found Uncle Craven and Grandfather had somehow used the opportunity to talk shit about Ji-hyeon even as he was exalting Sullen, had Sullen ripped the old baggage off his back? Other than their first night in camp he hadn't once given Grandfather a talking-to about respecting the woman he already intended to pledge his service to, come what may with his uncle. It had always seemed easiest to just ignore his crotchety ancestor, but maybe by doing so he was just feeding the fire of Grandfather's hubris. In any event, he wasn't doing himself any favors, letting Grandfather poison everything with that tongue of his.

It was time to talk to the old man, Sullen decided as he walked back to their tent. Grandfather had ordered him to follow Uncle Craven that night, to see what sort of a man this "Maroto" really was. From Sullen's reconnaissance, he seemed to be about the same as any other, still glum from his earlier shaming at the hands of Zosia, and hoping to hasten the healing process by slathering himself in drink, smoke, and companionship. Yet when Zosia had joined Maroto on his couch by the bonfire, Sullen decided he had enough to worry about for one night.

At least occupying himself with stalking his shady uncle and the woman a god had ordered him to kill took his mind off Ji-hyeon, and the return of her handsome lover.

Good for her. Good for both of them. He wanted her to be happy, after all. It's not like it would have ever worked out, a savage wooing a princess... Except for a minute there it had seemed like the princess was intent on wooing the savage.

Sullen realized he was approaching her tent instead of his own and abruptly changed course, much as he wanted to stroll past and see if lamps were lit inside. Would it be better if they were, if the sounds of talk and laughter came to him, or if all were dark and quiet?

Anyway, he had more important things to think about. Like thwarting Zosia. That was how the Faceless Mistress had put it: thwart her. That could mean damn well anything. Didn't have to mean murder. Then again, it might...

The rub was, he didn't feel much compulsion to do anything, now that he'd seen the woman in the flesh. He'd expected to feel some deep urge, some need to throw her down and do the god's will without a moment's hesitation…But he was having a real devil of a time getting too worked up about it. He didn't want a bunch of kids to die, of course, for a whole city to be consumed by liquid fire, but being real with himself, the whole situation made him melancholy rather than righteous or wroth. He mostly wished Zosia had never shown up at all…and not just because she had brought Ji-hyeon's lover back to her. He was happy for Ji-hyeon. *Delighted* for her.

He bumped into a pack of drunken, reeling soldiers and muttered an apology he didn't really mean. What a bullshit night. Here he was, halfway across the Star from the Savannahs, having traveled as far as any hero in the epics, and he felt just as small and stupid as he had back home. He could recite a hundred ballads, could tell you how Old Black had outwitted the sea devil of Zozobra, of Rakehell's lusty adventures in the Lair of the Minotaur and how he'd escaped that monster's bed, but when it came to his own song it was like he'd forgotten the words and bungled the meaning, clueless as to what canto ought to come next. They always seemed to know what to do, his ancestors, ready with a quip or a stab in just the right ear, learning from their mistakes and outfoxing their enemies…Yet Sullen could barely figure out where to take a shit without upsetting someone in this bustling camp of exotic foreigners, and if you don't know where to attend such basic business, what hope is there for navigating the real challenges set before you?

Maybe that was the problem—maybe Sullen was just in the wrong sort of song. Maybe instead of a great warrior or trickster his lot was always to play the dullard, bumbling into trouble to the amusement of any listeners. The Song of Sullen Half-wit, the Horned Wolf without a brain in his skull or a fang in his jaws. There was a song he could hum by heart, even if the words escaped him…

Stalking back to his tent, he saw Grandfather still set up in front of the small fire he had built for the old man before going after his uncle. Great.

"What's the word, laddie?" Grandfather asked as Sullen steadied himself and stepped out of the shadows.

"Nothing, Fa." Giving him a talking-to could wait until morning, or longer—why ruin a perfectly bad night by stirring up Grandfather? Sullen dipped into the tent, and closed his eyes in impotent frustration as the old man called after him:

"Come on out, laddie, we need to talk. Got a beedi rolled and ripe for the ripping."

Sullen fished around in the dark tent until he found his bandolier of sun-knives, then a water jug, and then a strip of cured horse to snack on, and only when he couldn't stall any longer he came back out and sat down heavily across the fire.

"My, but you're in a mood tonight," Grandfather said when Sullen took out a whetstone and set to sharpening the multiple blades on each of his branching knives.

"What?" Sullen said around a mouthful of meat, not looking up from his work.

"I don't expect nor welcome all the gory details of your courtship with that prissy girl, but if you want to tell me what's irked—"

Sullen stood, letting the bandolier fall into the dirt save for the knife he gripped in his fist. "Last time, Fa. Blood or no, last time. She's got a name. And she deserves better from scrawny old dogs she gave a place by her fire."

Grandfather sneered up at Sullen, but for once he didn't say anything smart, just gave a curt nod. That would have to do. Sullen sat back down as Grandfather set a braid of pinestraw aflame and lit his beedi.

"Shall we talk about your uncle, then?" said Grandfather, holding in his smoke and offering the smoldering cone. "Or that Zosia woman?"

Sullen turned down the sweet-smelling saam, much as he wanted it. He couldn't stand to be any closer to Grandfather at present. "Whatever you want. They got right, looked like. Drank 'round a fire. Like you do."

"Well, touching as that is, I'm mostly curious as to why you mean to murder them both," said Grandfather, taking another long pull, his fingers as dark and wrinkled as the leaf between them.

Sullen went all chilly, didn't know what to say. "Huh?"

"Huh," said Grandfather. "*Huh*. You might be black as the god of the Jackals to these pasty-arse fools, but you're clear as branch water to me, pup. You've been killing them with those lion eyes of yours ever since you first peeped 'em, same as you've been doing something else with your eyes to that...to General Ji-hyeon Bong, Second Daughter of Jun-hwan and Kang-ho, Future Queen of Samoth, and however the rest of it goes."

"You think if I give 'em a look it means something?" said Sullen, embarrassed that Grandfather had seen through him so fast and so sure. Embarrassed, and maybe a little relieved. It was the scariest thing out there, keeping your own counsel when affairs got complex. "You think if it *looks* like I give 'em a look, it means shit?"

"Heed me, Sullen," said Grandfather, but for a change his tone seemed conciliatory instead of chiding. "Whatever else they are, neither my son nor that friend of his are stupid. I seen what you were thinking, and you weren't even thinking it at me. I'd tell you to be wary, except I respect you too much to treat you as a child. You know what you're about. But I've been sitting here all night pondering your surly mug, boy, and for the life of me and the life of your mother, I can't reckon why you mean either of them trouble."

"For serious?" Sullen stopped sharpening his knife. "After hearing you yuck-mouth him every day since I can remember, you don't know why I aim to kick Uncle Craven's arse? You and Ma been telling me how bad he needs it since before he even left us! Probably whispered it to her belly before I even busted out, before he even came back."

"Ahhhhh," said Grandfather, puffing on his beedi. "That's it, then. You're *still* sore on him for leaving, eh?"

"Him leaving don't mean shit," said Sullen, wishing there was a way to make the words sound proud instead of petulant. "Good riddance. I mean, *we left*, didn't we? And we left on account of you thinking he did right, cutting out on the Horned Wolves that second time."

"I know what I think about my son, Sullen. I'm asking what you think, though I can guess."

"That's fleet," said Sullen, shaking his head. "What do I think, then, since you already know all?"

"I think it's the particulars of how he did it," said Grandfather, and there was some comfort there to soften the sting. Horrible a bastard as Grandfather could be, he was good, loving, and understood Sullen in ways he didn't always understand himself. "He cut out on us, left us to die on that battlefield, and all because he chose to stand with the Horned Wolves instead of his nephew. Instead of his own dad. We needed him most, needed him as much as anyone could ever need his kin, and he sided with the clan over us. That'll happen. My daughter did the same, which I don't reckon you need reminding of?"

"Nah, it was different for her," Sullen said quietly, still hoping after all these years that this time it would ring true to his ear. "Whole different thing."

"Sure it was," said Grandfather in a way that told Sullen the old man wanted to believe every bit as much as his grandson. "I don't reckon either of us can blame your mom for leaving us there, walking off with her brother and the rest. Shit, she's more Horned Wolf than anyone on that damned council, so her doing it the old way, that's fair. And what makes it so different, what this whole oryx chase comes down to, is that when you drug me back home after the battle, she was still there, part of the clan as always, but your uncle was long gone. And all these years later you're still raw-hearted he didn't stay with us—he was cutting out anyway, why not do it a day or three earlier, rather than leaving his kin to die on account of a principle he never lived up to nohow? That about the shape of it?"

Sullen eyed his shimmering reflection in the blade he held, nodded. "About."

"Yeah, I've wondered that, too," said Grandfather, and it felt like cold creek water washing the dust off your face to hear the old man admit that he didn't know everything. "Every day since it happened, and every minute since I looked him in the eye this morn. *Why.* Thing is, laddie, I don't think he knows himself."

"That makes it all right?"

"Hells no! But you always know why you do something, Sullen?

I sure ruddy don't, and I've had a good deal more thaws than you to get the measure of myself. What matters is that you, me, him, we all got the same idea, sooner or later, that those we came up with, those we'd given our lives to, they weren't worthy of our love, and so we all cut out on what the Horned Wolves had become. And now that we've finally run him to earth I think we owe our blood enough to put the question to him, and see if he can do better now than he did then. What happened when we were Horned Wolves means as much as yesterday's morning shit; what matters is what we do goin' forward. We're family, Sullen, and if that doesn't mean something, then we're no better than the rest of our clan."

It was quiet for a spell after Grandfather's wee speech, and Sullen put his knife down and went around the fire to sit beside the old man. Taking the dead beedi from him, he relit the half-burned saam and took a deep toke. Kept it in, absorbing the smoke along with the old man's words. Grandfather, man, that guy knew some stuff. Exhaled, and let out some of the bad air he'd been holding for most of his life. "You want to go have a verse with him now? I can take us."

"We weren't the only ones he'd given up for dead," said Grandfather. "If even one of those songs we heard about the two of them on the road here has even one honest refrain, they'll be talking till dawn. Him and that Cold Zosia are tendin' to their business, we'll let them tend. You're just hard on her 'cause of how she did your uncle this morn? You might hate him, but don't like seeing your blood whooped in front of half the camp?"

"Her? That? Nah." Sullen took another hit, held it till his eyes watered. "She...You don't wanna know."

"Thank the false gods and true ancestors I got a grandson so wise he knows me better than I know myself," said Grandfather, taking the beedi back. "I shiver to think what I'd do, I had to have a thought of my own."

"Nah, Fa...She...Look, you told me you didn't want to hear none of what that Faceless Mistress I met in that big-arse spooky temple had to say. The Soueast Arm, remember?"

"You think I'm so dotty I can't recollect where we was when you met a god?" Grandfather looked down at the beedi and then passed it back without taking a hit. "I wondered, after. Ever since, whenever we heard the name Zosia you got a hungry look on you. Hells, even the Horned Wolves knew about the Cobalt Queen, but you never seemed to take an interest in those songs... until that Emeritus temple. Yeah, I wondered."

"So you want me to spit or not?"

"Not, not," said Grandfather quickly, raising his palms. "These ears have done well by not having the words of the gods pass through them. But..."

"But?"

"But there's a lot of gods, Sullen, many more than just the Old Watchers who made our ancestors. The Star's got more gods down here than there are birds in the heavens, even with the Chain spreading their One True Faith shit all over. It ain't wise to rile any of them, sure, but that don't mean you have to take a knee before them all, or you'll never be able to stand on your own."

"But you always said a shaman had to listen, and I'm not saying that's what I am, but... shit, Fa, I don't know."

"Listening is always good," said Grandfather, staring off past the fire, into the dark between the tents. "But that ain't the same as always doing what you're told. You done that, you would have left me on the field and gone home with your uncle and the rest, and neither of us would be here right now."

Sullen nodded. He nodded a lot when Grandfather spoke. How the devils had Old Black or Rakehell gotten along so well without an ancestor to help them? "So... so as far as Zosia goes, what the Faceless Mistress said about her..."

"I told you, boy, I don't know, I don't want to know, and I don't envy you the burden you were born to. But where the gods are concerned, be very, very careful. You think Horned Wolves are petty, vengeful fuckers, well, our people don't have a patch on the gods... And this Zosia? She walks with one, or I'm no judge of devils."

"What?" Sullen swallowed, fearing where this was going. "Her coyote devil, you think it..."

"I know better than to think on such matters," said Grandfather gravely. "But that thing's as like to a mere devil as that Zosia is to an ape in the Bal Amon jungles. A devil king's just what we call the god of our enemies. So whatever other voices you heed, Sullen, listen to your grandfather here—stay wary."

The wind whipped down through the camp, the fire crackling. Sullen threw his arm around his grandfather and said, "Pretty sure I heard you say you weren't going to lecture me about being careful, on account I wasn't some kid climbing dagger trees."

"Old folk are allowed to break their word, laddie, and blame it on senility," said Grandfather, squirming away from Sullen's embrace. "One of the sole benefits of being too old to remember ever being young!"

Their laughter was short-lived, cut off by a canine whine from the side of their tent. A shadow detached itself from the darkness and tottered into their firelight on sleep-wobbly legs. Something shaped like a dog but weren't no dog at all. Zosia's devil. Its chalky tongue lapped noisily at its jowls as it appraised them, its black eyes swallowing the firelight instead of reflecting it. It barked once, what Sullen prayed was a friendly bark, and then strutted past their tent, disappearing into the slumbering camp of the Cobalt Company.

"That's us to bed, then," said Grandfather with a shiver. "If he's out prowling, who knows what else walks this night."

They went in, but for all the wisdom he'd found in Grandfather's words, Sullen found sleep to be as evasive a quarry as any he'd hunted across the Frozen Savannahs.

CHAPTER
19

Ji-hyeon slept alone. Well, slept was more of an aspiration than an accurate description. She pitched about in her sheets, occasionally punching a pillow.

Keun-ju had asked to stay with her, and she had wanted him to, but after her all-night plotting session with Zosia, who seemed as talented a tactician as her reputation implied, a morning nap had barely prepared Ji-hyeon for endless meetings with Choi, Fennec, and her other new captain, Chevaleresse Singh. So when she finally had time for Keun-ju in the late afternoon she was already yawning, and the three presses of kaldi they had put away during their long, draining conversation imparted twitchiness to her already rattled nerves, rather than bringing alertness and clarity. She felt better, after listening to his side of events. That Fennec and her second father had thwarted Keun-ju from accompanying her out of typical old-man objections to her being in love with her Virtue Guard wasn't all that surprising, but trying to convince her that Keun-ju had betrayed them to her first father was a dick move too far. If Zosia hadn't shown up when she did, Keun-ju would still be stuck on Hwabun, and Ji-hyeon might have given up on him altogether.

Yet even after hearing that what Sullen had suggested, what she had hoped, seemed to be the truth, her mood was somehow tart instead of sweet. So she had sent Keun-ju off, his pouting lip protruding through his sheer veil, to give herself time to digest everything. A good night's sleep would set her right...if she could ever manage one.

Keun-ju. How many times had she imagined their reunion? In her mind it had always involved a frantic stripping of clothing, jamming her tongue in his mouth to stop the flood of achingly earnest poetry, and then a furious fuck. This would be followed by a second, leisurely, completely relaxed undertaking, such as they had never been afforded under her parents' roof. As general of the Cobalt Company, she could bed whomever she wished, they could doze off in each other's arms, and no one could stop them...But their romance in Hwabun now seemed a lifetime ago. The Princess and the Virtue Guard was a song she knew by heart, but seeing him here, the same old Keun-ju he'd always been, while she had become a totally different woman...

As if that were true. Rolling onto her back, she stared at the dark dome of her tent where Fellwing clung. Loath as she was to admit it to anyone, herself most of all, she hadn't really changed all that much. She was still getting all gooshy over forbidden boys, wasn't she? Being real, as Sullen would put it, wasn't the truth that she felt weird about Keun-ju returning because she had finally gotten over him, finally felt the warm appeal of somebody else's regard? She loved Keun-ju, she did...But if that were true, why wasn't he next to her in bed? Why was she wondering how Sullen felt? Why did she miss the boy, when it had only been a day since she had last seen him? He had all but run from her tent as soon as he realized who Keun-ju was, and had made no attempt to call on her...Not that it had been very long, but still.

Also, hey, what about the war she was waging? What about all the lives that depended on her? What about all the lives she intended to claim in her quest? What about *that* shit? Rolling back over, she buried a furious shout into her pillow. She immediately felt better, but then a concerned voice called from just outside her tent:

"General?"

"I'm fine!" she replied, scolding herself for being so childish. She was lucky the guards hadn't stormed her tent, overhearing a muffled scream in the dead of night!

"Can we come in, or you come out?" called the guard, and Ji-hyeon sat up in bed, trying to keep her annoyance focused on herself rather than the people sworn to guard her life.

"I'm coming, I'm coming," she said and, fumbling around in the dim tent, found the bulky coat Sullen had forgotten in his haste the night before. Sliding her arms into its cavernous sleeves, she stumbled into some sandals and emerged into the night.

"Sorry, General," said the guard, quickly rehooding her lantern after blinding Ji-hyeon with it. "I thought I heard something. Very sorry."

"Yeah yeah," grumbled Ji-hyeon, hoping it was close enough to dawn that she could just stay up. "What watch is it?"

"Second, General," said the other guard. "Just after midnight."

"Hrmph. Look, I'm going for a walk, but I don't want you two crawling up my ass."

"Of course, General," said the first guard. "Let me grab somebody from the back of your tent to replace us."

Ji-hyeon stomped in place to warm up, the icy stars overhead casting a wan light over the camp. There was still a bit of revelry taking place, distant songs and laughter reaching her as they had back in the west wing of Hwabun, when her parents had sent her to bed before a party ended... But in this quadrant of the camp all was quiet. When the guard returned with two others, Ji-hyeon took off at a brisk pace toward a small but steep hill that stuck up from the tents like a single tusk jutting from a fang-filled maw. Fellwing reeled back and forth above her, a deeper swatch in the quilt of moonless night.

The tents fell away as Ji-hyeon climbed up to the overlook. Loose stones and damp grass made her slip a time or two, but she soon conquered the hill. The guards hung back enough to give her the illusion of solitude, but their constant presence was as exasperating as it had been back on Hwabun. The more things change, eh, General?

A pentacle of small stones garnished the crown of the hill, but

Ji-hyeon didn't know if it was an ancient site of worship or something recently erected by devote soldiers. The Lark's Tongue rose ominously above her, even the first low ridge of the mountain seeming to dwarf her and her humble hill. Her scouts had assured her that the other sides of the mountain and all of its immediate neighbors were even more treacherous than the face, but while that meant they couldn't be ambushed, it also meant they had no escape route. Zosia had insisted that making themselves so obviously vulnerable was the only thing that would provoke the Fifteenth Regiment into attacking immediately instead of waiting for reinforcements, but gazing up at the Lark's Tongue Ji-hyeon felt the uneasy dread that comes in the space between when a decision is made and its consequences revealed.

Sticking her hands in the pockets of Sullen's coat, she was happy to discover a stale beedi. He had seemed pleasantly surprised to find she had a taste for the same flowers he did, albeit of a lesser potency— maybe the varietals were different, or maybe the leaves he rolled them in added something; but whatever the cause, she found his smokes a little intense. Having forgotten her pipe back at the tent, however, she would take an intense burn over none at all. Besides, contemplating an imminent battle with a massive Imperial army probably warranted a little intensity. Doubling back to her guards, she lit the beedi on one of their hooded lanterns and then returned to the hilltop, savoring the taste of fragrant saam and bitter leaf, the mental weight of Sullen warming her all the way down to where her naked knees emerged from his coat...

She wandered into the center of the circle of stones and slowly twirled around, the camp laid out on all sides of the hill and creeping up the flanks of the mountains, dozens of bonfires and hundreds upon hundreds of smaller lights blazing even at this late hour. Thousands of soldiers, all ready to die at her command...or more accurately, thousands of mercenaries willing to kill to get her a crown, and all for a tael or two of silver. A few were volunteers who'd actually swallowed her song, true believers of the Cobalt Cause...a few, but probably not many. And the only thing her advisors could agree on was that the Imperials would be on top of them anytime now, and no matter how brilliantly they planned or fought, hundreds if not thousands of their people would die. Her heart began to canter beyond her reins, and she leaned down and stubbed out the beedi in the heart of the stone symbol, wishing she had something to focus on other than the enormity of her responsibility.

She looked east, beyond the lights of her army, where the hills rolled as black and vast as the night sea north of Hwabun, but without the flash of distant lightning where the Sunken Kingdom slept. Would she ever see that view again, leaning on the railing between her two fathers, her elder sister reciting poetry, her younger running around on the deck, working off the tiny cups of kaldi Kang-ho had talked Jun-hwan into allowing her?

The answer was obvious. She might see the Immaculate Isles again, but only from a distance. She'd tossed her family aside, and by the time this was over even her second father would be furious with her. Not that he deserved any better; the future he'd offered her was every bit as self-serving as the one her first father had. Actually, when you got right down to it, Kang-ho's invitation was far more selfish than Jun-hwan's—if she had done as her first father had asked and married Prince Byeong-gu, she would have still had her family, been able to visit Hwabun whenever she wanted. With Kang-ho's plan, though, there was no fucking way she would ever set foot in the Immaculate Isles again, and it was likely her first father would never speak to her again, either. Seizing control of the wall and then working with the Imperials to expand the fortification to protect her freshly conquered city-state of Linkensterne wasn't just an act of war against the Isles, it was an act of treason against her people, against her very family. Her second father had never phrased it like that, of course, he'd spun it as a grand adventure for his little girl, and wasn't he living proof that you could shame the shit out of your family and still make everyone happy in the end? It would serve him right to be disappointed by what she had planned, the conniving—

"Captain Fennec to see you, General," called one of the guards, her voice jarring up here above everything.

"Just the man I wanted to see," she said, and straightened to watch him huff and puff up the last dozen feet of the rise.

"You're up late, General," said Fennec. A few strands of dyed-black hair had escaped his ponytail, and he wiped them off his sweaty face, tucked them behind an ear. "Considering your counsel with Zosia kept you up so late last night, I would think you'd be abed."

"Were you watching my tent, Captain?" Ji-hyeon crossed her arms. "Or did you also happen to decide tonight was ideal for stargazing?"

"Hoartrap roused me," said Fennec, plopping down on a wide stone set in the pentacle's border. Now that her eyes had adjusted to the starlight, she could see the worry plain on his face. Had she ever thought this old devil looked young and handsome? "He wants a word with you but, since you're sometimes resistant to his uninvited appearances, suggested we come together. I told him to hang back down the hill until I'd said my piece and softened you up, then he could see if you felt like granting another audience."

"Tell me, Fennec, were you as relieved as I to see that Keun-ju safely found his way back to us?" Even in the dimness she could see he'd given up on playing her, making no effort to conceal a grimace.

"Ji-hyeon, you need to understand that it was for your own good that—"

"Oh, *fuck you, Brother Mikal*. It was for your own good, which is to say, my second father's—you never gave a shit about what was best for me! You still don't!"

"I do," said Fennec with that maddening sincerity he used to lubricate every lie. "Always have. I greatly prefer your company to that of your father. Either of them, as it happens. But we never would have gotten out of the Isles without Kang-ho's blessing. I wasn't the one to inform him of your dalliance, either—if you two had been more careful or, gods forbid, patient enough to wait until we were free to consummate your affair…"

"Enough," she said, glad the starlight was not so brilliant as to illuminate a blush. "You lied to me, Fennec."

"It's what I do best," he said with a shrug. "It never would have worked your way. To get you off Hwabun I had to convince Kang-ho I was on his side, not yours, and so that's what I did."

"And all this time I thought we were on the same side."

"I knew if Keun-ju truly loved you he would find a way back to us," said Fennec, peeling off one glove and then the other to let his clawed hands cool off in the night air—they must heat up something awful in the kidskin gloves. Watching him flex the grey-furred digits, Ji-hyeon gave silent thanks that only her hair had changed from their passage through the First Dark. From the panicked whimpers he'd issued when they'd emerged from the Raniputri Gate in Zygnema and he'd seen what his hands had become, their guide had not expected such a drastic transformation to his person. Yet nothing had changed about Choi—weird, but then Choi and weird went together. The beedi was catching up on Ji-hyeon now, and she found herself unable to stop staring at his altered hands, wondering what would have happened to her if she'd dared to open her eyes as they floated between Gates...But then he caught her staring and put his gloves back on sometimes. Between the snide comments he'd made about Choi's ancestry and the pride he took in his appearance, the man clearly didn't appreciate that a casual observer might now mistake him for wildborn. "It's all a moot point, though, isn't it? Keun-ju's here now, so I say there's no harm done."

"Moot point? No harm done? I spent the last year thinking he betrayed us, and he spent the last year trying to find a way back to me!"

"I swear on the devil I loosed, I wasn't convinced he wasn't secretly working for your first father. I'm still not, to be perfectly frank. It was safest to let you believe what you believed, rather than being distracted."

"I'm sure." Ji-hyeon crossed her arms, hating that a part of her still wanted to believe him. "How charitable of you."

"It was a selfish ploy, I'm not arguing that." Fennec sighed and hoisted himself back to his feet. "But be honest, if I had come clean as soon as we stepped out of the Raniputri Gate, would you have carried on with the plan, a plan that's going to drastically improve the lives of countless people...Or would you have turned straight back around and gone after Keun-ju?"

"I didn't think honesty was a word you were familiar with," said Ji-hyeon, refusing to admit he had a point. Vocally, anyway.

"The Burnished Chain says that everything happens," said Fennec, waving an arm over the camp beneath them. "I never put much stock in their teachings, and even less after I stole the habit of a missionary, but they might be on to something there. Everything happens. Whatever led us here, Ji-hyeon, we're all together now, you, Keun-ju, me, and Choi. Just like we planned. Life got in the way, as it always does, but in the end, here we are. Don't let the details trouble an already burdened brow, one responsible for the fates of thousands."

Ji-hyeon clapped slowly and softly, sufficiently buzzed to be amused rather than annoyed. "A beautiful speech, Captain Fennec. How foolish of me to focus on the details, when all they amount to is your betrayal."

"Don't be melodramatic," said Fennec.

"What do you want, Fennec?" she asked, really needing to know all of a sudden. And thirsty, so damn thirsty. "I mean it. I know what the others do, more or less, but what about you? What is it you *really* want? What would you take, if there weren't any...details to get in your way?"

Fennec's jagged smile broadened, but he didn't speak.

"What happened to your devil?" It was the most personal question you could ask, but after all the ways he'd made her squirm over the years she figured he owed her a little fidget of his own. "Father's wish was that Fellwing serve me instead of him, which was a clever way of going about it, but what about you? What did you want so badly that you gave up the most valuable treasure a mortal can possess?"

Fennec's grin had become a grimace, and he muttered something in his native Usban.

"What's that, Captain?"

"Doesn't matter," said Fennec, sounding as weary as she'd ever heard him. "Hold on to yours, Ji-hyeon. Whatever you'd trade Fell-wing for, you'll find it was a poor bargain."

"So you don't think I should see if she could get me a glass of wheat ale? My mouth feels dustier than your scruples."

"I would advise against it," said Fennec, smiling at her just like he used to when they were goofing off back at Hwabun, and she felt an urge to hug him. Smothered that urge with a pillow.

"Not even if it was a really cold one, with a slice of orange?"

"Not even for that. Now, it is very late and I am not as young as my beautiful and talented commander, so maybe I could trouble you with a concern or two that I harbor?"

"Maybe, maybe not," said Ji-hyeon. "Depends on the concerns."

"Zosia," said Fennec immediately. "I don't know what you two talked about, and I don't need to, but—"

"Ah, I'm afraid that's a 'maybe not,' Fennec, but rest easy; your name didn't come up more than once or twice."

"This isn't about me, it's about you, and it's about her—if you only heed one thing I tell you, it's—"

"Don't trust her?" said Ji-hyeon.

"If you would let me finish..." said Fennec, a wonder the words escaped between his clenched teeth. "You can trust Zosia, but only so far as her best interests lie. As soon as someone gets in her path, watch out—it doesn't matter if it's you, or me, or all her old Villains combined; if Zosia doesn't get her way, it's trouble for whoever disagrees with her."

"A happy thing that she and I are in agreement, then," said Ji-hyeon, remembering how radically the older woman's demeanor had shifted when she realized her impostor was eager for her help in a shared goal.

"For now, yes. But tomorrow, who can say? You've always been able to say no to me, Ji-hyeon, to Hoartrap or Choi or Chevaleresse Sasamaso...And even when we disagreed with your orders we carried them out. Zosia is not a woman you can rebuff and expect her to listen." Even in the darkness Ji-hyeon must have displayed her irritation fairly well, for Fennec raised his palms in peace, and said, "I'll say no more unless you ask me to. I could tell you stories…"

"I've heard the stories. She doesn't frighten me."

"No? She should!" Fennec glanced over his shoulder, as though Cold Cobalt were a devil to be summoned by repeating her name. "She frightens me, the other captains, even Hoartrap—a woman willing to lay low for twenty years before emerging like a cicada devil to enact her plans is capable of anything. She doesn't rush into things. She came here, came to *you*, because you have become part of her scheme, and I know from experience that Zosia will sacrifice anything or anyone to get what she wants."

"Unlike you," said Ji-hyeon. "Or my second father. Or Hoartrap. Or me."

"She—"

"She's off in her bed sleeping, where you should be, too, Captain Fennec—you've already snapped your trap quite a bit for one night, if you want it to be sharp for the morrow."

"May I share my other concerns with you first? They are urgent."

"If they were so urgent, why didn't you start with them?" Ji-hyeon groused. "Whatever, fine. Just be quick about it."

"I did start with them, days ago, and have repeated them twice daily since we made camp." Fennec was in his obnoxious listen-to-reason mode—she could practically predict the words even before they left his mouth. "We shouldn't *be here*, Ji-hyeon—that was the Fifteenth who met us in the mountains, and they'll be on top of us in two days, if not sooner. The whole point of our plan to lure them out of Cockspar and then have my allies in the city open the gates for us was to *avoid* fighting them. If we don't have their city, we don't have anything to barter with—why would the Imperials call off fighting and help us take back Linkensterne when they have us trapped and vulnerable?"

"They hate the Immaculates more than us, and are galled about the wall being built?"

"I'm not so sure about their hating anyone more than us right now. And you heard Choi's report—there were pennants for both the Fifteenth *and* the Ninth when she and Maroto brought a pack of monsters down on that Imperial camp. The Ninth are Myura's regiment, Ji-hyeon, meaning whoever survived the slaughter at their castle has combined forces with Azgaroth's regiment..." When Ji-hyeon apparently didn't show enough awe at having this intelligence repeated to her for the umpteenth time, Fennec's tone became almost frantic.

"We are about to meet the single most effective regiment in the Empire, on the bloody *Star*, and they're bringing with them revenge-minded Myurans. Add to that Maroto's cunning plan of being chased by wolves straight into the Imperial camp, where your subtle scouts apparently made no secret they were Cobalt agents, and you have one very angry army coming to bear on us, and you'll do what, exactly, to preserve our precarious position? Ride out and explain everything? Tell them we never really meant to kill all those Imperial soldiers and citizens, we just needed to get some practice before heading back to Linkensterne? Offer them a cut of the action if they start taking orders from you instead of the Crimson Queen?"

"Seemed like a good idea at the time," said Ji-hyeon, trying not to smile.

"*If* we had snatched the capital of Azgaroth out from under them, *if* we had strength of numbers, *if* we hadn't antagonized the Imperials quite so much up until this point, then *maybe* we could have parleyed them into helping us take Linkensterne. It was never a sure thing, but now, here, boxed in by hill and mountain, the only sure thing is that we die like devils in a trap. We should never have hammered down stakes, not here, but there's still time to pull them out. I can rouse the officers, give the order now, and we'll be safely away by dawn. If we're still here when the Azgarothians arrive, it will be *catastrophic*."

"We need supplies, Fennec, we'll never keep our strength marching to Linkensterne if we don't get more rations, rations that the Fifteenth has in abundance—it's as simple as that."

"It's as simple as liberating every town and farm between here and the Immaculate wall! It's as simple as losing a few hundred, maybe even a thousand to starvation and exhaustion, but the rest of us live long enough to resupply somewhere else. We send our terms of peace to Diadem and the Fifteenth, who will be hounding us every step of the way, and who knows, maybe it still works, maybe the queen is bitter enough over losing Linkensterne that she decides to back our play. Maybe not, but either way we're alive to regroup and think of something else!"

Seeing the spittle fly from his lips, it finally dawned on Ji-hyeon what was going on here. Fennec didn't know her intentions, of course, but even if he had, he wouldn't have been put at ease, because for all his experience and bluster, Fennec was scared. Terrified. He sounded like a condemned man pleading reason with his executioner.

"We're not abandoning camp, Captain—we're staying here until the Fifteenth arrive."

"Then we are utterly *fucked*. If only from bullshit chivalry and respect for their Myuran comrades, the Fifteenth won't listen to our terms, they won't, and so we will have to fight them. And if we fight them at our current strength, we *will* lose, and then the game is over, and nobody gets to go home."

"I am home, Captain," said Ji-hyeon sharply. "Any more concerns, or can I let my captain go get some beauty sleep, now that he's assuaged his conscience?"

"Nothing more," said Fennec, now playing the disappointed uncle as he turned toward her guards. "Pray sleep on it, Princess, and remember that everyone in this camp trusts you with their lives."

"It's General, not *Princess*," Ji-hyeon called after him, and, unable to resist, added, "But give it time, you might be calling me queen."

He stopped walking, looked back at her. "It's true, then. I don't know how Hoartrap does it. Well, let me say it again, in case you misheard me before—I'm with you, not your father. And assuming we live out the week, I'll be more help to you if I know your intentions, instead of only his. *General*."

Then he was just a silhouette tramping down the hillside, and Ji-hyeon looked up to where Fellwing wheeled above them. She felt the winter air, then, breathing its corpse breath down the mountains they had zigzagged up and down, and she pulled Sullen's coat tighter around her. It smelled of sweat and saam and the kaldi they'd shared, and she breathed it in, exhaling smoke of her own, and even as Fennec stopped for a word with the guards she heard a foot crunch the grass at her back. She turned, pleased with herself that she registered no surprise at seeing Hoartrap standing where she'd been minutes before, at the heart of the pentacle.

"Do you have a few moments to spare an old Villain, General?"

"For you, sorcerer?" Ji-hyeon tried to smile. "Anything."

"Oooooh, careful, careful," he said, rocking one of the stones with his foot. "One must always be mindful of how she words things, and never more so than when addressing my kind."

"Devils, you mean?"

"Well, we're both honest to a fault, but that's about as far as the resemblance goes. Come to watch the Imperials arrive, have we?"

"Hardly," said Ji-hyeon, but when she glanced back over the plains a shiver coursed down her spine. Far, far out in the frozen black sea of the night-draped hills, an orange glow outlined the southern horizon. She rubbed her eyes to make sure she wasn't just glimpsing a scout's campfire, but no—it was too remote, and that she could make it out at all from this distance meant it came from something far grander than a few scavenged logs. "That can't be...Why would they build their fires this late?"

"It's possible they've been marching late, and have just made camp," said Hoartrap, stepping beside Ji-hyeon and squinting into the south. "Or they're still at it, advancing by torchlight. In the old days, the Fifteenth had a real monster of a colonel—he'd trained his troops to live off a few hours of sleep a day, and march clear through blackest night. It was something to see, riding out with the original Cobalts. This great fiery wyrm, relentlessly pursuing you across the moonlit world...Brings back the memories, I tell you, seeing that right there. I'd wager cold coin that's the Fifteenth down from the mountains, and they're on the move."

It might have been her imagination, but the light did seem to waver as she watched. Now the dark hills really did look like the Haunted Sea beyond Hwabun, the fox fire in the distance completing the picture. Ji-hyeon's throat tightened as she stared out onto the Witchfinder

Plains. This was it, then—the Imperials had come to kill her and every single one of the people who had trusted her to keep them safe . . . the people she had ordered to make camp and build pickets, digging in for a battle that never had to happen. They could have packed up and moved anytime, she could have ignored Zosia's counsel and delayed this confrontation, like Fennec and all the rest had urged, but now it was too late. Even if she gave the order to move out tonight, to move out right fucking now, it would be well after dawn by the time they were packed up and moving, and how close would the Imperial regiment be then? Too close, was the answer.

"Eh, they're still leagues away," said Hoartrap, as though he was already bored with the subject. "I'd be surprised if they attack before tomorrow."

"Tomorrow!" Ji-hyeon felt sick. While they'd been bivouacking in the Kutumbans after leaving Myura, the days and nights had inched by, slow as arthritic snails, but now everything was moving far too fast.

"Don't fret, General, I'm sure you'll have scouts and advisors stalking your tent by the time you get back down, eager to deliver the intelligence you've already seen with your own eyes. But for now why don't we—"

"Cut to the chase, Hoartrap," said Ji-hyeon, ripping her eyes away from the hypnotic glow on the horizon. Turning from the beacon of an enemy army to the milky, misshapen face of a dangerous and unpredictable devil-eater wasn't much of an improvement.

"It's to be war, yes?" Hoartrap's smile was as warm and welcoming as the farthest frozen star. "You and Zosia were alone far too long in the command tent for it to be anything but."

"Hasn't that always been the goal, Captain?" Ji-hyeon watched the sinister bastard carefully, wondered if she could detect it even if he gave anything up. "I mean, you and Maroto stumbled on us quite by accident back in Myura, didn't you? So why would you expect the aim would be anything less than the conquest of Samoth? Of the whole Empire, in time? That's what we've been moving toward all along, isn't it?"

"Nothing could make me happier than learning you are sincere in your intentions toward our beleaguered opponents," said Hoartrap, nodding his head toward the light to the south. "Yet for all your talk of Samoth this and Crimson Empire that, where in your little war does the Burnished Chain fall?"

"They fall hardest," Ji-hyeon said with more passion than she meant to betray. Getting mad felt good; it made her decision to stay and fight seem justified. Besides, if you couldn't be honest with your devil-trafficking warlock, who could you be honest with? "The Crimson Empire is nothing but the carrier, the Chain is the sickness. The things they do to wildborn, to their own people, and all in the name of the *higher truth*...And their higher truth is spreading. I know that firsthand, growing up in the Isles, and coming in from Zygnema we saw whole Dominions that've converted. Hells, Sullen says even the Flintland tribes are taking a knee. The Chain's the real enemy, and always have been."

"A fine speech," said Hoartrap with exaggerated solemnity. "I'm just relieved you're not actually working for them."

"*Working* for them?" It was hard to tell when Hoartrap was being serious, and she didn't want to waste her indignation if this was just another joke.

"Oh, you know, a silent partner in your campaign against the Crimson Empire—the Chain's last rebellion failed, so perhaps they colluded with you to overthrow Queen Indsorith. You get Samoth, they get the Empire, standard stuff. Don't tell me you haven't even considered it?"

"*No.*"

"Good for you! Ethical standards are commendable in the young, though they can become terminal if left untreated. Of course, if the Chain's not secretly supporting you, then we're all in for some very, very bad times. The Fifteenth are going to come down on us like devils on fresh sin."

"That's been the plan ever since we made camp," said Ji-hyeon, barely able to keep her eyes on Hoartrap instead of the lights of the Fifteenth. "Have any other uncanny portents for the future, oh wondrous seer?"

"Ha! Well, maybe one or two. Would you heed advice, if I offered it?"

"First I'd have to hear it."

"Hearing can be harder than it sounds," Hoartrap said, and, following his gaze upward, Ji-hyeon wondered if he was eyeing her devil or the indifferent heavens beyond. "What do you think they want, I wonder?"

"Who, the Imperials or the Chain? Or the devils?"

"The devils, of course. I've been studying them my whole life, and the question is always what can we squeeze out of them? How do we bind them, everyone asks. And once we do, what will we accept in exchange for setting them free again? But there's so much more to it than that—why did they build the Gates in ages past? As a means of egress from their world into ours, surely, but to what end? To prey on mortals, but then turn around and grant our every wish once we shackle them? What sort of creature wields such power, yet is so easily captured by bumbling mortals? It's the question of our epoch, isn't it, lurking behind every faith and every fairy story, tugging at our curiosity... What do they want from us?"

"The Immaculates say they want to be left alone," said Ji-hyeon. "Nothing more."

"Oh, the Immaculate sages say quite a bit more than that on the matter!" Hoartrap clucked his tongue, and with a muttered word, the stars began to wink in and out of view. What at first caught Ji-hyeon's heart as witchcraft revealed itself to be something altogether more wonderful, and terrifying: dozens of other devils now shared the night sky with Fellwing, dancing with her owlbat. She didn't know if she should fear for her devil... or for herself. "The mysteries of the Forsaken Empire and the Sunken Kingdom are not so mysterious, when you've read as broadly on the subject as I; back when they were just plain old Emeritus and Jex Toth, those legendary combatants fought for the same stakes we do today. Do you know that until they destroyed one another the Frozen Savannahs had never seen snow? And the Panteran Wastes were more like a paradise than a hellscape?"

"What happened?" asked Ji-hyeon, scarcely able to believe even Hoartrap knew how the Age of Wonders had ended.

"What have we been talking about? War, a war that sought to harness that which cannot be predicted nor controlled. There are things far, far greater than the devils you've seen, lurking out there in the First Dark, beyond the Gates. Entities that could never squeeze through such a narrow doorway. But there are other ways to pass over, given enough time and assistance...And there are ways to keep them at bay, despite the machinations of their servants."

Ji-hyeon shuddered, though she no longer felt the chill of the night. "It's late, sorcerer, and I have a war to wage in the morning. If you wish to swap ghost stories with an eager member of the Bong family, I suggest you visit my first father."

"Oh, we go way back, Jun-hwan and I," said Hoartrap, arresting Ji-hyeon's retreat before she'd even taken two steps. This monster knew *both* of her fathers? "But it's you I'm talking to, isn't it, *General*? You know how the historians always talk about the great wars, like the one that claimed Emeritus and the Sunken Kingdom? They always come back to a very particular euphemism for all that blood-shed, all that killing. Can you guess?"

A tragedy. A waste. That was how her father had always referred to the war he waged with Cold Zosia, but Ji-hyeon didn't think these were the words Hoartrap spoke of, and so she simply shook her head.

"No?" Hoartrap smiled wide enough to swallow her, the Cobalt Company, the distant fires of the Imperials, and every star in the sky. "*Sacrifice*, General, a term with which you must acquaint yourself, if you wish to take the Carnelian Crown. No victory without sacrifice, ask any veteran officer. And if the sacrifice is great enough, well, that's how wars are won. That's how you buy back what was otherwise lost forever. That's how you demonstrate to your opponent that you cannot be defeated. With a mighty enough sacrifice, any obstacle can be overcome, no matter the odds. Anything is possible."

Whatever he spoke of, Ji-hyeon was sure it wasn't simply the imminent Battle of the Lark's Tongue. Feeling as vulnerable as she had as a child in a nightmare, she extended her hand and called for her devil. "Here, Fellwing. We're going to bed."

Looking up, it was hard to pick her devil out from the flock, and it only became clear which one was Fellwing when the others began to harass her. The small owlbat tried to dip away but the others gave chase, jostling her about, forcing her to climb instead of fall to Ji-hyeon's shaking hand. She looked to Hoartrap, desperate, and with another smile and a murmur the other devils were gone, and Fellwing quickly landed on Ji-hyeon. The devil squirmed anxiously into the wide cuff of Sullen's coat, shivering against her wrist. Without another word, Ji-hyeon wheeled away and hurried back toward her guards, the far-off blush of the Imperials definitely brighter now than before. As she fled, Hoartrap called after her:

"Don't fret, General, we're on the same side here. And when the time comes, I stand ready to make *any* necessary sacrifice."

CHAPTER
20

The Fifteenth marched all night, and as they raised their camp alongside the sun, Domingo used his hawkglass to survey all from a hilltop. He would have liked to stand in the bed of the wagon instead of sprawling there like an invalid, but propped up on his pillows he could still get a good enough view to know he had once again gotten the job done. Red canvas tents spread out across the surrounding foothills, and just beyond them the Lark's Tongue beckoned. The Cobalt Company was still hidden from sight behind those last few rolling hillocks, but the scouts assured him that only a league west the last foothill descended into a long valley, and on the far side of this vale his enemies waited. They had not retreated at the last moment, as he'd feared they might, and that meant as soon as he gave the order the decisive victory Cold Zosia had always denied him would finally be his.

Well, whenever his soldiers had gotten some sleep he could give the order; they had earned a little rest before the battle, yes they had. Domingo knew he had a reputation as a taskmaster among the other Imperial colonels, but what none of those gossips realized was that he didn't push his troops because he didn't value them, or considered them beasts of burden. He pushed his troops because he knew Azgarothians were made of sterner stuff, that they could take it, and when they'd once again risen to the challenge and proven their mettle, his heart swelled with pride. He loved his regiment, because they had earned his love, damn it, even that fellow there picking his nose as he sat on a hogshead. Go on, lad, mine all the silver ye may; you've earned it!

Domingo lowered the hawkglass from his eye, the instrument too heavy to hold up one-handed for long stretches. He turned it over, admiring the glint of the sunlight on its engraved surface, and let out a long, unhappy sigh. This was all that was left of Efrain; that blackened, thumbless thing they had put into the family crypt wasn't his son, it was just burned meat. If that anathema Portolés hadn't returned the hawkglass along with his remains, Domingo would have had nothing to remember his boy by, out here at the end of the hunt, with vengeance at long last within reach. He had never thanked her for bringing it back to him...

Nor should he have, not when she was at least partially responsible for Efrain's murder in the first place. That then was something for him to set his sights on, once the Cobalts were all killed—finding that witchborn war nun and bringing her the same justice he was about to mete out to Zosia and her army. Back in Diadem the Black Pope had made some noises about Brother Wan perhaps being able to help Domingo find Sister Portolés along the way, seeing as they were likely pursuing the same quarry, but that had been another exercise in frustration. Not that he had expected such a miracle from the hideous little monk; the Empire was a big place, and the only people you ever bumped into were the ones you would prefer to avoid.

A speck of movement caught Domingo's attention to the north, but when he raised the glass again nothing was there but a grassy hillock. Ah, no, one of his mounted scouts appeared in the eyepiece and then was gone again, riding damned fast, and here came another. Domingo dropped the glass to get a wider view, squinting north. The hills between him and the riders obscured most of the action, but a pack of his people seemed to be hounding a pair of dark riders, chasing them toward the western mountains. Cobalt scouts, obviously, rumbled as they sought a peek of the Fifteenth's camp—well, Domingo's riders would soon give them an eyeful!

He raised the glass again, but it was hard to track the fast-moving riders from this distance with his off hand. As they arced southwest, he caught another glimpse of the fleeing scouts, and he nearly fumbled the hawkglass. For a moment, the rear rider had almost looked like... but no, that was just an old man's mind playing tricks on him. From this distance what he had thought was a familiar face was just a pale blob that his imagination played with. The rider wasn't even wearing Chainite robes. Still, he looked again with the glass, hoping to calm his racing heart, but the riders were gone again behind some higher hills, and from here they would either make the Cobalt camp or be caught by their Azgarothian pursuers outside of Domingo's sight.

Not that it made much difference, really—either way they would be dead by this time tomorrow, along with every other member of their rebel army.

———

It was a scene straight out of the Chain Canticles, a lone believer and her doubting companion riding at breakneck pace toward their goal, the full might of a corrupt army rising behind them like a tidal wave of iniquity. If anything, it might be a little over the top, even by Canticle standards, especially as arrows fletched with cardinal feathers started whizzing past them when they refused to heed the final shouted warnings of their pursuers. Sister Portolés couldn't have asked for a more portentous entrance.

They reached the crest of another of the steadily steeping hills, horse froth running down their legs as they pushed their steeds beyond hope of repair, and then looked out over the final valley before the Kutumbans stabbed up from the plains. There at last they saw what both the war nun and her captor had taken on faith would be there, a camp nearly as impressive as the one at their hind, save here flew Cobalt pennants instead of Crimson.

If Heretic had not believed the gossip he heard in the last town that the Cobalts had come down from the mountains and made camp here, they never would have found them in time. If they had been spotted sooner by the sentries as they circumnavigated the Imperial camp, they would have been caught an hour ago, and all the prayers of Samoth's queen would go unanswered. If Heretic had not unchained her legs that morning so she didn't have to ride sidesaddle, or if the Imperials who pursued them were better shots—

"Fallen fucking Mother!" Portolés cried as an arrow embedded in the back of her calf, causing her to kick her exhausted horse all the harder. The fire burned its way up to her knee and down to her ankle, but all she could do was pray her horse had a little life in him...And then Heretic whooped in triumph, and glancing back she saw that the Crimson riders had stopped at the top of the hill, giving up the chase. Looking back into the valley, she saw a dozen of the Imperials' blue-blazoned cousins riding up to meet her, these outriders not looking much friendlier than the crimson ones they'd left behind...

Heretic seemed almost repentant as they were stopped in front of the command tent, the size of his eyes telling Sister Portolés he had never expected the Cobalt Company to be so enormous. From the point where they had been stopped by the mounted sentries in the vale, it had taken them well over an hour to reach the heart of the camp—the stop at a white pavilion to have the arrow pushed through her leg and a poultice tied on the wound barely took ten minutes, the rest of the time spent climbing steadily higher through the labyrinth of tents. Above them, Lark's Tongue Peak cast an imposing defense for the army's rear.

"Wait," said the burly chevaleresse who had intercepted them at the outskirts of the tents, sending the outriders back to their duties and escorting the prisoners into camp herself. She entered this final wide, nondescript tent without announcing herself, and from within came the sound of low voices. Heretic whistled nervously, rubbing his hands together against the morning chill now that the sweat had dried and the panic faded. The knight reemerged, flanked by more guards. "All right, these lads'll take any weapons you have, then you can come in and tell the command what you told us."

"Can..." Heretic looked guiltily at Portolés. "Here, hold up, let me take her chains off her wrists."

"You wish to unshackle your prisoner before taking her into the command tent?" The chevaleresse looked amused. "I don't think so."

"It was only to keep her in line until we got here," said Heretic. "She's not a danger."

"That true?" The chevaleresse's flinty eyes looked up into Portolés's. "Big woman like you isn't any danger? That hammer we took off your packhorse, suppose it belongs to your ferret here?"

"You heard the ferret," said Portolés. "I'm no danger at all. The maul's for shoeing our horses."

"Look—" said Heretic, but the knight shut him down.

"No, *you* look, son—I'm all kinds of curious to hear how an underfed thug like you put the manacles on a hoss like her. And I think you'll sing that song just as well with her in chains as not. Now get in the tent."

And just like that, Portolés ducked under a pole and found herself in the command tent of the Cobalt Company. Their maps and other papers had been flipped upside down, the whole rebel crew standing from their stools at her arrival, as though she were a foreign dignitary they hoped to woo and not a suspected spy, or worse. Heretic bumped into her as he came in, and the chevaleresse entered last. She and the other guards all had their steel drawn. Two empty stools were brought over to the other side of the table, and the young Immaculate woman who was clearly in charge waved them to their seats. In the lantern light, the girl's shock of darkly dyed hair could be cobalt, even, and Portolés let out a miserable sigh. Whoever led this army, it wasn't the mayoress from Kypck. Which meant her mission had failed, the weapon her queen had given her was useless, and she was about to be screwed in a big, bad way.

"Well, Boris of Diadem, the ditty you sang for my sentries intrigued me enough to grant you an audience," the Immaculate girl said, her cupbearer filling a bowl with hot kaldi and offering it to Heretic. "I am General Ji-hyeon Bong, commander of the Cobalt Company, and for the moment you have my full attention."

Bong? Sitting forward on her stool, Portolés peered at the girl, trying to see a family resemblance...Was Bong a common Immaculate surname? If not, if this general was the daughter of Kang-ho and Jun-hwan...

"Um, yeah," said Heretic nervously, "so she, Sister Portolés, I mean, I was a prisoner, in Diadem, but then she took me prisoner, but when I got free I took her prisoner. Shit. Let me start over."

Portolés sat back on her stool and took in the general's cabinet as Heretic blathered: an older Raniputri chevaleresse with an impressive mustache, a grotesque hulk of a man with a sickly smile on his wasted features, and a good-looking Usban fellow of middle age. Nondescript as this last member of the command was when seated beside the rest, his breastplate identified him, the prancing foxes embossed on its polished surface a dead giveaway. Here then were three of the Five Villains, straight from the forbidden songs of the Stricken Queen, all of them taking orders from a girl who was likely the daughter of the fourth. Interesting...

"Do you have a staring problem, Chainite?" said the general. "Or would you prefer to wait outside while your handler gives us a very compelling reason to believe you're not both Imperial assassins?"

"Whoa, hey!" said Heretic, standing so quickly he almost caught a sword to the spine before the guard standing behind him realized he was being foolish rather than dangerous. "That's not me, not at all. We nearly got nabbed by the Crimsons, trying to get to you—ask your scouts or whatever, your people who saw us being chased in here by them. They wouldn't be trying to kill us if we were with them, would they?"

"They evidently didn't do a good job of it," said the bewhiskered knight who had to be Chevaleresse Singh. "That bandage on the weirdborn's leg looks fresh, but it's obvious the rest of her injuries are weeks old."

"I'm on your side, I swear it!" said Heretic, prompting Portolés to wonder just what heretics swore on. "I was her prisoner, but then we were bushwhacked by some other Chainites, and she got tore up bad enough in the exchange I got the drop on her. Took her to you because you seem to be fighting the good fight, and I couldn't well risk trying to sneak back into Diadem with her, could I?"

"Yes, yes," said the man Portolés presumed was Fennec. "You told the sentries, one rode ahead and told us. What strikes the general as odd is your presumption that we are, as you say, on the same side. That, and the timing of your appearance, prisoner in tow, just ahead of an advancing Imperial regiment. And claiming to have invaluable information for us! How wonderfully convenient it all is."

"No, no, no, it's not like that!" said Heretic. "We came west from the Haunted Forest, and when I was buying food in Black Moth I heard it from some hunters that the Cobalt Company was laying down a camp here, in front of that big mountain. They said they'd seen you coming and cleared out just in time. This was a few days back, and those ignorant assholes said the Imperials from Thao were still a little ways off—last thing I expected was to come across the plains and see that nest of 'em between you and us. We went wide north to go around 'em, but their scouts—"

"Thao?" said the general, exchanging glances with her cohort. "You're saying Thao's regiment is already marching this direction?"

"That could be your disinformation," murmured the giant, loud enough for all to hear. "They've come to stir you up, push you into flinching first."

"I know what I heard, but I won't vouch for it being true," said Heretic, and it was quite something, to see the lad who had taunted his oppressors in the Office of Answers tremble under the gaze of his idols. "All I know is if you're fighting the Empire, then I'm on your side, it's easy as that. I mean, if I was a spy wouldn't I come with a better story? Maybe I'd have some claim to know what the Imperials are up to out there? I don't know shit, beyond what I told your people already, and that's the True Queen's truth!"

"You say this war nun rescued you from torture in Diadem, and fought her own people along the road, yes?" asked the chevaleresse, waving the cupbearer over to refill her kaldi bowl.

"I don't just say it, it's true," said Heretic, realizing he was the only one at the table still standing, and retaking his seat.

"And you also told my sentries you had information that would be valuable to any enemy of the Empire, but that you would only share it with those in charge," said the general, rocking back on her seat. "So ... what is it?"

"Right, yes," said Heretic. "So Sister Portolés here—"

"That's your name, Portolés?" asked Hoartrap the Touch. Portolés was more certain of his identity than any of the others. He was, by all accounts, a devil-eater and known witch.

Portolés offered the faintest suggestion of a nod. Things were about to get very warm in here, and she wondered how best to play this.

"So yeah, I don't know what she wants, or what, but she's working for the queen, not the pope, I'm sure of that," said Heretic. "Pretty sure, anyway. I searched her kit after she got all beat up by the other clerics and found some papers with the Royal Crimson Seal on it, and a roster, I'd guess. Names of soldiers, rank, that sort of thing."

"Ah, and here's that invaluable military intelligence our guest knows nothing about," said Fennec with a yawn. "Can't say we're in for much trouble from the Imperial command, if this is what they think passes for believable disinformation."

"Look here, all of you...you lippy churls!" said Heretic, jabbing a finger at each of the seated officers in turn. At the moment these four were the most dangerous people on the Star, and Heretic was barking at them like they were part of his petty resistance back in Diadem. Portolés would miss the lad, once they were both burned alive as enemy agents. "I'm not a spy! And whatever the sister is, I don't think she's a spy, neither. It was never her plan to come here and find you, far as I know—we started off and went straight up to the Isles, and then were coming down for the Dominions, I think, when—"

"The Immaculate Isles," interrupted the general. "She took you there? Which cities, which islands?"

"Well, we come up through Linkensterne, and then went to, whatsit...Hwabun, Hwabun Island, and then turned right around and—"

"What were you doing there?" the general demanded, not looking at Heretic anymore. Well, that certainly answered the question of the girl's lineage! Portolés doubted they'd need more than this girl's stare to get the kindling going underneath them. "I expect your full cooperation, woman, from this moment on. We both know that whatever royal errand you were on, it's definitely come to an end now."

"Has it?" Portolés couldn't help herself; perhaps it had been an early way of insulating herself from further harm or despondency, but whatever the source, there was no cushion nor chair she preferred to the hot seat. "With all due respect, General, I believe I'm the only one in this room who can speak with authority on that matter."

"Ah, so you do speak!" said the general. "And eloquently as any ambassador, I must say. Are you an ambassador, Sister Portolez?"

"*Portolés*, Sister Portolés, and I think you could say I am something of an envoy." It was so hard not to smile, but one look at how much pleasure the ancient Hoartrap was also taking in this exchange helped check her mirth. "The issue, General, is that I was not sent to treat with you."

"That so?" Ji-hyeon looked like she might throw her kaldi bowl at Portolés. "But you were sent to talk with my fathers, were you?"

Oh, but this was getting good! "It is an unfortunate clause of my assignment, General, but I am forbidden from discussing my business, which is to say Queen Indsorith's business, with any but the object of my inquiry. Your father King Jun-hwan seemed to be doing quite well, by the by—I found him most cooperative."

That did it, though Ji-hyeon clearly thought better of it at the last moment and hurled her bowl against the wall of the tent instead of at Portolés. Temper, temper, General.

Chevaleresse Singh cleared her throat. "I would remind the general that according to the Articles of Aghartha, all laws regarding the treatment of prisoners of war apply only to combatants, abettors, and commanders. When it comes to suspected spies, well, there really isn't as much errata as you'd think. An *unfortunate* oversight on the part of the authors. Whatever you deem necessary to secure the safety of your troops is permitted so long as—"

"Torture, is what the chevaleresse means," said Portolés. "And here my ferocious warden had led me to believe that the Cobalt Company was above such immoral tactics."

"Immoral, sister?" Fennec looked sad. "I'm sure you heard that word quite a bit, growing up as an anathema in some miserable Chainhouse. Did you find redemption after your first round of penance, or your fiftieth?"

That hurt a bit—how did they always know? Portolés didn't have wings or a tail, Savior knew she never even lisped anymore, hadn't for years after all her whispering to herself in her cell, getting every word right...Yet somehow, they always always knew, as though her impurity gave off the stench of rotten eggs.

"Nothing to say, race traitor?" Fennec pushed.

"No call to bring that into it," said Heretic angrily. "We're all meant to be equal, ain't we? That's the Cobalt Code, ain't it? Or is everything I heard about this new Cobalt Company being the same as the old just as false as its general?"

That was definitely the wrong thing to say. General Ji-hyeon was flushing red as an absolution candle, and Chevaleresse Singh stood with a flourish of her cape, drawing a mighty sword. Fennec was amused but mostly hiding it; Hoartrap was delighted and making no effort at all to conceal it. Good show, Heretic, good show—it always was the believers carrying the standard, volunteering for the front, while the cynics and the realists hung back in a command tent.

Come to think it, what did that make Sister Portolés?

"Right, sorry I'm late," came a familiar voice from the tent's entryway. "Tried to rouse Maroto but he's sick as a dog. Came straight back here, but met some frazzled scouts on the way, and brought 'em with me—you need to have them come in and report right fucking now, they say the regiment from Thao is creeping less than three days out from... *Hell.*"

Turning to the door, Sister Portolés felt a seesawing mix of relief and fear to see the old woman from Kypck...who looked pretty seasick herself, upon recognizing Portolés. She'd hardened up since last they met, and she hadn't been soft then, either. The dog was at her side, though he now appeared closer to an adolescent than a greysnout, his tail wagging enthusiastically as he trotted over to Portolés to say hello.

The war nun stood and bowed, the dog licking her face. She

smelled the wrongness on his breath, tasted it in her suddenly aching tongue—the two sides of the scarred tissue seemed to be trying to rip themselves apart again. She straightened up quickly to get away from the creature. A devil, no doubt about it, and, looking closely at the approaching woman, Portolés saw the jagged scar on her jaw that Queen Indsorith had mentioned.

It was as Indsorith had feared. This wasn't some random hillbilly mayoress with a chip on her shoulder; this was Zosia, the Stricken Queen. The long year since her people had been put to the sword didn't seem to have softened her ire much. And Fallen Mother bless them both, Portolés had found her in time.

"Lady Zosia," breathed Portolés, closing her eyes to better savor the sensation of salvation. "Lady Zosia, I have been sent by Queen Indsorith to—"

The first punch caught her in the throat, and the second nailed her tightening stomach. A month ago the nun might have shaken off the blows, or at least hidden the distress they caused her. A month ago she didn't have multiple puncture wounds to the chest, sternum, and belly. She went down, and would have gone down harder if Heretic hadn't been there to catch her. Fennec and the chevaleresse had scrambled over the table and pulled Zosia away, but only after she'd rabbit-punched Portolés's side four or five more times. The anathema felt the stitches tear with each blow, but did not cry out or resist. This was why she had come here after all.

"Get the fuck off me!" Zosia, spitting like a wildcat, threw Fennec across the table. Hoartrap snatched his kaldi bowl out of harm's way at the last moment, but did not rise to assist. Chevaleresse Singh got behind the furious woman and contorted a leg and an arm around her, then tightened her limbs, immobilizing her. It was something to see, what had seemed such a gently lined, welcoming face back in Kypck now transformed into a mask of the Deceiver himself, Zosia's teeth bared and her nostrils flaring. Splayed out in Heretic's arms beneath the wrathful woman, Portolés fancied she could feel heat emanating from her.

"Enough!" barked Ji-hyeon. "Enough! Do you want to die, Zosia?

Outside until you calm down, and if you can't act like a grown woman, don't come back!"

Hearing the general address the woman by name sent more waves of bliss shuddering through Portolés. She had not failed. Not this time. And now her wretched, cursed body could finally do something miraculous, could finally be used as her queen intended. Perhaps she had been destined for this, or perhaps it was all an accident, but everything happens, and the Crimson Queen of Samoth had bid her take any measures to ensure that it did.

"Whatever this fucking asshole says, don't trust her," said Zosia, trying to kick at Portolés and nearly carrying Singh to the floor with her. "Let me go, damn it, I'm all right now, I am. We got a history, is all. Bad, bad fucking history!"

"And a future," said Portolés, Heretic helping her back up. Even without the chains on her wrists the sickening aches in her stomach and side would have made it an arduous task. There was dampness under her habit there, but she couldn't worry about that now, not with the end of her quest at hand. She just had to live long enough to deliver her queen's will, and then there would be no battle between the Imperials camped out in the plains and these mercenaries, no war at all between the Cobalt and the Crimson. Everyone in the tent was staring at the battered war nun. "A short one, if you want, but we must talk. She sent me after you. Queen Indsorith."

"Think I don't know that, witch?" Zosia tensed again, but so did Singh. "Think I'm too fucking dense to see the starshine on the altar?"

"No," said Portolés, then repeated it, to her own mutinous body, "No, no, no..."

That heat spreading through her, numbing the pain, had begun creeping up her throat, and she tried to stay still, so as not to succumb to vertigo. Closed her eyes, but that only made it worse. She was so close, she could feel the warmth of salvation...but it was cooling now, drifting away, leaving her to steam in the frozen black center of the earth, where only devils dwell...

"Sister!" Heretic was shouting from above. "Sister!"

"Gods below, she's bleeding!" came another voice, from yet higher still. "What did you do . . ."

"Didn't hit her that hard." Zosia's voice was muted by the warm water as Portolés sank down and down, toward the Sunken Kingdom. The last thing she heard was the woman mutter, "Not so hard as she deserved."

CHAPTER
21

Zosia stormed out of the tent, ignoring the girl shouting after her, but didn't get ten feet before Ji-hyeon snatched her arm and whirled her around. The little princess almost got a fist to the chin, but then Zosia caught herself and let the arm drop. Good thing, too, for only as she let herself breathe and really take in her surroundings did she notice that Chevaleresse Sasamaso had the drop on her, glaive ready, and Zosia doubted the woman would take kindly to her beating on the general.

"Captain Zosia, I will have order in my tent, if nowhere else," Ji-hyeon said, meeting the older woman's hard eyes with some steel of her own. "Whoever that woman is to you, she is *my* prisoner. She knows something, maybe lots of things, but we can only make her tell us if she's alive. Do you understand?"

Being lectured by this blue-dyed child enraged Zosia almost as much as seeing Sister Portolés had. "That fucking witchborn and me have a history—"

"I didn't ask why," said Ji-hyeon, her fingers digging into Zosia's arm when she tried to pull free. "I respect you enough not to, just as I didn't ask why you looked so... *interested* when you heard the name of the Azgarothian colonel leading the Fifteenth Regiment. Tell me or don't, in your own time, but for now all I need is for you to tell me you understand."

"Oh, I understand," said Zosia, wrenching her arm free at last and making the Flintlander knight have to sidestep around the general to get a clean thrust at Zosia, if it came to that. Zosia looked past the two women, to where Choplicker came strutting up to her. If she disarmed the chevaleresse and used her own weapon against her, and then the general, her life would get a whole lot simpler—who in the Cobalt Company wouldn't prefer the real deal to an impostor?

"Good," said Ji-hyeon, letting out a big breath. "Good. I know you wouldn't act without reason, but please appreciate my position. That woman claimed to have valuable information, but now she's unconscious. This is a problem."

"Yeah, it is," said Zosia, letting out a big breath of her own, along with a shudder at the dark thought that had seemed so reasonable but a moment before. She'd gotten worked up at seeing that piece-of-shit nun Portolés, lost account of herself, but now she'd calmed down enough not to think that murdering her new friends would help her situation. From the way Choplicker was looking back and forth between General Ji-hyeon and Chevaleresse Singh, she supposed that ingenious notion might've had a little help slipping through her admittedly leaky sense of morality. "That woman's an agent of the queen, directly responsible for murdering hundreds of innocent people."

"She freely admitted to coming here on the queen's orders, to talk to *you*, Zosia, and you alone." Ji-hyeon rubbed her temples, and it occurred to Zosia that this brat was trying not to lose *her* patience—how was that for a change of pace? "I would very much appreciate it if you could get any pertinent information out of her when she recovers. If she recovers."

"Oh, I'll get it out of her, all right," said Zosia. "But I can tell you plenty about her now. She's the guard dog of Colonel Hjortt—you know, the asshole leading the Imperial army we're about to throw down on?"

"*They* are about to throw down on *us*, you mean—wasn't that the plan?" said Ji-hyeon, and Zosia felt another pang of guilt at encouraging the girl to go ahead with meeting the Fifteenth Regiment in open combat...but then it passed like an unwelcome burp. As soon as she'd heard which regiment was bearing down on the Lark's Tongue, and that Colonel Hjortt indeed led them, the temptation was too great for her to dismiss—she'd been overconfident to let the boy off with only a dethumbing at Kypck, and couldn't pass up a second chance to settle the debt he and his cavalry owed her. Besides, with her help, the Cobalt Company could probably take the Azgarothians. Probably.

"If there's nothing else, then?" said Ji-hyeon, and Zosia realized she'd been daydreaming of all the things she'd do to Efrain Hjortt once she met him on the battlefield.

"Not yet," she said. "I'll interrogate Portolés as soon as she's up."

"Delightful. Now, though, I need to send terms to the Imperial camp that's sprung up overnight—if you would excuse me?"

"Sure, don't let me keep you," said Zosia, not feeling abashed so much as . . . thirsty. Both the prospect of a vicious fight to the death and the niggling sensation of regret parched her something awful, always had. A drink and a smoke to wind down what might be her last day on the Star, a talk with the asshole who had helped assassinate her people, and then a good night's sleep before taking the fight directly to her old pal Colonel Hjortt, who'd evidently learned how to hold his reins without thumbs. That order.

———

"They've sent an owlbat, sir?" said Captain Shea, as though common practice was the most outlandish thing she had ever heard.

"*And?*" said Domingo, even the ordinarily pleasant thought of leaping off of his padded cart to assault her too painful to contemplate. Just sitting upright made him queasy and faint, but at least his subordinates hadn't tried to force him out of it into another tent. Sleeping under the stars to the lullaby of marching boots was an experience Domingo counted among the few unexpected pleasures of his return to command. "Surely the extent of the message is not *This is our owlbat, we await your reply*?"

"And they wish to have your agreement that at noon tomorrow we meet them in the valley for . . . um . . . *a combat both fair and honorable*?"

"Those riders who evaded our sentries must have delivered news of the Thaoan regiment's approach," said Brother Wan from his seat on the riding board of the small wagon. "Small wonder they want us to rush in before reinforcements arrive. They must think you very simple indeed, to—"

"Wheatley's people will be on the backside of the mountain by now," said Domingo, talking to himself more than the war monk or captain. Scowling at the map he had spread over his lap and legs like a blanket, he looked west to where the Lark's Tongue brooded over his camp and the countryside beyond. Not more than a single league to his reunion with Cold Zosia, and despite being wheeled up on a hillock overlooking the whole of the Fifteenth Regiment, a shiver went up his good leg, and a bolt of misery drizzled down the other. "Assuming Wheatley follows my one simple command and sends us no messages, there's no way the Cobalts will predict an ambush at their rear. Not one of such magnitude."

"It does look a good deal steeper on the face than it did from the mountains," agreed Brother Wan. "Presuming the Myurans don't have overmuch difficulty navigating those ridges on either side, they'll start down when they see us cresting the last hill into the valley?"

"Then, or when the Cobalt horns blow. Simple and elegant, like all the best stratagems," said Domingo. "This one is called the wolf trap—we snap them between our steel jaws and catch them fast. No escape, once we pour up from the valley and Wheatley's people come down the mountain."

"Wolf trap..." Shea seemed to have a thought stuck in her head like a stringy piece of meat catches in the teeth. He could see her worrying at it, brows knitted, then she said, "Isn't that the maneuver the Stricken Queen's rebel army used against the Fifteenth in the Shadow Deserts, at Wild Throne?"

"That was the place," said Domingo, remembering the battle like it was...like it was twenty-some-odd years ago, but he remembered the broad strokes. Said strokes were not pretty, not pretty at all. *Unrefined*, was the word he would use. Yet effective. "Our best tutor is often our enemy."

"Lord Bleak is the best, isn't he?" said Shea, and for the first time Domingo found himself intrigued instead of exasperated by his first captain. "There's poetry in *Ironfist* that I've not heard in any ballad. Ah. Sir?"

"Well put, Shea, well put," Domingo allowed. She was a student of war, then, if nothing approaching a scholar, but we all start somewhere. Efrain had never remembered a word of Bleak, despite Domingo's frequent quizzes. Alas, neither verbal lashings nor the more traditional sort improved the boy's memory or whetted his interest, to such an exasperating degree that Domingo had to ask if Efrain was making a mess of his lessons on purpose. Though why ever his son would do such a thing—

"Just a moment more of your attention, sir?" said Wan, leaning down from his perch over Domingo like a great raven prodding at a dying dog. His beady eyes were on the map. "If we are to agree to this luncheon with the Cobalts, which seems perspicacious, I should think we must do so without further delay."

"Excuse me? You think accepting their terms seems *perspicacious*, Brother Wan?" said Shea, perhaps coaxed into offering an actual opinion from the crumb of approval Domingo had tossed her.

"You don't, Shea?" asked Domingo, and when she began to balk he hurried her on with the stick since he never carried a surfeit of carrots. "I know you have a notion, so spit it out, damn you, unless you think a Chainite anathema knows tactics better than a captain of the Fifteenth?"

"Sir! Even with the rests we took along the way, the regiment's had over a full night and a day of marching, and with making camp here at the end of it all, most didn't get to sleep until the late hours of this morning." Shea's eyes were so bloodshot, Domingo wondered if she'd rested at all. "Pushing them onto the field less than a full turn of the sun from now seems...rushed? Especially with our holding every advantage save terrain, and the Thaoan regiment only two days out...sir?"

And he'd lost her again to indecision, but just for a moment there she'd shown some shred of competence. That shred had been thin from neglect and flapped about more as a handkerchief signaling surrender than a pennant flying proudly above an advancing army, but it gave Domingo an unexpected flash of optimism for Azgaroth's future after he had gone into that horrible endless night where nothing stirs, not even the regrets of a disappointed father...

"Sir?"

"Hmmm, yes, quite so, quite so. Excellent reasoning, Captain," said Domingo, imagining Shea wore much the same expression Efrain would have that fateful birthday, had he received a kitty cat instead of stern steel and a harder lecture. "A pity I cannot put it into practice. Accept their terms, Shea, noon tomorrow it is."

Ah, and there was the actual look Efrain had displayed, all resentment and confusion. It looked no better on Domingo's first captain than it had on his son, and he waved his one responsive hand in front of his face as though he could dispel her like an ill smell. She didn't question him, however, which was more than he'd been able to say for Efrain when the boy was in one of his moods.

"We attack at noon, then," she said. "I will inform the officers to prepare for—"

"We attack at first light, Captain," said Domingo irritably. "For the love of the living, don't go around giving orders I haven't made. We tell the Cobalts we will meet them at noon, but tell the officers to have everyone moving an hour before dawn."

"A fine and auspicious hour," said Brother Wan, as though Domingo's motivation stemmed from Chainite mumbo-jumbo and not pragmatism.

"An early hour, was my thinking," said Domingo, and, not wanting Shea to go away thinking the war monk steered anything but his command wagon, he added, "It seems underhanded, I know, but the Crimson Codices are quite clear—we're not officially at war with the Cobalts, which makes them insurrectionists, not combatants worthy of our usual chivalric standards. If I know Cold Zosia, and I do, she'll have the same notion—yes, come to think it, Captain, have our people ready to go *two* hours before dawn. Then we *might* get the drop on her."

"And so with your permission, Colonel," said Wan, "shall I anoint the regiment *three* hours before dawn, to make sure my people have ample time to complete the ceremony before we march? Everyone must have the holy oil upon their brow before we carry out the ritual, otherwise the effect could be...catastrophic."

"Catastrophic?" That was not a word Domingo liked to hear as regarded the safety of his regiment. "Explain yourself plainly so even an old blasphemer like me can understand, Wan. If you can't guarantee the safety of my people there's no fucking way we're using this oil of yours."

"The oil, Colonel, is not the weapon," said Wan patiently. "The oil is what protects our people, when the ritual is completed. The wrath of the Fallen Mother will fall upon the field, and anyone out in that valley who does not bear Her Grace's mark is at risk of being conflated with the Cobalt Company."

"Hmmm," said Domingo, all his doubts about this plan returning...but the scouts reported the Cobalt Company was even bigger than anticipated, and with Wheatley off on the other end of the Lark's Tongue, it would be far too dangerous to go forward with the attack and not use the Chain's weapon. Without it, and with the Cobalts dug in on the high ground across the vale, the battle could go either way, especially if Wheatley's attack on the rear was somehow delayed.

"I assure you they will be perfectly safe so long as they receive our blessing and anointment," said Wan. "All of my brethren will be down on the field with them—I would not ask your soldiers to undergo anything my people would not."

"If we waited for Colonel Waits to arrive?" Shea said, a pleading note in her voice, and that irritating doubt was what pushed him into it.

"Everyone gets the oil, then," Domingo decided. "We rest today, and three hours before dawn, anoint the troops and carry out your ceremony. We're using the Chain's weapon."

"Sir, I really think—"

"Dismissed, Captain Shea," said Domingo, looking out at the Lark's Tongue so he wouldn't have to see Wan's smug expression.

"Get that owlbat headed back to the Cobalts quick as you can. Mustn't keep my old friends waiting."

———

A pox on every graveworm, and a royal one on Diggelby. Maroto had felt worse—the gods of chance demanded such, given the life he'd led, the beatings he'd endured, the substances he'd abused. Still, he couldn't rightly remember such an occasion, whatever the gods of chance had to say on the subject. He didn't think of himself as one given to hyperbole, but he would rather, in all seriousness, be chopped to death by hatchets than feel this way a moment longer. Really dull ones, wielded by blind toddlers. He finally mustered the strength to produce a moan.

"Somebody drink too much?" Purna poked her head into the tent, delivering a blast of raw, corrosive energy directly into Maroto's brain, exploding his eyeballs in the process. He pulled the sweaty blanket over his head to block out the sunshine.

"Something I ate," he said. "I can handle my drink, woman."

"Sure," said Purna, and through the thin blanket he could tell she'd let the flap fall shut, banishing the hated sun. He poked his face out again as she brought a sloshing jug over to the nest he had made on the floor. "Brought you some millet beer—old Ugrakari cure, hoof of the yak that kicked you."

"Uhhhhh." Maroto shuddered, refusing to believe she could be that vicious.

"Snowmelt. Just the thing to get you up and ready to face the morning. Or afternoon, as the case may be. Hey, what's this? Thought you didn't smoke a pipe anymore—don't tell me you brought someone home in your state!"

Pipe? Oh yes, the pipe!

"That's the only briar I ever loved, the one I lost," said Maroto as Purna put the piece back down on his mound of shed clothes. "She made it for me, made one for all of us, and somehow . . . somehow she brought it back to me."

"No way, that's one of Zosia's pipes?" Purna whistled. "That'd make smoking one almost worth the trouble. Can you teach me? Can I smoke musk flowers out of it?"

"No," said Maroto, something even worse than the evilest hang-over of his life welling up at the thought of Zosia, a shadow in his aching skull. "Need something solid in me, Purna, or I'll fucking die."

The words brought another spasm; food was the last thing he wanted, but he knew from voluminous experience that it was a necessary devil.

"Maybe a nice slice of crow, since I warned you against eating that worm?" Maroto must have looked sufficiently pathetic for her to soften a little. "Choi and Zosia are scaring you up a plate of something hot."

"Zosia." It came out as a moan, the foreboding cloud at the edge of his awareness dispelled by the howling wind of reality. Maroto remembered everything. He dragged himself up into a sitting position, took the offered jug of deliciously cold water. After slurping some down, he tried to focus on Purna. "She's here?"

"Just missed her, champion—too busy blowing your guts out on yonder tent wall." Purna nodded toward the source of the stench Maroto only now realized was not rising from his own clammy body. Hey, he hadn't thrown up on himself—things were looking up! "Guess you two worked things out, yeah?" she asked.

"For now." Maroto shivered. Holy fucking devils, was this really all his doing? Had his sting-addled wish set in motion every bad deed that had led to Zosia coming here? Undoubtedly—this had Crumb-snatcher's tracks all over it. That rat loved nothing more than whispering in a sleeping ear, making it so you woke up thinking you'd had the greatest notion, or remembering something that had never happened...like receiving an order to execute a certain venerable citizen in a remote mountain town...Devils have mercy, Zosia had said her whole village had been murdered, a husband...That tore it, he was going to be sick again. This time he didn't make it to the side of the tent.

"I'm just going to see what's keeping Choi and that breakfast," said

Purna, talking in the stilted tone of one being very careful not to breathe through her nose. "There anything else I can bring you?"

"Yeah," Maroto gasped between retches. "Diggelby's fucking head."

———

Thrice Sullen had carried Grandfather to Maroto's tent so that the three generations of Horned Wolves could finally sing for one another, and three times the girl wearing the pelt of their people had rebuffed them at the flaps. Purna, something Purna they called her, and she hadn't been rude about it, more annoyed at her captain for being so hungover he'd spent the whole day getting out of bed just long enough to puke before collapsing again. But the last time she hadn't even looked up from the card game she was playing with her comrades, all of whom also wore horned wolf trophies. Instead, she had just waved them off and said:

"Soon as he's sensible I'll fetch you. He ain't been up for more than five minutes at a stretch, though, so don't expect poetry from the poot."

"The poetry of Maroto; now *that* I would like to hear!" said the duchess with the horned wolf tooth tiara perched atop her high wig.

"Yeah, thanks," Sullen muttered, carrying Grandfather back toward their tent. "With our luck he'll puke himself to death before we even get to hear his side of the song."

"We should be so lucky," said Grandfather. "He drops dead, we'll take his bones and grind 'em down to make you a weapon like the ones my mother used to wield. Iron forged with the ashes of your ancestors is the most powerful metal there is."

"Yeah?" Sullen hadn't heard this tale before. "Great-Gran had something like that?"

"One knife made from each of her mothers," said Grandfather, leaning in close to whisper in his grandson's ear, as though the camp was full of spies just looking to steal an old man's stories. "They never missed, Sullen, *never.*"

"Huh."

"'Huh' is all you ever say. *Huh.* Oi, laddie, see that hill there?"

Sullen saw it, all right: the camp backed into and partially up the base of a foreboding mountain, and right before the climb got really bad and the tents fell away was a tall spit of brown grass. Highest point around, short of climbing the mountain or one of the two ridges that came down like walls on either side of the camp, and without need for further clarification he tramped toward it as the Lark's Tongue speared the setting sun.

"There we are," said Grandfather when Sullen finally topped the hill, a crude symbol of stones at his feet and the whole world spread out beyond them. "That's something to see. Your Immaculate girl is in for it now!"

That she was. From down in the camp they could only see the ridgeline of the grassy rise across the low valley, but up here the foothills looked nearly as flat as the plains they melted into, and damned if the whole countryside didn't look like it had broken out in an angry rash. The Imperial camp wasn't twice as big as that of the Cobalts, but it was close. And from those Crimson tents to the valley floor it couldn't have been much more than an hour's march; from the valley floor to the first Cobalt tent was less than half that.

"Don't look good, does it?" said Sullen sadly. Their time was nearly out; as soon as tomorrow the battle could start, and what the hells would they do then? More specifically, what would Sullen do with Grandfather? He couldn't expect the old man to understand his need to fight in a war that they were no part of, nor could he leave Grandfather behind and go fight on his own—if he fell, what would happen to a Horned Wolf who hadn't walked on his own in over a decade? After all they'd been through, it looked like they might have squandered their only chance to talk to Maroto the day before, and now the battle might come before they could try again. Which meant they had to set out into the mountains that very night if they wanted to avoid a war between Outlanders, but it also meant leaving behind his uncle without giving him a chance to set things right... and leaving behind Ji-hyeon, which almost seemed worse. "Don't look good at all."

"Good?" Grandfather snorted. "Looks ruddy *great*, laddie. If I'd known they remembered how to fight a real war out here, I would've followed Maroto the first time he left the Savannahs."

"Yeah?" Sullen didn't think he'd ever heard Grandfather call his son by that name.

"Yeah," said Grandfather, "I'd near given up on the notion, but looks like there's still hope for me makin' it into Old Black's Mead-hall. If that many Imperial curs can't send me to the ancestors, then I reckon I might have to reconsider my whole mortality."

"You mean you want us to pledge our arms to the Cobalt Company?" said Sullen, half relieved to have the matter sorted in the best way possible, but only half, mind. He still hadn't seen Ji-hyeon since Zosia had brought the girl's lover back to her—as if Sullen needed more reason to be sore about the one called Cold Cobalt—and the notion that he now had an excuse to visit the general made him almost as happy as it did skittish.

"If that's what it takes to coax a smile out of you," said Grandfather, rapping his knuckles into Sullen's hair. "If the two sides are the Imperial dogs who dragged their Chain clear up to the Savannahs or anyone ruddy else, I'll raise my spear beside anyone ruddy else. Besides, that white witch wants us to leave, which is all the more reason to stay."

"Hoartrap?" Sullen gulped. If Grandfather found out—

"You did a lively dance keeping that from me, Sullen, though why you felt the urge I'll never guess. You think I'd be so ired over his bein' part of the crew that I'd wriggle after him on my belly, snapping at his ankles?" Grandfather's fingers burrowed through the hair that had caught his hand and scratched affectionately at Sullen's scalp. "Well, I suppose I might have, once upon a time. But he came by one of those evenings you were at your ease with that blue-haired . . . young lady. We had a talk, he and me, and we had a couple more since."

"Damn, Fa," said Sullen, impressed as ever with his grandfather's coolness. "You've known this whole time? I thought I was slick about it."

"Slick as pinesap."

"Huh. So what'd you talk about?"

"Never you mind," grumbled Grandfather. "You've kept enough of your secrets; I'm entitled to a few of my own. The relevant point is he wants us both gone, wants it in a bad way, which is why I've decided to stick around. I scare, the same as any mortal, but I don't scare by the likes of him. Now shake a paw, it's getting on in the day, and if we might die tomorrow I aim to get a good night's sleep first."

Even with the hardest battle of her life within spitting distance, Ji-hyeon couldn't help grinning as the four of them sat around the table in her tent. It was the first time in nearly a year that they had all sat together, sipping kaldi and passing a waterpipe, and for as much as the world had changed, they had not. Sure, she picked up more on minor frictions, like the glares Keun-ju would launch through his veil at Fennec or the saucy winks Fennec would fire back, or Choi's skepticism about both of her other guards, but those things had always been there, just swimming too deep for her to catch.

"Are you sure you wouldn't have the rest of your council in here for this?" said Fennec, nodding down at the map. "Just to make sure all qualified heads have a chance to take it in?"

"If she were worried about qualified heads, Brother Mikal, she wouldn't very well have you in here, would she?" said Keun-ju, sipping his kaldi.

"I've given a lot more people in this camp a lot more cause to wish me ill, Keun-ju, so I wouldn't make such a production about it," said Fennec. "Ji-hyeon seems to have gotten over it, so—"

"Enough barking," said Choi, which was enough of a burn coming from her to quiet them down. "Our general offers us paramount honor. Who else but her bodyguard need know her every movement?"

"I've done this enough times to know it's not as simple as we three keeping an eye on her," said Fennec, but he'd thankfully dropped some of the snide. "In a battle this big, if the general insists on leading from the field—which I still advise against, protective devil or no—the other captains need to know where to find her. An effective army is a coherent army, and plans we've spent a hundred hours perfecting may well fall apart in the first hundred heartbeats of the fight. If that happens we will need the command to regroup, and to do that the general *cannot* penetrate too deep into the front, and the other officers must have some idea of where to find her. *Does that make sense?"*

"If you bleating peacocks had let me speak, I would have told you that the rest of the officers have already gone over the plan. Several times, in fact." Ji-hyeon yawned, the gurgling pipe having counteracted the kaldi. "The Crimson agreed to meet us at noon, so I want everyone ready by dawn. No, make it an hour before light, just to be on the safe side. For now I think we'd all better assume this is our last night on the Star, and do some things we'll regret if we live out the morrow."

Fennec rolled his eyes, Keun-ju coughed and turned his face away, and Choi just looked befuddled. The more things change... However tomorrow's battle shook out, Ji-hyeon was glad these three were here to fight beside her, just as they had that fateful night of the Autumn Festival when she had found her calling.

"General," one of her tent guards called in. "Masters Ruthless and Sullen request an audience."

"Send them in!" Ji-hyeon realized she'd practically chirped it, and rubbed at her eyes in exaggerated fatigue to cover a blush of her own.

"Isn't the hour rather late to be meeting common mercenaries?" asked Keun-ju, and she'd been away from him so long Ji-hyeon couldn't tell if he was teasing her or actually jealous.

"Oh, I don't know," said Fennec, smirking at Keun-ju. "A general should always be accommodating for her troops."

"You *guys*," said Ji-hyeon, secretly loving the weird sensation of having her Hwabun crew here, providing a chorus to her new life just as they always had to her old. "They're probably just telling me they're leaving. They never actually pledged to . . ."

Ji-hyeon trailed off as the familiar shape of Sullen stepped into the command tent, the source of his delay now obvious: he'd had to unsling his grandfather from his back before entering the low-ceilinged tent, and now held the old man in his arms like the Star's nastiest baby. In all the excitement of the last few days, she hadn't been able to carve out enough time to see him, and now that he had come to her, was it really just to say good-bye? Their business was with Maroto, and if they had resolved it she might never see him again...

The old man said, "Sorry to interrupt, General Ji-hyeon Bong, General of the Cobalt Company, Second Daughter of some Immaculates I don't know nor ever will, but my grandson and I need a quick ear."

"Uh. General." Neither the presence of his grandfather nor Ji-hyeon's still-seated retinue seemed to be putting Sullen at ease, but then Choi clapped her hands together and rose to her feet.

"We will respect your secrets," said the wildborn, waving Fennec and Keun-ju to accompany her out. Ji-hyeon appreciated the gesture, but Choi's unique vocabulary proved especially mortifying—what was so bad about the word "privacy"? "Secrets" sounded...pretty damn appetizing, where Sullen was concerned, but that was beside the point. Choi was addressing Sullen now, of all people. "Has your uncle overcome his weakness?"

"Doubt he ever will!" said the old man, evidently appreciating Choi's turn of phrase more than Ji-hyeon. "If fear was a muscle, my son's would be bigger than his biceps."

"Choosing not to fight is not the same as fearing it," said Choi, taking the same chiding tone with this scarred-up geriatric as she always used to with Ji-hyeon. "I have seen how adeptly he avoids combat, how his eyes move when his body does not, how swiftly he strikes, when left with no alternative. When he chooses to spill blood, I believe he will prove himself undeserving of your scorn. When I asked of his weakness, I misspoke—I intended to ask of his injuries."

Misspoke? In all their years together, of all Choi's strange turns of phrase, that was one term Ji-hycon had never heard the wildborn use—she would clarify or translate, sure, but was as careful and precise with her language as she was with her sword. From the look Fennec and Keun-ju exchanged, they were similarly intrigued by this development.

The old man was less impressed. "The boy's certainly *adept* at avoiding fights, I'll grant you that. I guess all your tongue-wagging means the *Mighty Maroto* hasn't signed on for the big one, has he?"

"No, he has not," said Choi, and was that a trace of melancholy in her voice? "But it is honor that hamstrings him, not fear. You called him Craven, but that is incorrect. He is crude but strong. He is hurt but hopeful. He is loyal but conflicted. He is rash. Too rash. He has a devil inside him, but I think he can win against it. He will fare better with the tusks of his friends to face it."

Both the old man and Sullen looked taken aback at this, and they didn't even realize how rare a speech it was; usually prying that many words out of Choi required making an enormous error that demanded complicated correction. Then Choi gave them a nod and hustled out, but Keun-ju and Fennec seemed to have forgotten to leave.

"All right then, you two, if you'll excuse us—" Ji-hyeon began, but for the first time that she could remember, Sullen interrupted her.

"Nah, they can stay. General," he added quickly, eyes everywhere but on her. "We won't take but a minute, and I don't mind your captains or guards hearing what I've got to say."

"So say it," said the nearly toothless Ruthless. "Or I will."

"I knew you came to the Cobalt Company on your own business," said Ji-hyeon, feeling Keun-ju's gaze as she bowed to the two barbarians. "I have appreciated our time together, but unless you wish to be caught up in a war that you have no stake in, this is the time to go. I am...*delighted* you came to say good-bye."

"Nope," said Sullen, and he took a knee with his grandfather still cradled in his arms. "I do have a stake in this, General Ji-hyeon Bong, Second Princess of Hwabun, Daughter of Jun-hwan and Kang-ho Bong: you. I pledge myself in your name, because you're the first person I've met outside the Savannahs who deserves all my respect, and more than I can give besides. If you say this war is worth fighting, I believe you." Sullen was looking up into her eyes now, and without glancing at Keun-ju or a mirror, Ji-hyeon couldn't tell if she, Sullen, or her Virtue Guard looked the most embarrassed by his proclamation. It might have been a three-way tie. "If you'll accept my oath, I'm yours until you release me from the Cobalt Company."

Ji-hyeon nodded, doing everything in her power to keep the smile inside her mouth, but Sullen must have caught the edge of it like he always did, for his eyes lit up as he slowly rose. Grandfather gave her something that might have passed for a salute, and said:

"I go where he does, so that means you've got my word, too." He winked a rheumy eye at her. "I wouldn't have laid it on so thick, mind, but I approve the arrangement, if you follow. If we could discuss restitution—"

"Another time," said Sullen quickly. "We'll leave you to your planning, then, General. Just wanted to make sure it was all sorted, since there's noise around camp about tomorrow being the big day. General. Um, Captain Fennec. Captain Keun-ju."

"I'm a Virtue Guard, not a captain," said Keun-ju, meeting Sullen's guileless, friendly glance with a flip of his veil. "It was so nice to finally meet you, after hearing all of Ji-hyeon's tales—I hope when the day is won and we can all return to being civilized the three of us can sit down for kaldi. I'm sure we have so much in common."

"One thing, at least," said Sullen, bolder by half than Ji-hyeon had seen him since that first night he showed up in camp. But quick as the confidence came it fled, no doubt impeded by his grandfather's snickering and Fennec's loud snort. "See you both around out there, I guess."

"I guess we will," said Keun-ju, and then Sullen was out of there as fast as his tightly muscled legs could carry him. Keun-ju whistled softly as Sullen ducked out of the tent. "Oh. So that's what you see in him."

"Are you sure you don't want to ask him to be part of your bodyguard?" asked Fennec. "You can't buy the kind of protection he'd offer you; it has to come from the heart."

"Or somewhere lower," said Keun-ju. "What?"

"Both of you, go," said Ji-hyeon, shooing them out into the twilight. "After all that scintillating conversation I'm quite exhausted, and think I may actually get a good night's sleep for a change. Don't come back until an hour before dawn."

Fennec made tracks, as he usually did, but Keun-ju hung back, his veil rustling in the breeze as he leaned in and whispered, "What about that whole we-may-die-tomorrow business? Making lusciously regrettable decisions? I've missed you so much..."

"I've missed you, too," said Ji-hyeon, pecking him on the lace-hidden cheek. "Now, as soon as you fetch Sullen and get him to agree to a three-way split, we can get on with treating tonight like our last."

Keun-ju pursed his lips and blew, kicking up the edge of his veil. "*Really?*"

"Maybe for my next birthday," Ji-hyeon murmured, not really able to stop herself now that she'd gotten this close to him. She'd kept Keun-ju at arm's length when he'd first returned to her and they'd had their talk, because she still couldn't shake the doubt that his story was almost too plausible, that maybe he hadn't told her the whole truth... But then again, even if his allegiances were in question elsewhere, she knew she could trust him in bed. Oh, how she'd longed for him, every day since she had left Hwabun... Well, okay, most of them. "Tell you what, Keun-ju—let's go back inside and you can show me how much you missed me."

He'd missed her just as much as she'd missed him, apparently.

———

Zosia spent all afternoon with Singh and her kids and then ate dinner with Fennec, bullshitting her old friends nearly as much as they bullshitted her. Everyone had their doubts about the coming combat, but Zosia did her best to assuage them—she wanted all hands on blades when the day broke, and if people started losing their nerve now, an already dicey ploy would become unwinnable. In the end all it took was Zosia agreeing to pay the Raniputri mercenaries double what Ji-hyeon had already promised them, and telling Fennec that if he tried to change teams now she'd add him to her shit list. It felt good to know that threat still carried weight with people who knew her from the old days.

As the night wore on she went to check on Maroto again, but to hear his chums laugh about it the old bastard still hadn't recovered from his overindulgence of the night before. Diggelby had just given him something to help him sleep through the night, so after bandying a few words with Purna, Zosia ambled on. Not having much else to do, she took her time getting back to her cot, content to idly follow Choplicker as he snuffled along. In the morning thousands of people would die terrible deaths because a few narcissists were convinced they knew what was best for the Star, and one revenge-minded woman was willing to exploit them. Tomorrow old friends and new might die. Tomorrow the Star might be a very different place than it was this evening.

But tonight Zosia was going to sleep like a contented stinghound tucked in by his favorite centipede. Why shouldn't she? Melodrama aside, odds were the imminent battle wouldn't be the end of the matter; enough of one side or the other would retreat, gather their strength by preying on helpless villages who aided them from either fear or fervor, and then they would all go at it again. That order. Repeat as needed.

She could practically feel the tents humming with nervous anticipation. This was what they'd all signed up for, war...but to hear the other Villains tell it, and to read between the lines of Ji-hyeon's boasts, they'd yet to face a real engagement like this one. Whichever side was victorious, the devils would have more than they could eat on the morrow.

Choplicker seemed to be leading her somewhere through camp, looking over his shoulder to make sure she was with him before turning this way or that. She wanted him on good behavior during the battle, so she went along with him instead of reeling him in. It felt like a dream...no, not quite, it felt like she was wandering through a memory. This night, long as it already felt, might as well last forever—she'd paced camps like this before, the eve of a big tussle,

twenty years ago, twenty-five years ago, thirty years ago...and for all
the battles she'd won or lost, here she was again.

Ah, so that was what he wanted. The dog had backed his butt up
so a friendly guard could properly scratch his rump. The tent the boy
watched was the one they'd put the war nun in to convalesce, though
the sawbones hadn't thought much of the weirdborn's prospects. Had
Zosia known the sister was riddled with half-healed wounds before
laying into her that morning, it wouldn't have changed her course—
it was as overdue as it was richly deserved. Be that as it may, the
war nun's continued unconsciousness was getting irritating, with her
master Hjortt's army scheduled to attack anon and nary a confession
yet extracted. Zosia had already stopped by twice that day to see if
Portolés was alert, but whatever the barber had stung her with to ease
the pain had put her down but good.

"She up?" Zosia asked the guard, who looked up from Choplicker
and quickly snapped a salute.

"She came 'round and took some water when I got on," he said.
"She's asleep again, I think, but I can wake her for you, Captain. My
pleasure."

"Not just yet," Zosia decided, as much to spite Choplicker as to
give the witch more time to recover before interviewing her. Depending on what she had to say, it was probably best if she was able to take
another punch or two when the time came. "I'll be back for her soon
enough. Thanks."

Choplicker made to go in anyway, but at a sharp whistle he slunk
back, baring his teeth at her but not making a sound. Zosia offered
the guard a stiff salute, and from the grin on his face she supposed
she'd made the kid's night. Heading straight back to her tent, she
gave Choplicker a reproachful shake of her head as he whined again.
Whatever terms the queen offered now that she knew her assassination attempt at Kypck had failed, nothing could turn Zosia away
from her due.

Slithering out of smoky, sweaty clothes in the chill of her tent,
she supposed that was the real tragedy of it all. For all her musings
that night, the truth was that she was here because she set out to

bring down the queen . . . but even if she had died in Kypck alongside Leib and their people, this war would still be happening. General Ji-hyeon's plot against the Crimson Empire was exactly what Zosia had vowed and wished for, right down to the color of the flag on the rebel standards, but here on the cusp of successful retaliation, she was just another participant in a cast of many thousands. She had traveled to the far corners of the Star, only to find that the means to her end was doing just fine without her. She had become redundant in her own vengeance.

Crawling under her furs, she let out a long, wistful sigh. She had abandoned the Crown of Samoth precisely because she had concluded that it was beyond her power to change the world. Well, that and a guilty conscience over the realization that she had hurt just as many people as any tyrant before her, whatever her intentions. Now, twenty-some years older, she was all set to stir up the same crock of shit she'd thrown out the last time around, and for the same obvious reason—she thought the sovereign of the Crimson Empire was an asshole.

Except this time around she had only herself to blame for putting the crown on the queen's brow. Maybe she wouldn't sleep tonight after all.

CHAPTER
22

Portolés was dreaming of Brother Wan when her eyes began to burn. She stumbled out of her visions, into the glaring lantern light, and tried to rub the itchy crust from her eyes, but both her hands were shackled to the makeshift frame of the cot. She felt languid from more than sleepiness and injury, and remembered the biting centipede the sawbones had offered her when last she woke. Had she accepted? Probably, from the heaviness of her limbs and the lightness of her head, though she had no personal experience with such medicine—the Holy Barbers of the Church declared it a sin to distract an anathema from the material experience of its redemption, and so when they had corrected her tongue, teeth, and other failings she had felt every prick of stitch and rasp of file.

"You look well," said Cold Zosia, the Stricken Queen dragging a stool over next to the bed. The old woman shimmered, and Portolés closed her stinging eyes, offered a prayer to the Fallen Mother for strength. When she opened her eyes they had adjusted to the brightness of the room, and there could be no doubting the woman before was of flesh and blood, not dream and smoke. "Probably could have given you a few more taps and you'd be no worse for wear, big strong monster like you."

"Zosia." The name sent a shiver down Portolés's spine even now. "This is an honor. It's not often a lowly nun is granted audience with a god."

"Oh, it's not so rare as your people make it out to be," said Zosia, crossing her legs. "But I don't think Indsorith sent you all the way here just to talk theology."

"Not much time, now." Portolés licked her lips, amazed that even with the drug, simply talking was so painful. The sawbones who had tended her had told her to make peace with her Savior, but she hadn't reckoned on it coming so quick. She wondered if she'd been dying ever since Heretic had rescued her from the butte, if need alone had kept her alive this long, and now that her confessor had finally arrived she could be set free. "I provoked your general before. That was unwise. If the Immaculate girl truly commands here, if only in your name, you would do well to bring her here as well."

"Oh, the kid's in charge, all right," said Zosia. "But what makes you think she wants to hear anything out of a Chainwitch?"

"Queen Indsorith wishes to prevent war. I have the authority to broker a peace on her behalf, something the Imperial regiments harrying you lack. If I can convince your Immaculate general, if *we* can convince her, there will be no battle. There will be no *war*."

"Before Ji-hyeon hears word one of anything you have to say, *I* need to be convinced," said Zosia, not sounding as though that possibility were very likely. "So somehow dear Queen Indsorith got the idea that I was going to lead a rebellion against her? I wonder who put that notion in her head?"

"It wasn't her order," said Portolés, keeping her voice low. Given Zosia's demeanor, it was imperative she not provoke the woman's wrath, lest it overrule her reason. But how could you keep someone calm when discussing the crimes you had committed against her? "She never ordered Colonel Hjortt to Kypck, never ordered him to make an example out of *any* village. She never ordered him to execute anyone, not your lover, your townsfolk. None of this was her doing."

"Oh, well all right then!" Zosia threw her hands up. "I'll admit, I was a little worried on that account, but you've put my mind to rest. I will quibble with your choice of words, though—he was my *husband*, they were my *friends*, and you *butchered* them."

"You have no reason to believe me, I know, but—"

"But what?" There was that temper Portolés had been warned of, a temper that might ignite an empire. "She had her move, but she fucked it up. Or rather, her assassins did—that's really the only thing an assassin needs to do, assassinate the target. And now that she sees the plan got botched, she sends you here as a peace offering? I'm supposed to think that it was coincidence that her troops went rogue, coincidence that they happened on Kypck instead of any other of the Empire's thousand other backwaters? Does she think I'm a *complete* idiot?"

"No," Portolés said patiently. "She does not. She knows better than that, doesn't she? Something terrible happened to you, to your people, and now you are doing what anyone would expect you to do. And given your history, it is obvious that you would suspect the queen, even if it hadn't been Imperial soldiers who came for you."

"*Our history?*" Zosia raised an eyebrow. "I've told no one of what happened between us, even after everything at Kypck. Am I to understand she broke *all* of the oaths we made to one another?"

Devils take centipedes and all their soporific kind, Portolés was making a real mess of this. She had tried to talk the queen out of sending her for exactly this reason; that devilish tongue of hers always found a way to betray her. She bit the wicked flesh before trying again. "Given the graveness of the crime against you, and the importance of my mission, she thought it necessary that I know everything. So that if I found you in time you would know beyond any doubt that she sent me, and that I speak with the authority I claim. If I were acting on behalf of any other party I could not know what I do. I am her vouchsafe against further deception."

Zosia was listening now, really listening for the first time. "Prove it, then."

"Prove what?" Portolés wasn't stalling, she really didn't know what else to say that could convince this woman.

"Tell me the whole story, then, or rather, the version she told you. Then we can hear what I'm sure is a most convincing argument as to why she isn't the one I should blame."

"If you insist, Mistress Zosia." That foul curiosity that forever plagued Portolés's heart thrummed in delight at the prospect of having Zosia provide corroboration to the queen's most secret of songs. "Queen Indsorith was a lesser daughter of a minor noble in the Juniusian Court when you killed King Kaldruut and captured the Carnelian Crown. When your first mandate as Cobalt Queen was to disperse the Empire's wealth amongst the people, Junius was first to resist. And like all provinces who refused you, they suffered swift repercussions from your soldiers. What members of Indsorith's family survived your assault did not last long in the Ketzerel labor camps you exiled them to. Only when her last relations perished in bondage did the queen escape, coming to Diadem with a poorly conceived plan to assassinate you."

"She described it as 'poorly planned'?" Zosia smiled for the first time. "Well, I suppose it was."

"She was caught before reaching the second floor of the castle, but instead of a public execution you ordered that she be brought in chains to your throne room. Thereupon you had your private audience." Portolés waited, assuming this would be enough, but Zosia waved her on as she pulled out a curved black pipe and set to lighting it. "She said you looked... tired. You asked her what she intended, armed only with a sword and a grudge, and she told you what had happened to her people. Not to beg for mercy, but to be heard, but once, before her death. Everyone, even an Imperial noble, recognized that your reforms grew from a desire to help the people, but in doing so, countless innocents were paying the price. Instead of being ill-starred to be born a turnip farmer, they were ill-starred to be born noble, or landed, or devout."

"Your church, sister, was as corrupt then as it is now." Zosia blew smoke at Portolés. "I only wish I'd ignored my advisors and put every last one of your clergy to the sword. They said the Chain would help ease the transition to an egalitarian Empire, but those black-robed vultures conspired with the merchants and nobles to thwart me at every turn. That's my chief regret, that I didn't raze every Chainhouse before departing. But please, continue, this is all quite good."

"Yes, well..." Small wonder the church outlawed the mere mention of this woman's name. "After she had spoken her piece, you lectured her on the difficulty of ruling any land, let alone one in such desperate need of change. She responded with an insult, something about how Samoth would be hard pressed to find a worse ruler than you. That, she said, is when everything about your attitude changed, and you challenged her to the duel. And the rest is the rest, but you must believe that she would never, ever repay your—"

"The duel," snapped Zosia. "What did she tell you of it? I told you to tell me everything."

"My apologies," said Portolés, the sickeningly strong fumes of the woman's pipe filling the tent. "You told her... you told her you would grant her wish, as any devil would, and released her from her chains. You ordered her to resume her quest against you, then and there, but cautioned her that your duel could only result in death or exile. Then you fought, there in the throne room, on the edge of the precipice."

"Yes, then?" Zosia leaned forward. This woman was even prouder than Portolés, eager to relive her victory through the war nun's words.

"You defeated her—forgive me, I have not the tongue for describing whatever brilliant feint you felled her with. But after, as she lay disarmed on the floor, expecting you to deliver your hammer to her heart or perhaps kick her over the edge, to fall upon Diadem as an example, you dropped your weapon beside her. Lifted her up. Planted your crown upon her brow, and explained your meaning: she had accepted your terms, even if she did not rightly understand them, and as you were the victor she was bound to obey them."

Surely this was enough... but apparently not, Zosia waiting, a hungry smile behind the marrow-yellow stem of her pipe. Portolés concluded the tale in as colorful and flattering a fashion as she could manage.

"She was to learn firsthand whether ruling an empire and safeguarding the happiness and security of its subjects was as easy as she supposed. You drafted documents meant to guarantee the loyalty of your Villains as well as the rest of the governing bodies you had installed, and then you vanished from the Star. You even cunningly secured a fresh corpse from the pauper's field, and after the two of you dyed the dead woman's hair to match your own, she was hurled

over the edge of the throne room to prove the story of your defeat—
from that height, little remained of her features in the street below,
save long cobalt hair and your dress. Queen Indsorith had won much
more than she had set out to gain, and in exchange you were permitted to fade into the night, never to be seen again."

"Yessssss," Zosia said, savoring the telling of the tale far more than
Portolés would have thought possible. After an uncomfortably long
silence, and then, as if only just remembering more recent events, she
snapped straight up on her stool and pointed her pipe at Portolés.
"And Indsorith bided her time, patient as any devil, and only when
I had long stopped fearing any retribution she sent you after me, to
avenge her family. To take everything from me, just as I had taken it
from her. The only difference is I never intended to hurt her, never
intended to hurt anyone. I was healing the Empire, not harming it."

So says every tyrant, thought Portolés, but for once her tongue did
not betray her. "So you believe."

"So I believe." Zosia nodded, standing. "Thank you, sister."

"Hear me out," said Portolés, realizing the arrogant woman meant
to leave. "I...I beg you, Zosia, now that I have proven myself the
messenger, listen to the message. Believe what you will when I am
done, but pray, hear me out, in the name of your murdered people."

"I think I've heard enough," said Zosia. "Except, perhaps, why
Indsorith should send you, of all people, to deliver this message. And
why a war nun of the Burnished Chain would do the bidding of the
Crimson Queen instead of her Black Pope—it is true that you fought
your own kind on the road, is it not? Much as I'd like to claim the
credit, the wounds you will die from came not from my hands, but
those of your beloved church. Don't tell me you simply grew tired
of being treated as a beast by those who hitched the plough to your
back?"

"It wasn't Indsorith," said Portolés, praying her sincerity overcame
a devilish tongue and the false tranquility of the insect sting. "Anyone who wished to hurt the queen would set you against her. What
better means of harming her, of harming you both, than giving you
cause to war against her? If she'd wanted you dead, don't you think

she would have tried a little harder? Please, Zosia, you are too smart to be led by the nose like this, you know better than any that war will never—"

"That's not what I asked," said Zosia. "Now tell me, why are you the messenger of this tale?"

"Because I was the only one who knew exactly what you looked like now." Portolés closed her throbbing eyes. "And to convince you of her sincerity. I have not come alone."

"No?"

"No." Portolés looked up at the tear-blurred woman. "In my valise are writs that give me absolute authority to act on the queen's behalf, as I said, but there is something more. A manifest of the names of all the soldiers under Colonel Hjortt's command who were present at Kypck. A sacrifice. As soon as I reported what happened, how queer it all was, and what you looked like, and your dog, the queen realized what treachery was afoot."

"A sacrifice, eh?"

"Yes, Mistress Zosia, one to prevent a needless war. We are her gift to you, a token of her sorrow at your loss. I swear on the Fallen Mother, I was with Colonel Hjortt from the day he was given command of the Fifteenth, and not until we captured and killed your husband did he make any mention of such a plan. Queen Indsorith believes it was the Burnished Chain, and that must be why they sent agents after me, to stop me from alerting you to the truth."

"Hmmm," said Zosia, and to Portolés's elation she actually seemed to be considering it. "The Chain sent an Imperial colonel, knowing I would blame the queen. Interesting. That's why your Black Pope sent assassins after you, and why you fought them?"

"I...I can't say for certain why she sent them, but I fought them because they would have stopped me," said Portolés. "I don't even know for certain how the Chain found out my mission. I...A brother of mine, in the Chainhouse, he may have spied on my thoughts, after I met with the queen."

"So you have no actual proof that the Chain ordered Hjortt to target me and my people?"

"None," said Portolés, knowing that here at the end of her mission she mustn't deviate one step from what the queen had told her, mustn't stray from the truth even to better convince Zosia. Besides, Boris was right, she was a terrible bluffer. "The queen has no evidence to point toward the Chain or any other suspect; the single thing she is sure of is that she played no part in it. Allmother have mercy, knowing Hjortt as I did from serving in his bodyguard, it might have been as simple as that idiot hoping to seize an extra parcel of land for himself before the smoke cleared from the civil war. However he settled on his wicked course, it was not sanctioned by the queen. She is not your enemy. And unless you order your Immaculate general to stop, or talk reason to her if she in more than name commands this army, there will be another war, the worst war yet. She said that across all the Star, only you and she know just how pointless another war will be—even if you but agree to look over my writs and display them to whoever leads the Imperial army that threatens you, it will be enough to stop the killing before it is too late. She entrusted me with the most powerful weapon on the Star, and bid me deliver it to you, by any means: the truth."

Portolés shuddered, so much talk winding her as much as a jog up every flight of stairs in Diadem.

"That's only half my question, though, sister—I can tell you believe, I can smell it all over you...So why go against officers of your church, especially when you discovered that your queen gained her crown by treachery and deceit? She made a deal with a devil, Portolés, and yet you buck at your chains to serve her."

There was that hungriness again as Zosia pocketed her still-smoldering pipe and leaned down over the bed, no doubt hoping to catch a crack in Portolés's façade. There was no façade, so there would be no crack. For the first time, Portolés put into words the worm that had nested in her heart ever since Kypck. For all the orders and armies and schemes of mortals, it was true that nothing could destroy so absolutely as the truth.

"I came because I am guilty. It was I who carried out Hjortt's order. I was punished when I led the Fifteenth's cavalry back to the regiment, but not for the true offense. My superiors in the Chain told me that what I did in Kypck, to you and your people, was no sin, no sin at all. That I did no wrong there, for I am a vessel of the Fallen Mother, and that by killing them I had saved the souls of pagan peasants. But Queen Indsorith...alone, in her throne room, she told me that it was evil. That it was a crime, no matter what justifications I might present. And she is right." Portolés wept silently, her eyes becoming gummy as she shook with shame at what she had done, remembering how steady her maul had stayed as she brained the five Azgarothians who refused her order, one after another. Her faith had shielded her from this pain for so long, it was liberating to finally feel the full force of it. The magnitude of it was nothing short of heavenly...She had discharged her duty, and as she let the grief shake her she heard Zosia above her, crying as well.

No. She wasn't crying at all. She was *laughing*.

Unable to wipe away the thick film coating her eyes, Portolés blinked up at Zosia. The woman seemed to get ahold of herself, knelt down by Portolés's head, and murmured:

"You have acted with commendable bravery in the service of your Empire, Sister Portolés, and I cannot blame you for what happened at Kypck. I forgive you everything."

Of all the possible ends Portolés had contemplated, she had never dared hope for Zosia's absolution. An unexpected sob slipped out of her before she could stop it.

"There, there," said Zosia, stroking away Portolés's tears. "Was there anything else you wanted to confess, while you have such a sympathetic ear?"

There was. Portolés wanted to tell Zosia how good it had felt watching Efrain Hjortt burn alive, how the first step on her long road to the Lark's Tongue had come when she had decided to leave the little colonel to his fiery judgment...But here at last, her obligations met, she found herself finally free of the pride that had always governed her tongue. It was enough that she had done the right thing, she didn't need to crow about it, especially not to the woman who had set the fire in the first place; all Portolés had done was do nothing, despite the screams of a burning sinner.

"I...I thought I knew more than anyone in the Chain, even the Black Pope," she said, feeling the burden of this last sin rise from her breast as she finally articulated what had so long gone unsaid in the back of her warm heart. "I rebelled in every way I could think of, sinned for the sake of sinning. I did everything they expected an anathema to do, because I...because I wanted to prove they were wrong. That the Fallen Mother loved me no matter what they said. That if I pushed myself far enough, she would reveal herself to me. I just wanted to see her, to see the truth behind the Chain, before I went to whatever reward awaits me beyond this earth."

"Oh yes, plenty of rewards to go around, sister, and plenty of earth, too." Zosia laughed again, a malicious bark. "But since you're so keen to see some truths, maybe I can assist..."

The blur that was Zosia leaned down and ripped out Sister Portolés's left eye. An enormous, heavy hand fell over her mouth, and try as she did to keep her right eye shut, thick fingers dug under it. Another searing rip brought a gasp up her throat, only to be choked off by the palm sealing her lips, a thumb and ring finger pinching her nose shut.

"Everything all right in there, sir?" a voice called from just outside the buttoned flaps of the tent, and a masculine voice replied:

"Better fetch the barber, lad, the nun seems to have had a fit."

Portolés thrashed in her chains, but they had bound her well to the bed. The tent came back into blurry focus, and even being smothered she still shuddered with relief to realize her eyes hadn't actually been plucked out. They still burned, and, blinking the slime out of them, she saw not Zosia looming over her, but Hoartrap the Touch. He held her tight, suffocating her, and with his free hand waggled two shiny black leeches he held between thumb and fingers. Those must be what he had ripped off of her eyes. Tilting his head back, he dropped them into his mouth.

"Here's a little secret for you, sister, since you've been so free with yours," he whispered, his mouth full of blood as he chewed and talked. "Devils come in all shapes and sizes, and if you know what to do with them, any miracle is possible. The only difference between the Chain and my sort is that we sorcerers are honest enough to own up to our deceptions, once the parlor trick is over and the applause dies down. Would that all my audiences were chained down and drug-addled when I came calling with a pair of leech goggles!"

Portolés tried to bite him, but her teeth had been filed too close to the gums. The pain in her old wounds was nothing compared to the heat spreading from her chest, up her throat, pounding behind her eyes. She went limp, praying he would release her, if only to gloat a little longer. His hand tightened instead.

"At the time I didn't want to interrupt your little sob story, but I do think that having carried out your orders so diligently you're entitled to a little peace of mind where your church is concerned. I would hazard that you and Indsorith are absolutely correct about the Chain having sent Hjortt after Zosia to set this charade into motion. That's also why your own people tried to kill you before you could reach her, obviously, obviously. And the simple reason for all that plotting and scheming is that the Burnished Chain wants this war just as bad as me. That last little civil war of yours didn't claim nearly enough lives to summon the powers we're both after. This next one, though, promises to be a real corker—who knows what might happen, if the sacrifice is great enough!"

Black stars bloomed in Portolés's vision, the man rising rising rising away from sight, his voice still hissing in her ear.

"But do you know the biggest secret of all, my devil-blooded, witchborn friend? It's that none of you are devil-blooded at all, nor born of a witch, nor any of the other lies they spread around campfire and Chainhouse. You and your breed, my dear, are *divine*. There's a reason that more and more of you are born every year, despite there being fewer and fewer devils making their way into our world. It's because they're not where we've been, but where we're going. You're not some degenerate legacy of a corrupted ancestor—you, my child, are the future. Our future. There will come a day when your kind rules the Star, and whisper songs of savage mortals, the great fiends of antiquity..."

Portolés convulsed, felt something give in her chest, but even as she went to meet whatever gods or devils would have her, his fingers dug deeper into her flesh, his lips brushing her gnarled ear.

"But thank the Fallen Mother, that day is still a long way off."

CHAPTER
23

Since sleeping without cares was apparently out of the question, Zosia would have settled for sleeping at all, but it wasn't to be. She did have few waking dreams of Leib lying beside her on the cot, humming the old marching songs she'd taught him during their annual summer treks up to that icy lake on the far side of the divide, the only place on the whole Star where she'd been able to pretend, if only for a few days of camping, that she and her husband had truly escaped the whole Star, had found themselves a sanctuary. If they could have stayed there forever, swimming in mountain-cold water and then warming up in the grass, instead of always having to return to Kypck, pink from the high mountain sun and reinvigorated for their duties to the village...

Yeah, that didn't really count as sleep. Grumble, stub her toe in the dark, get her armor on backward the first time around, stumble out of her tent an hour or two before dawn, and make the barber wake up the weirdborn nun even if it took every bug in his bag. That order. Aside from the last, she executed her plan flawlessly.

They had already moved her corpse out of the tent, knowing the white pavilions would be overfull within a few hours, if the battle went off as expected. The man who had brought her in had apparently been tasked with her carrying her out of camp so that she wouldn't start stinking up the place prematurely. The guards Ji-hyeon had assigned to keep him in custody had scared him up a spade and accompanied him up the rise to the edge of camp, lest this be some bizarre part of their plot. Thanking the sawbones who had given her the disheartening information, she was glad for once to have Choplicker along, the devil leading her uphill without needing to be asked.

They found the man ankle-deep in his work, his two handlers sitting on their asses until one of them recognized the approaching woman and they both scrambled to attention. She didn't even bother returning the salute or acknowledging the grave digger, her full attention on the lump of sackcloth. Squatting over the corpse, Zosia couldn't unearth her satisfaction, deep as she dug—she should have taken more time doing it, she told herself, but no, that wasn't quite it. Nor was it the soon-to-be-resolved business with the cavalry of the Fifteenth and their Colonel Hjortt, business Zosia had told herself and her adversary would be a far longer time coming... Vengeance is something best enjoyed when it's piping hot on the plate in front of you, rather than hoping it'll still be there when it cools down a bit, so she had no intention of letting Efrain Hjortt off the hook a second time, assuming she'd land him a third. What it was, she decided, was that this was all coming just a little too easily, the war nun, the colonel, and the cavalry who had carried out the crime at Kypck dropping square in her lap, just as she joined up with an army big enough to help her seal the deal. Zosia didn't believe in destiny, but she certainly put stock in deviltry, and focused her full attention on Choplicker, who was staring up into the dark morning, toward the night-swallowed Lark's Tongue. Could it be...

"You're really her, aren't you?" said the prisoner, leaning on his shovel.

"Get back to work," barked one of the guards, but Zosia said, "It's fine, I want to talk to him. Both of you, piss off back to camp."

"The spy—" began the other guard.

"I'm not a fucking spy!" the man spat, but then that was what any spy would say, wasn't it?

"He's in my custody now," said Zosia. "Dismissed. If I hear another word about it, I'll have Ji-hyeon whip the both of you, but only when my wrist wears out from taking the first round. Now get."

Watching the guards shuffle back down the steep decline, the prisoner seemed even less happy than he had with them riding his ass. His rationale made sense, when he voiced it. "I'm going in here with her, aren't I?"

"Depends," said Zosia, a thought striking her, and she pulled back the sheet to see if . . . But no, it was indeed Sister Portolés under the cloth, eyes staring at her maker or maybe at nothing, who among the living could say for sure? "Barber said she had a fit?"

"Oh, I don't doubt it," said the man dejectedly. "Getting your fresh wounds beat back open by a madwoman will give you the fits something bad. Betting fellow would say I might be about to have a fit myself, soon as I dig a deep enough hole."

"Like I said, depends," said Zosia, about to rise back to her feet when the faint smell of stale smoke crept up her nostrils. Leaning close, she took a sniff of the woman's shroud. Especially noxious toilet water and strong tubāq, a blend she would have recognized even if the barber hadn't mentioned that Hoartrap had been the one to pay a call just before the run shuffled off the Star for good. His presence at her deathbed was damning enough, but that he'd evidently taken enough time to stink up the place with his pipe raised even more questions . . .

"What was she supposed to tell me?"

"Like I said in the tent, to the *general*, I don't know. Found some papers on her after she got beat on enough for me to slap the chains on her, but couldn't make much out of 'em: writs with the queen's seal and a roster of soldiers. That's the extent of it, so if you're going to put your devil on me to get the truth, do it quick and see for yourself I'm no liar."

"Devil?" Zosia rose to her full height, but Choplicker kept his attention on the unseen mountain, sniffing the dark as he took a few more tentative steps up the slope. "She told you that?"

"Lady, she never told me shit, other than a bunch of blather that sounded less like Chainite double-talk and more like the half-baked tracts I helped pass out back in the Jewel." The man was evidently the sort who liked sassing his betters, even when they held his life in their hands. Maybe especially then. "I know because I read those pamphlets, listened to the songs. Cold Cobalt has a devil to do her bidding, don't she? Or was that just another misprint, somewhere along the way someone scribbled down 'devil' when they should've wrote 'dog'?"

"We know which regiment is out there, so why wouldn't you come up with a better story, one where you rode in with the Fifteenth?" Zosia was talking to the dead war nun, but the man spoke for her.

"Hey, Cold Zosia, True Queen of Samoth?" She looked up at him, an already gaunt, dirty face made all the more hellish by the faint light of the lantern the guards had left. "Fuck you, lady."

"Fuck *me*?"

"Yeah." He nodded, as if warming to the idea. "Definitely. I believed in you, in what they said about your ways being better than those of the Chain or the Crown. I risked my life to keep your dream alive—maybe it wasn't much of a life to risk, but it's the only one I got, and maybe it wasn't my dream, just something I heard about secondhand, but it *meant* something to me. The only thing I hate more than the Crown is the Chain, so yeah, the Song of Cold Cobalt was something I believed in. And you know? I *kept* believing, right until I saw you lay into her. It took me lying and scheming and getting luckier than any devil to bring her here, to where I thought it might do some good, and what does the wise Zosia do? You killed her before she could even make a case for herself!"

"For a son of Diadem committed to the Code of Cobalt and dead set against Chain and Empire, you seem awfully broken up about a dead weirdborn."

"Her name's Portolés. Sister Portolés," said the man, staring at the war nun's winding sheet. "I never would have taken her here, I'd known you'd be just as bad to her as her kind would be to you, given the chance. So much for a fair shake. So much for a better world. You're no better than the Chain or the Crown, you just wear a different color and shit on different folks. Now, are you going to fuck off and let me bury her, or are you going to kill me? Because after the hours I put in serving the false memory of a dead woman who ain't even that, I'd appreciate the courtesy of not digging my own grave. Let the birds and beasts have me, maybe they'll find more use for a willing soldier than any of you lot ever did."

The lack of sleep must have caught up to Zosia, pried back her shell a little, because she felt his words like a snail feels salt. It wasn't just the speech itself, the final fist shake of a desperate, tired man who saw his own death not five paces away. It was that he obviously believed it, believed it as much as she believed the sun set in the west.

All across the Star, Zosia and her agenda had been championed by people she had never met, never even heard of, people who put everything on the line in her name...And all across the Star, she disappointed them, because at the break of day she was just as petty and stupid as they were. She felt an urge to tell the man to flee into the darkness and start over somewhere else, his mind scrubbed free from the oily film of idealism, while she finished digging a grave for the woman who had helped burn her world to ashes. She also felt an urge to snatch the shovel from his hands and beat him with it, a harsh lesson, but well needed, to never waste a breath praising a woman you know only from songs to her memory.

A horn blew from down in the valley, where the sentries had intercepted the man and the war nun the day before, sparing Zosia from having to choose between her urges. The man looked at Zosia, Zosia looked at the man, and then they both looked down at the dead servant of the Chain who had traveled so far to find her. Choplicker kept his gaze on the Lark's Tongue that only he could see, and then started barking fit to raise the dead, trotting up into the darkness. Yet the dead did not rise, and the man went back to digging as Zosia went after her devil.

———

Ji-hyeon was half dressed and less than half awake when she heard the first horn, and Choi and Fennec rushed into the dim command tent before the second sounded. Fennec helped himself to a bowl of kaldi while Keun-ju assisted Ji-hyeon into the rest of her armor—the plain but sturdy breastplate, greaves, and hauberk Zosia had helped her put together. Pulling the helm modeled after Cold Cobalt's over her head and feeding her long blue hair through the back, she took up the thick iron scabbard that housed her twin swords.

"How ready are we?" Ji-hyeon asked, her knees weak from more than the busy night she'd spent with Keun-ju. Maybe the day would be won and they would have plenty more time together, but they hadn't taken any chances. "How close are they?"

"They'll be most of the way across the vale before Singh and her riders are in position to support the rest of the cavalry, but that's all right." Fennec sounded like he was trying to convince himself as well as her. Not an auspicious start to the morning. "What good's the high ground if we leave it to meet them, anyway?"

"What good's fighting at all, before there's enough light to see the enemy?" said Keun-ju sleepily.

"They're trying to smother us before we're able to make the most of our defense," said Ji-hyeon. "A good thing we're early risers. If the other captains don't show up in five minutes we ride without refreshing, and hope they remember their roles."

"Tapai Purna's squad will reinforce your guard, General," said Choi, offering a curl of bone the Ugrakari girl had taken from a horned wolf. "She offers this horn as a token of esteem for the honor."

"Maroto's people?" asked Fennec. "What good are scouts at the front?"

"They are much better at fighting than scouting," said Choi. "Too loud. Too wild. They volunteered to scout for a reason, but without Maroto they'll have no cause to avoid honor-making."

"So Maroto never took the oath?" Ji-hyeon tried not to be too disappointed. It would have been something to have all the Villains with her, but if only two were sitting out the fight, her absent father and the grizzled barbarian would be missed the least. "I'd hoped he'd come around, especially after Sullen and Grandfather—"

"*Grandfather?*" Keun-ju tugged the last strap of his banded armor tight. "I didn't realize I'd missed the wedding!"

"Maroto swears too many oaths, rather than not enough," said Choi, whatever the devils that meant.

"General, I do think we need to reconsider your whole leading-from-the-front strategy," Fennec said. "Even with your devil protecting you, it's just too dangerous—"

"This isn't my first dance," said Ji-hyeon. "I know better than to wade in too deep. I'll just bust a hole in their front line, then fall back. Repeatedly if needed. But I have to be close enough to the action to see where I'm most needed, not hiding out in the rear."

"In that case you may wish to sound the horn, General," said Choi.

"What? Oh! Come on," said Ji-hyeon, rushing outside with her guards following her. Chevaleresse Sasamaso had their horses ready, five reins wrapped in her gauntlet. There was something surreal about the camp being this bustling and loud by torchlight, with not a star in the black predawn sky. More horns sounded from all over the camp, from all over the valley, and, lifting her visor, Ji-hyeon slid Purna's gift between the steel canine jaws to wrap lips around the horn and blow a high, mournful trill.

Now that it had begun in earnest, nothing could stop the Second Cobalt War.

———

"Nothing's going to stop me from finding her," said Maroto, although, swaying on his gelatinous legs in the blinding lamplight of his tent, he had to agree that Purna had a point. He couldn't risk breaking his oath to not raise arms against Queen Indsorith more than he already had, but he also couldn't hope to find Zosia in the middle of a battlefield without doing just that. Still, he couldn't let something happen to Zosia before he could come clean about his wish to Crumbsnatcher—she was about to go out and kill a whole lot of Imperials, all because she blamed them for something that Maroto had accidentally set into motion. It might not change her plans for the day, since Zosia had never turned her nose up at fighting Crimson soldiers, but she had a right to know. Not just for her future, but for theirs—he'd fucked up enough for ten lifetimes, and couldn't live another day knowing Zosia thought him a friend instead of the source of all her hurt…

"Still with us, big guy?" said Purna, and Maroto realized he'd almost fainted. Again. What had become of the insatiable sting-hound, that a single graveworm could lay him flat out for a day solid, and keep harassing him into the following morning? Only one thing for it, really.

"Diggelby, I need to see Diggelby. Right now."

"Don't blame him for your appetites, Maroto," said Purna, flicking him in the chin and nearly sending him sprawling. "You must be comfortable in that bed, since you were in such a hurry to make it. Now crawl back in it so I can get to work—we're riding out with the general, I just wanted to say good-bye in case... Well, I wish you were coming. It's going to be *epic*."

"I am," Maroto decided, everything making sense now. Giving Purna his best serious face, he said, "I swore an oath to protect you, Tapai Purna, and I don't break oaths."

"Except to the Queen of Samoth?" Purna looked skeptical.

"Not even to her. Now, help me to Diggelby's tent—he's been collecting shields from every encounter we've had, since clear back at that ambush in the Wastes. Says he's going to mount them in his den once he gets back home. I think he could spare a few in tribute to King Maroto."

"Whatever, man," said Purna, though she wasn't much of an actor—girl was over the moon her old hero had decided to get out of bed. "But if you can't walk out of his tent on your own, there's no way I'm letting you get in the fight."

"Don't worry about me," said Maroto as she helped him into the breastplate he'd mostly been using as a platter at the mess tents. "The Mighty Maroto's got a trick or two yet to impress the devils."

———

Sullen crawled out of nightmares and his tent, on his hands and knees beside the cold remains of their campfire while horns bleated and packs of bleary-eyed soldiers rushed all around, torches waving in the darkness. He focused on the dirt between his hands, terrified to look up at the black sky lest he see the Faceless Mistress looming over him, returning to claim him for failing to carry out her will. Yet when he refused himself another moment's fear and looked up, he saw only the darkest purple that preludes dawn. A dream, nothing more. Wiping his mouth and seeing the greasy black smear his lips left on the back of his hand, he allowed maybe it was a little early to call it.

A soldier rounded his tent at a full run and nearly careened into him before pivoting past. It was the other woman his uncle ran with, the duchess, dressed in what looked something like a scalemail catsuit. She had one of the weakbows Grandfather hated so much, though it was the largest specimen he had ever seen, all polished wood and inlaid metal gleaming in the light of the lantern her companion carried. Hassan was the bloke with the light, and in his other hand was the meanest-looking sword Sullen had ever seen, all serrated edges and hook tip. It provided a dull, earthy contrast to his frilly armor—Sullen hadn't even known you could dye leather pink, but it admittedly suited the man.

"Sullen!" said the duchess. "Just the moon-head we were looking for!"

"Moon-head?" Sullen touched his globe of white hair, too self-conscious to be mad.

"Your uncle Maroto extends his most sincere wish that you and your grandfather join us on the front," said Hassan with a bow, "where we may fight side by side, back to back."

"Huh," said Sullen, remembering what had happened the last time he trusted his uncle on the battlefield and not so sure he wanted to give him a second chance just yet. What if he was the one to end up crippled on the ground, begging for Maroto's aid?

"We shall be acting as the personal guard of General Ji-hyeon," said the duchess. "It is the most honorable of—"

"We'll be there in five minutes," said Sullen, hopping to his feet and ducking back into the tent without wasting another breath. Dark as the tent was, his eyes seemed to be getting keener by the night, and, giving Grandfather a firm nudge, he started fitting his gear in place. Only when he was all set and the old man had yet to respond to his patient muttering for him to get up did he take a closer look at his grandfather. His heart stopped, and his "Get up, Fa," never left his lips.

Only Grandfather's face emerged from the blankets, but that was enough to tell. The old man's eyes were wide, his face frozen in a contorted rictus, his tongue drying out in his slack mouth. Sometime in the night, he had...

"Sulllllllen." The voice drifted from Grandfather's slack mouth.

"Fa! Are you...What's wrong?"

"I...Cannnnn't..."

Even now his voice was fading, and Sullen put his ear to the old man's lips as tears began to well. "What, Fa? Tell me."

Grandfather cleared his throat, a gummy, smacking sound, and whispered, "I can't feel my legs."

Sullen slowly sat back, staring at his grandfather. The old man lost it, laughing until he coughed, and then laughing some more.

"Not going to be able to feel your arms, in a minute," grumbled Sullen, but he was smiling, too. It was time to see if they could find Grandfather a worthier end than dying in his sleep, a million miles from home. As if in answer, another horn sounded from the front.

———

"What the bloody shits are they doing?" Domingo demanded of nobody at all, but Brother Wan glanced back at his passenger and answered the rhetorical question anyway.

"I believe they are announcing our attack, Colonel Hjortt," said the anathema, his ghoulish face so pale it could be seen even on this Gate-black morning.

"That was one of our horns, not one of theirs," said Domingo. "Think I don't know the difference? Some dunce in the ranks is giving away our position!"

Another Imperial horn sounded, this time from the left flank instead of the right, and before Domingo could mount a proper splutter the damned cavalry issued a toot of their own from the vanguard. What was the point in sneaking up under cover of darkness if you blew your fucking horns the whole way? Was this the kind of cocksure madness Efrain had cultivated among the ranks? If so, good riddance to bad command.

"Perhaps the officers mean to alert the Myurans to the attack?" said Brother Wan.

"What attack? There is no attack, not until we can see something—oof!" A bump in the murky morning punctuated Domingo's point with bone tremors and a heaving stomach. "Stop the cart, Wan, this is more than close enough—I said take us down a bit, do you know what a bit means? At this rate dawn will find us in the bloody valley, bumping up against the rear, and I need to be able to survey the full field."

"I wouldn't have you miss that," said Brother Wan, tugging the mare to a stop with malicious abruptness. "No, I want us both to be able to see everything."

If only Domingo's body could be mended by willpower alone, he would have leaped from his bower in the wagon bed and punched Wan in his lipless mouth, and not stopped until his knuckles were full of splinters from the anathema's wooden teeth. If only, if only... Domingo was even more on edge than he usually was at the start of an encounter. He already regretted his decision to employ the Black Pope's weapon, though so far all he had seen was a disappointingly mundane prayer performed over his regiment while the witchborn clerics walked down the lines, dabbing oil on their foreheads. After it was all done and they started moving out he'd asked Shea if she'd felt anything during the ritual, and she said she'd felt bored, so apparently you got the same result from taking the oil as not. Wan had tried to talk Domingo into accepting the mark as well, but he had countered by pointing out that Wan himself had said only those on the battlefield would be at risk, and as Domingo didn't intend to set a single wagon wheel in the valley there was no need for him to find religion this late in life.

"It was wise to press on instead of waiting for the Thaoans," said Brother Wan, tying the reins on the wagon's unlit lantern post and stretching his thin arms. "What a pity it would have been, if Colonel

Waits had lived up to her name and insisted we postpone the attack until the queen sent her permission."

"Waits is a damn good woman, damn good," said Domingo, not much liking having his thoughts, however sensible, repeated back to him by this witchborn. "I appreciate her enough not to put her in a prickly position. And what did I tell you about sticking your nose into my nut, Brother Wan?"

"Do you wish to know a secret?" said Wan conspiratorially, twisting around and slinging his legs over the back of the riding board, so his dusty sandals brushed the edge of Domingo's padded command nest. "It's something I've never told anyone, not even Her Grace."

"Hmmm," said Domingo, not appreciating how chummy Wan had become ever since he'd come out of the horned wolf attack with a few bruises from a tent collapsing on top of him while Domingo was dashed near to pieces. Wan evidently took his grumbling for assent, as he usually did these days.

"You know why Her Grace entrusted this mission to me, and me alone, don't you?" The eagerness in the witchborn's voice was disquieting, but around them the black was finally giving way to grey, allowing Domingo to see his guards...Except even after suffering through the needles of pain in his neck to peer around, there was no sign of the six stout pureborn soldiers he had ordered to replace the two who had fallen during the wolf attack. He was alone with Wan on the dew-dusted hillside as light finally returned to the Star. "Besides my commitment to the Burnished Chain, and my ability to carry out this morning's ritual, there was another reason she blessed me with this sacred mission. Can you guess why?"

"Haven't the foggiest," said Domingo, cheering himself by focusing on the lack of mist this morning.

"It's because I share a...special relationship with Sister Portolés." At the mention of the queen's assassin Domingo spat over the side of the wagon. "Her Grace interviewed me after being apprised of my abilities by Cardinal Diamond, and of course my history with Portolés. It was then I was deemed essential for the job—the thought being that if we caught Portolés upon the road, I could plumb all her secrets, no matter how dearly she wished to keep them."

"This is not news," said Domingo, wondering just where this nonsense was going. He could see a bit farther down the hill now, and the silhouette of the Lark's Tongue was coming into view above the distant fires of the Cobalts, but he still couldn't make out the valley floor. He could hear distant shouts and the clang of metal, though, and it sent a warm thrum through him, just as that concerto does through every good colonel. "On further evaluation, take us closer, Wan, we're still higher up than I thought."

"I will take us down soon enough, Colonel," said Wan, and the casual refusal to follow an express order filled Domingo with a loathing quite unlike anything a civilian, or even a son, could ever inspire. "As I was saying, I entered into our pope's confidence in part because she assumed I might be able to dig into her mind anyway, and in part because she was sure I could look into Portolés's. Have you guessed my secret yet?"

"You're a bloody dull storyteller?" said Domingo, though they both knew that wasn't true, and the real reason was beginning to materialize; like the lightening landscape around them, even with large swaths missing a definite shape was taking form.

"The truth, Colonel Hjortt, is this..." Wan narrowed his eyes at Domingo, muttered something unintelligible, then grinned. "You blame yourself for Efrain's death. You regret not doing more to prepare him for the role he took on. You think that by punishing everyone else who played a part, however small, you can absolve yourself of the greater sin."

Domingo stared in horror at the anathema, then lurched forward to seize him by the cassock. He doubled over in pain without even getting upright, the jarring motion making him feel like a saw was slowly grinding across the back of his neck. Through gritted teeth, he managed, "I told you what I'd do if you looked."

Brother Wan clicked his horrible, inhuman mouth. "And that's my secret, Colonel Hjortt—I didn't. I couldn't, even if I wanted to.

No witchborn can, as far as I know. My secret is the secret of all anathemas, that we concoct excuses for the pureborn to treat us with respect or, failing that, caution. Like others in the Dens, I possess excellent intuition, something you and I share, but also empathy, in which most pureborn are deficient. No witchborn would ever disavow someone of the belief that we could peer into their innermost thoughts, for to do so would be to sacrifice one of our few advantages. But in truth, anathemas of my presumed powers are simply good listeners, good guessers, and good at altering our personalities to endear us to those we seek to convince—if you had seen me interact with Portolés, you wouldn't have recognized me, I don't think. Why do you think they say our abilities work best with those we know intimately?"

"But I felt you, I felt you rooting around in my skull—"

"What you felt was nothing more than your own paranoia, Colonel."

"Why are you telling me this, then?" said Domingo, wrenching himself back up into a seated position against the back of the wagon bed.

"You try it," said Wan. "Put yourself in my position, factor in everything you know about me, my desires. And *guess*."

Domingo had made the barber use the scabbard of his saber for the splint on his leg, but in this position there was no hope of drawing it. Meeting the anathema's too-friendly gaze, he said, "You don't think I'm going to survive long enough to tell anyone about it."

Brother Wan's bulbous eyes widened in mock amazement, and he raised his arms to the dawn. "Behold, an anathema in our midst! This witchborn mind-reader has passed itself off as Baron of Cockspar, but now reveals itself!"

"If you think you can take me, monster, I'm ready for you," said Domingo.

"Tut-tut," said Brother Wan, squirming back around on the riding board and untying the reins. "Maybe you don't have the sight after all. Or maybe your mind is enfeebled with age. Don't you remember that I wanted you to bear witness to the battle?"

The wagon jerked forward, and Domingo shuddered as another paroxysm passed through his spine. "Whatever mad schemes you've hatched, Wan, my regiment may surprise you yet, and their colonel most of all."

"I think you're the one in for a surprise," said Wan as he drove the wagon down the long hillside, the first light of day shining on the glittering masses of the Fifteenth, and the Cobalts who manned their pickets on the far end of the valley. "Before it's too late, are you sure you don't want to be anointed? It's not too late to receive the Chain's blessing."

"Think I'll manage without," said Domingo, offering a silent apology to his murdered son. For all his experience, for all his vigilance, he had fallen into the same trap as Efrain. Why had he ever allowed an agent of the Chain into his command tent? He had learned long ago to salvage wisdom from his failed efforts, but of all his unsuccessful plans, this was far and away the worst, and one he might never be able to learn from.

———

"This is the worst plan you've ever had, no mean feat," said Purna as Diggelby laid one jar after another on his tea table with all the pride of a new parent showing off his progeny.

"The best ones usually are," said Maroto, thumping the pot in his hand and provoking the finger-long centipede into striking the glass. "I'm telling you, Purna, I won't be any use like this—only cure is a bellyful of the worm that gnawed me. It'll make me better than new."

"Until you come off it again," said Purna. "How bad will it be next time, if you keep eating them?"

"Baaaaaad," said Diggelby. "I know from experience."

"Me, too," said Maroto. "I swear on my honor, Purna. This is the last time."

She gave him a look he knew all too well, and it would have broken his heart if it wasn't busy racing at the prospect of another worm. She wanted to believe him enough that for the moment she did. Or maybe he wanted her to believe enough that she was going along with it; the end result was all that mattered. "I'm going to see what's taking them. Hurry the hells up. We should've already rendezvoused at the command tent."

"Ack," said Diggelby, pulling a face as he chomped his worm and passed the box to Maroto. The bug-headed noble didn't even take his own advice; he'd told Maroto just the other night not to chew the things. Extracting one of the grubs that extruded from the piece of bamboo laid in the box, Maroto gulped it in one go, then had another for good measure. And a third; these were a lot smaller than the one Diggelby had given him before, so he had to make sure he took enough to overpower his hangover.

"You really should keep them in cemetery dirt," he said, passing the small box back over. "I didn't even know they could live anywhere else."

"Ah," said Diggelby, nodding with the air of a master imparting wisdom to a novice. "Graveworms require such soil, but these little fellows are only found in this rubbery bamboo that grows down in the Dominions, on the border between—"

"Diggelby," said Maroto, more focused than he had felt in memory, and not from ingesting the bugs. "Diggelby, what did you just feed me? A graveworm, right? Just some exotic breed?"

"Hmmm?" Diggelby's eyes were all pupil, and Maroto began to panic. The pasha was off his fucking gourd on grubs. "Oh no. Nothing like a graveworm. Bamboo worms are…" He grinned, showing teeth dripping with white goo. "Unique."

"Unique *how*?" asked Maroto, having no idea if his pounding heart and sweaty brow stemmed from the insects in his belly or his anxiety at what they might do. He could have just slit his own throat.

"Dreamy," said Diggelby, waving his hand back and forth and giggling at the tracers they left hanging in the air. Wait, what? Ancestors watch over him, Maroto was already starting to hallucinate. "Something to help you sleep, and see such sights as—"

"Diggelby, you dumb moron, I said graveworms, *graveworms*!"

"No," said Diggelby, sounding completely sober as he leaned forward and pointed at Maroto. "You said you needed another of the worms I fed you last night. Last night I gave you one of these, because you'd spent all day puking and I knew you'd never sleep through the night without it. The graveworm was *two* nights ago, so don't blame me if you can't communicate with language like most upright persons."

"Why would I want to take something to sleep right before a battle!"

"Because when you take a hit off of this guy, you'll be more awake than you've ever been in your life, and still get to see all the dream stuff from the bamboo worms." Diggelby held up an empty wine bottle with an enormous scorpion clicking angrily in the base. "I put him in when he was tiny, and he's grown too big to get out. I don't know what I'll do when his stinger won't fit through the neck." Diggelby inserted his pinky into the opening, and before he'd wiggled it twice the monstrous arachnid jumped clear up the side of the bottle, burying its stinger in the fingertip. Diggelby yanked it out with a yelp, his pale pinky turning as blue as the bands on the scorpion's back. "You have to be quick about it, or your finger will swell and you'll never get it out."

There was a time when Maroto would have tried to stick his tongue down the neck of the bottle to get the most out of the experience, but those days were mercifully gone. Well, not so gone, then, considering he was starting to feel a torpor in his limbs from the whatsit worms, and sleeping this one out was starting to sound pretty capital, as Diggelby would say...The dreams of last night were returning to him now, stranger dreams than any he'd ever lived, and going back to that place would be so nice...

No. He had oaths to keep, and grabbed the bottle from Diggelby. Tried to, anyway, but his numb arm just knocked it out of his friend's hand, and it shattered open on a steel spike protruding from the shield at Maroto's feet. There was a desperate moment where nobody moved, and then everyone moved at once. The scorpion scuttled out from the shards of glass, and Maroto managed to get a sandaled foot in its path just as Diggelby lunged forward to grab at it, inadvertently headbutting Maroto in the stomach. Bless the gods of the undergrowth, for the scorpion planted its stinger deep in Maroto's ankle before scurrying across the tent and into the heap of Diggelby's bedding.

"I'll find *you* later," Diggelby called after it in a come-hither voice. "He got you, didn't he?"

"Uh," said Maroto, vibrating all over. It felt like he had injected magma into his ankle, the hit unlike any scorpion he'd ever sampled. He definitely wasn't drowsy anymore, his thoughts coming faster than he could voice them: "WhatkindoffuckingscorpionisthatDiggelby?"

"I don't know the Classical Immaculate name for the species," said Diggelby thoughtfully. "I just call it *that brute I found in my slipper back in the Panteran Wastes.*"

Maroto stared at Diggelby, who seemed to be swelling like a puffer fish, ripples extending down his fleshy neck and across his padded caftan. He had just dosed Maroto with two separate exotic bugs, neither of which even an inveterate connoisseur of his experience had tried before, and one of which was presumably unknown outside of the wilds. They were both still giggling when Purna shoved her melting face into the tent and told them to move their arses. Snatching up the two heaviest shields in Diggelby's collection, Maroto glided after her. He had promises to keep, even though breaking them always came so much easier.

CHAPTER
24

So much for her esteemed personal guard. With first light showing but not a one of Tapai Purna's crew, Ji-hyeon mounted her charger and gave a final blow of her horn. With Keun-ju, Fennec, Choi, and Chevaleresse Sasamaso leading the dozen mounted knights that made up her bodyguard, she cantered through the camp, waving her flag-spear and picking up a wake of foot soldiers as she rode down the base of the Lark's Tongue, toward the bloody battle at its foot. Dark as it remained with the sun still hidden beyond the foothills, Ji-hyeon was pleased her army had been ready to meet their attackers, and begrudgingly impressed by the initiative of the Fifteenth Regiment.

The Crimson cavalry had attempted to crash through the pickets and pikers stationed just where the incline steepened, but before they'd reached the massed infantry more horns had sounded and the Cobalts responded in kind. Faaris Kimaera was an old sellsword Fennec had scared up in Nux Vomica, and the master horseman had led the motley Cobalt cavalry down from the southern ridge to intercept the Crimson riders. When the Imperials veered across the edge of the valley to meet them, Chevaleresse Singh's dragoons had swept down from the northern ridge, striking the Crimson cavalry across the rear flank. Beset on two sides by riders and with the Cobalt pikers jabbing at them from the slope above them, the Crimson cavalry nevertheless held their own. They defended their sides, repelling the Cobalts from penetrating their troop, and pushed hard up the hill, meeting rebel polearms with heavy lances and crushing the tightly packed defenders under hoof as they broke through the front lines. Behind them, the Crimson foot were charging fast, a wave of blood crossing the valley to wash up the base of the Lark's Tongue.

Avoiding the press of her main infantry, where she'd do more harm than good trying to break through and the soldiers jogging after her would be wasted, Ji-hyeon led her retinue and the several hundred infantry who had followed them from camp around to the north, where their fellows were thinner on the ground. Mostly deaf from the cacophony of the battle before she even joined it, she reached Kimaera's cavalry and skirted their edge, meaning to bolster their defenses from the charging red infantry while the Cobalt riders drove inward to meet Singh's contingent, squeezing the Crimson cavalry between them. Hoisting her spear aloft and giving the flag a final wave, Ji-hyeon set the weapon and spurred her charger into the oncoming horde, Choi on her left with an enormous crescent-bladed moon-spear and Keun-ju on the right with a long, tasseled trident. Fennec seemed to have fallen behind with Kimaera's cavalry, but her mounted knights and the crowd of panting foot soldiers still trotted behind them. Fellwing circled low over Ji-hyeon, and she tried not to be reminded of a vulture as her speeding horse delivered her to the fiercest battle of her life.

Arrows sped back and forth on either side of her, and then Ji-hyeon's charger crashed into the raging red sea. Her flag-spear punched through the breastplate of a bellowing woman in the front, and Ji-hyeon dropped the weapon just in time to avoid having her arm wrenched out of joint as the horse carried her deeper into the enemy infantry. She jerked the reins to wheel back out of the horde, but the Imperials were packed too tight all around her, with more pushing in all the time. Worse still, the Cobalt soldiers she had intended to lead into the fray had fallen behind, and now the front line was behind her. She had used this maneuver half a dozen times, but never driven so deep into the enemy. Shit.

Pikes jabbed at her, swords scraped across her horse's chainmail, bounced off her greaves. She fumbled her twin long swords from their scabbard, nearly dropping one as an arrow ricocheted off the side of her helm. Adept at riding as she'd become since leaving Hwabun, wielding a sword in each hand while surrounded by a furious armed and armored mob didn't allow for elegance, or much control of her charger. The warhorse was a better steed than Ji-hyeon was a rider, fortunately, his controlled bucking and kicking preventing her from being dragged down by the Imperials.

For now, anyway, the Crimson soldiers were throwing themselves at her, eyes wide under their pot helms and mouths flecked with froth as they careened at her, heedless of her horse's hooves or her steel blades. They were clearly mad with rage, behaving less like trained soldiers and more like fire ants swarming their prey. In the past her legendary appearance had instilled palpable fear in her foes, but here the soldiers betrayed no trace of anything resembling recognition or even understandable wariness, only a fury that was all the more disturbing for its presence on virtually every face. A man with skin as red as his tabard kept spitting and foaming after her sword jabbed through his throat, as though hate alone might keep him alive.

Two more men seized her leg on the other side, and as she swung around to beat them back, her faceplate was misted with blood as Choi's moon-spear hacked one of their heads off and embedded in the neck of the other. Still he clung to her greaves, trying to pull her down, and with a slash of a sword she completed the job Choi had started. Arms already sore, she spurred her horse's left flank, and the well-trained animal angled them back around as best he could in the tumult. Yet as he turned and Ji-hyeon saw Choi's spear blade fanning through the air to beat the red soldiers back, she realized in the press she had no idea which way they had come. This was exactly what Fennec had tried to warn her about; she'd done a very, very stupid thing, and was on the verge of panic when a chirp from Fellwing caused her to look up, beyond the chaos, and see the Lark's Tongue off to her left.

"Fall back!" she cried, but even as she gave the order she realized she couldn't hear her own voice over the raging battle, couldn't see Keun-ju or Chevaleresse Sasamaso or any of her other knights, only the turbulent waves of red curling with flashing steel and, impossibly distant, the ragged blue line of her infantry. A pike jabbed up, glancing off the snout of her helm, a sword pierced her charger's armor, causing him to rear up violently and nearly dislodge her, and Ji-hyeon cursed herself for the biggest fool to ever jump headfirst into hell.

———

By the time Zosia slid back down into camp, corralled the hundred confused foot soldiers Ji-hyeon had given her to command, and had them tap a like number of archers from the formation firing down into the valley, the Cobalts holding the front already looked to be in some serious shit. They'd be in a far riper mess if she didn't get things in hand on their rear, however, which she had to repeat three times to the lieutenant commanding the archers before the woman would let her take off with a hundred sorely needed shooters. Then it was a race back up the hill, through camp, keeping her eye on the exposed hump that marked where a small plateau jutted out of the Lark's Tongue five hundred feet farther up the mountainside. Any moment she expected to see the first Crimson soldiers crest it and come charging down the steep slope into camp, but nothing stirred among the rocks and cacti. The Lark's Tongue was bare to the hump and nearly bald from there to the summit, with only a few low bands of the pine that swathed the surrounding mountains, but she never would have scrambled high enough to spot the flashes of metal coming around the mountain's shoulder as the sun finally rose if Choplicker hadn't made such a stink about it.

There was nothing beyond the front of the range here but a lot of rough country, and ever since the Fifteenth had left the road fifteen miles south to follow the Cobalts' trail they'd been monitored by scouts, who'd reported no contingents splitting off to flank them. That meant the ambush had been set into motion before they even came down from the mountains, which bespoke a degree of tactical sophistication Zosia never would have credited to Efrain Hjortt—the boy must be taking things a lot more seriously since she'd cut his thumbs off. He couldn't have spared a large force for such a risky

course through the trackless wilds, but it might have been enough
to cripple the Cobalts, if Zosia wasn't there to help. She knew a clas-
sic wolf trap maneuver when she saw one, though she'd always led
the Imperials into them instead of building the gambit around an
existing camp; a lot could go wrong if you didn't already have both
units in position to crush the enemy between them, as she hoped to
demonstrate by taking that defensible plateau first and firing on the
Imperials as they came scrambling down from the pass above.

As they reached the upper edge of camp, the runner she'd sent to
alert Ji-hyeon of the ambush came huffing around a tent and waved
her down. He didn't look like he had good news.

"Let me guess," Zosia called, "our fearless general's decided to lead
from the front?"

"Uh-huh," panted the runner. "But I found these two, looking
confused, in front of the command tent, so I brought 'em, 'cause you
said bring any able hands."

The tallest figure Zosia had ever seen caught up to the runner,
looking a sight less winded. Zosia grinned up at them, and called
out in the Flintland tongue, "Well, you don't get more able than four
hands on two legs, do you?"

"Uh," said Sullen, not meeting Zosia's gaze. "It's you."

"Manners, laddie," said old man Ruthless, resting his hands on his
grandson's bulb of hair like it was a pulpit for his oration. "Anyone to
lay out my son the way she did is worth a nod, if not a drink. What
shall we call you, madam, since we've not been formally introduced?
On the road we heard a lot of titles, so let's see, is it Cold Cobalt
Zosia, Forsook Queen, Captain of Cobalts and Banshee of Blades,
First Among—"

"Zosia is fine," she said, seeing where Maroto had inherited his
love for the sound of his own voice. "I'll just call you Ruthless and
Sullen, since I hear those are your names. Fair?"

"More than," said Ruthless.

"What..." Sullen was staring at Choplicker, who'd come over and
rubbed his head against the man's leg. "What's your devil's name?"

"A devil's true name is a powerful thing, Sullen." A few concerned murmurs came from behind Zosia, but she didn't really mind his outing the fiend—if she didn't get to enjoy anonymity anymore, neither should her devil. "I just call him Choplicker."

"Huh," said Sullen, scratching behind the monster's ear to an appreciative yowl.

"I'm more concerned with mortal affairs than my grandson," said Ruthless. "Your errand boy said swords were needed to meet a pack of Crimson cowards stealing down the hill, that the shape of it?"

"Fa," said Sullen quietly, looking up from Choplicker but still keeping his eyes off Zosia. "We're supposed to fight with Uncle, help out Ji…General Ji-hyeon."

"And they weren't where they said they'd be," said Ruthless, "and the lady wants further proof against cowardice. What're you moaning about?"

"It's a big battle, Sullen," said Zosia. "You'll do more good for your uncle and friends by thwarting an attack on their rear than you will by wandering out into the field, hoping to find two fighters amidst twenty thousand."

"That many?" said Ruthless gleefully. "Oh, this ought to be a fine sendoff!"

"Yeah, all right." Sullen looked bashful as a virgin asked to dance by the most notorious rake in the room, and it gave Zosia a petty pleasure to see him squirm. Whatever Maroto thought about his motivations, it was plain to Zosia the boy either wanted her dead or in bed, or maybe he didn't even know which he wanted.

"I'm trusting you to watch my back, Sullen," she said, unable to resist, and that finally did it—he looked her in the eyes, and she saw the last thing she'd expect from a hard-looking Horned Wolf: he was scared of her.

"Yeah. All right."

"*Yeah, all right,*" his grandfather mimicked, and, reaching behind the boy's head, he pulled out one of the crazy-looking knives certain Flintland tribes used to throw at one another. "We've snapped and snarled enough, now let's put our teeth to some use!"

"Up we go, then," said Zosia. Raising her voice to address the archers and foot assembled behind her, she shouted, "I'll whittle a pipe for the first one of you to draw Crimson blood!"

A handful of huzzahs, and whole lot of confused stares. What was the Star coming to?

"Or a bottle of the best booze in camp, your choice!" That got a proper showing out of the ignorant blackguards, and Zosia set off up the escarpment, trying not to be too annoyed that the one skill she took actual pride in commanded such little regard. Oh well, a bottle was a lot easier to procure than briar and a lot less work once she had it; her hands would be busy enough in the days to come.

———

First Sullen and Da were a no-show at Diggelby's tent, and when Purna got tired of waiting and dragged the Moochers to the command tent they found Ji-hyeon had left without them. Suggestions that they stop off for another round were shot down by Purna, who had her meanest face on. Maroto didn't see what the rush was, considering that the swirling patterns of blue and red that flowed across the valley floor didn't show any signs of fading. Around that time, though, Maroto stopped being able to hear anything Purna or the others said, his one good ear filled with the grinding of insects beneath the earth, graveworms stirring from here to the far valley, rising to the surface to feed...

Purna led them down, but Maroto couldn't look at her anymore, couldn't look at Diggelby or Hassan or Din, because when he did he saw right through the garish makeup and the skin beneath it, saw all the way to their yammering skulls. He put all his attention on Prince, because Diggelby's lapdog kept looking up at him with this weird little smile as he trotted along beside the crew, and while he didn't look much like a dog anymore, at least he didn't look like a walking corpse with its face all chewed away by scavengers, and by Old Black's loose tooth, Maroto had never had a sting trip him out this bad. He was bugging *balls*.

"Will you stop!" Purna said. Maroto looked up from Prince, relieved to find the grinding riot in his ear had quieted, replaced by the good old-fashioned ruckus of countless people murdering each other. "Thank you."

"Eh?" But the sound returned as soon as he said it, and Purna's skull snapped at him again, a blackened skeletal finger pointing to her jawbone. "Oh."

Maroto stopped grinding his teeth, and the sound stopped, too. Funny how that worked. He closed his eyes, told himself when he opened them again the world would be back to normal. He gave it a go, and saw they'd come down the hill and were less than a hundred paces from the back of the press, bodies fucking everywhere, people wandering around them holding their limbs and where their limbs used to be and weeping and dying and sometimes both, blood welling out of the very earth, and Purna popped him in the cheek, like that ever worked except in the songs.

"Maroto!" The skull under the horned wolf hood sounded just like Purna.

"That'sdefinitelyme," he said, hoping he sounded convincing.

"Some people saw her ride in around there, but it's going to be a mess just getting through our people to the front—you wait right here until we come back with Ji-hyeon, all right? *Don't. Move.*"

Purna was gesturing off into the cloud of whizzing weapons and splattering gore that floated in front of them. As he squinted, it was like his confused brain thought he was already in the mix, because things started getting all precise the way they did when he was in real trouble, the incoherent blur of the battle coalescing into a hundred thousand crystal clear images: An ax cleaving an arm off. A woman bringing a shield up too slow to intercept the spear that was going to puncture her heart. A horse brained with a mace. The rider swinging his sword into another man before his horse even knew it was dead.

"Right, good. *Stay.* If you have to move, go back to the tent," said Purna, turning away, but before she'd taken a step an arrow launched from two hundred yards deep in the melee came hurtling down to skewer her face. Well, hurtling was selling the song a little hard; it just kind of drifted down, like it didn't have a care in the world, leaving a shimmering trail in the dawn sky, and so Maroto wasn't in a hurry, either; he just bumped past Hassan, apologized for the slight, and then long-stepped up beside Purna, raising one of his shields to neatly catch the arrow before it killed her. The point shivered on his side of the shield, having penetrated both steel and wood just above his sweaty grip. Could've planned that better; an inch lower and it would've gone right through his hand! He'd have to be more careful.

The human eyes in Purna's skull face wobbled at him, Hassan gasped in belated shock, and Din said, "Fallen Mother's mercy, I've never seen a mortal move like that."

"I'maVillainyeahdidn'tgetmyreputationleadingnoguidedtoursof thePanteranfuckingWastes," said Maroto, and Diggelby laughed and laughed, swooping Prince up in one arm and waving his crystalline cutlass around in the other like this one actor Maroto had run with who had this great mad pirate character he'd play, and Purna patted Maroto on the shoulder and sounded a little freaked out when she thanked him but didn't try to make him stay behind anymore, and they all started running to some quarter of the world-encompassing battle that was supposedly better than the rest of it. Leave it to the nobles to know where the best party is happening.

"Question," Maroto hissed back at Diggelby as they wove through the throng, not wanting to alarm the others. "We'rethebluesandthey're theredsyeah?"

Diggelby was still laughing when another arrow arced down from the clear morning sky, too fast for even Maroto to stop, an evil black tracer wavering in the air behind it, and it was a queer thing, to be looking at a laughing friend and know they were dead even before they were, to see them acting alive and hale but know they were a ghost and just didn't realize it yet. Yet instead of spitting the fop's lace-ruffled neck, the arrow was nudged over at the last moment by a breeze, the missile hitting some poor bastard behind them, snuffing out some stranger's friend instead of his. Maroto started laughing right along with Diggelby, because when you got right down to it, there wasn't anything more hilariously random than war.

———

Sullen had fought against the tide of the camp, a flood of eager, frightened, and resigned faces flashing past him as he made for his uncle's tent. It was empty, and when nobody returned after a few minutes he hustled Grandfather over to Ji-hyeon's tent, but he'd just missed them, too. It seemed smartest to wait there until someone came to tell him what to do, even with Grandfather harassing him to just run down the hill with the rest of the Cobalts and see what they could find at the bottom. The truth was, Sullen couldn't bear the thought of his leaving the command tent only for Ji-hyeon or maybe Uncle Maroto to wander over just after they'd left, so he made Grandfather promise to wait ten minutes, since the clashing armies in the valley wouldn't be going anywhere.

And once again, he should have listened to his grandfather, because the sweaty guy who had run up, poked his head in the tent, and then told Sullen to follow him back to some fight that was happening ended up delivering him right to Zosia. And now he'd gone and told her he'd watch her back, so there was another fool thing he'd blundered into—after giving his word, he wouldn't feel right carrying out the will of the Faceless Mistress. Not today, anyway. So that was maybe a good thing, gave him one less thing to worry about…Unless she'd somehow figured out he'd been sent to do her mischief, and meant to use the confusion of battle to move on him before he could move on her. Unless that.

"You watching that back?" whispered Grandfather as Sullen scrambled up the steep, grit-slippery slope. Above them, the ridge-line they'd called a "hump" poked out like the mountain's potbelly, but they still had a climb ahead of them to reach it. Zosia was a few lengths ahead of them, and yeah, being real with himself, he had been watching her back a bit; hard not to, from this angle, leather britches taut against her posterior.

"Shut it, Fa," said Sullen, but that must have answered the old man's question well enough, because he brayed with laughter.

Glancing back, Sullen promptly stubbed his toe and went down on one knee, gashing it open on a shelf of rock. He barely noticed, gawping out at the valley beyond the camp. Big a host as the Cobalt Company had seemed, the Imperials were bigger by half, at least— he'd only seen glimpses of the Crimson army after he and Grand- father had met Ji-hyeon in the mountains, when the Cobalts would get a vantage point to look back on their pursuers, and those peeks had barely hinted at their true mass. The two armies had collided right at the base of the mountain, stirring up dust, and while no ground seemed to have been given yet, the mass of red-dressed sol- diers stretched back and back from the front, blanketing the valley clear to the next hill.

Impressive a sight as it all was, what had put the slack in his chin was the shadow following fast behind the Imperials, a shadow that persisted even when the slowly rising sun was obscured by plumes of dust. Devils. The incorporeal ones that Ji-hyeon called "spirits," but still, a dire host of them, and Sullen prayed to Old Black and Boldstrut that they were merely scavengers looking for an easy meal. The only time he had seen so many swarm at once was when the Faceless Mistress had used them as her doorway into the world of mortals, and a dreadful thought slapped his heart into a gallop: what if she had come for retribution, to punish Sullen for siding with Zosia instead of carrying out her desire? They didn't appear to be congeal- ing together, though, so perhaps it wasn't as bad as that...

A tumult from just below reminded him of his immediate con- cerns, and he saw that the foot soldiers and archers were clumping up around and beneath him on the rock- and cactus-spined slope, shiny faces staring anxiously up at him...no, past him, to the lip of the escarpment that now obscured the rest of the mountain. Zosia had also paused her climb, flat on her stomach just below the summit, her devil slinking sideways along the crest of the scarp with a decidedly uncanine grace. Setting his boots in the slippery rock dust, Sullen hauled himself up beside her as she turned back to the trailing troops and put a finger to her lips before waving them up.

"They're here," she whispered to Sullen and Grandfather, eyes shining like her hair in the cold autumn sunlight. "Be on top of us any moment. Their archers catch us here, we're all dead. You ready?"

"Um," said Sullen, trying to think something nice, since it might be the last thing he thought. He tried to picture's Ji-hyeon's sly smile, but she melted into the Faceless Mistress. "Yeah. Okay."

Below them, one of their soldiers slipped, dislodged a stone, and it bounced down to camp, clattering all the way. Nothing stirred above them, most of their soldiers still a hard minute's climb from the top, minimum.

"You ready to see your ancestors, Fa?" Sullen whispered over his shoulder as Zosia nocked an arrow in her bow, her hammer strapped to her back.

"Hells no!" muttered Grandfather. "So make sure you keep that worthless melon of yours between me and the arrows—you're the only protection I got."

"Horned Wolves don't wear armor, Fa," said Sullen, and, glimpsing their shadow on the slope above, he saw that the old man had a sun-knife in each hand.

"Horned Wolves? In case you ain't noticed, boy, you and me been Possum People for well on twelve thaws—now move that pouch, boy, and let's show these red dogs how it's done!"

———

When charging any hill there's a dreadful uncertainty of where and when the curve of the earth will reveal you to those at a higher vantage. The operative word being "vantage"; the high ground was contested for good reason. As she rose slowly from her crouch, bow ready, what had seemed like such a sharp edge above her now became a gentle curve, the tops of a few pines coming into sight as she rose. Sullen stayed lower, taking those last few uncertain steps up to where the ground leveled off, his grandfather craning his neck for a peek from his own personal high ground.

There, across the grass and rocks of the plateau, was a shaded stand of pine, and Zosia let out her breath, relaxed her bowstring. Despite Choplicker's wariness, there were no Imperials. Yet.

She waved her troops up, and at her signal a shout came from the trees, followed by a half dozen arrows—Sullen had already broken into a zigzagging charge and they whipped past him; the one that would have struck Zosia's leg kicked up dirt at her feet thanks to Choplicker. Zosia steadied herself, drew, and fired on one of the silhouettes that had stepped out from the cover of the trees. It was easy to play hard with a devil minding your interest, but Sullen and his grandfather didn't seem to miss the advantage, both men howling as they quickly crossed the narrow plateau.

"Up and fire, up and fire!" cried Zosia, Choplicker whining as he ambled in front of her to take any more arrows that might come her way. A few more of them did as Zosia's troops stormed the hump, but went wide with a bark from Choplicker. One struck a young boy from Rawonam who had told Zosia he'd brought his own hunting bow when enlisting with the Cobalts. He died screaming on the ground as his comrades spread out on the ridge and drew beads on the pack of Imperials hiding in the dozen stunted pines that curtained the back of the plateau.

Their task was made infinitely harder by Sullen, who ran ahead, crashed into the pines, and fell among the Imperial archers like a panther that had been caged too long, only to be released into a paddock of red deer. A panther with a furious, armed monkey riding its back. The boy's spear was a wet, ruddy blur between the trees, and from his back the old man hurled a giant, multibladed knife at the startled archers. The two men resembled one of the Ugrakari gods Zosia had seen on the old headwoman's shrine in Blodtørst, a hulking, four-armed scourge of the iniquitous.

Blades alone rarely prevailed in a bowfight, though, and even as Zosia's arrow struck the crotch of one Imperial, another dozen arrows flew from her Cobalts, making a choice fucking mess of what would otherwise be a rather scenic grove. The situation managed, she hustled across the plateau, motioning her soldiers after her.

Sullen and his grandfather looked bewildered to be alive and unharmed as the last archer writhed screaming on the ground, a sunknife in her stomach, and Sullen finished her with his spear before retrieving the old man's throwing weapon and passing it up to him.

The wind rustled through the pines as she stepped into the copse, and all of a sudden Zosia remembered the musty smell of Leib's hair when that awful Azgarothian colonel had plunked his head down on the table where they had eaten nigh every meal for twenty years, and she stumbled, steadied herself against a tree. She gagged, and swatted Choplicker away as he pranced around her feet, merry as one of Maroto's fop friends.

Fast and hard as it had come, the dizzying sense of déjà vu passed. Glancing up to see one of her archers slit the throat of the wailing kid whose groin she'd shot, she straightened up from the tree, shook out her limbs, spit. It wasn't nice, it wasn't clean, but it had to be done. The bright-eyed young Imperials who had helped that asshole Hjortt murder her husband and village probably hadn't shed any tears, and neither would she. If someone was worth hanging her head over, it was Pao Cowherd, the boy Choplicker had dragged all the way up the mountains over Kypck just to die by her fire, not these well-armed scum.

"Thanks!" said Sullen, seeming relieved. Well, why shouldn't he be? He was alive. "That's one we owe you."

"My pleasure," said Zosia, trying to mean it.

"I know you didn't come all the way up here to stick a handful of dastards," said the bloodied old man. He looked like a vampire out of the songs, clinging to his victim. "So where's the hunt?"

"Huh." Zosia straightened up, trying to get it together. There were people here who were depending on her to keep them safe. If that wasn't the biggest joke of all... "See the crest on that one's tabard? A one-handed man with a greatsword is the seal of Myura. Your uncle's scouting party saw over two thousand of them in the mountains, and then saw their banners again when they brought the horned wolves down on the Imperial camp."

"I haven't heard that song!" said Ruthless. "Maroto did *what* with horned wolves?"

"Let him tell it," said Zosia. "Later. This is just a few of 'em, is the point, scouts sent ahead to secure the hump. Which means—"

"Yoo-hoo!" a high voice came down the mountain, and everyone ate dirt save Zosia, who recognized the greeting, and Sullen, who stepped behind a tree. Following the voice, Zosia saw that beyond the trees the Lark's Tongue resumed its steep grade up to another, higher hump, and beyond that, the peak. There was a cluster of red shapes on the upper ridge, but as she watched they began marching down the faint hunting trail that linked the two plateaus.

"It's all right," Zosia called to her troops, then to her whining, nervous devil added, "I think."

As the Cobalts watched them with ready bows, the Myuran regiment came down in single file from the upper hump, and even when they slipped and fell on the steep descent not a one removed hands from head. Zosia counted just shy of three hundred surrendered Imperials, and as the first shivering Myuran prisoner reached the pines, a lumbering figure took up the rear of the train.

"Line 'em up on the edge of the scarp back there," Zosia told her perplexed soldiers. "If they run down to camp, shoot 'em. Anyone without a bow waits here and escorts prisoners over to the archers."

"Is that..." Sullen didn't look so relieved anymore.

"Oi, that's him," said his grandfather, spitting over Sullen's shoulder. "If it's no harm to you, Zosia, we'll be headed back down to the real fight now."

"Sure. I don't like him much, either," said Zosia. "Good thing the Imperials weren't the only ones to cozy onto the notion of an ambush from the rear, or we'd have been in real trouble. I've learned every devil has its uses."

Ruthless nodded his agreement at that as his grandson carried him off, but the look Sullen gave her over his shoulder left a lot open to interpretation. Sometime soon she'd have to pry him open, one way or another, and see if the boy held a pearl for her, or something less pleasant.

"The wolves didn't wait for me?" said Hoartrap as he brought his last prisoner in, the Myurans looking ecstatic to be handed off to hard-bitten enemy soldiers. "Well, I'll catch up with them another time."

"A few thousand Myurans against one old greasebag?" said Zosia, ambling back across the saddle with her miserable devil, the misery-inducing sorcerer, and the final haunted-looking Imperial, a young man with iron on his chest but none in his step. "What happened to the rest?"

"I'm innocent, I swear!" said Hoartrap, the stumbling prisoner shuddering at this but not turning to refute the claim. "They lost most of their party getting this far; treacherous river crossings, sheer passes, and something involving an avalanche, is that right, Wheatley?"

The captured officer nodded curtly.

"I may have had a hand in the last, I admit it," Hoartrap stage-whispered loud enough for Wheatley to hear. Zosia rolled her eyes—if he was claiming responsibility, then he probably hadn't been involved. "We *did* lose a few coming around that last pass, to the saddle above, but I'm sure Cold Zosia will be fair in her dealings with the surrendered Myuran regiment."

This finally got Wheatley to look back at them. She hadn't thought it possible for him to look more frightened, but there it was. "You... you're her?"

"Hjortt tell you about me?" Zosia asked.

He nodded once, eyes growing even bigger.

"Good," said Zosia, the last traces of her temporary weakness flushed out in one heaving sigh of relief that Ji-hyeon's intelligence had been correct and Colonel Hjortt still led the Fifteenth. She quickened her step, eager to get down to the main event now. Hoartrap picked up the pace, too, forcing Wheatley to step lively indeed as they came up to the edge of the plateau where the rest of the prisoners sat, still cupping their heads in their hands.

"If I could ask one thing—" began Wheatley, but Zosia cut him off, looking out over the Cobalt camp and the battlefield beyond.

"You cannot. I'm a busy woman, and I'm sure Hjortt cautioned you against getting on my bad side."

"That's...interesting," said Hoartrap, and, glancing over at him,

Zosia was unhappy to see that he was as confounded by the sight as she was, sausagey fingers drumming on his lips.

"Interesting?" Zosia looked back to the battlefield. The ragged front line still held, if only by a few sturdy threads, but beyond it, in the massed Crimson infantry, the soldiers were aflutter with activity. Weird activity. It almost looked like they were... "That's really not your doing?"

"I'd be a lot happier if it were. We'd better get down there and pull our people back," said Hoartrap, a rare tremble of anxiety in his voice as he started down the mountain. "Or things will get a lot *more* interesting very soon. And not the good kind of interesting, like you want."

In another rare turn, Choplicker's mood improved immediately, despite the presence of the hated sorcerer. Of the two portents, Zosia wasn't sure which was more disquieting, and, ordering her people to bring the prisoners back to camp, she hurried down to see just what in all the fucking hells was happening out there.

CHAPTER
25

Such language!" Wan tsk-tsked in Domingo's ear. After delivering them to a small grassy hump partway down the last foothill before the Lark's Tongue, Wan had unhitched the horse to graze and crawled back into the wagon bed beside Domingo, so they lay shoulder to shoulder against the back of the cart, overlooking the valley. There was supposed to be a battle taking place, but instead...instead there was all *this*.

Domingo lowered the heavy hawkglass, hand shaking, mouth dry, lame arm and shattered leg forgotten. His thumb traced the etching of his son's name on the silver band set in the brass instrument, and most of the fight left him then. Until he'd seen the battlefield he'd held out hope of Shea or some other officer riding back to report, of managing to draw his saber despite his awkward position sprawled out in the back of the wagon, of anything...But the anathema had outfoxed and outfenced him at every juncture, and not a one of the Azgarothians he had brought to this place was going to come rescue him, because they were all too busy losing their minds and dying in droves.

"I'll tell you one last secret, Colonel," Wan said, throwing his spindly arm around Hjortt and giving him a comradely squeeze. "I had my doubts anything would happen. Or it would go halfway, and then...poof, nothing. That smoke, though, you can see that even without your glass, that means the ritual is proceeding just like Her Grace said it would."

"This...*this* is the pope's weapon?" Domingo tried to remember the particulars of the ceremony he had done his devil's best to ignore while it was taking place. "All that chanting about sacrifice, the Fallen Mother's kingdom ascendant...You fucking poisoned my people."

"Poisoned them? We *saved* them, Domingo—I may have told a fib or two to convince you to go ahead with the ritual, but I spoke true when I said it was the highest honor to be marked by the Fallen Mother. They will be the martyrs who end this war."

"I...I did this to them. I let you..." Domingo could say no more, his tongue as heavy as his heart. His soldiers had trusted him, and he had doomed them all.

"You did the right thing," said Wan, in the same patronizing *good-for-you* tone Domingo's wife had used when Efrain so much as pissed in the right pot. "Even after you agreed to take me and the oil along, there was initially some concern that you would raise...*secular objections* to the anointment of your soldiers, which was why I proposed using it as a poison for their blades instead. It seemed much more in line with your pragmatically disciplined bloodlust. I didn't know how to proceed when you declined both a blessing and a poison, but then those rebels brought their monsters down onto your smug shoulders, and a wolf's tongue convinced you of what my own could not."

"You smeared the same shit on my regiment's foreheads as you did on their weapons?" Domingo was still shaking, but no longer from fear and revulsion at what was happening to his people, at what they were doing to each other, or to see the earth smoking beneath the feet of his soldiers. He trembled because he had never wanted to kill anyone or anything as much as he wanted to kill the anathema that reclined beside him.

"Actually, most of it ended up on their brows, not their swords. We couldn't bring nearly enough of it for both, and if you can only consecrate one weapon, well...It's taken years to store up enough oil from the Chain's hives to make another go of it. The last time there wasn't enough, or something went wrong. I don't know. It was before my time, back when Shanatu was still pope, and a young one at that."

"Windhand," breathed Domingo, clenching the hawkglass in his fist.

"Oh, you were there?" Wan took his arm back from around Domingo's shoulder and sat up, all ears. "What was it like? Did it happen like this? What was different?"

"I wasn't there—it was the Fourth, out of Boleskine. But I heard stories," said Domingo, not afraid of dying, not afraid of much, but revolted to find the world was an even worse hell than he'd always thought. Soldiers he'd marched with for years were down there in that vale, and plenty of new blood that had flowed in during Efrain's short command, and now they were...

"*What* stories?" said Wan, desperate for it. Domingo sneered at his enemy, here at last some small victory he could claim. But then the anathema climbed on top of his legs like a child demanding a bedtime song from his parent, and the weight of even the slight monk on his broken leg caught Domingo's breath in his chest. "Quick about it, old man, I want to be able to watch when it happens. For all their gossip at the table before they sent me off, not even the pontiff and cardinals know for sure how it will transpire here, or what exactly happened at Windhand. We lost everyone there."

"Soldiers turning on one another," Domingo gasped through the pain in his leg. "Killing each other. Worse. Eating each other alive. Worse. Like...like they're doing out there."

"Oh," said Wan, disappointed. "Well, this time it's going to work—we have lit the beacons and prepared the offerings, and back in Diadem the Holy See will have worked stronger rites yet. She *will* bestow us with her bounty. The Day of Becoming is upon us, oh wretched doubter, and I'll even allow you to bear witness. She cares about you that much, Domingo—even after all your childish blasphemies, even though you refused her mark, you still get to be a martyr for the Burnished Chain. Saint or sinner, pureborn or anathema, the Fallen Mother loves us all!"

Despite her training, despite her youth, despite her skill, despite even her devil, Ji-hyeon was a dead woman, dead as her horse, dead as her bodyguards—the only time she found one of them in the churning flood of clashing metal was when she tripped over a familiar corpse. She could barely raise the one sword she'd managed to hold on to, and though Fellwing could eat well in such a place, the devil was exhausted, too, reeling drunkenly just above the melee. If not for whatever trick Hoartrap must have pulled to drive the Crimson soldiers mad she would have already fallen, but even with the wild-eyed infantry murdering one another as readily as they attacked her, there were too many of them.

The mob had thinned out substantially, but she was still surrounded by the enemy on all sides, and as she cut down one woman, a second looked up from where she squatted over a fallen comrade. Blood ran down this woman's chin, and from the gory chunk she clutched in her hand—Ji-hyeon staggered backward, realizing what the woman was doing but unable to accept it.

A hand knotted in the hair that flowed down from the back of her helm, yanking her off balance. She tried turning, stabbing behind her, but the hand held her too tight, and then something heavy slammed into the small of her back, popping links in her hauberk, a clump of her hair coming out by the roots as she fell facedown in the trodden turf. All her friends were gone, and if Fellwing could no longer protect her, that could only mean she had lost her devil, too... and it was entirely her fault.

She wanted to roll away and spring to her feet, to put her sword between her and her foes, but her body seemed done with the whole affair, scalp burning, ears ringing, head swimming, the world reduced to a tiny window between the steel jaws of her helm. Two men locked in an embrace tripped over her back and went down beside her, mouths snapping at one another's faces. From the black, bloodied soil between her and the wrestling soldiers, steam began to rise... no, black smoke, curling into phantasmal shapes as it rose, the earth warming the metal of her armor, and Ji-hyeon watched the fumes thicken, knowing she had to get up but wanting to stay down just a little longer.

This was why Fennec and all her other advisors save Zosia had tried to talk her out of leading a charge. What in all the Isles had she been thinking, ignoring everyone but a notorious madwoman? The front wasn't where you went to give orders, or intimidate your enemies, or rally your army. The front was where you went to die. A screaming wildborn war nun fell to the smoking earth just in front of her, and then the woman's bestial face exploded as a mace muted her forever. Ji-hyeon closed her eyes, just needing to rest, just needing to muster her moxie, and then, and then she would go back to the war...

She felt herself begin to melt into the black earth, and it made her skin prickle and her mouth water just like when she'd gone through the Gate, her body coming alive in a way it never had before nor since.

Then someone pulled her glove off her left hand, the chill air feeling so refreshing on her skin after being baked in her armor that Ji-hyeon moaned. She tried to look and see who was helping her out of her gear, but the helm was so heavy she couldn't lift her neck. Then a mouth closed lovingly around her middle and index fingers, sucking on the sweaty digits. It felt nice, letting her know the dream she was embarking on was shaping up to be a good one. Then the teeth closed, hard, crushing the bones as they chewed her fingers. Ji-hyeon screamed, rolling over and surprising the Imperial cannibal into scrambling to her feet. She took both of Ji-hyeon's fingers with her. That fucking settled it; Ji-hyeon tightened her grip on her sword and jabbed it up through the woman's groin, into her belly. The cannibal fell and Ji-hyeon rose, her heavy boots now feeling light as silk slippers as she kicked in the woman's horrible, thieving face.

"Take my fingers?" She shook the throbbing wet wreckage of her hand at the cannibal as she stomped her. "Take *my* fucking fingers! I'll give you my fucking toes, too!"

A man burst from the miasma at her side like an eagle diving at a trout, and Ji-hyeon pivoted out of his path, her backhanded swipe opening his throat as he passed.

"Fucking *eating* people?" Ji-hyeon demanded of the crowd. "Fucking eating *me*? Do you want to *die*?"

A woman glanced up from feeding to catch Ji-hyeon's blade across the temple, her skull splitting like a dropped pumpkin.

"Come on, then! Come take a bite!"

Two screaming soldiers covered in so much blood Ji-hyeon couldn't tell which side they fought for ran past her, flailing their weapons around but failing to cut more than the haze around her head. She sheared through one's ankle as they fled back into the chaos, then poked him through the back as he fell. Poked him again, harder, black ooze welling out of the holes she'd punched in his thin leather jack as she looked up for the next challenger, the world at last beginning to make sense again through the jagged mouth of her wolfish helm.

"I'll! Kill! You! All!"

Forms shimmied all around her in the cloud of smoke, the incense-rich fumes condensing, and then a dark silhouette came low at her. She brought her blade down, a wild cry on her lips—

Then twisted her sword away at the last moment when she recognized Keun-ju. In the dimness she had almost hacked his head off when he stumbled out of the haze. He was drenched in blood, a spear broken off in his left shoulder, but he still held the four-tiger sword she had given him: Keun-ju was alive, and he was here...And then Choi appeared through the smoke after him, the wildborn looking even worse off than Keun-ju, bleeding from every limb. In the crook of her arm she carried Fellwing, the owlbat shivering.

Ji-hyeon tried to greet them, but only a horrible laugh emerged from the canine mask of her helm.

"We have to go!" Keun-ju shouted in her face, as though Ji-hyeon were deaf, but then that was a sentiment that deserved an emphatic delivery. Her feet warming through the soles of her boots, Ji-hyeon, her Virtue Guard, and her Martial Guard cut their way through smoke and flesh as if they were the same.

———

"You see it?" Sullen asked Grandfather as they reached the upper edge of camp, the column of devils still hovering over the battlefield. He hoped they were just wild devils, anyway, and not something more material...an angry god, for example. Smoke was rising to join the swarm, but as they entered the maze of tents Sullen lost sight of the valley altogether, and couldn't tell if the black vapors were caused by a fire or something even less welcome.

"What?" said Grandfather, which was answer enough. "The smoke?"

"Nah, Fa, I—" Sullen began, but as they rounded a tent they nearly ran over a boy in a blue headband. The kid yelped, stumbling backward and firing his crossbow at them. The bolt went high, praise Rakehell for the luck he stole for his descendants, and Sullen skidded to a stop in front of the lad. "Ruddy hell, child, we're on your side! You could put a real hurt on someone, shooting off weakbows willy-nilly!"

The boy was still staring up in dread, and, following the kid's eye back over his shoulder, Sullen saw the line of Myuran prisoners coming down the mountain. That explained it, then; this runt thought the camp was being ambushed and had jumped at the first big shadow. "We captured them, kid, we took..."

But the kid wasn't looking at the hill behind them. The kid was looking up at Grandfather, who'd been too silent in the face of such bullshit, and then the first warm drops soaked through Sullen's hair, tickling his scalp.

"Ah, no, no, no," Sullen moaned, fumbling with the straps of the harness, but he knew before he even got them loose that Grandfather was too limp, an arm flopping against Sullen's face as he swung the old man down. Sullen had known it was coming for as long as he'd known what death was, but it wasn't supposed to happen this way, not for the man who'd taught him everything worth knowing, and a few more things besides. "Oh, *Fa.*"

A few feathers jutted out of Grandfather's open mouth, the rest of the quarrel lodged in his palate and skull, the glistening arrowhead punched through the top of his head. Already he smelled like he'd been dead for weeks.

Brought down by one of the weakbows he so despised. Brought down by a boy whose life they had just bought back on the plateau, before Grandfather had even had the chance to sing for his son.

"I'm sorry," the kid squeaked, and, looking up, Sullen saw the boy was crying almost as hard as he was. He dropped the bow as Sullen rose to his full height, then turned to run, but not fast enough. Sullen pounced on the boy, whipped him to the ground, and crouched over him, hand tight around his throat. He squeezed, the kid pissing his pants, and Sullen wanted to stop, wanted to let the kid go, was even more scared of what he was doing to him than he was heartsick about Grandfather, but his hand just tightened as he whispered:

"I'm sorry, too."

———

Just when Maroto thought the worms were wearing off, the shit got all intense and crazy again, the Crimson infantry looking a mite more human now, but behaving even more devilish. As Purna wrenched her kakuri knife out of a soldier's collarbone and Maroto deflected a thrust from another who would have stabbed his ward, he saw that the soldiers farther in had stopped fighting and started eating the dead. Of all the lousy times for a Windhand flashback... Nothing seemed funny anymore, not the good kind of funny, anyway, and Maroto told himself he'd never sting again. Just like he usually did at this point in a bug-out, when things turned scary. Smoke seemed to be pouring from the ground wherever he took a step, the smell like burning hair and pungent semen, and he barely got his shield up in time to block a pike that would've plugged Purna.

"Gotta fall back," she panted. "We'll never find General Ji-hyeon in this mist. You see the others?"

"Nah," said Maroto, his tongue working normal again now that he'd sweated out some of the scorpion. Three furious Imperials blasted out of the smoke at them, and Maroto performed the trickiest dance of his life; it would've been easy enough, if he could brain them with a shield in clear conscience, but he didn't want to push his oath any more than he already had. So instead he put himself between Purna and the raging soldiers, shield up, shield over, shield down, the girl darting through his openings and tagging the soldiers. In all the excitement he caught a few shallow slashes and scrapes, but credit where due, when he rolled out of the way and Purna leaped forward to hack into the last man's face with her curved blade, he saw she didn't have a scratch on her. Then he started snickering again, kept laughing as he clambered back up and they shuffled through the curtains of smoke to take the stage, because he had finally figured out what role he was playing in this strange new drama.

He was Purna's devil.

———

Zosia wheezed along after Hoartrap through the camp, a stitch in her side the size of the Agrimonia Trench. Even the camp follow-ers who usually laid low during the fighting lest they catch a stray arrow had come out to watch the baffling scene below, and a few had loaded heavy packs and were fleeing away up the slope, cutting out before things got any weirder. Zosia sympathized; she'd never seen Choplicker so happy, or Hoartrap so anxious. As the tents thinned out on the lower end of camp and they squeezed past the pickets, she saw that the black column of smoke rising from the battlefield was perfectly cylindrical, and extended as high as her eye could follow. Ripples of light began to appear in the heart of the pillar, and Zosia pinpointed the scent in the air she'd been trying to place the whole way down from the plateau: camping with Leib a dozen years before, they'd been caught out in the high country by a thunderstorm, and a bolt of lightning had blasted the stones close enough they could feel its energy tingling on their tongues and smell its hot tang.

The cylindrical cloud covered most of the valley, extending far enough outward to envelop the front lines, and Zosia saw that the Cobalt infantry in the rear were staring up at the black pillar in awe, weapons held limp when they were held at all. Hoartrap was curs-ing to wake the devils, and Zosia would have, too, if she'd had the breath—this was the worst deviltry she'd ever seen in thirty years of raising hell, the Chainwitches of the Imperial army calling up some-thing that no mortal could hope to put down again...and she was running straight for it.

Then Hoartrap stopped so abruptly she almost bowled into him, the sorcerer drawing up short just at the base of the Lark's Tongue. The slack shoulders of the rear guard and barber surgeons and officers and the rest of the remaining Cobalt Company were lined up between them and the swirling column. Choplicker sat back and howled for all he was worth, tail beating the dust around them, and...

Pop. Not a loud one, either, like some firearms made, but more like the sound and sensation Zosia felt when she came down to the lowlands after a long spell in the mountains. And just like that, the wavering pillar of inky darkness and flickering light sucked down into the battlefield, like smoke drawn through a pipe. As the crown of the column plummeted down from the heavens, though, something must have changed upon the field, for instead of being pulled back into the earth with the rest of it, the remaining smoke billowed out across the valley, stinging Zosia's eyes and making Hoartrap cough.

"That's gone and done it," the sorcerer managed. "There's not a devil in my bag that's going to escape my wrath for this oversight. Someone in there knew this was coming, mark my words, someone smelled it on the wind but kept quiet."

"What *was* that?" Zosia asked, Choplicker barking happily in response, headbutting her bottom to get her moving.

"I've got a pretty good idea," said Hoartrap. "But let's find out."

"Fucking devils," said Zosia, looking down at Choplicker. "First let's go find our friends. You willing to take me to Maroto and the rest?"

Choplicker strutted into the heavy clouds of smoke puffing up from the valley, and Zosia followed him down. No better guide for a tour of some new hell than your own personal devil.

———

"*Look. At. That*," breathed Brother Wan, still straddling Domingo but staring back at where the tower of blackness had collapsed to earth.

Domingo smelled it even before the wave of smoke rolling up the side of the valley reached them, his eyes watering as his nose recognized the orange sage oil Concilia had added to Efrain's bathwater when he was a child, when Domingo could still look at his wife with something other than desperation and his son with something more than disappointment. The grey shroud muffled the world, even the anathema atop him seeming remote and harmless as a memory of past failures.

"And the war's over," Wan said softly. "That which was prophesied in the Canticles has come to pass."

"What did you do?" Domingo asked just as softly, and because the hour was far too late for self-deception, he amended himself. "What did *we* do?"

"We've saved the Star, Domingo." Milky tears ran off Wan's chin and landed on Domingo's red uniform. "*You* saved the Star, by putting your faith in the Chain. Her Grace called it a weapon, because that was the only way you could understand it, but it was never a weapon. It was a gift, a gift to all mortals."

"I asked you what the fuck I did, you wretched monster!" Domingo's voice broke. "Stop talking Chainite madness and *tell* me. *Please. What did I do?*"

"Madness?" The fleeting softness of Wan's face set and his cheeks dried. "You still doubt her, even after all you've seen. All you've done."

"I just want to know," said Domingo, slumping back into his sweaty pillows, the monster that straddled him gazing down in scorn. "I just want to know."

"No you don't," said Wan. "You've never wanted to know. You've spent your whole existence denying the truth with one breath and demanding answers with the next. I was going to show you, I was going to take you through with me . . . But you're not worthy."

"You don't know, do you?" Domingo must be as mad as Wan, because it was so hard not to burst out laughing at this crazy, sad little monster who thought he had the whole game figured out. "You won't tell me because you don't even know what it is you've done!"

"I've saved the world, and now I'm going to pass through to my reward," said Wan. "But first I'm going to spare you from further pain. It will be . . . unpleasant, for the sinners left behind, and I think you have suffered enough in this life. You may despise me, Domingo, but I have nothing but pity for you."

Domingo groaned as the gaunt witchborn shifted his weight,

sending more currents of grief through the colonel's broken leg. From his cassock Brother Wan had drawn the black knife Domingo had declined back on the Azgarothian border, when he'd dispatched the Immaculate prince. What a long time ago that seemed, back when the Immaculates' conquest of Linkensterne had seemed a crime worth killing over, back when Domingo still had ambitions beyond dying better than he was probably going to, now that his time was up. He wondered if the foreign prince's family would respond to the news of their child's cruel death the same way Domingo had, with fury instead of grief...

"Safe roads guide you to her breast," said Brother Wan, clumsy enough with his dagger that Domingo didn't hold much hope for a quick end to this. "Time to let the angels take you, Colonel."

"I doubt either of us will be seeing any angels," said Domingo, tensing every fiber of his broken body as Brother Wan leaned down to slit his throat.

The witchborn came in, close as a lover, and Domingo clobbered his soft temple with the brass hawkglass. Wan reeled to the side, lashing blindly with the dagger and clipping Domingo's cheek. The blade ran back along the bone and nicked his ear. That was just the bit of extra incentive Domingo needed, and he cracked the anathema a second time, harder still, the glass set in the brass tube exploding out in a bloom of crystals, and Brother Wan slumped on top of him, their foreheads knocking painfully together.

"A wise general never leaves the battlefield," Domingo told the limp monk. "And I never gave the boy anything he couldn't use as a weapon."

Brother Wan had dropped his knife over the edge of the wagon when he blacked out, and so it required a bit more time and commitment for the broken-legged, lame-armed colonel to do what needed doing, especially with the crick in his neck. One wouldn't think it, but that was the worst, like a thousand thorns jabbing into his spine as he rolled the anathema off him and then dragged himself upright in the wagon bed. The fumes were thicker now, like he'd snuck into the steamy bathhouse to steal a kiss from Concilia while Efrain splashed around the tub, laughing the bright, sharp laughter of children, a sound that had never agreed with Domingo.

He should rip up this bedding, use it to bind Brother Wan before he woke up. Interrogate him when he came to, using methods reserved only for traitors to the Crown. Get a straight answer out of the crooked man. But there was an awful lot of blood running off Domingo's flayed face, and who knew how long he'd be able to stay awake. Who knew how long he'd be alive. So Colonel Domingo Hjortt did the only judicious thing he could think of, and bashed away at the back of Brother Wan's head until he had no more strength to lift the broken hawkglass. Then he slumped back in the bloodied, befouled wagon bed, hissing at the songs his ruined body sang for him, and stared up into the hazy sky, hoping the smoke would clear and he could see the sun one final time before he went into what the superstitious called the First Dark, but what Domingo knew was nothing more nor less than the cold, cold ground.

CHAPTER
26

Sullen held a boy of less than a dozen thaws to the ground, and choked him to death with one hand. Sullen smelled piss and shit, blood and old age, but that last was growing fainter by the breath, and as it faded he squeezed harder. The kid's eyes were bugging out, his legs flopping, feeble fingers latched onto Sullen's wrist. It was a dark task, but it needed doing, with Grandfather killed for no reason at all, murdered in a way to shame the ancestors. Vengeance had to be paid, and Sullen tightened his grip and looked away, for he took no pleasure in it.

"No." He dropped the boy as though he'd seized a snake and sat back on his haunches in the dusty lane between tents. The boy gasped, a dry, ugly noise that sounded like it hurt. And Sullen said it again, louder, trying to make it stick. "No!"

The whole reason they'd left the Savannahs was to find something better than the old ways, wasn't it? When you killed someone back home, you paid their family or you fought whoever came looking for revenge. Simple...but nothing seemed simple anymore. What good would come of killing this fool boy? What good would come of any of it?

"Sorry," the boy said it again, coughing on the word as he crawled backward on his arse, trying to get away, and, hearing that worthless word, Sullen wanted to jam it back down his neck. Hopping to his feet and advancing on him, he said:

"You think I give a *fuck* if you're sorry? You killed my grandfather!

I drag him all the way here, talk him into helping *you*, your people, and that's how you repay him? Fucking *weakbow*?" He raised his foot to stomp the cowering boy before he caught himself again, stamped the earth instead. "What the fuck do I do now, huh? Leave him here, after all he did for me? Let you run away, after what you did for him?"

"Plee...plee...please," the kid stammered.

"I'm asking you a fucking question!" Sullen bellowed, feeling like his brain was going to boil out of his ears. He had been mad, once or twice, and always to bad result, but he'd never had the devils in him like this. "I don't have anyone else to ask! 'Cause you killed him! So *what do I do now*?"

"Ca-ca-crimson, or...Immmmmaculate?" said the kid, and Sullen realized he'd been ranting in the true tongue, and wherever this child came from, it wasn't the Noreast Arm. That was just as well, Sullen could rage in other languages than his own, though fishing around for the right words made him lose some of his momentum.

"You murdered my grandfather," he said in Immaculate. "You murdered him because...because you're a stupid fucking arsehole. So what do I do now? How can I let you go, when you did that to him? How can I face him, my other ancestors, when I stand at the door of Old Black's Meadhall? How?"

"Please," was all the kid managed, making Sullen wonder if the barrier hadn't been language, if this boy was just simpleminded. He looked back at Grandfather's limp form in the dust, hoping that even in death he could provide wisdom, but all he offered was an appetizing meal to the flies buzzing around his bloody mouth.

"All right," said Sullen, closing his eyes, telling himself he knew this hour would come...But predicting something and being ready for it aren't the same, not by a stretch. He'd always imagined Grandfather dying to save him, or some worthier person still, the old man sacrificing himself to great honor. Taking on a hundred enemies and making them pay dearly for one grey wolf that couldn't even stand on his own legs. Using his last breath to boast or crack a joke or maybe just say farewell to his grandson. That's how it would have happened in the sagas. Not like this. What kind of sad, disappointing song would this make?

The thing was, there was more going on right now than just what had happened to Grandfather. A lot more. This wasn't a fucking song, with Grandfather's death the dramatic end to a night's entertainment; wars didn't stop for one old man...Or did they? All that ruckus down in the valley had gone quiet, now that he pricked his ears that way, and the faint whiff of charcoal mixed with sweet rice reached his nose just before a grey cloud of smoke flooded up through the camp on the breeze. Craning his neck, he couldn't see any of the ghostly devils that had gathered over the battlefield, couldn't see the valley at all. Ji-hyeon was down there somewhere, and so was Uncle Maroto, and while his motives for wanting them alive couldn't be more different, want them alive Sullen surely did.

"All right."

"Alllll right?" The kid tried to get up but was shaking too badly.

"Yeah, all right," said Sullen, settling on his own way, since there was no one here to give him a better idea. "Grandfather there? You carry him up that hill. On your back. To the hump at the top. You make him a bed of tree branches and grass. Lay him on it. Feet toward the plains, head toward the mountain. Then you stay there until I come for you. Do that, I won't kill you."

The kid jerked his head up and down.

"If you don't, if I get up to that hump and find the both of you aren't waiting..." Sullen was going to leave it unsaid, but seeing that this fucking piece of shit was too thick not to murder honest folk volunteering to help out his own army, he spelled it out for him. "If you don't do all that, I'm going to run you down, anywhere you hide, and I'm going to murder you just as dead as Fa there. Only it won't be fast. It won't be easy. You'll be begging your gods for me to finish it, to let you go on and die. Yeah?"

The kid nodded fit to snap his own neck and save Sullen the bother.

"All right then." And because he couldn't help the living if he watched the dead, Sullen launched himself down through camp without sparing a backward glance for the kid or the flesh his grandfather had worn. He tried not to notice how light and free he felt, how nimbly he moved, without the weight of the old man on his back.

———

"Holy... holy," said Purna, staring agog into the wavering smoke. They had turned to face another snarling Imperial soldier, only to see him pulled wailing into the earth, along with most of the thick cloud. Maroto had hoped this was just the last hurrah of his worms, giving him a few last visuals, but apparently not. "What... what."

"Fucking bugnuts," he said, squinting into the foul mists and seeing that ahead of them there was not a single other person, not upright, not dead on the ground. After the clangor of an epic battle, the eerie silence of the vale fairly roared in his good ear, like he'd put it up to a hermit spider shell. "So that happened, huh?"

"What..." Purna said it again, maybe hoping for a better answer. "What?"

Maroto got a squirmy, cold feeling in his belly, staring at where all those people, living and dead, had just up and vanished, like the whole world had gone to bugs. To either side and behind them there were still corpses aplenty, and he knew from long experience that it was always better to take your chances with the mundane dead than the devilishly mysterious. Tossing away one of his battered shields and wiping the sweat and grime from his face, he said, "Fight's over, one way or another. Let's move."

Booking it away through the thinning waves of smoke, he kept a close watch for their friends, both among the other dazed figures lurching through the haze, and at their feet. Just before they got separated in the press he'd seen Hassan take a bad hammer to the back, but then the man had been swallowed by the blurring clash. He hadn't seen what happened to Din or Diggelby... But speak of the devils and watch them rise, here came Diggelby swaying through the smoke!

"Digs!" called Purna hoarsely. "Did you fucking see that shit?"

"The smoke?"

"No, dummy, the fucking Imperials!" said Purna.

"What about them?"

"They're gone!" Purna's voice had the ragged edge of someone who'd just seen their first true devil. Then again, Maroto had seen a lot of devils in his day, and whatever had happened back there definitely still bugged him right the fuck out. "Like, all of them! Or at least all the ones back there—they just…*went*, right in front of us, and far as we could see the whole fucking army got took!"

"Sorcery," said Diggelby, in a tone that said it was *so* passé. He waved them over. "Take a look."

Joining their friend, Maroto saw that Diggelby's armored caftan had lost most of its padding, the garment shredded to the skin in places, but other than a lot of blood caked on his person, he seemed to have come out all right. He held a flask in one shaking hand, and Prince was cupped in his other arm. The spaniel looked even worse than his master, a bloodied foreleg spasming, a cut on his snout, and his collar missing.

"A war monk?" said Purna, looking down at the half-dead man in robes curled at Diggelby's feet, his breath coming in shuddering gasps, a javelin jutting from his abdomen. "What does that prove?"

"We'll put a few questions to him," said Diggelby, passing the flask to a grateful Maroto. "See what's what. They call them 'Chain-witches,' so maybe he knows something about all this obvious witchery."

"Nah," said Maroto, both to Diggelby's suggestion and Purna's snatching the flask from his hand before he could take a second pull. "Why the devils would they do something that wiped out their folk 'stead of ours? Purna and me were right there when the crazy went down, and the Crimsons got the worst of it by a country league."

"Can't hurt to ask," said Purna, tossing Diggelby the flask and putting a boot onto the war monk to roll him onto his back.

"Careful there, weirdborn—" Thinking of Choi's sharp smile, Maroto amended himself. "Shit, I mean wildborn, *wildborn* can be—"

"Maroto," said Diggelby peevishly, as if noticing him for the first time. "Maroto, where is my other shield?"

"Huh?" Maroto looked at the one shield he had left, which was no longer in any condition to be mounted in the nobleman's den once the war was won. "Oh balls, Diggelby, I totally forgot and—"

"Fucking bastard!" Purna yelped, staggering back from the prone Chainite, who had jabbed at her with a dagger. She gasped when her weight came down on her left leg.

"Told you to be careful," said Maroto, kicking the knife from the war monk's hand and snatching Diggelby's flask. "You tend that one and I'll see to Purna. Come on, girl, where'd he tag you?"

"I'm fine, I'm fine," said Purna, wobbling, trying to look at the back of her leg, and then she fell over. Maroto heard Diggelby grumbling as he drew his crystalline sword, a grunt and gurgle from the war monk, but didn't look back, his full notice on just how much red stuff was coming out of the back of Purna's thigh, leaking through the padded legging between the edge of her mail skirt and the steel cop protecting her knee. He fell to his knees beside her, rolling her on her side and slapping his hand on the narrow cut... But hot as her blood felt against his palm, ice began to spread through his chest— the pressure under his hand was bad, as bad as bad could get. She'd been stabbed, not slashed, and if her artery was nicked the girl would be dead in minutes. Maybe sooner.

"Diggelby!" he cried, trying to keep the terror out of his voice lest she catch it. "Your belt, Diggelby, right fucking now!"

"I'm fine, really," said Purna, trying to sit up on her elbow and slumping back down, blood flowing faster between Maroto's fingers. "Fucking jerk just... damn."

"Always talking me out of my belt, barbarian..." Diggelby started, but shut up as soon as he saw what had happened, stayed dead quiet as he slid down on the other side of Purna. A quiet Diggelby was not a reassuring portent. The fop fed his belt around her upper thigh with a junkie's steadiness, cinched it for all he was worth. The pressure barely lessened.

"I can get up," said Purna, voice quavering as she tried to see what they were doing. "I'm... fine."

Purna was dying fast, and there wasn't a fucking thing they could do to help.

———

"Hey, what's happened?" Zosia called, Choplicker having led her straight to a break in the smoke-choked valley. Given her devil's keen interest in sniffing the butt of a hurt spaniel that was inexplicably hanging out on the ruined battlefield, maybe he'd had ulterior motives. Beyond the wounded dog and the thing that pretended to be a dog, Maroto and one of his noble friends, Diggelby, kneeled over a fallen comrade. Purna, Maroto's cute, scrappy disciple—she hadn't recognized her at first, the girl too pale from all the blood covering her and her friends. "Shit, anything I can do to help?"

Maroto looked up at Zosia, obviously frightened out of his wits, and then, as though realizing this was all a nightmare and he would soon awake to find his friend unharmed, a rowdy grin lit up his dark, haunted face. Closing the last few feet of trampled grass, Zosia didn't see how the hells he could find any succor in her presence; she was worse at field surgery than he was, and the shuddering girl he held would soon be as dead as the countless unknown bodies she had stepped over in the course of getting to them.

"Zosia!" he said, sounding as close to broken as she'd ever heard him, which was saying something indeed. "Oh, thank every devil! Here, hold this, Diggelby, everything's going to be fine."

"Maroto, what the fuck!" Diggelby struggled to press his far smaller hands against Purna's slick red thigh as Maroto abandoned his post, lurching up and seizing Zosia's shoulders with his bloody hands. His face was right in hers, pupils filling his teary eyes, and he spoke with the measured composure of a bug veteran trying to convince a straitlaced stranger to lend him some silver.

"Shit, Zosia, Purna's real bad, you can see that..." He licked his chapped lips, gently squeezed her shoulders. "I know it's asking a lot, a whole lot, more than me or anyone's got any right to ask, yeah, but she's going to die, Zee, she's going to fucking die right here if you don't help her..."

Zosia's stomach dropped as she understood what he was driving at; even with Maroto managing to keep his eyes on hers instead of Choplicker, there wasn't a whole lot else he could possibly want from her.

"...and I swear, I fucking swear I'll do anything to make it up to you, break my vow to the queen, help you bind another, bind twenty more if you want, Hoartrap would help, I know it, so if you'd just—"

"I wish I could," said Zosia, making her words as precise as possible. "I can't."

Just like that, he got dangerous, friendly hands on her shoulders tightening down, fake smile turning into a genuine snarl. "Zee, I know it's asking a lot, and she's just one of thousands to get got today, *yes, of course*, but you need to do this. Please. I'm fucking *begging* you."

"And I'm telling you, it's not that I won't, it's that I *can't*," said Zosia, trying to keep her cool in the face of the heat he was throwing off. "He won't go. I offered him a way out, a long time ago, but he turned me down. He's not like other devils, he—"

"Try again, then, try it now," said Maroto, voice cracking. "Tell him you'll set him free if he saves her. Can't hurt to try, right? Maybe he couldn't before, but now, but now..."

Wouldn't that be a joke to wake the sleeping gods of the Sunken Kingdom with her laughter, if Choplicker refused to keep Zosia and Leib safe in exchange for his freedom, but took her offer now, for the life of some saucebox Zosia had spoken to once in her life? His very suggestion was absurd; even if Choplicker accepted and carried through, the world would be richer one smart-mouthed punk who'd get herself killed again soon enough, one way or another, and Zosia would have lost the greatest power known to mortals. If used wisely, a devil's wish could change the fates of empires, and Maroto expected her to dump hers on account of one girl he fancied?

"I'm sorry, Maroto, if I could help your girlfriend—"

"Try it!" he screamed, and then, realizing he'd shaken her, let go of Zosia's shoulders, tried to brush off the blood he'd smeared on her tunic. "Please, Zosia, she's not my girl, nothing like that, she's...she's my friend. She's my only real friend."

Maroto was blubbering now, and Zosia looked at the fallen girl, the fop trying to stanch her wound, and then her wicked devil, who was now giving the lapdog a look like he might eat it, if he thought nobody was paying attention. Quietly, Zosia said, "I'm your friend, Maroto, and I know how hard it is to let go—"

"You think you're still my *friend*?" He sneered. "You let me throw my life away on your account. Let me think *my friend* had been murdered. Let me think *my friend* needed someone to avenge her, keep her memory warm. You were a better friend dead than you ever were alive!"

Some of that stung, and some of it was horseshit for all kinds of reasons, but before she could stop herself the words were out of her mouth. Maybe she said it because she *was* his friend, for all his problems, or maybe because she just wanted to prove to him that she'd been telling the truth. "Choplicker. You save Tapai Purna there, make her healthy and whole again, with no kinds of sinister twists to the deal, and I release you from your bond. Onetime offer, take it or leave it."

Choplicker glanced over, and Zosia held her breath...

And then the devil yawned, and turned back to acting all stiff and tough with the lapdog. It was an odd feeling, to be disappointed and relieved all at once, and hating yourself for your uncontrollable emotions in the bargain.

"See?" Zosia reached for Maroto's shoulder. "I wish I could—"

"What a load of shit," said Maroto, flinching away from her touch, uglier than she'd ever seen him. "You have to *want it*, Zee."

"Excuse me?" Now Zosia was feeling her fire, too—he was in a place, obviously, but there were limits to how much she'd let go.

"You didn't want it, so it didn't work," said Maroto. "Everyone knows you have to want it, *especially* the devils. So why don't you want to save her?"

"I do want it," said Zosia, hoping she meant it but not so sure anymore—what if Choplicker had sensed her reservations and taken that into consideration? What if he'd seen into her selfish heart, and knew this wasn't her one true wish? What if when she'd asked him to watch over her husband he had sensed some similar doubt? What if this was all her fault, instead of his?

"Liar. You fucking liar." Maroto shook his head, snot and tears on his grubby face, and he poked her in the chest, his eyes black as Gates and just as warm. "We're fucking *done*, you and me. I gave up my life to help you, and you won't give up a fucking dog to help my friend? Fair enough, *Cold Zosia*, but after I bury Purna I'm coming for you, and not even that devil of yours will be able to help. You're a fucking dead woman."

Maroto wasn't in his right mind, and he'd made some fair points, shitty as it was to admit, but the day some asshole talked to her that way after she'd tried loosing her devil to help him was the day she was fit for the grave. She bit her lip, nodded like she was considering his threat, then hurled herself forward, headbutting him in the chin. He stumbled backward and nearly tripped over his dying friend, then launched himself back at Zosia—only to be swept off his feet by a figure who came barreling out of the smoke, one of the few people to make the Flintlander look modestly proportioned. Hoartrap actually lifted Maroto, clenching him in a bear hug, and, looking at Zosia, called:

"I'll help him back to camp, you mind the children here."

"Fuckingfuckbastard!" Maroto thrashed to no avail as Hoartrap clumsily carried him off into the smoke. Zosia scowled at Choplicker; now that Maroto was but an angry echo in the miasma, she realized she had never seen him that unhinged before, and all her wrath fled, leaving her as hollow as she'd ever felt. All she could do for her old friend was watch someone he cared about bleed to death in the dirt for no good reason at all, so that was what she did.

What she tried to do, anyway, but looking back at Purna's blanched body, she saw that Diggelby had turned away, his red hands stroking his lapdog rather than fighting the inevitable. The blood still trickled out from Purna's thigh, and her chest fluttered, but she was going fast. Then Diggelby jerked his hands back with a little scream, falling backward on his ass as his dog started having a fit. Choplicker licked

Zosia's hand, then plopped down at her feet with a whine, watching Diggelby's lapdog shake and shudder.

"What the fuck did you do to his mutt?" Zosia demanded, about at the end of her patience with her devil, but then Diggelby yelped again, and the worst stench imaginable overpowered the perfume of blood, metal, shit, and incense that permeated the ghostly battlefield. The fop's lapdog burst into green flames, and as it shook, burning hair came loose in stinking clumps, floating in the air like foul embers. What Zosia had thought was the poor animal squealing was its blackened skin roasting from the inside out, its boiling vitals whistling like a teakettle, and then the whole dreadful mass melted into the earth, giving off fluorescent vapors...vapors that snaked through the air, and plunged into Purna's nostril and mouth.

The effect was instantaneous, Purna's back arching and an ear-splitting shriek blasting from her mouth, her eyes rolling back in her head. The blood on her leg began to sizzle, and black ichors bubbled up from the ground beneath her, climbing her thigh in serpentine streams and plugging the wound. No, not plugging it shut—flowing into it, the current increasing as she bucked on the ground. The stench of burned hair now mingled with that of wet dog, and as Purna screamed again it turned into a howl, an impossibly long, black tongue curling out of her mouth.

Then she went limp, shivering, but her chest was rising and falling in orderly fashion, the color had returned to her skin, and when Diggelby cautiously approached her to remove his makeshift tourniquet, they saw that the wound had healed, and instead of a scab or scar there blossomed a patch of snow-white fur.

"You saved her," said Zosia, hardly believing it even having seen it. "That dog of yours was a devil?"

"I guess so," said Diggelby sadly, looking at the toxic stain on the flattened grass where it had disappeared from the world of mortals, back to the First Dark. "My father, he bought Prince for me. He always said he was a devil, but I never really believed it; Prince was such an angel! And Baba is easily taken in by bold claims, so I just thought... But when I heard you two fighting about devils and wishes, I thought why not give it a go and—say!" He brightened, pointed at Choplicker. "Will you sell me yours? I'll give you a more than fair price, and since I suddenly find myself on the market..."

"Not a bad idea, actually," said Zosia, earning a reproachful glance from Choplicker. "But I'd get the better end of the deal—in case you didn't notice, he's defective. Now, let's get miracle girl here back to camp before Maroto goes any crazier."

———

It wasn't like any of the songs Ji-hyeon's second father would sing. It was like something out of her first father's sutras on the many kinds of hells. Intense and bizarre as it had gotten during the combat, after the explosive or whatever it was had gone off across the valley everything had taken on an ethereal sheen, and if not for her aching back and hand, she might have been able to pretend it was all a nightmare, if only for a few moments at a time. Might have been able to let herself pretend this wasn't all her fault.

They had been close enough to the perimeter that when the bomb or trick or spell went off, she had heard the sudden termination of thousands of raging voices, the quiet that followed even weirder than their early shouting, wailing, and chanting. As Choi led them steadily onward, the Crimson soldiers who appeared through the smoke became less frequent, until they only encountered Cobalt troops. It made little difference, though, the fight having left both armies, and that in and of itself was unnerving—if the mysterious weapon hadn't been detonated by either side, what had caused it? And if it was an explosion, why hadn't she heard anything more than a distant pop?

Hoartrap's meddling was still the only explanation that made some kind of sense, but before she confronted him about experimenting on her battlefield without her say-so, she wanted something to drink. Maybe a ten-year-long nap. Looking at her battered guards, though, she felt the opening murmurs of her guilty conscience. Upright though they were, Ji-hyeon could see that their wounds were grave enough that both Keun-ju and Choi might never walk out of the barber's tent. Even Fellwing had used the last of her strength to find Ji-hyeon's friends in the fray, guiding the wildborn to their mistress, and now lay softly hooting in the crook of Ji-hyeon's injured arm, too weak to fly. And what had it cost Ji-hyeon? A couple of fingers of her off hand.

As they hobbled through the ruined pickets and started up the rise toward camp, Ji-hyeon looked back at where the fighting had been worst. A break in the smoke revealed that a new topography had formed in the Lark's Tongue vale, the piled dead creating wide hill and dales as far as the haze let her see. There was more red than blue on the ground, and more blue than red upright, mechanically trying to line up all the Imperials who had surrendered after their command and the bulk of their army had vanished in a puff of smoke.

"Ji-hyeon, was this..." Keun-ju began, following her gaze across the fume-filled valley. "Is this something you've seen before, campaigning with the Cobalts?"

Ji-hyeon shook her head, but then that wasn't quite true. The random people wandering around in shock, too scared to think anymore...*that* she had seen in the citizens of many of the towns they had sacked. And the smoke burning everyone's eyes and lungs, she'd delivered that at Geminides, when they'd sapped the wall of the castle to bust in the back. Then in Myura, Hoartrap had used deviltry and black magic to make the enemy officers go missing, although there had only been a few of them that time. And of course, of all the elements at work in this tapestry Ji-hyeon had helped weave, the one constant everywhere was death: dead friends, dead foes, dead animals, a dead land soaked in dead blood spilled with dead metal. So yes, she had seen this before, just never like *this*, never all at once...And if she had planned better, if she had listened to Fennec and had them pull out instead of making a stand, none of this would have happened. What the hells was she doing out here in the heart of the Star, anyway, running around playing soldier with real people for her toys? Dismissing the counsel of her advisors and throwing herself down on the front line, where most of her bodyguard could be massacred to protect their child general? She hadn't seen Chevaleresse

Sasamaso since her idiotic charge into the thick of it, nor the rest of her retinue...

"This is not your shame alone," said Choi, looking carefully at Ji-hyeon, as though she could really peer into her ward's thoughts just like Fennec always said. "Someone did this. Not you. We will hunt the truth."

"Of course we will," said Ji-hyeon, standing a little straighter and feeling it all the way from the goose egg coming up on her back down to the oozing rag Keun-ju had tied around her bitten hand. "First we discover where Fennec hid, since he didn't manage to keep up during our charge, and then...then..."

Ji-hyeon stared up at the blue tents arrayed on the hillside above her, tried to remember what was important and what was not, tried to consider everything that had just happened and how to proceed, but all she could think about was the look of feral abandon in the Imperial woman's eyes as she'd chewed off her fingers...That was something to focus on, anyway, and Ji-hyeon gestured with her crippled hand at the nearest white pavilion. "First thing we do is get tended by the barbers. Once we're there we'll have the officers brought in, figure out what happened, how many we lost, what our options are, with that other Imperial regiment no more than a few days out. Send sorties over to the Crimson camp and confiscate their supplies. Fennec can bide."

"Too well," said Choi, and they limped toward the busy sawbones, Ji-hyeon looking again over the murky field, wondering how many of the people who had trusted her when dawn broke that morning would never emerge from the smoke.

CHAPTER
27

Hoartrap, you fucking piece of fuck shit, put me the fuck down right now or I'm going to devote my life to fucking you up, too! I'm not fucking crazy anymore!"

"What a reassuring statement," said Hoartrap, tightening his grip on Maroto. "Definitely not the sort of thing a raving madman would tell his captor."

"Who captured who?" Maroto said slyly, unable to keep from shaking with silent laughter. The bugs were definitely still in him, but even with their aid he was too exhausted to fight Hoartrap, straight bushed from lugging those two shields all over, running game for Purna's unappreciative arse, but then that thought brought him back around to what had happened to her, and he started squirming again. "Just let me see her! Just let me see her before you murder my only friend!"

"Nobody's murdering anybody. Not yet, anyway." Hoartrap muttered the last.

"This is 'cause she found out, isn't it?" And there it was, the blazing insight into Zosia's evil heart. "She found out I killed her husband, so she's revenging on me."

"Husband, you say," said Hoartrap, though he didn't sound interested, didn't sound like he believed a word, was just trying to pass the time as he lugged his heavy cargo through the spectral landscape of dead folk and broken weapons and arrows sticking up from the dirt, everything beyond their immediate vicinity cloaked in the rank black air. Normally, scavengers would be all over a field this ripe, the humans coming for gear and maybe parts to sell to medical students, the animals and devils coming for a meal, but not so much as a fly buzzed in the dismal wasteland. "Whose husband was it you killed, Maroto?"

"I didn't kill him," Maroto moaned, sick with remorse and anger and a whole lot of bad bugs. "I didn't mean to, I didn't, but you know how they are, they'll take what you say and they'll mess it all up, they'll take a good thing and make it bad, they'll find a way to get back at you, when all you did was set them free!"

"Mmmm," said Hoartrap, slowing his pace. "Crumbsnatcher, that's who did it?"

"Who else!" Maroto missed his rat so much, especially now; if he'd held on to him, he could have saved Purna. "I just wanted to see her again, that's all, I didn't know he'd make it happen so bad. And I was going to tell her, I was, that's why I came looking for her, but she already knows, she has to, why else would she be so cold? Why else would she murder my friend? It's payback, and I deserve it, but not Purna! Not her!"

"My my," said Hoartrap, coming to a stop and looking around, as if even he couldn't orient himself in this infernal valley. "That's quite the story. You're sure it's all true, not a nightmare some bug laid in your brain?"

"Call me a fucking liar, Hoartrap, call me a liar and see what happens!" Maroto tensed, then gave what Hoartrap had asked some serious consideration. Through the mists of the battlefield and the worms and the sting and everything else, he had to wonder, now that the question had been posed... "I'm sure about it being my fault, from what I asked Crumbsnatcher to do. Not sure about Zee knowing it was me, because I wanted to tell her, *want* to tell her, 'cause she's got to know it wasn't the queen or the Chain or nobody but her old friend Maroto, but I didn't get a chance, and now... now Purna's dead, isn't she?"

"Did you tell her—Purna, I mean, or anyone else—about the terms of Crumbsnatcher's freedom? Someone else in camp Zosia could have heard it from?" Good old Hoartrap always knew the surest way to talk Maroto down when he'd worked himself up way too high; you just had to look at all the angles, and then sometimes you saw there was nothing to fret over.

"You're the first one I've told, ever," said Maroto, feeling relieved that Zosia couldn't know, and then shame at his relief. "No way she could know. Which means she didn't let Purna die as revenge, she let her bleed out because she's just a selfish old fucker who don't care about nobody but herself. I've got half a mind not to tell her at all, now, let her go barmy trying to figure out who sent the assassins, when all along it was—woof, what's the hurry?"

"Something I found over here that I want to show you," grunted Hoartrap, trotting off in a new direction. Through a gap in the smoke, Maroto saw the Lark's Tongue straight behind them, but when he tried to correct the old wizard's course he was reminded that they had something to see, at the center of the vale. Whatever it was, he doubted it was worth the bother; he was starting to crash pretty hard, but when they reached Hoartrap's destination he sobered up in one devil's breath of a hurry.

Hoartrap set him down on his own feet just as they stepped out of the smoke, and Maroto's knees almost went out on him as he surveyed the manifest impossibility. The miasma wouldn't cross the border of the enormous circular clearing, so here in the bull's-eye of what had been the battlefield was a perfect circle of fresh air, and beneath it, where crushed grass and kicked-up earth and a goodly many corpses ought to be, stretched a Gate. There were only six Gates on the Star, one for each Arm and the last in Diadem, everyone knew that...but here was a seventh, and it was wider than all the other six put together.

"This wasn't fucking here this morning," breathed Maroto, taking a step back from the edge where the flattened field gave way to absolutely fucking nothing. Made him feel ill, being this close to one, and he felt a powerful itch on his ankle. Looking down, he saw that the scorpion sting had started oozing grey slime down the side of his foot. Droplets peeled away from his skin and blew sideways into the Gate. "Where'd it come from?"

"I have a theory as to that," said Hoartrap, cracking his knuckles. "But I don't think you'll like it."

"Then you know what, don't even tell me. I've given myself enough black eyes, trying to see too far. If you think it's bad, I definitely don't—"

But then Hoartrap bum-rushed Maroto for the second time that day, carrying them both over the lip of the Gate.

It felt wrong, not having Grandfather's comforting weight on his shoulders, but then wrong was something Sullen would have to get used to. He slowed to a fast walk as he neared the edge of camp, not wanting to risk startling another kid into shooting his arse now that more and more roughed-up soldiers were moving between the tents. More than one of the grunts gave Sullen the iron eye, and he checked the cobalt handkerchiefs he'd tied on his bandolier, making sure his allegiances were right out there for everyone to see. There was a whole lot less singing and drinking than he'd expect out of returning victors, and given how idly they were all coming up the hill, they must have won, or come close enough—the fighting had stopped and they weren't being overrun by Imperials, so that seemed like it'd inspire a smile somewhere, anywhere... not a one. As he broke from the tight cluster of the camp and headed down past the white pavilions where most of the screaming was coming from, he saw the whole floor of the vale still blanketed in smoke, rising too high for him to see the far hills where the Crimsons had come in from the plains. He wondered if things were as grim on their side of the valley.

"Sullen!" Ji-hyeon. Fast as the relief bloomed at hearing her voice it wilted again, as he turned and saw how harmed she was. She looked like she'd been dunked in the giant bucket of chum from the Ballad of Count Raven and the Sea King, blood and bits of meat clinging to her from boots to forehead. The horned woman carried Ji-hyeon's helm for her, looking even more torn up than her mistress, and helping the general along was Keun-ju, the pretty boy's veil missing and his face caked in blood, a few shafts sprouting from his armor. They'd all made it out was what mattered, and Sullen sprinted over to meet the trio under the awning of a barber's tent. "Sullen, I'm so glad you're okay!"

"Oi," said Sullen, wanting to hug her, but reckoning that would've been low form even without her lover in the way, looking Sullen up and down like he was a butcher dubious if the animal before him was fit for consumption. Sullen wanted to tell Ji-hyeon straightaway about Grandfather, but with these two unfriendly strangers watching him, he just couldn't do it, and instead said, "You, um, you all right? All of you? Just missed you setting out, I guess. Sorry I couldn't help."

"We would have benefited from your presence," said Choi, not angry or mean about it, just telling it for what it was.

"Missed the whole engagement, did you?" said Keun-ju, and, not knowing if the barb he felt in the words was intentional or not, Sullen treated it as an honest question.

"Nah, she, uh, Zosia had us run up the mountain, to the hump up there? These...Myurans, they said, this regiment from Myura, they'd snuck around the back, and were trying to get us from behind, so we, you know. Stopped 'em."

"Must have been quite the clash," said Keun-ju, and Sullen finally kenned what this guy was driving at; unlike everyone else he'd passed coming down here, he didn't have a scrape on him, his clothes free of the blood, dirt, and the smoky stench that coated the rest of the Cobalts. That explained the looks he'd been getting from the soldiers he'd passed. "Were there many casualties?"

Sullen felt the straps of Grandfather's harness tighten across his chest, even though he'd taken them off and left them with the remains, and he took the first of three steps that would carry him to this smart-mouthed arsehole.

"Enough, Keun-ju," said Ji-hyeon, smiling wearily at Sullen. Her eyes were glassy, and she had the shakes even worse than most of the other troops he'd passed on the way down here. "That's great, Sullen. I wondered where the Myurans got to, since they weren't with the Fifteenth. I'll have Captain Zosia give me a full report, so don't worry about it now. I've got...I've got some other stuff to do first."

She lifted a bandaged hand, and he saw that the cloth was dark and sopping. Fellwing lay cradled in her elbow, the charcoal black owlbat now turned grey, and diminished somehow, but the devil would be fine, in time. It was feeding on something intangible that Ji-hyeon was giving off, he could tell somehow, and once it had enough strength to return to the air it would find plenty more nourishment in this place.

"Yeah, definitely, get yourself looked after," said Sullen. "Anything I can do? Not here, right, but just...anything?"

"Oh sure, lots," said Ji-hyeon, but then she just stared past Sullen at nothing at all, lips pursed.

"No one from Purna's squad arrived at command this morning," said Choi. "The general orders any able officers to report here, so if you know where she or your uncle is, you could tell them that."

Did he know where his uncle was? The eternal question. Whenever Sullen thought about how his uncle had abandoned the clan but not tried to help him and Grandfather, he would get a sad, sour stirring in his stomach, and his heartbeat would quicken unpleasantly. He felt the old symptoms now, but ignored them—he hadn't met Ji-hyeon and her people at the command tent in time, either, and big as the camp was, big as the fight had been, Maroto had probably just missed them, same as Sullen. He was around here somewhere, he wouldn't just disappear as soon as the threat of violence revealed itself...He wouldn't do that to Sullen again, not now that he'd finally tracked him down, and they were going to hear his explanation, just like Grandfather had always wanted. The old man had died for something after all, then: to give Sullen this opportunity.

"I'll find him. I'm good at that."

Keun-ju muttered something about what Sullen was good at, and he was glad he'd missed it, because Ji-hyeon looked to be having a tough enough day without Sullen beating her boyfriend's arse.

"Yeah, that would be helpful," said Ji-hyeon, sagging a little in Keun-ju's arms. "Thanks, Sullen."

"It's my honor, General," said Sullen, knowing a dismissal when he heard one, and wishing he was good for something other than chasing after his no-account uncle. "Feel better."

"Thanks, Sullen," she said again, but her eyes were back on nothing. "And thank your grandfather for me."

Sullen set off quick as he could, so she wouldn't see his face, wouldn't see that for a frost-cold boy from the Frozen Savannahs, he couldn't think about Fa without melting. He iced himself back over by focusing on the task at hand, what sometimes felt like the only task he'd ever known. Though his gut told him to look for his uncle back in the rear of the camp, hiding out in his tent, he decided to give Maroto the benefit of the doubt one last time, and started his search down on the hazy battlefield.

———

Instead of waiting for Hoartrap and Maroto to fall into it, the Gate swam up to catch them, and Maroto instinctively closed his eyes as he felt the textured blackness press its slick, cool membrane against his face and chest. It accepted him, and he was sinking into heaving mulch, fronds or cilia brushing against him, pushing him along, pulling him up, and just as he pondered if he'd rather drown in deviltry with his eyes closed or open, his ears popped and he felt solid ground beneath his feet, cool air on his skin.

After the Gate, the sensation felt all wrong, *he* felt all wrong, unable to balance, and even as he tried to slowly lower himself to all fours lest he fall, his injured, overworked, and heretofore bug-numbed knee gave out on him. His eyes flashed open and his hands came up to break his fall, but he couldn't even see the ground as he toppled forward, the smoke thicker than ever. Hoartrap caught one of his arms and jerked him to the side, so instead of landing on his palms he cracked his ribs into toothsome rocks. Some improvement. He was about to roll away from the treacherous sorcerer, so he could spring up and pay him back proper for shoving Maroto into a fucking *Gate*, like *that* was ever acceptable, when a stern wind whipped up from the ground just in front of him, dispersing some of the smoke...

Not smoke. Fog. Sea fog, to be particular, as evidenced by the emerald waves crashing far below, against the dark ankles of the cliff he had nearly fallen over. He gingerly edged away from the rough precipice where he'd sprawled like a cat on a windowsill, and only when he had a few good feet between him and the cliff did he rise to his good knee and look around for Hoartrap. The sorcerer hadn't gone far, inspecting the bloated eucalyptus trees, sap-dripping vines, and greasy-looking bushes that closed in tight around the tiny scrap of open rock overlooking the sea.

Wherever they were, it was a very long way from the Lark's Tongue. The Bal Amon jungles, maybe. Hopefully. He knew how to get back from Bal Amon, once he'd thrown Hoartrap over the edge of the cliff. He tried standing up, but it wasn't happening, his equilibrium still trying its best to roll him into the sea. Woof.

"It's hard not to be impressed," said Hoartrap, turning back to Maroto.

"Well, I'll manage it somehow. Where in the bleeding holes I'm about to put in your face are we?"

"Your new home," said Hoartrap, fishing under his heavy robes and pulling out a foot-long centipede that had nested somewhere in the vicinity of his groin. When he was on a bender it took a lot to disincline Maroto from begging a hit off a bug, but that did it. Holding the unnaturally docile arthropod up in his fist and raising his other hand in the air, Hoartrap looked all set to carry out some more of his witchy shit, when he paused and gave Maroto a glum smile. "I do wish it had turned out different, Maroto. You were always my favorite."

"Are you going to kill me, is that what this is?" Maroto lurched up to his feet, then stumbled back down to a knee. "You promised, you treacherous dick! Back in Emeritus, when all that crazy shit with the Faceless Mistress happened, who stuck his neck out to save you? And this is the thanks I get?"

"Yes, Maroto, this *is* the thanks you get," said Hoartrap, shaking the centipede at him. "More than I'd do for most. I swore I'd never kill you, and I take my oaths every bit as seriously as you do. You have nothing to fear from me. It's whatever creatures who dwell in the sea caves and jungles that I'd be concerned about, were I you."

Maroto looked down at his befouled, bedraggled armor, his single sandal, his empty knife sheath, and then raised his hands in disbelief. "You're breaking your oath, Hoartrap. This is murder."

"Oh tosh," said Hoartrap, crushing the centipede in his fist. "You're a resourceful boy, I'm sure you'll be back to troubling me in no time."

Maroto dove up from his crouch, hoping to take Hoartrap to the ground where his screwy balance wouldn't be as much of a detriment, but even moving in the right direction proved beyond him: instead of connecting with the sorcerer, Maroto landed beside him, squarely on a big succulent plant. By the time he'd removed himself from the spiny vegetation, Hoartrap was gone, only a ring of blackened rock and vegetation to mark where he'd disappeared.

Even when his balance finally returned, Maroto balked at blundering straight into the alien jungle. He was in that strangely sober liminal space between a powerful binge and an equally powerful hangover, and he didn't want to rush into anything. Instead, he limped back over to the cliff, dangled his legs over the side, and thought about Purna, and how she was dead right now, dead for nothing more than wanting a crack at glory and trusting him to show her the way. He sat there for a long time, feeling the sun-warmed limestone against his legs and watching the mist thicken, mourning her, missing her already. Then he rose wearily to his feet, and set out to kill every single person who had in any way contributed to his exile on this far-flung seascape, and to the death of his dearest friend. No excuses, no second chances. No devil in hell as bad as the Mighty Maroto, now that he sought vengeance for Tapai Purna.

———

"That's, uh, Tapai Purna, yeah?" said Sullen as he reached the two familiar figures who were carrying a third between them as they slogged up the hill toward camp. "Is she..."

"She's something," said Zosia. "But dead ain't one of 'em."

"Sturdy's the word I'd use," grunted the only member of Maroto's party who had always looked smooth and soft rather than tough and scarred. Diggelby, that was his name; no way Sullen would have come up with that handle on his own. He didn't look so smooth and soft anymore, and the little devil dog that he'd always carried around was nowhere to be seen. "Sturdy or, oof, well built—sounds nicer than heavy as lead shot. Be a chap and lend a hand?"

"Can't, on orders to bring my uncle to Ji-hyeon." Noticing Zosia's amused expression, Sullen explained, "Bring Maroto or Purna to the general, I mean, to give their reports. But Purna don't look able. She also wants you to tell her about the Myurans, ma'am."

"*Ma'am?*" Zosia ignored the chuffing sound her devil made. "Don't you mean Captain Zosia?"

"I did mean that," Sullen said quick-like, anxious to be away. He didn't like her looking at him now any more than he had before, feeling more exposed than ever without Grandfather to literally cover his back. "Better be away, though—you two seen him around?"

"He went off into the smoke with Hoartrap," said Diggelby, looking back down to the hellish field. "If they're not back yet they must still be out there."

"Thanks," said Sullen, trying to get shy of Zosia as fast as possible. Having her watch him so closely felt much like being under the eyeless gaze of the Faceless Mistress; that he'd blundered into a feud between the two inscrutable, overly interested powers was a tragedy fit for the singers. "I'll sniff him out, then. Meantime, the general wants all able officers to report in at the barbers' tents, so you two could, um, do that."

"Sullen?" Diggelby looked in the dumps for the first time since Sullen had met the man.

"Yeah?"

"If you see Duchess Din and Count Hassan... We lost track of each other, and I don't know if they're back at the tents, or..."

"I'll keep a watch out for 'em," said Sullen, one of Maroto's cronies the last person he would have predicted himself relating to when this awful day had started.

"And if you find Maroto, give him a message," said Zosia.

"Sure," said Sullen, thinking maybe he should have learned Immaculate letters just like Grandfather always said, so he could've jotted down a list.

"Tell him to quit being such a scared little crybaby and get back to camp. I've got a surprise for him."

"Um...sure."

Zosia and Diggelby resumed carrying the unconscious girl up the hill, the silver-haired woman's devil dog giving Sullen the side-eye. Getting a gander at Purna as they hauled her past, she didn't look to have a mark on her, so she must've been knocked upside the head. Sullen hadn't previously noticed that the girl also had the blood of shamans, and he asked himself how'd he miss something obvious as that. If he was to survive on his own, he'd need to get out of his thick skull more, start paying attention to everything, instead of waiting for Grandfather to tell him what was what.

South a ways on the hillside, some folks with the red tabards, shields, or other heraldry of the Crimson Empire were sat on the ground, surrounded by soldiers in blue and being talked at by one of the many Cobalt captains whom Sullen hadn't met. He wondered what they'd do with them, or with the Myurans they'd captured on the mountain. Found himself hoping they'd just give them a word and let them off, like Silvereye had done with the unnamed pups who had climbed a rope of moonbeams up to her kingdom in hopes of earning their names. Kind of doubted it would play like that.

Coming down toward the point where the slope got real sharp just before leveling off into the valley, he figured this must have been where the worst of the fighting went down. Too many dead to count, and the living didn't look much better, some just standing there, blinking into the smoke, or sitting on top of corpses that might have been their friends, heads in their hands. The worst were the laughing ones, their strained cackles even less welcome in this solemn place than the moans and screams and sobs. The smoke flowed in high, thick currents down here, and Sullen stopped walking, contemplating the veiled valley from whence gloomy figures emerged like devils from darkness. Sullen felt like Rakehell, after he'd evaded the Eater of Mortals by hiding in the Land of the Coward Dead, watching the blind specters march past him in their everlasting retreat from the honor of the battlefield...

Except that was all a great heaping pile of shit, wasn't it? Sullen had seen enough fights by now to know a battlefield was the last place on the Star you'd find honor, only heartache and horror, which were hardly the same thing. And as for the rest of it, that was shit, too, Rakehell and Old Black, Boldstrut and Count Raven, the whole stinking pile of them. They were all just songs the Horned Wolves made up to boast about how great they'd been, back in the day—all those places their ancestors went, all the Star-shaking deeds they'd done, why hadn't anyone heard of 'em outside the Savannahs? Sullen had asked everywhere they went, hoping their travels would take them past the Altar of Plagues or the Kingdom of the Oblivion Eaters, but even after he'd gotten the hang of the Crimson tongue everyone just looked at him like he was a fucking idiot. *Are we anywhere near the Lake of Satsumo? There's a tomb someplace 'round there where my ancestor laid out Old Man Gloom and his child... No?*

Of course not. Because none of it was real, it was a stew of half-truths and full lies bards ladled out to quiet down unruly brats and feed the fancy of overgrown children like Sullen, who could recite a hundred sagas but didn't know enough about the real world to be of practical use to a single other person. If he'd spent more time taking things on their face instead of puzzling over their secret meanings or how they'd fit into the song of his days, maybe his life would have been a lot easier back in the Savannahs. Maybe Grandfather would still be with him. Maybe he'd have told Ji-hyeon what he thought of her before Keun-ju showed up, or even after, instead of avoiding her and hoping all the while she'd come to him. Maybe he'd have come at Zosia head-on, demanded to know if she was really planning to light up a whole city with liquid fire. Maybe he wouldn't be alone, utterly, completely alone, with not a soul to miss him if he never came back to the camp, never came back to the Savannahs, never went anywhere but into the barrow beside Grandfather.

Looking at the great wavering wall of grey mist before him, Sullen felt helpless as ever—where to begin, that was always the question. What was he supposed to do with himself, when his whole ruddy existence amounted to this, trying to find solid ground in a world of smoke and shadows? Nothing to do but what he always did, put his head down, wander ahead, and hope he either got lucky or somebody showed up to point the way for him. Like the Faceless Mistress had, far as that went—she was the one to tell him where to find his uncle, and if he hadn't run into her he'd still be wandering the Star, Grand-father in tow...

The colorless haze and the unnatural stillness of the place as Sullen pushed through the smoke brought Emeritus back to him, all right, what had seemed so dreamlike again as hard and real as the ache in his chest, the sob that still lurked in his throat. They'd had some good days in that place, him and Grandfather exploring a realm that almost made the old songs seem plausible. Here, in this unearthly field, he felt that same sense of giddy uncertainty, of being in a place between the real world and that of heroes, and he half expected the Faceless Mistress to appear behind the next bank of smoke. Wouldn't that be an ending to please any teller of tales, if his reflexive fear when he'd looked over from the hill and seen a flock of devils had been justified? If all the pandemonium and this sinister quiet that came after was the result of a vengeful god come to punish him for not following through on his quest, for raising spear and knife beside Zosia instead of against her?

"Stop it," he told himself, back to his old habits already. "It's not a song, Sullen."

"Oh, but all the Star's a song, isn't it?" came the melodious voice of Hoartrap, smoke sliding off his robes as he stepped atop a dead horse, took a bow. "Careful, laddie, I hear this field is crawling with Horned Wolves."

"Don't call me that," said Sullen, cursing himself for the careless wish that somebody would show up to help him. "Somebody" could mean a lot of things, and Grandfather used to say the only gods who listened were the tricksters. "Where's my uncle, witch? I know he was with you."

"And I know my dear Ruthless friend was with *you*, last I saw him, and yet he is gone, too," said Hoartrap, eyeing the empty space over Sullen's shoulder. Oh, but it hurt that in Sullen's trek down through camp this witch was the only one to remark on Grandfather's absence—Ji-hyeon was in a bad way when she'd seen him, they all were, but still... "Perhaps they are off together, having some long overdue father-son bonding?"

"He..." Sullen closed his eyes and gulped down the foul air, poisoning the sob before it could hatch. Hoartrap was trying to distract him, was what was happening, and when he opened his eyes again they were clear. "My uncle Maroto was with you, witch. Do you deny it?"

"Of course not! He was in my company, yes, he was," said Hoartrap, hopping down from his perch on the dead horse and putting a hand over his breast. "I fear the Mighty Maroto is gone, Sullen of the Horned Wolf Clan."

"*Gone?*" There it was, the last fucking stitch that held Sullen together snapping. "You mean dead, or you mean he *left*? If he's dead I'll see his body, *now*. If...if...if he..."

"I almost think you'd prefer him dead!" said Hoartrap.

"Fucking right I would!" Sullen was on top of Hoartrap before the witch could summon his devils or his brawn, and if Sullen hadn't needed answers more than he needed satisfaction he would have ripped the giant's arms off instead of merely shaking the shit out of him. "Where? Why? Where? *Why?*"

"Let. Me. Go!" bellowed Hoartrap, and Sullen felt an evil warmth in his chest to see the witch lose his calm, if only momentarily. He did as he was asked, lifting his palms off the man's broad shoulders but not backing up an inch. Hoartrap didn't budge, either, his stale breath hot in Sullen's face. "Very well, very well, though I only know his motive, not his objective."

"Speak."

"I *am*," said Hoartrap haughtily, stepping around Sullen and bumping his shoulder, forcing him to walk alongside the witch lest he be walking after like an obedient devil. "You've met Purna, Maroto's disciple, haven't you?"

"Just saw Zosia and Diggelby carrying her up to the sawbones. What about her?"

"You mean she pulled through?" Hoartrap's giggle sounded as genuine as it was uncalled for. "Good for her, but no thanks to your uncle. She was gravely injured in the battle, but when she needed Maroto's help, he turned his back on her. He can be ... exceptionally *cautious*, your uncle, and I suspect his baser instincts got the better of him—none of us know what happened, all this smoke, all those Imperials blinking away to devils know where. It could spook any-one, and he said carrying her would slow them down."

Sullen tried to breathe, but nothing came in or out. He was so full of wrath there left no room for anything else, even air.

"Zosia fought him over the matter, right there with Purna dying on the ground at their feet. Fortunately for all parties I was able to overwhelm Maroto and escort him from the scene, which I suppose allowed Zosia and the pasha to carry Purna to safety. I walked with him a short way, whereupon he informed me he was done with all of us—he'd already sworn to kill Zosia, ask her if you don't believe me. I would have stopped him, but the truth is I owe Maroto my life from something that happened long ago, and could never bring myself to harm him. He's long gone by now, and didn't inform me of a destination."

They walked on in silence, and only when Sullen was positive a howl of rage wouldn't leave his lips, he quietly said, "You don't know where he went. But you tracked him before. You'll help me find him."

"I will, will I?" said Hoartrap, but one look from Sullen and he dropped the attitude. "Of course I will, Sullen, of course I will. But what you have to keep in mind about your uncle is that he gets this way sometimes, leaving his friends in a pinch. But he always comes back, tail between his legs, and we let it go because, well, we don't expect anything more from him. I think if you wait a day or two he'll come back to camp on his own, full of excuses for his bad behav-ior, promising to do better, finding loopholes in the oaths he swore against us in a moment of passion ... the usual."

"Three days," said Sullen, as the smoke parted before them and he saw the Lark's Tongue high above, the Cobalt camp nestled on its knee, and the hump where his grandfather's corpse had better be waiting for him, if that kid didn't want to be eviscerated ere the moon rose. It was as though the fog inside him had burned away, too, from the least likely of suns; thanks to Hoartrap the Touch, Sullen had finally found a purpose that made sense, something he could follow through on without overthinking it, without doubting, without hesitation. What to do about Zosia and the Fallen Mistress, about Ji-hyeon, all that could wait until he'd done what most needed doing in all the world.

"He's not back in three days, I hunt him. He comes back sooner, we settle it then. There'll be no song swapping. No more of his treachery. Uncle Craven's fled his last fight."

CHAPTER
28

At the third or maybe fourth polite whisper from the guards stationed just outside, Ji-hyeon hauled herself upright, temples pounding. Another whisper, and she gingerly disentangled herself from Keun-ju's bandaged limbs, taking stock of her tent. The kaldi warmer she had left burning revealed scattered clothes, busted armor, and dozens of stained dressings and washrags from where they'd changed one another's wrappings before collapsing into bed that afternoon. The poultice on her disfigured hand needed changing already, and she got queasy just looking at where her fingers should be.

"General," came the whisper again. Fennec. At last. "General! An emissary to see you!"

"Coming," she answered, pulling on a grimy skirt and jacket and groaning as her throbbing tailbone and bitten hand protested the exertion. Either the bugs they had given her for the pain had worn off or she was in an even worse way than she'd thought. Stuffing her hair back in what was probably a lopsided bun, she took another survey of the room and decided she just didn't care. If her visitor was the envoy who had announced his coming via owlbat while they'd been laid up in the barber's tent, he could choke on his indignation for all she cared... But, pausing at the flap, she changed her mind. No matter the point it would make, and as few shits as she had left to give, it was just too damn embarrassing. Old habits and such. She stepped into her slippers, hurried over and blew out the kaldi warmer, then quietly slipped out of the tent, careful not to let the guard's lantern light sneak in past her. It was after dark, but that was about all she could tell; it might have been anytime between sunset and dawn.

"Ah, General," said Fennec, rubbing his gloved paws together. "If we could talk inside, it is a matter of—"

"We'll walk and talk, gentlemen." She used her snottiest tone to address Fennec and the Imperial emissary at his side, the guards behind them exchanging a bemused look. "I need to stretch my legs."

Which was the truth; they felt like they'd been threshed by farmers with a personal vendetta against wheat, and hopefully a stroll would help.

"I think you can stretch later, Ji-hyeon," said the envoy, raising the visor on his owlbat-shaped helm. "I need a sit and a smoke, and your tent—"

"It's a little messy right now, Dad," she said, and, mad as she was at him, it was good to see his face. She hugged him, the studs of his armor cold through her hanbok. "I wondered if your old gear would still fit you!"

"It's possible I had it let out," admitted her second father, stroking her hair. The obvious pride on his face softened her a bit toward his betrayal... but only a bit. "Damned if you don't look the part. Fennec says that you've been a real handful, for him and the Imperials!"

"I bet he did," said Ji-hyeon, not terribly miffed—they both knew Fennec's biscuit was best buttered by whoever was closest to the plate. "You want to light your pipe before we get moving? There's a lookout spot I'd like to show you."

"You really aren't going to let me sit down for five minutes?" Had she actually missed that peevish note in his voice? "I sent word earlier, so you'd be ready for me—didn't you get it?"

"Oh, we got it," said Ji-hyeon, waving her bandaged hand at him and blinking away tears from even that little motion. "I've just been too busy waging your fucking war to set out kaldi for you like a good little girl."

"Oh, Ji," he said softly, reaching for her hand but thinking better of it. "Fennec told me, but... but what the devils were you doing out there, anyway? I've told you once I've told you a hundred times, a general leads from the rear, the rear! Fellwing's protection isn't some magical bubble you can step inside and then jump into a volcano! If you *ever*—"

Ji-hyeon jabbed his chest with her good hand, got right in his face, and said, "If *you* ever speak to me like that in front of my troops again, I'll have you run out of camp and close all future negotiations. Is that clear, Kang-ho?"

"Really, this is too much," he blustered, lifting her hand off his armor, when one of her guards took a step behind him, asked:

"General?"

"It's all right, soldier, the emissary is from foreign lands and his ways are strange. We'll acquaint him with Cobalt discipline soon enough." Ji-hyeon beamed at her father's gobsmacked expression. "Now, oh welcome ambassador, I am eager to hear the Empire's terms. The vantage point is this way, if you would be so kind?"

"Here, Kang-ho, mine's already packed," said Fennec, ever the peacemaker. In his glove he held out the thick briar billiard he was so proud of, the one whose mix of straight grain and birdseye made it appear to have two many-branched trees on the side of the bowl. "I believe you and the general have much to discuss, so the sooner we stop debating the location the better."

"Hmph," said her father. "I see you've done a fine job of keeping her in check."

"I live to serve my general," said Fennec with a bow, and as Kang-ho snatched the pipe away Ji-hyeon caught Fennec winking at her. If he thought a little ass-kissing now would spare him a harsh reproof for his desertion of the general's bodyguard during the Battle of the Lark's Tongue, the old fox was in for an even bigger surprise than her second father. Well, maybe not quite that big...

———

"I hope I didn't keep you," said Hoartrap, ever the gentleman as he flicked his fingers and the unlit lantern flared up, blinding Zosia after the dark of his tent. "If I'd known you wanted an audience, m'dear, I wouldn't have tarried. Oh, and you've brought my favorite little doggie-woggie in all the Star!"

Zosia was pleased to see her pep talk had done some good, for Choplicker didn't twitch, lying on the floor by her stool and watching the sorcerer as casually as he'd observe any other mortal. She puffed on the corncob pipe she'd bought off an old-timer earlier that evening, since she'd been fool enough to do the right thing and give Maroto back his briar. Someday she'd have to carve herself a real piece, but for now it was back to loaner pipes and cheap cobs.

"I'm in no hurry, Hoartrap, I've only got one more stop to make tonight."

"And here I hoped that handsome outfit was for my benefit," Hoartrap said wistfully, eyeing her dirndl. "Ah, but you've tied your apron wrong! If the knot's in the back like that everyone will think you're a mourning widow, Zosia. Let's move it around to the front, so the suitors will know you're available."

"If I tied it in the front they'd think I was a virgin," said Zosia, trying not to betray her annoyance with Hoartrap's damnable perceptiveness. "It's fine where it is."

"Well, whatever your status, you still look good in a dress, old friend. Far better than I did at your age."

"Oh, I'm sure your calves are as shapely now as they ever were," said Zosia. "Now, unless you've got any more beauty tips for me, why don't you pull up a seat, pack a bowl, and let's have us that blather you proposed the other day. I want to talk devils and secrets."

"I heard what happened with Diggelby's pet and dear Tapai Purna—was that the first time you've actually seen one set loose?" Hoartrap had a hard time keeping his eyes off Choplicker whenever the devil was around, Zosia could see that now. "Not pretty, I'd expect, but then passage from one world to another never is; death, birth, other roads..."

"Not pretty, but effective. She's good as new. More or less."

"I'd say improved. More or less." Hoartrap wasn't sitting, which was good, too—she was making him nervous. "Considering your options for our mutual friend, now that you've seen the efficacy of a devil's wish?"

"Hadn't occurred to me," said Zosia, and Choplicker drummed his tail on the dirt floor of the tent. "Not that he'd listen if I did."

A bark from the devil, and a chuckle from Hoartrap. "Yes, yes, I remember your difficulties in that regard. I've been pondering it, and I wonder if he isn't a special sort of creature, just as I've always said."

"A special wart on your vag is still a wart on your vag," said Zosia, and pulled in a mouthful of hot ash. She never could get the hang of cob pipes.

"You know, there are other ways of getting what you want than ordering one about." The pipe she'd made Hoartrap appeared in hand, already smoldering with the familiar aroma of cheap perfume and burning garbage. "Asking nicely. Begging. Offering something in trade beyond the usual terms."

"And here I thought you just ate them," said Zosia, and Choplicker growled at the laughing magician.

"I've never been lucky enough to catch one as fine as your specimen," said Hoartrap, puffing his pipe back to life. "But I have been looking into the transfer of devils. Our beloved general and her father put me onto the topic. I think I may have found a way, if you were so inclined, to take that troublesome fiend off your hands, in exchange for a more obliging devil. Maybe even several."

Choplicker's cold nose urgently nuzzled Zosia's dangling hand, and she rubbed his snout before wiping her damp palm on her checked apron. "You always were the helping kind, weren't you?"

"There's nothing I wouldn't do for a friend," said Hoartrap, blowing a smoke ring at Choplicker. The devil snapped at it.

"And what would you do with him, I wonder? Some sort of a roast?"

"Zosia, Zosia, Zosia," said Hoartrap. "I'd win the war, of course."

"All to help Ji-hyeon gain the Crimson Throne? That altruistic streak is going to get you into trouble someday."

"To help us all. The entire Star is in danger, or haven't you noticed? The Burnished Chain is too strong, its ambitions too grand. Do you have any idea what they called down this morning, what their ritual accomplished? It's too preposterous to even say aloud."

"I'd wondered where Ji-hyeon picked up her disdain for the church," said Zosia, her curiosity piqued despite her reluctance to be drawn into Hoartrap's schemes. "Is that why you murdered the war nun before I could talk to her? Sparing me the danger of an audience with a bound weirdborn?"

"I *knew* it was eating you up, not knowing!" Hoartrap crowed. "You've finally mastered your temper, after all these years, but I knew you wanted to know!"

Zosia shrugged. "For all the good knowing has ever done me. But let's hear it all the same."

"Let's just say she was dangerous, and you're better off without her," said Hoartrap. "But getting back to the far more interesting issue of the evening, I've had a peek beyond the veil and those mad Chainites have—"

"Choplicker," Zosia said, heart pounding at what she was about to do. So much could go wrong... "Choplicker, I want Hoartrap to tell me the truth about why Sister Portolés came here, what she wanted me to know. I want it so bad that if he doesn't tell me, now, of his own free will, I grant you your freedom to secure the facts by any means necessary."

It went as quiet as the smoky valley in the tent, Hoartrap not doing a good job hiding his amazement...And then he chuckled, shaking his head. Zosia's gambit had fallen flat, as all of them did, when they involved her worthless, disobedient devil, and from here until the end of the Star she'd never again be able to put the screws to Hoartrap with the threat of an unfettered Choplicker.

"Oh, Zosia, you do keep me interested!" said Hoartrap. "A clever ploy, but devils don't work that way. I only wish that poor nun had told me something you'd find interesting, then—"

The lamp went out, its glass mantle exploding in the black tent, and the cacophony of a thousand bones splintering and snapping filled the air, the smell of lightning mingling with the scent of rich earth, and Zosia felt a wave of icy air brush past, her cheeks and shaking hands tickled by a thousand probing threads, and then—

"I'll tell, I'll tell," squealed Hoartrap. "Just call him off!"

Then the tent was still once more, though Zosia continued to feel minute pricklings all across her skin. After a few shaky breaths, Hoartrap tried an incantation, but stumbled over the words a few times before he calmed down enough to say them properly. When he finally completed it, light returned to the tent in the form of what appeared to be a small phosphorescent jellyfish floating in the air between them. Hoartrap stared down in horror at Choplicker, and Zosia had a look, too; same dog as ever, but his lips were pulled back in an uncanny approximation of a human smile. Strands of dog hair floated through the charged air, settling on everything, and Zosia brushed them off her dress, trying to slow her racing heart.

"You were saying?" she said, but it came out as a croak. She couldn't bear to look at Choplicker any longer, couldn't stop her legs from shaking like she'd missed a toehold climbing up a cliff. She'd almost gone and loosed the devil.

"Yes, yes, I was. I will. I am," whispered Hoartrap, still staring at her devil, and seeing Hoartrap so rattled was as thrilling as it was foreboding. What would have happened to the old sorcerer if he hadn't elected to come clean before Choplicker forced him?

"Let's hear it, then," said Zosia. "Starting with Portolés and everything she told you, and ending with whatever fell deviltry happened out there on the battlefield. Tell me that, and we'll call it a night."

"As you wish," said Hoartrap, finally taking a seat.

———

Kang-ho softened a bit when Ji-hyeon asked him about the family, and as they marched through the dark camp she felt an unexpected pang of homesickness. Come what may of the coming war, if every engagement resulted in such havoc as this one, Hwabun would remain apart from it all, safe from harm at the ends of the Immaculate Isles, and that gave her succor as they climbed the hill where she had parleyed with Fennec and Hoartrap but two nights before. Once the guards reached the crown of the hill and hung back out of earshot, though, her second father laid straight into her.

"All right, Ji-hyeon, you've had your fun," he said, puffing furiously on his borrowed pipe. "Now, just what the devils is the meaning of all this! You were supposed to use my silver to hire a crew big enough to secure the attention of a regiment or two, not the whole Crimson Empire! And now this...this *madness*, provoking the Azgarothian regiment into open war? You're lucky Hoartrap was here to help you, or you'd never have carried it."

"Hoartrap didn't have anything to do with it," said Ji-hyeon, trying not to lose her temper; the louder she spoke, the worse her hand hurt. "We're still trying to figure out what happened—seems like a ploy by the Imperials that blew up in their faces. I've ordered everyone to stay off the field until that smoke clears and we can see what happened out there; it went dead quiet, right in the middle of things, and I've heard reports from soldiers close to the action that the earth opened up and swallowed the whole damned regiment. None of the Azgarothians or Myurans we captured are talking, if they even know what it was, but I've got one of my best captains interrogating the Azgarothian colonel as we speak."

"You took their colonel?" Her father sounded impressed in spite of his best efforts to the contrary. "How'd you manage that?"

"He was leading from the rear. When my people rode out to pillage the Imperial camp somebody found him hiding in a wagon on the far side of the vale."

"Well," said Kang-ho, trying to work up his ire again. "It still sounds like chance carried the day, such as it is, and by the look of things you gave up a lot more than you gained. How many heads did you lose?"

"Too many," said Ji-hyeon quietly. "Far too many."

"You're lucky, daughter, very, very lucky I arrived in time, and luckier still that my old buddy Waits is leading the regiment out of Thao. She still thinks we can work something out."

"She does, does she?" Ji-hyeon peered through the misty haze that still hadn't cleared off the vale. She wondered if it ever would, or if she would be forced to send a scouting party in to discover the truth behind the smoke. "Well, then I suppose you're both in for a disappointment, aren't you? There's been a change in plans, I'm afraid."

That got him flushed, all right, and for a moment he just scowled at Fennec, who shrugged and said, "You were the one who always said she took after you."

"Ji-hyeon . . ." her father began, but then a horn sounded from the direction of the command tent, two long blows to signal an arriving messenger. She sent Fennec to fetch the news, and as he left, her father tried again, his voice softer. "Ji-hyeon, listen to me. You've had your fun, but the reality is that you've gotten yourself in an awfully tight spot, and unless you want to have an unstoppable war on your hands by lunchtime, you need to get smart, and . . . and . . . oh no. No, no, no, Ji-hyeon, you're smarter than this!"

Evidently she wasn't doing as good a job of hiding her excitement as she'd thought. "It's too late, Dad. You offered me one role, which I thank you for, but I'm taking a better one."

"Ji-hyeon, I never would have let you go if I thought you'd be in real danger," said her father, looking down at her missing fingers. "This isn't a game anymore, this is—"

She socked him in the chin before she knew what she was doing. He stumbled back, more from surprise than the blow. She harried him, putting her face in his, and snarled:

"You and Fennec love saying that, but this was never a game! Never! People died, lots of people. Some of them I knew and some of them I didn't, but there was never a way for your plan to work without hundreds, hells, *thousands* of people, innocent people, going to the grave. I've killed people, I've lost friends, and you lecture me about playing *games*? Fuck you, Kang-ho! Fuck you!"

He looked abashed. Nodded. Squatting down to pick up the pipe he'd dropped, he quietly said, "Please don't call me that. I'm still your friend, I hope, but I'm also one of your fathers. Call me names if you must, so long as 'Dad' is always one of them."

"Urgh!" She closed her eyes, breathed deeply, and when she opened them again she waved away the guards who had begun creeping closer. "Okay, *Dad*. But let's be real here. We both know what the stakes were. And now I'm raising them. Substantially."

"Hear me out, I beg you," he said in that pleading tone that always got under her first father's skin. "Let me broker a truce with the

Empire. You said you know it's not a game, and I believe you, so you know that my plan involved a lot less risk for everyone. A lot less death. A lot less pain. I can get my people in the Empire back on board, if we act fast, color what happened here as unprovoked aggression by the Fifteenth. We can still take Linkensterne, which means you still have a choice to do the most good for the most people."

"We both know I don't have a choice anymore," she said, hoping reason would cut through his emotion. "Even if the Empire was willing to look the other way for this and every other crime I've committed against the Crown, I've got my own house to worry about. If I roll over and tell the troops we're teaming up with the Imperials they've been fighting all year just to take some shitty Immaculate border town, half of them would walk. The good half."

"They're mercenaries, Ji-hyeon, they'll do what you pay them to do." Her father smiled knowingly. "Don't pass the blame on this, Ji-hyeon—you want to take on the Empire, because you're young and ambitious and naïve enough to think you can swing it. Nothing more."

"There's a lot more," said Ji-hyeon angrily. "The Crimson Empire is a plague on the Star, and—"

"Oh please!"

"They are, and you fucking know it! The Black Pope rules in all but name after their last civil war, and what do you think that bodes? Her missionaries have been gnawing away at every Arm of the Star, and as soon as the Empire recovers from its infighting there isn't a power in the world that will be able to stop them. They've found a new way to win wars, Dad—by not fighting them. You get enough converts, and pretty soon the whole Star bows before Diadem… This could be the last chance for anyone to stop them!"

"Spoken like a true believer." Kang-ho shook his head. "Jun-hwan will never forgive me for singing you all those old songs."

"Listen to me, Dad, for once, listen! If I did things your way we'd have Linkensterne, a free state, a bastion of liberty…But for how long, before Diadem and all the Immaculate converts decide we're another Sunken Kingdom, in need of spiritual cleansing? We walk away now, when the fight's hard but not unwinnable, and we'll never have a second chance—never!"

"God of the Seas, but I was wrong about you," said Kang-ho, delivering the lowest blow yet doled out: "You're *exactly* like your other father."

"Yes, well, say one thing for him, he never tried to murder my boyfriend." Ji-hyeon crossed her arms.

"Your what?" Her father looked honestly confused.

"Keun-ju! You stopped him from leaving with me, and would have had him executed, if Papa hadn't stopped you!"

And there was the recognition she was looking for. Kang-ho pulled on his pipe to stall for time, probably trying to decide between acting contrite or superior. Fortunately for him, he decided on the latter; Ji-hyeon preferred her second father when he was being an honest asshole rather than a deceitful charmer. "So Fennec spilled the rice, eh? Well, whatever the fox told you, yes, I kept Keun-ju on Hwabun, but I never planned on hurting him. To say nothing of an execution! Does that really sound like me?"

When she didn't answer, he said, "Look, you can ask him yourself, if you listen to reason and do things my way. Once we're all back on Immaculate soil, I'll send for him to meet us in Linkensterne, and you kids can carry on in whatever way you wish. What do I care if you want to piss on five hundred years of tradition and elope with your Virtue Guard? Jun-hwan may never forgive you for bringing such dishonor on our house, but *I'll* always love you."

"So he's still safe on Hwabun?" This was fucking it, right here, if her dad lied to her one more time…

"Wellllllll…no, no he's not," said Kang-ho guiltily. "But he's safe, I promise, he's with the best swordswoman the Star has ever known."

"Zosia?" When her dad gulped she poked his armor hard enough to feel the iron plates beneath the canvas coat. "The woman you tried to pay Chevaleresse Singh to murder? I wonder what instructions you gave her about how to deal with Zosia's companion?"

"How…Gods shit on my face, she's not…"

"One of my captains, now. I'm sure she'll be delighted to see you, catch up on old times."

He looked all around, as though the specter of Cold Cobalt was about to leap out of the darkness, and when he turned back to her there were tears in his eyes. "You're breaking my heart, Ji-hyeon."

"Just like you broke Grampa's heart, to hear you sing it."

"She'll murder me, Ji-hyeon, she'll fucking murder me, right here, in front of you!" She actually felt bad for her second father, even after all his bullshit, so she patted his shoulder and said:

"No she won't. Not without my order, and big a jerk as you've been, I'm not a monster." She hoped both clauses of her statement proved true before the end. "You wait here and think about whether you want to ride with us, against Samoth, or if you're going to get back on your horse and get the fuck out of my camp. But if you turn your back on me, Dad, I can't make any promises. Now, if you'll excuse me, I have to take a message from my captain."

It would have been nice for him to say something supportive, like maybe he was a teensy bit impressed at what an amazing general she obviously was, but instead he just stared at her, beyond words. Well, that would have to do for now—Fennec looked ready to drop from running up the hill. Her father stayed behind, watching her go, but when Fennec whispered the report in her ear, and then repeated it, as she commanded in a surprisingly steady voice, she was glad he hadn't left.

As she plodded back over to him, a wild giggle burst out of her, every ache in her body forgotten and the day's dire battle suddenly small. The expression on her face must have revealed something of the message's tenor, for her father looked as concerned as if both her arms had fallen off.

"What is it?" he asked. "What's happened?"

Her voice broke when she tried to speak, because even though she'd only met the man a handful of times, even though she'd fled the Isles in part to escape him, she never would have wished him harm beyond the sting of rejection. Who could have done such a thing? Other than her, of course.

"You're scaring me, Ji-hyeon, what's happened?"

"I..." Horribly enough, another giggle came out. "I..."

"What? What did you do?"

"I killed my fiancé," said Ji-hyeon, trying to remember what Prince Byeong-gu had even looked like. She recited the rest as precisely as it had been told to her. "I killed him, and I cut off his head, and I stuffed the white scarf he had worn in mourning for me into his mouth, and then I wrapped it all up in one of my Cobalt pennants and delivered it in a box to the Linkensterne garrison under cover of darkness."

Her father opened and closed his mouth several times, but when nothing came out she answered his unvoiced question:

"I mean, I didn't. Obviously. *No.* But tell that to Empress Ryuki; she's just declared war against the Cobalt Company. Oh, and offered governorship of Linkensterne to whoever brings her my head. So there's that."

Like everything else about her adventure in the Crimson Empire, it sounded so simple when she said it out loud. Instead of yelling at her, like she expected, her second father stepped forward and held her, and though her hand started hurting worse than ever and her back ached under his embrace, she did not join Kang-ho in shedding tears. She was too busy planning what to do next.

———

After her meeting with Hoartrap, Zosia had a powerful need to be away from Choplicker for a spell, and so before she entered the prisoner's tent she stopped in the darkness between campfires. Kneeling down, she scratched behind the monster's ears, scratched like she'd never scratched before. He groaned happily, licked her shaking hand.

"We've got a history, old devil," she told him. "I hope our future goes better for both of us. Now go treat yourself to whatever you want, so long as it harms no mortal."

He was off like an arrow, not giving her so much as a parting bark as he loped away. Zosia instantly regretted her carelessness—just what treat would he be able to secure for himself; how far might he range from their camp to obtain it?

Near on twenty-five years she'd had the devil bound to her, and after all this time she didn't know much more than she'd started with. Going forward she'd have to be a hell of a lot more specific with what she offered him, like she'd done in Hoartrap's tent. It had taken hours of pondering her wording before she'd dare to say it, and considering how well it had turned out, that had been a lesson, albeit an obvious one. Nothing with devils should be done rashly.

As she picked herself up, the chill of the looming winter cut through the dirndl she had not worn since the last time Efrain Hjortt had graced her with his presence. The dress no longer fit her as well, the woman who had sewn it with the help of her husband having a bit more weight on her bones, and a whole hell of a lot more on her heart. She tried to recall what Leib had said to her as they worked by the light of their hearth, what it was that had made her laugh so hard she'd pricked herself with the needle...She couldn't remember. Could barely remember the sound of his voice, though it had been but a year since he'd been taken from her. Murdered. In all that time, Zosia had spent far more hours intentionally *not* thinking of him to spare herself the hurt than she had cherishing the good memories. Hardly seemed right. And now she had no earthly fucking idea why he had died; if Portolés had told the truth to Hoartrap and Queen Indsorith wasn't involved, then just what in every hell was she doing out here, waging war against the Crimson Empire? What had she been doing for the past year, if not preparing to avenge him?

Doing what she did best, apparently—making a lot of people dead for no damn reason at all.

The guards saluted as she approached the tent, probably having expected her earlier in the evening. Looking at the dark flap, she almost turned around and went back to her own tent, utterly drained now that the shock she'd suffered in Hoartrap's tent was wearing off. What a fucking day: climbing mountains, fighting Imperials, fighting her friends, trafficking with devils, and to top it all, learning credulity-straining revelations. That the first new Gate in recorded memory had opened right at their feet was dire enough, a signal that forces more powerful than she could imagine were actively seeking to reshape the world. The other part of the ceremony, though, the thing that Hoartrap believed was the true purpose of the Imperial sacrifice, with the opening of the Gate but a part of the price they paid to complete the ritual... could she really believe such a thing was even possible?

Yes, she decided, she had to. Hoartrap was in fear of more than his life when he'd told her everything. If he believed it had happened, then it had.

Which meant that the Star of today was unlike the Star of any day before it, stretching back for five hundred years. The world could never go back to what it had been this morning, when she'd bandied words with an avowed heretic digging the grave for a sister of the Chain. Word would spread quickly of the miracle that happened this morning, and then the entire Star would shudder before the supreme witchery of the Burnished Chain. Everyone would become a believer. What did Hoartrap say the Chainites called it? The Day of Becoming?

It almost made what had happened to Leib and everyone else in Kypck seem small. Almost convinced her to go check if Maroto had come back to camp yet, licking his wounds. She wanted to see the look on his face when he found out Purna was alive, and all because some spoiled fop from the old capital had been nicer to his dog than Zosia had been to hers. Almost made her stagger back to her tent, so she could bury her head in her cot and sleep for days, hiding in dreams that couldn't possibly be as mad as the waking world.

Almost, but the last time Zosia had put off interrogating a prisoner who would supposedly speak only to her the woman had been murdered in the night. It was time to get the truth out of Efrain Hjortt: assuming Portolés was right and Queen Indsorith hadn't sent him to Kypck, who had? The obvious suspect was the Burnished Chain, but Zosia was done with suspicions. She was ready for facts. When the Gate had opened beneath the Imperial army the entire Fifteenth Cavalry had disappeared along with most of their regiment, which meant Hjortt was the only one left alive from that day, save her.

A day hadn't passed that she hadn't cursed herself for not finishing the job, for giving Hjortt's people the chance to save him from the fire, but now she praised the stars overhead and the devils beneath them that she'd stuck a pin in him for another day. Who knew, depending on what he told her, she might not kill him now, either—wouldn't it be something, if every time she caught Efrain Hjortt he gave up some new secret, and then she could toss him back in for another day?

"Evening, Captain Zosia," said one of the guards as she shook off her thoughts and accepted his offered lantern. "He's in a bad way, barber ain't sure he'll live the night. He doesn't seem able to move much, but we chained him to a post to play it safe."

Just like they'd bound Sister Portolés, apparently; it was enough to make a girl wonder if somebody liked her, upstairs or down. Everything happens, according to the Chain, and maybe they were on to something. "Thanks. I won't be long."

Hjortt groaned as the light of Zosia's lantern reached the foot of his cot, and exhausted as she was, much as she'd thought she'd changed over the last year, the sound of his discomfort brought a smile to her face.

"Good evening, Colonel Hjortt," she said, taking her time crossing the room. An old trick for getting the prisoner's heart moving before you even started. "It's been a while, hasn't it? And yet it seems like only yesterday."

"A very long while, but not long enough," he said, his voice hardly anything like she remembered. "I wondered how it was possible... Even after everything, I wanted it to be true, but I had my doubts. But... but it's really you."

Zosia was glad she'd saved the dirndl for him. The light reached the top of the blankets, the prisoner closing his eyes from the glare, and she nearly dropped the lantern. Whoever this beat-up old man was, he wasn't Efrain Hjortt, and she came closer, holding the lantern up as though his wax disguise would melt away, revealing her nemesis. She could almost see a resemblance in his nose, despite all the bandages on his cheek. But then she was just confused, because she did recognize him, but hadn't seen him for so long she couldn't place it...

The Fifteenth. Of course. The fucking Fifteenth Regiment out of fucking Azgaroth.

"Nicely played, Cavalera," she said, sitting down on the edge of his cot and hooding the lantern so he could open his eyes again. Disappointed though she was at being tricked, she had to respect her adversary's cunning. "They pulled you out of retirement to lure me in, huh? The disinformation was a nice touch; I would've eventually gone after the Fifteenth Cavalry, but if I thought that awful boy was still in charge I'd never be able to resist."

He slowly opened his bloodshot eyes. They were wet with tears. He looked so old. "You...you remember me?"

"Remember you? Motherfucker, you rode me worse than every other regiment combined! Why do you think I ended up on that lunatic suicide mission to storm Diadem? You'd have kept us in the high country for years without getting a crack at King Kaldruut." Zosia shook her head in amazement. Twenty-odd years ago she had cursed his name almost as much as that of the king he served, but seeing him down all the days, she recognized that he'd just been playing his part, the same as she had played hers. He'd always fought fair, too, which was more than could be said for most of his peers. "Domingo Cavalera, Colonel of the Fifteenth Regiment out of Azgaroth. I understand you probably don't believe me, given the circumstances, but by the six devils I bound, it's damn good to see an old face."

"Forgive me if I don't share your sentiment," he growled, blood leaking through the bandage on his face.

"Shit, let me get that," said Zosia, dabbing his chin with her sleeve, unable to stop smiling. What she wouldn't have given to see him laid low like this back in the day, but now...now she just felt bad for him. He was just like her, a relic of days gone by trotted out for one last job. "This is ridiculous, keeping you in irons in your condition. I'll have them unlock you immediately. Anything else I can bring you, Colonel Cavalera? Food, drink, smoke? A bug for the pain? Anything at all, I'll fetch it myself."

"Yes," he said, the words falling hard as a hammer shaping a sword. "You can give me back my son's thumbs."

Zosia froze. "*What?*"

"His thumbs, woman—you took them, didn't you? Bad enough you burned him like a witch, but he went into the crypt looking like a fucking thief."

Zosia stared at her old opponent, tried to speak…but nothing came out.

"And it's Hjortt now, Domingo Hjortt. I kept my wife's name, even after she left."

"Colonel…Hjortt?" Zosia sank back down to the ground, and seemed to keep sinking, all the way down to the lightless reaches beneath the earth, where the Flintlanders say the First Dark gave birth to all the monsters and devils of the world, the worst of which were named mortals. She couldn't open her eyes, couldn't do anything but let out a long, miserable sigh. She had killed Efrain Hjortt after all, had killed him first, and hadn't even realized it. Now that the hour had arrived, Zosia found herself unable to keep the promise she had made to him back in Kypck—not a single tear fell to mark the passing of the young colonel who had set her on this blood-drenched road, the path that had seemed so obvious a year before now lost in shadow.

And now she was the only one left alive from that day in Kypck, with no more answers than she had started with. She would never hear from Efrain Hjortt's lips who had sent him, because she had been so convinced she had known that she hadn't even asked him before cutting off his thumbs and setting him on fire. Leib forgive her, she was every bit as mad a monster as her enemies had always said. It didn't matter if it was an empire or a village, everything Zosia touched fell into ruin—even if the younger Hjortt were here to give her one answer, she knew that behind it would be the deeper truth that her husband and the rest of his village were killed because of Zosia. If she had never gone to Leib after abdicating the Crimson Throne, never convinced him to retire with her to his childhood home, he and every other villager who had died in the massacre would still be alive. That was why the six devils were first drawn to her, before she and her Five Villains bound them: because no matter where she went or what she tried to do, Zosia sowed misery and death.

Opening her eyes and staring into the dark at the corner of the tent, she at last understood why Choplicker hadn't granted her wish to protect her and Leib all those years ago. Not even a devil can save you from yourself.

"Will you tell me something?" Domingo asked her, sounding just as tired and heartbroken as she was. When she shrugged her heavy shoulders in response, he said, "Out there on the field...what happened? What did I unleash, letting those Chainites perform their ritual?"

"That?" Zosia looked over at Domingo and saw her grief and guilt reflected back on his wracked features. At least it wouldn't be lonely in hell. "Oh, not much. Just the end of the world."

"Oh," said Domingo, as though he'd rather expected that but still wasn't happy to hear it. "Well, where does an unrepentant old sinner go from here, then?"

"Where do you think?" said Cold Zosia, because there was only one direction left, and only one way to get there. "We go down swinging."

EPILOGUE

The sloop cut through the fog, no one aboard making a sound lest the Immaculate turtle ships be right on top of them in the pale miasma. You had to be just as ruthless as a pirate to sign on as a customs officer, and twice as greedy, so it wasn't surprising the two turtles hadn't given up the chase even when it became apparent where the smugglers were fleeing to. What did surprise the captain of the vessel renamed the *Queen Thief* was that the Immaculates had followed them into the eternal fogbank that hovered over the sea where the Sunken Kingdom had vanished so many hundreds of years past. Usually Immaculate ships were too skittish to get anywhere near the perpetual storms of the Haunted Sea...but then again, most smugglers were too smart to risk it, too.

Whether there was actually a continent-swallowing whirlpool at the heart of the rain and fog, as the old salts claimed, made little difference, since a scant mile into the mists the seas grew so high and rough that even a much larger ship than the *Queen Thief* could be tipped in short order. The captain knew, because she had fled here once before under similar circumstances, and been followed in similar fashion, only to give their pursuers the slip once things got choppy. As if to warn her against future trespass, the fog had lifted just enough for them to see the customs ship capsized by a massive wave, the screams of her crew drowned out by the turbulent sea and the crack of furious lightning. Yet the captain wasn't the superstitious type, and so she'd tried the same trick twice...only to find the Immaculates hot on her heels, and the Haunted Sea calmer than a stoned sloth underneath all the mist.

"Cap'n Bang," the lookout hissed down from the crow's nest. "Got a glimpse through the glass when that breeze blew through, and they're coming in on either side. No hope of turning in time."

"Hells," said Bang, chewing on her pipe. "Can you get a look north?"

"North?" Dong-won, her boatswain, turned the color of the fog. "Cap'n, I know it looks calm now, but..."

"Sew buttons on your butt, Bosun," said Bang with more bravado than she felt. "You give me a clear sea and I'll sail it, no questions asked. It clear up there, Hae-il?"

The lookout said nothing, but his hawkglass fell from the mist-obscured crow's nest. Bang neatly caught it out of the air and tucked it into her belt. Trying not to look as impressed with herself as she felt, she hissed, "Hae-il. Hae-il!"

When the lookout didn't reply, Bang nodded up at the crow's nest. Dong-won took a step back, raising his palms, but with another hard nod at the mast, Bang cajoled him into climbing. She slapped his rump as he went up, just so he'd remember who was boss the next time an order was given.

"He's fainted dead away, Cap'n," Dong-won called down a moment later.

"Well, there's a welcome omen," muttered Bang. "What do your hungry gull eyes see, Bosun?"

"See, Cap'n? Not much. It's clouded up again. Here, I'll see if I can wake him up," said Dong-won.

"Double time, Bosun, double time," said Bang, and took another long draw on the pipe she'd stolen from Cobalt Zosia herself. Well, given the toll of years and all, she ought to be called Silver Zosia these days, but credit where deserved—the cutty smoked better than any pipe Bang had ever set her lips to. "Bosun?"

"Oh shit," Dong-won moaned. "Oh shit, oh shit, oh shit."

"Another welcome omen," said Bang, trying to bluff herself through the sardine scales rising on her neck. "What's the song, Bosun? Sea monster? Whirlpool? What?"

"Uhhhhhh," said Dong-won, followed by what sounded suspiciously like a prayer to the Sea God. Bang didn't like prayers on her boat; it was asking for trouble from whatever gods you left out. Knowing two in the crow's nest was already tight, she shoved her way past her nervous crew, down to the front of the boat. Snapping out the hawkglass, she peered over the prow in imitation of the crane figurehead just below her.

Thick as the fog had been a moment before, as soon as she put her eye to the hawkglass Bang was blinded by sunlight reflecting on wet rock or metal. Stowing the instrument and rubbing her eye in irritation, she looked back up to see what blasted spit of rock was threatening her ship now...and nearly lost her grip on the prow. Her jaw dropped wide as a customs officer's pocket. Zosia's pipe fell from her teeth, but treasured though the cutty was, Bang didn't even notice.

The *Queen Thief* broke through the last few curtains of fog, and instead of a storm or maelstrom at the heart of the Haunted Sea, there was an entire coastline. They'd come perilously close to the sea cliffs that rose a thousand feet into the air, the island steaming in the bright sunshine and light breeze. Impressive as all this was, what smacked Bang square in the gob were all the enormous caves yawning in the cliffs, caves from which swarmed enormous, many-legged creatures the likes of which she'd never conceived, even in harpy-fish dreams. The monsters dove down into the calm sea, one close enough to splash sense back into the captain.

"Tack!" Bang yowled, running back across her ship, slapping any of her stunned crew in striking range. "Tack, you poltroons, tack tack tack! Get us out of here!"

Already, though, Bang could hear the scratch-scratch-scratching of something at the hull...After all these centuries, the Sunken Kingdom of Jex Toth had returned, and she hadn't come back alone. Off the starboard bow, Zosia's bobbing pipe was knocked under by a violent splash, and sank into the busy darkness.